IN DARK SERVICE

THE FAR-CALLED

Volume One

STEPHEN HUNT

The right of Stephen Hunt to be identified as the author
of this work has been asserted by him in accordance with
the Copyright, Designs and Patents Act 1988.

First published in Great Britain in 2014
by Gollancz
An imprint of the Orion Publishing Group
Orion House, 5 Upper St Martin's Lane,
London WC2H 9EA
An Hachette UK Company

This edition published in 2015
by Gollancz

A CIP catalogue record for this book
is available from the British Library.

ISBN 978 0 575 09207 5

Typeset at The Spartan Press Ltd,
Lymington, Hants

Printed and bound in Great Britain by
Clays Ltd, St Ives plc

The Orion Publishing Group's policy is to use papers
that are natural, renewable and recyclable products and made
from wood grown in sustainable forests. The logging and
manufacturing processes are expected to conform to the
environmental regulations of the country of origin.

www.stephenhunt.net
www.orionbooks.co.uk
www.gollancz.co.uk

To my wife.

The love we give away is the only love we keep.

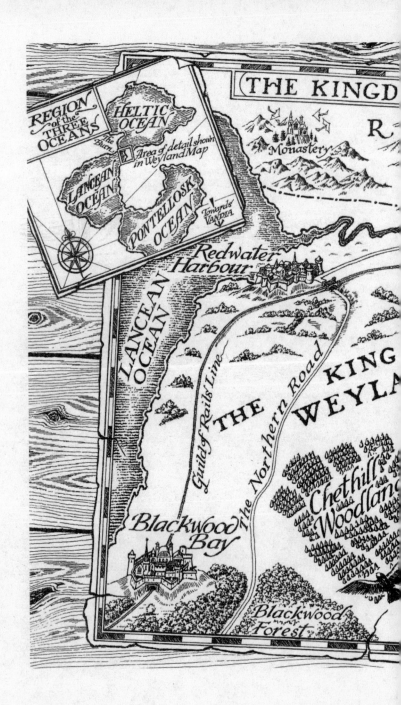

THE KINGD

R

Monastery

REGION of the THREE OCEANS

HELTIC OCEAN

The Burn

Area of detail shown in Weyland Map

LANCEAN OCEAN

PONTELLOSK OCEAN

Towards VANDIA

Redwater Harbour

LANCEAN OCEAN

Guild of Rails Line

The Northern Road

THE KING

WEYLA

Chethill Woodlan

Blackwood Bay

Blackwood Forest

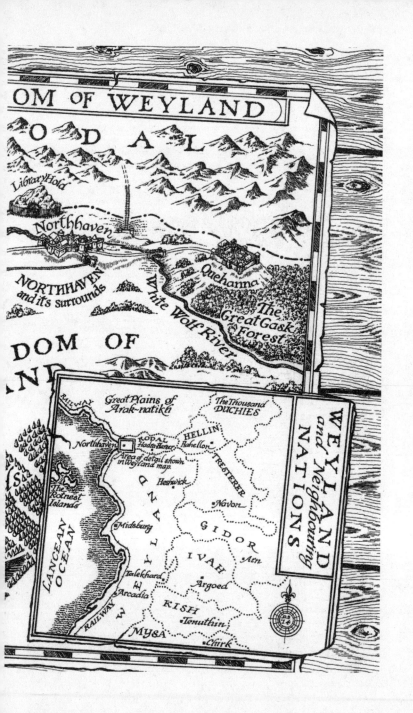

ONE

THE ABACUS BOX

Northhaven Township.
The Kingdom of Weyland

Jacob Carnehan could tell there was going to be a whole mess of trouble. A hush fell across the crowded street, stillness as sharp as a razor. That was when the constable appeared sprinting around the corner, his silver badge clipped to a belt jangling with a pistol on one side and a long-knife balancing the gun. This trouble didn't involve Jacob, but from the look of urgency on Constable Wiggins' face, Jacob was going to be involved in it anyhow. Wiggins was old for the job, late sixties and running around after street thievery and sheep rustling at his age. No wonder he was sweating; rivulets of the stuff running down the skin of his shiny white skull, white tufts soaked at the side.

'Jacob,' the constable puffed, drawing to a stop and placing his hands on his knees as he recovered.

'Constable Wiggins. You planning on taking retirement any time before the call of God puts you in a box before the congregation?'

'What would I be doing then?' Wiggins coughed, clearing his throat and spitting across the street. 'If you are what you do, when you don't, you ain't. I finish with my job, I'll be in that box by the end of the week anyway. We've got some trouble in old lady Kalem's inn, the *Green Dragon*.'

Jacob sighed. End of the harvest season, naturally there was going

1

to be trouble. Wheat and corn being shipped out along the train line, moved down the river to the port. Farm workers with money, dockers with money, sailors with money, just about everyone looking to spend that coin too hasty or steal someone else's. Northhaven reaped a whole crop of aggravation this month, and if people were sitting in the pews of Jacob's church with just a few black eyes by the end of the week, not lying at home with bandages covering stab wounds or worse, then he would consider himself a lucky man. 'Who is it this time?'

'Sailors up from the coast,' said Wiggins. 'From a schooner called the *Venture*. They were playing cards against a gask. He won of course. Sailors claim he's cheating, using one of their people's abacus machines to hoodwink them.'

Jacob had to stop himself from laughing. Gasks didn't have much use for gods or preachers, given how they worshipped probability. It was a brave man who played cards against one of their people. 'I don't suppose they've heard how dangerous a gask can be?'

'Reckon they've heard how almighty peaceful they are,' said Wiggins.

Up to a point. And when push came to shove, that point could be damn efficient.

'I've left that green-behind-the-ears probationer, Jay, holding the line,' said Wiggins, raising a hand placatingly to encompass the simple black churchman's tunic Jacob was wearing. 'You've got a way of calming men down, Jacob, that's rare to behold. If it's not you settling the trouble, then it'll be the high sheriff, and then there'll be caskets at the front of your church for sure.'

That was true. The high sheriff was up for re-election soon. Coming down hard on rowdy out-of-towners was just the kind of crowd-pleasing that would be going on if the shallow, politically-minded dolt arrived in Northhaven's new town district.

'I'll see what I can do,' said Jacob. 'Where's the sailors' skipper?'

'Crew's captain stayed downriver,' said Wiggins. 'I've already been to the radiomen's hold and sent word to the harbourmaster at Redwater to have him take a boat up here. His sail-tuggers have been creating problems in town all week as it is, but this is the first time they've actually pulled a knife on anyone.'

'Do they speak any language I can understand, Mister Wiggins?'

'They sure curse in trade-tongue well enough for a man to understand.'

Jacob walked fast, his long legs pacing as the short constable struggled to keep up. *I wonder if Wiggins knows the other constables call him Stumpy behind his back?* 'Sometimes I don't know who it is I'm working for here. The church or the high sheriff?'

'Hell, I could just shoot them,' said Wiggins. 'But then I'd be at the front of your church having to listen to you sermonise about the natural harmony of the universe and how it don't include shortening another's natural span.'

Jacob snorted. 'You haven't drawn that gun in years. You shoot, you'll lose your fingers when the barrel blows.'

Wiggins patted a retractable baton belted next to his long-knife. 'When I give my sermons with this, the cuss receiving the Word of Wiggins stays alive long enough to learn better. Weren't we all young once?'

The constable's philosophising reminded Jacob that this wasn't the only predicament he was facing this morning. *If only rowdy sailors were the start and end of my troubles.* 'Never a truer word spoken, friend.'

They arrived where they needed to be. The *Green Dragon* inn was part of Northhaven's outer ring, a sprawl of buildings spilling beyond the high battlements that protected the old town. It was a lot easier to apply for a licence from the city's aldermen to sell liquor this far out. But *this* far out also meant visitors never reached constables on the gates into the town's centre, where the ordinances to hand over weapons were enforced. An angry buzz resonated from behind the tavern's open doors. Jacob noted the flow of foot traffic moving away from the three-storey tavern. Those were the sensible ones. Fleeing the trouble. *So, how come I'm the only one heading towards it?* Jacob stepped up to the entrance; brownstone bricks, half-covered by climbing ivy, sunlight on windowpanes obscuring the drama unfolding within. Jay stood inside the tavern, a contemporary of Jacob's son. His blue constable's uniform seemed a couple of sizes too large for his frame – someone at the station with a sense of humour pranking the cadet officer. His pistol appeared equally out of place. The Landsman five-shot as jarring as finding a timberman's saw in the fingers of an infant – equally as dangerous to the boy wielding it as the patrons of the inn he was threatening.

The quarrelsome sailors had overturned the drinking hall's tables. One of their number held the gask from behind, a second man in front had a dagger pushed up against the twisted man's leathery brown neck. The gask looked young to Jacob. You could tell from the ridge of quills running along the side of his arms. Orange, not black, as a mature adult male's would be. His fingers were coiled around a little silver box; which, apart from its illuminated dials, might have been a tinder-lighter. Jacob noted the ring of patrons, farm labourers mostly, standing nervously apart from the rowdy seamen. Behind the long serving counter, old lady Kalem's staff crouched out of aim of the cadet constable. Old lady Kalem was as fearless in the face of the destruction of her drinking house as she was about anything else. The tavern's owner hurled abuse at the sailors from behind the heft of her heavy scattergun, her weapon seesawing on the counter with the best part of a small cannon's menace.

Jacob and Wiggins walked forward, the constable pushing down the cadet's pistol while the usual patrons moved aside for Jacob. There was a stillness and calm about the pastor ... the quiet before a stormfront. Some people called it a church aura, though not all the church's pastors possessed it. You didn't have to have met Jacob Carnehan before to feel it. There were many in the room that had never met the churchman before, but they fell aside with the same hesitant wariness. This pastor in his black jacket and his serious face and penetrating green eyes. No hat to cover his curly mop of dark hair. It was as though he carried an invisible lance before him, a space clearing, all eyes fixed upon him.

Jacob stopped just short of the puddle of spilled beer. He spoke to the mob of sailors, maybe twenty of them, his voice deep and resonant. 'You've been out at sea a long time, I know. The Lancean Ocean, more than half a year's sailing, with only the occasional island to steady your feet in between. Curled up so tight. A watch spring, ready to snap when it tries to unwind.'

'This one cheated us!' cried the sailor holding a knife against the gask's neck, his indignant tone wavering in the face of the pastor's still, quiet demeanour.

'I assure you, I did not,' said the gask, with the slight watery accent of all his people, his vocal cords jouncing against each other.

'I know,' said Jacob.

'He was counting cards on that abacus machine of his,' spat the knifeman.

Jacob shrugged. 'Of course he was. But not to rig your game. When a gask gambles, he has to make sure he doesn't offend against the laws of probability. If your friend here were winning too heavy, he'd have needed to fold his hand. Too much luck for him in the game would bring bad luck to the rest of his people out in the forests, right?'

'You are learned,' said the young gask. 'It is not wise to offend the harmony of averages.'

'And I appreciate your forbearance,' said Jacob, 'with these gentlemen of the ocean.'

'I'm the one with a blade pushed up against this dirty card-sharping leather-skin's neck,' said the sailor. 'Maybe you should be appreciating me more, here, in this arrangement?'

Seems like these fellows fresh off the boat don't know how hard adult gasks work to teach their young kin to master their temper. Or why. Jacob lifted up one of the cards spilled across the floorboards during the fracas. He nodded at the gask before tossing the card into the air. The muscles along the gask's brown arm swelled taut and an orange spine flicked out from the quills along the twisted man's forearm, impaling the card quivering against a wall.

'That's the reason gasks don't boil over,' Jacob told the astonished sailors, the man holding the gask from behind releasing his prisoner. The idiot had just realised how easily he could have been turned into a human pincushion. Jacob's words and the gask's demonstration both served their purpose. 'There's poison on a gask spine that'll have you dead on the floor in seconds.'

All fight fled from the sailors. The mob believed they had been in control, but in reality, they had been balancing on a precipice, dulled by drink and anger and too blind to see the fall in front of them.

'Set those tables back up,' ordered Wiggins. 'You lads can pay for any breakages before you leave.' He patted Jacob on the arm as the pastor headed towards the bar. 'They sure are as dumb as dirt.'

'They've never seen a gask before,' said Jacob.

'You ply foreign parts, you learn caution,' said Wiggins. 'Or if it ain't a gask to teach you better, it'll be someone else.'

'Like you said, they're young and ignorant.'

'Never seen a man talk 'em down like you can,' said Wiggins. Behind him, Cadet Constable Jay glowered at the sailors. Probably disappointed that he hadn't got to fire off a warning shot or bust some heads with his lead-weighted baton. 'Not all pastors got the way like you have. Maybe that wandering monk that comes begging through here every few years with his rice bowl stretched out. He can talk up a storm, or whistle a tornado out of existence like you can. But have you ever heard the pastor out at Redwater sermonise? Dry as tobacco in a curing chamber.'

'Better words than sharp steel,' said Jacob. 'Without words, people become wolves. Without words we forget ourselves.'

'Them words in the Bible?'

'All words are. All learning.'

Wiggins drew out a long noise at the back of his throat, something close to doubt. 'You know, I warned you that your boy would buck. Apprenticing him to the Librarians' Guild, sticking him in that windowless shelter below the hills. A boy like Carter, that's the same as burying him. I could've got him onto the high sheriff's rolls. If I can turn that young blockhead Jay into police, I surely could have done it for Carter Carnehan.'

'My son needs to reach for words more,' said Jacob. He tapped the grip of the constable's holstered pistol. 'I won't have him treating *that* as a tool of work. Violence solves nothing.'

'If you'd given the boy a little more of the back of your hand when he was younger, maybe ...' muttered Wiggins.

Jacob said nothing. It was too bad. *If my son had his way, he'd sign on with one of the captains in port as quick as a flash. But what kind of life would that be for Carter?* No roots in his life, years sailing the ocean, running short of drinking water and chewing on biscuits with more weevils than wheat. Storms flashing out of the immense waters, capable of ripping masts off a vessel and sweeping her crew into the depths. In exchange for what? Seeing strange lands? However far you travelled, wherever you landed, you always ran into yourself. Travel only ever offered the illusion of escape. A trick. A distraction. Human nature was the same everywhere.

Old lady Kalem had slipped her artillery piece back under the counter. The tavern's owner manoeuvred her large bulk opposite Jacob and Wiggins. 'Whisky, my dears?'

'A little early in the day for me,' said Jacob. 'A rice wine instead, perhaps.'

'I swear you must be part-Rodalian,' laughed the *Green Dragon*'s proprietor, bringing out a bulbous pottery decanter alongside a bottle of the local firewater. She dropped them both on the counter.

Deputy Wiggins rubbed his hands together approvingly. 'Sweet and warm.'

'Just like my soul,' Jacob smiled.

The young gask appeared at the pastor's side, requesting a lemon juice. Alcohol was a pure poison to gasks. Poison for most common pattern people too, but then Jacob had never met a man half as clever as the stupidest gask. The gask brushed the sawdust off his simple white cotton toga before he leaned across the counter to drink.

'You're a little early in town, friend?' said Wiggins. 'The monthly caravan from the forests isn't due in for another couple of weeks. You arrived early for the market tomorrow?'

'I am called Kerge among my people and I've come here from Quehanna in search of my mean,' said the gask. 'I thank you for your assistance.'

'Well, hell, you found a whole pack of mean among those sailors on shore leave.'

'He's talking about a spiritual journey,' Jacob corrected the constable. 'His people's wandering as they pass from child to adult. Kerge is seeking to weigh himself against fate, against probability.'

'Well, your luck nearly ran out on you here,' said Wiggins, downing his tumbler. 'Did some of that wandering myself when I was a pup. King's Cavalry, posted in the east; bandits and marauders like weeds out there back in the day.'

Kerge bowed towards Jacob. 'You are my balance. Fate led you to my path when my mean fell short.' He showed them his little silver box, pointing to a small screen flickering with moving numbers. For the gask it was his tarot deck.

The equations didn't mean a whole lot to Jacob. 'Life has a way of sending you what you need, Kerge, not what you want. You can call that fate if you like.'

'You are a priest in the church? I've heard there is some similarity of philosophy between the fates of the gask and the harmony of your god. May I have your name, manling?'

'Father Carnehan,' said Jacob. 'The ugly fellow here is Constable Wiggins, and I'll give you some more advice. In a town like North-haven, you're not testing your luck, you're pushing it. You need to journey on up through the old town's gates. Climb the hill. There are a few more constables and a lot less weapons behind the old city's walls.'

Kerge sipped at the lemon juice, his bear-like eyes blinking in appreciation at the tartness of the liquid. 'You are kind to a traveller. And your advice should shorten my journey.' He slipped his abacus machine into a simple leather satchel hanging across his shoulder.

Wiggins shook his head as the young gask left the tavern. 'Forest men blow into town as bare-assed as a monk with a begging bowl. Beats me how those leathernecks ever got so clever with machines, or find the money to make them. Reckon they've got an alchemist's mill out in the glades of Quehanna turning wood into gold?'

Jacob finished his rice wine. 'No police. No politics. No army. No brawling. No crime. No riots. No drinking or lighting up weed. The gasks put their passions into thinking and arts and invention, Mister Wiggins.'

'Life as quiet as all that, you won't live to reach two hundred years old, but it'll sure feel like it.'

'I believe that's called serenity.'

Wiggins looked at the sailors clearing up the smashed-up tavern. 'The forest people sure can gamble, though.'

'That they can.' The men of the forest didn't have much to do with the rest of Weyland, that much was certain. They had been separate from the main branch of mankind for so long that any union between a gask and a Weylander resulted in children born insane. *Too many twists on the spiral*, that was the midwives' old piece of wisdom. Damned if Jacob knew what spiral they meant, unless it was the serpent wrapped around a staff, the old healers' symbol, but he understood the sentiment. Forest people's minds were too different now; the gasks' prophetic gifts too dangerous to be held in common pattern flesh.

Jacob heard a train of horses pulling to a halt outside the inn and the pastor suspected *his* fortunes were about to take a turn for the worse. Confirming his premonition, one of the few men in town who could afford a private carriage with six horses on train came barrelling through the entrance. *Benner Landor.* The largest landowner in Northhaven. Probably the richest in the whole prefecture. *With enough ambition to propel him even further.*

'Father Carnehan,' said Benner, his eyes settling on the pastor next to the constable. 'Where do you think your son's at?'

Jacob lifted the fob-watch on his tunic. 'Well, I'm hoping he's at work in the library by now.'

'Try again,' said the landowner. 'There's a duel being fought over at Rake's Field this morning, and unless I've been misinformed, Carter and Duncan are both out there. Not—' he sucked in his cheeks '—mark you, as seconds.'

Jacob groaned out loud. 'Pistols or sabres?'

'Given there're two cavalry swords usually crossed above my fireplace that are missing, I would say the latter.' He looked at Wiggins, the constable's wizened fingers floating over a second whisky. 'And I think you'll find that duelling is still listed on King Marcus's statute books as an offence, even in a town as out of the way as Northhaven.'

'Only if someone dies in the duel,' sighed Wiggins. 'If they live ... well, there's nothing the girls find half so attractive as a duelling scar or two to mark that puppy fat.'

'Father,' growled Landor. 'Do you think Mary's going to share this ex-battalion roughhouser's view of one or both of our children ending up on the surgeon's slab?'

No. Jacob's wife would surely give him a few scars of his own if he let a duel involving their son go ahead.

'Make sure reparations are made,' Wiggins called back to Jay.

The constable hobbled after Jacob, looking to reach the coach. Wiggins sure wasn't about to walk out to Rake's Field at his age.

It was crowded in the carriage, bouncing along towards the woodland at the edge of town, rocking like a cradle on the rough roads. As well as Jacob, Wiggins and Benner Landor, they had the company of the landowner's daughter, Willow. Her warning about the duel, it seemed, was the spur behind their speedy departure to Northhaven's outskirts. Willow's long red hair swayed with the carriage's bumpy passage over the dirt track, the woman flashing little daggers of anger towards her father when she wasn't biting her lip in worry about her brother's plight.

'I should've packed the two of you off to an academy in the capital,' complained Landor, his words momentarily lost under the crack of the driver's whip and the clatter of hooves outside. The footman at the back of the carriage called out warnings to those on the road to leap aside. 'The promise I gave your mother on her deathbed was a mistake. Honeyed words about learning the running of the business here and staying close to the family. *This* behaviour is all that Duncan's learned at Northhaven. Brawling like a river-boatman over a spilled glass of rum.'

'It's a girl they're fighting over,' corrected Willow.

'Then you should've told me earlier,' said Landor.

'I only discovered the news from one of the staff an hour ago when I couldn't find my brother,' said Willow. 'You knew as soon as I did.'

'Which one?' asked Benner Landor. 'I mean which girl is the duel over, not which member of staff told you about this foolery?'

'Adella Cheyenne.'

'The daughter of old Cheyenne who keeps the minutes of the town's aldermen?' said Landor, his temper not best improved by the news. 'A clerk's daughter. *That's* who he's quarrelling over?'

Willow nodded.

'Your brother,' hissed Benner Landor, a finger poking the rich red upholstery of the carriage's interior as if it was his boy's ribs. 'Your brother. And what does he think he's going to do if he wins his duel? There's a whole season's worth of society beauties who'll be throwing themselves at Duncan for just a sniff of our wealth. Earls, barons, counts – fancy titles, draughty baronial mansions down south that need their roofs repaired, and not two farthings to rub together. That's the wife Duncan will be taking, not a *clerk's* daughter.'

'High hopes and great expectations,' snorted the constable. 'From a man that sweet-talked a timberman's daughter into going down the aisle with him. You sure you been distilling your corn for fuel, Benner Landor, not drinking it raw?'

'When I married Lorenn, we were starting out with nothing,' said Landor throwing an angry glance at Wiggins. 'We were equals and what we built, we built together. You think any nobleman's daughter would have taken *me* when I was a farmhand? Swans swim with swans, ducks swim with ducks, that's just the way it is.'

The constable spat out of the open window. 'You should've told me that's the way it is. I would've got the radiomen to send a message to King Marcus to set a princess aside for you. You don't want all the royal family married off before your boy gets to court.'

Landor looked to Jacob. 'What about you, pastor? You've not got an opinion?'

'You know I travelled here after I married Mary.' *And it doesn't matter how many years I've stayed. I'll always be an outsider.* 'Families want what's best for their children,' added Jacob. 'That's a natural yearning. It's not for me to pontificate to anyone else on what their *best* might be. I've got trouble enough convincing Carter of what constitutes a good path.'

'You could try letting himself find his own way,' suggested Willow, tartly.

Jacob's hand slipped down to a handgrip by the seat as the carriage twisted to one side. 'When you know where the bends in the road are, it is an unkindness not to call a warning to someone driving too fast.'

Benner Landor nodded. 'That's the way I'm thinking too. I wish there was some of your wisdom in our young men, pastor.'

Jacob held his peace. It was exactly what the son *had* inherited from the father that had him worried.

'And am I also expected to be married off to some earl's drooling, half-wit heir?' asked Willow. 'Or is one coat of arms to hang above the fireplace enough to satisfy the family's honour?'

'We'll see how that goes,' growled Landor. 'The Avisons of Grovebank have two sons who need to find matches, and the end of their land is only two hundred miles down the coast from the corner of our last farm.'

'Of course, why go to the expense of sending *me* to court, when there's a local idiot adjoining our corn fields?'

'When you've got four fool-headed grandchildren arguing about whose gambling bills the sale of our estate is going to pay off first, you'll be glad your long dead father had the sense to marry the Landors into a title they can't trade away as easily as their land.'

'You can always get your sons to marry a timberman's girls,' the constable winked at Willow. 'At least that way they'll always have wood for the fire as well as between their ears.'

The creaking of the carriage lessened as the six horses slowed. They were arriving by the woods. Benner Landor was out before the coach had even stopped, leaping down into the meadows in front of the woodland, the traditional setting for local duels. Far enough outside town that a stray bullet wouldn't catch a bystander; near enough that a wounded man could still be carried back to Northhaven's surgeons without bleeding-out more than a pint's worth of blood. *Grass before breakfast*, that was what the tradition was called. A polite euphemism for a brutal settling of so-called honour among dunces. And here were two of them, surrounded by a crowd of their jostling, jeering peers ... cheering on the clash of swords as Carter Carnehan and Duncan Landor parried and thrust at each other. A corded duelling line across the field was all that separated the pair, a boundary neither combatant was meant to step over. Nominally, it was to ensure the duel was to the first blood and not the death. Although much good that did the gallants frequently pulled wounded from Rake's Field.

'Thought those two were meant to be friends,' said Wiggins. 'Leastwise, it was always that pair trying to sneak into taverns together on the wrong side of the age ban.'

'They've moved on,' noted Willow, the sarcasm dripping from her voice. 'Now they're finding trouble with women who should know better, rather than at the bottom of an ale glass.'

Carter Carnehan and Duncan Landor might have been much the same in temper and temperament, but in looks they were poles apart – all they really shared was their height and frame – both tall and raised barn-strong by country living. Carter was dark-haired, his mane tending to unruly twists like his father, while Duncan possessed an untidy straw-coloured mop. Carter was dark-skinned and swarthy, a face all hard lines and as jutted as granite; Duncan's features fairer, the angelic suggestion of his handsome countenance undermined by a slight curl of superiority that often crinkled around the edges of his lips. Duncan waiting for the whole world to be given to him on a plate, Carter with nothing but an ageing pastor's hopes and worries. As dissimilar as they were, it had seemed natural to Jacob they had become fast friends growing up – two halves of a coin snapped apart and joined to make a whole. How had it come to this, their friendship spiked by the pressures of looming adulthood? *Well, their friendship might be skewered, but damned if I'm going to let these two young fools do the same to each other with sabres.*

Jacob could see the young woman Willow had mentioned on the side-lines. From the flushed look on her face, her hands clasped together in anticipation as if she was praying, she seemed to think that it was terribly exciting to have two beaus crossing blades on her behalf. Willow had Adella Cheyenne pegged straight all right. At their age, men needed a good woman's common-sense to stop them cracking antlers. A lady with as little insight as a man was as dangerous as a crowded inn on payday. Blockheads like Carter and Duncan needed civilising, not encouraging behind a duelling line.

Benner Landor was ahead of Jacob, bellowing his way through the onlookers, his large farmer's hands seizing members of the audience and shoving them out of his way. Not all of the onlookers were contemporaries of the two young men … new apprentices. There were gamblers and roughhousers aplenty; the kind of rascals who would've turned up to any duel, morning, afternoon or evening, just for a chance to view spilled blood. They sounded angry curses at the exertions of the barrel-chested estate owner cutting a passage through their ranks but the mob quietened down quick enough after they saw Constable Wiggins trailing in the landowner's wake. If this combat took a fatal turn, the audience could be locked up for incitement to murder. It took Benner Landor getting to the front of the circle of jeering brutes before the two participants realised that unwelcome company had arrived at their duel.

'You fool,' bellowed Benner Landor striding out, 'you damnable young fool. What are you doing here? Have the stealers got into you this morning?'

Stealers. Benner had used the old formal name for the demons that could worm a way into a man's soul and twist it to evil. Give Duncan

13

Landor his due; he seemed willing to brazen it out. 'It's a matter of *honour*.' Duncan said the last word as though it had been passed down to him on a scroll by an angel to protect him from his formidable father's wrath.

'Honour! Whose honour would that be, boy?'

Duncan pointed toward Carter and then Adella. 'This ruffian's slighted Adella. Says he's going to throw his post at the library and take passage on a ship at Redwater Harbour.'

'So what?' Benner Landor's voice wavered angrily. 'So this girl's the harbourmaster of Redwater is she? Making sure every Northhaven man fresh out of schooling has valid papers of apprenticeship with the seaman's guild? That's her job?'

'Carter said,' Duncan went on, faltering under the intensity of the large man's gaze, 'that Adella didn't matter to him as much as travelling.'

'You draw your sabre every time some Northhaven man gets bitten by the bug to see what's over the horizon and a girl takes hurt at it, I'd better build a log cabin here for you,' said Landor. He jabbed a finger at Adella and the slowly dissipating crowd. 'Because you'll be cracking steel here for the rest of your dumb life. A town clerk's daughter takes hurt; there are plenty of lamp-lighters and circuit riders around to pick up a sabre on her behalf. You want to fight duels for fun, you find a slighted countess from a good southern family to draw your blade out over.'

From the crestfallen look descended upon Adella's face, Jacob had a shrewd idea what game was playing out here. The pastor had spent enough afternoons drowning worms along the river with a rod and line to know that sometimes to snare the river's big fish you had to use a minnow as bait. Carter Carnehan was being played, and Jacob's young fool of a son was too full of fight to realise that he was the lure. The look of melancholy crossing Adella's young face was the river's big catch about to be yanked from her menu.

'What have you got to say, pastor?' demanded Benner Landor.

'That I raised my boy better than this,' said Jacob. 'Any fool can fight and most fools usually do. Violence is the last refuge of the incompetent. It solves nothing and only ever comes back to cut the hand wielding the blade.'

14

'Get into the coach,' Benner Landor ordered his son. 'Before I have the constable toss your tail in the gaol.'

Wiggins rested his hands on his hips and called out to the dwindling number of onlookers. 'Sabre practice is over ... back to your homes, all of you!'

Duncan reluctantly sloped off towards his father's coach, sliding his sword back into its scabbard. Carter passed his blade to a man who had been acting as his second, trying to ignore Duncan's sister who was fixing him with a stare strong enough to burn wood lacquer off a cabin's walls. The second carried Carter's borrowed weapon over to the carriage.

'This wasn't my doing,' Carter protested to Willow. 'Duncan challenged me. What was I to do, be known as the biggest coward in Northhaven?'

'I don't know who's the *biggest* idiot out of you two,' said Willow. 'It takes some choosing.' Willow shook her head wearily before following her brother to the family carriage.

'I'd offer you a lift back to the town,' Benner Landor told Jacob. 'But I reckon these two should be kept apart for a while.'

'We'll walk,' said Jacob, his gaze hardening on his son. *Carter's showing mighty little repentance for having come within a hair of running through a boy he used to call a friend.* 'And use the time to discuss this foolery.'

Carter watched the carriage depart with nonchalance. 'You mean you'll talk, Father, and I'll have to listen, same as it ever was.'

'You got something to say, boy?' said Jacob. 'Maybe about why you're out here brawling and not working at the library where you should be? About how you're planning to ship out from Redwater? Your mother agreed to sign your papers for the seaman's guild apprenticeship has she? Because I know I haven't.'

'You don't need an apprenticeship to sign on with a skipper. There are plenty of ships that will sign you on without papers.'

'Sure there are,' said Jacob. 'If you don't mind lighting out on some tub loaded down with twice as much cargo as she can safely carry. There're sheets on your bed more sturdy than the sails those seabed-scrapers venture out with. Use your head, boy. I want a son, a living son, not a collection of bones scattered on the bottom of an ocean.'

'Standing in the river tickling trout twice a week doesn't make you an expert on matters nautical,' said Carter. He looked around, noticing they were almost the last people left in the clearing. 'Where's Adella?'

'She got onto the Landor carriage. Old Benner might be tighter than bark on a tree but he's got a gentleman's manners to go with his self-made fortune.'

Carter angrily lashed out at a sod of grass with his boot. 'Damn!'

'Nobody held a gun to her head to make her accept the ride,' said Jacob. 'You think on that, boy. Then you think what your mother would have done to me, if I'd been the one out here.'

'You? What have *you* ever fought for?' said Duncan, bitterly.

'Only that which counts,' said Jacob. 'This is the trick of getting through life. Only stand up for what counts. Give it a few years, maybe you'll start to mull on *what counts* might be.'

'Why does everyone believe they got the right to tell me what to think and how to act and who to be?' spat Carter. 'You, that rich little turd Duncan, Adella, Willow, the Master of the Codex at the library. Do I tell any of you how to behave? Do I wake you up to nag you every minute of the day with your shortcomings? No! I keep it to myself; because I figure how you act and live is your concern. I think it's time I got some of the same courtesy!'

'And I think it time you finish the day where you should've started it. Working at the library. And to make sure you get there, I'll be walking with you every step of the way.'

In the end, Jacob and his wayward son only had to walk half the ten-mile journey to the library. They hitched a lift with a cart coming out from the Radiomen's Guild in town. Both men sat on the cart's tail, behind a pile of wooden crates, each box holding dozens of message tubes. The sun grew hotter. Jacob rested under the shade of the cart's tarpaulin cover – raised on four poles above the flatbed – while Carter swung his feet lazily in the bright light. Carter rode in silence. *Content to hold his tongue, or just annoyed with me?* As always, Jacob wondered about the contents of the messages. The colours of the wax seals indicated how far the messages had travelled to date. Most would have started their journey far beyond the Kingdom of Weyland's borders.

Some would have already travelled millions of miles ... far further than any man could hope to travel in his lifetime. Distant librarians passing knowledge on to faraway guild brothers, slowly updating the universal indexes and ancient encyclopaedias of knowledge. *A worthy and noble calling.* Unfortunately, Carter Carnehan seemed unable to share Jacob's enthusiasm for their mission.

Fertile golden fields of corn stretched out in between the woodland, slowly swaying in the gentle breeze. All owned by the Landors. Occasionally Jacob could see the mist of smoke from a fermentation tower, spherically stacked processors distilling corn oil into various strengths as well as producing ethanol. Landor's improved fermentation process had been the source of his fortune, his invention allowing him to squeeze out as much as a quarter more refined ethanol than any other landowner. Allowing him to buy up most of the farmland around Northhaven, too. It would be the landowner's son and daughter's fortune, one day. And the expanse of cornfields a reminder to Carter of all he didn't have to offer the girl he had set his heart on, every day he went to work. An hour out of town, Jacob caught sight of the library, their cart rounding a rise cut through pine woodlands. The road wound down through a valley and then up towards a series of foothills. Cut into the opposite slope stood the library's concrete entrance, big metal blast doors locked into place, a series of circular air vents rising out of rocks overgrown by shrubs and vines. In front of the entrance lay an area of flat dirt where travellers could draw up, a caravan already resting there. It must have arrived recently. A couple of wagoners waited outside the doors, speaking to library staff through an intercom. The caravan towered two storeys high, their living and home, both.

Carter had arrived late for the day's work and the staff inside weren't in the mood to listen to Jacob's apologies on behalf of his son, ordering Carter to handle business with the wagoners while his father repaid the cart driver's kindness by helping him unload message crates.

'I need sale prices for sheet glass,' the older of the two wagoners explained to Carter, his accent making the words hiss slightly on each 's'. 'For coastal towns within four months' travel from here, as well as the dates and locations of market fairs that will be held along the route.'

'Raise your right hand,' said Carter, sounding bored. 'Do you swear to carry no fire within the halls of the guild, and—' he indicated a brass plate in the corner of the archway imprinted with the library's rules '—abide by our ordinances and charges, as listed?'

The two men grunted affirmation.

'And payment?' asked Carter.

'Copper trading coins or rice,' said the wagoner. 'I'd prefer to pay from our rice sacks, see. Even dried, it's not going to keep forever.'

'Rice is fine,' said Carter, having to work to keep the sarcasm from his voice. 'You can never have too much rice.'

Carter went to the intercom and had a brief conversation with the staff. A small sally port inside the blast doors opened, a librarian emerging with a metal detector which she passed quickly over the clothes of the travellers. She made a snide remark about Carter's timekeeping before, satisfied the visitors were unarmed, allowing them access.

Jacob hefted one of the message crates towards the open entrance, nodding at the librarian. 'The most dangerous thing I've got is my son.'

'Pass,' said the librarian. 'He's more annoying than he is dangerous.' She glanced at Carter and tapped her blue tunic and the guild emblem sown there – a courier pigeon hovering above two open books. 'And *you* had better be dressed appropriately when you stand before the Master of the Codex, Carter Carnehan.'

There was no natural light inside. Oil lamps illuminated a long stone corridor beyond the door. The corn oil smell made Jacob's stomach rumble for the comforts of lunch. Inside – safe from fire, flood and bandits – the library's subterranean labyrinth was laid out like a wheel. A massive six-storey chamber for a hub, shelf-lined corridors as its spikes. Corridors led to reading rooms and lifts and stairwells down to lower levels where non-guild members were not permitted. All libraries, Jacob understood, were built on a similar pattern, always defended as carefully against nature as against man. A second librarian came out to meet the two wagoners. He escorted the travellers down a spiral stairwell to the floor of the main chamber. There, they sat at a wooden table that could have hosted fifty for supper, the librarian leaving to retrieve ledgers with the requested calendars and trade prices. Carter came back a couple of minutes later looking ill at ease dressed in his formal tunic and was dispatched to unload the remaining message crates, piling them inside a dumb waiter where they were winched out of sight. When the Master of the Codex appeared he nodded towards Jacob, and, as the churchman hoped, pointed down a book-lined passage to one of the reading rooms for a private meeting. Whereas Carter made his librarian's tunic look slovenly and ill fitting, Lucas Lettore wore his as if it had been hand-tailored to his short, fastidious frame.

Jacob started with an apology when they were out of earshot of the central chamber, but Lucas was having none of it. 'You warned me what to expect of your son, and he's certainly lived up to expectations.'

'He'll settle,' said Jacob, trying to keep any note of pleading from his voice. 'Given time.'

'Well,' sighed Lucas. 'If a churchman can't have faith who can?'

They ended up in a reading room, wood-lined walls concealing bare rock, a line of large map tables filling the centre of the room. The oil light from the lamp glass was just warm enough to make a man forget he was buried out of sight of the surface, standing here. Its illumination painted the wooden panelling a burnished orange, the arms of brass page-holders glinting across the tables.

'There are plenty of young men kicking up, now they've been cut loose from their studies,' said Jacob. 'You can go into any Northhaven tavern and see the trouble that comes from apprentices downing their first pay packet in a single night.'

'My guild hold isn't a tavern,' said Lucas, his eyes widening. There was something of the snake about those eyes, spiral-like. Sometimes Jacob expected them to spin if he stared too closely, trying to hypnotise him into taking his son back. 'The guild offers more than a simple apprenticeship. Our life is a calling. After Carter's first year probation, he will be expected to live inside the dormitory here, with home visits once a month or less. He could be assigned to another library.' Lucas leaned over the map table, running his fingers across the contour lines of coasts and mountains on yards of paper unrolled before them. 'You have to love what you do, Jacob. Your boy doesn't have a passion for books and I can't see him giving his life to preserving knowledge within the order. He can't lay out type on a letterpress to save his life. When I ask him to update a ledger with what arrives from the radiomen, there are as many mistakes as words in his entries – and that's if we can even find any volume he's re-shelved. You can lock Carter's body down here with us, but his mind's been far-called. *These* are the only thing he's ever paid any interest to inside the library. Our map tables.'

'He's not a traveller,' said Jacob, 'and my rectory is no caravan.'

'Well,' sighed Lucas, drawing the sound out. 'Your son certainly isn't any librarian. Those two wagoners you came in with; you know their accent isn't the same as the one they were raised with, nor what they'll end up speaking on their deathbed? The journey changes their accent, slowly, inevitably, with every mile they travel.' Lucas tapped the long unfurled map. 'This is a single tube's worth of charts laid out here. About two-hundred million square miles. I've got another seven-hundred tubes in just this map room. I've lost track of how many map rooms we have inside the library. And what we have here is only a tiny slice of all that lies out there.'

The journey changes the mind, but the mind can never change the journey. Jacob took the librarian's point, but the nearly infinite size of the world outside Northhaven was precisely what he was worried about. 'There's a horizon full of land to swallow a soul out there, Lucas. What's one man in the beyond, without friends or family to give him the foundations he needs to rely on?'

'The furthest update I've ever received was from somewhere called Jhark,' said Lucas. 'The transmission stamp on the message puts it at about ninety million miles away. Physically, I could ride a horse only a fraction of that distance in my lifetime. But up here—' he tapped his head '—with our archives, I can make a fair stab of understanding what life is like there – or at least, what it *was* like when that message first started to pass down the radiomen's relays. For you and I, that's more than enough. For your son, it is not. He wants to see a piece of the infinite for himself. To feel it under his boots and experience it.'

'Things are the same any place you travel to, consistent ...' Even as Jacob said the words, he knew he was trying to convince himself.

'Consistently appalling, you mean, Pastor,' smiled Lucas.

'Carter's talking about sneaking down to the harbour and trying to ship out unregistered,' said Jacob. His hand passed west over the vast waters on the map, towards the blackened patchwork of feuding states along the opposite shore of the seven-thousand-mile-wide Lancean Ocean. 'He's liable to get himself drugged and sold to some mercenary company over the water. Enslaved in the Burn as cannon fodder for one of their warlords.'

'My library isn't a prison,' said Lucas. 'And there are safer ways of working the wanderlust out of a young man's system.' He passed his fingers over the countries of the Lancean League, the nations hugging the eastern coast. 'Why not consider an apprenticeship for Carter with the Guild of Rails? He would be away a couple of years travelling the mainline circuit on a train – every league member as boring and civilised as we are in Weyland. He'd be back soon enough, after he realises that the water that runs through our neighbours' land is no sweeter than the streams of home.'

'What if he doesn't come back? Things are meant to be better down south. Bigger cities, wealthier living.'

Lucas laughed. 'That's merely a function of our kingdom's position at the far end of the caravan routes. They still have resources somewhere down south, metals and ores and chemicals, and the caravans don't have so far to travel to bring raw materials up to trade. Are you worried that Carter will be seduced by a life of ease? Do you think he is the sort of man who cares if he owns a machine that can cool and preserve food, or another that can steam his clothes clean?'

'He might.' Even as Jacob said the words, he heard the uncertainty in his own voice. How much of that was true and how much of it was an excuse? He and Mary had lost Carter's two brothers to the plague, lost them far too young. The pain was meant to pass, eventually. Everyone said it would. But after a decade had gone by, there wasn't a week that passed when Jacob didn't think of his dead sons and mourn their loss. How much of what he and Mary did now was just trying to clutch onto Carter too tight for his own good?

'In this matter, at least, I think you underestimate Carter,' said the library hold's master. 'He yearns for adventure. I would be more worried about him heading north, to the real edges of the caravan route. There are northern states where they carry only swords and bows to repel the nomadic hordes of the Arak-natikh steppes. Countries situated too far away from the passage of ores to build even the simple life we enjoy in Weyland. No metal for machines in their towns. Not even lead type for a printing press. Only iron for the swords that protect your village. That's what Carter thinks he wants. Not lanterns lit by the pulse of electricity, but the life of an adventurer or a sailor or a caravan guard. So, you must both compromise. Secure Carter a position with the Guild of Rails and point him towards the civilised heart of the league. Let him travel.'

'Mary worries about Carter's wild ways when he's no further than a cart ride away from our home,' said Jacob. 'How can I sell her a couple of years riding a railway carriage?'

'You're a good man, Jacob Carnehan, but you worry too much. Sometimes matters just have to run their course.'

Jacob sucked in his cheeks. *Two years.* And was he going to raise that little matter before or after he told his wife about having to drag Carter away from crossed sabres with the Landors' heir?

Carter trudged down the gallery of shelves as if the weight of the world was on his shoulders. Actually, it wasn't the world's weight. It was the barrel of water strapped to his back, a rubber hose attached to a spigot on its side ... a wooden nozzle to refill humidifier boxes mounted on the wall like bird feeders every hundred yards.

'Dry paper is dead paper,' muttered Carter, aping the Master of the Codex's voice as he soaked the sponge-like filling of the nearest box. 'And books with dead paper will eventually die. Control the environment, limit the sunlight and the archives' pages will prosper.'

Hell, I'd be better off breaking my back in one of Benner Landor's fields. At least I'd feel the wind on my face and the sun on my neck, watering something other than these old tomes.

A librarian poked his head through the archway into the chamber, snapping Carter out of his mood of despondency. 'Got a job. The master says you're the lad for it.'

'Really? Then I'm betting it's not one of the better tasks on today's rota.'

The other man grinned. 'I was late three days in a row during my apprenticeship. Master Lettore had me humping re-shelving crates for so long I thought I was on probation with the longshoremen, not the librarians.'

Carter clipped the hose back onto the barrel. 'Well, I've already unloaded the last message cart of the day, so I know there's nothing heavy that needs humping.'

'There's an old tramp at the entrance, hollering and banging on the gate. Sounds as mad as a sailor marooned six months with only sun and seawater for company.'

Isn't that fine and dandy? Another way to punish me. 'And what would the master like me to do?'

'Deal with the vagrant, Mister Carnehan. Use your initiative.'

Carter left the chamber, racked his humidifier in the storeroom and walked the stairs up five levels to reach the entrance. He slid open the sally door's metal hatch to see what he was dealing with. Outside, the tramp had abandoned his attempts to communicate via the intercom and was dancing a mad jig around the caravan's traveller children. Wide, watery eyes blinked as he capered and croaked a badly out-of-tune song. Happy to have new company, the children seemed delighted to frolic with the lunatic, although an old matriarch was keeping a wary eye on this exuberant newcomer. The object of Carter's attention wore a bright brown leather coat that flapped around his riding boots, kicking up dust. Carter had never seen a coat like the one worn by the tramp, carefully etched with hundreds of intricate pictures as though they were tattoos in leather. In his hand he thumped a sturdy walker's staff into the dirt, using it as a maypole to lift his legs off the ground. Hanging off the man's jutting chin, a long straggly white beard swished through the air that surely would have benefited from the attentions of a bath and comb.

Carter was half-tempted to leave him outside, cavorting for the travellers, and tell the Master of the Codex he had dealt with the vagrant. But the traditions of courtesy to strangers were too strong in Carter's blood to allow him to lie, even if it meant having to talk to this odd-looking lunatic. Unlocking the sally port, Carter stepped outside in the sunshine and felt the brief joy of being in the open, not stuck in that badger warren of desiccated learning behind him.

'Old man!' Carter called to the tramp. 'Over here.'

Glancing up, a look of surprise creased his features. He halted his dance around the caravan, lurching forward towards the entrance. 'Am I old?' The tramp's voice creaked like his words were being dragged over gravel, too many nights spent out under the stars with mossy woodland clearings for his mattress.

'I'd say you are. Maybe sixty, seventy years?'

'Oh, I shouldn't count that as old. Are you the baron?'

'Baron of what?'

The tramp jabbed his walking staff towards the metal gate buried in the hillside. 'Of yonder castle ...'

'Isn't much of a castle. That's a guild hold, old man. The Guild of Librarians. You know ... archives, knowledge?'

'Ah, reading!' smiled the tramp. His teeth gleamed white and perfect. He'd clearly never wheedled enough coins for tobacco or whisky to stain them properly. There were dentists in Northhaven with poorer sets of dentures than his. 'I do so love reading. And food, of course. A *good* meal. Nothing fortifies the soul more than reading a good book having first been served with a hearty stew.'

Carter took the hint. 'If you're claiming visitor's poverty, I can enter you in the *Ledger of Salt and Roof* and give you a drink and a feed.'

'Poverty? Why, young man, I am insulted! Yes, I am. I shall pay, naturally.'

'You can pay?'

'Of course, through the telling of fine tales.' He ran a finger along the images on the leather coat. 'All of these are stories. I have recounted them to kings and presidents and sultans and princes and emperors the length of Pellas – *all* have been entertained and none have been left disappointed.'

Well, the hobo hasn't met the Master Codex; there's a man who'd surely slid out of his mother's womb with a disappointed look on his face. Pellas. The hobo had used the archaic, formal name for the world. Not a word you often heard. *A bard then, with a sideline in panhandling.*

Carter reluctantly led him through the entrance. 'Let's just enter you in our *Ledger of Salt and Roof*, and call it quits. One meal, mind, and you can't sleep inside. Only the guild's members are allowed to sleep underground. There are a couple of log shelters down a path behind that caravan there. They belong to us. You're welcome to bunk in one of them for a while.'

'If I do that, I won't be able to see the stars, and I do so enjoy the stars' company.'

'I'll need your name for the ledger, Mister ...'

'Sariel, that's what the stars call me.'

'They do?'

'Oh yes. They often whisper to me during the long nights, recounting new stories to illustrate on my coat. It was the Duchess of Krinard, a courteous lady and a great scholar, who taught me how to communicate with the stars. She owned a telescope cut from a single great diamond and she kept two hundred ravens to drag it into position every night. Perhaps I could teach you the trick of communicating with the heavens, Mister ...?'

'Carter Carnehan. That's kind of you, but I'll pass. If you walk through Northhaven, maybe you can show my father. He's a great one for watching the sky at night.'

Sariel ran a hand through the hedge of wiry white hair above his wrinkled forehead. 'The stars undoubtedly whisper to him, too. He must be trying to hear the heavenly orbs better.'

Carter led the tramp through the most indirect route he could think of to avoid the other librarians. The *Ledger of Salt and Roof* was really intended for wandering monks, maybe merchants who had fallen on hard times and were reaching the end of their supplies as they passed the guild's hold. It wasn't meant for any lazy rascal who fancied a free supper at the guild's expense, but here was Carter, using his 'discretion' in a way guaranteed to rile the Master Codex when he asked how Carter had dealt with the tramp. *I guess I just like making mischief.* Carter avoided the hold's refectory, seating the tramp at a reading table in the corner of the nearest map room, leaving him there while he slipped into the kitchens – liberating a jug of water, flat bread, cold ham, cheese and a bowl of rice along with a glass vessel filled with soy sauce. It wasn't the hearty stew the hobo had hinted at, but the librarians preferred rations as plain and bland as their lives. Balancing the food on a wooden tray, Carter carried it back to the map room.

As Carter slipped through the doorway, he found Sariel leaning over one of the map tables, swaying from side to side and banging his temple with his left hand. 'It's so big, so large, so much of it.

I remember the size now, how could I ever have forgotten? I'm no better than a fobbing, evil-eyed horn-beast.'

Carter felt a twinge of nerves. Just how unbalanced was his unpredictable guest? Carter hadn't swept him for matches or a flintbox, either, before allowing him inside the hold. Carter's apprenticeship might be miserable, but he didn't want to end his tenure with the first fire in the library's recorded history. 'I've got your meal here, old fellow. Sit down.'

'I apologise. I suffer headaches sometimes. So many stories cluttered inside my mind, plotting and planning with each other. Which nation does your castle lie in, Lord Carnehan?'

'Come south over the mountains, have you? Through Rodal? This country is Weyland, old fellow. We're part of the Lanca, just like Rodal. You understand? Part of the Lancean League? You will be walking for a couple of decades before you're free of the league. Every country south of here and a few more out to the east, all part of the Lanca, all as quiet and peaceful as a church social in the meadows with the picnic blankets laid out.'

'No, I don't think I recall mountains. Sea, there was a significant surfeit of sea. Waves as big as mountains crashing down on top of us … of those there were plenty.'

'Worked passage on a vessel, did you? Shipped in from the west? Know how to rig a schooner as well as spin a yarn?'

'A schooner? Twenty-five sails hung across seven proud masts,' said Sariel, tugging his silver beard as if he could wring information out of the hair. 'No, of course not, don't be ridiculous. I crossed the ocean on a pod of whales, borne by the noblest of those great mammals of the sea, the Prince of Baleens. He was grieving for the loss of his favourite cow, what we would call his wife. He sang only songs of sorrow for the entire journey. So many tears shed, my lord, sometimes it was hard to know where the tears ended and the ocean began. I'm not embarrassed to say I wept for his loss.'

Whatever sense of sadness Sariel felt, it didn't seem to make much difference to the old beggar's ability to work his way through the pile of food Carter had delivered. His gnarled old fingers tore into the bread, using the knife Carter had fetched to hack at the cheese and ham. Then he emptied half the soy sauce over the cold rice, letting it drown, before rescuing it with his spoon.

Sariel raised a mug of water, regarding it suspiciously. For someone who'd supposedly crossed an ocean of it, he didn't seem much inclined to drink the stuff. He tapped the mug. 'Nothing stronger?'

'Once a year, to celebrate the day when a whole year's worth of radio messages have been entered in every journal, tome, history, codex and atlas racked on our shelves. Then we start again. Come back in eight months and I'll be glad to serve you some rice wine. We're holier than monks down here.'

Sariel reluctantly swigged from the mug while demolishing the meal's remains, chasing crumbs with his knife. As mangy as the down-on-his-luck bard was, Carter felt a surge of sympathy for the sly old devil. *Is this what people warn about when they talk of young minds being far-called?* Wandering without finish across lands that never ended. Bereft of friends and family. Letting empty spaces and the almost infinite wilderness fill your mind with madness, until the day came when you turned up at a town and all you could talk was nonsense about riding fish and your good friends the stag and the hare? No job, no prospects, no kin. Was Carter looking at himself in sixty years times if he abandoned his stultifying apprenticeship? *No, surely not. I'd be stronger than Sariel. It isn't a crime to want to see more of the world than the dust on top of the guild's atlases.*

'What did you find out there, Sariel? Did you really cross the ocean? See anything of the war on the far shore ... travel through the Burn?'

'Oh, surely,' said Sariel, wiping crumbs out of his wiry white beard. 'All the countries and kingdoms of the Burn at each other's throats, killing and murdering for longer than most empires have stood. Lands as black as night, the very ground murdered by continual combat, unable to push out more than a single stalk of corn from their field, and that a sickly weak-whore weed of a plant. Brigands for princes and killers for police and cannibals for judges. It was in the Burn that I met Oak-legged Andal, his legs so powerful he could vault into the sky with a single bound. He tied sails to his arms and loved to glide so high, where the world's pull is less than the tug of a feather. Together we fought an evil warlord, the Sultan Gram. Ah, the sultan! Never have you met such an impertinent, fool-born bombast. Gram had enslaved a host of nations, setting them to building a massive firework as tall as a mountain, a rocket to carry him and his court far from the Burn's ruins. But Oak-legged Andal and I foiled the sultan's scheme and paid him back for the millions of peasants the devil had worked to death constructing his grotesque folly. We sabotaged the rocket's mechanism and when he mounted the vessel, it kept on going straight up.'

'And what happened then?'

'The firework melted, of course. Turned to a slag by the sun, and he fell back, landing in one of the neighbouring states. There, refugees who had survived the sultan's predations fell upon him, tied him to a spit and cut slices of him off to feed their dogs, just as the sultan's soldiers had done to their families.'

Carter felt a pang of disappointment. *This old beggar probably hadn't travelled further than the Marshes of Hellin.*

'There are no happy melodies sung in the Burn, only lamentations. Nobody in the lands is willing to honour the traditions of salt and roof to deserving strangers such as I.'

'If you're finished, Sariel, I'll guide you to a cabin down the valley. If you're found here by the others, I reckon it'll be the tradition of salt and boot up the back-side that's offered to you by my guild master.'

The mad old bard pushed his empty plate aside. 'You lead, Lord Carnehan, and I shall follow. What did I say my name was again?'

'Sariel.'

'Yes, that's it. So much to remember, so much that's forgotten.'

'If you're still here tomorrow, I'll fetch you another meal to see you on your way. But I'll bring breakfast out to you, old fellow, understand? Better all round that way.'

'Your nobility is a shining beacon to lesser men, Lord Carnehan.'

'I'm no lord, old fellow. Not unless I'm lord of refilling humidifier boxes.'

'An outrage!' said Sariel, his voice growing dangerously loud, a magnet for any passing librarian to investigate. 'But you are in luck. It was the Tsarina of Nera-ka herself who installed me as the Secret Master of the Grand Order of Protectors. I shall knight you forthwith, indeed, that is what I shall do. Kneel ...'

Carter sighed and dropped to one knee. Better to humour the old beggar than be found out and forbidden to bed him down in their guest cabins. Sariel lowered his walking staff on Carter's shoulders, the left first, then the right. The wood felt heavier than granite, and for a second Carter had the oddest sensation he was being pushed into the ground. As quick as the strange feeling arrived, it fled. The old tramp incanted, 'Carter Carnehan, you go to your knees as a commoner, but you shall rise as a knight of the order of the Grand Order of Protectors, lord of this hold, most beloved of the Tsarina Nera-ka. May her blessings straighten your aim and give strength to your arm in defence of her code most chivalrous.'

Carter got to his feet and murmured an insincere-sounding thanks to the beggar. *If my arm had been a bit stronger and quicker this morning, I could have taught Duncan Landor a fine lesson about poking his nose in another man's affairs.*

Sariel leaned conspiratorially across as Carter led the bard back out through corridors and stairwells rarely traversed by the library's journeymen. 'Now you are a fellow brother of the order, perhaps I can tempt you to our cause? There is a wicked emperor who plots dominion over all things. And only those of good heart may band together to stop him.'

'I'm afraid the duties of my hold are currently a little heavy right now, old fellow. The good people of Weyland need their knowledge transcribed, codified, copied and bound. But maybe another day ...'

'Of course,' said Sariel. 'Any noble who does not rule for the people hardly deserves their office. I believe the family of travellers camped outside will be only too eager to join me in my quest. I once did a considerable favour for the goddess of that particular clan, Lady Gameesh, and ever since, their descendants have held me in considerable regard.'

'No doubt,' said Carter. *Yes, no doubt.*

Carter led the beggarly bard to one of the guest huts outside, settled him and his impossible tales in for the rest of the day and started to walk back to the hold. He had just reached the hold's entrance in the slopes when he spotted Willow riding fast through the valley on her favourite sorrel mare. Carter raised his hand in greeting, hoping that she might have forgiven him for this morning's fracas with her brother. When Carter had been fast friends with Duncan, he had developed quite a crush on the boy's sister, but a chance remark from Benner Landor when Carter had been visiting their great estate had made him realise that Willow was destined for better things than a dirt-poor pastor's son. What had it been? *Swans swim with swans, boy.* Something like that. A simple enough remark, but at the time it had kicked the foundations out from under Carter's feet, leaving him feeling miserable and wretched for weeks. He was older now. He knew how the world worked. Willow Landor would marry some rich landowner's son – or maybe one of the southern mill owners. A dynastic match. While Carter's family expected him to drown in boredom out here, little better than a monk taken a vow of poverty and chastity. Of course she wouldn't look twice at him – what had he been thinking? He should have resented Willow and her wealth and her perfect future mapped out with such precision. But somehow, he still couldn't. What Carter had once felt for her was a wound he had cauterised, bound and would never uncover again, its ugliness a reminder of how he had been a big enough fool for taking it in the first place.

Willow drew the chestnut-coloured horse to a halt in front of him, its nostrils flaring with the excitement of the canter. Corn-fed, of course, the best you could breed and as fast as lightning. Carter's father kept one old nag in a rented stall in the new town's stables, a gelding called *Icabob*, for the times when he needed to visit parishioners outside the town. Blind in one eye and well past its prime. Carter had learnt to ride on it but the other children had called out jokes when they saw him swaying on the elderly nag. He'd rather walk or hitch a lift with the regular message run to the library than be seen riding Icabob, now.

Willow raised an eyebrow. 'The Master of the Codex hasn't cancelled your apprenticeship yet, then?'

'I'd need to burn a few books to get booted out,' said Carter, knowing the very idea would be sacrilege to Willow. 'Hey, maybe that's an idea!'

'If you value learning so little,' said Willow, rising to the bait, 'maybe you could take off to the north and join one of the nomadic hordes beyond the mountains? Of course, you'd have to leave off burning an atlas or two to actually *find* the steppes.'

'Oh, I can navigate well enough with a compass and the stars,' smiled Carter. 'It'd be a novel experience anyway, walking across an acre of land that *doesn't* belong to your family. Nice afternoon for a bit of leisurely riding. Or are you off to count the full fuel stills over those hills?'

'I'm off,' said Willow, a little irritated, 'to see why one of our land agents thinks a family should be evicted from a farm close to the forest. I've heard rumours that the father's been ill out there and that's why they've fallen behind with the rent. If I left such decisions to you *men*, then they'd be out on their ear without a second thought to what's really happening on the farm.'

'Well, there are always more tenants where they came from.'

Willow scowled. 'With an attitude like that, if you do get tossed out of the librarian's guild, you should travel to Hawkland Park and ask my father for a job as a land agent. He'd be glad to have you.'

'What and end up working for Duncan? That's why I'm getting out of Northhaven, one way or another.'

'And you don't think *I'm* worthy enough to inherit the estate on my own terms?'

'You wanted that job; you should have let me fillet Duncan with a sabre this morning.'

Willow snorted. 'Really? Do you think so? Good day to you then, Mister Carnehan.' She put the spur into her mare and the horse galloped away.

Carter exhaled slowly, trying to suppress his anger. That hadn't gone quite as well as he had hoped. *Oh well.* Willow was her brother's sister, that much was certain. Every month, Duncan Landor became more like his grasping self-important father. It was no wonder the heir to Hawkland Park wanted Adella so intensely. Duncan's gaze had rested on something he didn't have, couldn't have, and it itched him like a bad shirt. Adella was about the only reason for Carter to stay in the prefecture, or was it the need to deny her to Duncan? Damned if he really knew. Or maybe he did, and he didn't want to recognise the answer. Sadly, Adella had shown no interest in leaving Northhaven. But that was Adella for you. Home and hearth close to their family and the familiar was what she yearned for, not new sights out in the infinite. Carter knew exactly how matters would develop after he left the prefecture. Duncan would sweep Adella off her feet and every-thing would be fine for a year or two. But then some rich southern girl would show up, a match 'worthy' of a Landor, and poor Adella would be tossed aside like a rusty nail, bitter and broken as the Landor heir discovered a fresh itch that needed scratching. If Duncan was this competitive and hostile when the pampered pup was waiting in the wings to take over from his old man, how bad would he be when he finally sat on Benner Landor's immense pile of wealth? It didn't bear thinking about. *You'll be long gone by then, Carter Carnehan. It'll be some other fool's problem.* Carter cursed his father's intervention out on the field. Didn't the pastor understand there were some matters that couldn't be settled by prayer and good intentions, only blood? The two of them should have settled their hard business there and then. Carter could have skewered the rich young idiot's leg and left Duncan Landor a limp to remember him by every time he hobbled across one of the House of Landor's numerous holdings. That would have been the best way imaginable for Carter to sail away from Northhaven for a new life. Duncan Landor left lame and with a lesson in manners that would surely teach him a valuable lesson about the true nature of his fellow Weylanders. They were free men in the north, not vassals or serfs. The pockets that the House of Landor filled with their coins in the prefecture entitled the paymaster to an honest day's labour, not the recipient's life and soul. Who the hell did Duncan Landor think he was, ordering Carter around like one of his damn stable boys? They could stick it up their arse, the whole bloody house … the controlling patriarch, the haughty daughter and the arrogant prick of a son.

Carter slapped his leg in anger, relishing the sting of it, something real as he watched Duncan's snappish sister disappear over the hill on her horse, towards some poor unsuspecting farmhouse filled with tenants who were about to get a tedious lecture in proper economy and their own good business. 'Goodbye, Willow Landor.'

Back to wiping the dust off damned bookshelves.

Carter lifted his fork, letting it toy with the pork crackling on the side of his plate. When his father said nothing, that is all it was. His father saying nothing: an absence of noise, maybe tinged with a vein of solemnity. When his mother said nothing, she could make the silence more intense and far worse than any shouting fit.

'Maybe some more gravy?' said Carter.

His mother reached across the table and banged the hefty pottery jug down in front of him, still saying not a word.

'What was I going to do?' said Carter, giving in and breaking the uncomfortable silence. 'I was called out. I didn't start the duel.'

'Walk on by,' said Mary Carnehan. 'When trouble comes, you just walk on *by*. Nobody that matters would think any less of you.'

'Only everyone I know,' hissed Carter. 'My friends, all of our neighbours, even those dusty bookbinders buried under the hillside.' He looked across the table at his father. 'You told me that a man's honour is like his soul – his to keep and no one else's.'

'It's like a knife, boy,' grumbled his father. 'It's got to grind up against life to stay sharp and stay in its guard until its edge is truly needed. That means holding your temper, treating your neighbours well, helping strangers, and not looking to sink a sabre into the gut of a man you were calling friend up until last year.'

'What, you afraid old Benner Landor will forbid his tenant farmers to come to church on Bible day?' laughed Carter. 'Their family might hold every acre worth owning out to the sunset, but Duncan Landor doesn't own me. *He* doesn't get to push me around, he doesn't get to order me about!'

Mary Carnehan banged the table, making the heavy plates jump across the polished oak. 'Do *I* get to tell you what to do, under my roof, my own blood?'

'I'm working out at the library, aren't I?'

'And saving your money for a riverboat ticket down to the coast by the sounds of it,' she added, raising her fork towards Carter. 'Is that the way it's going to be? I wake up one morning and your bed is empty and your clothes are packed in a roll tied to your back?'

'I've respected your wishes well enough,' said Carter. 'I even withdrew my name from the rolls of the territorial army. Two weeks with the home regiment, filling in as marines for an exercise with the royal fleet. It was a couple of weeks away and I couldn't even do that.'

'It's dangerous,' she protested.

'Dangerous?' retorted Carter. 'Redwater hasn't seen a lick of pirates' masts for centuries.' Carter was used to his mother lecturing him. As one of the teachers at the local royal free school, she had pretty much been doing it since he had been able to talk. When he got his lessons right, the others in his class would rib him about his parents ... the teacher and the pastor. When he got them wrong, they'd lay into him even worse. Much like his duel with Duncan Landor, life always seemed determined to damn him for a coward if he ran, and brand him a scoundrel and hothead if he fought. A big pile of *lose* at either end of the street.

Mary Carnehan wasn't about to back down. 'Clumsy drunken idiots from town playing at being marines for two weeks, tumbling down from masts, letting cannons roll over their toes and toasting each other's foolery with rum before falling over the side of a ship.'

'Sounds better than filing paper for the Master of the Codex.'

Mary Carnehan jumped out of her chair and yanked open the kitchen curtains. Across from the rectory lay its graveyard, the church silhouetted against a velvet night embedded with pale stars. 'When the plague took your brothers, I made a vow before the saints that nothing would happen to you.'

'Well, your vow's been kept,' said Carter. 'Nothing's ever happened in my life. That was over ten years ago.'

'Ten years,' his mother seemed startled by the truth of it, sitting down as if she had been struck. That was often the way with his mother's fire and passions. They would bloom and flare before petering out as quickly as they had risen.

'Corn oil isn't Northhaven's main crop,' said Carter. 'It's boredom we're growing out in our fields.'

'Boring's just fine,' said Jacob, poking at a roast potato.

Yes, his father, the pastor, was more of a river. Slow, steady, but relentless. Able to wear boulders down to pebbles given enough time. 'Although I appreciate it takes time to grow into that conclusion. How about we take a stroll as a family? Look at the stars and see how many of the constellations' names you can remember?'

Carter shrugged. What was the point of learning to navigate by the stars if you never went further than the woodland on your doorstep?

'No, it's late and getting cold,' said Mary, drawing on a shawl hanging on the back of her chair. 'Throw some more woodchips in the heater.'

Carter's father stood up. He opened the door of the box nesting inside their fireplace. 'We're running low. Need to lay in a couple of barrels' worth before autumn and the prices start to rise.'

'Market week begins tomorrow,' said Mary. 'Best we don't get any from the Chethill timbermen this time. Don't know what kinds of trees they cut for lumber in Chethill, but their chips smell worse than cigar smoke when you burn them. If we wait for the end of the week there'll be a caravan in from the east. Gask wood chips, those I like.'

'I saw one of them earlier today,' Jacob smiled. 'A young gask rolling his luck around like dice and calling it holy. Plays cards a mite too slick for the patrons of the *Green Dragon*.'

'Short-root Tobacco Cedar,' said Carter.

'What?' Carter's mother looked intently at him.

'That's what they grow in the forests down at Chethill. You know. Library. Archives. Atlases.'

What type of woodchips to lay down for winter – damn. 'The excitement never stops,' Carter whispered into his plate.

TWO

WHAT YOU HAVE TO SELL

Much like the Landor mansion itself, the family's dining hall at Hawk-land Park was massive, rising through two of the mansion's three storeys; well, four, if you included the maze of basement rooms and storage chambers below. The hall floor had been lined in dark brown wood, polished up to a mirror shine. A mahogany gallery ran all the way around the second storey, hanging off castle-thick grey limestone, walls mounted with colourful metal shields and the stuffed heads of stags and deer and mountain lions. Duncan Landor never much saw the point of that gallery; enough helms and crests to keep a chamber of heralds busy for a year studying all the mantlings and coronets. Were the Landors expecting to invite a couple of hundred locals inside to fill the gallery anytime soon? A hungry crowd to watch the feast below, scrutinise the Landors stuffing themselves on silver platters full of more sliced meats and garnished fish than a wharf full of hungry dockers could be expected to finish? That was the thing about great wealth. Most of it seemed to bring no comfort that meant anything to Duncan Landor, and the rest just seemed to deliver duties and responsibilities which none of his friends were required to shoulder as burdens. Didn't seem much point in having an army of retainers in dark tunics and starched white shirts either, just because they were *expected*. Expected by whom, exactly? The same people who seemed to think that the best way to get a chuck of steaming beef on your plate was to ask the head butler who would ask the footman, who would carefully serve it across Duncan's plate in twice the time it'd take him to reach out and pick the piece he wanted. The people with all those expectations didn't seem to inhabit Northhaven. *Maybe they live down south in the large cities and the capital, Arcadia? God knows, my father seems to talk about them enough.*

Willow didn't seem too bothered by the ridiculous formality of dinner at Hawkland Park. Seated so far down the table for supper that Duncan might as well have commissioned the radiomen to pass his sister messages, rather than hear his voice echo around the cavernous space. People said Willow took after their mother, but with Lorenn Landor in the grave from the fever from almost before Duncan could remember, he only had the oil painting of his mother hanging up above their fireplace to go by. Same red curls, maybe. Same pert lips and quizzical look as she chewed thoughtfully, but he doubted if his tall sister took after their mother in character. There were plenty of people in Hawkland Park who still fondly remembered Lorenn Landor, and from the sound of it, she'd had none of the pretensions of her husband. A simple woodsman's daughter who had appreciated the luck that had brought her family to this position. A mixture of hard work and common-sense. Unlike Willow, she wouldn't have played along with all of this – every meal set like a court banquet; formal clothes laundered daily and passed on as soon as they began to wear. She would've told Benner Landor to shut his face and patch the kids' jacket sleeves the same as everyone else, and what the hell do you mean we got to go through this pomp and circumstance just to get some victuals down you? Northhaven ain't the royal court and you, Benner Landor, you squat old fool, you ain't King Marcus, so get over yourself.

Willow took matters at her ease, calmly, serenely, as if it didn't affect her. Nothing fazed her. Calm, always so damn calm and logical about matters. As though this was normal, which it surely was not. Did she think that cold-hearted fool Carter Carnehan was sitting at home right now, asking three ranks of servants if they could maybe, please, pass some horseradish for the steak? No, he'd be talking and laughing with his parents like a real family. Probably boasting about how Duncan Landor couldn't hold a sabre worth a damn because his father expected him to hire a fencing master to stand in his stead as champion, rather than facing Carter down like any normal man would. Saints, it would have been good to have given Carter Carnehan a fine cut or two at Rake's Field. It was a lesson he sorely needed. And Duncan knew the bull-headed fool well enough to see that their business hadn't been cancelled, merely postponed to another day. Just the thought of it made him shake with anger; want to send the plates and glasses flying off the table as he seized one of the ornamental swords from the hall and set off to avenge Carter's slights against Adella. That's how it would have been done in the old days. Blood for blood, until one of them was finished.

'You need to travel to the wharves tomorrow morning,' said Benner Landor, bringing Duncan back to the present. 'Early. We need to take an inventory, every tank of ether, every barrel of oil accounted for. And when that's finished, same needs doing in the yards at the rail-head.'

'It'll need maybe fifty clerks to do all of that,' said Duncan. 'Fifty-one makes no difference.'

'The difference,' said Benner Landor, his voice heavy and weary, 'is that a Landor needs to supervise the count. So that some half-arsed yard-hand and his wharf rat friend isn't tempted to pull our cargo and re-stamp the manifest with the name of their cousin's damn farm, rather than the House of Landor.'

'So you don't trust our staff to run an honest inventory?'

'I trust our people to act like *people*. When you're not minding the shop, you're hanging a sign up asking the next customer through the door to dip their hand in your till and walk out with a pile of what's yours by right and effort.'

'I'll manage the count, Father,' said Willow.

'You can *both* do it,' said Benner Landor. He raised a fork towards his son. '*Early*, you hear. You need to take more of an interest in the estate business now you're of an age, Duncan. And I don't mean carousing along the river with the last crew of sailors to fall off the Redwater ferry. The harbour barges will be sailing towards us tonight along the White Wolf River and it's the first day of market tomorrow. There'll be travellers and peddlers in town from places that aren't even on the map. And if our barrels aren't rolling through the auction gates along with every other landowner's by sun-up, then those gypsy merchants won't be waiting around for Landor oil to show up before bidding for their cargoes.'

'I'll be there,' grunted Duncan, raising his hand in surrender as a servant moved forward to refill his empty glass with ginger-root sugar water. He'd drink the cup and it would refill as if by magic every time. Truly was a wonder he wasn't heading to the bathroom twice an hour after he turned in for the night.

'And when it's time to head up to the old town with the auction shipment,' added Benner, 'it can be you that goes, Willow.'

Duncan glared at his father, although with the table being so long, where Benner was sitting he might not even notice. 'You're pranking me! Please tell me that you are?'

'Does this look like my mischievous face, Duncan? The clerk of the town's going to be at the auction. Which means that fool daughter of his I gave a lift to in my carriage is as like to be there also.'

'Do you really think you can stop me seeing Adella Cheyenne?'

'Count on it. You will be going to court as soon as we've cleared this year's harvest business. The season will be starting in a couple of months. I think I've honoured your mother's last wish for long enough – you've been educated here, rather than the academy in the capital I wanted for you. Duelling and drinking with ploughboys is all you've learnt at Northhaven.'

'This is my home!'

'Ambition and drive has no home!' shouted Benner, standing up. 'It travels on the seas where there's wind to fill its sails and carry its cargoes. It grows in the land wherever a man has got the wit and gumption to work it. It travels to the capital where Landor oil lights street lamps and heats kitchen ranges; where that fat lazy rascal of an assemblyman, Charles T. Gimlette, sits in the national assembly with his expenses greased by my purse for a goddamn decade. That's where it travels. And it does so obediently and gratefully for a chance no one else in his *home* is ever going to get.'

'You started with nothing but a hoe and a strong back,' said Duncan. 'You don't think I'm man enough to do the same?'

'The Landor name means something now,' growled Benner. 'And that means you've got to be man enough to live up to it. Maybe that's harder than I ever had it, maybe it's not. But it's the way things are; I can't change it and neither can you.'

Duncan shook his head in disgust and said nothing. *Our name means more to my father than I do. Me and Willow, both.*

'Old Cheyenne's girl is a pretty enough flower, but when all's told and tallied, that doesn't count for a single thing. Down at the court there'll be daughters just as fine – ladies who call counts and dukes and barons, *father*. You're expected to marry well and by the saints you *will*. Long as I'm drawing breath, I won't have you travelling to the palace with rumours of a mistress trailing behind you. Maybe a couple of bastards wailing in the wings to sour your inheritance.'

The old hypocrite. It was fine for Duncan Landor to be moved around like a pawn on his father's chessboard, shuffled to fulfil an old man's vision with hardly a thought of what the son's dreams might be. *But what about father?* Benner Landor had seen his fill of suitors since their mother's death. Fine matrons and noblewomen – young and old – travelling up to Hawkland Park by train and carriage, paraded like a travelling tailor's shirts in front of the head of the house. But he had never appeared even the slightest bit interested … just going through the motions to keep dynastic relations open with other houses. Too loyal to the memory of their mother to ever commit to a second wife. But were his children to be afforded the same dignity? *No. Of course not. We're expected to bend to his will, same as everyone else in Northhaven.*

Duncan laid down his cutlery. His meal was over. He made to get up.

'You can wait for us to finish,' ordered his father.

'My courtly manners are lacking, I know,' said Duncan. 'But if I need to wake as early as you say, I'll skip heading to the tavern to see my friends and turn in now.'

His father grunted something that might have been approval and Duncan left, the servants tucking in his chair and briskly removing all trace of his presence at the dinner table. There was something very fitting about that. *Home isn't really home, is it?* Hawkland Park was more an idea how the Landors should be seen to live. Half the time the estate never seemed real to Duncan, so why shouldn't all signs of his existence automatically fade after he left? Perhaps the manor house only existed when he was there to watch it. There was only one thing that felt real in Duncan's life, and she – naturally – wasn't allowed to impinge on his existence, any more than his presence was allowed to mark the mansion. Turning in for the night was the last thing on Duncan's mind right now.

Duncan made sure none of the servants were watching as he slipped into the main library. Outside the tall windows he could just see the silver river in the moonlight, forking silently through the bottom of their valley. Landor territory all the way out to the horizon's scattered stars. Their neatly trimmed formal garden lay outside, an acre of lawn rolling down to the river, orchards on the hillside opposite, the tenant farmers after that, a rollcall of wealth and territory growing longer every year for the family. He slipped through the shadows. Nobody used the books here except for Willow. Just a display of how all-fired educated the Landors were. Most of the titles were volumes you had to be seen to own, rather than enjoyable enough to want to read. Histories and philosophies and treaties and dry learned journals from the capital, leather-bound by the finest local bookbinders, but otherwise ignored by Northhaven eyes.

All Duncan's father wanted was a little more than he already possessed. All that Duncan wanted was waiting for him, concealed in their garden. It seemed a fact of life that what was forbidden to you was what you burned for, and so it was with Adella Cheyenne. Duncan quietly unlatched the patio door and slipped away from the grand house. Adella was waiting in their sunken garden, tucked inside an alcove within a tall dark hedge. This particular alcove was Duncan's favourite, a line of vases on plinths, each twice Duncan's height. You could have concealed a company of royal marines inside. Adella emerged when she saw he had come alone. Duncan quickly checked behind him. The mansion was well lit tonight. Smoke from its chimneystacks coiled into the air, but its light didn't spill far enough to reveal their assignation.

Adella took a seat on the alcove's stone bench and patted the limestone surface beside her. 'What you did for me today at Rakes Field, Duncan. Nobody's ever stood up for me like that.'

'I did what I thought was right,' said Duncan. 'Someone so careless of your feelings needs to be wakened to their duties.'

Adella's long delicate fingers reached down to rest on his knee. 'What if it wasn't his duty, what if it was yours instead?'

Her words awoke mixed feelings in Duncan. Carter Carnehan's behaviour towards Adella was shameful. The pastor's son knew exactly how much Duncan had always loved Adella, and had clearly resolved to barb Duncan by stealing her away from him forever. After Carter had grown old enough to understand the wealth and power of the House of Landor, the previously amiable heart of the pastor's son had turned bitter and hateful with jealousy. Duncan wished he could say it was an uncommon reaction to his family's success, but it wasn't. Duncan and his father might have their differences, but even he could see that what Benner Landor had built, he'd built from scratch, from thin air and nothing. But his success only served as acid to those who hadn't worked as hard or as cleverly over the years. It was sad that it should be so, but his father's almost limitless wealth just reminded lesser people of their limited natures. Some Weylanders turned obsequious and fawning around the family, others foul and resentful. Carter was one of the latter. Carter should have listened to his father's droning sermonising about sinning against the saints through jealousy; as it stood, sooner or later Duncan would have to leave the selfish dog with a duelling scar down his cheeks to carry with him as a reminder that this Landor was his own man. Not some damn symbol of the house that could be slighted and shoved into the mud to make a pastor's son feel better about his common means.

Duncan returned his attention to Adella. And what father had achieved, so could the son, and all the easier with the right woman by his side. 'Then you've thought on what I said?' He indicated the tall mansion glinting in the night. 'That doesn't mean anything to me, it never has, and a lot less since I've known you. There'll be a guild train loading up at the railhead in a few days. We can jump on it, travel someplace where my father's not got the pull to stop us getting hitched.' Duncan was so lost in the excitement of the idea that he didn't notice the brief frown of alarm Adella cleared from her face.

'This is your birthright, Duncan. I won't have you throw away your life just for me.'

'There's no *just*,' insisted Duncan. 'We can start over, you and me. I don't need Hawkland Park and an army of tenant farmers tugging their forelock to me every time I ride past, asking me how I am, when they don't really give a damn if the answer's good or bad. We can build our own life, free of all of this. That's where the joy of life is ... in the *building* of it, not the *having* of it. If it were any other way, my father would've slowed down years ago and be spending time with Willow and me. Doing something other than locking himself away in an office with nothing but a gaggle of clerks and a mountain of papers and schemes.'

'You're not a quitter,' whispered Adella. 'And what you're speaking of, that isn't freedom, it's quitting. You walk out on Hawkland Park and everything would go to your sister – and if something happened to her, who then? Some distant cousin seven times removed; a stranger you've never even met inheriting everything that should be yours? I've seen you stand up for what's right this morning, Duncan. It's no time to stop now ...'

This is what Duncan loved most about Adella. She wasn't like the others. She didn't fawn around him, and nor did she cower. Adella could see what Duncan was capable of and encouraged him with a passion. If only he could make her see how Carter Carnehan was playing her for a dupe, using her for his own ends. 'Hell! You know nothing's ever going to happen to Willow. We're safe here and my sister would actually have to leave her library and lift her nose out of a book to get into a scrape. Listen to me, Adella, as long as you and I stay here, we're never going to be together. The old man's given orders I'm not to set foot in Northhaven market tomorrow, just on the off-chance that you might bump into me. I'm going to be kept buried all day counting barrels and checking they've been stamped with the correct order numbers.'

Adella's features crinkled in annoyance. 'Then I'll sneak out to the wharves to see you. There'll be barges in for your oil as well as riverboats up from the harbour port, hundreds of travellers milling around. Who's to spot me with a docker's cap pulled over my head?'

'I'd spot you,' Duncan laughed. 'Won't be much of a disguise.'

Adella's hand moved up to tug his shirt playfully. 'We could *really* be together, right now. Just slip behind the hedge and show Benner Landor that his son doesn't take orders, that he's his own man.'

'What if I put a child inside you?'

'It's not my time for that.'

'From what I've seen, those matters always move in their own good time, not any calendar you keep by your sideboard,' said Duncan. *Saint's teeth, sometimes it's almost as if she wants to get pregnant.* 'Don't think that I'm not aching for it, Adella, worse than a furnace fire, but it'd be wrong. Northhaven is a Landor town and there's no church here that is going to make it right without my father's blessing. Besides, Carter Carnehan might not deserve a minute of your time, but until we do the proper thing, or Carter really does up and run for the sea—'

'I'm not minded to throw Carter,' said Adella, petulantly, 'not until you can stand up to your father and make him give you what's yours by right.'

'What's mine by right, well, there we are,' sighed Duncan. *There's not often that I feel like I know what that is anymore.*

Adella stood up, brushing the hedge's leaves off her skirt. 'You're as good a man as your father, Duncan. I know you'll find a way to make him see what you want works, and do it without turning tail and ducking out of your house like a burglar caught rattling the windows.'

Duncan watched Adella disappear down the slope, heading for the copse at the bottom of the slope where she'd have tethered her father's old nag of a horse. Changing Benner Landor's mind? That was quite an act of alchemy. Might as well ask Duncan to turn grass into blades of gold, for all the chances he stood of achieving that. The shadows of the staff moving around behind the dining room curtains told him that dessert was being served. *Time to head back to my room before my absence's noticed.*

Carter stalked angrily along the pavement of the North Road, ignoring honking geese being driven down the middle of the street by a pair of drovers. The drovers' long walking sticks whirled like windmills; streams of curious geese trying to duck down side roads before the whirling canes dropped in front of them, encouraging stray birds to keep with the main flock. Heading for the central market and slaughter at dawn, not that they knew it. Behind Carter and his father a string of flat-bottomed carts creaked, loaded down with corn oil, the Landor crest carefully stamped into each barrel. Every one another pocket full of profit for their family. *What's Duncan done to deserve it? Except being born to a man with ambition in his belly, not a sermon in his throat?*

'You don't have to come with me,' Carter told his father. 'I'll be at the radiomen's hold in time to catch their first message run of the day out to the library.'

'I need to pass through the market, anyway,' said Jacob. 'I promised I would buy some fresh milk to take along to the Hanniels' house. He's nursing his wife and doesn't leave her bedside as near often as he should.'

Carter didn't know what to say to that.

'Be with the angels soon enough,' continued Jacob.

Carter grunted. There was no shortage of old people in North-haven. Anyone young enough to still have some spark left in them usually jumped on to a train to look for work in the teeming cities down south.

'Both of them, probably. Seen it before,' Jacob added. 'Get to that age and with half of you gone, the other half just ups and follows.'

Carter said nothing. He noted the way shopkeepers opened their shutters and nodded towards his father, everyone with all the time in the world to exchange a friendly greeting. That's all he would ever be here, the child of Jacob Carnehan. *The preacher's son.*

Northhaven was built on a hill, and the closer they came to its centre, the narrower and steeper the streets became. There had been a church inside the old town once, centuries ago. Now it was gone, the valuable land sold off and the churchyard relocated to the sprawl outside the old town's walls. Carter found the forest of towering radio masts rising over the cramped streets, partially obscured by wash-ing lines hung between buildings, the guild's hold safely within the town walls. A central minaret concealed the main radio mast, the tower circled by booster spikes. Carter hadn't even reached the top of the street when he spotted something was wrong. The radiomen's delivery cart was outside their hold, a flatbed half loaded with mes-sage crates, but its two horses were off the train; being saddled up individually while a gaggle of radiomen stood around outside. The armoured entrance to the hold stood gaping open. They never left their door open! You'd think a person would go blind for glimpsing the guild secrets inside that sanctum. There was something you never saw in Northhaven, too ... urgency and fear written across the faces of the guild's members.

'Why are you saddling outriders?' asked Jacob, addressing a guildsman with gold stripes sewn onto his black leather radioman's jacket.

'We're getting word out fast,' said the radioman. 'An aircraft's been spotted heading our way, not answering any guild hails.'

'How many rotors?' demanded Jacob.

'Three hundred, at least,' said the radioman. 'Maybe five, hugging the coast before turning east. Blackwood Bay called it in, but the station there was down for maintenance. It took them two hours to get back up and pass the warning along the relay.'

Jacob's mouth drew into a thin line, as close as Carter's father ever got to showing anger. 'I'll warn the wall's western keep, you run your horses out to the other two gates. Have you sent runners to the lord mayor and high sheriff?'

The radioman nodded.

'What about transmitting word up to Rodal?'

'Of course,' said the radioman, growing irritated at the pastor's questioning. 'But it's a waste of battery acid. Their skyguard squadrons are out with our fleet, dropping rocks in the sea and pretending target barrels are pirate galleons. Our luck's as empty as the territorial army's barracks.'

Jacob shouted at Carter to stay where he was, before running down the same road they had just climbed. Carter ignored his father, sprinting down the hill after him. *Damned if I'll stay back there.* Carter called after the pastor. 'What's this about? Just a plane in the air. Aircraft pass over from Rodal all the time.'

'This isn't a single-seater kite, boy. Even aerial nomads answer ground hails from countries they're overflying. And you only travel wave-skipping over the ocean to avoid being spotted by radiomen until it's too late.'

'Bandits?' said Carter, astonished at the alien sound of the word in his mouth. Bandit raids were something that happened to other people. Distant parts far away in the sparsely populated east, not boring backwaters like Northhaven, quiet boondocks nearly fallen off the map. Carter was growing short of breath, even sprinting downhill.

He had never run through town so fast before. 'What the hell we got that they might want?'

'You mean apart from the entire harvest of corn oil filling the Landors' warehouses along the river? The engines on a bandit's rotors would drink Benner's crop faster than a sailor downing whisky rye.'

'We've got to warn mother,' said Carter.

'And I need to ring the church bells,' said Jacob. 'Warn everyone living outside the battlements to get up into the old town. Bandits like their pickings easy. They won't be here for a siege. Just what they can pillage before the sea fort at Redwater sends frigates up the river.'

Despite Jacob Carnehan's protestations, Carter arrived at the battlement's western keep close behind his old man. He watched his father put the fear of god into Constable Wiggins and the other policemen manning the customs gate. Wiggins might have been the oldest of the group, but he was faster on the uptake than the two younger constables, shouting at his men to fetch more officers to the wall and bring heavy rifles to drop on the rampart's tripod mountings.

Wiggins spat onto the cobbles under the portcullis. 'Sitting here since sun-up, playing cloakroom attendant for all the traders and travellers coming in. Turns out I should have been handing out guns and swords, not collecting them in.'

'Are the barrage balloons along the wall in any state to be raised?' asked Jacob.

'Damned if I know,' said Wiggins. 'They only go up during the annual wall drill. More patches than fabric, and that's if the cylinders to inflate them haven't leaked. Well, we'll find out, I reckon.'

'You've got pistols collected in there?' asked Carter, pointing to the guardroom. 'Let me have one.'

'As far as my son's concerned, you keep your guns racked,' ordered Jacob. 'I know you, Carter. You get five rounds in a chamber and you'll be charging the first bandits that hit the ground as though they're no more than paper targets at a fairground stall.'

'Your old man's got a point,' laughed Wiggins. 'I've seen how that drunken sot of a sergeant in the territorials teaches you kids to shoot on cadet days. One hand on a bottle and the other like this—' Wiggins formed a gun barrel with his fingers and clicked off shots straight up into the air '—when he gets overexcited.'

'Stick it,' said Carter, his temper flaring at both of them. 'I'll fight them with my fists and harsh language if I have to. This is my town; I'll do what I need to defend us!'

It was the distant droning that caught Carter's attention first, like a flight of hornets stirred up and ready to swarm the dunderhead who'd banged their nest. Staring through the keep's open gate, he could just see a black dot against the sun, little bigger than a coin. *Have the radiomen marked the size right – don't see that having a couple of hundred propellers?*

'No perspective that high in the sky,' said his father, guessing what his son was thinking. 'Their sound tells you the size of it, though.'

'So far out, and she's still humming like a flight of locusts,' said Wiggins. 'More like a goddamn flying city than any Rodalian flying wing; pardon my language, Father. Ten minutes and they'll be on top of us.'

'Keep the gate open as long as possible,' Jacob told the constable. He was off, under the walls and sprinting towards the church with Carter following as fast as he could.

'Stay inside the battlements,' his father shouted back.

'You got your congregation at church and I don't know about it?' asked Carter, ignoring his father and catching him up. 'Ringing the bells is a two-person job at least.'

'You take your mother out,' hissed Jacob, relenting. 'That's your job. Just stay alive.'

They fair flew through the streets, yelling warnings at everyone they passed to head up the hill to the old town. Given the size and noise of the approaching aircraft, their warnings were fast becoming irrelevant. The flying machine approached like a dark black dragon filling the sky, eight long wings stacked on either side at the front; another four wings towards the carrier's rear, the spinning discs of its propellers – each a dozen times bigger than any Northhaven windmill – far more numerous than Carter could count.

'Won't be much left of Landor's fields after they've landed that monster,' panted Carter.

'Doesn't land,' said Jacob. 'That's their mother bird up there, a carrier. See those dark oblongs running along the bottom of her fuselage. Those are hangars. They'll launch gliders to land raiding parties, and it's those that'll come down in our cornfields. You need flats to land a glider. We'll see their fighter kites first, though, looking to give us something to worry about other than bundling up the family silver and running for the forests.'

'What, the saints wrote some passages on bandit tactics that I missed out on?'

'Don't be smart with me, boy. That's the way it'll happen. Don't look to fight them. They're not some pony-riding barbarian horde aiming to settle here. They're raiding for the corn oil and any trade metals and valuables not nailed down or buried. They'll hit hard and fast and brutal. Anyone that stands against them is a corpse. Their reputation is all the baggage they've got up there.'

'What's the point of me passing through the cadet force if I can't take a stand?'

'I'm glad the territorials aren't here, boy. They're good for scaring off wolves from the livestock in the winter, but bandits like those devils up there, if their raiders haven't left a trading caravan looted and dead on the road at least once a week, they're not pulling their weight.'

Despite the chill in the air, Carter was sweating by the time they arrived home. His father banged on the door and got their mother out, pointing to the sky and growling out the town's predicament in a quick, terse explanation. Mary Carnehan sucked in her cheeks, shielded her eyes with her hand, looking up at the approaching air-craft as if this was just one more thing sent to try her patience this morning. Might as well have been a cloud of locusts looking to strip the town of its harvest. Carter had to admit he was impressed; secretly proud, even. *No hysterics. No flapping or cursing or tears.* Just a couple of seconds to get a handle on the situation and then she was straight to business.

'What tune will you be ringing?'

'There's only plague bells or fire bells,' said Jacob. 'And people hear the former and they're as like to lock themselves inside their house as scurry out for the old town.'

'Ring them loud.' She thumped Carter on the arm. 'Don't just stand there, boys, get to it.' She started to go back inside the porch, but Jacob grabbed her. 'Leave the cutlery and altarware.'

'Stick the church's finery,' said Mary. 'I'm going to grab my school bell and rouse the neighbours. The Littimer boys have just left for the distillery and Leanna Littimer sure isn't going to be good for pushing her old man up to the gates in his wheelchair.'

Jacob shook his head as she ran back inside. 'Just once, maybe someone could do what I ask.' He produced the key for the bell tower and they sprinted for the church. Above the woods where Carter had duelled Duncan Landor, the massive bandit carrier was circling slowly, lazily, clouds of smaller planes beginning to drift away from her black belly. Monoplanes with a single propeller up front, as larger gliders slid into the sky from their hangars – silent and gull-like as they rode thermals rising from the valleys. The attack was happening just as Jacob Carnehan had described, as if the saints had sent his old man's predictions as a vision. From the north, a more familiar sight arrowed towards the city-sized bandit carrier, a tiny triangle, bright blue with two friendly red stripes on its fuselage, a single small rotor spinning at the back. It was a Rodalian aircraft, a solitary flying wing from the mountain people's skyguard.

'Look, Father!' called Carter. He pointed out the diminutive dart vectoring in against the storm of raiders discharged by the carrier.

'Sweet saints,' whispered Jacob as he unlocked the bell tower. 'There goes the unluckiest man in the whole Rodalian nation.'

'Or the bravest,' said Carter.

'Won't make any difference,' said his father. 'A single flying wing against twenty bandit squadrons.'

'Have the element of surprise, though.'

'Surely will have that. Let's get it done, boy. Fill the streets with our people.'

Carter entered the gloom of the belfry and grabbed one of the bell-pulls, putting his back into the work as counterpoint to his father – two peels to every three his father was pulling, sounding the fire warning until the ropes were practically lifting him off his feet. They went at it for a good few minutes, raising hell fit to wake the dead in the graveyard out back, ringing the bells until Carter's skull throbbed from the sound. Their fire warning was to prove prophetic. Carter and his father traded the bell tower's twilight for the churchyard, finding the first fighters from the bandit carrier diving down, trailed by banshee screams as they descended. Dark packages unlocked from under the planes' wings and continued plummeting as the aircraft pulled up. Geysers of flame erupted as each bomb struck, columns of burning embers settling and sparking fires across the timber roofs. Carter recognised the ordnance, remembering the day the old territorial sergeant had brought along a variety of cannon rounds to show the cadets. One cannonball in particular, packed with tar and cloth fuses trailing like mouse-tails. *Incendiary shot.*

'We've rung our alarm true,' said Carter, watching people gathering in the street beyond the church's walls.

'They're landing bombs on the new town, not inside the battlements,' noted his father, looking up at the screaming gull-winged dive-bombers, 'where the buildings are stone and won't catch alight so quickly. That's where we need to be ... up the hill. Find your mother!'

Two fighters zoomed overhead, hardly higher than the bell tower; a couple of seconds in the air above and then they were gone. Carter ducked at the low pass, the propellers on each nose a circular blur. Just enough time for Carter to see them passing as gaudy as a traveller's caravan. Not neat and uniform like the Rodalian Skyguard's flying wings. These aircraft had been painted with bands of rainbow colour, unfamiliar animals pictured on the fuselage as elaborate as a sailor's tattoos. Their engines reverberated louder than any machine Carter had heard before, the deep roar of beasts, throaty and powerful. Any other day, Carter would have loved to watch such aeroplanes passing over their backwater. *Don't look half so wondrous when they're raining destruction down on you, though.* In the distant sky a handful of their brethren twisted, dogfighting with the Rodalian flying wing, planes rolling and barrelling around each other. The battle was fought like crows mobbing a hawk, the small swift triangle falling through the flock whirling around it, seemingly too tiny to be torn out of the sky. Carter could just hear the distant thud of guns mounted along their side, bullets traded invisibly at this distance. Plaintive fingers of black smoke from the burning town reached up towards the duelling aircraft, black spirals blown into shreds by passing bandit fighters. Higher still, the massive carrier circled, extra waves of gliders launching from its hangars. When the carrier's shadow fell on the edge of town, it was as though a stormfront was passing over; sunlight cut off, the only illumination from the fires spreading and raging across the new town.

Chaos reigned in the streets. Almost everyone had come out to see why the bells were sounding, finding not a single fire but dozens burning across the houses and shops and mills of the new town. Some of the Northhaven citizens had formed fire lines, buckets passed from wells and troughs and public fountains. Others dragged panicking horses out from stables; attempting to load up with as many personal possessions and family members as their beasts could bear. A few people fled along the roads out of town, even as the circuit of the huge bandit aircraft passed directly over the woods and fields beyond, bandit gliders drifting down towards the cornfields and river landing. In front of Carter, the balance of the town surged for the old city and the relative safety of the hill's battlements, streets congested by people. They jostled an exodus in the opposite direction as wagons and carts full of goods tried to head away from town. Northhaven wasn't home for the travellers and peddlers – they'd only feel safe on the open road or concealing their trading caravans under a forest canopy. Northhaven's market day would be one to remember. Now local historians would have something to record to liven up their journals. Northhaven, a town where dropping a cornhusk was an event most years.

'Get moving into the old town!' yelled Jacob, shepherding people up the hill and towards the battlements. 'When you pass the gate, head for basements and storm cellars!' He began shouting at families desperately loading up carts, wheelbarrows, horses – anything that moved – with as many of their belongings as they could lay their hands on. 'This is your wife's lucky day, Rufus, she's getting new plates this year. Dump your cart and haul your family through the western keep while it's still open. Mary Frances, you planning on moving house this afternoon? Then leave now. Cole, you born in a sheep pen? No? Then quit wandering around the street like a lost lamb and move with a *purpose!*'

Carter's mother appeared, pushing old man Littimer, the gnarled invalid cursing and hollering in his three-wheeled hospital chair, its pine frame bumping over the cobbles set in the road. Mary Carnehan steered it around abandoned wagons and through the scared jostling mass of townspeople. She had Carter helping in a second, the wailing Littimer grandchildren – no more than three years old – one under each of his muscular arms, thrashing about as they fled up the slope for the battlements. It got more and more crowded as roads narrowed towards the wall and the old town. Occasionally the bandit fighters overshot him, colourful streamers on their wings angrily flapping as they roared over low. The raiders appeared empty of incendiary bombs to release and didn't seem inclined to waste expensive wing-gun ammunition on the panicked mobs below. The fires in the new town grew worse higher up the rise. Maybe due to the buildings being packed in tighter, maybe because the high sheriff's men manned the wall, heavy rifles mounted on iron stands tracking planes and loosing off the odd shot, and the raiders retaliated by smoking the defenders' aim. Barrage balloons bobbed at intervals along the ramparts, big brown canvas bags shaped like cigars. They had each been stitched with the royal crest of Weyland, the black boar, as if to tell the bandits which nation was doing the defending in this town. Hell, if they had heard the corn oil harvest had just been collected, they knew that much already. Probably didn't care either way. Just pockets that need picking, and easier to steal from someone already kicked down to the floor. Up above, the mismatched aerial defence of the town finally ended, the remains of the Rodalian flying wing corkscrewing towards the woodland leaving a black coil of burning smoke in its wake. There was a nest of contrail tentacles where the brief combat had been fought. He hadn't gone alone. In his wake he'd left half a dozen bandits scratched out of the sky, as many more fighters desperately limping back towards the carrier streaming smoke and flames. The Rodalian pilot had experienced one small piece of luck, anyhow … surviving for now. A white parachute drifting towards the town, caught by the suction of fires raging across the town in the chilly breezeless morning. Bandit planes arrowed past the chute, not bothering to plug the Rodalian pilot with cannon fire. A display of gallantry between fellow pilots? *Doubtful.* The bandit fliers were probably running light on ammunition after their aerial duel. Carter could see where the parachute was heading – a couple of streets over and lower down the hill's slope. The Magnus Brewery, burning brighter than any of the surrounding rooftops, green-painted boards spewing flames from its high windows. Down the chute floated, catching on a loading beam poking out a third storey warehouse door. The pilot was left hanging like a puppet with cut strings, boots thrashing. *Can't cut the chute from that height. It's a choice between plummeting to death or staying put and being roasted alive.*

Carter pointed the pilot's predicament out to his parents.

'He's still alive,' said his mother.

'That flier risked his life to help the town,' said Carter. 'I'm not going to leave him strung up there like a chicken dangling on the spit.'

'Don't suppose there's any point asking you to stay here?' Jacob asked his son.

Carter shrugged. His father already knew the answer to that question.

Mary Carnehan pushed the wheelchair over to one of their neighbours, Carter passing the care of the children tucked under his arms to the same family. His mother returned to stand in front of his father. 'You fixing to head over there and pray him down, Mister Carnehan?'

'Not if I've got you to nag him down, Mrs Carnehan.'

Trying to head back down the hill was like wading against a tide. People were desperate now, shoving and shouldering each other as the fear of fire became panic. Some yelled angrily at Carter and his family as they pushed through, others not even seeing him, eyes fixed on the safety of the old town. Carter and his parents had to avoid the smaller passageways between buildings; many already blocked by burning debris. Taking one of the larger cobbled roads that circled the hill, they came back on the brewery, flames lapping around Ale Hill. Street lamps were still burning, too early in the morning for the lamplighters to have finished their circuit extinguishing the previous night's work. Little fire risk from those lamps now, not with the windows of the brewery building crackling and exploding. Something about the scene put Carter in mind of sitting in the stalls of the town's theatre. Maybe it was the back of the street hollowed out so just the frontage was left standing, like a flat piece of scenery in the wings. He gazed at the surreal sight of Northhaven burning and imagined the leaping blaze as red tissue paper waving from windows, an actor struggling and twisting in the tangled remains of his parachute.

There he is. The pilot looked to be male; stranded three storeys up and suspended from a gantry crane, its wooden arm creaking as the rest of the brewery crumbled. One of the building-fronts came tumbling down ahead of Carter, landing across the street in an outrush of burning timbers and sparks. Carter glanced inside the brewery entrance. Too much fire and smoke to even begin to see the staircase inside. No way up to the roof to try and release the pilot. The interior of the brewery was a death trap.

'I don't think we can get to the roof to bring him down,' said Carter.

His father gazed up at the figure. Carter could watch the pilot's kicking legs growing weaker, enveloped in waves of black smoke from the burning brewery. *Brave devil's going to suffocate from smoke inhalation before he burns.*

Jacob pointed to the drainpipe fixed to the brewery wall. 'Could climb up that. But how to bring him down safe?'

Mary Carnehan was rifling through the contents of an overturned wagon, someone's hastily packed possessions strewn over the street in their dash to safety. She emerged from the mess with a blanket roll and a small hand-axe. 'Isn't that just like men? Yakking when you should be doing. We'll cut him down with the axe, slow his fall with the blanket, just as if the three of us were the real fire service.'

Jacob took the axe and passed it to Carter. 'Can you make the throw? Seen you practising out in the trees when you think I'm not around, tossing those three throwing knives you bought last summer.'

Carter was briefly astonished. His father actually trusted his son to do something by himself. The old man had seen him throwing at targets on the trees and *rated* his aim?

'If I thought I could make the throw better than you, I'd do it,' said Jacob. 'But I've never been much of a one for throwing cutlery about.'

Carter tucked the axe's wooden handle under his trouser belt and started to shin up the drainpipe. The boards the drainpipe was nailed to felt scalding hot, the back of his fingers burning as they scraped the wall. *Wouldn't take much to buckle now, bury you and your parents, both.*

Coughing from the acrid backwash of smoke crackling inside the building, Carter halted, dangling two storeys above ground. Down below, his mother and father had spread the blanket out wide, holding it drum-tight at chest level, waiting below the Rodalian pilot. Could have done with a few more hands to catch the flier, but just his parents would have to do. The pilot was wearing a purple-dyed sheepskin aviator's jacket edged with golden fur and he was getting smoked pretty good. *You could cure bacon in less than that.* His head lolled to one side, covered by a leather pilot's helmet with the Rodalian's Asiatic features partially hidden by wide flying goggles. Carter got the impression, though, that the flier might just be conscious enough to be aware of the suicidal young man clinging onto the drainpipe across from him.

Carter tugged out the hand-axe, his right palm so sweaty that it nearly slipped out of his grip. His left hand clung to the gutter's increasingly hot surface. *Here goes nothing.* His eyes focused on the parachute cords wrapped along the loading arm. The flier's line had become tangled with the warehouse pulley's ropes. Carter let his mind clear, trying to forget the precariousness of his situation. The ridiculousness of it. His town ablaze around him. A bird's eye view of townspeople fleeing up the hill along parallel streets. The thunder of bandit planes strafing the town. *Just focus on the parachute lines. That's how you strike bark with a throwing knife. Nothing else. Just you and the target, not even thinking about it. The thinking only gets in the way.* The throw was made. The hand-axe left Carter's hand before he was aware it had gone, its head rotating lazily before thudding into the tangle of pulley rope and chute lines, the whole mess exploding like a nest of kicked snakes. The pilot was suddenly freed from the loading arm. A loud ripping noise as what was left of the pilot's chute took wing in the hot draught, flapping away as if the fabric were alive. The Rodalian plunged down, arrow-straight, taking the tension out of the waiting blanket below. After he'd slapped into it, the pilot was left lying in the middle of the street while Carter's parents made a stretcher out of the blanket. Then they dragged the Rodalian away inside the roll to the other side of the road. They were both shouting something at Carter that he couldn't hear. But he heard the smash of exploding glass in the surviving windows, the roar of collapsing floors giving way inside the brewery. He was getting good at shinning his way down the wall, sliding and slithering towards the ground. *A spooked lizard couldn't do it any better.* The wall Carter had descended collapsed behind him even as he was throwing himself to the ground. He rolled once, then came up in a cloud of dust to sprint for the side-street his parents were retreating down, dragging the Rodalian flier with them. How Carter escaped was a pure-born miracle, the lick of burning timbers and rubble a wave of surf chasing him every step of the way. It was as though he outpaced a storm, the heat of burning dust and wooden cinders stinging the back of his neck. Carter barrelled in front of his parents. His father had the flier up, limping and leaning against his shoulder. Dazed, the man's yellow cheeks covered in soot, the Rodalian hacked his guts out.

'Ankle's twisted with the fall,' said his mother, 'maybe broken.'

'Take the man's weight on the other side,' Jacob ordered his son. 'He's not climbing up to the old town by himself.' *Not a word of admiration for my aim, not a word of thanks for what I've just done.*

'Surviving's the only medal worth being pinned with,' said Jacob, reading his son's face. 'And that was forty or fifty people's livelihoods that just went crashing down. Nothing worth celebrating. Now, let's move.'

Well, stick them, anyway. He'd have something to tell his friends, now, something more than just running and hiding in old town cellars. Bravest man to ever take to the air, and he was only alive thanks to Carter.

'You did okay,' his mother whispered across to Carter as they hauled the flier away. The pilot wasn't taller than five and a half feet, but he sure did weigh some for such a diminutive figure. It was like dragging bricks up the hill. She wagged a finger at her son. 'But the only thing knife throwing is good for is a circus act, and I haven't raised a Carnehan boy to turn circus tricks for pennies, you hear me?'

'They're good for other things too ... I can draw them pretty fast.'

'The *other* things I'm not even going to pass comment on,' she warned.

The flier mumbled, but it didn't sound like anything Carter understood. Maybe some local mountain dialect. The pilot had been concussed pretty hard, cuts and bruises all across his face. Must have taken a mouthful of fuselage bailing out of his flying wing.

There was no sign of refugee numbers abating on West Hill Road, a whole street full of hysterical townspeople throwing themselves onto the cobbles every time a bandit plane buzzed by. The town was full with visitors in from the countryside for the market, every hotel and guesthouse already packed. Seemed like the raiders had run out of incendiary bombs to drop and were relying on the screaming sirens built into their engines to inflict terror on the people. *Robbers softening up the householders before looting their property, that's all they are.* Just give Carter a rifle and he'd show the bastards what you got for attacking good Northhaven folk. Gunfire rippled along the ramparts, heavy rifles bucking on tripods with the recoil from large-bore shells. If one of the bandit planes had taken damage from the defenders along the parapet, Carter had yet to glimpse it.

Carter's family had just reached the gate's shadow when his mother collided with a figure pushing the wrong way through the fleeing residents – a woman Carter recognised. It was Caroline Ormund. She always seemed to be bustling about town with more children than anyone else in Northhaven, a couple of them hanging on to her coattails right now.

'Where in the name of the saints are you heading with your two youngest?' demanded Mary, stopping the woman from heading down the hill. 'You want to be putting some strong walls between you and these murdering devils in the air.'

'It's my boy, Felix,' cried the woman. 'He's down at the school. His class started early for archery practice … some woodsman in town for the market going to teach them. I've just seen one of the girls from Felix's class – she says all the adults are dead, half the children hiding in the classrooms under their desks. Sounds like chaos down there!'

Carter grimaced. The school was at the edge of the new town where the farmland began. Flat land leading out to the river road where those bandit gliders would surely be looking to land.

'Damn that fool of a master,' spat Mary. 'Always angling to beat the Redwater Royal Free School at the thirty yards line. You'd think arrows in the gold were more important than making sure children get their letters and numbers. Call them in early for history and maths, *no*. But dangle an archery prize for our trophy cabinet …'

'What am I going to do, Mary? He's my little boy, what—'

'You focus on your responsibilities to the rest of your family,' said Mary firmly. 'Keeping them alive.' She looked at the two terrified girls hugging her leg. 'You keep your head together for them. Because they need you, and you need your wits about you this day.'

'There's going to be bandits in town soon, ripping up houses for whatever's not nailed down,' Jacob told the woman. 'You take those two little ones to shelter, Caroline. I'll bring the children at the school back here.'

'*We'll* do it,' said Mary. 'It's my school.'

'We'll bring little Felix back,' promised Jacob.

Mary Carnehan's eyes shone like two flints in a rockface. 'We'll bring them *all* back.'

Jacob turned to Carter. 'Take the flier inside the walls.'

'I'm—'

'No arguing, boy. When you save a man's life, his soul's on you to care for. He's not walking up the hill by himself. Take the flier to safety and tell Wiggins to hold the western gate open, you hear, keep it open until we get back.'

'He'll do it,' said Mary. 'Old Wiggins' granddaughter is in the same class as Felix.'

'But the raiders won't be shooting at children?' questioned Carter.

'The bandits'll want to put the fear in the town, keep the citizens bottled up and behind those walls and too scared to take offence at the looting outside. No better way to do that than a slaughter,' said Jacob. 'And youngsters don't shoot back, which, for bandits, makes them the best target of all.'

Then Carter's parents were gone. He was left with the weight of the semi-conscious pilot as well as the burden of his family's slim chance of returning alive. As Carter hobbled forward with the stumbling Rodalian, it was hard to know which of them bore down greater. *Well, you wanted your life livening up, Carter Carnehan. This lively enough for you, you idiot?*

The school was in as bad a shape as Jacob had feared. Bombs had flattened the furthest of the four long buildings joined at the centre by a teachers' block. Where the bandits had dived down, the classroom had been left a burning wreck. Children's bodies lay scattered lifeless around the fenced-in fields, a couple of straw-filled archery circles stripped of their target cloth, overturned and smouldering from a strafing run, sods of grass torn where planes had passed overhead with their wing guns blazing.

Mary hissed in fury as she saw the corpses, her fingers bunching into a fist. 'How could anyone do this?'

Jacob had nothing to say by way of explanation. *Why does the sun come up each morning? Why does the rain fall and soak people?* Why did bandits choose the life they did, preying on those weaker than themselves, rather than toiling in the soil and working with nature to provide a living? Why did hawks hunt hares rather than grazing the meadows beside their prey? Some things just were. Jacob scanned the skies from their hiding place, crouched in the vegetable patch of one of the homes bordering the school field. The aircrafts' hornet buzzing sounded from behind them, raiders still driving townspeople up the hill as though this was a cattle drive.

'I can see movement in those windows over there,' said Jacob, trying to keep his wife focused on something other than her anger. *It's a fickle thing, anger. You can ride it like a log down a river. Sometimes it takes you where you want to go, other times it just dumps you down perilous rapids.* Any angrier and Mary was likely to do something dangerous. *Well, more hazardous than this morning's business, anyhow.*

Jacob and his wife jumped the fence and ran across the fields, keeping low. Adults lay mixed among the children's corpses, the head of the school, another teacher and her young assistant – a boy barely older than Carter. The headmaster had a couple of nine-year-olds clutched under his bloody body. Jacob stopped, turning the man over to check the children for life. *No good.* Not with bandit fighters pumping out shells large enough to tear apart an enemy aircraft's fuselage. The strafing run had ripped the schoolmaster apart and his body had proved as much of a shield as rice paper for the pupils he'd scooped up to sprint to cover with. Tears sprang into Jacob's eyes. He could barely stand to look at the two youngsters, fear left frozen on their faces as they had died. *This isn't glory. This isn't war. Just shortened lives with as little point behind their end as—*

'Come on,' Mary urged. 'I can hear crying inside.'

Jacob stepped through the wreckage of a blackened wall. Mary climbed behind him, kicking aside the building's smouldering boards to gain access to the part of the school where they had seen heads bobbing through shattered glass. Two of the surviving classrooms were empty. Inside the third, they found desks overturned by the blast, whimpering heads quivering behind furniture. Frightened little faces stared out of a makeshift camp. An adult lay slumped against the wall under a window. A spreading pool of blood slicked out from his body where the left leg should have been, and Jacob saw where the archery target fabric had ended up. Ripped off and bandaged around the stump of limb which remained. Not one of the teachers, and from his size and workaday green jerkin, this was the woodsman who had come in for the market. He was still alive, just, his right hand clutching his bow as though it was a walking stick … a queer-looking contraption, a cam at the end of each limb supporting a sophisticated system of pulleys and cables. Jacob recognised the weapon for what it was. *Haven't seen one of those for a while.* Mary raced to calm and gather the school children while Jacob ducked below sight of the shattered window to reach the man.

'Didn't see my leg outside, did you?' growled the woodsman as Jacob bent down.

Jacob shook his head and checked the bandaged stump. 'Reckon a wolf must have had it away, Mister …?'

'Folks just call me Hamlet. You can take your choice of wolves out there. Sneak a peep out of the window behind me. Careful you're not seen, man.'

Jacob lifted his head and glanced through the broken glass. Long lines of townspeople marched down the river road, their legs manacled together, just enough play to allow them to shuffle forward. Their captors were twisted. The bandits strutted a head taller than most of Northhaven's men and women, green-scaled and lizard-snouted to boot. Twisted far beyond the common pattern. Short powerful tails swayed behind the raiders as they cursed and poked their prisoners forward with the business end of rifle-mounted bayonets. Before the Weylanders were chained in the cornfields, Jacob saw some locals being removed from the line, and he choked back his bile as he saw what happened next. Prisoners made to kneel, then one of the bandits – who must have been large even for his nation – walked the line with a scimitar, decapitating the hostages from the start to the end of the queue.

'It's the old 'uns they're murdering,' said Hamlet, hearing the catch in Jacob's throat. 'And the ones too young to work.'

'Not just bandits, then,' said Jacob. '*Slavers*.'

Hamlet nodded. 'Oh, they're raiding the town's corn ether too. You can see their transport planes landing near the wharves on the river. But out in those fields? Any Weylander over thirty-five isn't worth the fuel it'd cost to fly them to the slave block. Wouldn't survive long enough under the whip to fetch a good price. And anyone under ten years is too small to do a day's hard labour.'

Off on the horizon, Jacob could see blimps hovering where the river ran. Skyhooks connected to grounded gliders, every craft filled with captured townspeople. Squat triplanes dipped down, all engines and wings, catching lines dangling from the balloons and pulling the gliders back into the sky, towing them up to the bandits' monstrous carrier. *Slavers*. Jacob felt a dagger of fear jabbing in his side. How many people did Jacob know were chained inside one of those bandit gliders? Good people, terrified and bloody and cowed. His parishioners. His friends. *Thank God I got Carter out.*

Mary came over behind Jacob with a wooden pole. 'You can tie this on as a splint. Got a longer piece of wood you can use as a crutch.'

Hamlet snorted in amusement. 'Seen enough lumber come down the wrong way and crush a fellow to know this is only going to end one way for me.'

'We're not leaving you here,' said Jacob.

'Sure you are. Because those ugly twisted brutes have raiding parties tearing up houses for silver and anyone hiding in storm cellars, and they're going to be rolling right through here any minute. Then you two lightweights are going to need a mighty powerful distraction to see these youngsters safely up to the town's walls.'

'What can we do for you, friend?' asked Jacob.

Mary began to protest. 'We're not—'

Hamlet raised his hand, silencing any argument. 'Wedge me up here on a chair and pass me my quiver. Come on now, be about it – I'm shy a leg, not my arms.'

Jacob heaved the woodsman's body up onto a chair, feeling the tremors in the man's chest. *He's right. Too much blood lost. Dead soon enough, even without the slavers helping him on his way.* Hamlet's life had narrowed to a single, slim path, that wasn't leading anywhere a sensible man wanted to travel. Hamlet hefted his bow, a tight grip on it, laying it across his leg and stump. 'This here is *magic* wood.'

'I know what a compound bow is,' said Jacob. 'Though they're rare enough around these parts.'

Hamlet pulled an arrow from his quiver, fitted the string around it, and locked the arrow back in one smooth motion. The weapon's pulleys held the arrow taut without any extra effort on the woodsman's part, ready to be loosed with a finger's worth of pressure. 'Bought it from a caravan that passed through town last summer. They told me it had been in their family for twenty generations. Think about that, travelling millions of miles, just to end up in my hands. End up here on this day. It's almost a miracle.'

'Maybe it is,' said Jacob.

'You see those children to safety up the hill and I'll know it travelled true,' coughed Hamlet. 'Know it got here with a purpose.'

'Trick bow like that,' said Jacob, 'Maybe I ought to cut your other leg off to make sure it's a fair fight.'

Mary had the children lined up and ready to leave; fourteen of them, only half the class that had turned up early for competition practice. Some of them still had the school's practice bows in their hands, clutching them tight like totems to protect against the fate that had befallen their friends and teachers.

'We'll head up Prospect Rise,' said Mary. 'That's where the fires are worst. Bandits'll leave that end of town last; those devils came here to start fires, not put them out.'

'Sounds like a plan.'

One of the little girls peeled away from the line and offered her quiver to Hamlet, intent green eyes in her smoke-blackened face looking up at the dying woodsman. 'Thank you for our archery lesson, Mister Hamlet.'

'That's a mighty kind gift, young lady. I'll see if I can put some of those bolts where they need to be.'

Mary hustled the girl back into line, placing a finger against her lips. 'We're going up to the wall and playing silent rabbits all the way. Even if you see fires or other things on the way, you'll be silent, won't you? There'll be a prize for the quietest when we get there.'

'And there might be ugly lizard-faced strangers about who're looking to trick you into making a noise,' added Jacob. 'But none of you are to fall for their pranks.'

'You know the archer's tradition,' Hamlet said to Jacob before he left, 'the final shot?'

Jacob nodded.

'What's that?' Mary whispered as they ducked through the wrecked part of the school.

'Something for later,' said Jacob. *And sweet saints, let there be a later for us.*

They had slipped beyond the school fields, winding their way slowly, quietly up the hill, when a coughing snarl of rifle fire broke out behind them, short bursts of fire. Jacob couldn't hear the twang of arrows being returned, but the angry discharge of guns told its own story. *Sell yourself dear, woodsman.*

Supported by Carter's shoulder, the Rodalian pilot grew a little more coherent as they limped together through the Western gate. His face was a work of art, all right, and not just because he was Rodalian. His eyes were like a crow's feet turned on their side, a line-apiece for eyebrow, eyes and the bags underneath, all three razor-thin. His hair might have been a twelve-year-old's, as thick and bushy as any Carter had seen, and probably unnatural for a man who must've been in his late forties at least. Two prominent smile lines hung off a nose slightly too wide for the face, twitching above a clear white set of teeth that would've looked unnatural doing anything other than smiling. Even allowing for the man's injuries, his movements were awkward and ungainly, like a mime pretending to be a pilot. The saints only knew how he had twisted and turned that flying wing of his with so much skill during his outnumbered duel above the town. Desperate refugees streamed all around Carter and his pilot, citizens grabbed by constables standing duty and pushed down the streets that branched out into the old town. Anything to hurry the townspeople along and keep the portcullis entrance unblocked.

'What's your name?' murmured the pilot, using the back of his leather flying gloves to rub a streak of soot away from his cheek.

'I'm Carter Carnehan.'

'Where are your two friends, the ones who caught me after you cut my chute?'

'My parents. They're helping people down in the new town.'

The flier glanced towards the sky; the noise, but not the sight of the bandit raiders still rolling about up in the blue. 'I have failed in my duty.'

'You're kidding me, right? Bandits must have sixty fighters in the air. You went right at them, flew into their squadron like the bravest fool I ever saw.'

'The number of foes does not matter. You win or you do not win – one enemy or a hundred, no difference. If your soul is pure you will triumph. What chance now for the name of *Sheplar Lesh* to be entered in the skyguard's rolls of honour after *this* defeat?'

Sheplar Lesh continued mumbling about losing his plane and his honour as Carter stumbled with the pilot towards an aid station set up in the lee of the wall. A gang of young men stood in the road, milling around uncertainly. Many of them faces that Carter recognised from his final year at school, others from the taverns and river when the ferries sailed up from Redwater bringing sailors who'd pay to be guided to good rooms and amiable company. It was obvious the mob wanted to do something. *And it sure isn't hunker down in some cellar and let the most interesting thing to happen in Northhaven for a couple of centuries pass on by while they're quaking in the dust next to old jam bottles and spare blankets.* The men moved aside for Carter, a jabber of excited voices talking fast and breathless.

'Heard they dive-bombed a crowd outside the Five Horseshoes and put thirty into the grave.'

'No, that was along Blists Hill.'

'Flattened the Pickerell house, killed Amy Pickerell and her little sister too.'

'Bastards.'

'Hey, is that the Rodalian—?'

Carter slipped past before the group could try and detain him. A makeshift surgery had been set up inside an ironmonger's store, merchandise tables swept of goods and wounded constables stretched across the counters, burnt and gunned by the bandit planes wheeling through the sky, civilians too. Just townspeople out minding their business and looking to make an honest living when death had come screeching down on them. *Damn the bandits to hell.* Unexpected, uninvited and looking to steal what they had no right to.

Auxiliaries from the town's hospital quickly stretched the Rodalian flier over one of the cleared tabletops, pulling away his flying jacket. Carter watched their practised hands at work. 'You fix him up. This man's the Rodalian who flew for us. He's called Sheplar Lesh. One pilot against a whole bandit horde, that's a name worth remembering.'

'I'm not a head doctor,' said the orderly, wiping bloody hands on his butcher's apron. 'But I'll tend to everything except his madness.'

'Can't cure a man of being Rodalian,' said the medic next to him. 'You head up north and cross the mountain border; I hear they're all like that.'

Carter ignored their mortuary humour. This flier had nearly died for them, a stranger in a flying wing honouring the ancient compact of the Lanca. *Attack one, attack all.* Well, now it was Carter's turn. He was boiling as he pushed his way past the stretchers and blood and bandages and the stench of wounds soaked in pure alcohol. His temper wasn't much improved by the sight of the high sheriff arguing with Constable Wiggins in the shadow of the keep. The squat leader of the town's police was demanding that the portcullis be lowered; old Wiggins squared up to the officer as though he was planning to wrestle his commander to the ground.

'There's still too many down in the town,' insisted Wiggins.

The high sheriff appeared unmoved. 'We've got a care to keep the people inside these walls safe. There's more on this side of the battlements, now, old man. Northhaven can't afford to have a gate sitting wide open when the bandits' ground forces push up the hill. If there're stragglers still outside, that's just how it is.'

Carter pushed past two officers behind the high sheriff, big men squeezed into blue uniforms with hands resting on holstered pistols. 'Stragglers be damned! My parents are still out there. They're coming up from the school with children.'

'You're the pastor's son, aren't you? What's that you say … children at the school this early?' The high sheriff dug his pocket watch out of his jacket pocket, taking in the time. 'Damn, but I'd like to know who's got our luck today; this is a hell of a mess!'

Carter stuck a finger up towards the enormous bandit carrier looping lazy circuits below the clouds, her engines a distant drone while fighters, gliders and transporter tugs passed in and out of her belly, a cloud of midges buzzing around their massive host beast. 'Not a mess for the raiders. They know what they're doing, right enough. Hit us on market day when we've long lines of oil tanks ready for shipment, the town fat with trade metals and travellers. The territorial force off with the fleet, and Northhaven a chicken fat on corn and clucking for a plucking. In at sun-up to maximise daylight for looting, catching us at breakfast.'

'They know their business, that I can see. Clumsy bandits wouldn't have lived long enough to fly this far out.'

'They've got a map of the town is what they got,' said Carter. 'Striking Ale Hill and every part of the new town that's tinder to burn. But they don't really *know* the streets, not the way we do.' Carter indicated the mob milling in the shadow of the ramparts. 'You've got a guardhouse full of weapons handed in for market week. You give them to us and we'll keep the bandits away from the walls. Give them something to think on 'sides rolling up all of Northhaven's silver into a sack.'

'That's crazy talk,' spat Wiggins. 'You think I'm going to let you—?'

Carter jabbed a hand towards the battlements. 'You've got new signings the same age as us up on the wall, only difference is most of us can shoot worth a damn. Hell, how old were you when you signed on as a constable? All those tales you tell of the old days, they just hot air or did they actually happen the way you told?'

'This ain't the old days, Carter.'

'He's got a point, old man,' growled the high sheriff. 'We did as bad back in the day. And if these wharf rats and tavern brawlers raise half as much hurt for the raiders as they do for us on pay day, then the stragglers in the new town'll have a good chance of making it up the hill.'

Carter looked at Wiggins. 'I know where the raiders are going to be heading, Constable, and I know your daughter's kid is down at the school with my folks. And right now, we're what you've got.'

'Damn your soul, Carter.'

'Damn the bandits', first.'

'Wait in line,' sighed the high sheriff. He beckoned the gang over, young toughs spilling over each other to reach the front of the guard-house. 'Raise your right hands. Higher, there, boys. You're not asking your mother for an extra helping of stew. Do you swear to obey, uphold and maintain the statutes of King Marcus and the lawfully constituted Assembly of Weyland, to keep the charter of the Lanca, protect the Northern Prefecture of Weyland and obey lawful orders from its duly elected officers – that would be me, you little arseholes – its magistrates and courts, and execute your powers and duties honestly, faithfully and diligently without fear of or favour to any person and with malice or ill-will toward none 'cept those flying, thieving bastards up there?'

Eager assent roared back towards the high sheriff.

'Then you are hereby deputed by the Royal District Police as special constables and extraordinary regulators, saving this young fool here—' he pointed at Carter '—who is deputed as acting cadet leader, on account of this lunacy being his idea. I have just four orders for you. First one is to stay alive. Second one is to make sure any locals coming up the slope stay alive. Third is that when we torch the yellow signal fire on top of this keep, you light on back to the gate before it shuts. Final one, and I reckon this is going to be the most popular, you see a bandit, you make the son-of-a-bitch a *dead* bandit. Are they four orders you can carry out?'

Carter nodded as the men cheered.

The high sheriff indicated the guardhouse inside the keep. 'Then fill your boots.'

Carter followed Wiggins and his constables into the room as the mob began to empty the racks of rifles and shelves of pistols, holsters, bandoleers, knives and swords. 'I still got time to run over to the gaol,' grumbled Wiggins. 'In case that bunch outside isn't wild enough for your tastes. Maybe add a few knifers and highwaymen to your crew.'

'Just doing what needs to be done, Constable.'

'Reckon that's what Mary Carnehan's going to say when she comes after me for letting you idiots loose outside the wall.' The constable passed Carter a lever-action repeating rifle along with a satchel of bullets. Seven shells for the chamber and a brass trigger latch set into the front of its stock to eject spent cartridges and load the next shot. Carter read the legend engraved on the barrel. *Landsman Weapons Works of Arcadia, Weyland*, all the way up from the capital. *Finest gunmaker in the nation, maybe the whole damn league.*

'You're not in a duel, Carter. You drop your sabre out there, ain't no bandit going to be bowing to impress his friends and let you pick it up for a second try. You see a raider, you put one in their stump.' He thumped his chest hard. 'No trick shots, no hesitating. Put one in the centre of the body; then even if you pull high, low, left or right, you're going to hit something.'

'Is that why the other constables call you Stumpy?' asked Carter, loading the rifle. 'I always thought it was because you were shy of a few inches.'

'Man's got to be called something. I don't draw my gun often, but when I have to do it, the villain goes down and ain't much for getting up again. That's the art of it.'

Carter glanced around the guardhouse. The mob hadn't left enough weapons inside the room to ambush a pilgrimage of nuns. The town's rowdies had cleaned the keep clear out. Would the travellers and merchants in town for market thank the gang or curse the ruffians for taking their expensive weapons? *Guess that'll depend on how we do down in the new town.*

'I'm not afraid of bandits,' announced Carter. 'Not with a chance to pay them back a slice for all of this.'

Wiggins stepped out after the boy, gazing with weary eyes at the wild mob loading up and eager to be at the raiders. 'That's what I'm afraid of. Only two types that fall that way ... the foolish and the dead.'

Cater levered a charge into the rifle's breech. 'You've sat through enough of my father's sermons to know there's a third sort. The *righteous*.'

Carter glanced around at the faces in the mob standing in front of the battlement, looking at him for a lead. *This must be what being born a Landor is like.* Maybe after all this was over, the Carnehan name would shine for something other than a hell-fire sermon and probity among the pews in Northhaven.

'Here's how it is,' said Carter. 'The bandits have got a map of Northhaven. Must have, to hit the brewery, drop all their incendiaries on the new town, and leave the old town untouched to corral the rest of us. But out there are *our* streets, right? We've been running them and slipping past constables and angry fathers for years, unlike those sky-born locusts. And a map doesn't mean much when you are at eye level and the place is filled with smoke.'

'So how do we play it?' someone at the back called.

'Those of you who've put your time in with the territorials, remember what we were taught about guerrilla warfare. We move out in small groups of four or five; split up, keep to cover, keep leaping and hopping, and cut up the bandits wherever we make contact.'

'I heard they're twisted,' said one of the men. 'People coming from the outskirts talking about how they're green-scaled dragons walking on two legs.'

'Well, that's good to know in advance. I've watched caravans containing people of all shapes and sizes roll on through the town over the years, all friendly, and I've smiled back at every one. I don't care how many twists on the spiral they're removed from a Weylander, but when they arrive burning and stealing, me and Mister Landsman here—' Carter pulled out the rifle '—we've got a point to take up with them about that.'

The crowd cheered and rattled the weaponry cleared out of the guardhouse.

'Don't see too many of their planes overhead now,' said one of the irregulars.

'No matter. We don't bunch up, keep moving, they'll have nothing to dive-bomb,' said Carter. 'We'll fan out and head for Wallace Hill. Every bank, metal smith, and jeweller in the new town runs along that road. If I wanted to get rich on a raid, that's where I'd go. Got to figure these bandits are at least that smart.'

'Ain't smarter than me!'

'If that was true, fool, you'd be up on that battlement with old Wiggins and his constables,' laughed Carter. 'Well, let's see if we're for taking some pain, or giving some out.'

They jeered good-heartedly and split into groups, cousins with cousins, friends with friends. Three men that Carter knew, Joah,

Eshean and Caleb, attached themselves to him. Eshean, the largest of the three, slapped a short-sword against his palm. 'Maybe if we take some skulls, the mayor'll let us stuff them and mount them next to the stags he's got up in the town assembly?'

Joah kicked the man in the shins. 'Hell, Eshean, since you've been working in the abattoir, all you think about is carving meat.'

Carter looked at the stragglers still struggling up the slope, panting and frightened and desperate. The people were coming in with faces and clothes blackened by soot, fires spreading and fewer and fewer left to fight the blazes. *Won't be much left of Northhaven outside its battlements when this is over.* 'We're doing it for them, not the mayor's hunting trophies.'

'Is it true, Carter, that your folks went down into the new town to bring up the school?' asked Caleb.

Carter had been trying not to think about that. What might happen to his mother and father if the bandits came across them before … still, at least Adella was safe. This early, she would still be in bed in her parents' house near the centre of town. Trying to ignore all the banging and shouting in the streets outside, thinking the racket was market week starting, rather than a bandit raid. *That'd be her all right.*

'Yeah, that's what they're doing, Caleb.'

'That's some beans they got,' said Caleb. 'No disrespect to your father, but he caught me taking a catapult to a squirrel in a tree once. You'd have thought I was trying to assassinate King Marcus, the talking he gave me. That's some beans, though.'

'Where do you figure they'll be coming up with the school?' asked Joah.

'Where there's smoke to throw off the bandits' aim. Other side of the brewery, Prospect Hill.'

Joah stared at Carter through a thick, cheap pair of spectacles, his eyes made owlish holes by the distortion of the lenses. 'That's the other side of the banks and jewellers.'

'I know.'

'Then if we raise some hell, we'll cover their escape on the way up too.'

'Ought to be due some luck today,' said Carter. *We must be owed it by now.*

The four men kept to the narrow passages between buildings, sprinting through smoke and skirting the worst of the destruction. Carter's clothes were only going to be fit for giving to the charcoal burners to wear by the time he was done here. The stink of the devastation would stay with him quite a while, he suspected, frequenting his nostrils long after the fires had died away. *The scent of market week.* It was eerily quiet as they ran, only the sound of crackling timbers and the occasional complaint from birds abandoning rooftop nests for the safety of the sky. Getting to Wallace Hill and finding the street relatively unscathed, Carter selected an antique shop midway up the road. The door had been left banging open; its owners fled for the old town. They checked inside, climbed upstairs and unlatched windows on the second storey, a storeroom, waiting by the wall to see if the bandits were going to follow Carter's predictions. Carter stared up. He could hear the distant drone of the bandits' carrier circling Northhaven, that big ugly vulture the size of a city.

Caleb opened the chamber on his rifle and rolled it nervously. 'Handed me an Accuracy Armoury 54 calibre, what you got?'

'Stag and Robinson percussion system,' said Joah.

Eshean brushed the soot off his pistol. 'An old Emory five shot. Good sword with it, though.'

'Landsman repeater,' said Carter.

'Hell, that's a guild boy for you,' laughed Caleb. 'Even gets the best rifle.'

Carter kept a watchful eye on the deserted street below. 'Guild of *Librarians*. Stuck out in the hills, where a tramp banging on the gate is the highlight of the day.'

'Soft, easy work,' said Caleb. 'Good salary and pension. There's me hauling luggage up at the Grand Hotel, dressed like an admiral but sweating like a sailor. Eshean swinging a blade all day to carve steaks off cattle and Joah lugging a mason's level and trowel around, mixing mortar with his dad.'

'I like being a stone mason,' said Joah. 'At least I do in the summer. Feet get as cold as chunks of ice in the winter, no matter how many socks you pull on.'

'Well,' said Caleb, 'there it is. Getting into a guild isn't to be sniffed at. You're the top of the heap, Carter.'

'It's a small heap.'

'Yeah, I figured you for itchy feet,' said Caleb. 'But you don't need to travel much further than the custom gate for a wild time today, pastor's boy.'

By the window, clutching his pistol and short-sword, Eshean started shaking softly, tears rolling down his cheeks.

Carter leant forward. 'Are you—?'

'He's okay,' said Caleb, spinning the chamber on his rifle.

'He was sweet on Amy Pickerell,' explained Joah. 'Her house took a bomb right through the roof. Just matchwood left.'

'Never did tell her,' said Eshean. 'Never will now. I don't even want to think on the waste of it.'

'That's too bad,' said Carter.

Caleb shrugged. 'Got a town full of "too bad" now.'

And something else moving out there. Carter raised a finger to his lips and whispered. 'Four raiders coming up the hill. Three in front. One of them's riding something ugly as hell.'

The something in question resembled a salamander so large it could have swallowed a pony. Four big stocky legs, its body undulating as it moved. Panniers hung off a saddle that began at the nape of the lizard's neck and ended by its tail. Its rider and the raiders on foot were twisted lizard-snouted men, just like the refugees had claimed, muscular tails emerging from dark leather uniforms. Carter marked the one riding the beast as their officer. He sported a bicorn hat shading his face. A pole with three triangular standards fluttering from it stood strapped to his back, similar to the multi-coloured streamers tied to the wings of the bandits' fighters. They were all carrying rifles except the officer, who sported a belt hung with a brace of pistols and a sword, just the same as if he'd been serving with the king's cavalry. *The damn nerve of them! Raiders swaggering up the hill as though they were born in Northhaven.*

'Man,' whispered Caleb, 'and I thought the gasks were ugly.'

'Your sister's a leatherneck.'

'No, that was the last girl you stepped out with.'

'Saints, if that's what the men look like, I'd hate to see the women.'

'Hold it down,' ordered Carter.

Caleb gently pulled the hammer back on his rifle, a soft click inside the storeroom. 'I'll take the rider.'

'Wait a second.'

Outside, the bandit officer dismounted, all four raiders checking the door on the goldsmith opposite. Finding it locked, one of them booted open the door, an explosion of splinters as wood collapsed inwards.

'Four guns here and four of them in the street,' said Caleb, 'and you want us to sit on our backsides?'

'I do. Hold off until they come out loaded with all that they can carry,' whispered Carter. 'Hands too full of silver to be reaching for iron.'

'That's cold, no better than a bushwhacking.'

Carter remembered the old constable's words. 'We're not going down there to challenge them to a duel! They come out loaded with silver, we give them lead.' He raised his rifle and hugged its stock tight against his shoulder to absorb the recoil. 'Gun them down when they come out.'

Caleb raised his rifle. 'You sure you've not been apprenticed with a highwayman out in the hills, rather than those librarians? Carter Carnehan, Northhaven's greatest bushwhacker ...'

'Don't waste your time gassing. Don't waste any bullets, either.'

They exited two by two, only the bandit officer without any booty, his soldiers staggering under the weight of sacks stolen from the workshop out back. They hadn't taken more than a step towards their riding beast when all four men opened up – a shot apiece from the rifles – two of three bullets bracketing out from Eshean's pistol, his hand working the hammer fast. *Isn't much effort to take four lives, feels like it should be harder.* Four bandits threw back against the shop's boards, the officer jouncing forward and flipping over the rail in front of the store. Hitting the cobbled street, his bicorn cap fell off and caught in the wind, skipping past the rearing, panicked riding beast. It broke its ties to the rail and went stampeding down the hill, a strange wailing from its jaw, panniers spilling the product of earlier looting across the road as it fled.

'I don't feel a thing,' said Eshean, reaching for his sword.

Carter stopped him as he realised what the abattoir worker wanted to do. *No trophies.* 'We're not savages.'

'They're just meat now, that's all they are to me.'

'We better change location quick,' said Carter, chambering another round into his rifle. 'We need to be down the street when their friends come visiting.'

'Bushwhacking, bushwhacking,' sang Caleb. 'For our picnic they came packing, and when down they were sitting, we got the lot bushwhacking.'

He's running high on the tension ... maybe far too tight. 'Keep it together,' growled Carter as they ran down the stairs, checking the street, then lighting out for a pottery overlooking a crossroad.

'One shot.' Caleb raised a finger, laughing. 'Just one shot. Wish I could do this to the head doorman at the Grand. This is living.'

No, you idiot, it's dying – it's them, or us.

'Save it for the bandits,' said Joah, glancing worriedly at his friend.

They took up position in the pottery. As before, they climbed upstairs for height, sliding the windows open on the second storey. They had a view of its terrace, a striped canopy over the pavement and a sniper's sight of the street; Caleb laughing and joking, Eshean as dour and brutal as a block of granite, Joah blinking through his big milk-bottle glasses and Carter maybe as cold as they thought he was. They waited for the sound of their ambush to bring more of the twisted bandits running, but come the raiders didn't. Guns crackled in the distance, brief bursts of fire being exchanged.

Sounds like the four of us aren't the only ones having luck ambushing bandits. 'There should be more raiders,' said Carter.

'Saint's teeth, Carter,' said Joah. 'What you hoping for? A cavalry charge of those horse-sized lizard monsters?'

'I mean, if the bandits were serious about looting Northhaven, they'd have put more boots on the ground. You don't commit a light scout force to a raid.'

'They were landing gliders on the river flats, mostly,' said Joah. 'I guess their main targets are the goods stored at the warehouses and the railhead? Those four we gunned could've been chancers, just dipping in from the main raid to see what they could loot?'

'Not enough people inside the old town,' said Carter, thinking out loud. 'You've seen how busy it gets during market week. People crushed so tight you can hardly take a step without getting cursed by some old girl out shopping. We've been here maybe twenty minutes and we've not seen a single straggler heading up the slope.'

'You saying we're not going to be bushwhacking any more raiders?' asked Caleb.

'I'm saying it doesn't make sense. The bandits are dive bombing us to keep us hunkered up in the old town. But why bothering corralling us if they're not going to bother to loot Northhaven properly?'

'If all you see is a fist, ask yourself where the hand with the knife is,' said Joah, quoting one of the territorial sergeant's favourite maxims.

'Don't think we've seen the knife hand yet,' said Carter. And that had him worried, but not as much as at the sight that greeted him the next second. His parents sprinted out of the fumes from Prospect Hill, a gaggle of children behind them screaming and yelling. Carter didn't need to be told what would be pursuing them. Caleb, Joah and Eshean jolted up and started to run back to the stairs, but Carter yelled to them, 'Hold and shoot – keep the high position, or we'll be setting up a crossfire with those youngsters catching bullets in the middle!'

Carter vaulted the windowsill, jumping out onto the store's wooden terrace. He aimed his rifle towards the swirling sea of black smoke. Joah leapt behind him, then the other two men. In the street, Carter's parents turned the corner of the crossroads, driving the gaggle of school children up the hill, so focused on hurrying the youngsters along they hadn't spotted the four young men on the second storey of the building opposite. *They'll hear this, though.* Six or seven bandits came sprinting out of the wall of smoke to meet a hail of bullets, the painful buck of the rifle butt slamming against Carter's shoulder as he worked its brass lever. He worked the trigger guard so hard his finger blistered up. Smoke from the others' guns drifted across Carter's vision, sulphur filling his nostrils. Through it, he could just see raiders dropping to the cobbles, bandits holed and a few still thrashing. His fusillade hadn't made any difference to the pupils from the school … the kids pelting up the street, each one following the next.

Carter's parents glanced to the rear as the four young men swung down over the canopy, hitting the raised wooden walkway in front of the shop. They retreated backwards with their guns ready to cut down the next wave of raiders.

'I see signal smoke coming from the keep!' shouted Joah, pressing a fresh round into his rifle's breech as he fell back. 'They're going to drop the portcullis on us.'

Please, not yet! Other men from the deputed mob came running out of a side-street, attracted to the violence like trout to a fishing lure. The melee quickly became a nightmare. Bandits emerging from the smoke and fires burning in surrounding streets, the Northhaven men retreating, dodging behind water butts and columns, firing wildly, and none of them faster than the slowest school children. Carter shouted with excitement and fear, the bandits shooting back, bodies dropping. More men sprinted out ... some behind the raiders, others in front. Bullets zipped past Carter's ears humming like hornets, wood splintering, masonry cracking amidst screams of rage and fear and wild exuberance. Hard to tell if Carter's shots struck anything, there were so many bullets in the air. Bandits spun off their feet, men dragging bloody bodies out of the street and into cover, some rushing across the street with their rifles jolting, others fanning the hammer on pistols. It was madness. Fumes and puke and fear and bravado. Who could see this carnage and call what happened tactics or strategy? Just random death and hate and killing mixed with blood. More men appeared, these ones in the blue uniforms of the town constables and running down from the ramparts. Wiggins' constables must have seen the battle breaking out and ducked in from the old town to help cover their retreat.

Carter dodged behind an unharnessed cart, using its cover to slide a fresh chain of shells into his repeater's breech, pieces of wood splintering from the wagon as the bandits tracked in on his dash to shelter. He lifted the reloaded rifle. Carter's eyes settled on the other side of the street and caught a sight to still his heart. His father dragging his limp mother out of the road, onto the shops' raised walkway opposite. Children rushed away from them, a couple of locals backstepping and covering the pupils' flight up the hill. *Mother!* Carter followed a strangled yell of anguish that might have been his own out across the road, bullets drifting around him as thick as rainfall and not one touching his tall, haring body. Jacob Carnehan dragged his wife into cover through the open door of a general store. Carter nearly slipped on the slick trail of blood her passage had left on the planks. Inside, his mother moaned something, the words croaking out through a froth of spittle and it was only when he knelt by her side, opposite his father, that he could hear what she was saying.

'Get — the children — up — the hill.'

Carter clutched the hand his father wasn't gripping. 'Wiggins' men have got them. They'll be through the gatehouse any second.' Carter could hardly keep his eyes off his mother's stomach, ruined and bubbling from where a volley had caught her.

'Thought I — told you — to — stay put?'

'I carried that Rodalian pilot to safety,' whispered Carter. 'But who else was going to come down here and make sure everyone in the school got up the hill?'

'Who else?' She was staring up at Jacob, her eyes as clear as stream water. 'You look — after — my boy now.'

Jacob Carnehan was so pale, the old man's skin might have been whitewashed. 'What am I going to do without you, Mrs Carnehan?'

'I refer you — to my — previous answer, Mister Carnehan.'

'Just hold on,' Carter begged. 'We can carry you up the hill. Hospital staff are working right behind the battlements.'

'I need to rest — now, Carter. That — spot — behind the church — with your — two brothers.'

'Help me carry her!' yelled Carter.

The warmth drained from Mary Carnehan's hand. And just like that she was gone. His mother had shut her eyes and was speaking no more. It was easy to tell. The illumination in her soul, the warmth … it had moved on. Carter's father wasn't in any state to register his son's words – just clinging to Mary Carnehan and crying. *No, not my mother anymore, just her body.* Whatever warmth had been in Carter's blood drained away too. He had never felt anything like this before. The pain was unbearable, welling up and twisting his heart into a helpless knot. Part of him couldn't believe that this was happening. That he had actually watched it. Mary Carnehan must have experienced something similar when Carter's brothers had been buried. But he had been too young at the time to understand. Too young to share the pain, to try to offer comfort. Not now. Death carried everyone away, always missing Carter by inches. *Time to give it another chance.* Carter stood up and checked his rifle. Seven rounds heavy. It wasn't a gun. It was just a tool, and its work lay outside. All his feelings wasted away, along with the fear and the adrenaline and the worry and the anguish. What was left? Just a hungry void. And it needed feeding. Carter stepped out of the general store. The street filled with Northhaven men running and dodging, bandits advancing up the hill and mixed in with the town's defenders. Carter stepped through the smoke and the flying bullets of a bad dream, sending one of the twisted men whirling with his first shot.

'How do you like that? Here I am! It's my turn!'

It was a start, a single pebble tossed into the pit, and he had a canyon that needed filling. Eshean was ahead of him, the abattoir worker out of bullets for his pistol and taking his short-sword to the raiders, a company of them alongside one of their riding beasts, two raiders on top, big iron pipes on either side of its scaly green flanks. Carter worked the brass lever under his rifle, bandits dropping around the abattoir man as his gun bucked. Eshean was lost to the world. The big man had his own void that needed filling, no doubt.

'Come on! Is that it?' Bullets whizzed past him, but they always missed. *A bullet for everyone but me.* 'How can you sons-of-bitches keep on missing me?'

'Carter!' Jacob Carnehan stood in the doorway of the general store, shouting towards his son. Carter levered a shell into one of the ugly twisted raiders sprinting towards him. The pastor had the saints and angels and maybe even God to fill his void. But this was all Carter had. *Let me be.*

'Carter, get—'

The rest of his father's words were lost in the double explosion from the weapon tubes on either side of the riding beast. The creature bucked, nearly throwing the two bandits – its gunners – over their mortar. Carter just had time to glance around and mark the collapsing cascade of timber where the general store had been located, smoke and vapour and fire where his father should have been standing. *Father! No!* Both parents dead. His mother and then his father. *Murdered.* It wasn't pain he felt now. It was anger. An endless boiling sea of it. Pure white-hot fire. Every one of these murdering bastards was going to die. If death wouldn't take Carter Carnehan, he'd keep on prodding and poking the grim reaper until it damn well took notice. Until every raider in the prefecture was a corpse. *Or I am.* He strode forward; ignoring the inhuman screeching until he realised it was coming from his own throat. His gun bucked and the nearest raider went down, shot in the spine, even while it struggled with a Northhaven man. That was a fine sight. Carter took aim again, but then a second mortar's shell impacted forward of the first. Another storefront came tumbling down, its explosion lifting Carter up and forward. He flew wingless, just like so many dreams that had been mere premonitions of this moment. Carter hardly felt the cobbles of the road scouring his body into a bloody mess as he struck and rolled. *Still time, to fill the hole.* Still time to kick death until it turned round and took notice. He staggered to his feet. Carter's eyes settled on his Landsman – the finest rifle in the Kingdom of Weyland – split in half as clean as if it had been designed that way. His ears rang, the sounds of the raid distant and tinny. His lips split and mouth full of dust. Something red filled Carter's eyes. As he blinked away the sticky, gluey liquid, he was just in time to focus on the end of the rifle butt growing massive in front of his face.

After that there wasn't much of anything.

THREE

LOSS IS CHANGE

There wasn't any particular moment when Jacob Carnehan regained awareness. If his body was a beach then his mind was a tide, rising and falling, steadily dipping in and out. A bare awareness of light and broken wood being pulled off him, faces drifting backward and forward, voices, darkness, more whispering, memories and pain – physical and of the soul and heart – tugging him below the undertow. Time passed. Jacob's body would twitch and his eyes would blink, water being spooned through his parched lips, something warm that might have been soup, the taste of carrots and barley, before the darkness grew cold and total and he could not stop shivering.

Finally, something built within him, an ache, a pain so sharp, swelling and growing, that it finally carried him to full consciousness. Sweating and weak and light-headed. Jacob lay in bed – his own, the room with a view over Church Lane, the weight of a dozen blankets pressing down upon his body. There were two people in the room, waiting on chairs on either side of his bed – Constable Wiggins on the left. On the right, another familiar face. Brother Frael from the old monastery in the mountains, a place of peace overlooking the Lancean Ocean's green depths. As always, the brother seemed to carry the smell of the sea on his simple grey habit. A sallow, wide face, an open and friendly countenance with skin as tight as dried seaweed.

Jacob summoned enough energy to speak, the whisper rustling out over chapped lips. 'Where's Carter?'

'Stay down,' advised Brother Frael, reaching over to lay a hand on the rough woollen blankets.

'Where is—?'

'As close to death as I ever seen a man sail,' said Wiggins, 'and he comes out of the other end just as stubborn as he fell.'

'You need to rest,' said Brother Frael, scratching the bald scalp of his tonsure.

'Man needs the facts,' said Wiggins, 'and he won't be much for resting until he gets them, if you ask me.'

The monk clicked his teeth in irritation.

'Truth is,' said Wiggins. 'As far as Carter is concerned, we don't know. Almost all of the new town was burnt to ash. After your school children were brought in, the raiders took umbrage at the bloody nose they'd been given on the hill. Flew in again with dive bombers and flattened what wasn't already burning.'

'I have seen where you were pulled out,' said Brother Frael. 'It is the only part of the street not torched to embers – a miracle, truly.'

Wiggins shrugged. He obviously didn't share the monk's sentiments. 'Not much of a one for the rest of our people, Brother. We've come across hundreds of bodies in the ashes, too burnt to identify. The cruel truth of it, Jacob, is that Carter's either dead or one of the quarter of the town's people unaccounted for.'

'Slavers,' hissed Jacob.

'Ain't that the truth of it. Anyone my age they rounded up, they left on the other side of the river road minus their skulls. More corpses out in the fields than we've recovered from the new town's wreckage.'

'How long?' moaned Jacob. 'How long have I been like this?'

'This is the sixth day since we dug you out,' said Wiggins.

'I and the other friars came down from the monastery on the train,' explained Brother Frael. 'To handle the burials and services.'

On the train? The monks' vows included travelling only by foot and eating wholly from the wooden begging bowls they carried with them. That was enough to tell Jacob how bad things were outside his room.

'I'm sorry, Jacob,' said Wiggins. 'We had to do Mary's service already, you understand? We put her next to your two kids out back. Figured that's what she would have wanted.'

'The mayor demanded we dig mass graves,' said Brother Frael. 'But he relented when we refused and said we would carry out only individual services. Mary's final candle was lit by my own hand, as gentle as any service ever conducted.'

Jacob pushed himself up. *Mary*. He had almost been able to imagine that her death was a bad dream. A premonition never come to pass. But it wasn't. He tried to speak, but only a dry keening noise left his lips. *My wife, my darling wife. What am I going to do without you? How will I live? How can I go on from here?* Where would there be, indeed, to even go to? She had been his anchor, his rock and his conscience. His best part. He recovered his composure for a second. 'I need to see.'

'Lie back down,' commanded the monk.

'Where my wife is buried,' said Jacob, pushing his legs out from under the mountain of blankets enveloping him. *I need to see her*.

'Listen to the man,' urged Wiggins.

'Hold my side,' ordered Jacob. 'Bear me up. I'll see her grave *now*.'

Grumbling, the constable took Jacob's weight, ignoring the monk's despairing gaze and Jacob slid his heavy, trembling weight, step by step, down the rectory stairs.

Brother Frael opened the door of the boot room and Jacob felt the raw slap of cold outside. Northhaven was a sight to see, the hill bare and black. Only the wreckage of the occasional store or home stood, a grid of grey in the black where streets had once been, the walls of the old town streaked dark with soot. Smoke coiled from the chimneys of buildings hidden behind the ancient battlements. Up in the air, barrage balloons still swung in the wind, as if the town expected a second raid.

'Sweet saints,' coughed Jacob.

'The slavers stayed here a night and a day,' said Wiggins. 'Ambushing everyone coming in for the market. They left in the afternoon of the second day, an hour ahead of a couple of river frigates packed with royal marines from the sea fort at Redwater. The bandits' carrier flew straight over their sails, heading back towards the ocean.'

Jacob limped to the plot at the back of the rectory where he had once buried two of his three children, finding a freshly-turned hump of dirt. Unlike the other two mounds, its marker was staked in simple wood rather than marble. The town's masons were probably dead, tools looted and destroyed. Jacob stumbled forward, numb with cold and exhaustion, sinking to his knees by the freshly turned dirt. He read the jolting words. 'Mary Carnehan, mother of three.' *How many funerals have I presided over as the pastor of Northhaven? All those words, all those people.* 'This is my family.'

'Get up, Jacob,' said Wiggins. 'This isn't any good for you.'

'I should be with them.' He wanted to be. This was a terrible wound. Being gut-shot would be a mercy compared to this pain. Losing an arm, losing a leg, they would be nothing. Scratches he would trade in an instant to bring his family back. *Mary dead. Carter dead.* 'I'm dead, too. My body just doesn't know it.'

'On your feet, Father,' said Brother Frael. 'Your son might yet be alive.'

Jacob's eyes cleared of tears enough to look up at the blasted ruins of the city on the hill. 'No, he's up there; his ashes are in the new town, where mine should be. I'm cursed, all I've ever loved is here, on this plot.'

'It's time to rebuild,' said the monk.

'Not for me,' whispered Jacob. He could travel to the ocean one last time. Find the shoreline and keep on going. Let the waves cover his body, claim him. Their weight was the only peace he would be able to find. 'Leave me here. Just going to be with them.'

Wiggins knelt down beside the pastor. 'You saved my granddaughter the other day, Father. It'd be on my soul mighty heavy if I was to repay you by letting you freeze to death here tonight.'

'Mary saved them, not me. All that I am was her. What am I now? Not even the right words to speak here, over her body. There should be more than five words carved on her grave.'

'Father, I've got a platoon of royal marines fifty feet from here digging fresh graves in the grounds of your church,' said Wiggins. 'Damned if I'm going to let one of those holes become yours. So you can get back on your feet and tuck yourself under your blankets, or I'm going to order a company of those blue-coated man-mountains to come over here and carry you back, as undignified as that'll be.'

Jacob rose to his feet and let the monk and Wiggins lead him back inside the rectory. *So tired now. Sleep.* Sleep was a form of death, the little death. Something other than cold to numb him and carry him away from this.

Brother Frael came into the bedroom, a look of irritation creasing his normally calm features as he saw that Jacob had his hands on a newspaper, the *Redwater Post*. 'Who gave that to you, Father? There's nothing inside but lists of the dead and missing.'

'The woman you've been sending to force a spoon in my mouth passed it to me,' said Jacob.

'You saved her child, Father. Her little boy wouldn't be alive without you.'

'Maybe that's why she passed me her newspaper, even though you've forbidden it.'

'You are not an easy man to get along with, Father Carnehan.'

'Guess that's why I'm here and not in the monastery.'

'You have a visitor, Father.'

'I don't want to see any more parents, Brother.' *Let me be, just let me wither away here in peace, in silence.*

'This one, I think you will want to meet,' said the monk. He turned and opened the door, admitting a broad six-foot figure. Jacob took in the leathery brown skin of a gask – a fully-grown adult man, the black spines along the backs of his arms as taut and proud as an oiled porcupine's. He placed a hand over his chest, resting his fist against his white toga and bowed slightly. His sad, bear-like eyes met Jacob's. There was something knowing in that gaze, expectant.

'The manling Wiggins told me you would be here.'

'And here I lie.'

'My name is Khow,' said the twisted forest man, producing one of his nation's metal abacus boxes, the green light of its screen washing across his face with the bedroom curtains closed. He presented Jacob a book with his other hand, laying it down on the blanket above Jacob's chest. It was a tome the pastor recognised. The novel had been taken from Carter's room, one of the few he and Mary had got the lad to love out of so many brought home from the stationers. *Tales of the Overland*. A couple of centuries' worth of outlaw tales committed to paper.

'Khow is a mystic of his nation,' said Brother Frael. 'He has come to Northhaven with three of the forest men. Their presence here has been ... useful.'

Khow was drifting the silver box up and down above Jacob's blankets.

'What are you doing?' growled Jacob.

'All things are weighed in numbers,' said Khow. 'Time, events, people, all of them bound and described only through maths – and that influence can be traced and felt.'

'I don't understand?'

'Of course not. The minds of common pattern men do not resemble ours. I did not need my calculator to lead me to yourself or the manling Wiggins. I followed my son's thread to yours.'

Son? 'You're the father of that little gask, out on his wandering? Kerge?'

'I am,' said the twisted man. 'Kerge, son of Khow. He has been taken, Jacob Carnehan. The slavers have snatched my son.'

'How do you know? Maybe he's here? His ashes scattered in what's left of the new town?'

'I know,' said Khow, 'because my son has a weight on the universe. A pressure. And that weight is undiminished, even as it rolls further away from us with each new hour. All gasks know where their children are, and can follow the trail with their heart, their instinct and this—' He held up the silver box. 'Your son too. My child's life is bound to your son, as your life is bound to my son since you rescued him.' The gask pushed down on Jacob's chest with his long fingers. 'And I believe your child's weight is still upon the world. Even with your manling minds and strange lives, my calculator's results indicate that much.'

Could it be true? Jacob could barely dare to hope. So many strange tales circulating about the forest people and their superstitions and legends. *It sounds like madness ... clutching at straws. Is this just a herb-induced vision spun from their woodland magic ... encouraged by this damn monk to give me a glimmer of hope to cling to?*

'The four of them have been doing this all over town,' said Brother Frael. 'Survivors bringing in things that missing family members were fond of ... flutes, books, hats, anything that wasn't destroyed during the raid. Most times, the gasks have been able to tell our people whether their loved ones are dead or alive.'

'Where is Carter now?'

'That I cannot say with certainty,' said Khow. 'Only my child's soul may I track with accuracy. The bond I have with your boy is where his threads cross with those of Kerge. It would be logical to assume they are still together, as prisoners of the slavers. They were taken as a group. They will in likelihood end up sold at the same slave market.'

'Do you believe this?' Jacob asked the monk.

'I have faith that the gasks believe it,' said Brother Frael. 'You live closer to their forests than I do. But even up in the mountains, there are things to be seen that make little sense to the rational mind. You remember your time with us in Rodal? The way that spirits guide the skyguard pilots … fliers riding crosswinds ferocious enough to tear a flying wing into tinder. I cannot explain that. I cannot explain how gasks know where their children are.'

Jacob pushed the coffin-like shroud of blankets away from his sweating body. 'Where is your child, Khow? Where is Kerge now?'

The gask raised a spined arm and pointed to the wall. 'That way.'

'I've sent Wiggins to the library,' said Brother Frael. 'He's coming back with the master librarian and a large-scale atlas. Gasks don't seem to have much sense of distance. But Khow here believes he can indicate where the snatched people are on a map.'

Khow steepled his brown fingers together, the back of his hand covered with a soft down of fur. 'Time and distance are closed together, like this, perception and reality. When you are *of* the flow, you can never correctly *perceive* the flow.'

'If you're fixing to follow your son,' said Jacob, 'the existence of those miles will seem a mite realer to you.'

'I was in two minds as to whether to tell you about this,' sighed Brother Frael. 'You needed to know about Carter. But following? Have you ever heard of success in such matters? You will die an old man out in the infinite world and never return to us.'

'A man's got to die of something,' said Jacob. He held a hand out to Khow, and the twisted man helped him sit up. Even that made him feel dizzy. 'How far you figuring on travelling, Khow?'

'Only to my son,' said the gask.

Only to my son. That's as good a way of looking on it as any other. All thoughts of allowing the ocean to take his life had fled from Jacob's thoughts. Carter could be alive. There was a chance he was *alive*, survived along with hundreds of other frightened, terrified Northhaven townspeople. Taken as human beasts of burden. Part of Jacob hated how easily he grasped at this single, measly thin thread that had been thrown to him. How easily he could believe in the forest man's superstitious mumbo-jumbo. *God, tell me that this is real. Tell me that this isn't just some survival instinct kicking in, looking for an excuse to go on living, living for nothing but a fantasy?* He heard a voice answer inside his mind. *'Mister Carnehan, you damned fool. If our son is alive, you can drag your carcass out of bed and bring him back home. I don't care if he's one mile away or ten million. You haul yourself after him and keep going until you've brought our boy back home again. Him and every other man and woman that was taken from our town. There is no distance too far; no force too strong to stop you.'* That voice sounded a lot like his dead wife's. Jacob brushed the tears out of his eyes. Damn his self-pity. Those would be the last tears he would allow himself until Carter was safe once more. Jacob shoved the weight of blankets away. He might as well have been sliding the lid off his coffin.

Brother Frael tutted and Jacob caught a glimpse of himself in the mirror on the sideboard, a skeleton swaying in white underclothes. 'I'll have some real food now, brother. Not chicken broth.' Jacob limped downstairs, ate and waited for the librarian to arrive. Filling up on meat and cheese and bread and milk and everything that had been dust in his mouth until a few minutes ago. He was still eating when Wiggins came into the rectory with the library's guild master by his side, a leather tube bulging with maps tucked under the old man's arm, along with a large book. Jacob realised this was the first time he had ever seen Lucas make a house call. He was probably violating half a dozen guild oaths in carrying his precious maps beyond the hold's security.

'Shoot,' grinned Wiggins, seeing Jacob out of his bed and sitting at the table. 'Always said Northhaven needed a cathedral, the size we were getting to. And here we are ... a gaggle of monks moving around the church and a walking corpse crawled out of his coffin and stuffing his face fit to be a fully titled bishop.'

Jacob ignored the constable's sardonic humour and nodded to Lucas. 'Master Codex. I was happy to see that none of your people were listed among the dead and missing, apart from Carter, of course.'

'Not for a lack of trying,' said Lucas. 'Seventy bandits turned up outside the library with barrels of blasting powder for our gate – intent on looting the hold of its works. There are, I am sorry to say, plenty of libraries outside the guild that would pay handsomely for contraband titles plundered from my shelves.'

'They couldn't get past your metal doors?'

'It was the strangest thing,' said the librarian. 'As the bandits arrived, a mist fell over the valley. It turned so thick that an aircraft circling in support of their raiders flew too low, destroying itself against the valley's slopes.'

'I have heard that can happen in battles,' said Jacob. 'The fires from Northhaven, the weapons smoke. It can play games with the weather.'

'When we came out to check, there were bandits' corpses scattered everywhere. Reckon the explosion from the plane's payload must have taken them out. The rest had fled.'

'It was surely the hand of the saints,' said Brother Frael.

'Perhaps. When Carter was small, I always used to tell him that there was nothing God loves so much of an evening than settling back in a comfortable chair and reading a little.'

'Poor Carter,' sighed Lucas. 'I certainly am sorry the way things have worked out. And for your wife, may the saints watch over her treasured soul.'

Jacob lifted a fork towards the window of the kitchen, the crunch of the marines digging fresh graves carrying over the rectory wall. 'How much sorry have we got to go around for this?'

'Always enough,' said the monk.

'You're a better man than I, Brother,' said Jacob. He pointed at the librarian's tube next to the red leather-bound tome he was carrying. 'The map holder I recognise, what's the book?'

'Volume seven hundred and twenty-six of the *Bestiary Physicallis*,' said Lucas. 'The one where the raiders' nation is referenced.'

'You're sure you've got the right people?'

'Indeed I am,' said Lucas, tapping his volume. 'The hospital has already dissected a corpse. The physical drift of their internal organs matches the people recorded inside this volume, as does their physical appearance. The bandits are called skels. Millennia ago, their nation lay millions of miles southwest of here. It was destroyed and overrun when their neighbours tired of the skels' continued brigandage. Since then, they have lived as aerial nomads. Slavers, as we know to our cost.'

'How up-to-date is that entry?'

'It was recorded three thousand years ago,' said Lucas. 'But the devastation of Northhaven indicates their society is still based on brigandage and blood.'

'A long way from home,' said Wiggins, pulling up a chair at the table. 'Never heard of them before.'

'Unfortunately, Weyland has,' said Lucas. 'Three years ago, a town out in the east by the great lakes was attacked by slavers. No bandits' bodies were taken, but the raiders' description matches that of our attackers. And this is only what my archivists have managed to turn up in the archives with a few days of searching. There may have been many similar attacks across Weyland. On other league nations, too, perhaps.'

Jacobs scratched the stubble on his cheeks. 'If there's a pattern to their raids and we can spot it ...' *Our soldiers can be waiting for them next time.*

'If the assembly and the king know of this, then they wouldn't want panic,' speculated Wiggins.

'I'll take informed caution over a slaughter,' growled Jacob. *If they knew, they should have told us. Warned the prefecture.*

Lucas lifted up his map tube and removed an old parchment from inside, unfurling it over the tabletop. A patchwork of a thousand thumbnail-sized nations and countries, all squashed together so tight there wasn't even room to fit in their names – only numbers: an index on the side to identify each nation. Down the middle of the map lay the long boot-like shape of the Lancean Ocean, the feuding nations of the Burn on the western shore, the countries of the Lanca along the eastern seaboard.

Khow leant over the table. 'Where are we on your representation?'

Jacob reached out and touched the Kingdom of Weyland.

'Then my son is here,' said the gask. His hand stretched out, a finger coming down on the border where the last nation of the Lanca lay.

'Heading south?' said Wiggins, not able to hide the surprise in his voice.

Jacob felt the disappointment rising within him, crushing his heart. *Nothing but woodland magic and mystical nonsense after all.* 'I think you're mistaken.'

'I am not. He is *here*,' said Khow, tapping the map again.

'I do not think that is likely,' said Lucas, gently. 'As a rule, the nations of mankind grow more civilised the further south you travel.'

'Ain't that the truth,' said Wiggins. 'Out west, across the water, they'd sell your hide in a second. Don't have slave markets out in the Burn, just markets, you understand? And north of Rodal, well, you go far enough north and they ain't even got swords to beat on each other, just bows and flinthead arrows. Slaves are as good as horses and cattle to the nomad hordes.'

The gask shrugged his shoulders. 'We have never kept slaves among the gasks. But where I have indicated ... that is where my son is. He is still being moved away from us, I fear.'

'It's possible, theoretically,' said Lucas, as much to himself as the others in the room. 'If you flew far enough south and travelled past the rumoured origin point of the trading caravans, resources would grow scarcer again. You'd eventually end up flying over countries where keeping slaves could be considered an economic proposition.'

'Years of flight, half a lifetime to travel that far,' said Jacob. 'All that time ... the bandits feeding and watering their slaves, fuelling their carrier's weight as they travelled. It makes no sense? The skels have to be looking to sell Northhaven's people as slaves in the Burn. Only a week's flight across the sea; plenty of demand out west for slaves to bear spears and muskets for some Burn warlord.'

'Do you have a representation of Northhaven similar to this document?' asked Khow.

Jacob walked to his shelves in the parlour and returned with a local map. Khow examined the layout of the town for a second. He tapped the outer circle of the old town by the walls' eastern keep. 'One of the gasks in my party is my niece, Khbar. She is presently here, in the middle of the street, and is walking towards here.' He placed a finger on the end of the road.

Wiggins pulled a signalling mirror out of his belt pouch and left to flash a message towards the battlements. He returned a few minutes later with a crooked grin on his lips. 'Right on the money, damned if he ain't. One of my boys saw the lady gask outside the general store at the eastern end of the outer circle.'

'If you wish,' said Khow, 'I can sit here with you, and at a time of your choosing, I will show you again where Khbar is travelling.'

'I believe you're not selling us a confidence trick,' said Jacob. 'Forgive me my surprise. I have seen enough lies in my time to know the truth.' *Even though it makes no sense. Flying south? Travelling that far? Well, I'll travel to hell without a compass if it means saving Carter.*

'I know what that look in your eyes means, Father,' said Lucas, the librarian's hypnotic gaze fixed on the pastor. 'I might fold you into a frequency wave and have the radiomen fling you across their relays, and you would still have a job catching up with the bandits' carrier. And even if you can overtake the raiders, what then? Will you convert the skels into sainted followers of the church; have them renounce brigandage and make a gift of our kidnapped people back to you?'

Jacob pushed his now empty plate aside. 'What do you say, Khow?'

'That what a father feels for his child has a distance that cannot be measured. You are a manling and I am a gask, but in this matter, as in many others, the equations of our existence are bound together.'

Jacob nodded in agreement. The gask's words reflected how he felt. But there was a faint voice of doubt within him, too. One that said that setting out to rescue Carter and the others was as much a death wish as walking into the ocean. But he had nothing else to live for, now. Only this. *You always were a stubborn mule*, said the voice in his mind. *Now you're going to put that to a purpose, you hear me?* The old librarian leaned across the table, passing Jacob a piece of engraved stone set in a rectangle of soft black leather.

'What's this?' asked Jacob.

'If you truly are set on this madness ... your son is a member of the guild, pastor, albeit reluctantly. Show this at any hold of ours, however far you need to travel, and you shall be given any and all assistance our libraries can provide.'

Jacob was touched. He had a feeling he was going to need all the help he could get. 'Thank you, Lucas. I don't know what to say.'

'You don't need to say anything. In this matter, actions speak louder than words – and that is from someone for whom words are his business.'

Jacob pocketed the seal. 'Carter never was going to be much of a librarian, was he?'

'That which he has been sent will help him understand who and what he is to be.'

'Troubles do have a way of doing that.'

'That's something to be afraid of,' said Wiggins. 'A stubborn fool with a plan. You want to let me in on it?'

Jacob lifted up the newspaper, a long list of dead across its pages. 'Here's my plan. It's time I started thinking of people who have suffered other than myself.'

So light, floating in heaven. Carter groaned as pain flared across his ribs, his face a crackling web of agony. *Not paradise, after all.* He pulled himself up from a warm wooden floor, into a dim, crowded pen stinking of sweat. Joah was there, the young stonemason's face a bruised swollen mess. A mirror of Carter's own? 'Where are we?'

'Slave hold of that bandit carrier,' said Joah. 'You were banged up pretty hard. Still, reckon we're lucky. One of the bandit officers stopped his soldiers kicking us to death; figured he might as well turn a profit from our sorry hides.'

Carter focused on their surroundings. They were inside a mesh-walled cage in a gloomy, cavernous chamber packed with hundreds of young Weylanders. One of many cells in the sizeable space, all filled to capacity with produce for the slave block. Only two portholes in the wooden fuselage inside Carter's pen, people crowding around both viewports for a chance to see something other than the dirty bodies of their fellow unwashed prisoners. A walkway crossed outside their cage, dividing them from an identical pen opposite.

'Who else is here?'

'Hell, Carter, might as well ask who isn't here. Most of the people in your graduation year, most of the people in mine. Eshean and Caleb are about somewhere. Nobody much older than us, though. No one young enough to need coddling, either. Only prime meat. The rest, I hear the bastards left as fertiliser in the fields out to the river.'

Then it came back to Carter, the terrible memory bursting like a dam. His mother dying. His father blown apart by a bandit mortar. The fuselage shifted slightly and Carter choked, his stomach heaving. His family was dead. How could he go on, now? *You don't have a choice, fool. You've been taken for a slave.* His gut retched again and he shut his eyes. Even with them closed he couldn't take away the image of his mother dying of her horrific injuries; the mortar shell exploding where his father stood.

'Hold it down if you can,' said Joah. 'Nothing to mop up puke with in here except our own clothes.'

'My mother and father, Joah, they're dead.'

'I know. We've got to be strong for each other now. That's all we got left, one another. They left the new town as ashes after we flew away from home. Us here, we're all that's left of Northhaven now.'

Carter could hold down his gut, but not hold in his tears. He lay down and sobbed for what might have been minutes or hours, until finally he drew himself up. Joah was still there. How long had the man been waiting? Carter hadn't even noticed. 'I'm done now, Joah. Where are the guards? I'm going to kill—'

'Anyone enters the cages, it's usually other slaves,' said Joah, holding up a placatory hand. 'The slavers are called skels. They're as ugly, twisted and mean up close as they are at a distance. And escape? Well, take a peep out of the porthole. We're way above the clouds. That's why it's so hot up here – the radiation belt is cooking us. And do you feel how light we are? Maybe a quarter less than we were on the ground. Unless you can pilot one of the slavers' gliders, only way we're getting off this carrier is when they sell our hide.'

'Then we take the whole damn carrier,' said Carter. 'Stick a bullet in the skull of every twisted bastard on board until we find one willing to land us.'

'Sure,' smiled Joah. 'Maybe then you can run for assemblyman when you get back home, catch the eye of one of the king's daughters, marry her, and accept the crown when he passes over. If we're going to stay alive as slaves, Carter, I think we're going to need to inject a little realism into our schemes.'

'I'll be a corpse before I'm a slave.'

'Well, at least that's realistic. You want a victory in this hellhole? I reckon staying alive will do.' Joah pointed to a wooden box-like affair in the corner. 'That's the only head, just a hole down onto the sky. Try and reach it if we hit turbulence and you're feeling delicate.'

Carter was about to reply when a gask in a dusty white toga came up to him. 'I beg your pardon, but might you have some paper upon your person you could spare me?'

Carter looked into the gask's green, bearish eyes, as if the twisted man was insane. 'Paper?'

The gask flourished a charcoal-burnt needle of wood he must have scavenged from the fall of Northhaven. 'Our captors have stolen my calculator, manling, but they cannot imprison my intellect.' He tapped the side of his head. 'I can evaluate probabilities solely with my mind, but I am faster with a pencil and paper.'

'Kerge here's been asking everyone inside the cage,' said Joah. 'You might as well check.'

Carter emptied his pockets, coming out with his half of the receipt he had given the travellers at the library for their trade data. *Sure had been meaning to archive that.* 'It's not much, but it's blank on the other side.'

The forest man's leathery face bobbed in appreciation and took it from Carter, his hand juddering as if the receipt was electrified. 'I know *you*. You are the child of Jacob Carnehan, one of the priests of your people's faith.'

'Yes, I'm his son,' said Carter. 'How the hell can you tell? Sure didn't see *you* in church!'

'Your father preserved my life on the great fractal branch, along with the manling Wiggins. Our means are bonded by his actions. Your father is a noble soul.'

'He was that, before the bastards flying this slave carrier blew him to pieces.'

'I do not think that is so,' said the gask. 'I could make a truer reading if my calculator was returned, but I do not think the threads between us would appear so heavy if your father's weight was missing from the world.'

'You're saying he's alive?'

'It may well be so.' The twisted man waved the receipt. 'Your presence here is significant to me. I must see what I can determine using pencil and paper.'

Carter watched him push his way gently through the crowd of prisoners to the other side of the cage, squatting against the fuselage and scribbling across the paper. Could it be true? *No, the gask's mistaken, as much as I want to believe him. I saw father's building take a direct hit from a mortar. My old man might have been a pastor, but if God provides those kinds of miracles, I haven't seen many of them so far.* Carter listened to the distant drone from hundreds of propellers muffled by the fuselage. Every hour, they put more and more distance behind them. Carter felt a well of desperation surge inside his chest, as though he was choking. He wanted to run to the cage's walls and shake it free. *Do something. Anything!*

'The gask's a little mad, isn't he?' said Joah. 'I wouldn't put too much faith in that woodland magic of his.'

'I saw my father die, right after my mother ...'

'You saw what you saw,' said Joah. 'You *know*. Hell if I do. My family might be holed up in the old town, weeping over me. They might be stretched out in the fields minus their skulls. Like as not, we're all going to our graves not knowing what happened to each other. Odd thing, though ...'

'What?'

'Check the sun outside. We're flying south, have been ever since we left home.'

Carter stood up. 'You sure? Not east? Not north?'

'Might be flying higher than eagles, but the sun still sets and rises in the same place. Straight south, I swear it.'

'Sweet saints, but that makes no sense?'

'Well, they're slavers, right? Must be a slave market out where we're heading.'

Carter's stomach sank further without the need for gravity's light touch. *We're going to be travelling further than anywhere I've ever heard of, right off the map.* And Joah was right, damn the man. The chances of their ever coming back were slimmer than pine needles. His eyes drifted to his right just in time to see the fist coming towards him. Carter side-stepped by instinct, the punch swinging wide, revealing Caleb at the head of a gang of young men – many of them the recently deputed irregulars he'd led out from the town's battlements. He backed off as far as he could, bewildered by the sudden attack.

'This,' shouted Caleb, raising his other fist, 'this is on you, Carter Carnehan!'

'You've got to be pranking me ...'

'Get back,' Joah shouted at the mob, trying to shove them away. 'What did he do? Invite the slavers to Northhaven? Sell them the blasting powder to burn it to the ground? You followed Carter out of the old town, and nobody had to hold a pistol to your head to make you do it.'

'You stand aside, Joah. This isn't on you. Without this fool, I'd be back safe inside the old town.'

Joah tried to stay in their path, but the mob was too strong, flinging him aside. Then they were on top of Carter. He lashed and punched and kicked at them. But the mob shoved Carter into the mesh, giving him the sort of pummelling fit to finish the job before the slavers had taken their turn. Carter could smell the stench of smoked clothes, punch after punch landing. Suddenly there was an abrupt brightness, as if someone had turned on a sun inside the slave pen. This was no natural illumination. Long arclights activated along the chamber's roof, blinding Carter after the cage's murky half-light. It had blurred his attackers' vision too. They stumbled about, all animosities briefly abandoned. Then something Carter struck in the back, flung him forward in a tsunami of water. As Carter slid across the soiled floor, he blinked water out of his eyes to watch a team of leather-clad slaves standing outside the cages wrestling with high-pressure hoses, knocking brawling prisoners down in the torrent. Tall skel guards waited behind the newcomers, well-armed and hissing orders at their house slaves. The servants turned their hoses off, leaving Carter and the others soaked and bruised from the pressure gunning. Carter watched a bandit officer step forward, a large coiled whip tied to his belt. His cruel snouted face turned to either side, examining his produce with contempt. Words came out, mangled by a forked snake-like tongue flickering through his twisted throat. The length of red flesh quivered back and forth over serrated teeth. 'Me am Si-lishh, slave master of this most noble vessel. Weyland vermin now have the honour of belonging to Duke Si-meliss. Blessings be upon the duke.' He raised a gloved fist towards the Northhaven mob sprawled in the lake of water.

'Weylanders young, full of vigour. That is why you selected to serve. But mob cannot be allowed to cull itself. That am job of Si-lishh.'

At his command, a gate in the cage was opened, and a line of the skel guards moved in. As they entered, they lashed out with black rods twice the length of a constable's truncheon, oily-looking batons sparking as the weapons connected with slaves. Men were flung back, landing writhing on the deck in agony.

The officer raised his voice loud enough for every crowded cage within the chamber to hear him. 'Some Weylanders grow sick and die. Weylanders weak … they always perish. Skels allow for natural wastage. But skels not allow for bad discipline. Not allow slaves to be fighting each other. This too wasteful. And now, Si-lishh must also be wasteful to demonstrate Weylanders not wild anymore. You am property!'

Carter moaned as he was picked up from the floor by a couple of slavers. The ugly twisted soldiers loomed a foot over his height, muscles as solid as the flanks of a rhino. They pulled Carter and his assailants out of the cage, not a word spoken by the guards as angry, sibilant breaths rasped over their forked tongues. In the cage opposite Carter's own, he glimpsed faces he recognised pressed against the mesh. *Duncan and Willow, Adella!* Shocked faces and eyes opened wide in recognition at the beaten, bloody form being dragged away before them. What a sorry sight he must appear. Pulled down the chamber's central gangway, Carter was lugged in front of three cells. Unlike his previous lodgings, these pens couldn't accommodate more than a handful of slaves inside. The stalls weren't mesh-walled, but formed from some transparent substance – translucent but as thick as a farmhouse wall. The skel guards threw Carter into the middle of the three cells, then tossed struggling Northhaven men after him, each cell soon packed to capacity with miscreants. Transparent doors slid shut, the voice of the slave master carrying through tiny air holes dotted across the walls. Carter swayed on his feet, steadying himself against the enclosure – cold and oily to the touch, like fish scales.

'Set timers!' boomed Si-lishh. His soldiers jumped to it, laying gloved hands on some kind of clockwork mechanism embedded in the wall. Si-lishh turned to face the prisoners caged in the rest of the chamber. 'Normally Si-lishh set timers to a day or two, to keep things interesting. But slaves' fight has interrupted meal of Si-lishh, so slaves only going to stay inside punishment cells for five minutes.'

Carter glanced around his cell. *Punishment? For only five minutes?* They were packed inside a little more crowded than they had been in the main cages, but with the air holes, Carter wasn't about to suffocate any time soon. He glanced to the cell on his left and saw Caleb staring at him in hatred from the other side.

'You're a dead man, Carter Carnehan!' Caleb yelled, banging the enclosure. 'There's not a cage thick enough to protect—' Caleb's words were cut off as he stumbled back, the wooden floor opening up beneath him like a bomb-bay hatch. One second he was here, the next he wasn't. Falling away, a tiny black dot tumbling towards the clouds below. Just like that ... maybe seven prisoners sent plummeting into the sky. *The man was an idiot, but he didn't deserve that!*

Carter's face snapped up when he heard the laughter hissing from the slave master. 'Guards set punishment cells' timers. Two hatches open at random. Third cell will stay closed. But even skels do not know which one. This gives guards of Si-lishh something to wager on.' Si-lishh leaned back rocking with amusement outside the enclosure. 'Of course, sometimes Si-lishh set all three cells to open. Just for change.'

Carter began trembling. He tried not to, but it was as though he just walked out into a winter night wearing only his underwear. Carter tried to get a grip on himself. He wasn't going to give the slave master the pleasure of seeing how hard he had to work to keep terror and panic at bay. Around him, men went wild in the two remaining cages; banging on the armoured walls, flinging themselves at the doors.

Si-lishh pulled out a watch on a chain fob from his belt. 'Three minutes am left. But is it to be one cell or two today?'

Twisted alligator-faced bastards. Punishment cells. You might as well load a single shell inside a pistol, roll the cylinder, point it at your head and squeeze the trigger to see what happens. Northhaven men threw themselves up the wall in the adjacent cell, fingers digging into the air holes. But the gaps were no bigger than a pencil lead, not enough purchase to hold a piece of paper, let alone a man's weight. One of the men inside Carter's cell lurched back at an imagined crack appearing in the floor – his screams mirrored from the cell on their right.

Carter dragged his gaze across. Their neighbours had been flushed. Whistling wind from outside beat through the air holes. He could see white clouds through the open hatch; hear the distant humming of hundreds of vast rotors keeping the city-sized slave ship in the air. *And then there was one.*

'Two minutes left,' laughed the slave master. 'What Weylanders think? Did Si-lishh set two or three hatches to open this afternoon?'

Carter smashed his fist against the door. He felt the same burning anger he had back at the fall of Northhaven. A desire to break free and crush the eyes out of this twisted man's skull with his bare hands. 'Why?'

Si-lishh bent forward, close enough that only Carter could hear the reply. 'Why? Why not, am better question. Common pattern scum overrun skels' motherland age ago. Driving survivors into sky. Make nomads of all skels. Am not fitting that skels now make their living from people on ground? Most proper that Si-lishh send Weylanders back to it.' He checked his watch. 'One minute left.'

Inside Carter's cell, the other slaves ran at the walls, trying to hang on for dear life before they met the same fate. Carter slammed his fist into the wall. 'You're going to kill me, do it and get it done, but don't bore me to death.' Carter slipped to the floor and stared up at the slave master, his face a mask of cold hatred. Si-lishh did not break his gaze, but just stood there, tapping his watch every few seconds. Carter tried to keep calm, each passing second as long as a full day. After an eternity, the cell door cracked open and the guards stepped forward. They smashed back the wave of desperate Northhaven men trying to flee, the spark of weapon prods filling the air.

'Slaves lucky today. Yes,' said Si-lishh looking down at Carter, the man's legs still folded, 'Si-lishh get fine price for this Weylander.' He turned to the slaves carrying hoses. 'Clean Weylanders' piss out of punishment cells.'

Carter left the cell. Sometime over the last few minutes his body had stopped trembling, but inside he was still shaking. Carter took deep, controlled breaths to still his pounding heart as the skels shoved him back along the passage, laughing. A small, useless victory. He was alive, but he might as well have been flushed into the open sky rather than face the fate waiting for him beyond the slave market.

Back in the main pen once more, Carter squatted on the cage floor opposite the gask. Kerge had run out of paper and was scratching formulae across the wooden planking, concepts that went far beyond Carter's understanding. The gask hadn't seemed much amused by Carter's suggestion that they could use what was left of his charcoal for a game of noughts and crosses. Behind the Northhaven man, slaves stood pressed up against the mesh, silently gazing at prisoners in the cage opposite. Slaves weren't allowed to call across the gantry to neighbouring cages. That was classified as a fracas, drawing a beating from the slavers' pain rods. At least the skels hadn't thrown anyone else in their transparent-walled punishment cells. As far as small mercies were concerned, nobody was foolish enough to try to attack Carter again. The slave master's meals were, Carter suspected, going to be uninterrupted by his captives in future. Behind Carter, people gazed silently at friends as though they were statues that had been sculpted opposite each other ... family at family, cousins at cousins, separated by chance, keeping vigil over the familiar, hanging on to anything they could from their old life. Carter had already played that game, spotting Adella in the press of the cage opposite, her usually mischievous face dull and blank, hardly seeing him at all. And then she had turned and slipped through the press towards Duncan Landor, leaving Carter kicking the mesh in anger. *Even here, even here.* Landor's heir had to prove he could take anything that mattered to Carter. *How the hell was Adella taken anyway?* Adella should have been protected behind the walls of the old town, nowhere near the slavers. *Somehow, I can't imagine her leading the charge against the raiders.*

Joah lounged across from Carter, sweating inside the hot, humid cage. The man misread the cause of Carter's brooding face. 'Caleb just needed someone to blame for this. He was always like that. Any shit he pulled, it was always somebody else's fault. Never his. He could run into a wall and blame me for laying the bricks. Nobody who grabbed a gun from the guardhouse back home had any right to think bandits were handing out picnic blankets and lemon drinks for us on the slope.'

'What Caleb was, he was,' said Carter, raising a tired hand. 'Don't matter much now, does it? The skels dropped him and the others like they were goddamn rocks.' Carter tilted his face back to the mesh, searching for Duncan Landor in the cage opposite. 'He had one thing right, though. Beating on the right person makes you feel better.'

Across from Carter, the gask muttered something about incomplete sets, setting Carter's nerves on edge. Carter reached out and stilled the charcoal the gask was using to sketch numbers across the floor. 'Trust me, Kerge, as someone who used to sit in a maths class with his brain pounding and his ears aching, some equations just don't have an answer.' Blinking rapidly, the gask stared at Carter as if he was mad. *Well, one of us is, anyway.* The gask's presence only added to the surreal atmosphere in the slavers' pens.

There came a commotion by the cage wall, but not another brawl this time. House slaves had appeared in the corridor outside, thin and rangy and wearing simplified grey versions of the slavers' leather uniforms. They carried bag-like water bottles, and unstopping the sacks, the house slaves pushed drinking spouts through the cells' mesh. Eager prisoners pushed and jostled for water like so many swine at a sow's teats. Skel guards unlocked the cage door and allowed six house slaves into Carter's pen, tall men, all of them dragging full hemp sacks. They approached a circular depression in the centre of the cell's floor. Into this hole they emptied their sacks.

One of the slaves raised his hand as well as his voice so that everyone in the cage could hear him. 'These rations need to last three days. Water will come once a day. If you hoard food and water, if the strongest steal food and cause deaths – wastage – among the weakest here, then the slave master will issue his soldiers a set of scales. They will weigh everyone once a week and the fattest ten among you will be placed in the punishment cells. So share these rations fairly.'

Carter crossed to the house slave emptying his sack, his shining black face sweat-beaded in the heat. Joah followed, gazing at the food with disgust. *I know how he feels.* Their rations appeared to come in two flavours. Fist-sized domes of stale biscuit and small pellets that might have been chipped-off tree bark.

'And which day do you bring the steak?' asked Carter.

The house slave shrugged. 'The day you die and end up in paradise, friend.'

'That's a Weyland accent,' noted Carter. 'You're an easterner?'

The house slave nodded. 'James Kurtain, like curtain, but with a "K". Been stuck here three years, ever since the skels raided Heshwick by the lakes. Sold most of my people. Kept me. Used to be a clockmaker so the skels set me to stripping and cleaning their engines. Skels are as sharp as flint but as dumb as dirt – wouldn't get very far without their house slaves. Best I can tell, they've been keeping us common pattern types as vassals since records began.'

'Well, James,' said Carter, 'when you've finished emptying that chickenfeed out, how about you leave your sack here?'

The house slave laughed. 'Right, so you can make a parachute, smash the head and slide down out of the shit pipe. You're not the first person to think of that. It feels light up here, but it gets real heavy, real quick, nearer the ground. You want to stay alive, let the skels sell you off, Northhaven boy.'

'Sell us down *south*?'

'Guess rich people like having folks to do the fetching and carrying as much as the skels do.'

'And it's common pattern people doing the buying?'

'Same as you or I,' said the house slave. 'Same set of people doing the purchasing, too. Skel order-book is always full, even when their slave pens are sitting empty ... what they're about, you see, is raiding to order.' James finished emptying the sack and moved in between the foraging mob so that none of the guards would spot him idling. 'The skels' customers turn up in a craft twice as long as this carrier; looks like a large firework. No rotors on her wings, just rockets at her rear, smaller jets on the side. She can hover like a hawk hunting above a meadow.'

Carter looked askance at the house slave. *Perhaps too long in captivity's unhinged him?* 'And the rockets don't set fire to the fuselage, how?'

'Because she's made of metal, brother.'

Joah laughed at his outrageous claims. 'Solid gold or solid silver?'

'Steel, if I had to say. I shit you not. But I guess it's something you'll need to see for yourself.'

Carter shook his head in disbelief. The house slave had to be wrong. What the hell kind of nation could produce something like that? He turned his mind to more practical matters. 'How easy would it be to send a woman from over there—' Carter pointed to the cage opposite '—and get her in here?'

'A lot easier than sewing a parachute out of sackcloth. Only the slave master down here has a practised enough eye to tell any of us common pattern types apart. But,' the house slave warned Carter, 'a word to the wise. Wherever it is our people end up, the slavers require everybody fit to work. Men and women alike. Not too young. Not too old. And definitely not sick or pregnant. Your lady arrives with a bun in the oven, and it's not light duty for her, it's a one-way trip out of the hatch. That's why the slavers never touch any of the Weylanders they take. A skel half-breed kills a common pattern woman on the way out of her womb.'

'I just want Adella released from that cage and across here with me.'

'Okay, Northhaven boy. You point her out to me and I'll see what I can do. In return, you get to wherever they're taking you, keep your eyes peeled for a woman – she'll be two years younger than me. Anna Kurtain. My little sister. You look out for her, maybe. Do what you can for her.'

'That's fair.' Carter stuck his hand out and James shook it. He pointed Adella out to the house slave and then the man left, still calling warnings to the packed pen about fairly distributing the food.

'What you think about him and his talk about a massive metal aircraft?' asked Joah.

'I'll hold judgement. Sounds mad, but if you'd told me a few days ago I'd be caged like a hog in a slavers' carrier, I would've said you were crazy too. James is lying about one thing, though. Passing out the food fairly is *his* idea, not that bastard Si-lishh's. The skels might not want their slaves cracking horns unnecessarily, but culling the weak out? They'd probably think it was good herd management.'

Joah stared despondently at the dry rations in the pit. 'You're not planning to get killed over Adella, are you?'

'I'm getting out, Joah. One way or another, I'm getting out. I'm just not slave material.'

It felt cold outside, colder than it should do; Jacob was a ghost moving through a town he barely recognised. Houses burnt and broken, whole districts reduced to ashes. Jacob wasn't the only phantom drifting through the landscape, plenty of others were wandering around – locals lost in their own home, so many familiar landmarks removed. Some were just standing still, faces wan and shiftless, looking as though they were trying to remind themselves that this was where they lived. From a town where nothing ever happened to a town where nothing was left. Companies of blue-uniformed marines marched in columns through the wreckage. *More troops still arriving down the river from the coastal port. Nothing they can do now, though.* No bandit in their right mind would be heading for this town ... filled with soldiers, plucked of most of what was worth plucking. Everywhere the smell of old burning drifted. A charcoal stench left in the wind, until a man's nostrils were filled with nothing else. Acrid veils of it clinging and following Jacob around – sleeping, waking, eating; no difference. The men of the town's territorial regiment were returning now. Back from the fleet, after looking for pirates when they should've had their eyes turned to skies closer to home. Their houses gone. Livelihoods gone, families gone. Not much of anything left for anybody.

Flying wings drifted overhead, arrow-like formations of triangular aircraft. The Rodalian Skyguard trying to reassure the nervous survivors below. Wiggins hobbled along on Jacob's left, his old eyes sweeping across the ruins without comment.

'How is Benner Landor taking matters?' asked Jacob.

'Frankly,' said Wiggins, 'you're lucky he's made time to see you. With Duncan and Willow missing, he's only living for the honour of the house. Rebuilding wharves along the river, getting his tenants to try and lay in a late-squeeze crop to make up for what's been stolen.'

'People react to grief differently.'

'Ain't that the truth. I hear there are fine ladies from down south showing up again at Hawkland Park, sniffing around for a wedding sometime down the line. Maybe the wharves aren't the only things he's looking to replace.'

'Don't judge him too harshly.'

'Just saying, is all. Before Lorenn Landor passed, Benner was a better man. Money and power and prestige are all he's been left with, so he figures he might as well fill up on as much of it as is going.'

Jacob traded a stony look with the constable.

'Hard to open my mouth without putting my foot in it. Can't even say good day to a fellow without checking for a mourning band on the arm first.'

'The saints carve the course a river must flow. It's different for each of us.'

Up ahead, a party of marines stood stripped to the waist, hacking at the broken remains of the royal free school, cutting it into tinder and filling cart beds with the rubble. At least there was enough of a school left standing for classes to be opened after they'd cleared the wreckage. Children needed the comfort of routine more than anything else. On the other side of the school was a single fresh grave, a boy and a girl tending it, laying a ring of flowers around a simple wooden cross driven into the mound as a marker. *Hamlet*. They've got that much right. The archer's tradition. Buried where his last arrow fell.

Jacob detoured towards the grave. 'Do you know how many skel bandits the archer took with him?'

'Seven, as I hear it,' said Wiggins. He held up his hand, measuring a couple of inches between thumb and finger. 'The young'uns' practice arrows mostly, too. Strangest-looking bow you ever did see. The other lumber folk down from the woods insisted we bury it with him. Undertaker took enough lead out of that man to re-roof your church.'

Jacob stopped a second by the grave, resting a hand on the marker, watching the two children lay a ring of flowers around it. 'I heard your arrows,' Jacob whispered to the dirt. 'I remember you.' Jacob could no longer pass a grave without thinking of Mary, or worrying that Carter might soon be heading for his – if Carter wasn't dead already and everything he was about to attempt, everything he was planning, could just be written off as the long, slow suicide of a grieving father? The uncertainty of his son's fate, not knowing whether he was truly alive or dead, ate at him like a cancer, a slow jabbing burning. He couldn't clear his head of it. As much a part of him as the perpetual stench of his sacked town. Jacob had a feeling that the reek of burning would fade a lot sooner than his pain.

'We'll bring flowers to his grave every week,' announced one of the children.

'Hamlet saved us,' said the other.

Jacob patted their heads. 'Yes, he did. He lives through you, now. You remember that when you tend his grave. You live your life in a way that brings honour to his soul.'

'That was a man's death,' said Wiggins, as they left the mound. 'Damned if I'd want any less when it comes time for me to pass.'

'You're too ornery to die, old man.'

Jacob and Wiggins walked wordlessly down the river road. Halfway to the warehouses on the waterway, they came across a strange sight. A large pit had been dug out in the cornfields, and the wreckage of a Rodalian flying wing was being lowered into it with ropes, a dozen burly men that Jacob recognised as wind chanters down from one of the Northerners' mountain temples. *Heard about this ritual, but never seen it before.*

'There's that flier ... Sheplar Lesh,' said Wiggins. He pointed to a pilot in a purple aviator's jacket. 'He came to try and see you twice when you were laid up in the dark, feeling sorry for yourself, but you turned him away both times.'

'Did I? I don't remember doing that.'

'Shoot, are they actually burying what's left of his aircraft out there?'

'To ride with the winds is a holy thing to them,' said Jacob. 'They believe their planes have a soul, given to it in a temple blessing after it's built.'

'Hell, now I *have* seen everything.'

Noticing the two observers by the side of the river road, Sheplar Lesh detached himself from the funeral party and marched over. He gave a deep stiff bow towards the pastor and Wiggins. 'Our second meeting, sir. With the first, you save my life. With the second, you see my shame.'

'I know you're meant to die with your kite,' said Jacob. 'But I am glad you're standing here with eyes to weep for your flying wing. There's been enough death in Northhaven, don't you think?'

'I stand unworthy before you,' said Sheplar Lesh. 'My soul should be protecting your family on their journey through the afterlife.'

'My wife has passed,' said Jacob. 'My boy is still alive. And Mary, well, if there's a wind demon fixing to ambush her on the way to paradise's gates, then I hope it's brought a pack of friends to protect its tail.'

'*Alive!*' Sheplar's narrow eyes widened in surprise. 'Your son is alive?'

Jacob reached out to touch the aviator's arm. 'My son called you the bravest man in Rodal and I don't think he was wrong. I know how your people feel about a life debt and I'll be coming back shortly to give you a way to repay it. You and the skyguard, both.'

'What honour I do not bury here is at your service, Jacob of Northhaven.' The pilot bowed again and walked back to the chanting Rodalians casting silk streamers into the pit.

Wiggins limped after the pastor, spitting into the corn as he caught up. 'Why do I get the feeling I'm out walking with the biggest fool in Northhaven?'

'Because it takes one to know one, old man.'

Wiggins glanced back at the bizarre burial being conducted. 'The pilot; I think I know what you will be asking him for. But what of Benner Landor?'

'Only what he's got to give,' said Jacob. *No more than that.*

The wharves by the river hadn't been intentionally burnt, that much was clear. Where damage had occurred, it was the incidental sort caused by Benner Landor's warehouse guards fighting it out with the bandits. But numbers hadn't been on the locals' side, and the House of Landor's two-storey warehouses, where they stood at all, now lay empty and looted, a few carpenters tearing out smoke and battle-damaged walls and re-planking them with fresh timber. *Landor's staff. Brave or foolhardy, depending on your take.* The warehouse guards were only armed with swords, but still they had resisted hard against the raiders. Luckily, the piers hadn't been touched. Riverboats from Redwater still landed, bringing travellers up from the large coastal town. Distant cousins and kin disembarking with food and supplies for relatives. Mingling with troops from navy barges and a couple of shallow-draught frigates, four masters with single rotating turret cannons up front, a line of eight pounders in gunports along the sides of their hulls. Benner Landor stood amidst the empty halls of his warehouses, a table laid out in front of him, filled with contracts for corn oil he no longer held and plans for resowing, rehiring. Schemes for everything except what Jacob was here to propose.

'Father Carnehan,' said Landor, extending his hand to shake Jacob's. He had aged since they had last met at the duelling field. Still as tough as granite, but weathered stone now, crumbling around the edges. 'I was going to come and see you next week. I'll be needing a plot in your graveyard to put up a monument to Duncan and Willow.'

'They're not dead,' said Jacob.

'I hope you've not been talking to those leathernecks from the forest? You're not putting your faith in their superstitious woodland sorcery, are you?'

'Carter, Willow, Duncan, they're alive,' insisted Jacob. 'Because all this—' he indicated the warehouse '—wasn't what the bandits came for. Every headless corpse we've buried speaks for what they really were. *Slavers.*'

'My children are dead,' said Benner. He paused a moment before gathering his thoughts. 'You're right, in that I don't know if their ashes are in that warehouse behind me, or mingled with dust on the town's ruined slopes. I don't know if my children are among the blackened corpses that your monks are burying nameless. I don't know if their bodies are packed in some slave pen on that bandit carrier ... fading from thirst, starvation and dysentery, living only to be put to work in some hellhole thousands of miles away for the scant couple of years they might survive. I don't know *that!*'

'But you'll know if you've got any love in your heart left for Duncan and Willow?'

'Love!' spat Benner. 'Is that the love of the God and saints and angels that lets this foul shit happen to us? Did you get an answer on that when you buried your first two kids from the plague, or when Mary was gunned down? I know I didn't when Lorenn died. I didn't when Willow and Duncan were snatched from me. I haven't got time left for your God or your leatherneck fairy tales. What I do have are thousands of workers who won't get paid again this season, half of whom are still grieving for the murder of their family and friends. The House of Landor stands, you understand? Our name still stands and it counts for something in this prefecture. There's not a bandit crew big enough to steal that, or to break us.'

Jacob grabbed the landowner by his lapels and shoved him against the table. 'This is your lucky day, Benner Landor, because I'm only here for what you've got. I want your money! Enough to buy every one of our people back, one slave at a goddamn time if I have to. And I want that tame assemblyman you've got sitting in your pocket. I want Charles T. Gimlette's support when I arrive at the capital and beg King Marcus to give us a company of the meanest, hardest bastards he's got in the national army, to make sure we arrive alive at wherever we need to get.'

Benner pushed the pastor back angrily. 'You've lost your mind! Every Northhaven man and woman will be dead decades before you catch up with them. *You'll* be dead before you travel half the distance they've been taken.'

'Man's got to die of something. I need your money and I need your tame politician for my pursuit to work. Do I have them?'

'You write me that letter you've always refused to write,' hissed Benner. 'The one where you agree to the synod's plans to build a cathedral in Northhaven. I'll be reconstructing the town at twice its old size and we'll need a cathedral here. You write me that letter and I'll give you two in return – one telling the assemblyman to support you at court, another ordering my bank to make funds available to you.'

'Is that all you feel for your children?' asked Jacob in disgust. 'A cathedral?'

'I feel they'll be better honoured by a tomb in a cathedral's crypt than a plot in the back of a rickety old church.'

'You'll have your letter,' said Jacob stalking away. Leaving the landowner to his name and his glory and his empty sheds.

'I'll build a crypt inside for you,' called Landor, 'next to my dead children's. The last pastor of Northhaven, right next to an empty one for the first bishop of Northhaven.'

'You figure he'll put one in for me too?' said Wiggins, chasing after the pastor. 'Here lies the biggest fool in the prefecture. Lost, presumed missing in parts foreign.'

'Only the biggest fool gets a crypt,' said Jacob. 'The second biggest? That's an urn in the wall, at most.'

'Shit.' Wiggins spat against the side of a wagon. 'Figures.'

★

Brother Frael moved through the graveyard, homing in on the sound of digging. Dusk made the vastly extended field of mounds an even sadder place. But Jacob Carnehan wasn't digging a fresh grave to go alongside the hundreds recently dug by the marines. He was unearthing one.

The monk stopped by the pile of dirt thrown up from the oblong pit where the pastor worked hunched over. 'I know I told you we were going to have to triple the size of the churchyard, Father, but excavating old graves?'

Jacob looked up, slowly wiping the sweat from underneath his mop of dark, curly hair. 'This'll be a bishop's problem soon, Brother, not mine.'

'Ah, yes. Some self-assured politician of a priest dispatched from the synod in Arcadia. One who will no doubt regard our monastery in the hinterlands as part of their domain and be only too keen to flex their newly minted authority. Are you really going to attempt this mission? Try to buy back those who were taken? Fight their owners if they will not sell?'

'In the Bible, Brother, the three saints gave their life as martyrs for God the Father. Isn't it time a father gave his life for his son?'

'The saints sacrificed their lives for peace, lifting not a fist in violence towards those advancing on their pyres with lit torches. What you're digging up here is not peace, is it?'

'It is ... what it is.'

'But nothing of what I've taught you. When I found you on that beach amidst the planking and sailors' corpses, as near to death as you were, I told the others in the monastery at Geru Peak that it was not your body we must heal, but your soul.'

'You've saved me twice, Brother, once in the mountains of Rodal, the second time when you brought that gask to my room.'

'I wanted you to hold out hope for your son, not this. Do not exchange your body with the one in that coffin.'

Jacob's spade struck the wood of the lid. He knelt down to brush dirt off it. 'There's no body in here. This was my first funeral service at Northhaven, a pauper's grave – not even a name.'

'It's what *is* in there that worries me, and I think we both know the name of the man you buried.'

Jacob clicked open the cheap rusting clasps along the side of the coffin. Before he opened the lid, he glanced up at the monk. 'To get my child back, Brother, I will crawl through every black yard of every circle of hell. I will swim through a sea of tortured souls. I will shed every pint of pumping blood in my veins. There is no distance I will not travel, no enemy I will not face, until Carter is back where he belongs. He will not die as a slave. I promised Mary this. I promised myself. I promised God!'

'Mary is dead, Jacob. Please. If you have made a promise, make sure it is not one of vengeance.'

'I will not break. I will not let my son down.'

'Think how far our people are being taken,' pleaded the monk. 'Our world is endless.'

'Then that will be my journey. I shall travel to the very edge of Pellas if it has one. If all I have left is the pursuit, then that is what I shall do. *Pursue*. Nothing will stop me. Not even death.'

The monk gazed sadly at the old grave being violated. *Not even death*. Could a man die twice? Brother Frael sighed. 'There's an old saying, Father. It's not found inside the pages of the Bible. I have a feeling it's much older even than the good text. When you seek revenge, you must dig two graves. One of them should be for yourself.'

Jacob levered the coffin's lid up. There were no bones, no rotting flesh. Just a small blanket wrapped around something pillow-sized. A shroud to conceal what should have stayed buried forever. The pastor lifted the bundle out, then re-sealed the coffin and picked up the shovel, ready to refill the plot. He was trembling with an unholy fever. 'Pray for me, Brother Frael.'

The monk nodded curtly and turned away, saying nothing as his boots carried him far from the sound of dirt being flung down onto faded pinewood. He would pray for the pastor, but there weren't enough monks in the monastery to pray for the slavers who'd burnt Northhaven. To the untutored ear, it sounded like the pastor was refilling the hole he had excavated. In reality, Jacob Carnehan was digging deep. He was heading down for hell's own ceiling, and Brother Frael trembled as he imagined what might emerge from that pit.

FOUR

THE SKY ON HIS BACK

Jacob gazed around Rake's Field. It seemed like only yesterday that he had arrived at the woodland to stop his son's duel. The crowd here today weren't rakes and rowdies, just families waiting to see the departure of the town's sole chance of retrieving their kidnapped loved ones. The pastor could tell from their grim, worried, pallid faces what Northhaven's survivors really thought of his chances of success. With Jacob, Khow and Wiggins all arrived at the field, the pilot Sheplar Lesh broke away from the line of parked Rodalian flying wings, the pilots practising their empty fist fighting art in front of the aircraft. It was a hypnotic thing to watch, the line of aviators in their purple flying jackets turning slowly, gently in unison; a single living organism of mirrored reflections moving softly, without pause. A slow dance that, when speeded up, would result in snapped bones and burst sinews.

Jacob bowed to Sheplar, then indicated Wiggins and the gask mystic. 'Why four aircraft, Mister Lesh? There are only three of us that need taking to the capital.'

'The additional plane is carrying two pilots,' said Sheplar. 'The pilot in the spotter's seat will fly my kite back to Rodal so that I may travel on with you.'

'It's a hard road we're embarking on. May only be travelling one way.'

Sheplar's artless grin only grew wider. 'So it may prove. But those that are missing are also my responsibility. It was my failure to repel the slavers that allowed them to land and take captives.' He stared at the gask and the two Northhaven men. 'Have any of you ever flown before?'

Jacob looked around. None of the party had. 'Hell,' spat Wiggins. 'If Weyland had its own skyguard, that bandit carrier wouldn't have dared attack us in the first place.'

Clearly the constable wasn't looking forward to taking to the air. Jacob, by contrast, was curious and felt no nerves. Flying wings had regularly swept past Jacob's old monastery high in the mountain peaks, riding storm winds strong enough to rip a shutter off a window. There wasn't a weather system in Weyland that would prove a threat to the Rodalian skyguard. Sheplar checked the weight of the three travellers' backpacks, and judging them light enough to be stowed, left to fire up his triangular-winged craft's rotor.

'This will be a new experience,' said Khow, his fingers nervously clutching the box of his calculator.

'Just ain't right,' said Wiggins, 'that's all I know.' His grizzled eyes scanned the crowd. People waved handkerchiefs towards the aircraft or held up lockets with portraits of their missing family members. 'Already said my goodbyes to my daughter and her young'uns. You can imagine what she thinks of this foolery. Don't see Benner Landor over there, or your monk.'

'Brother Frael?' shrugged Jacob. They began walking towards the aircraft. *Well, the church never did smile much on suicide. As for Benner, I reckon this is just another business deal for the landowner.* The port at Redwater was already shipping stonemasons in from far and wide to begin construction on the new cathedral. Jacob felt inside his pocket. *I've got what I need.* Benner's draft instructing his bank to pay Jacob's expedition a tidy sum. A second letter instructing the prefecture's assemblyman to extend every assistance to the rescuers.

Wiggins limped after the gask and Jacob, the vibration of spinning propellers filling the meadow. 'What are our odds then, Khow?'

'The future is fractal, manling Wiggins. Too many branches for me to scry true.'

'Well, I'd say our future's something that begins with an "F", all right, but fractal it ain't – nor anything else that's fit to say in front of a churchman. At least I'll get to see the capital before I die. You ever journeyed to Arcadia, Pastor?'

'First time for me,' said Jacob.

'Always meant to take the train down there one day, when I'd retired. Me and the wife both. When she passed first, I never saw the point of travelling to the capital by myself. Guess I've got the two of you, now. And by air, too. Never did think that day would ever dawn.'

The flying wing carrying its pair of Rodalians pilots had already turned around on the grass, taxiing towards the Northhaven Road to take off. It bumped along, perched on three tiny rubber wheels, one apiece under the wings with a larger third wheel at the rear – the layout of a child's tricycle reversed. Jacob approached Sheplar's flying wing. He stopped short of the aircraft to admire it. A cigar-like fuselage made into a triangle by the curved sweep of its wings, its single rear-mounted wooden propeller a blur; an engine coughing out cooking-smell smoke from a pair of exhaust pipes. With the pilot's cockpit forward of the spotter's position, there was nothing to protect either of the aircraft's occupants from the elements. It sported something well capable of preserving them against enemies in the air, though. Two steel guns protruded from its wings, an empty cage either side of the spotter's hole for the passenger to launch small bomblets towards the ground. From nose-cone to rudder it couldn't be more than twenty-four feet. 'She seems too small to carry even one of us.'

'This is the largest kite in the skyguard,' laughed Sheplar, affectionately patting its wooden fuselage. 'She carries two! A Tomlar Brothers *Nomad*. Produced by the finest craftsmen in my country. People travel months to a temple to see a new *Nomad* given life during her blessing ceremony.'

Jacob dropped himself into the spotter's cockpit, just enough space behind the seat to stow his backpack. Once inside, his only cushioning was a parachute. Two belts hung off the seat to cross over his chest; all that was going to hold Jacob inside the plane if Sheplar had to manoeuvre suddenly. After Jacob belted up, Sheplar turned around lifting a leather facemask connected to an air tank, large goggles built into the apparatus. 'When I tell you, Jacob of Northhaven, pull on your mask. You will find one similar to this under your seat. We travel a long way, yes? We must travel high to minimise gravity and drag. You will need to breathe through the mask.'

'I understand.'

'Yawn frequently as we climb. Otherwise your ears will ache as if you are being beaten. Also, try to keep your skin covered at all times. Sunburn at altitude is very bad.'

'I used to live in a monastery up in the mountains,' said Jacob. 'I know about covering up when you're exposed on high.'

Sheplar laughed and gave him a thumbs up. 'Then we fly, Jacob of Northhaven, we *fly*.'

Jolting and bouncing over the grass, the kite rolled past the town's crowds, a ragged cheer rising from their throats. The huzza had a surprised quality to it as it emerged from their throats, as though the townspeople hadn't been expecting to cheer. Khow's flying wing bumped along in front of Jacob's aircraft, Wiggins' to the rear, and the small squadron picked up speed down the slope of the simple dirt lane, leaving the woodland behind, the distant spread of North-haven in front. Trees on either side flickered past, faster and faster, the engine's drone becoming a roar, and then the flying wing in front began lifting off, Sheplar's aircraft tilting back as it followed suit. *How peculiar*. It seemed the most natural thing in the world to watch the landscape falling away, cottages and orchards shrinking to a toy-like patchwork, cold air rushing past Jacob's head. He sank lower in the seat to cover himself from the whipping draught, but as Sheplar's kite climbed higher, so the heat increased, while Jacob felt the weight of his body lightening. *How flat and infinite everything looks from up here.* It was no wonder Rodalians boasted that even the priests of the wind temples envied their skyguard's pilots. As the squadron gained altitude so the temperature climbed. The higher they flew, the hotter it grew. Jacob looked up at the blue heavens. There was no sign of the radiation belt that circled the world like a girdle during the daytime, but if you looked up after dark you could clearly see its distant crimson shimmer, obscuring the middle section of a night sky. Pilots told tall tales of aircraft that had ascended so high that their engines melted while their frames caught fire. Jacob doubted the stories were true. You flew that high; you'd pass out from heat-stroke long before you burnt up like a struck match head. At one point in their ascent they

116

passed a flock of honking geese, Sheplar careful to stay clear enough from the birds to prevent a stray goose running through their propeller. *What would Mary have said about this sight, I wonder? Her fool of a husband flying with the angels.* Jacob had to remind himself that she was gone. He kept on expecting to see her appear and berate him for how ill-prepared he was for the pursuit. Their four aircraft locked into an arrow-shaped formation as though they were imitating the geese, two abreast in a 'V', Sheplar's flying wing at the head. *It's tidy flying.* As good a start to their journey as could have been hoped by Jacob. When would the point come when that would change? Sooner or later, it was inevitable. Things would get real chaotic real fast.

I'm coming for our son, Mary. Every day from here on in; a bit closer, every day ...

Duncan Landor pulled his hand back a little too slowly, cursing as his fingers were trampled. Pain not withstanding, he had accomplished something that a few days ago he would have believed impossible – escaping Hawkland Park and the weight of the estate's duties, absconding with Adella by his side. *But if anyone had told me that on this day, success in my endeavours would taste like ashes in my mouth, I would have damned them for a liar.* Duncan shifted again as another surge of prisoners pushed past where he squatted with Adella and his sister. It was worse inside the badly lit slavers' cage than any market day press. Stuck inside their monstrous captors' city-sized aircraft, people throwing up through a combination of airsickness, fear and hunger. Some captives brooded, imagining what horrors would be waiting for them at the end of their flight. Others continually paced the pen's confines. Of the two groups, Duncan was definitely a squatter and a worrier. Fighting to hold himself together in front of the two women. That's what you did, wasn't it, when you were a Landor male? Set the example, even when you were terrified and working harder than anything to stop your hands shaking. Back at the manor house, the head of the kitchen kept a blue and red parrot in a cage. Duncan had watched that parrot shuffle nervously from one end of its swinging perch to the other every waking moment of the day, the bird pulling rainbow feathers out one at a time, until it was as bare as a plucked chicken. Now Duncan was a captive, he knew how that parrot felt.

Water, when it arrived for the newly taken slaves, came pushed through the cage's mesh in pigskins, Northhaven's townspeople reduced to the status of cattle as they pressed and jostled for a drink – none left for washing or clearing out the stinking wooden toilet hole in the corner. That stench was a funny thing. After a while, it just seemed to burn its way out of your consciousness. Your own stink mingled with everyone else's until you couldn't tell the difference.

Duncan was only just holding it together, so he could have done without the pointless arguments with an increasingly peevish Adella. 'As bad as it is in here,' said Duncan, being shoved by the press of bodies around them, 'I don't see things being better in any of the other cages.'

'That house slave only asked me to go,' said Adella. 'It's *you* insisting you have to come across too.'

'What I'm saying is, I don't see why any of us are going to be better off inside another cage rather than just staying put?'

'I know you don't like Carter Carnehan, Duncan. But he was the only one who put up a real fight back at the town. We're safer alongside Carter than separated from him.'

'Listen, Adella, there's plenty of folks in this cage who'd like to see Carter swing for his foolishness. He's a reckless halfwit. He led our people straight out into the slavers' hands when they should have stayed safe behind the ramparts.'

'I'm sure that Carter did what he believed was best at the time,' said Willow. 'You need to be fair to him, brother. If you read between the lines, how many of our people reached the safety of the town's walls who wouldn't have if Carter and the others hadn't been fighting a rearguard action?'

'Reading between the lines,' sneered Adella. 'Your books aren't here, Willow, and they wouldn't help you if they were. What I've got to say isn't written on paper, but it's the only thing *you* need to understand. If there's a way out of this slave pit that doesn't end with some fat, sweaty barbarian chief trading a bag of coppers for our tails, then Carter Carnehan is the man who's going to come up with it.'

Duncan's heart sank as he heard Adella's words. *Just the same as it ever was.* When people met Duncan, all they ever saw were the wealth and riches of Hawkland Park, not the man standing in front of them.

Every time that happened he tried to master his resentment. Duncan Landor was a bigger man than his father's reach, he knew he was. But how to get anyone else to realise the truth? He had to resist grabbing Adella by the shoulders and shaking her until she saw sense. 'There *is* a way out of here, and Carter's already found it.' He jabbed a finger towards the three punishment cages. 'Doors open, and straight down. If you have anything to do with Carter's schemes, you're going to end up leaving that way too.'

'You don't have to come,' said Adella, her eyes narrowing slightly as she glared in Willow's direction. '*Either* of you.'

Willow ignored her hostility. 'Kurtain has his numbers now. Three people in the pen opposite with family inside our cage. When James sneaks them over here, the three of us need to leave our cage so the guards don't notice. Look on the bright side, brother, at least opposite there's a porthole to stare out of.'

'Less crowded over there, too,' said Duncan, 'after Carter's brawling dropped half a dozen Northhaven men into the clouds.' He reached out to rest a hand on Adella's soiled skirt, but she pushed him away.

'Carter risked his life to save the town. What did you do? Lead the three of us along the river for those monsters to toss nets over us and bag us up like turkeys for a butcher's counter.'

Duncan could barely contain his temper. 'If I'd had a gun I would have fought with something other than my fists.' *And maybe have stood half a chance against the dozen slavers who jumped us.*

'The Landor warehouse staff only had swords to fight with. It doesn't make sense to keep rifles and pistols at an oil warehouse,' said Willow, as if she was explaining to a child. Exasperation crossed her face. 'A single stray shot and you would be riding an explosion fit to send you flying all the way to the Redwater shoreline.'

'I'm sure there's a lot that doesn't make sense to *you*,' retorted Adella. 'But where we are is where we are. Those monsters have the Landor harvest stolen and stored in their hold, and they've taken the Landor family and most of Northhaven for slaves.'

'You're not family,' said Willow. 'You're hardly even a passing fancy.'

Adella rocked slightly with the impact of Willow's words; she looked as though she was going to launch herself at his sister. Thankfully, the arrival of James Kurtain distracted the pair. The house slave dragged in a sack of food for their trough; behind him staggered three prisoners from the cage opposite, two women and a man, also weighted down with feed sacks.

James halted in front of the three of them. 'When the bags run half full, grab one and follow me across to the cage opposite. Empty what remains into the food station, then you stay over there while I carry the sacks out.'

'How safe is this?' asked Duncan.

'I've brought three people across from your friend's cage,' said James. 'As long as three go back with no fuss or bother, nobody will care.'

Duncan scowled. 'Damned if he's my friend.'

'Boy, you better get friendly. The skels'll kill you just for looking at them funny.'

Duncan watched the new arrivals emptying the food. The three visitors' family and friends were already clustering around them, trying not to draw any attention to their obvious happiness at being reunited. Willow was right, as she so frequently was, God preserve her soul. *Too late to back out now.* With the sacks half emptied, Duncan shouldered a feedbag from one of the visitors, leaving the grinning Northhaven man to his kin while Adella and Willow did the same with their counterparts. Then the three of them followed James out of the cage, past a band of armed skels holding the door open, crossing the gantry and entering the pen opposite. The portholes in the fuselage here seemed a poor exchange for Carter Carnehan's bruised mug. And by the look of surprise giving way to anger on Carter's face as he saw the two unasked for additions to the prisoner exchange, Carter felt precisely the same way. *At least I've made the right decision, then.* Letting Adella come across on her own would have been tantamount to pushing a lamb into a wolf's cave and hoping for the best. *Duncan Landor never hopes. He plans ahead.*

Carter stood there glowering at Duncan, Adella and Willow, as they emptied their sacks into the feeding circle, prisoners already jostling for the first chance at fresh rations. James collected the empty sacks with a nervous glance towards the skels guarding the cage door before leaving with the hemp bags slung over his shoulder.

Carter spoke to Duncan's sister. 'No disrespect to you, Willow, but it was only *one* I was counting on receiving.'

'Well, you've got all of us,' said Willow. 'Do you have a problem with that?'

'Probably wouldn't make much difference if I did, would it?' said Carter.

'As far as friendly greetings go, yours could do with a lot more work,' said Willow.

'My apologies, your ladyship. I guess I don't have the benefit of an expensive finishing school to educate me.'

'And *I* do?' spat Willow. 'I'm Northhaven raised and bred, the same as you Carter Carnehan. Don't you be hanging any false airs and graces on me.'

Their needling was getting on Duncan's nerves, but not as much as the bare-faced arrogance of this man. 'We might have been taken as slaves, but we're not sold yet,' said Duncan. 'It's not on you to say who gets passed around like tobacco in an ale house.'

Carter snarled. 'But it is for *you*? Your father's money doesn't mean shit up here and neither do you.'

Adella positioned herself between the two of them, but Carter was already moving around her to square up to Duncan. She was actually trying to reason with the idiot. Adella would have more luck arguing with a rock. 'We're all came over, Carter. And that's because the best chance we've got of staying alive is by sticking together. I would never have crossed if I thought you felt differently.'

'You're wasting your breath on him. This is my currency, Carnehan,' said Duncan raising his fist, 'same as it was back in Rake's Field before your father showed up and saved you from a much needed lesson in manners.'

'You think you can teach me?' laughed Carter, ignoring what Adella had said, neglecting her, just like he always did. 'How's that work, like this—?'

Carter swung a punch into Duncan's gut, knocking him back into the mesh and winding him. Quicker than Duncan could react, Carter was on top of him, the metal of the cage pressed against his spine. Ignoring the pain in his stomach, Duncan lashed up with his knee, catching Carter in the groin, and then kicked one of the man's feet out from under him. They went down to the floor together, locked and lashing, rolling over the wooden planking while the other prisoners made room, yelling and hollering. Duncan could hear Willow and Adella screaming at them, the house slave James calling a warning too, squawking through the mesh. There was even a gask among the crowd of slaves, shouting, 'Peace! Peace!' *Only peace that leatherneck is getting is a piece of Carter Carnehan.*

None of it mattered. Duncan could taste blood and salt in his mouth, his lip cut and swelling, and all he could think of was how good it was to have Carter Carnehan on the floor, Duncan's fist driving repeatedly into his face until he wasn't able to curse or mock him anymore. They rolled across the cage, punching, kicking and jabbing at each other, wild and looking to maim, struggling for purchase. Duncan so enraged that he hardly felt the burning impact of the first blow from a slaver's electrical prod, the second and third strikes just enough to separate them, the next few lashes swelling with the agony of an amputation as he tumbled away from Carter. By the time it dawned on Duncan that this fracas wasn't the best way he could have greeted the arrogant knucklehead, both men were hanging in the guards' reptilian arms. Sparking truncheons had temporarily numbed all animosity the pair felt towards each other.

Si-lishh marched down the stairs onto the gangway between the pens, the slave master's thick green tail swinging irritably behind him. His voice was an irascible, sibilant hiss as he stopped in front of the two Northhaven men being dragged from the cage. 'Does Si-lishh not feed slaves enough? Is something special about this cargo, that Weylanders must always drag Si-lishh away from meals?' His tail swished around and jabbed Carter's chest. 'Second offence for this slave, Si-lishh thinks. Not learn before? Well, Weylanders selected for size and age, not brains.'

Held firm by the pair of guards, Carter's contemptuous gaze tilted up towards the slave master. 'When you visit a zoo, Si-lishh, you must buy two tickets. One to get in, one to make sure they let you out again.'

The slave master struck Carter across the face, audibly cracking something in the man's jaw. 'Not take you as slave for the making of insolence. Throw these two Weylanders in same punishment cell. Set hatch opening for five minutes.' Si-lishh kicked Carter in the ribs as the arrogant delinquent was dragged past. 'Si-lishh would make time longer and see how many more jokes boy can think up, but Si-lishh still hungry.'

Carter's face drew into the sneer that he did so well. 'Why, are you eating your mother's kin out there, you alligator-faced bastard?'

Duncan groaned. The dolt was actually making things worse, if that was possible. *Don't think an apology is going to cut it now, though.*

Willow banged her fist on the other side of the cage, running alongside the mesh as the guards dragged Duncan and Carter towards the punishment cages' transparent walls. 'Let them go! That man's father is the richest man in Northhaven. He'll pay for these two to be ransomed. Gold, silver, any trading metal you want!' Duncan gazed at his sister's panicked face, his anger completely evaporated now, its place taken by a fear almost as strong. Just the thought of being dropped out of the aircraft – the skels' mocking version of walking the plank – was enough to turn his legs to jelly. *Who's going to keep Willow and Adella safe when I'm a shattered mess on the ground below?*

The slave master laughed as he strode after the two prisoners. 'When skels need wealth from Weylanders, skels steal it on next raid.'

'Please,' Adella begged, 'don't do this.' She was left clinging to the mesh, her face as white as baking powder. 'Don't leave me here alone!'

Beaten close to semi-consciousness, Duncan didn't even have the wherewithal to wonder which of the two men Adella had been shouting at. He struggled futilely in the hands of the two muscular slavers grasping him. 'I didn't start the fight. He came at *me!*' The guards tossed him into the punishment cell, before manhandling Carter inside.

Standing in the corridor, the slave master glared at Duncan through the wall. 'Si-lishh sees why you want to kill other boy. Kill rival before hatch drops and Si-lishh will open punishment cell door for you. Kill boy quickly, or two bodies drop into sky.'

Duncan balked as he realised what was being asked of him. Kill Carter? He had burned to a minute ago. But like this, for the slavers' amusement? *Even if it means you'll live to look after Adella and Willow,* a sly voice whispered inside him. *He deserves to die, doesn't he? Before he gets any more good people killed.*

'Willow and your father can't buy you out of this one,' said Carter, getting to his feet from the corner of the punishment cell where he'd been tossed. Duncan stood up as the door sealed behind them both. A violent clacking sounded from the wall's timer as the guards set it.

'Maybe five minutes,' laughed Si-lishh. 'Maybe one, if slaves unlucky.'

Carter steadied against the wall. 'You might as well come for me, unless you think you can fly.'

'I'll gut you for the way you treat Adella. Damned if I'll do it for the amusement of a slaver.'

'Then you're going to get what you got coming before you die.' Carter lowered his head and charged Duncan, smashing him back into the wall and unbalancing both of them. Duncan chopped at the man's neck on the way down, an arc of pain along his body as he struck the floor hatch, the bruises left by the slavers' cattle rods lighting up in agony.

Carter laughed at Duncan as they briefly separated, both rolling over on the hatch, staggering back to their feet at the same time. 'Let's show everyone what the heir of Hawkland Park is good for, with only his daddy's fancy clothes just rags on his back.'

You low bastard. Howling a roar of rage, Duncan headbutted Carter in the face, sending him rolling to the side. He followed up and elbowed Carter in the stomach, leaving him sucking for breath as he closed his fingers around the man's neck, his fingers tightening. Carter's hands struggled to find the purchase necessary to break Duncan's hold as he was pushed down towards the hatch doors.

'Two minutes left,' Si-lishh called from outside the punishment cell. 'Kill boy faster!'

Duncan barely even heard the slave master's spitting laughter, lost in his fury and the quickening of his blood.

Arcadia was as impressive as Jacob had imagined it from all the newspaper illustrations. Having flown all night and landed with sunrise, there could be no more impressive view of Arcadia than the one afforded to Jacob as the Rodalian squadron corkscrewed towards a landing on one of the roads outside the capital's margins. The constant howl of the wind along the aircraft's wings dwindled as they dipped lower. Sheplar had been flying at altitude, riding furious tailwinds to arrive here as fast as they had, aerial currents as strong as tornadoes, catching the Rodalian kites and making flying arrows of the squadron. Now they were descending into silence as the ground magnified below them. Jacob slipped off his breathing apparatus, enjoying the smell of fresh clean air free of the mask's leather and rubber. His face had been left red-raw where the straps had chafed for so long. Below, the capital's harbour lay spread out in a crescent, the bay filled with hundreds of ships and sails, water sparkling with the first orange glint of the sun creeping upwards. At this height, the city's streets resembled the exposed mechanism of a clock, a single vast dial with concentric circles of sea-fed canals tightening to a bull's-eye in the centre. The bull's-eye's centre was a verdant green, the gardens of the royal palace backing on to parade grounds and white stone buildings of the king's residence. To the southeast, a pair of steep hills rose next to each other, breaking up an otherwise flat landscape. Jacob spotted the pale marble outline of what must be the People's Assembly on top of the closest hill. Every prefecture of Weyland represented under its vaulted domes, and one of those seats occupied by the man that Benner Landor had helped to office. Charles T. Gimlette's pockets stuffed with Landor money and a ballot box filled with the votes of all the citizens who owed Benner their living. But now Charles T. Gimlette wasn't just Landor's man. He was Jacob's. The second hill had a smaller construction at its apex – an older structure, although no doubt still equally impressive when you were standing in its shadow rather than skimming over it upon high. Arcadia Cathedral, home to the archbishops of the Synod. Jacob doubted the church council could even find Northhaven on a map, but as long as they never troubled him, he always tried to return the courtesy. Maybe now there was a new cathedral and a vacant seat for one of their cronies going begging in Northhaven, that was about to change. *No matter. I'll be hundreds of thousands of miles away by the time those politics are played out.*

'Bigger than your other cities, I think,' called Sheplar Lesh from his cockpit in front of Jacob. 'I mean you no disrespect, but such a place is too flat for anyone born to the mountains to want to live there.'

'None taken,' replied Jacob. *All of Weyland must seem like a millpond to a Rodalian flier.*

Jacob gazed down with interest. Arcadia was at least ten times the size of the largest town they'd passed during their flight. And most of those cities had made Northhaven look like the provincial market town it really was. As their four flying wings circled lower, Arcadia's streets and inhabitants came into focus. Close enough to hear tram bells ringing, Jacob gliding over wide boulevards still empty so early – a few tradesmen opening up shop fronts, lamp-lighters on ladders snuffing out their previous night's labours, carts making the first deliveries of woodchips, cooking oil and milk. Fumes from brick chimneys drifted up from a thousand breakfasts, each of those families oblivious to the squadron cutting through their smoke. *Families getting ready for the day. Didn't seem so long ago I was among them.* As was so often the way, there wasn't a thing he saw that didn't remind him of his wife and son, of all that he had lost. It was good to feel the pain, though. Jacob used it like a spur to keep on going. Whenever he doubted. Whenever he wavered, he just had to let the grief come flooding in and carry him forward.

The buildings were high compared to Northhaven. Some rising six storeys with tall apartments and roof terraces and gardens above the shops and stores. Jacob had heard there was a law forbidding construction any larger in the capital. Six floors were plenty when you didn't have enough metal girders to build safer and higher. There was no airfield at the capital for the squadron to land at. The National Assembly didn't want its citizens reminded that their nation was a distant backwater without the resources necessary to field its own skyguard. The only airfield in Weyland was the city of Talekhard, close to the south-eastern border with the Republic of Ivah. And that was a free port for merchants and aerial nomads to land and refuel and conduct whatever trade they needed to with the kingdom. No, for Weyland, for the whole Lanca, the league's lifeblood was the sea. The capital's harbour was where all freight that mattered embarked and disembarked. Weyland was a maritime nation, where proximity to the water equated to wealth and life and cargo. Sheplar put his aircraft down on the capital's outskirts, the landing commonplace to Jacob after their refuelling stops – no thoughts now of how easily a flying wing could be blown off course by a sudden gust of wind, to roll and crash and burst into flames. The squadron taxied down the main highway, finally coming to a halt in a line as neat as a parade ground formation. Arcadia lay half an hour's walk away, a mass of white shimmering in the distance. Wiggins and the gask dismounted from their planes, and Jacob followed suit. *Good to have real ground under my feet again.* He looked around. Set back on either side of the road were vineyards, grapes climbing trellises and swaying in the sea breeze. Jacob could taste the salt from the direction of the ocean as he walked away from the flying wing.

'The city by the sea,' said Wiggins, his spirits obviously restored now they were done with the flight. 'You think it looks as impressive up close, Pastor?'

'Just bigger and noisier than home.'

'Never seen a man love the quiet life as much as you; that I ain't. You love our country acres so much, it's still a surprise to me when I recall you weren't born there.'

Khow raised a sinewy hand to cover his eyes as he gazed at the city before them. 'There are few trees here to speak of. No forests. No woodland. You set yourself apart from the bark, living like this.' He sounded doleful over the way the Weylanders lived, sad for Jacob's people.

'Drinking what these fields produce is as close as most of the capital get to living on the land,' laughed Wiggins.

'It is not the gasks' way.'

Don't think it's mine, either. Jacob watched Sheplar bow to the pilot who would be flying his small aircraft back to Rodal. There was a short ritual, as the care of the diminutive fightercraft's spirit passed between the two fliers. The other Rodalian pilots patiently watched, sitting cross-legged. After the ceremony was over, the pilots began checking their machines' engines, each man trained as both mechanic and flier. Sheplar sighed as he watched his plane attended to by the spare pilot, but his lopsided grin quickly returned. It was a lot to ask Sheplar Lesh to leave his duty behind, but he was following his honour with the two Northhaven men and the gask. Jacob already had his traveller's pack strapped to his shoulders, a small bedroll tied on top. They would enter the capital looking like the supplicants they were, four backwater hicks stumbling into the nation's centre. One letter in Jacob's pocket for Palmstruch General Bank, another for Assembly-man Charles T. Gimlette.

Halfway to the capital proper, they came across a large open market, traveller caravans of all sizes setting up in a fenced-in enclosure, pens filled with livestock and stalls piled high with merchandise – everything from rolls of silk to gilded glass mirrors and crates of dried nuts heaped next to each other. The market hadn't opened to the public yet, but the smell of roasting meat from the food stalls preparing for breakfast reminded Jacob how long it had been since he'd last eaten. That would have to wait, though.

'Reckon every day's market day here,' noted Wiggins.

'It's not like home, that's for sure,' said Jacob.

Outside the market they found a cabbie, surprised at his good fortune in filling his two-horse cabriolet with visitors so early.

'We need to stay near the hill, friend,' Jacob told the driver after they were rattling towards Arcadia.

'Nothing too fancy or expensive,' warned Wiggins.

'You want to stay on the hill,' smiled the cabbie, 'expensive is the only flavour of hotel you'll find. Cheap lodgings are at the north-eastern end of town, furthest from the bay and government buildings.'

'Are there any woodlands in the northeast?' asked Khow.

'You're kidding me? You want greenery, you better camp out here. No, sir, the cheap end of town has lots of artists and singers and stage types,' explained the cabbie, directing a lazy flick of his reins towards his horses. 'But I don't figure you boys for any of those.' He didn't seem fazed by Khow's question or the gask's appearance. But then, with so many foreign ships in harbour from distant ports, he had probably given rides to stranger people. Wiggins' police uniform was probably more of a curiosity than Khow's presence here. As long as they spoke trade tongue, commerce could be done, and that was all that counted in the capital.

'Somewhere good for a quiet night's rest, no crowds,' said Jacob, tapping the pocket where Benner Landor's bank draft was tucked. 'The rate's not a problem. Someone else is paying for our stay.'

The cabbie happily stroked his walrus moustache as he steered the coach through an arch, the first city marker, and rolled them down an avenue lined with gleaming white statues. 'That's the best kind of stay there is!'

Charles T. Gimlette was a big man and from the way he ordered food in the fancy restaurant Jacob had booked for the assemblyman, he gave every appearance that he was fixing to stay that way. It was a tribute to the expensive tailoring of Gimlette's high-collared dark jacket that it held in the man's paunch as effectively as it did. Even when the politician wasn't feeding, his wide jowls moved up and down, chewing air as if he needed to exercise his jaw in preparation for the next course. His skin had a good healthy gleam despite being upwards of fifty, and his long dark hair shone as slick as the glazed chicken legs and peppers piled up in front of the politician. He hadn't confined himself to meat, though. There were dishes of seafood spread across the table too. Gimlette used his fingers while he talked, his hands adding emphasis to each statement. You'd have thought he was on the floor of the assembly, rather than just filling a chair above the restaurant's rich green carpet. With Sheplar Lesh visiting outfitters to secure supplies and passage for the next leg of their journey; Wiggins and Khow returning to the bank to ensure that the ransom money would be released on time; dealing with the assemblyman had fallen to Jacob.

'Father Carnehan, I was shocked, I say. Shocked to the core when I heard about the raid on Northhaven. Had to send one of my staff over to the radiomen to make sure it wasn't some fool prank being played on me by one of the other assemblymen. They would love that. Have me standing up and making speeches about a disaster that never happened. This city's ablaze with the news and fixing to mend what's broke.'

Except that the disaster was no prank. *Not that it's enough to put an assemblyman off his lunch.* 'The newspapers in my hotel lobby seem to have a Northhaven-sized hole where the story should be,' said Jacob.

'Wrong sort of newspapers where you're staying, Father. Only boring political stories. But that's what you get when you lodge on the hill.' His eyes – just a little too small for that wide face – drifted to look out at the view of the city spread out below them; a haze of sparkling stone buildings in the full heat of the day. The prices of the food that Benner Landor was paying for seemed to suit the politician just fine, though.

'Is there anyone in the government who can even find Northhaven on a map?'

'Now, I know that our prefecture seems small and far away down here, Father. But even if the government don't know it, they know me. And Benner Landor is my good friend. It breaks my heart when I think of his two children – and yours, and all of our people's young men and women – in the hands of goddamn slavers.'

'So you'll help?'

'Without a doubt, you will have everything I can arrange to assist you. But what happened during the raid, sad as it is, is part of wider considerations too.'

'Wider?'

'You have to view this through a political lens. There are two main factions in the assembly, same at the court too. The gaiaists and the mechanicalists. Hell, the whole Lanseatic League is divided down the same lines, even if they're called something different.'

'Those that are content with what they've got and those that want a little bit more,' said Jacob.

'That's just gaiaist cant, Father. You think if we had more mills here and were importing the coal and steel to fuel them, fielded a skyguard of our own, the slavers would've dared to strike Northhaven? Hell no, they would have headed north. Gone for easier pickings at the far end of the caravan routes. Hit some poor devils where a witch doctor's dance is the only medicine to save you when you're ailing.'

'I can see why Benner Landor throws his votes behind you.'

Gimlette made a steeple of his fingers, his elbows resting on either side of a plate of steaming crab. 'A little bit of progress, that's not much to ask for, is it now?'

'What does either side of this squabble care about the raid on Northhaven?'

'The mechanicalist side of the assembly can use the raid as an argument for advancing things. Building a stronger, more industrialised Weyland. That means the gaiaists will look to frustrate us at every turn, just on principle; and they, Father, sadly hold the majority in the assembly. That's the bad news.'

'And the good?'

'King Marcus is on the forward-thinking side of this argument, on our side and Benner's too. He can't use his royal veto in the assembly without provoking a constitutional crisis, but that doesn't mean he's without feelings for his people. People that we can barely protect anymore. Northhaven isn't the only town that's been hit by slavers. Lots of towns have been raided over the last few years. All small and too far away for the army to get to in time. Now the slavers are growing bolder. Mostly it's been dirt-poor out-of-the-way places to the east that have been raided. Now the skels are heading west towards the coast, where the arteries of the league's trade runs thick and fat. If we don't arm up soon, it won't be long before those flying savages are passing over Arcadia itself and raiding for slaves.'

'I never read of other sorties by the slavers in our papers?'

'The Lanca is a big place, Father. Unless you're in the radiomen's guild, all news is local news. But the king, he knows.'

'And what is his knowing worth?'

'You and I, we're going to find out, Father. Because I have secured a royal audience for us. Already radioed Northhaven to let Benner know how well his people are being looked after and his interests represented.'

'What can the king do?'

'He's still the king, Father. You want to go after the slavers? Well the royal guardsmen report directly to the monarch. The gaiaists can't vote the king down if he backs your mission out of his own pocket, however much they might want to.'

'Royal guardsmen,' said Jacob, trying to suppress the flicker of hope before it was prematurely snuffed out. 'I've heard they're good people in a fight.'

'The best,' Gimlette smiled, forking a piece of crabmeat between a wall of white teeth. 'Strongest, fastest, most accurate with any weapon from a crossbow through to a sharpshooter's rifle. Recruits have to stand over six-feet tall just to join. It'll be like having a regiment of giants marching behind you.'

'Good,' said Jacob. 'I'll need soldiers like that.'

This was as much as Jacob could've hoped for, with the king only a few years on the throne himself. He still remembered when

Northhaven had been flying royal standards from every window for the funeral of the old king and half the royal family had been swept away in a winter hunt's avalanche. Then bunting stretched across the narrow streets for the coronation of King Marcus. Jacob bit his lip at the thought of himself and Mary and Carter together at the celebrations. *Those were good days. I wish I had known how precious they were at the time. You never appreciate what you have until it's gone. Damn fool.* Nobody in this room wanted to see a churchman's tears falling onto a dining table. Not the staff, or the other patrons or this avuncular gourmand of an assemblyman.

'You will, I say you will have them. Prayer can only take you so far, Father. Against the slavers, a repeating rifle will carry the day and bring our people back. Where will you go after Arcadia, though? That's what the king will ask.'

'Wherever I have to. I figured I'd ride the railway to Talekhard and book a commercial passage on board one of the big carrier planes. Follow the slavers wherever I have to.'

Gimlette raised his wineglass, one of the waiters rushing over to refill it. If the powerbrokers at court knew this assemblyman as well as the waiters here, then the expedition from Northhaven would be off to a fine start.

'How are you going to follow the slavers? Could be anywhere by now. Across the sea to the Burn, east, west, north? Can't track a weeks-old contrail, not even on a couple of hundred propellers. They're nomads of the air, Pastor. You have to go back to ancient history before you find a chunk of land those skel savages called home.'

Jacob brushed his simple black church tunic. 'They were last seen flying south. But I'm a pastor, assemblyman. I figure God's going to show me the way.'

Gimlette looked at Jacob, his eyes wet and glistening and his brow sweating slightly, the man trying to work out if Jacob was being serious or not. Then his paunch rolled as he laughed. 'You had me going there for a second, Father. Hell, the guardsmen got the best weapons and the best men, probably got the best trackers too, right?' He pointed at the glass of red and caught the waiter's eye again. 'Some white wine too, to go with the crab. You should have some, Father, it's as fine as fine can be. All the best wines come from Arcadia.'

'I'll stick with water. Meeting the king's not an everyday experience for a simple country preacher. But don't mind me. Benner Landor's paying for a cathedral, now. What's a bottle or two of white wine compared to the cost of that?'

The politician chortled and held his glass up high. 'That's the right attitude. As sober as a churchman, I say. But don't you worry about the king. His Highness knows who supports him in the assembly. Just as I know which landowners support Charles T. Gimlette.'

Jacob raised half a smile in return as he heard the creak of wood from under the assemblyman's seat. *A stout chair with the best view in the house, and it just needs to hold you up for as long as it takes the king to sign over a company of his finest fighters.*

Jacob stared at his clothes in the mirror. The finery of the hotel room only reinforced the simple cut of his pastor's clothes; threadbare compared to the expensive curtains, elaborately-woven carpets and polished walnut furniture. Simple blacks and greys that would no doubt look even plainer against the pomp and colour of the court. Well, he was who he was. *Never felt like apologising for it before. Isn't any time to start now.* Jacob looked over at Wiggins sitting in an easy chair twice his size and whittling with his knife at a piece of wood. His legs rested on one of the crates of coins drawn from the bank. Filled with a small fortune, each freshly minted coin stamped with the black boar of Weyland on one side and the House of Landor's crest on the other. A final little vanity for Benner – even his currency reminding those whose hands it passed through of the wealth and power of the man who had first paid it out. *Hell, the slavers will only care about the purity of the platinum – not the crest sitting on it.* Behind the constable, Sheplar and Khow examined the map that the Rodalian flier had picked up, a square booklet unfolded over the entire width of their table.

'It's not too late, old man. You can come with me to the palace.'

'You want me travel to court in this here police uniform? Some fool is just going to try to post me on guard duty. What the hell would I say to the king anyhow?'

'How about "Nice army, do you mind if I borrow it?"'

'That's a fine try, but I'm fixing to stay here. Why don't you drag Khow or Sheplar along with you?'

'Our Rodalian brother would only remind the court that Rodal has a skyguard and doesn't require big smoking factories to churn out its planes. And Khow, well, I just have a feeling ...' *About how eager the assemblyman seemed to be to discover how we were following the slavers. Khow's a card I'm keeping tucked up my sleeve for now.*

'Way I see it, Father, they're more likely to throw behind us if they see one fool rather than four anyway. Besides, I'm for staying here and guarding our money. If one of the cleaning maids discovers this lot left on the carpet, we might need to radio Benner and beg for a second fortune.'

'You guard it, then. I'll do what I need to do.'

'Nobody can talk them down like you,' said Wiggins. 'Whether the court or Northhaven, that ain't changed.'

'What are you carving over there anyway?'

'Started off as a Rodalian kite, but the wings sheared off. So now, I thought I'd carve a traveller's wagon. Maybe bring us some luck on our voyage.'

Jacob sighed. 'You never could carve worth a damn.'

'That's why I need to practise so much ...'

Sheplar and the gask seemed distracted leaning over the map. Jacob went across to see what had engaged the pair's attention. Khow kneaded the furrows on his forehead with one hand while the other tapped at the calculator resting on the map. 'Something has changed, I can feel it in my soul, I can see it in the numbers here.'

'Change for the better or the worse?' asked Jacob.

'The weight of my son's soul is drawing away from us faster now. Much faster. I do not understand how such a thing is possible. This development worries me.'

'The greater the altitude you fly at, the fiercer the world's currents,' said Sheplar. 'The slavers could be riding a fleet trade wind. We may follow them using the same skill.'

'The velocity I see here is of an order different, akin to the difference in speed between bullet and bird,' said Khow. 'How can that be? How can he retreat so quickly?'

Jacob rested his hand on the gask's bony shoulders, the quills under the twisted man's toga flat and still. 'If you can feel him, we can follow him. It doesn't matter the distance or speed. We're going for your son, just like we're going for mine.'

'Your presence registers as an outlier in my numbers, manling,' said Khow. 'Your very being disturbs my equations.'

'If that's all I have disturbed by the end of this evening, I'd say it was a good night's work.'

Assemblyman Gimlette's black lacquered coach had driven Jacob to a scene every bit as grand as the setting the pastor had imagined. Each ceiling in the palace higher than the steeple of his church, a ball busy with thousands of guests, velvet gowns and long elegant silk gloves for the women – a riot of colours: crimsons and greens and ivory whites – the men in dark tailored suits and uniforms with more braid and piping than cloth visible below. Everyone whirling in clockwork precision to the waltz-like crescendo of an orchestra seated below tall windows in the largest ballroom. Oil-fired chandeliers dangled from a high ceiling, constellations of crystal casting yellow beams into the vista, marble floors and medals and jewels sparkling across the dance floor.

Assemblyman Gimlette sported a black frock coat with tails that flapped as he strode alongside Jacob, pressing palms and returning greetings as they passed through the crowd of courtiers, politicians, businessmen, military officers and nobility on the fringe of the dance's smooth rotations. He wore a colourful line of medals above the crimson sash bisecting his gut, although the Lord knows what they had been awarded for. Territorial officer service, or just keeping the restaurants on the Hill in trade, it was a tough choice.

'It's a sight, isn't it?' said the assemblyman.

'You could fit Northhaven in a corner of the palace gardens,' said Jacob.

'Yes, I believe you could. I was arranging to have Duncan Landor presented at court next year. A buck that handsome, what a figure he would've cut. A shame, a damn dying shame, I say.'

'You can reschedule the ceremony. If he's alive, I'll bring him back.'

'Of course, of course. Let's see what we can do to expedite that noble endeavour. Standing by the conservatory doors, do you see him? That's our King Marcus.'

Jacob followed the line of the politician's podgy forefinger. The man he pointed out was an unlikely monarch. A figure in a simple dark jacket only a little finer than Jacob's, the man standing a couple of inches shorter than the pastor. If it wasn't for the two red-uniformed soldiers with golden brass helmets standing discreetly against the wall behind the man, hands resting on tall sabres, he might have mistaken King Marcus for one of the footmen taking a breather on the conservatory steps.

They approached the steps together and Gimlette bowed, Jacob following suit. 'Your Majesty, I have the honour of presenting Father Jacob Carnehan of the parish of Northhaven.'

King Marcus had an open, contented face, early middle age drawing silver lines across the sides of his straight dark hair. The royal stretched out a hand towards Jacob, and when they shook, he covered the pastor's hand with his own, a nod back towards the conservatory. 'The honour is mine, assemblyman. If you would excuse me, the father and I will discuss what we need to outside.'

'Of course, Your Majesty.'

King Marcus smiled towards Jacob. 'Walk with me, Father.' He crooked a finger towards the two soldiers behind him. 'Please find Major Alock for me and have him join me in the lake garden.' He turned back to Jacob. 'Do you dance, Father Carnehan?'

'Truth to tell, not much, Your Majesty.'

'Excellent. You can never trust a man who dances to be sensible.' He opened the door to the conservatory and Jacob followed the king outside. Lanterns burned across a neatly trimmed garden, turning the green space as bright as the ballroom they had left behind. Stones on the path crunched underfoot. Neat lines of trees concealed the sight of the distant palace walls, only the lights on the twin hills beyond to indicate the two of them weren't strolling through the wilds of Northhaven. They followed the path to a lake. Dark green waters sparkled from the shimmer of lanterns dotted around.

'Your Majesty, I can't promise that what I've come to the capital for is going to sound anywhere near sensible.

'I have the bones of your story from the good assemblyman,' said King Marcus. 'And I know some of the rest from the reports I receive from the radiomen and our secret service.'

'You're making your two guards nervous by leaving them behind,' Jacob pointed out.

'I noticed their annoyance too,' said King Marcus. 'But who in Weyland would want to assassinate me? King of a constitutional monarchy. Too weak to rule, too strong to be ruled? And the slavers are not yet so bold, I think, to attack the nation's palace.'

'It's true, then, Your Majesty? Northhaven isn't the only town the skels have raided?'

'Sadly so. And that's the last "Your Majesty" I want to hear from your lips tonight, Father. Haven't you heard up north? I am the accidental monarch. The burden of my crown should have stayed my cousin's and so on down his line.'

'Yet you still wear the crown, sir.'

'The collapse of snow on a slope brought it sliding towards me. You know what they call me behind my back inside the assembly? The *cobbler*. Four years ago I owned and operated the largest shoe factory in the capital. My wife and I designed half the boots and shoes on show in that ballroom. An avalanche. Of all the foolish capricious strokes of fate. It sounds insane, doesn't it? A year after my brother died, I was installed and invested here. I saw the look on your face when the good assemblyman pointed me out to you. The reason you don't recognise me is that I have so far resisted the mint's attempts to put my face on our nation's coins and notes. Finding my features on the back of a penny will feel a little too final as far as my fate is concerned. You see, Father, if I had my way, I would organise and modernise this nation. Weyland would have a skyguard of its own to claw those murdering skel raiders from the air. The Grand Army of the Lanca would form and we'd sail out to whatever Burn hellhole the slavers are operating from and torch their fuel depots and hangars. But the national assembly does not want a monarch to run the country like a well-tuned factory. They only require an ornamental fop to host parties for the wealthy and reward politicians with ill-earned titles when they retire.'

'I have come here for a king's help.'

'Then for what it's worth, you shall have it.' He indicated a tall officer crunching down the path towards them. Much the same age as Jacob, the man wore the red uniform of the royal guards, a brass helmet with a dark brush atop the helm. A sabre swung on his white patent belt, a holstered pistol on the opposite hip. As the officer got closer, Jacob saw the newcomer must have been close to seven feet tall – probably the same weight as the assemblyman, but all of it granite-hard muscle.

'This is Major Justus Alock,' said the king. 'Before serving in the royal guards, he was the most highly decorated officer on the eastern frontier. Bandits and nomads and outlaws were his daily bread. His men are experienced and loyal. Their talents are wasted here. I think most of them look upon service in the palace as their retirement, in truth.'

Jacob took the officer's gloved hand. His handshake offered Jacob an experience not far off pushing his fingers into a mountain fissure and twisting. 'A happy retirement, Major?'

'We serve His Majesty. Where he commands, we follow,' said the major, stiff and formal. There was a faint web of scarring on his face that whitened when he spoke. The trace of a grapeshot load? Having the major in train would be like having a pet boulder following Jacob around, but hard men were what he had come here for.

'But following where, that is the question?' said the king. 'The assemblyman mentioned you were planning to pursue the skels to the south, Father?'

'That's the direction the slavers were last seen heading by our sailors.'

'Initially, perhaps. But a ruse, surely? I am willing to wager the raiders will have turned east across the sea,' said King Marcus. 'Our army intelligencers believe the skels are based somewhere in the ruins of the Burn. It's the closest market for disposing of human cargoes.'

'You may be right. We'll follow wherever we need to go.'

'How many guardsmen will be required?' asked the major.

'Just a single company,' said Jacob. 'I need to move light and fast. Enough rifles to protect the money we're taking to purchase our people back. Enough to mount a raid of our own if it comes to it. Where folks are friendly, we'll buy supplies; where they're not, we'll live off the land.'

'Father, my men and I spent most of our professional career fighting outlaws. If it comes to it, we can live like them too.'

'I'm going to save blood, Major. I'm not aiming to take it.'

Alock nodded in agreement. 'That sounds more than acceptable to me. Once a soldier's spine has felt a soft warm cot in the palace barracks, returning to it is a far more preferable alternative to leaving his corpse in the dirt of some foreign field.'

'Excellent,' said the king. 'It actually feels as if I've achieved something for the nation this evening. I suppose it wouldn't do to grow too accustomed to that experience. Have your men provisioned and armed tonight, Major. I think it's best you leave quickly, before the gaiaists in the assembly get a whiff of our scheme and wangle a way to have you posted back east, while Father Carnehan suddenly finds himself appointed abbot of the most distant monastery in Rodal.'

FIVE

TO PLEASE A PRINCESS

Carter rolled across the floor of the punishment cell, trying to find the purchase he needed to wipe that smug self-satisfied expression off Duncan Landor's face before the hatch floor swung open and spilled both of them into the clouds. It wasn't going to feel like much of a victory for Carter unless Duncan put his heart into the fight, though. *Come on rich boy; show me what you've got.* Duncan pushed Carter away with a boot just as Carter jabbed his rival low in the gut. Carter swayed back to his feet, every second of solid footing below his boots a bonus. The slave master and the other skels hissed excitedly from behind the cell's wall, jabbing fists in approval as they urged Duncan on to murder. Would the slavers make good their promise to open the cell door, if Duncan killed his countryman? *Guess that's one of those abstract questions as far as I'm concerned. I'm leaving dead, either way.*

'Come on Duncan. Your fancy unwashed clothes don't look any different from mine now. Show me what the man inside is worth ...'

Duncan lowered his mop of straw-coloured hair and charged Carter, roaring his anger, striking him in the chest and carrying both of them against the wall. Carter could see the timer in the wall. *Only a minute left.* He struggled against Duncan's hands as they closed around his neck. The random switch on the trapdoor might just give them both the time they needed to murder each other. Carter snaked his arms past Duncan and squeezed back at the man's neck – like trying to throttle a tree trunk – both of them locked in a contest of raw strength, choking and pressing. Carter slipped, both of them falling forward through the – *open door of the punishment cell?* He struck the passage between the slave pens. Carter immediately noticed the hush. No more jeering guards, no screams and shouts from the prisoners. It was as if they'd fallen to the floor of a church in the middle of a service. Carter's eyes drifted up as Duncan broke the silence, grunting and getting to his knees. The surprise of their survival had temporarily shocked both men out of the fight. In front of Carter, the skel guards and the slave master also knelt. A number of tall soldiers stood outside the slave pens, elaborately engraved golden breast plates covering muscled chests, heads protected by brass helmets topped with red brushes, cloaks enveloping the back of their greave-plated thighs. One of the newcomers had opened the punishment cell's door. It was clear these men weren't Weylanders, but Carter's heart leapt at the thought that this was some League-sponsored rescue force come to save them. *Are we free? Free!* His heart soared at the thought of returning home. Discovering if his father was alive or not. Eating real food, not caged like a swine and beaten worse than one every time a skel guard required amusement. *I swear I'll never complain about working in the librarian's hold again.*

That idea evaporated in agony when a shining black boot landed on Carter's spine, pinning him to the floor. One of the other soldiers crushed Duncan with a boot too. A woman stepped out from the escort of fighters, as tall and dark-haired as Carter, a sharp-cheeked beauty marred by the cruel set of her wide blue eyes. She was dressed in a feminised version of the soldiers' uniform, a platinum chest-plate shaped to flatter her breasts, but without a helm, her dark hair curling over the armour's engravings. Two golden shoulder clips shaped as eagles' claws held an ermine-trimmed cloak in place, long legs bare, apart from the short-sword strapped to one hip and a pistol holster strapped to the other.

'Now I know why you only ever send us weaklings,' said the woman, addressing Si-lishh, the slave master quivering as he knelt. 'All the ones with spirit are flushed into the sky before you ever reach me.'

'These slaves fight, mistress, even after seeing punishment cell working,' hissed the slave master, keeping his head bowed. Carter noticed the way his thick tail trembled. The twisted man was terrified by these newcomers. *Who the hell can throw a scare like that into the skels?* 'Si-lishh must punish, must set example for others.'

The imperious woman walked past the skel officer, unclipping the whip from his belt and fondling it with her flared leather gloves' long fingers. 'Slow learners, then? Or perhaps they simply don't care what happens to them?' She halted in front of Carter and Duncan. 'What do you think? Shall I toss you back inside the punishment cell and let you walk the sky?'

'Answer!' yelled the soldier behind them, his boot crushing painfully into Carter's spine.

Carter winced as he spoke. 'You're the one standing in front of a company of men armed with guns and swords, is what I think.'

She prodded Duncan's head with the tip of her boot, an even larger soldier crushing the heir to Hawkland Park. 'What about you, slave?'

'I figured I'd say as little as possible, on account of the boot on my back. '

'There we are, Si-lishh. Arrogance and caution. They will need both to survive the work that my slaves are given. I believe I shall keep them ... for now.' She turned away, then wheeled back, the whip cracking out and cutting Carter's face open, an ear-splitting snap chased by Carter's yell.

Damn, but that hurts. Carter moaned in agony, finding it difficult to fight for air with the weight of the brute bearing down on his back. What was the point in being spared if they were going to keep on treating him like this?

'I liked your friend's answer better,' she said. She clicked her fingers and her brutes dragged Duncan before her. She knelt down, examining Duncan's face like a horse broker checking the goods. 'Yes, it would be shame to mark a face this handsome. Whatever would it do to the resell value? He's a keeper.' Carter had to suppress a laugh. Money obviously recognised money, even up here. Maybe rich people smelt the same? The woman cast the whip down in front of the slave-master. 'Chain them all, Si-lishh, and have them transferred across to the *Primacy of the Sky*. How many slaves have you taken this time?'

'More than five hundred, mistress.'

'The wastage rate is still increasing in the sky mines. I'll need far more slaves from you next time, even if you have to keep some of the older ones alive. Even if you have to start raiding larger towns.'

His reply hissed towards the deck. 'Your will shall be done, mistress.'

She swivelled on her heels and departed, the guardsmen marching behind her. The slave master got to his feet, yelling orders at the skels to shackle the prisoners. He pulled Duncan and Carter off the corridor decking. Pain burned across Carter's slashed face.

'Slaves think they plenty lucky being spared fate of punishment cell, being spared to work for Princess Helrena Skar? Lucky would have been left to drop into sky. That would have been your luck!'

Carter wiped the blood off his face with the back of his sleeve. 'One day, friend, I'm coming back for you. And on that day, I'll see this aircraft and every one of you thieving, raiding, twisted bastards burn just like you torched my town. You remember that. I'm going to kill you!'

'Only if Si-lishh trips over your corpse and breaks neck,' laughed the slave master. 'What princess has in store for little slaves is better than punishment cell. Is very *slow*.' Dozens of skels marched into the passage, accompanied by house slaves. They locked tight metal clamps around Carter's ankles, chains with no more than a foot's play to shuffle forward on.

Si-lishh tapped the side of his pocket, the rattle of a handful of coins. 'Sold!' He walked away hissing in amusement as the survivors of Northhaven were dragged out of the pens and bound together in a long line. The skels roughly shoved Carter into the chain gang and shackled him to the others. James Kurtain arrived before Carter, checking the pins in the locking mechanism around his ankles. The house slave passed Carter a square of wet cloth to press against the blazing wound on his face. *It burnt*. Whatever the cloth had been soaked in, it sure wasn't water.

'If you had let me know you fools wanted to kill each other, I could've slipped the two of you engine cleaner for poison. Would have been quicker. Remember our deal, Northhaven.'

'I'll let your sister know you're alive,' said Carter. 'Do what I can for her. Are those armoured sons-of-bitches the same ones who took your town's people?'

'Same ones.' James glanced nervously down the lengthening

columns of chained slaves. 'Just stay alive. That's the only victory we're allowed now.'

'I surely plan to.' *At least long enough to keep my word.* 'You look after yourself, James.'

That was the last Carter saw of the house slave as the prisoners stumbled forward through the wide, wooden corridors of the aircraft. Wasn't much of a guided tour – only skel crewmen to watch them being hauled to their new owners. The twisted men rocked and hissed in amusement at the sight of the bedraggled Weylanders. It was clear they felt only contempt towards their common pattern stock. Eventually, the passage opened out into an empty hangar. James' words drifted back to Carter as he caught a glimpse of the incredible sight outside. *Damn, but it's true.* There were no gliders or transport planes waiting with blurring rotors to carry them away from the skels' town-sized carrier. The slavers' huge aircraft still soared high above the clouds. Outside, matching the aircraft's velocity and joined by a docking bridge, flew the miraculous warship that James had talked of. Twice as long as the skels' carrier, hazing the air from hundreds of thruster nodules angled towards the ground, and, incredibly, every yard of the flying vessel composed of gleaming steel. It was clear to Carter that this behemoth was designed for war. Firing gantries had been constructed into the vessel's hull, ant-sized soldiers moving along the ramparts, past turrets where cannons slowly turned and tracked from side to side. There was a Gothic ornateness to the vessel's design, as if someone had ripped out the bell tower of the largest cathedral in the world and tipped it on its side. A cathedral devoted to destruction, burning more fuel than Benner Landor's tenant farmers could grow in a season. What was it Princess Helrena Skar had called the craft back in the slave pens? *The Primacy of the Sky*. Well named.

'Sweet saints,' whispered Carter, despite himself. 'Dear sweet saints.'

Duncan Landor lurched behind Carter in the chain gang 'There isn't that much metal in the world.'

'Reckon they've found it, anyway.' Maybe that's why there were no ores left to mine inside in the league. They had all been stripped out in the past to construct this hovering leviathan of the air.

Slavers hauled Duncan aside into a second line while Carter was roughly pushed forward. The cattle were being lined up, readied for a stock transfer. Shouts sounded and the prisoners started moving; the astonishing warship their destination. Carter shuffled slowly across the gantry between the two vessels, the shackled clink of hundreds of prisoners passing across a mesh floor, as solid and immovable as the bridge over Mill River back home. Segmented metal railings stopped just shy of chest height. Carter felt giddy as he peered over the edge. Only clouds below, the distant brown smudge of land passing through gaps in the cover. There was no sign of the sea. No hint of where they might be. He glanced back across the gangway. So many faces he dimly recognised from Northhaven. He couldn't see Adella, Willow or Kerge. Even Duncan Landor's ugly mug would be welcome right now. For the first time since Carter had been taken, the abysmal reality of his situation sank in on him. *This is my fate from here on in. Not Carter Carnehan, master of his own destiny. Just a slave to be traded like cattle in a market.* Desperation overwhelmed him: the unfairness of this. If only he had left home a little earlier, he would have been safe inside the library when the attack began. His mother might still be alive, without the gunfight he had started. He could be enjoying a real life with his parents by his side. If there hadn't been a wall of steel mesh between him and the sky, Carter might've jumped at that moment.

The gantry ended with a large air lock. As Carter entered the warship, one of the plume-helmed soldiers encouraged him forward none too gently with a rifle butt. He passed into a semi-circular chamber, two levels high with large mounted guns on the second-storey gallery. More soldiers stood by, rifles ready, stationed in case the slaves became troublesome. They wouldn't get much fuss today. Carter felt as broken and as hopeless as any man on Pellas, and he was as wild as any of them snatched from Northhaven. Everyone said so. *Is that all it takes to break a man? To crush all the hope from him?* A series of tunnels fanned out in front of the prisoners, each with a steel path leading into the warship's interior – but there was something strange about the floor. As Carter stared, he saw that each walkway was moving. A house slave cut Carter out of the chain gang. His ankle manacles, he noted, were left locked. Silently, the house slave guided Carter to one of the walkways, preventing him from stumbling as he was led onto the sliding floor. Carter was propelled into the tunnel, a few seconds of darkness. He briefly lost his vision as a harsh light flared on. The moving belt beneath his feet had halted. Carter's sight returned just in time to see three house slaves advancing on him.

'Don't move,' one of them ordered, 'or you'll be cut.'

Carter watched his crumbling shoes tugged off his feet by the closest house slave, while his two colleagues ran humming metal boxes over the Northhaven man's body. Carter shuddered as he realised all his clothes, already ripped and blackened and falling apart, were being peeled away. It didn't take them long to shear him of his dignity. He was left naked apart from his ankle chains. A hatch in the wall opened and the house slaves tossed his dirty rags into a blast furnace inside.

'What are you—?'

'Keep your cake-hole shut,' barked one of the house slaves. He slammed a rubber button on the wall and the floor began trundling forward again. In the next section of the tunnel, Carter flinched as nozzles in the wall's sides began squirting an oily yellow mist over his body, a fine layer of gel coating his bruised, bare skin. He attempted to rub the gunk from the burning scar on his face, but it just seemed to cling all the harder. He was still wiping it away when the gel was followed by a steaming wet smog that washed the grime away. The walkway kept trundling through into darkness. Carter yelled in shock as a cold metal vice pressed in on him from either side, clicking in place and locking around his body, forcing his arms down by his legs. *What the hell are they doing? Trussing me for the oven? Are these devils cannibals or slave owners?* Lights flared on again and Carter saw prisoners ahead of him on the tunnel's moving floor; dripping water onto the walkway, metal caskets stamped around them concealing most of their nudity. They could no longer collapse. They couldn't wriggle an inch, little more than living components in this bizarre mill. A metal arm swung down ahead, striking the nearest slave on the arm near the shoulder. A female screech sounded. *Branding! We're being branded, no better than cattle.* Someone cried behind Carter, calling out words lost among the rattle of machinery. Carter stifled a yell as burning hot metal slammed into his side, a second of agony and then nothing. Compared to the cold lingering pain of being whipped across his face, this new discomfort was hardly anything at all. A whine of machinery deafened Carter as he was lifted off his feet, the moving walkway falling away like a waterfall's edge. A rail carried him now, hanging, through the air and into a chamber so large it must have occupied a good part of the warship's interior. Vast metal shelves filled the space. Carter had to stop himself from laughing when he saw people being racked below by the machinery. *I'm a book. A human book. Back to being a librarian again after all. Carter Carnehan, a volume of meat stored in a library of slaves.* Carter grunted as he was lowered into a cell, a blank metal wall in front and behind, only the distant, muffled whimpering to tell him that he was one of many prisoners being stored in this flesh-filled hold. Down he went, a wet slap as he plunged into a pool on the cell floor, a viscous jelly rising around his body, the impact of a hard surface beneath his bottom as he was forced to sit within the liquid. The well's liquid stopped at his chest, lapping around his skin.

'Open your mouth,' commanded a tinny voice, echoing disembodied around his cell. Carter did as he was instructed. A small pipe rose up from the pool, snaking into his mouth and stopping an inch above his tongue. 'Slave rations will be dispensed twice a day. Water, followed by nutrients. A sewage removal cycle will be triggered after each feed.'

'Damn you to hell!' Carter yelled, trying not to gag with the tube in his mouth. 'Damn—'

He fell silent as the pressure on his chest increased, the warship's extreme acceleration blurring his vision, the cries from hundreds of stored slaves smothered as a red mist descended over his vision.

Carter's journey had truly begun.

Jacob waited for the green-uniformed conductor to fold down the train's stairs, dropping them towards the platform. He listened to his bones creak from weeks of confinement on the train as he stepped down. The sign on the station platform read *Brinkdalen*, over halfway to the commercial airfields of Talekhard. The expedition had left the main line that followed the coast, heading southeast now into the nation's wide heartland. A landscape of spectacular scenery, high mountains and chilled alpine lakes; lush meadows and pine forests as deep and endless as the ocean. Towns were further apart now, the train's refuelling stops becoming infrequent. Some days, all Jacob saw outside were royal cavalry patrols protecting the rail guild's investment in laying down tracks within the kingdom. Six or seven soldiers on horseback, their packs jangling as they cantered alongside between army staging posts. Any nation foolish enough to allow thieves to rip up its rails would soon discover how hard it was to prosper without trains running through their territory.

'One hour,' the conductor reminded Jacob as he stepped off the train. 'Then we depart Brinkdalen.'

Jacob smiled in acknowledgement. *And you can set your clock by that.* Behind the pastor, Khow received a similar warning. Jacob felt for his wallet. It contained Weyland shillings, rather than the small fortune in platinum trading coins they had withdrawn from the House of Landor's bank. Jacob was a thousand times richer now than he'd ever been, yet he had never felt poorer in anything that mattered. He glanced behind him. Their train ran three-storeys high. More like a ramshackle mobile township. Cabins mixed with exhaust manifolds and the windows of dining rooms, wooden viewing decks shaded by tarpaulin, long oak doors sliding open to expose cargo chambers. Animals driven off, goods rolled on, crane arms swinging over to pick up stacked bales, conductors trying to bring order to stevedores, porters and passengers moving in and out. A crowd of peddlers and merchants, trays of knives and matches and fruit and piping-hot chestnuts strapped to their chests, accosting passengers or attempting to board the train without paying. The whole train quivered on jet-black antigravity stones, the rail guild's greatest secret. Big menhir-sized stones that buoyed the train's carriages above the land, the train clutching the rails below with just a few curved clamps.

'All this way and we've hardly even begun. It still seems like magic to me, Khow.'

'Airflow acceleration, inducement and entrainment across an airfoil-shaped ramp with minimal drag,' said Khow, 'combined with magnetic levitation through superconduction. Such principles are known science, manling, not supernatural forces.'

'And that's different from magic, how? I never did understand your people,' said Jacob. 'Smartest men I ever met, and all you ever do is hide in the woods. Always seemed a contradiction to me. Simple lives and complex minds.'

'To my people, our manner of existence seems the most intelligent way of living,' said Khow, taking a deep breath of high clear air. He indicated the forest on the other side of the train. 'I will return before the train's departure.'

'Do the trees ever reply?'

The gask tapped his ears, more like a bat's than a Weylander's. 'In very subtle ways, if you know what to listen for.'

Jacob was hard pressed to tell whether the gask was pranking him or not. Major Alock's troops were easy to spot as they dismounted from the military carriage coupled into the train. You just searched for caps raised a head higher than everyone else. The royal guardsmen kept themselves to themselves mostly; regarding, Jacob suspected, the two chests of coins they were minding and the civilian members of the party as a fool's mission into the back of beyond. But then, they were pragmatic men. The troops had swapped the bright stiff uniforms of royal guardsmen for the practical khaki of the border riders they had once been. Green cloaks with grey edging that could be pulled over a crouched body as camouflage. Each soldier sported a modern Landsman-pattern sharpshooter's rifle slung over his shoulder, its stock weighted down with the slim brass tube of a telescopic sight. Good for more than opening holes in paper targets, Jacob reckoned.

Sheplar Lesh climbed down the folding steps, tripped and stumbled forward into the crowd of peddlers, his fingers ending up in one of the boxes of steaming hot chestnuts. Withdrawing it with a yelp, he flapped it in pain and sent a pile of folded journals flying into the air from a stationer's tray.

Wiggins landed on the platform behind Jacob. 'You tell me how a fellow that can find and hug the only updraft in the whole prefecture, soar on it like a hawk, becomes the clumsiest fool I ever did meet on the ground?'

'Gills maketh the fish and eyes of night maketh the owl,' quoted Jacob.

'That they do,' said Wiggins. 'But I've a feeling that when it comes to the kind of scum who trade in human flesh, your good book ain't going to mean a whole lot more than kindling.'

'For the slavers we have Benner Landor's money.'

'I saw that woodland magic of the gasks back in Northhaven just the same as you: who's alive, who's dead, and where's Auntie Mabel out a-walking today. But still, I don't know ... this pursuit. You've got to wonder if Khow knows what he's talking about? Every piece of common sense inside me says that we should be sailing across the ocean to the slave markets of the Burn, not pushing south.'

'Four points in the compass, old man. If one direction don't work out. We can try the others in a few years' time.'

'You figure I've got a few years left in me?'

'At least.'

'How you doing, Sheplar?' Wiggins called out as the pilot advanced on them, shaking and blowing on his wounded hand.

Sheplar pointed to the snow-tipped peaks in the distance. 'I see mountains, but this land still feels flat to me.'

'Nothing ever feels like home,' said Jacob.

'Perhaps if I was in the air ...'

'Don't worry, we'll be at Talekhard soon enough. We'll be relying on you to find us a merchant carrier whose propellers won't drop off while we're in the air.' Jacob indicated the soldiers disembarking across the platform. 'Your nation would have needed to strip out every border squadron in the skyguard to lift these man-mountains. And as good as I know your people are behind a kite, even you've got to admit, your flying wings are short on range.'

'The winds are only strong to carry us home,' said Sheplar. 'That's carved on the temple walls. I never understood what it meant until I found myself riding a train so far from Rodal.'

Jacob cast his eyes over the town, locating the tip of the radiomen's guild near the centre. 'Let's head to the radiomen's hold. Might as well make a show of getting our "mysterious updates" on the slavers' position.'

'You know,' said Wiggins, 'your "secret" source is really scratching at Major Alock.'

'You think the guardsmen would follow us if they knew we were chasing nothing more than wood magic? Hell, the king would probably have asked if Arcadia's most secure head hospital had four spare cots with a sea view.'

'Hell, Pastor, we're crazy enough to be far-called. The king's mad enough to back us, and the major's mad enough to follow us ...'

'I'm not mad yet,' said Jacob. 'So far, I'm just mildly irked.'

'You think I'll be alive when you lose your temper?'

'I surely do hope so, Constable.'

Sergeant Nix peeled off from the milling troops and walked towards them. The only one in the company who had been anything other than taciturn towards the civilian members of the expedition. The sergeant looked a long lost twin for Wiggins – including his height, but what the man lacked in stature, he made up for in orneryness. Two people wide and, despite his age, fit enough to drag a plough behind him. A midget among giants, he must have turned mean just to survive among the royal guardsmen. The sergeant adjusted the angle of his bush hat against the sun, a gap-toothed grin directed towards Jacob. 'You know, I'm sure we've met before, Pastor. Just can't place the where and when of it.'

Jacob shrugged. 'Unlike Constable Wiggins, I've never ridden with the cavalry on the eastern frontier.'

Wiggins just laughed. 'And you sure ain't spent any time sitting on Northhaven's pews, or any other church, unless it be the house of the holy hangover.'

'You got that much right, Stumpy.'

'Well, Sergeant.'

'Well, Constable.'

'That over there is the Railway Hotel and those windows on the ground floor belong to the Railway Tavern.'

'And that sounds like a plan.'

'An hour only,' said Jacob. 'Otherwise you had better hope that the local mounted police are hiring.'

'An hour?' said Wiggins. 'Hell, I thought I had a few years left just now.'

Paying for a private suite on the train had proved a good investment of Benner's money ... spacious enough to accommodate all four travellers, and not part of the military carriage. Jacob sat on the sofa's upholstered leather in the first of three connected cabins. In front of him stood a small fold-out table. The cabin had been converted to its daytime configuration, beds tucked away behind the oak panelling. Situated on the train's third storey, their cabin's window was high enough to peer over the endless forests passing by. Sheplar and Khow played cards, a gask game with rules that seemed too complicated for common pattern minds to comprehend. But the Rodalian pilot would nod and smile, repeating each new explanation of play and expansion of the rule-set as if he had known them all along and was only having to be reminded.

A knock at their door sounded and Jacob slid it open. A cabin steward stood waiting in his blue-and-gold uniform behind a cart with four covered meals. Their tickets to Talekhard included food from the dining car, to be taken in the restaurant carriage or served in their cabin. Jacob was glad for it, now. Railway lines stretched across millions of miles. Too long to provision for even a small part of the journey with a single delivery; so the trains took on supplies as they rolled, favouring local dishes. It was said the rail guild's chefs ran the best kitchens in the world, and what they'd served to date hadn't made a lie of that boast. It was the same young man who'd served them all week. Every time Jacob saw the apprentice steward, he had to stop himself from wincing. *Could've been Carter here working the guild routes in safety, if Mary and I hadn't tried to hold on to him so damn tight.*

'Good afternoon, Father,' chirped the boy, oblivious to Jacob's grief. He pushed the cart inside and went over to their four large cardboard tickets, hooked to the wall, punching them with an extra hole to indicate another meal delivered. He glanced down at the folding table in front of the window where Wiggins had his pistol in pieces, the constable meticulously cleaning each piece.

'You preparing for Dog-rider Pass, sir?'

'What's that, son? You fixing to run a whippet race down the corridors to liven up our journey?'

'No race, sir, though things might get livelier than anyone cares for. Before we reach Talekhard, the line leaves the country to bypass the highest peaks. We cut through a corner of the Kingdom of Ivah. That's bandit territory.'

'And these bandits ride dogs?' asked Jacob.

'Mega-wolves as big as horses, Father, but that's not why they're called dog-riders. The bandits are like your friend here—' He indicated Khow. 'But even more twists on the spiral removed from us. Fur, long snouts and red eyes. Their faces look like dogs if you squint at them right. Not the friendly kind, though. They're cannibals and they'd have all of us for a meal quick enough, if they could.'

'Do soldiers patrol the railway line in Ivah?' asked Khow.

'The Queen of Ivah's dragoons perform that service, sir. Although the land's sparsely populated, more bandits than villagers. We should be fine. A train of our length is usually left alone ...'

Wiggins pushed a brush through his gun's rotating cylinder. 'My daughter once owned a terrier, black as the space between the stars. A right sweet little fellow he was.'

'If there's one thing the dog-riders aren't, it's sweet,' said the steward, lifting the lids off their meals. 'They're bloody savages. But they're smart enough to know that sentry ports on a carriage means we're running with a barracks car in the train. They don't like guns. Their tribes don't have the art of metal working – spears and clubs tipped with flint are all they have to attack travellers with.'

'Not that I'm complaining, mind, given how good this tastes. But how come your food always smells of corn chowder?' asked the constable.

'The hot plates are part of the engine car, sir. Everything from the kitchen smells of oil.'

'That'll be why, then.'

Halfway through serving, their steward spilled a splash of gravy as the train began braking hard.

'Next stop is a day away?' said Jacob. *We don't need delays.*

Sheplar Lesh opened the compartment's window and leaned out, the sound of the train's engines dwindling to a sigh as it slowed. 'Signal flags are being raised over the lead car.'

Their steward abandoned the meal cart and poked his head out too, reading the pennons. 'Says there's a rail missing ahead. We'll need to stop, then take out one of the rails behind us to replace it.'

'Missing?' said Jacob.

'Stolen,' said the steward. 'Some traveller caravan riding around with bootleg trade metals in the back of their wagon, I'd guess.'

'Fools if they are,' said Wiggins. 'If they're caught, the guild mark will be placed on their heads. Nobody willing to trade with them or their descendants for as long as there's earth to roll over and air to breath. Might as well sign up with a gang of outlaws now.'

The steward returned to the cart. 'It'll take at least an hour or two to swap the rails out and re-test the line, sir. You might want to stretch your legs after you eat.'

Jacob groaned inside. Every hour lost was another hour for his son to be carried further and further away. *It feels like I'm losing him, Mary. God forgive me, but it feels like our chances of success are being stretched thinner and thinner. Every day we lose is another day for Carter to be worked to death by the slavers.*

A stairwell close to their suite led down through second class, steerage and cargo. Jacob took the stairs to the doorway and climbed down from the halted carriages. The train had stopped in the grasslands of a wide valley. At least they were clear of the snow in the high passes. It had only been a few weeks ago when the plough at the front of the train had been running into drifts the engine car couldn't cope with. All the passengers had been forced to disembark, shivering in the cold under as many layers as they carried, helping to clear a passage with shovels. At one point they had come up behind a goods train in front of them, and they'd had to clear its route and then dig their own train free too.

Fifty feet away from the halted train, Jacob could see the ruins of an overgrown village, little more than grassy mounds. A few mossy rocks to indicate people had once lived there, a light green patterning in the meadows indicating where streets had once run. Wild goats chewed brambles on the mounds, eyeing the resting train and its disembarking passengers with suspicion. It was at times like this that the immensity of the world shook Jacob. Good grazing land that had once supported families, long abandoned and swallowed up by the infinite for reasons that were dust now. *Will the land devour our cause without trace too? All this way, and we haven't even crossed the border yet. Everything that's left of me is slipping through my fingers, lost to the world, further and further away each day.*

Jacob rubbed a hand through his dark curly hair, feeling his sweat from the sun. His legs creaked as he walked forward, ligaments cracking. *I'm getting old. And what I'm doing isn't an old man's game.* He decided to take a stroll before climbing back on board and headed for a copse of trees, five minutes from the ruins of the village. As he got closer, he saw the trees masked something older than the village's remains. A stone circle, menhirs rising twelve feet high. The trees hid their ancient presence. Everywhere you went in Weyland, other nations too, similar stone circles could be found. Jacob pushed through the undergrowth to see if these stones matched the others he had come across. *Just the same.* Dark obsidian-like stone, polished enough to see your face reflected on its surface. Their bases lay overgrown with lichen, but above the reach of the grass, the rune-covered menhirs seemed invulnerable to the depredations of time, weather and nature. *But here's something that doesn't look familiar.* The grass inside the circle had been blackened and burnt, as if someone had reached down and stamped the circle's interior with a giant branding iron. Jacob touched the ground. Warm, even in the glade's shade. *Maybe travellers set up shelter here, recently?* Possibly the same rascals stealing rails off the track. These ancient circles were fey places. Jacob felt a cold shiver pass down his spine. That feeling only faded after he pushed his way out of the trees' half-light. The sun floated hot in the sky. Fellow passengers from the train waded through the long grass, men and women dotted around the valley like farmers in a field. With a single glance back to the copse and what it concealed, Jacob cursed his superstitious hackles for a child's fear and headed back to the train. There was something of a commotion sounding on the other side of his carriage as he arrived. Jacob slipped under a walkway joining two carriages to discover the argument's source. *Aha.* Two train guards blocked the passage of an old man. He sported a scraggly white beard which could've nested robins in its growth. The stranger carried a stout walking staff, but he wasn't using it to threaten the men, merely resting his chin against it while the guards manoeuvred themselves to stop the stranger reaching the carriage's steps.

'Back you, back,' growled one of the guards.

'Isn't this man a passenger?' asked Jacob.

'Wants to be, Father, but without the botheration of paying,' said the guard. 'He came walking down from the side of the valley when he saw our train halted. Watched him with my own eyes. Just an old beggar.'

'A beggar!' said the old man, his voice filling the meadow. 'Damn *you* for a rapscallion, sir. You are no better than a hell-hated foot-licker. Do you not recognise Sariel, the Prince of Players? I am a bard! A noble recounter of tales!'

'Well, you can recount them to the next caravan you come across, friend. Guild rules – no panhandlers to ride on board and disturb *paying* passengers.'

'It must be a thousand miles to the next town,' said Jacob. 'You can't just leave him out here.'

'He walked here well enough in the first place, didn't he? With the berries on the bushes and the mushrooms in the forests, he's probably feasting fine every night. And rules are rules.'

'What about the traditions of salt and roof?'

'Father, the guild of rails only has one commodity to sell. *Passage*. If I let him on board free, I figure I'll owe a refund to the other three thousand souls on our train. This is the express to Talekhard, not a mercy mission.'

'How much?' sighed Jacob.

'We haven't stopped at a guild station, Father, and our other passengers still have their sense of smell ...'

'If the train master asks, I'll vouch that he got on at Brinkdalen. You can split the ticket money between you and pay for a couple of nosegays.' Jacob jingled his wallet. 'We're still in Weyland, gentlemen, these shillings of mine are tested pure by the national mint.'

'The old fool rides steerage, and your silence, or it'll be my job.'

'Steerage and meals, and my discretion can be thrown in for free.'

'Done. You've more money than sense, Father.'

'For once, I think you're right. I'm having a cathedral raised back home, boys. I'm feeling flush.'

'Ah, sweet charity,' smiled the old man, pumping Jacob's hand. 'You will surely end up sitting on one of the synod's golden thrones for your kindness.'

'I believe I've been punished enough already, Mister Sariel. Up the steps with you, old fellow, before one of the guild's journeymen catches you and decides your ticket's invalid.'

'You have a fine deep tenor, Father. A northerner I would say, Northhaven perhaps?'

A bard's ear for detail at least. 'Of late, I have been. You visited the town?'

'Why, of course,' Sariel enthused. He climbed up before Jacob, taking the side door into the cargo level. 'Northhaven's like a second home to me.'

Was like a first one to me. 'You can't have visited recently. All the way out here, you must have been hiking for a good few years.'

'No indeed, Your Grace, I was carried here a short time ago by a giant eagle. Wild Pohierax, a monarch among birds who has reason to remember me kindly. Pohierax bore me most of the distance, calling to his friend the moon as we flew.'

'Just Father Carnehan, if you please. No "Your Graces". I'm not an archbishop yet.'

'Are you not? A disgrace, Your Grace, if not a travesty! God is surely weeping over that cruel offence. Tell me, good sir, where does this train of ours travel?'

'Talekhard's the end of the line.' Jacob glanced around the cargo chamber. The oil lamps hanging from the ceiling weren't burning, but there was enough natural light slanting in from ventilation slats. Bundles of sacks marked with merchants' crests lay piled around the space, a maze of crates to navigate and the passengers' racked luggage sitting safe behind a locked cage. Things could be worse for the tramp; it could have been a livestock wagon he bedded down in.

'Ah, the great free port of Talekhard, the town that goes to sleep every night to a lullaby sung by a thousand rotors.'

'You know your geography, Mister Sariel. But I guess you don't have much calling to use aircraft, not with your feathered friend Pohierax.'

'Ah, it must be said that my acquaintance with matters geographical is no accident. I shall share with you a confidence, Your Grace.' Sariel stopped amongst the crates. 'I was not always a bard. Once, many years ago, I served as the royal mapmaker to King Butembo. I was a cartographer without equal. The king had married a thousand wives and, sadly, he dismissed me after we quarrelled over which of them was the most beautiful ... Yakini or Nabila. It was an impossible choice.'

'Never choose between beauties, Mister Sariel.'

'Will they really bring me food, do you think?'

'With what I've just paid for your passage, they had surely better.'

Jacob left the tramp brushing down the cargo netting and rearranging crates and bales to make himself a cot. Jacob returned outside, content to sit on the grassy mounds and watch the rail being removed from behind the train and bolted down in front. After an hour or so of peace, he returned to his cabin. The steward arrived back with water and fruit, clearing away the dishes. Wiggins had finally relented and joined in the game of cards with the other two.

'They've finished swapping the rails,' said Jacob. 'We'll be moving soon.'

'Just a little bit longer, now, Father,' said the steward. 'One of the passengers stumbled across the missing rail in the meadows up ahead. Damnedest thing. It'd been ripped out and cast aside. Train master has ordered it to be re-laid behind us before we leave.'

'Ha,' snorted Wiggins, flipping a card down on the folding table. 'Couple of young bucks must have stolen it; probably caught hell when their caravan chief discovered what they had done. Tossed the rail quick and rolled off at a gallop before the next patrol turned up. What do you think, Pastor?'

'I was wondering whether flying by giant eagle would be quicker than passage on an aircraft.'

'Depends on what kind of bull you're feeding it.'

'That was my line of thinking too.'

Jacob opened his bleary eyes, a couple of seconds to remember where he was, blinking away the sleep and placing his position in the world. A first-class compartment on the express to Talekhard. He felt a pang of disappointment. For a confused second, he had thought himself at home in the rectory. Mary by his side, Carter down the corridor and all that had happened a bad dream. Her presence had seemed so vivid. *Hell, I guess this must be the bad dream, then. And I'm still living it.* If the light outside was any guide, it was early morning. Apart from Khow, the others still lay asleep in their connecting cabins. The gask, though, was sitting on the floor cross-legged, his mind lost to meditation and the calculations running through his mind. *We've stopped; the train's halted again?* Jacob asked Khow if he knew why they had halted, but the gask just shook his head. When the gask was like this, Jacob could have cut off one of his fingers and the twisted man would be hard-pressed to notice. He stuck his head out of the compartment's window. Thick dark-green forest. And a smell ... a foul one that Jacob recognised. A lot like the ravening of Northhaven.

'Get up, Khow,' said Jacob. 'I think something's happening. Better wake the others'

They soon discovered the reason for their off-schedule halt. Major Alock turned up outside the compartment, his eyes serious slits under a kepi – the circular-topped cap's peak throwing his granite jaw into shadow. Alock's khaki uniform appeared as crisp as if the creases had been beaten flat with a hot sabre edge. The officer's news was enough to wake Wiggins and Sheplar quick enough. They dressed fast, all four of them emerging into the cold morning air. *And there it is*. Another train sat in a siding to their right, three carriages long, a smoke-damaged engine car trailing a single carriage, another flatbed truck loaded with rails and equipment at the rear. Beyond lay the forest, every tree facing the siding with a blackened body tied to its trunk, the smoking remains of a bonfire by the feet of each carcass. The major's troops filtered out warily across the treeline, checking the corpses. The dead soldiers wore a grey uniform Jacob didn't recognise.

Jacob addressed the major. 'A track maintenance train?'

Major Alock nodded grimly. 'Those soldiers are crossbowmen from Ivah. Tree-stake burnings ... I understand this particular execution is a dog-rider speciality.'

Jacob turned his nostrils in disgust from the evil stench of burning. *Too close to the smell of the devastation at Northhaven.* 'We're travelling through Ivah, then?'

'Have been all night. This attack creates a problem for us.' The officer indicated the train's staff swarming over the damaged locomotive. 'The train master has examined the bodies and the rail guild's men are missing, it's only the military escort accounted for among these casualties.'

Wiggins came up behind them, overhearing the exchange. 'This is foreign soil, Major. Sure as hell ain't our fight. Ivah isn't even a league member and we can't be more than a day from rolling back across the Weyland border.'

'The train master has made his request officially, Constable. The guild would no more leave their people behind than the regiment would consider abandoning its own.'

'Your job is guarding our two moneyboxes and going after Northhaven's missing, not this,' said Wiggins.

'There's a reason why the rail guild won't run a full service across Ivah, and,' said the major, pointing to the half-wrecked train, 'it's *this*. If you can't protect the guild's trains, then services don't run through your country.' He picked up a discarded crossbow from the grass. 'No trains mean no goods moved around. No goods means less industry. No trains mean commerce slowing to the crawl of a wagon. If I ignore a formal guild request for military aid, then *this* toy is all the next major of the royal guards is going to have to defend the king. You want to try and keep the peace with no ammunition for your pistol, Constable?'

'And going after them is the right thing to do,' said Jacob. *Though not for Carter or our people, damn it*. He was torn between helping the ruined train's crew and keeping fast on his son's trail. *Can you ever do the right thing by doing the wrong thing?*

Wiggins obviously didn't share the pastor's view. 'This is unlikely to be the worst sight we see before this trip is done, Father. You aiming to help everyone we come across? We got to think about what's important. Those poor devils on that train, they got to be dead by now. Just not dead *here*.'

'Then we'll cut them down from the trees and bury them,' said Jacob, coming to a decision. It was painful and hard, but Carter wouldn't want them to continue their pursuit by abandoning others. *Nor Mary, for that matter*. 'These ashes are still hot. It shouldn't add more than a day to our travels. You don't have to come, old man.'

'The hell I don't. Your Bible's just so much kindling to the beasts that did this. It's my gun that needs to do the sermonising on this jaunt.'

Jacob looked at Khow and Sheplar. The flier tapped the pistol holstered on his belt. 'Two guns are better than one.'

The gask looked uncertain. 'This is not a good forest. Too much blood has been spilled across its roots.'

'I know your people are peaceable. There's no shame in it. You'll be safe enough on the train. The major will leave half his force to protect the passengers.'

'Where the bowers run dark,' said Khow, sadly shaking his head, 'you will need one who understands the paths and ways. I must come with you, though I would rather not. Our fates are linked by the mean.'

'You just ask the trees where the dog-riders have put a match to these poor bastards,' said Wiggins. 'And while you're about it, ask them if we're a rescue party or a choir of goddamn missionaries.'

Major Alock's troopers assembled with full kit in front of the train, water canteens passed out to each of the party by a commissary. 'Drink that down, then refill your canteen until it spills,' ordered the major. 'We'll need to make our water last. Wait as long as you can for us,' the major turned to the train master. 'Should you need to withdraw, will you head for Talekhard or Brinkdalen?'

'Back to Brinkdalen, sir,' called the train master. 'It's closer by two days. We have to radio news of this massacre to the brotherhood as soon as possible.'

'Remain on station here as long as you can. We may well be return-ing with wounded. Lieutenant Benteen, you have command of the barracks car and our remaining men. Mount heavy weapons on every port and keep the train, crew and passengers on a high state of readiness. The dog-riders' scouts might well be watching us this very second. Withdraw if you come under heavy attack and you believe you can't hold.'

With a full water canteen, Jacob and others from Northhaven took position in the middle of the column of soldiers and moved out, fol-lowing the trail into the darkness between the trees. What Jacob found was nothing like the woods back home; no trace of morning in the gloomy twilight, trees as silent as a cathedral around them. Nobody talked, not even the normally gregarious Sheplar, the soft crunch of dead leaves under their boots the only sound as they followed the army's tracker. There was only one piece of luck about the guild of rails' workers being taken prisoner, and that was their trail clearly written in disturbed foliage across the forest floor. There was no other sign of the dog-riders, though. They might as well be following a fog of malicious forest spirits. After half an hour of moving through the forest, Khow slowed in front of Jacob to whisper. 'There are manlings ahead.'

'You're sure?'

'I can feel their presence. They do not belong to the trees, to this place.'

'Alive?'

'Yes.'

Jacob turned to see where the major was in the line, but he couldn't find Justus Alock, couldn't focus on the soldiers' faces, all of them blurred, all of them the same. Jacob's tried to breathe, but found he couldn't. The spray of leaves and dirt against his face was the last thing the pastor saw as a dark curtain slipped across his vision.

Duncan Landor woke up as the suffocating pressure began to lift from his chest, the surface liquid of the well he sat restrained in flattening to calm stillness. How many times had the bruising strain driven him into near unconsciousness? It was hard to tell. Nobody to talk with, only the muffled moans of those nearby on his ledge of imprisoned slaves. The lights never dimmed inside the warship's slave pens. Day as good as night and night no different from day. There were no portholes to contemplate the sky outside … sun, clouds and night's canopy all hidden from him. If Duncan stretched his neck around, he could just see the chasm of space separating him from an identical wall filled with Northhaven's human produce. Apart from the occasional faint cry of wretchedness, the only other sound to mark the tedium of Duncan's imprisonment was the hiss from his feeding tube prior to it squirting out a gluey oatmeal-like gruel, the bland substance followed by a fountain of biting cold water. All Duncan had to mark the passage of time was the disembodied metallic voice that sounded twice a day, usually an hour or so after each feed, intoning 'Muscle stimulation', followed by a burning jolt of pain which left his trapped body quivering for an hour after. All around the chamber the distant, unseen cries rose at this unnecessary torture. At first, Duncan thought the shocks must be punishment for some infraction of the pen's unexplained rules – the hours he'd spent yelling out for his sister and Adella, in the vain hope one of them might hear him and draw some small comfort from his presence nearby. But the regularity of the chastisement made Duncan come to believe there might be some medical purpose to it. People bathed in electrical waters in Arcadia to rejuvenate arthritic limbs. Perhaps this cruelty served the same purpose, keeping the slaves' flesh fresh for market? With the two steel segments pressed around Duncan's torso like a mould, he had to sleep in a sitting position when tiredness overwhelmed him. Tilting his neck back against the steel behind his neck – as poor a pillow as a rock on a camping expedition. He dozed off in two-hour segments, spinning back into a perpetual weariness every time the warship banked or changed altitude. If Duncan had fallen asleep when feeding began, he woke up choking and spitting, his mouth filled with gruel from the metallic teat. Days gave way to what must have been weeks, and even the open slave pens of the skels' carrier began to feel like the finest rooms in a Northhaven hotel. How Duncan missed the luxury of speaking with fellow slaves, grubbing about in the food pit for supper, even getting into a fistfight with that scoundrel Carter. At times he drifted into self-awareness and realised the warm salty water falling down his face were tears. *Not for me. Not for self-pity. For Willow, all by herself in this dark place. For Adella and all the others. For father, left alone in the echoing vastness of Hawkland Park, without his family. For all of them, not for me.* This wasn't living. It was existence. Not wounded. Warm enough. Fed and watered. Was this his tuition in what it took to be an acceptable slave? For surely anything that happened after this would be preferable to what had gone before. *They have to sell us, don't they? They have to have some labour for us to do, however unpleasant.* That bastard skel slave master had hinted as much. You took slaves for a reason, not to torture them like this. Duncan's chance to explore the next stage of his captivity arrived when a long metal gantry lowered down, clanking to a stop at the same level as his alcove. There was a draining noise underneath his feet; not the cleaning cycle disposing of his bodily functions, but the whole pit emptying of the viscous fluid that surrounded him. Duncan looked down at his legs, his flesh as wrinkled as a skinned beaver after being so long submerged. He felt as light as a feather, gravity's clinging embrace reduced to half its normal force. *We're still in the air, then, and at high altitude too. Are we to be sold on, transferred to a third owner?*

A rattling sounded in the distance, growing closer and louder, until a metallic cart stopped in the gantry outside Duncan's alcove, two house slaves pushing it along.

'Male, size seven.' One of the house slaves removed a pile of clothes. The garments looked identical to the suit the slave wore. White single-piece underwear covering crotch and chest, a grey skirt-like affair and a simple slate grey, armless tunic. Along with the simple uniform, Duncan was tossed a pair of sandals with cross-webbing to fix the shoes to his feet. On the house slave's right arm lay an identical brand to the one burnt on Duncan's own skin. An upside down triangle with two eagles' heads facing away from each other.

'Don't jump,' said one of the slaves.

Duncan cleared his throat. It had been so long since he had last used his voice in conversation, it was as though he had forgotten how to speak. 'Jump where?'

The slave indicated the chamber's void on the other side of the cart, no railings to stop a man from falling if he slipped.

'I want to live,' said Duncan.

'Me too, brother. Me too.'

'Put those clothes on after your restraints unlock,' instructed the second house slave. 'Dress quickly and move to the left. Follow this gantry to the exit at the front of the pen.'

'But—'

'No talking with the other slaves,' said the first man. 'No questions. Obey all instructions instantly.'

They pushed the cart forward towards the next alcove and Duncan could do nothing but wait. Outside of the warming fluid and sitting naked, he began to shiver. Eventually, the two halves of the frame that had trapped his chest unlocked with a loud clack, the metal prison withdrawing on crane-like arms. Duncan hauled himself weakly out of the now empty well, catching a glimpse for the first time of his seat and a circular well containing a metal faucet. Whatever the substance that had filled his well, its residue had already evaporated from Duncan's wrinkled body, leaving him as dry as if he had been towelled down. Duncan fitted on the undergarment, then squeezed into the skirt, too tight until he realised there was a belt built into the side of the garment that could be adjusted. Lastly, he slipped on the sleeveless tunic. Simple clothes to cover his nakedness. *Such a basic thing.* He almost felt like a human again, not an animal. Outside Duncan's alcove, the other prisoners were already shuffling past, house slaves on the gantry loudly repeating the same instructions given to Duncan. As Duncan turned to the left, he heard the scream from the other side of the chamber, someone casting themselves off one of the walkways, a flash of naked skin and then a crunch on the metal deck below. *A slip?* But there was another scream from his wall, a figure from a gantry below rushing out of their alcove and willingly hurling themselves into the open space. This death was close enough for Duncan to see that the prisoner had taken the trouble to get dressed. A woman, he thought, from the glimpse of long dark hair before gravity caught her and broke her body against the deck far below. *Why did she get dressed, if she was going to kill herself?*

'You can always jump,' noted one of the house slaves standing along the gantry. 'That's one freedom they can never take from you. Keep moving. Turn to the left. Keep moving.'

'Don't jump,' whispered Duncan, understanding the instruction at last. *Adella, Willow, please, stay alive, stay strong.* He tortured himself, fretting that his sister and the woman he loved might succumb to the madness of being confined for too long. The two women had to stay alive. Even life as a slave had to be better than being dead, didn't it? The mocking words of the skel slave master, Si-lishh, returned to haunt him. *'Slaves think plenty lucky being spared fate of punishment cell, being spared to work for Princess Helrena Skar? Lucky would have been left to drop into sky. That would have been your luck.'*

The gantry ended in an open door, steel as thick as a safe vault. Stepping through, Duncan shuffled along a long metal corridor, nobody he recognised, although from the way some of the other townspeople were looking at him, a few seemed to know whose son he was. *Duncan Landor. The most privileged slave in whatever hell we've landed up in.* He had to stop himself from laughing maniacally. The Landor fortune would have been hard pressed to afford the metal in the decking he was walking down. Duncan kept his eyes open for his sister and Adella, glancing around even as he stumbled forward. But neither of them was to be seen, curse his luck. Eventually, he filed into a wider part of the corridor. A pair of house slaves sat behind a metal desk, its surface cluttered with unfamiliar machinery.

'Name and occupation,' demanded the house slave on the left.

'Duncan Landor.' He hesitated as he struggled for words to summarise his profession. *Ex-landowner? Most disinherited man in the nation?* 'Farmer.'

'Another hayseed,' laughed the house slave, not bothering to disguise his disappointment. He fiddled with one of the machines for a minute, and then nodded to a large man standing behind Duncan. The giant seized Duncan's left arm and shoved it inside a rubber circle on the bank of machinery. There was a brief sensation of heat on the underside of his forearm, and when Duncan withdrew it, he gawked. A line of numbers and black bars had been etched into his skin. The tattoo looked as if it might rub off, but his bare skin burned as he massaged the surface.

The man behind the desk raised his own arm to indicate a similar line of script. 'That's who you are now.'

Duncan touched the tender area on his shoulder where the brand had been burnt. 'I've already got one.'

'That's the brand of the Princess Helrena Skar – your mistress, fool. The number on your arm is your identity stamp. It gets you food, if you work hard enough.'

'What if I don't?'

'You ever been hungry, boy?' asked the house slave. 'I mean really hungry, not just ready for dinner? Get out of here, idiot.'

Duncan had to hold back a snort of disturbed laughter. *Well, I've been trying to escape from the shadow of all that I was heir to. That much I've managed. And I'd trade it all back in a damned second, if I could.* The processed queue of slaves continued to shamble forwards, heading down the long corridor. They marched until they reached another armoured door, a house slave waiting with a small box, clicking the trigger on the device and counting each slave out. 'Eight more. Keep on moving.'

Duncan ducked his head through the archway. Immediately the intense light blinded the young Weylander, his vision blurring with sudden exposure to sunlight. It was like stepping through a curtain of heat. The sun burned hot and prickly on his skin after so long in confinement. As Duncan's sight returned, he saw that he stood on a platform docked to the outside of the warship's hull, caged in by wire. It was some kind of aerial craft, a mobile cage. The deafening clamour of the warship's jets kept her hovering in the sky, engines roaring, the smell of her exhaust overpowering. On either side of Duncan, similar platforms had docked, flying metal cages with an open pilot's cockpit up front, their undersides a blur of turning rotors. The aerial pens filled with slaves, all of them prisoners offloaded from *The Primacy of the Sky*. Northhaven men and women, packed in tight inside the transporters. *Steers in a cattle truck.* Duncan pressed through the crowd to reach the craft's side, trying to catch a glimpse of the landscape below. Squeezing through the rabble, Duncan's heart hammered in his chest as he caught sight of ... 'Willow!'

His sister angled around, hearing his shout, then shoved her way through the scrum of bodies to throw herself into his arms. Duncan was overwhelmed with loathing for their captors as he caressed the scarred brand burnt into her shoulder. *Thank God. I never thought I would see you again.*

'Duncan! When I saw people jumping from the gantry back there, I was so—'

'I'll never jump, and nor will you. We're still Landors. No brand on our skin's going to change who we are.'

'Thinking like that will get you killed,' said Willow. 'We need to keep our mouths shut and our heads down, until we learn what this means for us. Our name's as useless to us as our family's money this far from home.'

The metal deck under their sandals started to vibrate as the flying cage disengaged from the prodigious warship. With the rotors' whine below growing louder, the transporter dipped from side to side, sending slaves sliding against each other. Only the density at which prisoners had been packed inside stopped Duncan and his sister tumbling to the floor. The two of them reached the craft's mesh wall, clutching tight to the wire and trying to work out where they had ended up.

Duncan held onto Willow's hand; so tight it began to go white. 'You stay close to me. Whatever happens now.'

'We're going to end up on a slave block, probably sold to different owners.' She sounded panicked at the notion of being separated from him.

His heart ached. *So powerless. Sweet saints, just keep us together, that's all I ask. I can bear this as long as I'm around to protect her.* 'I think we've both got the same owner,' said Duncan, feeling the brand on his arm. 'And it's that woman with the whip, the princess ... Helrena Skar.'

'The bitch! She nearly blinded Carter.'

'Only after she pulled the two of us out from the skels' execution cell. She was making the point in front of her people that saving us wasn't an act of weakness.'

'We're not animals, Duncan.'

'I figure we've been traded like beasts. But for what work, that's the question? When the princess was talking to the slave master, I thought I heard her say something about a mine.'

'A mine? I thought there was nothing left to dig out of the earth?' said Willow. 'Out in the Burn they use slaves for everything. Farming, working in mills, serving inside a house. It's a sign of status; the more slaves you keep, the grander a warlord you are.'

'We've been heading south, not over the ocean,' said Duncan. 'I always thought the southern nations were said to be more civilised than Weyland, not less.' He grabbed the mesh and hauled himself higher, catching a glimpse of the vast warship rising away behind them. Then the transporter entered a bank of haze, nothing visible through the murk. Above, the sun was just visible as a blurry orb of light through the vapour. 'We're still flying high. Feel how light we are. And that sun! It's like standing next to a blacksmith's forge in the middle of the summer. My skin's prickling, even in the fog.'

'We're off the map,' said Willow. 'The speed that vessel must have been travelling. How far have we come?'

'Far-called,' agreed Duncan, 'that's what we are.'

'Well, they must be every bit as rich down south as the records suggest,' said Willow. 'The size of that warship. The cost of producing such a monster would bankrupt the kingdom, even if we had the science to put one together ...'

'If you'd told me you'd seen that steel monster before we were taken, I'd have called you a liar.'

Below them the haze turned thinner for a second, allowing Duncan to catch sight of a dark, cracked landscape as empty and featureless as a desert. The ground lay in shadow as it pushed up towards a fiery red surface, all steam and fury, the outline of a lake of immense size ... a reservoir filled with undulating magma rather than water.

Duncan whistled in amazement. 'What the hell was that?'

Willow pulled back from the transporter's mesh side, shocked by what she had seen. 'I think it was a volcano.'

Duncan felt a moment of doubt. *Have we travelled east across the ocean after all?* 'That's the way I've heard the Burn described down there ... empty and barren. Pools of fire as big as lakes.'

'It can't be the Burn,' said Willow. 'We've travelled thousands of times further than an ocean crossing. That's what those pits of liquid we were imprisoned inside were for, I think. To cushion the pressure of extreme acceleration. The speeds we've been travelling at, we could have navigated half the world.'

Duncan fought to hold down his misery. The terrible realisation that they would never see the fields and forests of home again. *I have to keep strong, for Willow if no one else.* Wrapped inside the haze the transporter suddenly banked. A wall of rock climbed up to meet them, the craft's engines roaring as the pilot gunned the rotors and sent them diving below the ledge. Duncan's first thought was that this was a mountain peak, spearing into the clouds, but they kept flying. He was mistaken. This was something far more bizarre. *We're passing underneath it!* Duncan noted the rock had been studded with the black oblongs of antigravity stones. This was a vast chunk of ground, kept aloft high above the land by artificial means, a castle in the sky. What bizarre manner of people had taken the Weylanders as their property? Warships that could power across the sky at crushing velocities, a nation which could keep an island of rock hovering above the ground for its amusement? The transporter followed the curve of the stone, twisting and slowing, hovering in the air for a second, then launching forward towards a hangar cut into the rock's side. Skids unfolded from the bottom of the craft. It touched down on a flat bare surface, a cavern lit by crackling electrical lights. Other transporters settled next to theirs, the whole hangar filling with a squadron of mobile slave pens. Wind from the craft stilled as their propellers slowed to a halt. A group of slaves appeared at one of the hangar's cave-like entrances; a man in front, old and wizened and holding a walking stick. Duncan was struck by the slave's appearance, like a biblical prophet, a saint come to lead them to a promised land. *Except*, a voice whispered inside him, *you know this place will be the opposite of that.*

The old slave's tired voice boomed out, echoed and repeated by speakers around the hangar. 'My name is Thomas Gale. This is where your new life begins. Follow me to the assembly hall and I will tell you how to survive here.'

At the rear of the transporter, its bow swivelled down onto the rock floor, becoming a ramp. Northhaven's stunned and disoriented masses followed the other slaves into a rock-hewn tunnel, unadorned except for circular lights flickering and casting a wan illumination over the gloom. They were led into the assembly hall, a high-ceilinged chamber cut out of stone, its floor flat and smooth. Thomas Gale waited at the far end, raised on a granite platform. When he spoke, his voice carried over the heads of hundreds of prisoners gathered in front of him. 'You are the property of Princess Helrena Skar and the mining of rocks similar to this one is how you will fulfil your duty to the Vandian Imperium that has enslaved you. This rock you stand inside is Station Forty-three. It's mined-out, but acts as our base of operations. This will be your home until you die. Such rocks are ejected during the eruptions of the stratovolcano, the monster you will have glimpsed below on your flight over here. Your work is to capture ore-bearing rocks, stabilise them, mine them, and when they are mined out, send their remains to the ground below. How effectively you do this will determine if you are fed, and how well. It is hard, dangerous work. Later on today, experienced slaves will be transported here to begin your training in everything that you need to survive in the sky mines. Those who complete their training satisfactorily will eat. Learn well. Learn fast. Questions?'

'Where are the guards?' someone shouted out. Duncan tried to locate the voice, but it was impossible inside the echoing cavern. It had sounded suspiciously like Carter Carnehan.

'Ah yes,' smiled Thomas Gale. 'Thoughts of escape. I remember those. The stratovolcano we hover above is nearly seventeen miles high and four hundred miles in width. You will find a further thousand miles of dead zone surrounds us; where life is rendered impossible by poison gas venting from the volcano, pyroclastic flows and the rain of fire and rubble. Beyond the dead zone you will find two hundred thousand miles of the Vandian motherland. On foot, even unaccosted, you will die of old age before you are ever clear of the imperium. Beyond the empire lie countless thousands of countries that are completely dependent on the imperium for the metals and resources that sustain their civilisations. In all those endless miles, the penalty for aiding—' he tapped the brand burnt on his shoulder '—an escaped slave is execution. The rewards for handing in escaped slaves are substantial ... dead or alive.' He gazed across the mob. 'Do not misunderstand me.

There *are* legions of heavily armed Vandians patrolling the sky mines' perimeter. But they are stationed on the edge of the dead zone to shoot local thieves attempting to steal residual ore-falls. The legions of Vandia will happily kill you if they discover you trying to escape, but it's a lot less effort to simply halt food and water supplies to disobedient slaves. You require two gallons of water a day merely to survive here. So you need to learn your place ... the imperium has a caste system. All slaves are part of the fourth caste, *hostile*. Each caste has three levels – lower, middle and upper. You all start your service as *lower-hostile*. I'm *middle-hostile*. *Upper-hostiles* are the favoured house slaves you see trotting behind a Vandian. Work hard and survive and you might one day be promoted to middle-hostile. Anyone in a higher caste can order anyone in a lower caste demoted or executed without any more justification than their say-so, so never piss off a Vandian.' His voice grew serious. 'Those are the imperium's rules. Here in the sky mines, on this station, we slaves have our own rules. If you steal another slave's clothes or possessions, you'll be beaten to within an inch of your life. If you steal another miner's food or water, you'll be thrown off the rock. Any slave who tries to murder or rape a fellow slave, likewise. Trust me, the stations that don't have those rules aren't places you want to land up. Follow the maintenance staff to a dormitory. If you have kin or friends among you, you can arrange to swap bunks to be with them. Having something to live for will help keep you alive. And staying alive will help us meet our quotas.'

'Sounds like there's not much apart from working hard and obeying orders that won't see us executed,' whispered Willow.

'It's a good thing our old man's not here,' said Duncan. 'He might get ideas about rearranging the common law for the tenant farmers.'

Willow glared at him. 'Don't you dare make light of this. The way these Vandians keep slaves is pure evil. Their nation has so much, yet they treat people like chattels. As backward as the league may be in comparison to these people's science, our frigates carry orders to chase slavers across every point of the compass rather than let them ply their trade in sight of our shores. You ask yourself, who are the barbarians and which is the civilised nation?'

The meeting chamber emptied, the prisoners marched out a hundred at a time, green-shirted slaves leading Duncan and Willow through the warren of stone corridors – identical; each new passage only differentiated by the numbers painted on its walls. Duncan made sure his sister stayed close to his side at all times, as though taking his eyes off Willow for a second might cause her to disappear. *No, it makes sense for families to be kept together. Less likely to run. More likely to look out for each other and work for these pigs. It's the ones with no one and nothing to live for that were throwing themselves to their deaths back on that warship.*

'So, I guess these passages used to be mine tunnels,' said Duncan. 'They look like the works that our old man financed that time on the border of Rodal. Do you remember? Up in the mountains …'

'Hard to forget,' said Willow. 'It was the only time the house lost serious money on a venture.'

Duncan nodded. People had lived in the world for so long there were no minerals left to mine, no fresh seams of resources to be found anywhere. No metals, no oil, no coal anywhere near the kingdom. These sky mines were a far cry from what Duncan had experienced in the Rodalian hinterlands. Engineers begging their sceptical father for more money and extra time to dig further and deeper, despite the fact that the tunnels and shafts were already at a depth where the additional gravity was like having to carry twice your natural weight with every step. Miners emerging exhausted and empty handed with nothing to show for their labours except the shovels and picks that they had gone down with.

'When you dig a mine it's always you who gets shafted.'

'Maybe for us back home, but not here, though,' said Willow. 'That stratovolcano must be throwing out ore from the bubbling core of the world, deeper than any mine works can reach.'

'God,' said Duncan. 'No wonder Vandia has the steel to build that warship. They must be the richest country in the world.' He had to marvel at their ingenuity, wicked though it was. Vandia had even tapped the perfect resource to undertake the backbreaking, dangerous labour of working the sky mines. Slaves. Well, what was the point of being rich if you had to do the hard work yourself?

It felt cooler inside the station than it had been outside on the transporters, but the heat still weighed down oppressively. Duncan's tunic was soaked with sweat by the time they reached their dormitory – a large featureless oblong of a chamber, fifty cots on either side, iron beds with mattresses cut from some soft cork-like substance, no sheets or blankets or pillows. There were hollows in the wall with spigots and a foot pedal to release a stream of drinking water. Duncan and Willow took a turn at the nearest tap, slaking their thirst. The sky miner in charge of the dormitory was a man called Cannelle Ram, hailing from a country called Attijaf that Duncan had never heard of before meeting the man. He bore a calm, learned expression. As head of the dormitory, his advice to the new slaves was simply to learn what they could until their work assignments came down, duties to be allocated based on their previous trades. Their tutors were to be fellow slaves who had survived long enough to be counted old hands in the techniques of sky mining. Cannelle Ram began the task by calling for silence. He approached a blackboard where teams and quota numbers had been chalked up for the previous occupants of the station. He rubbed out the numbers and outlined the basics of sky mining for the new slaves.

'Okay, all you greenhorns, listen up. Stratovolcanic eruptions are graded into seven levels of significance. Anything above a level three discharges material large enough for us to mine. Rocks are ejected at high velocity. Where an initial assessment of a rock shows promise, we intercept it with transporters, slow it down and attach antigravity stones to stabilise it at a neutral buoyancy. Then we land prospectors on top to confirm our initial appraisal, locate mineral veins and calculate where shafts and tunnels can be safely dug without causing fatal fracturing. Everything that follows is raw, backbreaking work.'

'Why not let the rock land and mine it on the ground?' Willow asked.

'An intelligent question,' said Ram. 'Princess Helrena is the owner of more than just our sorry hides. She holds title to a sky mining territory, a sector of the firmament where she controls the imperial licence to mine what she stakes. There are similar territories on the ground that belong to rival nobles; minor houses, because surface mineral fall is not as valuable ... all the ground worms are doing most of the time is panning dust-rain. They receive little, because, with the volcano left to its own devices, eruptions push ejecta mass higher than the sky mines can operate, where the sun's hot enough to melt rocks, gravity so light the rocks can stay up there for months.

There's high-altitude cross winds fierce enough to drag them millions of miles, landing them somewhere other than Vandia. The empire will not allow that to happen, which is why we intercept ore-bearing rocks first. The imperium's monopoly on metals is what keeps them wealthy. Rich enough to pay for nations to act as the empire's lackeys and enforcers, rich enough to buy slaves to work the rocks. A monopoly that allows the imperium to turn off the spigot of resources to any neighbour who might be tempted to try and seize control of the stratovolcano. The sky mines *are* Vandia. Without them, the imperium would be nothing. This is the original source of trade metals that reached you with the caravans and the travellers and the peddlers. The iron you haggled over back home left the empire centuries ago, acquiring scarcity value with every mile travelled away from the sky mines.'

'What if we refuse to work?' asked Duncan. 'Demand freedom in return for our labours?'

'A *dangerous* question,' said Ram. He drew out a circle, sketching a smaller one inside, and then bisected the outer ring into twenty different segments. 'A high-ranking member of the imperial family, one of the *celestial-upper* caste, controls each of these sky mines. Our territory is this one here—' he filled in one of the sections, '—but the princess is one of many children. The imperium's emperor is a mad old goat called Jaelis Skar who keeps a harem of hundreds of wives and thousands of feuding offspring. His children's relationships mirror those of Vandian society – they loathe each other; they compete with each other; they plot and scheme against each other. Not a single mining force, but twenty separate ones. If our station stopped working we would be abandoned to die of thirst, while the sky mines of the princess's siblings worked on, no doubt clashing to see how they could turn Helrena's woes to their own advantage. The Vandian caste system, the slaves, the power, it is a web of internecine loyalties, shifting alliances and infighting. Everything designed to keep the emperor secure at the apex of Vandia, with the imperium at the apex of all nations. Vandia is power without limit and she maintains her grip with ruthlessness and cruelty. If that ruthlessness ever fails, Vandia is surrounded by nations who have endured millennia of subjugation, countries who would gladly step into the breach and assume the imperium's mantle. It has happened in the past. Once the skels controlled the stratovolcano's resources. Now they are little more than itinerant nomads and paid lackeys of the conquerors who overthrew their rule. History has many lessons to teach, and few of them are gentle.'

'What happened to the last group of slaves who worked here?' asked Willow. 'Why is the station empty?'

Cannelle Ram looked pained at the memory. 'The rock we were working broke apart and fell into the dead zone. It happens. There was an accident in the blasting powder stores – a detonation that blew our claim into pieces. Some survived, but not many. Most of the dead were Weylanders, the same as you, but taken years before. Sky mining is dangerous. You can choke on poison outgassing or be torn apart by shrapnel blasts of lava. Bad mining or plain bad luck can shatter a rock with too few antigravity stones to hold each piece stable in the sky, sending hundreds plummeting to their deaths. There are cave-ins and natural gas explosions and blasting powder deaths and limbs lost to machinery. But all of that pales in comparison to what happens here.' He tapped the inner circle he had drawn. 'This central area is where the ejecta mass is blown from each new eruption. It is open sky for any station to stake a claim to new rocks before we tow them into our territory. And out there, there are no rules or laws to protect us from the ambitions of Helrena Skar's siblings. When we find a good claim, we must fight to keep it.' The head of the dormitory noticed the look of horror on Willow's face. 'That's the real danger of working in the sky mines. Not the stratovolcano or working the rocks, but our fellow slaves from neighbouring territories. You must fight to survive, or the rock you land on will become your grave.'

Duncan and Willow settled into the bare dormitory as best as they could. The station was only used as a barracks, long since mined-out but retained as living quarters because of its structural integrity. Princess Helrena Skar's territory held no more deposit-bearing rocks captured to mine. Her new slave force from Weyland had arrived for training during the fallow period; waiting for the next eruption to bring them a stake. There was little natural light inside the warren of passages and vaults. Most corridors were bare of portholes, only the transporter hangars and a few air vents on the top of the station to give a view on to the stratovolcano's all-enveloping smoke and the fetid humid air outside. With the heat clinging to every corner of their chamber, Duncan never missed his sheets. The loss of privacy was another matter entirely. Even the lowliest servant at Hawkland Park had more seclusion than they did in the dormitory here. No sanctuary in the shower chambers either, where water blasted you clean for all of a minute until the sweating started anew, men and women expected to shed all modesty together. The place was clearly designed to break slaves down, discard the last vestiges of being a free citizen. *Property, not people.* Also unfamiliar to Duncan were the day-to-day tasks they were expected to perform alongside their training. Washing tunics and clothes in massive stone tubs, uniforms stirred like soup with paddles. Cooking the food issued to them, preparing it in communal eating areas shared with the other dormitories, those spaces made unbearably hot by ovens and gas boilers. Strange-looking root vegetables and pulses and tiny quantities of meat, all boiled together in vats that were little different from the vessels where the slaves' rags were cleaned. Evenings spent fixing rips and tears and darning their clothes. Acclimatising to the enforced novelty of being kept constantly busy by menial tasks, surrounded by people all the time – and none of them Duncan's servants. But keeping busy was necessary to stop yourself dwelling on what you used to be; on what Duncan might be doing now if only he had stayed at home that day, rather than visiting the warehouses. When he wasn't attacking the array of common chores, he divided his time between searching the station for Adella and learning everything he could about the sky mines. Anything that might help him, the woman he loved and his sister survive. Strangest thing were the flies. You couldn't leave your rations for a second without insects buzzing around the gruel. How the hell they flew this high, he would never know. Maybe they just followed the stench of so many sweating bodies crammed into a hollowed-out rock.

He explored the station's maze of mine tunnels with Willow, following numbered passages in search of the other dormitories. There were graffiti in every corridor, chipped out of rock with hammers and steel gouges designed for mining. Insults, prayers, names, art, dates, declarations of love, declarations of despair. Their presence gave every passage its own character and helped the new slaves learn to navigate the labyrinth of tunnels, stairwells and chambers hewn out of the rock. Eventually, Duncan found the chamber containing Adella.

Willow grabbed Duncan as he caught sight of the man by Adella's cot. Carter Carnehan! The smug look on Carter's face as he saw Duncan enter the dormitory was just a little more than the heir to Hawkland Park could stand. 'Enough!' Willow hissed at him. 'Didn't you learn anything back in the skels' punishment cell?'

I learnt how good it felt to stick my fist in that selfish fool's face. 'I won't swing for him if he doesn't go for me first. That's more than he deserves, Willow.' Duncan strode up to Adella's cot. 'I was wondering why you hadn't come looking for me. I guess now I know.'

'This is just where I ended up,' said Adella. She met his gaze without a trace of shame or embarrassment. 'After the fight the last time we were together, staying out of your way seemed the safest thing.'

'Safe,' snorted Duncan. 'People who hang about with this hothead don't end up safe; they end up like the idiots who followed him down into the old town.'

'Not much that's safe here, as far as I can see,' said Carter. 'Apart from a handful of maintenance staff on the station and a few old hands, you notice anyone over forty? We're equal here, Duncan. Both shit. Just the muscle behind a pick and shovel, all owned by the same folks who paid for the spade.' He pointed down the dormitory and Duncan recognised the others from the skels' slave pen – the gask, Kerge, a few of the men from the town ... Eshean and Joah. 'We're going to have to stick together to stay alive and we're going to have to keep our wits about us to escape this flying prison.'

'Carter's making plans,' said Adella. 'He's already talked to the sky miners, trying to learn how people have been caught escaping before.'

Duncan shook his head in despair. 'Escape? Escape to where? Even if we could get past the dead zone, we'd die of old age fleeing through foreign lands; places where every man and woman would know our brand and turn us in for the bounty on our heads.'

'Not if we learn how to fly one of those Vandian warships and get home the same way we arrived,' said Carter.

'Would that be one of the big metal ones with thousands of heavily armed soldiers and crewmen? The kind patrolling the edge of the sky mines, just itching for a chance to turn their cannons on a handful of bare-arse slaves bearing shovels?'

'Well, there's the thing,' said Carter, slapping the brand on his shoulder. 'Doesn't make me a slave. This is just a scar on my arm, and I'm going to make the bastards that put it there pay for every inch of the thing.'

'Talk sense, Carter!' interrupted Willow. 'Listen to yourself. There might well be a way for us to escape, but you've got to take your time, not do anything rash. Learn how the imperium works, learn what you would be escaping into. You'll need maps, knowledge of their society, supplies, clothes to blend in – a plan that's more than flinging a stolen pickaxe at the first Vandian soldier you run into.'

'There's not a library in the station with a section on slave escapes,' sneered Adella.

'That's fine,' Willow snapped back. 'Because you'd have to be able to read it, and not just use the pages as toilet paper.'

'I'll leave when I'm ready,' said Carter. 'One thing's for sure, I'm not going to die here like a worked-out plough horse in harness for these Vandian sons-of-bitches.'

Duncan looked pleadingly at Adella. 'Are you going to switch cots to my dormitory?'

She shrugged. 'You can switch across here if you want.'

Those weren't the words Duncan needed to hear. Couldn't she see Carter was still using her? Just another weapon in their long, on-going duel. He struggled for an argument he could throw at Adella to change her mind, but he had none. Duncan felt the bite of shame, of being bested in this mean manner. Being a Landor was currency that only worked at home, it seemed. Out here, his name was worthless. *He* was worthless. 'I crossed cells for you on the skel carrier, and that didn't work out so well, did it?'

'All that we've got now, I reckon, is each other,' said Carter. 'You bunk down here if you want. As far as I'm concerned any fight we had is behind us, in Northhaven.'

'I'll stay where I landed,' spat Duncan, trying to keep hold of his temper. 'And if you get Adella hurt or dead in your wild schemes, we'll find out how far our fight travels.'

'You're still a Landor, all right,' said Carter. 'Nurse a grudge for a million miles.'

'You've got the distance about right, if nothing else,' said Willow.

'We're a long way from your family's fine and mighty name, Willow,' said Carter. 'The slave drivers running the sky mines don't care if you're a Landor or a Smith, just the tonnage you can dig out for them.'

'At least they care about something that *matters*.' Willow tugged Duncan away, back into one of the connecting tunnels. 'Leave them. This isn't helping anything.'

Duncan followed reluctantly, another lump taken out of his pride. Willow shook her head, exasperated. 'Of all the stubborn, pig-headed ...'

'I can't believe that man,' said Duncan. 'All this way, so far from Northhaven and he still treats her like a gun dog on a hunt. Only fit to trot along behind him, while he makes up his mind which way he's going.'

'I think you should take a second look at which one's the master and which one's the hound,' said Willow. She seized him by the arm. 'I need your head fixed on staying alive in this hellhole, Duncan. *Please*. Not a single thought or tear or regret wasted on Adella Cheyenne. Not with us held prisoner here, no better than stolen ponies.'

She was right. They were still family, still together, whatever else fate threw at them. 'I'll look out for you, Willow. You have my word on that.'

'We'll look out for each other, and I mean more than just the two of us. Because if we really are alone out here, every Northhaven man and woman on the station is going to need to pull together.'

Hell, I couldn't even save us back at home, could I? All three of us plucked from the riverbank by slavers. It's no wonder Adella feels safer with Carter. I've driven her back into the arms of that blockhead. And, eventually, he's going to give these Vandian slavers all the excuse they need to toss her corpse into their ugly damn volcano.

SIX

A RUDE AWAKENING

A heavy splash of icy water brought Jacob back to a groggy conciousness. His hands had been bound behind his back, his legs tied tight near the ankles with rope. The pastor's first thought was that he must have been captured by dog-riders, but as his eyes focused on the surroundings; he saw he was seated in a forest clearing. A line of army tents in Weyland colours had been pegged out in front of a rocky outcrop, four or five royal guardsmen on sentry duty. A groan to Jacob's right drew his attention. Wiggins was tied to a tree with coils of rope, his face a patchwork mess of blood and bruises. Beneath the constable, Sergeant Nix was building a pile of kindling. Each of the trees in the clearing held a body, blackened and burnt remains of rail guild uniforms smouldering on the corpses.

'What the hell is this?' coughed Jacob, the hands of a soldier reaching down to grab Jacob's black duster and drag him across the grass towards Sergeant Nix. The soldier emptied the rest of the cup of water in Jacob's face by way of an answer.

'This, Father,' grinned Nix. 'Is what we call ... an interrogation.'

'Where's Major Alock?'

'Oh, he's gone back to the train to announce that you all died as heroes, courageously attempting to bring back the railway men's bodies.'

Jacob stared in horror at the burnt corpses ringing the clearing. 'Sheplar, Khow!'

Nix just laughed. 'The leatherneck and your Rodalian friend are still snoring off the sleepy juice we slipped into your canteens. Don't want you all awake at the same time.' He raised a piece of kindling. 'Only got two hands to work with, ain't I? Roused Stumpy here first, thought he'd tell me what I need to know, and then we could just put bullets in the rest of your sleeping heads, do you the favour of a dog-rider bonfire *after* you're dead.'

'You're a real friend,' spat Wiggins, from the tree. His voice sounded hoarse, probably exhausted from screaming.

'Sure I am, Stumpy. Remember you can stop it if you talk to me.'

'I talk and you're going to kill us all anyway.'

'True enough,' Nix smiled. 'Otherwise you'd only go and tell everyone how those two money chests on the train weren't lost to the dog-riders when it was taken to ransom the guildsmen.'

'You're ex-cavalry,' spat Wiggins. 'How the hell can you do this to us?'

'Only served a year on the frontier,' said Nix. 'But that was all the time we needed to show the bandits it was healthier for 'em to move on to parts foreign.'

'What are you talking about?' coughed Jacob.

Nix turned around and booted Jacob in the stomach, sending him rolling across the grass. 'That's not how a questioning works, is it, Father? But I'll tell the both of you, just so you know how far this is going to roll. A few years ago we were a mercenary regiment, Weyland men, fighting in the Burn for princes, dukes, barons, bishops – lots of fancy titles and most ruling over not much more land than the range of their best brutes' guns. They called us the Army of *Bad Justus*. That's a play on words, right. Bad justice. In the end we got ourselves more than just a name, we got an offer from the government at home too. To come back to Weyland with full pardons for all the shit we'd done over here that had made us cross the sea in the first place. All we had to do was get rid of the nomads, raiders, bandits and ne'er-do-wells plaguing the country out east. Easy work, because the one thing you get out in the Burn is an education in real soldiering.' He indicated the blackened corpses tied to the tree trunks. 'You think this was hard? Radioing ahead, getting a few friends to come down from Talekhard to bushwhack a train and that patrol of amateurs from Ivah? Taking a torch to a living soul is nothing compared to what we did in the Burn. Land's seen centuries of blood spilt on the other side of the water, warring just for the pleasure of it. Hell, we really got to hone our craft.' Nix plucked out a long, heavy lump of wood from the kindling under the constable. 'Here's the thing, Stumpy, I know you won't talk to save yourself. I can tell the sort of man you are. But how about you watch me work the pastor over, just Mister Oak and me, before I light you up? Will you talk to save the churchman?'

'You've already stolen a fortune in rare metals,' said Jacob. 'What the hell else do you want from us? The recommendation of a good bank back in the capital to stash your plunder?'

'I need to know who's supplying you with the skel slavers' location. Not much to ask, is it? Don't like leaving mysteries behind us, not the sort that might come looking for a couple of pilfered money chests.'

'You can keep our money,' pleaded Jacob, 'but in the name of God, leave the four of us alive. I have to find my son. Please, I'm the only chance he has ...'

'Alive,' snorted Nix, amused. 'Your boy's dead meat and you know it. So are you, your way or mine. Hell, none of my men are going to do it your way. We didn't survive years soldiering in the Burn to die for you on a suicide mission.'

Jacob hating pleading with this murdering thug. He knew what the answer would be, but he had no pride left. They had to stay alive to find Carter and the others. They *had* to. 'Just let us go back to the train.'

'It's already left with the major. The six of us will be heading back on the maintenance train after we've finished "unsuccessfully" tracking the dog-riders. You and your friends only got two choices, Father. Slow or quick. Which is it?'

Jacob moaned, rolling over across the grass. 'I'll tell you how we were tracking the slavers. Bend down, so I can whisper it – your men must never know.'

There was a spark of greedy curiosity in Nix's eyes as the sergeant knelt down in the clearing's damp grass.

'I wrote the answer down on a piece of paper. Then, last night, I crept into the barracks car and stuck it up your arse.'

Nix stood up, face grim, and tested the heft of the wooden club in his palm. 'All you've got to waste is my time, Father.'

He whiled away the rest of the afternoon on Jacob's body.

Carter sat in his dormitory, still savouring his moment of triumph when Duncan realised that Adella had no intention of following the big man of Northhaven. His reverie was broken by the arrival of more station staff. Sky miners had arrived to allocate work to the newcomers, one of the slaves carrying a machine on a strap around his neck – a scanner able to read the marks tattooed on their forearms and match slaves to their names and previous occupations. The sky miners showed great interest in Kerge – the gask's mechanical talents meant he was a perfect candidate for the engineering pool – helping keep the station's machinery oiled and running; as well as operating the survey equipment. Even Joah in the bunk opposite attracted their attention with his stone mason's training, though with Joah's shortsighted gaze peering at them through his thick spectacles, a more unlikely miner was hard to imagine. *So, what opportunities are there for Carter Carnehan, son of a churchman and a reluctant librarian?* He didn't have to wait long to find out. Two sky miners stopped by his cot – the woman maybe four years older than Carter, the male slave the same age. The man carried the arm-scanning device while the woman had a pad of paper with work assignments listed. The female slave didn't look old enough to be a sky-mining veteran. Adella eyed the woman suspiciously from the bunk next to his. Was it apprehension at the duties she might allocate Adella, or a hint of jealousy at the new woman's sharp, beautiful cheekbones, her skin as dark as polished ebony? That was one thing even an unobservant lunk like Carter had cottoned on to … as far as Adella was concerned, other women were always potential competition, never a potential friend.

'Don't worry, darling,' the female slave told Adella. 'Just hold your arm out, the scanner won't burn you. You'll be glad enough to get scanned when you're mining. Those bars on your arm will match you up to your team's quota. The harder you work, the better you'll eat.'

Adella nervously extended her wrist. The male slave raised the gun and flashed a beam of red light against her skin, then checked the readout. 'Adella Cheyenne. Apprentice seamstress. Biological age, eighteen. Blood type, AB. Clean for diseases, predisposition to diabetes beyond the age of fifty.'

'May you reach that age, Adella,' smiled the other slave woman. She felt Adella's arm as if she was evaluating horseflesh at a fair. 'May we all.'

'How do you know my family has a history of diabetes?'

'The imperium can read your blood sample like a book,' said the male slave. He sported half a beard, dark stubble on his jutting chin and the outline of a moustache. The hair on his head was as dark as Carter's own, but thick and bushy, as were the eyebrows over two narrow, clear eyes – like fire slits in a fortress. 'A lot of the tricks they can do seem like magic to us.'

'But they're not magic, are they?' said Carter.

'You're damn right,' said the slave. 'Even if their science sometimes appears that way. The ironic thing is, it's not even the *imperium*'s science. Most of the empire's technology is traded by other nations in exchange for the minerals blown out of that stratovolcano smoking down there. Anything new in the world gets to be traded here for a couple of tons of gold and iron, eventually.'

'What work am I going to be given?' asked Adella.

'Only two sorts of labour for women in the sky mines,' said the female house slave. 'Working the processing belts, grading and sorting rocks; or climbing into shafts too small and narrow for men to work. You're lucky, darling. Too tall and light for serious digging, so your butt is going to be warming a conveyor belt's stool.'

'There's a third sort of work too,' said the man. 'But you'll want to keep your head down for that duty.'

'What do you mean?'

'He means,' said the woman, 'when one of Princess Helrena Skar's celestial-caste friends comes to the mines, checking up on our quotas and work, the pretty ones like you could get selected as house slaves. Get yourself bumped up to upper-hostile caste, although what you would need to do to earn the promotion isn't anything a decent Weyland girl should contemplate.'

She seemed amused at Adella's look of repulsion, and pushed Carter back down on his cot as he rose to complain on Adella's behalf. 'That goes for you too, pretty boy. Though with that weal across your face, you're probably an acquired taste, now. That's a slaver's whip, right? I think I already have you marked down here somewhere, as the *feisty one ... trouble*.'

There was something about the woman's voice and manner. Carter suddenly realised that he recognised this woman – or at least, he knew *of* her. 'You're Anna Kurtain, aren't you? James Kurtain's sister?'

Her jaw dropped, as shocked as if Carter had tried to punch her. 'How—?'

'Your brother was on the skel carrier plane that raided Northhaven, working as an engine mechanic and tending the slave pens. I gave him my word I'd look after you in the sky mines.'

'James!' She wiped away a sudden spill of tears rolling down her smooth cheeks. 'When I couldn't find him here, I thought he'd died in transit. Just wastage. He's really *alive*? All this time ...'

'Alive and well,' said Carter. 'Way he told me, he was taken from the pens when the skels found out he was a clockmaker. They put him on engine maintenance duty and kept him for themselves. He's still flying around up there in the clouds.'

'James! He was always lucky. I'm glad he's not here. If he's keeping that bandit carrier in the air, he'll be alive long after our corpses have been tossed off the station.'

'I wish I could let James know you're still alive,' said Carter.

'So, you're going to look after me are you? Let's have your arm and I'll read your tea leaves for you. Bushy-tail here, his name is Owen Paterson. He was with me when we were attacked back home.' Carter held out his arm and the male slave, Owen, scanned his forearm while Anna examined the readout on the device's screen. 'Yeah, you're down here, Carter Carnehan, gold-grade trouble. Got a mark from an upper-celestial on your ticket for you and your friend, Duncan Landor. A little too feisty and full of beans? You're both down as hitters.'

'Hitters?'

'There are only three real stages in the sky mining process, Northhaven. Finding the rock, keeping the rock, mining the rock. Hitters do the "keeping" part. There's one good piece of news; after you've completed your general training, your specialist training is going to be real quick. As in: take stick, swing stick. Training complete.'

'Don't listen to her,' said Owen, playfully prodding Anna in the back. 'You'll get plenty of training in how to fight to stake a claim. She thinks that anyone who can't fly a transporter is only fit to swing a stick.'

'Why the hell would I fight with just a stick?'

'You're sky mining labour, Northhaven,' said Anna. 'You think the empire's going to give you a gun out here? You'll get a pickaxe minus its axe head, because imperial law states no slave can fight with a bladed or ranged weapon outside the arenas, either that or called up as cannon fodder for the legion.' She mimed swinging with a bat. 'So, which celestial-upper marked you down for that duty?'

'Princess Helrena Skar.'

Anna Kurtain snorted with amusement. 'And you're planning to look after *me*? Damn, we'll see how that works out.'

Adella watched the two slaves moving on down the line of cots allocating work details, her eyes narrowing in anger. 'She's haughty *and* obnoxious.'

'She knows her way around. Three years jump on us, learning how to stay alive in the sky mines. Time to work out the escape routes too, maybe.'

'Escape? The woman's still trapped after all those years, isn't she, Carter? Just like us. Don't trust her so easily.'

'We'll see.' *Going to have to trust someone*, said a voice in Carter's head. *Survival is a team game.* It sounded a lot like his father's.

Carter turned up to the hitters' training session with low expectations that might just be about to be exceeded. Owen Paterson was one of the old hands allocated to train the intake of new sky miners. There were more survivors from the previous batch of miners arriving in the station now, experienced workers reassigned from other holdings to bring the new recruits up to speed. Weylanders for the most part, with a handful of other nationalities mixed in. Carter was a little shocked to realise how long Weyland had been raided for slaves. And angry too. That his nation hadn't proved better able to protect its people. But then, bandits, brigands, pirates, nomads and slavers always picked away at the margins of Weyland's vast territory, especially along the eastern frontier. You never really thought about the victims until you became one yourself. The green Weylanders lined up in the high heat of an empty chamber to learn the craft of bashing in skulls; murdering other slaves to ensure their mistress won in the claim-jumping stakes. Like the others in the room, Carter clutched a pickaxe handle without its metal head attached.

'Would it cost so much to put a cutting edge on the end of this?' asked Carter, holding up his heavy length of wood.

'Vandians would consider it a bladed weapon,' answered Owen. 'And that'd cost you your life.'

'Seems to me that Princess Helrena Skar is the one asking us to fight. Least she could do is to send us into the fray properly armed.'

'The Vandians are big on their caste system,' said Owen. 'Even the lowest caste of citizen is allowed to carry a dagger. If a low-born Vandian saw a slave bearing a bladed weapon, it would be like that slave claiming they were the equal of an imperial citizen. They want a sky mine up here, not an armed camp of slaves that might spark a revolt. That's something they really fear, because there's a *lot* of slaves in the imperium.'

Carter shook his head. 'I'm not their equal, I'm better than a dozen of them.'

'Got an ego to match theirs, for sure,' said Duncan from down the line.

Carter shot him an angry look.

'Never underestimate the Vandians,' said Owen. 'They live by their duelling code. It's intended to weed out weaklings, make sure the sons and daughters of empire never get fat and complacent. Allows feuds to be settled without the empire collapsing into civil war every few years. Princess Helrena can be challenged by anyone of equal caste, or receive a challenge from above. No champions permitted; she has to be ready to fight to the death to keep what she has, every minute of every day. You face an adult Vandian in combat; you're fighting a proven survivor.'

Carter dropped the wood into his palm with a thud. 'And am I allowed to challenge up?'

'No,' said Owen. 'And the princess wouldn't dirty her honour by challenging anyone lower to a scrap. Vandians don't duel with slaves; they apply whips to our backs.'

'You know a lot about their kind. Ever been off the sky mines?'

'The easiest way off is to die, get wrapped in a shroud, and be tossed over the side. Try talking to the house slaves when they visit the station with the princess and her allies,' said Owen. 'You might pick up a few things to help keep everyone alive.'

Carter swung the makeshift club around. 'So this is it?'

'This is it ... and be glad of it. In the Vandians' gladiator combats they'll throw you bladed weapons inside an arena, for the few days you survive. Compared to a gladiator's fate, labouring in a sky mine is a weekend fishing trip.'

'I've fought with steels,' said Carter.

'And you think a pickaxe handle is below your station?' said Owen. 'Then we'll start with you, Mister Carnehan.'

Carter stepped out of the line, testing the heft of the wood, feeling the balance. 'You want me to hold back?'

'I want you to take this seriously. Just pretend I'm one of the Vandians that purchased your sorry hide for a handful of coins. If that doesn't make you mad enough, let me know. I'm sure I can come up with some insults to help you along.'

Carter laughed and faced off against the bushy-haired slave. Owen held his length of wood two-handed, one fist at either end of the handle, circling Carter as they manoeuvred around each other in the chamber. Carter kept his club clutched in his right fist, holding it forward, ready to jab and strike when he saw an opening.

There was a shout from one of the other training groups – someone taking some lumps, and Carter thought he saw Owen's eyes slide away for a second. He rushed in and aimed his club at the old hand's gut, a blow to knock the air out of his lungs, then a tap to the head, and Carter would have made his play. Unfortunately for Carter, the distraction was simply a ploy. Owen stepped forward, moving to the side, tripping Carter up with the club and letting him sprawl onto the hard rock surface. Owen brought the weight of wood down towards Carter's head, halting it a hair above the back of his skull to make the point.

'Looks like I'm a survivor, too,' said Owen. 'One of my uncles ran a fencing hall back home and I helped with the business. Sabre and staff weren't strangers to me when the skels came raiding. The corpses I planted in the ground just hung a higher price around my neck.'

'You're quick,' said Carter, carefully picking himself up from the stone floor. *Quicker than you look.* The thing that smarted the most was his pride.

'If I wasn't,' said Owen, 'I wouldn't be here.' He turned to the other slaves ringed around the two of them. '*Never* underestimate your enemy. When you're out there in the sky, trying to stake a claim to put rations on the table of your friends and family, you won't know anything about the slaves attacking you. Not their names or their country. You certainly won't know if they're old hands or as green as a Weyland meadow. You want to stay alive, you'd better act as if they're superior to you and plan accordingly. There's no such thing as easy up here. Only dying is effortless. So make *it* and *yourself* damn hard.' He pointed to a series of air masks stacked inside wooden crates against the wall. 'Pull those on. You'll be wearing oxygen breathers when it comes time to scrap, so you need to get used to fighting with restricted vision.'

Carter took one of the masks by the strap and slipped it on, then spent a second or two getting over the smell of stale air from the air canisters on either side, choking down his gag reflex. Everyone else milled around, jostling for masks, some of the slaves swapping sizes until they got a respirator with straps that could be adjusted for a half-comfortable fit. Carter tapped the clear visor. Not quite glass, lighter and with a slight oiliness to the touch.

'It's called plastic,' said Owen, his voice slightly muffled behind the air mask he had slipped on. 'It's shatterproof. Okay, Duncan Landor, you seemed to find the sight of Northhaven here falling on his tail amusing. Step forward. Let's see if any of you northern country boys have anything to teach me.'

Carter was pleased to see the heir to the Landor fortune hadn't, and the harsh 'instruction' the rich boy received made Carter glad he'd cleaned his visor for the lesson. Until now he would have laughed if anyone had told him there could be so much finesse and craft behind swinging a club. Owen could make that simple shaft of wood a short staff, a wooden sabre, a billy-club or a stave. And he made it dance in his hands, as well as painfully administering cracks and impacts across his victim's form. The trainees went at it for long hours, and by the time they'd finished, the new slaves were limping back to their barracks with a constellation of purple bruises across their bodies. The next day the training began anew, and the next day, and the next. Owen was as underfed as the rest of them, nothing but water and subsistence rations to keep him going – he was hungry, and always absorbing blows on his lithe, bony body when someone, usually accidentally, connected with him. *He's putting his heart into it, that's for sure*. It was obvious that it meant something to Owen to help his fellow Weylanders becomes as skilled as possible, ready for the day they would need to fight. Carter doubted he would have been as passionate, if he had seen so many fresh intakes arrive from home and then disappear into the heartless maw of the sky mines. It was obvious that with a few exceptions – Owen and his friend Anna among them – most of the old hands had been blunted by life out here. Carter would have to survive for a good few years or so before he would be considered worth talking to. As far as the veteran sky miners were concerned, getting to know Carter Carnehan would be an emotional investment in a walking corpse.

Training on the station wasn't easy for any of the greenhorns. Willow and Adella had been set to learn the sorting lines. They were given a crash course in identifying minerals being run at speed down conveyer belts. For every valuable ore they missed or failed to sort correctly, there was a sharp lesson from an overseer that Adella described as a bitter old harpy. Another long-term survivor, but one without Owen's core of decency, it seemed. Only Kerge seemed to have landed on his feet – his uncommon mechanical skills bringing him a job in the repair bay, maintaining the heavy mining machinery.

If there had been any fat on the slaves when they were been taken, there certainly wasn't now. Carter got used to getting up hungry, training ravenous and collapsing, sweating, on his cot with his stomach still grumbling. The training was exhausting, especially on short rations. When the slaves weren't learning combat as hitters, they were taken to mining training – fewer lumps, but it was even more back-breaking. Cutting new tunnels in the station's rock just for the hell of it. The skills of tunnelling and shaft sinking, ore haulage and hoisting, stopping supports for the passages, air pumping, blasting powder safety. Adella, Willow and many of the women captured at Northhaven were taken away to master the grinding and crushing lines, classification and screening. They came back with their hands and arms raw and bleeding, complaining about lessons in electrostatic separation, gravity separation, dense medium separation, magnetic separation and froth flotation. The distracting effect of this harsh regime was, Carter realised, probably largely the point of it. No one had time to brood over their lost lives, though from the sobbing he heard rising from cots at night, that strategy wasn't always successful. Sometimes, Carter had to work hard not to join that sad night chorus. Agonising over his last moments with his parents. Remembering his mother's blood pooling around her stretched-out body, his father's body vanishing in the exploding shell flash. It was odd. He could feel pain for the family he had lost and the comfortable life he had known. But the station's grinding toil didn't really leave much room for self-pity or fear. There wasn't hope. Or ambition. Nor much in the way of glimpses of joy. There was just a weary grind until Carter lost track of the days, each the same as the last. Until it was a relief to let fatigue prise him from his thoughts and send him spinning into darkness. And asleep he dreamed of food. Real meat and vegetables, not the thin barley gruel that barely covered the bottom of the bowl pushed across the counter towards him in the station's refectory cave. The dreams seemed far more tangible than his meagre rations; memories of the wholesome smell of his last meal in Northhaven. But you couldn't live on happy reminiscences, and the contrast with life back in Weyland and his existence here in the sky mines was too stark to dwell on without going mad. In the end, his former life drifted away into the perpetual mist of volcanic vapours surrounding the station. This was his life, here, or at least it was base survival.

And then at last, there was something new …

Carter stood in the station's hangar, rubbing the stubble on his face while Owen rummaged around in one of the aerial transporters, returning with a handful of leather masks, round biscuit-tin-sized canisters on either cheek to hold air tanks and a voice amplification device built into its shaped mouthpiece, lending the speaker a tinny machine-like burr. Carter blinked the sleep from his eyes, leaning on a length of thick, heavy wood … a pickaxe with its head removed.

Kerge was with them, too, the young gask trained in the use of the transporters' survey equipment.

'You'll need this to breathe,' said Owen, the slave checking the masks' seals. 'The stratovolcano pumps out pyroclastic flows and gases strong enough you can smell them up here on a bad day.' Anna Kurtain was the pilot who would take them down to the edge of the caldera to check the ground sensors for seismic activity. She arrived in the hangar accompanied by an unwelcome sight: Duncan Landor, swinging his wooden club as if he was a constable rotating a truncheon.

Anna laid a palm on Carter's chest, the other on Duncan's. 'You can both save it for the other houses' hitters, right? '

'No problems from me,' said Carter.

'I'm not planning on starting anything,' growled Duncan.

'Good,' said Anna. 'Because between Old Smoky down there and the princess's rivals trying to kill us, I'm going to need you watching for anyone coming after us, not fixed on each other.'

'I find your people's proclivities towards violence quite disturbing,' added Kerge.

'You don't get any argument from me, there,' said Anna. 'Be a lot better if the ores erupting from that stratovolcano were fairly parcelled out by the gods. But being as we are where we are, us Weyland slaves are just playing the bad hand we've been dealt. Walking away from the game isn't a choice anyone gets to make.'

'It's why the princess raids the same country, rather than mixing too many nationalities together,' said Owen. 'It's easier to make her slaves pull together as a cohesive force – easier to fight off a rival house's miners when they come swarming towards your claim.'

Carter noticed the gask was carrying something that looked very much like the small calculating device he had lost back in Northhaven. 'You found a new one?'

'I constructed it,' said the gask, 'from spare pieces in the machine shop.'

That's a useful skill to have, Carter mused. *Reckon it's one worth cultivating for an escape, too.*

'Yeah,' said Anna, 'we lucked-in, getting you, spiky. We've got slaves that've been on the station's maintenance team for a decade, and they know less about imperial gear than you do.'

Owen, Duncan, Carter and Kerge climbed into the transporter, slipping on masks, while Anna climbed into the cockpit up front. There was no roof on top of the flying cage, so Carter could stand up and glance around at the hangar as they prepared to take off. Rotors under the platform spun into action, and the craft hovered, shaking in a cloud of oily smoke above the hangar floor before tilting forward and powering out into the sky. In the back, all four slaves held on to the metal benches, pieces of equipment sliding about the stowage area under the seats.

'We'll be making more and more of these trips over the next few weeks,' said Owen. 'There hasn't been an eruption for a while – we're overdue. Late. After the last rock blew apart under our feet, we've been mining nothing but vapour up here. There's a lot of pressure from the princess to score a good claim with the next eruption. She has plenty of rivals in the imperial family out to stop us getting one, too. They scent weakness. A chance to remove Princess Helrena from the emperor's favour and yank her sky-mining concession from her hands. It's going to cut up rough, that much I can tell you.'

'If there's an eruption due,' said Duncan, 'then what happens if the volcano goes off and we're checking sensors down there?'

'If we've got time, we'll just light out back to the station in the transporter.'

'And if we don't?'

Owen bent under the bench and pulled out a metal crate. He unlocked it and lifted out a strange silvery suit that looked like it might be made of metal ... but it was too light in his hands to be. It was as shiny as a mirror and had a transparent panel up top on the full-face mask. 'This is a survival suit. If the volcano is throwing out poisonous vapours and you're working on the surface of a sky-mine, you'll need to wear one of these.'

Carter reached out and felt the flimsy foil surface of the survival suit. 'And how well does this fabric stand up when that beast is spitting fire?'

'There are caves on the stratovolcano's slope,' said Owen. 'Shallow, formed from old air pockets. Look for shiny black rocks, find a cave and hunker down inside with the suit on. As long as you're not covered by a pyroclastic flow or directly hit by ore fall, you might stay alive for long enough to signal a friendly transporter.'

'How long can these transporters stay up in the air?' asked Carter.

Owen laughed. 'Not long enough, Northhaven. Not nearly long enough. That greenhorn's speech you got on the station, it's the God's honest truth. Unless Kerge here can build us a warship twice as fast as anything the Vandians can muster, we're never getting back to Weyland. Best you could hope for is dying on the road, an old man with a price on your head.'

'What's the range of one of these aircraft?'

'Quarter of the way out of the dead zone, maybe, before it runs out of fuel. Good luck walking the rest of the way out with just the water and food you can carry on your back. Plenty of burning magma to rain down on your skull and not a lot to hide behind when the guards come flying overhead.'

'There's got to be a way out of the sky mines.'

'You really are fixing to get yourself killed,' said Duncan.

'I'm a Weylander, damn you,' said Carter. 'I was born a free man and I'm fixing to die one too.'

'The empire can only enslave your body,' said Kerge. 'Your mind, manling, is always free. It is your greater part, your own domain and nobody else's.'

'I can see how that's a helpful way of thinking, given how we're imprisoned here,' said Carter. 'But I never was much of a one for philosophising. Back home, I was stuck in a hole with the guild of librarians. Now I'm stuck on a sky miner's rock anchored above the Devil's own acres, and I find neither situation is much to my taste.'

'There are strange attractors at work,' said Kerge, tapping his makeshift calculator. He sounded puzzled. 'There is no certain fate to be found in my numbers.'

'If that's the gask way of saying we're up shit creek without a paddle, I have to say, your numbers are pretty much the same as mine,' said Duncan. 'And I didn't need one of your abacus boxes to work it out.'

Owen raised his air mask briefly, tilting the canteen to his mouth and gulping water down before passing it to Carter. 'You greenhorns need to be careful who you speak to about trying to escape. Slaves who mouth off too loudly about escape tend to be snatched by the Vandians and never seen again.'

Carter raised his mask for a second to rub away tears of sweat. *God, it's a furnace out here. And I thought it was hot inside the station. It's got nothing to the air outside.* 'How the hell do they hear about escape plans? From what I've seen, the imperium snobs let the slaves get grubby and don't dirty themselves too much with the mining business.'

'As long as our quotas are met, that's true enough. But the empire has informers among us. The way things happen up here, you just know it.'

'Vandians?'

'No, Carter. Slaves. Our own people. Traitors that want a promotion, people who're looking to wangle serving inside an imperial household – they inform on us to get it. There's a radio room in the station, only Thomas Gale's staff are allowed inside. You see any of your Northhaven people slipping off towards the radio room, you let people know … quietly.'

'And then?'

'Sky mining is a dangerous business, lots of ways for a slave to die doing it.'

'Nobody from Northhaven would turn informer,' said Duncan.

'I used to think the same thing about my prefecture,' said Owen. 'Then one day a man called Will Kamber, he was a constable back home, gets taken as a house slave for Helrena Skar. We worked it out afterwards; all the people he tried to buddy up with. Some of them were killed trying to run, others snatched – vanished without trace from the station. He wasn't the first and he won't be the last to sell out.'

'Nobody from Northhaven is like that,' said Carter.

'There's a little of *that* in all of us. We've all got a choice to make here. Your gask friend is correct; the empire can't change who you really are. There is only one person who can parcel off your honour, and that's yourself.' Owen stood up and stared through the transporter's mesh walls. 'There's something else to think on. It's not always the princess our people sell us out to. There are rumours that our last rock was lost that way: blasting powder was filched, set on a slow fuse and detonated. All so some son-of-a-bitch slave could get a ticket out of the sky mines from one of Helrena's rivals.'

Carter was about to protest, but Owen cut him short. 'We're a couple of minutes out from where we hid one of our lines of ground sensors. Eyes peeled for enemy transporters and ground scouts.'

As they neared the land, Carter caught sight of a hideous, stomach-turning sight across the black wasteland. What he had first taken for discoloured lumps of stone a shade lighter than the dark plain, were, as they dove in closer, clearly bones – skulls and ribs and vertebrae protruding from the landscape, melted into dried flows of magma that had cooled and left rivulets and gullies; bones emerging like macabre flowers seeded by stealers broken free of hell. Bones large and small, familiar and unfamiliar scattered everywhere. He didn't have to ask whose bones they were. Carter had watched dead slaves' corpses dragged from the fever room and rolled off the station. There had been no churchmen taken as slaves to say words over the deceased, so it was for the survivors to remember the dead's life. How many millennia had the empire existed? How many corpses had rained down here over those years? Carter had presumed the sky miners called this the dead zone because of the impossibility of escaping it alive. But they hadn't; *this* was why. It was a sobering sight. The whole institution and might of the Vandian Imperium existed to ensure Carter and his friends would, one day, end up here. The very sight made him sick and angry and weary, all at the same time.

'Get ready to leap off. Carter, Duncan, keep your eyes on the clouds – any transporter you spot will be unfriendly. Kerge, you're with me – check the boxes for magma damage and grab the readout rolls for all the sensors, regardless.'

In front of them, the stratovolcano's black rocky slope loomed up, barren of life – not even lichen clinging to the rocks. For all of the volcano's height, the inclination of its slope was as gentle as millennia of erupting magma could make it. Carter jumped from the back of the transporter while they hovered, grateful for the cooling air from the slowing rotors. Duncan came next, then Owen and Kerge. They had landed near the beast's base, where the seismic sensitivity for the sensors was supposedly strongest. Carter might've jumped into hell for all that he could see. Endless black, blasted slopes cloaked in steam; nothing moving, the stench of the place unbearable even with the mask clasped to his clammy face. He was momentarily stunned by the silence and brooding violence of the bone-strewn landscape. He and Duncan just stood there, enmities forgotten, leaning on heavy wooden handles like old men watching a street back home. The optimism Carter had felt about his chances of escaping from the sky mines dwindled as he faced the reality of this hellish scenery. *Nothing to eat, nothing to drink. The mother of all volcanoes ready to rain fire down on anyone trying to escape across the black flats. What was I thinking?* He clung to the memory of his mother dying, murdered, so he could be sold into this existence. The hate was enough to rekindle his fire. Damned if it wasn't just as fierce as anything this fiery anthill could vomit out.

Four skids hit the dirt, Anna settling the transporter on a flat area of slope.

Duncan grunted. 'You ever saw anything like this before?'

'Not even in my worst nightmares.'

'Nothing can survive out there,' said Duncan.

'It won't all be like this. Your heard the boss slave's speech. The dead zone lasts just as far as this volcano spits. After that, it's real country again.'

'*Hostile* country,' said Duncan. The way he pronounced the words, you could tell all hope had drained from his heart. Guess that was one thing his money couldn't buy.

'A rich country. Rich on *our* labour. Wealthy enough to build those steel-hulled giants they fly around in. Must have normal aircraft, too. If we can get our hands on a flying wing, it can't be more than a few decades in the air to get back home.'

'You steal it,' sighed Duncan, the irony dripping from his words, 'I'll get my father to pay for the fuel.'

'To escape,' spat Carter, carefully scanning the sky, 'you have to want to leave. You have to feel the need to get out coursing through your blood like a fever.'

'Don't have a problem with leaving. Leaving and *dying* is another matter.'

Carter despaired. It didn't take much to knock the fight from a Landor. Deprive them of their butlers and stable boys and they went to pieces, it seemed. But anything was better than staying here to die. *Anything*. He wandered along the incline in high dudgeon, until something caught his eye. There was a small flat plateau where the stratovolcano's slope met the dark plain beyond, with a circle of twelve dark menhirs raised there. He had seen standing circles back home, but this one's presence here was an oddity. They were ancient works, beyond the memory of his people, and if druids had set up here to practise blood sacrifices, the massive stratovolcano surely would have granted the builders their wish at some time during the circle's construction. He went over to take a closer look. The bases of the stone sentinels were partly covered by molten rock flow solidified into rivulets, but despite the damage, the dark black material seemed to glitter like starlight in the heavens. *An oddity*. A curiosity that put him wistfully in mind of home. He sighed and turned his back on the stones. Duncan was inspecting something behind the circle, and as Carter got closer, he noticed that it was an entrance to a cave, its mouth as impenetrable as night, a foul stench of burning hot vapours steaming out from somewhere inside.

'Smells like a hound died in there,' said Duncan.

'Only fumes from inside. This rock's got more bubbles in it than a bath-scrubbing stone. Reckon this must be one of the caves Owen was talking about.'

'Feel that heat rising out of there – I wouldn't want to try to hide inside it during an eruption.'

Carter looked around. Owen and Kerge had headed a few feet down the slope, inspecting equipment left hidden under the overhang of the ledge of volcanic rock supporting the menhirs. An ominous rumbling sounded from the stratovolcano, growling like Carter's empty stomach, but about a hundred times louder. The ground trembled below his boots, dislodging a dusty shower of rubble down the slope. It was as though the great satanic stealer who had created this hell was sending the party a warning to depart; mount their transporter and return to their rock in the sky.

'Sweet saints,' said Duncan, 'I really don't want to put one of those silver survival suits to the test. Not on my first visit to the ground.'

'It'd be just our luck, so far,' said Carter. He eyed the transporter. Anna had kept the engines running, and was bobbing up and down in her cockpit as she glanced around the slopes for potential landslides. Further than a hundred yards, though, the slopes were wreathed in steam from a variety of stink-holes; they might well hear a landslip before they saw it. Despite the tremors, Carter considered exploring the cave, but Duncan got there before him, squeezing through the rock, disappearing for half a minute, then reappearing.

'No bears sleeping inside, then?'

'They'd have to like eating rock to hunt around here. I've slept in bigger tents,' said Duncan. 'We could all fit inside it if we had to, though.'

Kerge and Owen's checks only took another minute, and then both of them were sprinting back, a single roll of tape clutched in Owen's hands. 'Every sensor box smashed!' Owen yelled to Anna, still in the open cockpit. 'Someone's found our stash.'

Carter stumbled as Owen pushed him and Duncan away from the stone circle and back towards the rear of the aerial platform.

'Aren't we going to plant new ground sensors?' asked Duncan.

'Not around here. Back on board. Someone could be watching us – hoping we'll lead them back to the rest of our sensor line.'

Anna swivelled around in the cockpit to call across to them. 'We could take out the camouflage netting, try and hide the transporter while we get the job done.'

'Might as well break out the fire-suits, too, then,' said Owen. 'Find a cave and hole up. Use your nose. If it smells this bad down here, Old Smoky is going to start belching fire real soon.'

'Okay, bushy-tail, you've got my vote. Tails up, gentlemen, we're making for the station!'

The four of them mounted the transporter. Anna lifted them up in a blast of cutting dust, the volcanic slope dropping away beneath the vehicle. Any unvoiced thoughts Carter entertained that Owen might be being over-cautious vanished when he saw two transporters dipping behind them, vanishing in and out of the thick clouds of steam. As the enemy craft grew larger, Carter made out the crest on the transporters' nose cones: a spider, not Princess Helrena's two-headed eagle, and the craft's flanks had men clinging to its sides, heavy wooden staves attached to their belts.

'They're running light and stripped!' Owen shouted to Anna.

'You think?' she called back. 'I hadn't noticed.'

Owen ducked under the equipment bench, bringing out two pick-axe handles. He kept one and threw the other to Kerge. 'Well, looks like we're all hitters today.'

'My people's way is one of peace,' protested the gask.

'This isn't my preferred way either, but if we don't hold them off they'll roast us over a burn hole to discover where the rest of our ground sensors are hidden. I've found our scouts dead, tied like that, before.'

Anna banked and angled their transporter, throwing them about in the rear, engulfing the transporter in clouds so thick that Carter could hardly see the cockpit. But her aerobatics were no good. They weren't flying a Rodalian kite here, as manoeuvrable as a hawk on the hunt. They were in a box which was designed to haul flesh and ore, with their pursuers so tight on their tail that they had to be tracking the Weylanders with equipment other than a pilot's eyes and ears.

'A few months ago I would've taken this handle to your skull myself,' said Duncan.

'Reckon these boys are fixing to save you the job,' said Carter.

'Who would've thought it? You and me swinging on the same side again.'

'If the saints aren't laughing at us, the devils and stealers surely are.'

They pulled out of a bank of vapour. For a second, Carter couldn't spot the two enemy transporters and allowed himself a brief shiver of elation – but that fell away as a set of rotors whizzed overhead and he realised their pursuers had been climbing for height. Five men leapt down, sweating muscles on their attackers' bare arms bulged with the spider's brand. Anna's transporter rocked from side to side with the sudden impacts and new distribution of weight. Owen yelled in fury, first to wade into the melee, one of the brutes blocking his strike and lashing out with a club. Carter pulled back as a bludgeon whistled past him. Kerge knelt, mumbling some gask mantra, his pickaxe handle abandoned, but for Carter and Duncan, the induction to their terrible new trade had well and truly begun.

Jacob came to consciousness coughing up blood. It was his own. He was in one of the army tents and screams hung in the air. Wiggins, his voice reduced to an animal-like keening. *They're still torturing him.* The pastor's body drifted in and out of agony, his bruised flesh a shifting mesh of pain. Sergeant Nix knew his business all right. It took an artist to dish out that much punishment and keep the man being questioned alive. Jacob's head lolled against the tent post he was secured to, arms tied behind the pole and legs lashed in front. Jacob was insensible enough that it took him a minute before his gaze fell upon the bindings around his hands and ankles. *Is this a joke? A trick?* When he'd been worked over, the ropes had been as tight as though the bindings had been sewn shut. But now the ropes were tied in an exploding knot, a double carrick bend, same as any rowboat on the river. Ready to be given a yank and fall off. And like a gift from the saints, there was the rolled-up blanket Jacob had dug out from Northhaven's graveyard. That blanket had been well-hidden in Jacob's compartment back on the train. There'd been no time for anyone to travel to the train, retrieve the roll, and return to leave it here. Nor would any of Nix's men be crazy enough to have done such a thing, even if they could. The roll sat by the side of the tent, rebuking Jacob. Tempting him. Whispering to him. Wiggins' cries carried across the clearing again, bringing Jacob back to the world. He twisted his legs and arms, the exploding knots falling away like a conjurer's trick, and reached for the roll. Jacob tossed the rough fabric across the tent as though he were a merchant laying out wares in a market: hell's own trade. A leather belt as black as night, riveted with shells, the wicked patina of twin Landsman navy pattern single-action pistols holstered inside. Corruption in stamped, nickel-coated steel. Six centre-fire rounds apiece within each rotating chamber; the weight of mountains ... the weight of the dead. Never so heavy, strapping it on below his grass-stained duster, the silver barrels glinting with pure evil while the ebony grips rested in near invisibility against the pastor's black jacket. *You followed me from the grave where I buried you. Down to the capital ... down the rails to this clearing. You were never going to leave me alone, were you?*

Jacob staggered into the glade, using a split second to take in the scene. Sergeant Nix stood in front of a tree where Wiggins burned. Five soldiers with rifles were dotted around the clearing to deal with any natives who might come to see who was setting pyres on their territory. The troopers saw Jacob and turned, five men working rifles and chambering rounds into their guns, Nix tossing aside a burning branch and reaching for his holster. Depravity sucked the twin pistols into Jacob's hands, the cold press of their ebony handles against his palms as the guns rocked, one soldier flung back, two, three, four, all hit. The fifth got off a shot – his rifle spurting smoke – before somersaulting back into the tree line, his spine blown out by the heavy slug. Nix had almost cleared his gun from his holster; in the same moment his chest absorbed the full weight and velocity of a sixth shell, and he was tossed back into the fire around Wiggins' feet, before collapsing forward and hitting the grass. The pistol in Jacob's left hand was as light as a departing soul, the pistol in the right still leaden … not a single shot loosed.

Jacob yanked the knife free of Nix's belt, tossing the sergeant's pistol into the trees as he walked to kick out the fire and cut Wiggins down. It was a slow, damp fire. Designed to linger and loosen a man's tongue. As the constable fell against Jacob, it was clear that he'd only have lasted a couple more minutes.

'You should have talked,' said Jacob.

'And we'd – all be dead,' coughed Wiggins. 'Who'd save the children – then?'

Jacob lay the constable's body down on the ground. 'I won't leave you here for the dog-riders to find. I'll carry you back to Weyland soil.'

'Never — did — see anything like — that. Six shots in the ·— stump. Six. All down — fast as lightning.'

'Rest yourself.'

Wiggins pressed something cold into the pastor's hand. 'On — my — marker — just write — second biggest fool — in Northhaven.'

'Maybe you're the first biggest.' Jacob stared at the shining silver badge sitting in his palm. The constable's badge. 'I'm not nearly good enough for this.'

'Try — to — be.'

Jacob sat in the grass, holding Wiggins' hand as the man passed away. How many people had Jacob sat with like this back in Northhaven? The old and the sick. Two of his three children. Mary. You only ever continued for the living. Not many of those left now. *I'm cursed. And this is my fault. I was the one who wanted to go after the missing train crew; Wiggins all for staying.* Jacob rose up and crossed to the other tents, splashing water across the face of Sheplar Lesh and Khow. He sliced their bonds and helped them into the clearing. Khow needed a lot of assistance … his canteen had been laced with a strong dose. Both of them stood there for a second, swaying, sick from the drugs and the vista of carnage.

'A dark wind,' muttered Sheplar. 'What happened here?'

'My muscles are paralysed,' whispered Khow, checking his satchel still held his precious calculator. 'My spining reflex is dead.'

'It'll come back to you,' said Jacob. 'Can you follow the trail back to the maintenance train, Khow? Maybe between you and Sheplar you can carry Wiggins' body.'

Sheplar was still in shock. 'He's dead. Wiggins is—'

'He went saving us. Didn't go alone. I'll explain as we move, just bear in mind that if you see one of our military escort, the bastards will try to kill you on sight. Don't think there's any troopers left out there, but …'

'The woods *are* cursed,' said Khow.

'Not as damned as these troopers' souls though. Take a gun apiece and head off. I'll strip the guardsmen of supplies and follow you. What's left here is all we're going to have for a while.'

The gask and Sheplar did as they had been asked. Jacob collected four of the five rifles and a single backpack, filling it with food, water canteens, ammunition and, as he'd hoped, a few of Benner Landor's coins which Major Alock had scattered around his troops. *Thieving devil.* A little taste of what the troopers could expect from final divvy of the loot. *A little heat for the branding iron.*

Jacob bent down by the sergeant's body, frisking him for coins, when he realised Nix was still alive, even gut-shot. He sure was a tough, mean little bastard.

'I've fought you before,' Nix moaned.

'Then I should've done a better job the first time around, saved us both some bother.'

'Jacob Carnehan, my arse,' he spat. 'I knew I'd seen you before. Jake Silver, that's your real name. Quicksilver is what they used to call you. *Quicksilver's Rangers*, the nastiest damn regiment in the Burn, and that was quite a contested title.'

'You're wrong. That man's dead. I held his funeral myself.'

'All this time, hiding behind a dog collar.' Nix spasmed as he laughed. 'Put one in my head before you go, for old time's sake. Don't let me bleed out here. The dog-riders are going to turn up sooner or later to see who's been setting fires on their territory.'

'Anything they do to you … hell, you fought in the Burn. You've seen worse. You've *done* worse.'

'Do it!' Nix shouted.

'There's been enough killing.'

'Put a bullet in me!'

Jacob slipped out one of the spare pistols he had taken from the guardsmen, dropped five of the six shells from the chamber into his pocket and then tossed the pistol on the grass in front of Nix. 'That's all the mercy God has for you, today. One bullet. You can kill me or save it for yourself when the dog-riders turn up.'

'God's *mercy*,' called Nix, crawling for the pistol as Jacob left the clearing. 'Compared to you, I'm one of the three saints! Blood follows you, Jake Silver, it follows you like it's a river a man can wade through.'

Jacob wasn't listening. Reloading his pistol with the guardsman's shells, he walked after Khow and Sheplar, the weight of his pistols dragging him down more than the backpack slung over his shoulder. *Only ever light when I'm using them. Never could work that one out.*

Jacob heard a volley of shots as he got close to the rails and for a moment he had a terrible premonition that Nix had lied to him about the train departing – imagined his two friends gunned down by the barracks car. Lurching forward, Jacob sprinted through the woods to the beginning of the trail, but when he got to the siding, he found Khow and Sheplar still alive. A dead guardsman hung out of the maintenance train, Sheplar's pistol smoking in the air. On the ground the trooper had dropped his rifle as well as a silver metal box the size of a doctor's bag.

'He tried to shoot us, just as you said!' For all that Sheplar had been forewarned, he still sounded shocked.

'The troopers were mercenaries from the Burn before they became guardsmen,' said Jacob. 'Landor's loot was enough to tempt them back into old habits.' The pastor felt his heart sink even as he said the words. Their task had been impossible enough to begin with, funded by the richest man in the north. What were they without the money to buy back the slaves? Just itinerants on the road; minstrels with a sad story that nobody would pay to hear. The wheels had come off their wagon before they had even left the country. His old friend from Northhaven dead and murdered. How long before Sheplar and the gask either joined him or abandoned their mad, impossible pursuit?

Sheplar looked down at Wiggins' blackened face, then at his hands, sooty from where he had been carrying the dead constable. 'The guardsmen did *that* to him for money? Just for—'

'It's not something you ever want to understand, Sheplar.' Jacob went to where Khow squatted, the gask's long fingers examining the metal box dropped by the soldier. It had a control panel on the front like an oversized version of the gask's abacus machine, a silver dish on top and a metallic needle protruding from the basin. A strange fizzing emanated from the device.

'That sound's not a fuse burning, is it?'

'No, manling. This is a radio transmitter.'

'It's too small. The guild of radiomen's equipment fills an entire hold. Just one of their batteries is fifty times the size of that box.'

'Nevertheless, radio communications are this device's function.'

'That's crazy. The guild mark would be placed on anyone caught with such a thing. Who would be stupid enough to risk that?' Dangerous for the people found carrying it, equally as dangerous for any nation attempting to develop its own network. Having the guild of radiomen withdraw its services was not something any sensible state invited. It would force them to rely on slow message riders. Cut them off from foreign news. Which nation wanted the first tidings of a nomad horde coming its way to be when their border posts were overrun?

'He was speaking into the machine when he saw us emerge from the woods,' said Khow. 'Whoever the trooper was talking to at the receiving end, it is likely they're aware we have survived.'

Jacob ran his hand over the steel casing, mystified. *Well, the guardsmen didn't find this in the Burn. Grapeshot, muskets and sharp sticks are all they've got to poke each other across the ocean.*

'What do you think?' asked Sheplar.

'That we had better get this maintenance train heading towards Talekhard,' said Jacob. He unslung one of the rifles and caved in the sides of the radio with his stock, its fizzing cut off in a fury of spitting sparks. 'Before Major Alock comes back to ensure reality matches up to his story of the four of us getting butchered in the wilderness.'

'How could mere killers afford this wonder?' brooded Sheplar. 'And why would your nation employ murderers in the first place?'

'The first – hell if I know. The second, well, men like this are effective enough in their way. Sometimes, you just need the business end of a sharp sabre and not being too fussy about who's been run through with your steel beforehand.'

From the distance, the echo of a single lonely shot drifted on the wind. Sheplar craned his head but there was no more gunfire from within the forest. 'What was that, I wonder?'

'A little bad justice,' said Jacob. 'And time for us to travel on. I have a feeling there are dog-riders nearby.'

The three of them walked back to the tree line to pick up Wiggins' body and carry him towards the train.

There was an explosive crack of wood as Carter blocked a blow that would've caved his ribs in if it had struck true. The flat rear of the transporter was a tumult of jostling, thrusting bodies, the advantage of raw strength telling in the cramped confines of the small aerial vehicle. And that edge lay with their huge attackers. Carter heard a yell of pain from Kerge as the praying gask was knocked off his knees, falling sideways with the impact of a bat. Duncan and Owen were lost behind the mass of swinging, jostling brutes dropped into their transporter's open cage. Carter could no longer see Anna in the cockpit at the front, still weaving and swooping their craft as hard as she could, attempting to shake off the two enemy transporters dogging their tail. Whatever nation these hostiles came from, their country sure turned them out large. Carter gripped his handle with both hands, thrusting it at the face of the man-mountain confronting him, but the slave whipped to the side and rotated his own club, bringing it around against Carter's hand, cracking into his clammy fingers. Carter yelled in pain, fingers numb and dead and his weapon dropping towards the craft's metal deck. The miner from the rival house moved around for another crack at Carter's ribs, but Carter stepped forward and seized the handle first, only to be shoved back against the transporter's mesh wall.

'You're all they've got?' snarled the slave, crushing his handle against Carter's chest. His words were exotic and guttural, the meaning only coming to Carter a second after the man had spoken, the brute's breath hot and fetid. *What do they feed them on in the other station?* 'Your territory will belong to us when the next eruption leaves you with nothing but dust.'

Carter had nothing to say. Nothing he *could* say, as the slave's pick-axe handle moved down, slowly, inexorably towards Carter's throat. The Northhaven man couldn't stop it. The muscles along the slave's bare arms bulged as hard as iron. He was at least twice as strong as Carter.

'Little chicken, little chicken,' clucked the brute, 'let's see how well you peck after I've crushed your windpipe.'

Carter hollered in rage, the heavy length of wood forcing him down, his knees close to buckling under the weight upon him. If he fell here he would only last the few seconds it took the giant slave to kick him to death.

'Cluck, cluck, cluckkk-*aahhh!*' The brute's ruddy face froze solid as his mocking call throttled in his throat. The silence was filled by an inhuman cry – a strangled screech like the fox-song that haunted Northhaven's woodland after sundown. It came from Kerge, the gask coming into view as the enemy slave slid sideways, gask spine needles embedded in the back of the man's skull. Not the only one dropping towards the deck either. All five enemy borderers tumbled down, puppets with their strings cut.

'Wash me,' yelled Kerge, standing in the centre of the bed of corpses, his voice strangled and pained. 'Water!'

Carter grabbed the ring of canteens under the equipment bench, throwing one apiece to Duncan and Owen as he tore a cork out and tossed its contents across the gask. Uncomprehending, the other two did the same, Kerge's wild trembling body calming as he was soaked.

Owen watched the gask sink to his knees, moaning and whispering to himself. 'Saints' blood! What was that?'

I guess father was right. 'An angry gask,' said Carter, watching the twisted young man wailing with some degree of sympathy. *It wasn't his fault – it was these fools'.* 'Pain makes gasks sweat something that sends them into a killing fury. Kerge needs water to wash it away and regain control.'

'I thought the forest nation were peaceful,' said Owen. 'Good with machines and—'

Anna's transporter banked steeply and the four of them nearly spilled off their feet. They were still being pursued. Carter unlocked the rear door of the transporter's cage, careful he wasn't thrown out into the sky. 'Toss the bodies over the side.'

'I'm sorry,' wailed Kerge as he helped to drag his victims towards the craft's open rear. 'This is shameful.'

'This is just survival,' Carter gently told the twisted man, hauling a dead slave towards the back. 'I reckon they would have pulled out every spine you've got, along with our teeth, to find out where our ground sensors are hidden.'

'They have made a beast of me! They have made beasts of us all.'

'I've seen cattle face down a wolf when their calves were threatened,' said Duncan. 'That's just the way it is. You saved us all, Kerge. Think on that, if you have to dwell on something.'

'Don't speak of this,' Owen told the other two men, assisting Carter and Duncan in lightening the transporter's load. 'Not to anyone back on the station. He's the only gask the Vandians have taken. If they find out what he can do ...'

Carter saw the problem. The imperium didn't even allow their slaves metal axe heads to fight with. The Vandians would have their own solution for Kerge, and it wouldn't be anything good for their friend. With the last of the attackers' corpses jettisoned, Carter was locking the transporter's door when he heard a cannon-loud crack, then a second and a third report. His eyes darted around the sky, trying to locate the pair of dodging enemy transporters – but they were still weaving in and out behind Anna's tail. Neither had the ordinance to account for the cannonade. As Carter looked on, humid clouds of vapour around them began to be punched through by black, bird-sized projectiles, hot steaming trails of smoke scratched behind each dart.

'Brace!' screamed Anna. 'Brace for shield flying!'

Carter had just processed their pilot's words when the deck began to slide underneath him.

'Grab the benches!' yelled Owen.

Carter and the others followed Owen's example, arresting their slide as the vehicle's angle of inclination increased. The transporter engine's pitch changed; two of the rotors slowed, the remaining pair screeching angrily as they spun fast, close to burning out. Around them, the thick cloaking clouds of vapour were split by hundreds of flying pieces of rock. Most no bigger than coins, all burning white hot, bigger pieces crackling as they punched past.

'It's a proto-eruption,' yelled Owen. 'Hold on tight. We're flying the transporter like a shield all the way back home.'

'Saints,' whispered Carter, digging his feet into the bench opposite and tightening his hold as the craft's deck sloped even steeper.

'Lucky,' called Owen through clenched teeth. 'If those dogs hadn't chased us off, we might have been too close to the stratovolcano to survive this.'

Yes, lucky. I guess this is what luck feels like, when you're a slave.

To the side, Carter saw the two enemy transporters angling away, heading for the safety of their own territory. The pattering of rocks against the underside of his vehicle grew louder, heavier, turning from a hail into an angry, blazing mad hammering. Off in the corner of the sky, Carter watched the nearest of the enemy transporters dip into a spin, smoke and flame pumping from the rear of the craft. Then, suddenly, the flames leapt higher and brighter, engulfing the transporter, tiny burning figures tumbling off the rear of the platform as though it was no more than a tree shedding leaves in autumn, before the craft was lost inside the thick cloud cover.

'Fuel feed holed,' said Owen. 'It's pumping out flammables like a cut artery.'

Those sky miners had been coming after Carter and the rest of his party, looking to murder the Weylanders in a cold-blooded ambush. Still, he couldn't find any pleasure in their fate. What choice did the slaves have? Back home they might have been labourers, mill workers or shopkeepers. Here, they were merely meat to advance the ambitions of their Vandian masters. A mangled whine sounded from below, an abrupt shaking, and then Carter's craft started to shudder under his sandals.

Duncan Landor twisted around to try and locate the vibration's source. 'Is that—?'

'Propeller blown,' Owen called. 'Burnt out, or holed by ejecta mass.'

The air was becoming increasingly inhospitable. The ubiquitous smog giving way to a hot, burning dust, stinging every piece of Carter's exposed skin, clinging to his branded shoulder and scorching like hell. Anna Kurtain's comments about how Carter had arrived to look after the pilot floated back into his head. She was going to save them all, with her flying; either that or send them all crashing towards the ground, where Carter's present difficulties weren't going to matter a whole lot anymore. Carter was nearly blinded by a steaming chunk of ejecta mass twice as large as their transporter. Passing yards from the craft on their port side, the rock's surface whistled with escaping gases as it creaked and cooled in the air. It was followed by a drumbeat of smaller rocks against their slanted hull, the dying scream of one of their remaining rotors chasing the sound of the volley. Carter's aerial platform started seesawing violently from side to side. He dug his feet and hands in deeper on the rapidly failing transporter. 'Can we fly on two rotors?'

'We can crash gracefully,' said Owen.

'There!' shouted Duncan.

Below them, the clouds had cleared enough to reveal the station's roof, marker flags whipping around from the turbulence of the eruption. There was something docked in its lee – a Vandian warship, smaller than the *Primacy of the Sky*, but still close to the width of the station she was attached to. Carter just caught Anna's words over the whining pitch of their last two propellers. 'Not – enough control – to land – in the – hangar – we'll ditch – on top.'

Corkscrewing towards the station, the four passengers were whipped around. Hanging on desperately for dear life, Carter tried to keep the contents of his stomach down as they spun crazily, lashed at by the eruption's opening salvo, the tiny craft aiming for the rapidly closing-in wall of rock. Ramming the station was their only chance. A miss would launch them into the magma-tossed inferno below.

*

The maintenance train rattled above the rails at a fair old speed. Jacob, Sheplar and Khow had uncoupled the third car, leaving it behind with a small fortune in iron rails and repair equipment. They sped forward at a rapid clip; an engine car capable of dragging an entire train pulling just a single carriage. Forests that stretched to the horizon surrounded them on either side, the dark rise of a basalt mesa hiding the sinking sun. Khow had been able to get the engine car moving. The gask had climbed into the train's cab, running his fingers over the dials, levers and control wheels and firing up the engine. Before they left, Khow had helped Jacob and Sheplar push a spare antigravity stone from the maintenance flatbed into the carriage. He had activated it, leaving it floating above the floor. After a few minutes it had grown as cold as winter ice on a lake, as Khow had known it would with no load to tax it. They'd laid Wiggins' corpse on its flat surface, the constable stretched out, his arms crossed by Jacob as if the policeman were the main attraction at an open casket funeral. Jacob could hardly bear to step in the back and sit with the body, with the guilt that he felt about the constable's death. *The old man would be alive if we had followed his instincts.* Jacob tried to set his remorse aside. Khow had his prayer mat unrolled, a rough bamboo oblong embroidered with odd-looking flowers nested inside each other. He was on his knees fiddling with his calculator. Three times a day, as regular as clockwork.

'You know,' said Jacob. 'In my time I've seen travellers come into town with religions that pray to the north, the east, the south and west. But I swear, I've never seen you go to your knees in the same direction twice. Is that all part of worshipping chance?'

'It is not chance I bow to, manling Jacob. It is the great fractal tree, from which all branches flow. And the direction I face is the true direction of the universe. We are all required to move towards our true direction.'

'Maybe we are, at that.'

'And this is not prayer, as such. It is mindful consideration,' said Khow. 'The fractal tree extends as myriad branches and we must carefully choose the branches we walk. Especially when the numbers are so against us.'

'Well then,' said Jacob. 'That's a pity. I figure we could do with a

211

prayer or two. Just enough of Landor's coins left to buy third-class passage at Talekhard; the troopers meant to be protecting us aiming to kill us ... and our children are lost on the other side of beyond. But we've got the three saints standing behind us, the great fractal tree, and enough wind spirits to fill a Rodalian canyon.'

'We have our minds,' said Khow.

'And we have our hands,' said Sheplar, glancing at the twin guns belted around Jacob's waist. 'Where did those come from? The guardsmen?'

'No. From a dead man,' said Jacob. But how much longer will he stay dead? *As long as he needs to,* a voice inside answered.

'A dead man,' said Sheplar. 'This is not a simple matter. I realised as much when we discovered that peculiar radio device. I do not think it wise to trust anyone in Weyland to assist us with our mission from now on. No, I do not think so.'

'Fight to win and only fight what you understand,' said Jacob. 'And hell, we were running away to start with, right?' He held a pair of fingers up. 'Two stops. One to bury Wiggins, when we spot the first Weyland border flag fluttering by the trackside. The second to ditch this maintenance train in a siding close to Talekhard. We'll walk in and do our damnedest not to look like a country pastor, a mountain flier and a gask, right up until we've booked a flight south.'

Khow finished his prayer, or whatever he called the mantra. 'You have changed, manling. I don't need to examine the numbers on my calculator to know this – I can see the hardness around your eyes.'

'Maybe being tortured gives you a new perspective on life. Losing a good man like Wiggins.'

'No, it is more than that. A priest must witness the passing and share the sorrows of many of his people. It is as if you are forgetting who you are.'

No. Sadly, I think I'm just remembering. 'My wife was my anchor, Khow. My son too.'

'Perhaps that is why you want him back so greatly ... why you need him.'

'No, that's love – that and the fact it's the right thing to do.'

'He will be your anchor again, manling. But you should remember your love more. Otherwise you will not be the one that reaches him. Not your boy's father. It will be someone else entirely.'

Jacob grunted. 'Did you ever consider the irony, that God created men so all-fired dangerous as yours, only to make you such pacifists?'

'Why else would God cover us with spines and swell our barbs with neurotoxins, if not to teach us to live in peace with each other?'

'Maybe it's your females who are the fierce ones. Is there a Mrs Khow back home, waiting to brain you with a saucepan if you don't return with Kerge?'

'More than my son's mother mourns his loss,' said Khow. 'Kerge is significant to our people – mathematically significant. He carries a golden mean.'

'You are talking of prophecy?'

'The weight of his presence is greater than anyone elses in our nation. It has always been so, from the moment of his birth. Kerge is the pivot around which we will swivel.'

'Well, we're following in his wake, right enough.' *And glad I am for it.*

'Your fate was bound to Kerge when you assisted him in North-haven,' said Khow. 'And now I am bound to you as my son's journey is bound to your child's. Always has it been so around Kerge, from his very youngest years. He is a strange attractor.'

'I don't know about signs and portents, but I've had a bellyful of random chance, and of what people turn into when they follows their lusts.'

'Those weapons are not yours,' said the gask, indicating Jacob's brace of pistols. 'You should lay them aside.'

'They're my spines,' said Jacob. 'Maybe they're how God is going to test me, too.' *And maybe I'm going to need to get real prickly again, real fast.*

'I can see the Weyland border flags,' said Sheplar, calling from the front of the engine car. 'But there are other eyes out there ...'

Jacob moved to the window. His heart quickened inside his chest when he saw the mesa's flat top lined with hundreds of mega-wolves, each the size of a warhorse and each bearing the tall silhouette of a rider. A vast echoing blast sounded as many of the figures raised curled horns to their mouths. *The signal to attack? How quickly can those monsters run? How fast can we travel if we drop our rear carriage?* Jacob bolted to the cab's rear, grabbing a rifle leaned against the wall. 'I don't see any tree trunks cut down forward of us, and the rails look intact.'

Khow pushed aside Jacob's rifle. 'They do not mean to attack, look.'

All along the ridge top, dog-riders raised spears with their right hand, then dipped them down in unison, their mounts joining the coyote wailing coming from the riders' throats. The twisted riders struck their weapons fast against large round shields; the rhythm rising and falling eerily; plaintive, mournful, an ear-splitting beat of spears against shields.

'Are they saluting us?' asked Sheplar.

Jacob clung suspiciously to his rifle. 'They don't even know who we are.'

'Their song suggests otherwise,' said Khow. 'Can you not feel its power?'

He could. Jacob could see the truth in the gask's words. *This inhuman hymn is for us; as little sense as that makes in the world.*

'Leave manling Wiggins' body here,' said Khow. 'The dog-riders will bury him on the Weyland side of the border.'

'They burn our people,' said Jacob. 'Mutilate our bodies.'

'In the normal course of things, perhaps,' said Khow. 'But this is the way it is to be.'

Khow slowed the train to a halt, and Sheplar and Jacob pushed the antigravity stone out of the rear carriage, leaving it hovering to the side of the track, stone and corpse both as cold as ice. Khow came to join them as the dog-riders passed down a switchback path along the ridge, a slow funeral pace as mega-wolves picked their way down from the heights.

'We can stay and see him buried,' said Khow. 'We will be safe among them.'

'I've buried enough good men in my life,' said Jacob. 'And I can surely hear Wiggins up there in paradise, the old man laughing his arse off at all of this foolishness.' Jacob laid his hand on the antigravity stone's freezing surface. 'See you around, Stumpy.' He removed the constable's silver badge from his pocket and pinned it across his belt's brown leather. 'Let's go.'

By the time the train started rattling towards Talekhard again, the antigravity stone with Wiggins' remains had been roped to two riders, pulling him sedately towards the border while the beasts formed up into a double line behind, the constable's very own cavalry cortege. As the mounts came forward, they began a hyena-like chattering between each other. At a distance, you could almost mistake it for laughter.

When the ground rose up to strike Anna's transporter, it was as though the whole weight of the station had been picked up by a gargantuan hand and thrown full-pelt at Carter. There was a quickly stilled crack of splintering rotors; a screeching explosion of breaking metal, and then Carter was thrown sideways as the whole craft rolled over and over. A fleeting collision with Kerge's body, before the rockface slammed into Carter, spitting him out to spin away from the velocity of the crash while a burning pain stabbed at his side. As Carter came to a stop he nearly passed out, but the burning hot rain scouring his face was enough to hold him back from unconsciousness. He tried to get to his feet, and was nearly failed by his body. Carter was gripped by a sudden desire to go to sleep, the heavy weight of tiredness ambushing him. Moaning in pain, he forced himself to his feet, rising up as though these were his first tentative steps. Their transporter had split into three sections. Anna Kurtain was in the open cockpit, struggling at an angle to release her belt and fall sideways. The young gask pulled himself away from the rock a couple of yards in front of Carter, moving to Owen who lay still. But of Duncan Landor there was no sign. It was as if the surface had swallowed the heir to Hawkland Park. Duncan couldn't have been thrown into the sky, could he? The transporter had crash-landed near the centre of the station's topside, too far from the edge to toss a man into the void. Carter stumbled towards the gask and Owen. He reached Owen a couple of seconds after Kerge, the gask turning the body over to inspect the man.

'He is alive,' gasped Kerge, 'although bleeding badly from a scalp wound.'

'Looks worse than it actually is,' said Carter, gently pulling back the matted hair. He glanced towards the nearest air vent, a door in its side leading down into the station's tunnelled-out heart. 'Are you up to heaving him out of this storm?'

The two of them levered Owen up onto Kerge's shoulder. The gask shuffled forward with the man's weight; Kerge limped badly himself, but he did the job without complaint. A hardy, noble young man for sure; however many twists in the spiral separated his people from the Weylander's. You couldn't ask for better man at your side. Carter crossed to Anna, beating at her belt, the locking mechanism holding her into the pilot's seat and jammed by the crash. She was dangling off the floor, looking fairly trim for someone who had rammed them into the station with just two dying rotors left working.

'I can see where the clasp is bent,' said Anna, rubbing burning ash-fall from her dark curls. 'Grab that sensor spike and use it to lever the metal up.' The sensor spike had spilled from the cargo onto the station's dark basalt surface. Carter scooped it up and returned to the cockpit.

'I get to save you, after all,' rasped Carter.

'You've not done it *yet*, Northhaven. Belt's bent inside. Push the spike through the lock without impaling me, then twist it up to free the release.'

He located the bent lever behind the central disc, steadying it with one hand while he pushed the tip of the sensor spike in. It was just narrow enough to slip through the mechanism, but would it hold when he tried to spring Anna? The pilot wrinkled her nose in disgust as a black wash flowed over Carter's sandals.

'You've not just soiled your trousers, Northhaven?'

'Not unless I'm leaking engine fuel,' said Carter.

'That's what I was afraid of. Doing it fast would be good. Before some chunk of magma hot enough to put a match to the stove lands by your toes.'

He ignored the lancing pain in his arm as he applied pressure to the spike, sweating like a pig in the fierce haze of volcano dust. With a clack, the lever bent back into shape and Carter caught the slave woman as she fell out of her seat.

'*Now* you've saved me.' She stood up, leaning against the upended cockpit. You, me, Kerge and Owen, where's ...?'

Her question was answered by a moan from the other side of the fragmented craft. Duncan Landor lay trapped underneath the middle section of the aerial platform, pushing vainly against the weight of metal. A large boulder off to the man's side held up enough of the craft to have stopped it from crushing him to death – a lucky rock. Without it, Duncan's body would be paste. Duncan's legs and lower chest were pinned under the mangled metal, only his head and arms free as he struggled to lift the wreckage.

'Sweet saints.' Anna's breath sucked in. 'That's a hell of an umbrella you've found yourself, man.'

'I'll swap it for the bunkroom below.'

'We need to find a strong length of metal, lever the debris off,' said Carter.

Anna shook her head. 'Not even if you were a circus strongman, Northhaven. That transporter's made from reinforced steel. We'd need a hydraulic shaft jack to lift it – there'll be one of those in the mining stores.'

Carter looked at the pool of fuel spreading in the pelting rain of burning rubble. It was only a matter of time before the inevitable happened.

'I'll break off the corner of the boulder, make enough room to slide him across, then pull him out.'

'That boulder is all that's holding up a couple of tonnes of metal. If it crumbles …'

'So go inside. Find that shaft jack and bring some extra hands back with you.'

Anna shook her head angrily, but ran for the air vent anyway, calling out. 'I'll bring some buckets of water too, to douse the flames leaping across your crazy head.'

Carter knelt by Duncan and began striking the boulder near the ground, the sharp metal sensor spike clattering against the rock.

'Why?' moaned Duncan. 'Back at Rake's Field you would have run me through.'

'You were the one who called me out, remember? Besides, this might be the end of you, yet. You could end up flatter than a daisy in a flower press, wouldn't that be a cheery sight?'

'Maybe that'll make you happy. Take off, you fool. You're just tickling the rock. And those sparks are likely to cook us both in this lake of fuel.'

'Damned if I will.'

Duncan's tone became more urgent. 'Why?'

'Because it's going to annoy you to owe me something,' said Carter. 'And because any one of us that dies in this hell is a victory for the Vandians. I'll be damned if I'll give their empire anything they don't take at the point of a gun.'

Cracks began to finger out from the section of stone Carter was attacking. There was an angry creaking from the platform, as if the wreckage was moaning.

'Trying to get inside your mind is worse than understanding a damn woman's.'

Raising the spike with both hands, Carter brought it crashing down against the boulder. 'I'm real simple to understand. Get out of my way or get flattened. If I've a motto, that's it. One day soon these Vandians are going to find out they didn't take a slave. They just bought a whole mess of trouble and shipped it home.'

'They're probably regretting it already. You're going to get us all killed, you son-of-a-bitch.'

'The Vandians first, Duncan. Them first.'

Duncan yelled as the boulder began crumbling while the weight pressing in on him shifted; but the wreckage held in place as the boulder's side fell away. Carter grabbed the largest loose piece and pitched it behind him, reaching in for any other chunks of chipped-off rubble he could dislodge and remove. He worked as fast as he could, blinking away hot, dusty sweat from his eyes. Carter tossed every lump of rock he could find, ignoring the warm puddle of incendiary liquid pooling across his knees.

'Damn!' yelled Duncan as the sound they had dreaded hearing began crackling on the other side of the debris. 'Don't let me burn, God, please ...'

Carter's heart sank. Scarce seconds left. He grabbed Duncan's arm and started to pull him free, the man crying out in agony. 'What, and have Benner Landor pissed at me for letting the heir to Hawkland Park crisp up on some mined-out rock?'

Both of them screamed as Carter dragged Duncan clear of the

wreckage, inch by inch: Duncan's teeth clenched in pain while Carter yelled in rage at the fiery rubble raining down on them, at the broken transporter, at the Vandians and every slave in the sky mines who had goddamn ears to hear. Flames leapt up the edges of the broken craft as Carter dragged Duncan backwards and out of the tangled mess. A noisy fart cracked from Duncan as Carter heaved the young landowner wobbling up to his feet, bearing the man's weight against his shoulder. 'Hell, Mister Hawkland Park, I thought that was the volcano!'

'This is going to go up like blasting powder,' growled Duncan, the two of them limping towards the air vent.

'You're not wrong. Still, better out than in.'

They nearly collided with Anna, a gang of men hauling mining gear up the steps as they popped the air vent's door. The second it unlocked, what was left of the fuel tanks met the flames behind Carter, spinning steel wreckage peppering the landscape as a flower of fire reduced the crashed transporter to fragments.

Anna laughed to see the two of them alive. 'Carter Carnehan. Hero of the dispossessed. King of the slaves.'

'I'm nobody's slave. Just a Weyland man stuck on a rock.'

'That's as maybe, but you're going to sweat like a slave, Northhaven, we all are.' Anna pointed to the increasing tempo of fiery rain outside. 'That's building up to a full-scale eruption, and Princess Helrena, she'll be wanting herself a nice fresh rock full of something expensive. Trust me: she's one lady none of us wants to disappoint.'

SEVEN

OUT OF THE NATION

If Talekhard was a city that never slept, it must be, Jacob mused, because of the constant roar of aircraft landing and taking off. Visitors might as well adopt the consensus view and sup on the teat of the non-stop stream of vice and licentiousness available to the city's guests. Jacob needn't have worried about a pastor, gask and mountain pilot drawing inquisitive stares arriving at the city. They might as well have painted their maintenance train red and ridden the line all the way into the town's central station while dancing naked on top of the engine car for all the notice anyone would have taken of their arrival. Abandoning the train in a siding and walking in the remainder of the journey had been, it transpired, overcautious. Talekhard sprawled across a flat rocky saltpan, hemmed in by canyon walls twenty miles distant – empty ground ideal for planes to land, take off and taxi across. But the city made up for the remoteness of its location by importing all the taverns, gambling dens, bawdy houses, fighting pits and race tracks that any aircrew on leave could desire. It made Northhaven and its visiting sailors look like a serene saints' day service in front of Jacob's altar. All the constables Jacob spotted wore port authority uniforms, and short of arresting locals stabbing someone for their wallet, there didn't seem much in the way of enforcing the laws going on. Maybe that's what being a free port meant. *Free* to do anything shy of murdering a fellow reveller on ground leave. Stevedores from the freight yards mingled with aircrew from a hundred nations, every colour and hue of humanity weaving and wobbling and deaf to the roar of arriving aircraft kicking up clouds of dust from the flats. Space to land even the largest of flying machines – six-hundred-propeller carriers filled to the gunnels with cargo. The landing staff had their work cut out, galloping across the flats on geldings and flashing landing pennants at circling craft. Trying to clear space for bigger craft. Keeping the ground organised for a mosquito storm of smaller planes acting as shuttles for those carriers too large to land. Fuel traders dodged through the field staff, flashing signs that advertised their prices and fuel purities towards the air as though they were penitents waving prayers at heaven. Jacob and his friends arrived from the direction of the salt flats, mingling anonymously among passengers and crew leaving their parked aircraft.

They briefly stopped for Jacob to pump one of the landing-field men for information on where the cheapest ticket agents in town might be found. Then they entered the free port proper. Talekhard's crowded streets reflected the diversity of visiting carriers. Transients from nations that were just names on the maps in a library hold. Women in thick fur stoles with bare tattooed arms, dancing wildly outside a tavern; twisted seven-foot giants tight in neat military-style uniforms with extendable javelins strapped to their backs; aircrews wearing an eclectic wardrobe of clothing collected during life-long one-way passages across the endless surface of the world. Among these eccentric, exuberant crowds, the twisted people seemed almost tame. Street hawkers yelling their trades assailed Jacob, the din of horse-drawn cabs and rickshaws trundling through the busy avenues, touts for the music halls and taverns and gambling dens trying to outcry each other. Drunks ejected from paradise with their funds exhausted. Doxies for the molly houses calling crude entreaties from the windows above. Preachers from a dozen religions and sects proselytising to the lost – and very few visitors showing much interest in what the priests had to sell. It was hard to tell who, between Khow and Sheplar, was the more shocked by this sin city's peacock flash of feathers ... as far removed from the quiet life of the forest people and the hand-to-mouth living of the mountain folk as was possible to imagine. There was another difference from Northhaven. A free port meant free to carry weapons too. Most of the travellers and passengers strolled around the streets with the weight of knives, swords, pistols and rifles strapped to their person. There were no guardhouses at Talekhard to hand in weapons. Jacob felt for the brace of pistols beneath his duster. *The uniform of a pastor or the uniform of a bandit. Which suits me better, in a hole like this?*

'How can an entire population function intoxicated?' wondered Khow. In many matters, the gask was as wise as a woodland owl; but faced with the works of man, he was often left stupefied.

'They're just visiting for the most part,' said Jacob. 'This is the first time most of the visitors will have walked solid ground for months. This isn't so much a city, Khow. Think of it as a pressure valve on one of those boilers your people are so adept at fixing up.'

'It's a wonder they're fit to return to the air after shore leave taken here,' said Sheplar.

'You just judge the air-worthiness of their craft,' said Jacob. 'Find us a reliable carrier. Leave the state of the crew's souls to the saints.'

Sheplar patted the pocket where he had secreted his share of the remaining money. 'I fear we will end up sharing a pen with goats.'

'We don't have time to visit the radiomen and send to Benner Landor for extra funds. Major Alock and his troops are going to be riding the next train that comes in.'

Jacob hadn't forgotten the matter of the strange miniature radio set. The one thing that made less sense than all the rest of this affair. An illicit device that could signal ahead to Talekhard. Whatever waited for them here, whoever might be coming from behind, Jacob didn't have time to deal with it – not with his child taken to the other end of the globe.

'The comfort of our trip is of no importance,' said Khow. 'We must book passage south and begin to close the distance.'

'And you're sure our people have stopped travelling?' asked Jacob.

'Yes, they have halted. I believe they have reached their destination,' hummed the gask. 'My son's position has remained unchanged for too long for their layover to be a mere refuelling stop.'

'A slave only has value when he's put to work,' said Jacob. 'Until then, he's just a food bill and the cost of a cage. Well, we've got money enough to rent a hotel room here. No more than a night, to be on the safe side.'

'Major Alock's men ...' said Sheplar.

'Yes, they'll be coming for us. We need to get ourselves a berth in the air before they get here.'

'He's a serpent,' spat Sheplar. 'For an officer to betray his oath so easily—'

'There were a couple of thousand good reasons inside Landor's money chests.' *Round, metal and shiny.* Jacob's mind drifted to the impossibly advanced radio the guardsman had been using. *And if we're real lucky, robbing the party is the only motive for silencing us.* 'Alock's people are going to want us dead before we stand before an honest magistrate. We need to find a flight broker and see how far we can get on what we've got left. Then we can make the decision whether it's wiser to stay and wait on fresh funds from Benner Landor or light on out of here.'

'Will your rich friend in Northhaven send more money if you radio him?' asked Sheplar.

That's a real good question. 'I don't doubt Benner loves his children.' But he'd already written them off as dead and the pursuit as a fool's errand. And given how matters had begun out here, could Jacob really blame the landowner?

Not for the first time, doubts welled inside Jacob – not only their pursuit, but the direction he was following. The gask's understanding of maps had increased with familiarity, but the distances he described made absolutely no sense to Jacob. The slavers had flown far further and faster than the range a bandit carrier should be able to cover in the time between the raid and Jacob's arrival in Talekhard. *If Khow's correct, we could be flying south for decades.* What if the distances involved had skewed the gask's homing instinct? Maybe Carter really was languishing in a slave market in the Burn ... being whipped into the service of one of the local warlords, handed a rusty sword and marched onto a distant battlefield? Jacob could hardly stand the thought. *My son maltreated, while I'm heading off in the wrong direction, chasing wood magic.* Jacob hadn't even left Weyland yet, and he had already lost Wiggins. Jacob couldn't afford to leave three more graves scattered across the world's endless acres, while a slave's brutish existence whittled Carter's life shorter, day by day. *Dear God, Mary, tell me that I'm doing the right thing by him. Just give me a sign.* But none came. Only the raucous free port's revelry. A thousand drunken strangers pressing through the streets, and not one who gave a damn for the look of agony creasing Jacob's face.

Sheplar returned to Jacob and Khow's table, the sad look on the flier's normally effusive face speaking volumes for his luck in finding a crew willing to take the three of them on as passengers for what they had to pay. Jacob glanced around the lobby of the *Red Roof Coffeehouse*. The lobby looked more like a livestock auction than the ground floor of any coffee-house back home; brokers mingling with passengers, merchants with freight that needed shipping. Wasn't much coffee being consumed, either – not compared to the beer and spirits available. Mirrored walls made the throng appear a dozen times larger. Staff manoeuvred through the tables and a fog of cigar smoke, carrying the orders that were the price of entry to this de facto trading pit. *So many brokers, and not a sniff of a damn passage south to be had for the slim funds we've got.*

'They are asking for twice as much as we have left,' admitted Sheplar.

'I've booked passage on ships before, and I seem to remember them being a lot cheaper than this,' said Jacob.

'The wind that fills a clipper's sails is free, Jacob of Northhaven,' said Sheplar. 'Sadly, that is not the case for the fuel keeping a free trader in the air … even running at altitude with a fast trade wind behind its wings.'

'Couldn't we offer to work out our passage? A pilot as good as you – there must be airmasters in the port willing to take us on?'

'Merchant carriers are owned by clans,' said Sheplar. 'They might accept me as crew through marriage and blood – but no other way. Pilots are the elite. It is an honour jealously reserved and guarded.' Sheplar lifted one of their remaining coins. 'If we are to fly, only *these* will gain us our cabins. If only we had more …'

'I can send that message to Benner begging for extra funds. But I reckon Major Alock's killers will be here hunting us long before another chest of money turns up.'

'Money,' said Khow, 'is a troublesome concept.'

Jacob shrugged. 'A lot of the world's problems come from too much of it, friend, and the rest from not enough of it.' *Not to mention coveting it too fiercely. Poor Wiggins lying dead on the border speaks volumes for that.*

'I have never begrudged a warrior's meagre salary until now,' said Sheplar.

'Well, we are where we are. Wishing won't make it otherwise.'

Even so, neither of Jacob's companions voiced doubts about continuing without the ransom money. *Rich in mettle, if not in more material matters.* Jacob looked at Sheplar. 'If we had the money, who would you choose to transport us?'

Sheplar indicated a couple of men in simple grey jackets that Jacob might have mistaken for monks' habits, save for the heavily tattooed arms emerging from the sleeveless sackcloth. Both airmen had identical long black beards with their remaining hair cropped short. 'They are crewmen from Touriel. Their carrier is called the *Night's Pride*, rated at seven-hundred rotors. Large and safe. Pilots from their state are said to be solid and reliable. Best of all, they are flying towards the far south. Few layovers, no diversions.'

Jacob grunted. That was the sort of flight they needed. His nightmare was that they'd use what funds they had to begin the trip, only to end up in a foreign port down the line without friends, money, influence, or any idea how to complete the rest of the journey. To catch up with Carter and the others, they had to travel fast, go by air all the way. Otherwise, the three of them would end up fulfilling Benner Landor's doubts. Living off the land, travelling by caravan and sailing ship, and dying of old age before they got within a thousand miles of any child of Northhaven. There was no helping it. Some things you couldn't plan for – you just had to do. *Find Carter. Free my son. Return with my son.* Any one of those tasks seemed impossible, right now. But they always would be, as long as he believed they were. Jacob lifted the bottle of wine he and Sheplar had been drinking from. 'It's not too late for you, Sheplar. If Khow and I divide the money between the pair of us, we can pay for a flight south, even if it's only to the end of the league. Out there we could radio begging messages to Benner Landor from relative safety. You could travel north back to Rodal.'

Sheplar shook his head. 'The vow of a skyguard officer is not circumscribed by distance, Jacob of Northhaven. Any more than the bond that exists between father and son.'

Jacob shrugged sadly. Without the protection of the soldiers and Benner's funds, this was looking less like a rescue mission, and more like two parents following their grief on a suicide mission.

'We are with you in this, manling,' said Khow. 'To the bitter end.'

I don't want a bitter end. I want Carter home with me, whole and safe. An upsurge of voices rose to their side. Someone stumbled back into their table, spilling drinks across the lacquered floor. The broker who had fallen into them drew away, apologising profusely, and Jacob started as he saw the figure at the centre of the altercation. It was the vagrant bard, Sariel. A party of gold-uniformed airmen had thrown him to the floor, one of them pointing an angry finger at the rascal. 'When you sing songs, old man, take care you do not impugn our country!'

Sariel's walking staff had fallen to the floor, along with the tramp's tattered backpack. From where Jacob sat, he could see the money piled inside the sack, a solitary coin rolling out for him to stop with his boot and scoop it up. On one side was the royal boar of Weyland, on the other was the all-too familiar crest of the House of Landor – twin maize stalks resting against a seashell.

'Did I say your king was a syphilitic madman?' spluttered Sariel. 'A thousand apologies, good airmen, I misspoke, indeed I did. I surely meant your neighbours to the east, Magdouf. That tale was about Magdouf … my age, you see, and I am so thirsty, having just arrived in town. Hunger addles the details of my otherwise splendid tale.'

'A pox on your tales, you leprous dog!'

Jacob was out of his chair, placing himself between the bard and the irate airmen before they advanced on him and kicked a few lumps out of his flesh. 'Peace upon you, gentlemen. Forgive this old rascal. I've warned him many times about entering coffee-houses and begging when the church is already extending alms to him.'

'Better that you throw this dog in a house of work, Father,' spat the airman, 'rather than allowing him to slander noble dignitaries.'

'Oh, I will,' said Jacob. 'I am afraid our bishop is far too merciful; too soft, allowing such layabouts out of the poorhouse. Allow me to take him away and add a few stripes across his back for the nuisance he's caused you. The local police shouldn't disturb your rest for a brawl with a lowborn scoundrel like this.'

The airman made a dismissive wave of his hand, as though he was a duke dismissing a pauper. His crew turned on their heels and Jacob grabbed Sariel's collar when the bard tried to exit with the backpack clutched in his hands. He dragged the beggar back to their table and sat him roughly in a chair.

Sheplar's nose wrinkled in distaste, as he smelt the unkempt man's clothes. 'Charity only goes so far. You have averted a fight. Must we also share our wine with this dispossessed devil?'

'Oh, but this is one devil I recognise,' said Jacob, reaching over to pluck a coin from the tramp's bag. 'This gentleman of the road is the same traveller whose fare I paid to ride our train.' He turned over the coin to show Sheplar and Khow the crest on the other side. 'And while you don't know Sariel here, I'm sure you recognise this ...'

'Thieving serpent!' shouted Sheplar, restrained from leaping up by Jacob. 'How did you come to lay your hands on our money?'

'Why, through the ants, of course,' said Sariel. 'And this is *my* money, you shallow man.'

'Ants, you treacherous serpent, tell us the truth!'

'I was sleeping in the cargo hold of the Talekhard express. I woke one night to see a line of ants carrying these coins into my bag. Many ants hold me in considerable regard, you understand, ever since I was of some small assistance to their empress during the great war between the ants and the beetles.'

'Or maybe those light fingers of yours found a little opportunity for theft in the garrison car,' said Jacob, 'when half the troopers had headed out for the forest and the rest were standing sentry against a nomad attack?'

'You impugn me, Your Grace,' spluttered Sariel. He reached for the bottle of wine as the pilot tried to stop him from grabbing it. Sheplar was too slow. The bard slurped from the bottle as Sheplar turned his face away in disgust.

'You didn't arrive here on the express,' said Jacob. 'It was heading back towards Brinkdalen. It hasn't caught up with us, yet. So I'm guessing that after you raided the strongbox, you jumped the train before the troops found they'd been robbed. Another service rolled past and you jumped a ride here. Freight hopping is the least of your crimes.'

'Nonsense,' insisted Sariel. 'The red ants' generosity is renowned throughout the world. And a ghost train provided my passage here.

What a sight she was, manned by the unquiet spirits of all the departed railmen. And my fellow passengers ... spirits from the afterlife that have met untimely ends on the endless lines. The ghost engine stopped to pick up the maintenance train's poor, slaughtered souls. I painted my face as white as a sheet with ashes from the attack, then boarded, pretending I too was naught but a wailing spirit. I was assisted in my endeavours by the spirit of the lawman you travelled with, Sir Wiggins, newly arrived after crossing the River of the Dead. How he cursed and railed against his assassins.'

'I will make you wail, scoundrel,' said Sheplar. 'You are not fit to mention our poor friend's name. How did you know he was dead? What sorcery have you used?'

'A confidence man's eye for detail, is all,' said Jacob. 'Wiggins isn't with us and the obvious conclusion ...'

'We should see this vagabond thief hung,' said Sheplar.

'I am no thief,' insisted Sariel. 'Damn you if you claim so, you spur-galled cutpurse. And if you try to steal my money like perjured, false and disloyal brigands, I have only to call for the city's constables to take you into custody.'

Jacob moved his coat aside to show the tramp the two pistols belted around his waist. 'That depends on how quickly you can call, don't you think?' This was the best chance they had of leaving the country without getting involved in an all-out war against Major Alock's company of barely reformed brigands. Damned if Jacob was going to let that opportunity walk out of the door carrying away their passage to some distant slave market. God had taken away their money and God had given a portion of it back again. Maybe the Wiggins' spirit was involved somewhere in the affair after all. He'd be laughing himself hoarse at how things had worked out.

Sariel scratched nervously at his straggly white beard. 'What business does a servant of God have with those evil tools?'

'Let me acquaint you with one of my favourite passages from the good book of the saints: *And the hammer of the lord shall fall on the unright-eous.* As you can see, old man, I'm carrying *two* hammers by my side.'

'You make a fair point, Your Grace. Perhaps the ants carried the money to me so I could act as its temporary guardian, until such time as I could reunite the funds with their rightful owner?'

'That's a right healthy way of looking at things,' said Jacob, dragging the pack from the tramp's arms and placing it on the centre of the table. Khow lifted the flap up to examine the heaped coins inside. *The old rascal – it's a wonder he could stagger after a freight train carrying that much weight.*

'Half our funds. Not enough to ransom back all of those taken by the skels,' said Sheplar. 'But sufficient to carry us to the skel slave market.'

'Skels!' Sariel fair jumped out of his chair. 'What business do you have with those foul beasts?'

Jacob patted his pistols. '*This* kind of business. They've kidnapped my son for a slave. Khow here's son, too.'

'And they carry with them my honour,' said Sheplar.

Sariel shrugged. 'Such a small thing for a mountain man. It's a wonder they have not already mislaid it.'

Sheplar grinned evilly and patted the sword belted to his side. 'The same may happen to a thief's hand, when he is not careful.'

'I know little of being careful,' said Sariel. 'Although I know many stories about the virtues of caution – including how the Rodalian Skyguard was only formed to allow the mountain warriors to retreat faster than they ever could riding horses.'

'Enough,' ordered Jacob. 'I've already got all the trouble I need in my life. What are the skels to you, Sariel?'

'I had a wife once,' said Sariel. 'The skels arrived where we lived, and then … I didn't.' He said the words with sadness. No boasts or hyperbole. So simple that Jacob knew here, at least, he had a nugget of truth out of the raggedy old bard. *Maybe that was the start of the old man's wanderings?* How many of Jacob's parishioners had he abandoned at Northhaven without a living or family or life, people who would wander out of the prefecture and keep travelling. As if casting off their old existence could ever be the same as forgetting their pain.

'Then we have something in common,' said Jacob, 'beyond the fact you're sitting there with a pile of coins which are mine.'

The sadness faded from the vagrant's face almost as quickly as it had appeared. A twinkle of mischief settled again, as though Sariel had remembered all that he needed to of the truth. 'The skels' ruler, the Great Khan of the Sky, is my mortal enemy, as I am *his*. If this

money is to be used against the skels, you can have every last coin ...
and I shall travel with you to make sure it is well spent.'

'We do not need your stench along with us, thief,' said Sheplar.

'Yet, you appear to need my money.'

'*My* money,' said Jacob.

'For the cause,' said Sariel, 'for the cause. And I know much about
the skels and the nations they sell slaves to. You are going a *long* way
on this journey, Your Grace. You have been far-called.'

'You don't need to be a bard to know that much,' said Jacob. 'Everywhere on Pellas is a long distance away.'

'So it may be. But your journey will be longer than most.'

'What do you say, Khow?' asked Jacob.

The gask fiddled with his abacus machine, tapping the calculator's
buttons. 'This is extraordinary. The probabilities of meeting in this way
are inconceivable. Yet, this manling holds no weight within my calculations. It is as if he does not exist, as though he is insubstantial as mist.'

'Ha!' said Sheplar, pouncing on the gask's conclusions. 'No
weight ... no purpose to our mission.'

'Naturally, dear gask,' said Sariel. 'You calculate an infinite deal of
nothing. I have travelled so far and cheated death so many times – do
you think mere sums are capable of describing Sariel the Magnificent?
No mortal but Sariel has ever travelled the ghost train, leaping from
her engine car before she sank down to the underworld, whistles
keening with the screams of a thousand souls.'

'If you know the skels,' said Jacob, 'tell me one real thing about
them. Something I can use. Something besides the pain you claim you
feel about losing your wife.'

Sariel laughed. 'I shall tell you two things, Your Grace, and those
two things are all that you will need to know. The skels have fallen
very, very far, and what has supplanted them in the world ... well that
is far worse.'

'And how is that?'

'Because they've been replaced by *man*.'

Duncan squatted in the back of Anna's transporter. Slaves moved around
the station hangar wearing masks against the burning squalls blowing
in through the opening. Outside, the sky was a crazy swirl of crimson

230

clouds, the air filled with firecracker rattles – sleets of rocks cooling as they powered up from the erupting caldera. On either side of the transporter's cage sides, slaves with drills screwed in a series of metal panels as protective armour. The extra weight meant the transporter would have less flight time, but at least the sky miners would have a chance of reaching a fresh claim alive. Only two days for Duncan to recover from the crash the last time he ventured out. Allowing the stratovolcano to vomit out the worst of its fury. Duncan sat on the craft's bench with bandages wrapped around his ribs. But a claim rush loomed … with Princess Helrena's zones of the sky mines as bare as a beggar's cupboard. Duncan could have had both his legs amputated in the accident, and he'd *still* be sitting in the back with crutches. Carter hardly looked any fitter than Duncan, the man's breathing mask covering a web of bruises around his face. Anna limped around the new transporter, checking and rechecking every bolt of the shielding, her rotors and fuel lines. Only Kerge and Owen appeared unaffected by their previous outing. *We've already been caught by the volcano and sent crashing into the station. How much more dangerous is it to enter the eruption in its dying stages?*

Owen tried to reassure the nervous miners in front of him, twenty slaves racked in the transporter's rear for the flight. 'I know this is the first time for most of you. I know you haven't been given all the training you should. But we're dry, just dust left to process, otherwise we wouldn't be heading out so hasty.'

'Damn this waiting,' said Carter. He fiddled with his green armband – something to distinguish the Weylanders from any rival crews they encountered during the rush for fresh stakes. 'We doing this, or going back to our dormitories?'

'If there's an art to sky mining, *this* is it, Mister Carnehan. Getting the balance right. Put out too early and we'll lose every transporter we've got along with everyone on board to the storm. Light out too late, and any rocks worth staking will either belong to someone else, or be caught in a trade wind heading for Vandia's neighbours.'

'I'll just settle for coming back alive,' said Duncan. There were nods of agreement from the other slaves. He was glad of that … it made him feel a little less like a coward. He was meant to be on light duty for a few weeks after having half a transporter sitting on his ribs. That meant pushing a cart between the supply chambers and any strike they brought back with them. He guessed that bringing the fresh rock home was going to prove the most troublesome part of that equation.

'When we take off, that'll be Thomas Gale's decision. Princess Helrena and her entourage have shown up to make sure he doesn't call it too late. We're in for a hard pounding out there, no doubt. From that smoker, as well as every rival house with an interest in undermining the princess's standing within the imperial family.'

Duncan felt a ball of tension tightening in his gut. He had already tasted the stratovolcano's fury once. He had little desire to push his luck by risking his life a second time. At least Willow and Adella were safe inside the station. Their work wouldn't begin until a new rock had been captured and towed back. Tethered next to the station, for the slaves to swarm over it and begin the slow, unrelenting task of weeding out every vein of metal-bearing ore. If there was any consolation to this situation, his sister and Adella waiting out of harm's way was it for now. Duncan had to stay alive for the two women. Who else was going to look after the pair if he went down in the eruption spewing outside? Those worries wormed deeper into him than any consideration of his own safety. *God, I haven't asked you for much before. Seemed I already had everything and didn't much appreciate any of it, anyway. But just keep me safe, please, to watch out for Willow and Adella.*

'We're heading out first as lead scout,' said Owen. 'And you remember this: what we're doing, we're doing for every Weylander here, not for the imperium. You think the rations shipped in by the Vandians have been bad so far? You see how hungry our people will get if we fail to come home with a stake. Princess Helrena doesn't see much margin in greasing the cogs on her mining machine if it isn't running, you understand?'

Grunts of assent rose from the sky miners on the transporter's benches. Only Carter maintained a sullen silence. That fool would probably eat rock if he thought it would piss off the Vandians. *That's the fool you owe your life to*, a nagging voice reminded Duncan. *Yeah, well, that was only to piss me off too.* Showing courage when matters turned difficult was no substitute for a pinch of caution and common sense. A bit of yield, given their current miserable circumstances. *That's as maybe, but a life saved is still a heavy debt.*

'The way you talk,' said Carter to Owen, 'people'd think you were responsible for feeding the whole station.'

Owen turned around, a look of seriousness visible behind his mask's visor. 'The person behind you, the person in front, that's all you have to count on in the sky mines.'

'I *am* the person behind him,' said Duncan.

Carter nervously swapped his pickaxe handle between his hands. 'And that about sums up my situation.'

Owen shrugged at the pair of them. 'You'll learn to work together, or you'll die out here. One of the two.'

Shouts echoed down the hangar, orders passed from slave to slave. 'Tails up,' called Anna, banging the side of the transporter.

'If we make it back, try aiming for the hangar this time,' said Owen.

'Hell,' laughed Anna, adjusting her mask and pulling a poncho-style cape over her body as protection. 'I crash another transporter, my next assignment's going to involve a blunt shovel and a real narrow shaft.'

A warbling drone rose up around Duncan, then the rotors' updraft as they lifted off. They flew out of the station, the loud clatter of rocks falling on their newly installed roof.

Owen jabbed a finger towards the ceiling. 'More rocks coming down than going up. This is early ejecta mass. Same stuff that we were pushing through to get back to the station. Just coming down, rather than going up.' He indicated a clip on his leather tool belt; identical to the belt Duncan had been issued with, and then pulled out a line from under the bench. 'Tether up like this. We're hunting high, and I don't want any of you Weylanders floating away on me.'

Duncan did as he was ordered, connecting his line to his belt. Owen and Kerge squatted at the back of the transport, hunched over a nest of unfamiliar-looking machinery bolted into the survey craft's floor, all pertinent to the business of finding and evaluating a new stake. Racks filled with surveying gear. A steel console with buttons and levers and dials; telescope-shaped tubes on tripods surrounded by thick, coiling cables. Evil-looking needles protruded from saucers that hummed with electrical power. Half of their crew were hitters. The remainder were older hands with experience in the evaluation of stakes, the slaves that Duncan and Carter were along to protect. A squadron of transporters followed Anna as she climbed for altitude, other formations banking away to sweep adjacent sectors for claims. Also pulling away from the station was one of the vast metal craft that belonged to Princess Helrena.

'That monster's following us?' asked Duncan.

'Only to ensure no rivals stray into the princess's territory. We bring a rock back; the princess's enemies will get real motivated to snatch it out from underneath us. Her ship can't venture out into the free sky to support us. We're on our own until we return. The emperor might be playing a game of divide and rule, but he doesn't want the fruits of his noble loins openly shooting it out up here.'

'So we do the dying for them,' observed Duncan.

'Slaves to do the digging, slaves to catch the blunt end of a pickaxe handle. Rich people back home keep staff on retainer to do the fetching and carrying for them. Except for our lack of choice in the matter, it's not that different here.'

And I was one of them, Duncan thought. It was a measure of guilt made worse by the longing for his old, comfortable life. *I just want to be home with Willow and Adella.* Carter's very presence was a reproach to him. *You want to be home, but you're not willing to risk anything to do it. Damn you for a coward, Duncan Landor.* They climbed higher and higher, running into banks of thick rolling clouds. Anna navigated solely using her instruments, now; only brief glimpses of the squadron following through the fog bank. Duncan felt the increasing lightness of gravity's embrace. The mask he wore sensed the thinness of the atmosphere, its canisters releasing squirts of air into his leather mouthpiece. The transporter bounced in the currents. Duncan jolted up from the seat and came down so slow he swore there was a layer of invisible cushioning between him and the bench's surface. His gut filled with queasiness, riding this high, freed from gravity's tyranny. The sound of rotors died away, and the transporter's movements became gentler, gliding. The pelting of ejecta mass on the roof fell away too as their transporter moved with the whistling wind, buffeting fingers reaching out for the fuselage and toying with their aircraft.

A large rock suddenly peeled out of the cloud cover, coming straight for them, and Anna threw the transporter up, barely clearing stone by ten feet; a complaining roar from their engines at being overtaxed. With a shock, Duncan realised this find wasn't from the eruption – it was a mining station, sides embedded with antigravity stones to give it additional lift, the roof pockmarked with rusty air vents and a top-side landing hangar, its doors half open.

'What the hell's that doing floating out here?' yelled Duncan. 'In unclaimed sky? We could have flown straight into it!'

'Station sixteen,' said Owen, pointing to white rubble piled across the rocky landscape below. 'The ghost station. There was a slave revolt there, long before our time. The Vandians left it anchored here as a warning to the rest of us. Position must have shifted with the push of the ejecta mass; our charts show it to the south of here.'

With horror Duncan realised the white debris was bones. Hundreds of dead slaves littering the station's roof. 'The Vandians assaulted the station?'

'Just cut off water deliveries and blockaded it,' said Owen. 'Why waste bullets and blood on slaves when you don't have to? Legends say the Vandians' patrol ships kept on dropping cans of food for the slaves, though. Real good stuff, the kind of rations we never ever see up here. Salted beef, salted fish. Alcohol too. Anything that would make them thirstier than they already were.'

'Bastards!'

'If you look real hard among the bones, you'll see the remains of the transporter fuel drums they were drinking from by the end. If it had been me, I would have jumped before it came to that. But I guess everyone's different when you're choosing how to die.'

'I can hear something,' said Carter, gripping the transporter's cage sides opposite Duncan. 'Whistling?'

'Air vents left locked in open position,' explained Owen. 'Funnelling the wind. Just a bit of theatre for the rest of us rubes in the sky. You don't really believe in ghosts do you, Northhaven?'

'I believe that Vandians make them out of their prisoners.'

Owen nodded grimly. 'That, at least, is no camp-fire tale.'

Duncan watched the ghost station pass behind them, claimed by the clouds. Maybe that was the true purpose of the mines – a mill to process the Vandians' slaves into the shades of the dead. Even after death the unfortunate slaves still served their masters, like corpses swinging inside a crossroads gibbet.

Anna called something out from the cockpit. Kerge and Owen started to rotate a tripod-mounted piece of surveying gear. Duncan realised the team had come across their first potential sky mine: a large grey slab tracking upward through the almost non-existent gravity. Their transporter slowly circled the rock while the rest of the squadron took up a holding pattern behind them. The stake appeared little different from their home station, although the rock's surface was still boiling hot – surrounded by a trail of steaming moisture as it rotated its way through the thick clouds. After a minute attending the survey equipment, Owen turned round and attracted Anna's attention, making a cutting gesture across his throat. 'Nothing to justify a ground survey. Next ...'

They banked away, leaving the mass to waste a rival crew's time. Similar results were discovered from a smaller rock, a real smoker moving fast as it scratched skyward. Owen and Kerge located signs of iron ore inside, but at that size, the strike wouldn't last long enough to keep the princess happy, so they cut it loose too. Anna shrugged and banked away in search of another strike. Their third find, though, that was the charm. A rock so hefty that the cloud cover was left clinging to its margins, concealing its true width.

Owen punched the air, whooping. 'This is the one! Copper, iron, silver, gold, platinum. It'd be easier listing all the metals she doesn't contain.'

'You getting paid commission?' asked Carter.

'We bring this stake home; there'll be well-fed Weylanders in the station for a year. That's as much a pay packet as we ever get to see.'

That probably didn't cut much ice with a bull-headed fool like Carter Carnehan. *Brave, bull-headed fool*, a voice noted inside Duncan. *Shut up. What one man calls bravery, a wiser man would label as recklessness.*

Owen rummaged under the bench and withdrew a flare, pulling its firing pin, billowing green smoke left trailing in the transporter's wake. Shortly after his signal, the rest of the squadron went into action, not landing – just hovering above the rock's surface as teams of men dropped out of the transporters' rear, lugging the antigravity stones they'd need to stabilise the stake against gravity's eventual summons. At the same time, other men leapt from the platforms with spear-long rods of steel topped with thick hoops. These were driven into the rock with hammers, cables unwound from the mining crafts' fuselage and clipped into place. Anchors to turn the squadron into a flight of tugs.

It was amidst this flurry of activity that Anna's transporter set down, settling on the rock's surface just long enough for Kerge and Owen to offload their survey equipment. As soon as Duncan, Carter and the others had helped drag the gear out, Anna lifted off in a cloud of dust, heading for the rock's edge where towing cables were being secured. Heat seeped through the thick soles of Duncan's survival suit, making his feet itch. It was hellish hot at this altitude. Like standing above a spit roast and volunteering to be steak for dinner.

Duncan and Carter rested against their wooden clubs, looking to Owen for what was to come next.

'We've got to secure this claim fast,' Owen told Kerge and the two men. 'Help me shift the gear. No need to watch the skies yet. Anybody planning to jump our claim will let us do the hard work of fixing antigravity stones and anchoring it before they move in and try and snatch it.'

Duncan lifted up one of the cases. Not heavy at all in the light gravity. He followed after Owen, every step given an extra spring by their altitude. The wind had picked up by the time he got to Owen's camp location. Eddies of burning dust carried around Duncan, whipping his tunic and making him glad of the mask's protection. 'Quite a gust.'

Owen pointed to the clouds above. 'That's where we're heading. High altitude trade winds all the way to heaven, from here on in. We need to get this rock stabilised and heading down again real quick.'

Duncan didn't last long before he had to raise his mask and spit out the grime seeping through its seals. *Sure would be good to take a swig from my canteen about now.* Instead, he helped Owen, Kerge and Carter drill holes large enough to accommodate survey sensors. Owen appeared satisfied that the ground equipment backed up his preliminary findings. That was of less concern to Duncan than the tornado-strong gusts he had to fasten his feet against. But the sound and fury of the winds they were rising into gradually abated as more and more transporters leashed to the rock, beginning to drag the stake back down. Finally, a tipping point was reached when gravity's natural course worked for them rather than against them. Cries echoed around the rock, and the sky miners' antigravity stones activated at the buoyancy point. The rock's passage through the volcanic storm had become a simple matter of being hauled by their transporters.

Duncan spotted a transporter dipping above them, marking its passage with red flare smoke. One of their own craft spotted the intruder and peeled away to chase it off. 'Why do I think that's not Princess Helrena signalling there'll be a red carpet laid out for us when we get back to the station?'

'Birds in the air without a nest, Northhaven. They've spotted us and they're going to try to take ours.'

'I don't want to do this,' said Duncan.

Owen laid a hand on his shoulder. 'I feel exactly the same. Everyone here does. But what we want, well, that doesn't count for a whole lot. The princess's enemies will try to land near the anchors, cast off our cables and then attach their own tugs.'

Carter made a noise in the back of his throat that mirrored what Duncan felt.

'Kerge and I will remain here and protect the survey equipment,' said Owen. 'If it's any consolation, you'll find it easier to defend your rock after the hostiles have landed and are trying to add a few busted ribs to the injuries you received on your last outing. Until then, just think about your sister and girl and everyone else back at the station. Stay alive for them.'

Shouts echoed from all over the rock, Weylanders congregating at the rim, bunching around anchor points. There was a bounce in Duncan's step that didn't reflect the way he felt. His heart as heavy as lead he walked towards the edge.

'This is wrong, Carter.'

'There's nothing personal in it. The same as when the miners attacked us down by the volcano.'

'We're not animals.'

'Isn't that exactly what slaves are? Men have choices, slaves don't. Protests from us are no more worth listening to than a swine squealing as it's hauled to the abattoir.' Carter looked meaningfully at Duncan. 'That is, as long as you accept being a slave. If you've changed your mind about that, maybe you want to throw in with me after all.'

'I don't want to get Willow killed. And what the hell are we going to do about Adella?'

'We're not children anymore. Everyone in the sky mines can make their own minds up. Willow and Adella too. A man's got to die of something, right? That's what my old man used to say. Those Vandian bastards, they've stolen more than our bodies. They've snatched our hope. Made us think we're just possessions to sweat and die at their pleasure. If the road home is all that's out there, I'll take my end on it. Chased, pursued, hunted. At least it'll be the death I've chosen, not getting my skull cracked by another poor sod starved into desperation by the Vandians. So are you in, or out, Mister Landor?'

'We'll see,' said Duncan. 'We'll see.' He looked up at the sky. Waves of enemy transporters broke through the filthy clouds, a web of red smoke trailing in their wake, too many invaders for their own aircraft to discourage. 'I reckon the hitters on the back of those birds are fixing to solve all our problems for good.'

Jacob's hand rested on the window of the hansom cab as it pulled through the crowded streets of Talekhard. Sheplar Lesh was right about one thing. With the pungent smell of the bard in their carriage, the first order of the night when they got back to their cheap hotel would be to get the traveller a bath and avail themselves of the establishment's laundry service. With the evening approaching, more aircrews spilled into the street; merchants and travellers the worse for wear after their carousing. The two horses up front shifted slowly through the press of carriages and carts, oblivious to the siren cries of women leaning from doxy house windows, yelling obscene suggestions to the crowds below. Jacob sat next to Sariel, the vagrant humming and tapping his walking staff on the cab's floor. Khow was lost in thought opposite, next to Sheplar, who was doing his best to ignore the tramp. A hatch opened in the cab behind the gask's head, the cabbie on their driving step bending down to speak. 'Roads are thick with drays heading for the warehouses. Your hotel is only at the end here. It'll be quicker for you to get out and walk the rest of the way. Could take me ten minutes to push through this traffic.'

Jacob poked his head out of the open window. Carts piled with barrels and bales stood stalled all the way up the street, the impatient clatter of hooves on cobbles as traffic waited along the boulevard. Jacob spied their cheap lodgings ahead. A gang of street vendors weaved through the carts, beseechingly lifting trays of food and knickknacks up to captive riders and wagoners. Jacob saw what he wasn't meant to, as well. Three men sitting at a table outside the eatery next to their hotel, incongruous among the families seated around them, gossiping over evening meals. A carriage had drawn up down the street, its driver feeding his two horses and waving away a prospective passenger trying to buy a ride. The canvas bundle tied up top, just the right length to hide rifles. The two men pretending to window-shop at the general store opposite. *Six outside the hotel. How many inside, to close the trap?*

'Take the turning over there,' said Jacob, pointing to the next street corner. 'We're not going back to our rooms. Head for the airfield.'

'What is it?' asked Sheplar.

'A feeling in my water,' said Jacob. He patted his pocket, touching the tickets Sheplar had negotiated for them in the packed lobby. 'There's an ambush waiting for us outside our hotel. That strange radio set we found on the guardsman ... I don't think the receiving set is limited to Major Alock's hands. I reckon there's one in town, too.'

'Enemies in front of us, enemies behind,' said Sheplar. 'This conspiracy runs larger than a single corrupt regiment.'

'Which explains why the weight of numbers is against us,' said Khow, holding up his abacus machine. 'The branches of the fractal tree are far narrower than they should be.'

'Do you speak of skels, Your Grace?' said Sariel.

'Maybe their common pattern equivalent,' said Jacob.

'What do the tardy-gaited mites want?'

'They'll settle for taking the money in our pack and putting a bullet in our heads,' said Jacob. 'But it's the *why* of it that's bothering me. If I could see how whoever is behind this is benefiting from the situation, I'd be a lot more comfortable about taking them on.'

'I can see you are a master strategist, Your Grace,' said Sariel. 'You realise the need to understand your enemy and battlefield to triumph. I once served in the staff of the Grand Marshal Fourou. That courageous officer won many battles with the assistance of my suggestions.'

'And what fount of advice do you have for us here, smelly one?' asked Sheplar.

'That you must never engage an enemy on his terms, only on your own,' said Sariel.

'The best victory is the one you never have to fight,' added the gask.

Jacob checked his pistols. *That may not be in my gift.*

As the cab halted by the field staff at the edge of the flats, Jacob leant out of the door to talk to the men. 'We need to get to one of the shuttles taking cargo up to the *Night's Pride.*'

'Over there,' said a field hand, pointing to a line of stubby tri-wing planes, their nose cones open while wagons unloaded stacks of wooden crates in front. 'Those are the tugs from the *Night's Pride.* Not much comfort on a Tourian bird, though. She's no liner up there.'

'We require range,' said Sheplar. 'Not vases with flowers in our cabins.'

'You'll have a long journey with her,' said the field hand. He indicated a series of buildings off to the side. 'Pull up over there for a customs' check before you leave.'

'We're going out, not coming in,' said Jacob.

'That's what I told the bosses,' shrugged the field worker. 'Most months they don't give a turd about what's coming in, either. Why do you think the traffic's so backed up in the city? These extra checks are throttling operations. We'll be working into the night at this rate, and not with any extra money for us, of course.'

'How long has the port been operating like this?'

'Only started today. Maybe the prefecture wants extra paperwork to justify the revenue service's next pay rise.'

'That'll be a clerk's idea, all right,' said Jacob, watching the official turn and walk towards the wagons drawing up behind them. Jacob spoke to the cabbie on the coach step. 'Head straight for those triplanes over there.'

The man on the footstep grunted and with a flick of the reins, the small black carriage rolled across the salt flats, kicking up a trail of dust from its wheels.

'Ah, that's the spirit, Your Grace,' said Sariel. 'Not a fig for bureaucracy! I have travelled through a thousand countries and never once seen a line painted across the dirt delineating where one state ends and another starts. Nor found entry duties written in the grass of the meadows where I wandered.'

'It's coincidences I don't care for,' said Jacob. He could feel the wrongness of this, like a fist clenching around his heart. He sensed the desperation of the forces trying to murder him before he left the country. Someone didn't want the expedition to succeed, and they were going to any lengths to stop it dead. No sooner had the cab halted outside the line of stubby transport planes and cargo wagons, than a rider caught up with them, his horse panting from the gallop from the customs house. 'You there!' he shouted at their cabbie. 'Over to the buildings! Are you deaf? You can't follow simple instructions?'

Jacob leaned out of the open window and snorted in derision. 'Don't take that tone of voice with us, sir. We've already had our papers cleared by the Mayor of Talekhard himself.'

'What's that, you say?' The official drew his horse alongside. 'Present them.'

'Here they are,' said Jacob. 'A gask, a mountain pilot, a tramp and a pastor.' As the custom man's eyes widened seeing the passengers inside, Jacob slammed his door open, smashing into the official and sending his horse clattering back into a wagon. The wagon's team of horses took fright and jolted forward. Shouting in anger, one of the wagon's stevedores stumbled and dropped a crate. It smashed open on the ground below. Sariel hooted in approval at the mayhem.

Khow looked aghast as Jacob swung out to the dirt and booted the struggling officer in the gut as he attempted to get to his feet. 'Manling, have you taken leave of your senses?'

Jacob reached into the semi-conscious man's duster and pulled it aside, revealing a shoulder holster with a pistol that he tugged out and tossed away across the salt flats. Then he lifted up the man's leg and tapped his shoes. 'Look at this ... soft, expensive leather. Customs men wear stout boots with steel caps; at least, the ones who want to keep their toes attached to their feet do. Doesn't take long checking piles of lading before a crate slips and falls on your boots. Only two breeds of wasps that hide their stings. Criminals and secret police.'

'And with only a police badge's width to be slipped between the two careers,' announced Sariel, prodding the downed official with his walking staff. 'Not much backbone in this doghearted clotpole. Fewer morals. I can tell.'

Jacob tossed their fare to the cabbie and slapped the nearest horse's flank, sending the cab skittling away from the triplanes. He glanced up at the wagon and the cursing stevedores. The crate the men had dropped lay broken across the dusty ground, a spill of straw, and among the packing material … a pile of heavily greased rifles. The stamp on the broken crate was still legible: Landsman Weapon Works. *Gunrunners? I thought Sheplar had pegged these people as an upright crew?* A female pilot ducked out from under the nose of her transport plane, the same colourful tattoos on her arms as on the pair of brokers he'd seen earlier. She waved angrily at the stevedores manhandling her cargo. An idea flashed into Jacob's mind. A way to expedite their exit and have the aircraft above ignore all commands from the ground to land its passengers. Jacob picked up the semi-conscious official and one of the oiled rifles, tossing gun and man to the ground in front of her as the pilot ran forward. 'It's not your wagoners' fault! Where's your export licence for these weapons?'

'What are you saying?' demanded the pilot.

'I'm saying that the customs officers are going to require you to land that—' Jacob's hand jabbed up to the sky where the *Night's Pride* circled '—and unload your cargo until you've secured valid export licenses and paid transfer taxes on every gun and bullet you've taken on board. And you better be able to prove that these crates aren't going to be sold to any warring nation. The league has strict rules about exporting weapons into combat.'

'War, war?' the pilot repeated, her features growing crimson and incredulous. 'Of course *war*. You think we plan to sell rifles to fishermen with broken nets to shoot fishes in the waves? Your government are thieves. Let us buy first from your friends' factories, pay your officials their finder's fee, then *problems*! Then *confiscate*? No!'

Jacob pointed to the man on the ground, jabbing a thumb back to the customs house. 'He's just the first of them. Be plenty more along in a minute.' Jacob pulled out their stiff oblong boarding cards. 'And we need to travel out. We haven't got the money to spend on another month's rent in Talekhard's hotels while you trade paperwork and grease government palms here.'

'On board!' The pilot clapped her hands together. 'You workers, load, load! We leave now.' She sprinted down the line of triplanes, yelling instructions at the crews in their cockpits; pilots opening windows in glass bubbles above the landing doors, shouting to each other. Airmen came running down loading ramps to spin rotors into coughing life. Ribbons of smoke began trailing from their engines as stevedores struggled up the ramps with the last of the crates.

'A magnificent performance, Your Grace,' said Sariel, his face glowing with admiration. The vagrant stooped down to inspect the contents of the downed man's pockets, flourishing a couple of paper notes as happily as if he discovered a small fortune. 'I doubt if I could have done better myself, not if I was treading the boards of the Imperial Theatre with the beautiful gaze of the Tsarina of Nera-ka on me as my motivation.'

'You are not always a truthful man,' Sheplar told Jacob, his tone a lot less admiring. He tried to snatch the stolen money off Sariel, but the tramp danced back out of reach.

'I know how much fuel they burn landing one of those city-sized carriers and taking off again. They have to stay flying at high altitude if they're to turn a profit this side of winter.'

'In that much you're correct,' said Sheplar.

Jacob kicked one of the rifles left dropped on the ground. 'And I thought you said the Tourians were an upright crew?'

'Tourians, upright?' laughed Sariel. 'You are thinking of their southern neighbours, the Touresekians. These people are of base descent who would hawk their grandmother to a skel slaver if the price were right.'

'Be quiet, smelly one,' Sheplar swore. 'Your mind's been addled from drinking too much rotgut.'

Jacob dipped down and grabbed the lapels of the customs officers, pulling out one of his pistols and shoving it against the bruiser's skull. 'Who're you working for?'

'Go to hell!'

'You've been told to look out for the three of us, haven't you? Who set you up to it?'

'You're dead men, all of you.'

Jacob slapped the officer across the face with his pistol's ivory-handled grip. 'Quite possibly, but you're heading to hell first.'

'You won't shoot me, churchman.'

Jacob cocked the pistol. 'How sure are you of that?'

'Go to hell.'

Jacob slapped the man harder and pushed the barrel between his teeth. Khow appeared and rested his long gnarled fingers on the pistol. 'This is not you, manling. Do not do this thing.'

Jacob hesitated, fighting the anger surging up inside him. 'You tell whoever set you to this that they'll find out who I am. And when they do, they won't much care for the discovery.' He rammed the pistol butt into the man's nose, his head crashing back in a fountain of blood.

'It's not people such as this you have to fight,' said the gask.

'One battle at a time. Until the day is ours.'

'Quickly, now,' urged Khow, pointing towards a frisson of activity centred on the customs house. Officers sprinted out of the warehouse doors, arrowing in on the sound of the triplanes' roaring engines, angry armed men shoving their way through a queue of wagons lined up for checks. 'Our paths are narrowing.'

Narrowing like the end of a noose. 'To the *Night's Pride*, then. For better or worse.'

Jacob and the others followed the pilot inside the triplane, a windowless cargo chamber filled with wooden crates, all of them stamped with the Landsman Weapon Works' legend. She climbed a ladder and disappeared behind a simple curtain sealing off the cockpit. Outside, the engines built up to a throaty crescendo as the triplane's nose doors began to swing down, sealing off their view of the salt flats. Benches had been built into either side of the fuselage, just enough room to sit down and hold on to the freight's netting as the aircraft turned, jouncing along the flats, its bouncing speeding up with the clamour of its engines. Then the stout transport angled up into the air, accompanied by the crack of gunshots from the ground. Fuselage splintered towards the rear of the plane as one of the bullets broke through and found a home inside the freight, and then they were spiralling and twisting upward. Jacob felt the clutch of gravity lessening as they climbed towards the *Night's Pride*.

'I think we have worn out our welcome in Weyland,' said Sheplar. 'That was a strange experience for one who is used to being the hunter, rather than the hunted.'

Jacob clutched the webbing as the triplane spiralled ever higher. *I wish I could say it was a novelty for me. If just leaving home alive is this hard, how difficult will it be to find Carter out there?*

Carter shoved back the brute of a man he faced. He spotted another slave trying to slip behind Duncan and brain the man. *How long before we have to abandon the anchor point?* The Weylanders hardly needed green armbands to distinguish them from their attackers. The rival mining force had similar features to Rodalians, their curses so mangled they hardly registered as words at all. Whatever land had been raided to take these hostiles for slaves, that country hadn't short-changed its sons on ferociousness. Enemy sky miners dropped off the transports in seemingly endless waves, screaming unintelligible war cries at the Weylanders, their aggression cold enough to turn a man's blood to stone. Would it have made a difference to Carter if his enemies had hailed from one of the league's neighbours, a fellow member nation of the Lanca? *Probably not.* Carter stepped in and shoulder-slammed Duncan's attacker, knocking him sprawling over a boulder. Unlike the station's exterior, the battleground on this new rock was anything but smooth-surfaced. Cracks and pits and miniature valleys a man could tumble into, falls that would kill you as sure as an opponent's club finding its mark. Carter saw Duncan trade blows with the man facing him, blocking the pickaxe handle, turning it and bringing the club down on the attacker's knee. A crack of heavy wood sounded as Carter fended off a pickaxe handle, then he ducked on instinct as an enemy transporter buzzed down, nearly giving him a haircut with its humming rotors. Two of the rival house's slaves pushed forward with an anchor cable lowered from their craft, waiting for the defenders to be distracted enough for them to rush in unopposed and trade lines. A group of Weylanders guarded the anchor point, yelling muffled abuse through their masks and waving their clubs menacingly towards the invaders, bravado and fear fuelling their challenges in equal measure. This brawl had degenerated into a mad, deadly game of tug-of-war; the *war* part of the game given extra emphasis by the violence. Their rock was still heading towards the princess's territory, its motion not yet arrested by enemy transporters trying to drag the stake towards their own slice of sky. Owen's words proved prophetic. It wasn't difficult to hate this rival slave force when they were landing blows on you, Carter's bruised and bloodied body pitted against the yelling banshees. *Not in the slightest.* Two invaders jumped Carter simultaneously, one of them slipping an arm around his neck while the other ripped off his mask. Trying to suck in the almost non-existent air at this altitude, Carter half-fell as he was brought to his knees by the two assailants' weight. Another slave with a pickaxe handle rushed forward to cave in Carter's skull, but Duncan appeared from nowhere to clash sticks with the screaming slave. Undaunted, the two holding Carter dragged him on his knees towards a chasm ... a gap in the rock that ran all the way to the open sky. He couldn't breathe, let alone fight them off. It was as though he inhaled fire, his lungs burning every time he gasped vapour and smoke. Carter's chest heaved as his body convulsed, hopelessly gasping the thin air. With a last, desperate burst of strength, Carter kicked his way to his feet, grabbed the man trying to hold him down and lunged forward, using the momentum to flip the fighter over his head and into the chasm. The remaining slave grappled with Carter, working hard to send the Weylander after his comrade. Then he hesitated a second as a siren began to drone from the rear of one of the transporters, the slave's head urgently glancing from left to right. Carter kicked out at the man, but it was too late, the hoary little slave had discontinued the wrestling match and was running full pelt towards a landing transporter. Carter pulled back from the rim and staggered towards the boulder where his mask lay abandoned, still pumping out little spurts of air. He shoved it against his mouth, sucking greedily for a full minute before he had the wherewithal to slip the straps around his head. All around the rock, enemy transporters ditched their cables and pulled away.

The attacking force ran almost comically in the weak gravity towards their craft, although there was nothing funny about the cruel way they were pursued by the defenders, smashed down from the rear and bludgeoned to death by the princess's vengeful sky miners. At the opposite end of the rock hovered the reason for their desperation. Princess Helrena's ship floated in a cloud of engine smoke, loitering on the margins of her licensed territory, a brooding steel gigantean with all her gunports and turrets swivelled and ready to open up in defence of the prize her labour force had hauled home. A second after the ugly rock nosed across into home territory, Carter heard a drone in the air as a large squadron of transports broke through the clouds. More of the attackers or allies of the same – for no sooner had they appeared and spotted the princess's ship ahead, they wheeled away, climbing for height and twisting and turning back into the clouds. *We were that close to dying. If they had landed a second wave, we'd have been beaten into a pulp.* Carter was overwhelmed by competing emotions. Sickness at the carnage and death ... elation at surviving. Shame, too. The guns on the princess's ship let loose a broadside, gobs of flame arrowing towards three transporters too slow to depart. The craft were trespassing inside her territory now, and they were going to pay the price. All three invaders exploded into oily black flowers, not enough debris left to tell transporter wreckage from burning flesh as their remains expanded into the sky. A cheering sounded from the Weylanders on the strike. As Carter turned around, he saw Duncan walking forward, the heir of the Landor acres dragging his bloodied wooden club like a gamekeeper having dispatched a downed flight of partridges.

'You not raising a huzzah?' asked Duncan.

Carter lifted the mask a second to touch the red weal of the whip-lash he'd received. 'Hell no. Maybe the Vandians will cheer *us*. Maybe that princess will come out and kiss me when she sees the strike we've brought home for her.'

'Maybe she'll kiss my arse, first.'

They walked back to Owen and Kerge, crouched by the intact survey equipment and their bodies untouched by the bloody battle across the rock.

'Feels like your stake, now, don't it, Mister Carnehan?' said Owen. 'Just remind yourself that it's only ever theirs.' He nodded towards the long silvery warship hovering on a spear of fire.

Guess my arse isn't going to get kissed, either.

Carter was sitting on the edge of his bunk in the dormitory, his arms extended for Adella to remove the old bandage around his ribs, his body cracked and smarting from the battle to seize the sky mines' new claim.

'I was so worried about you,' said Adella.

'Nothing's going to happen to me,' said Carter. Even as Carter mouthed the words, he knew they must sound like a lie. There were

248

a lot of promises a slave could make that couldn't be kept. And that had to be the greatest of them all.

'I don't think I could go on living if you died,' said Adella. 'What would be the point?'

'You'd find a way,' said Carter. 'Everybody here has to find a way of going on.'

'They discovered another dead slave this morning in the barracks,' said Adella. 'Loretta Popham. She died of poison. She was from Northhaven, too, just like us. I knew her back home. She worked as a maid in the hotel.'

'Where the hell did she get her hands on poison up here?'

'Mogo tubers,' said Adella. 'You can unearth them from the soil at the foot of the volcano. Slaves dig them up and bring them back to exchange for food rations, or lying down with the people that found them.'

'Sweet saints!'

'You get to travel down to the surface to run eruption checks,' said Adella. 'I was going to ask you to dig around for some tubers for me. Just in case it gets too much.'

'Don't be stupid. I'm not going to do that.'

'You can't stop anyone checking out from all of this, Carter. I could climb the steps to the top of the station any day I wanted and leap. But boiling those roots and drinking it down is meant to be painless. You go to sleep and you never wake up. That has to be a better end than falling.'

'We're going to get out of here!' protested Carter. 'You and me both.'

'They'd hunt us down,' said Adella. 'All the guardsmen and their warships. Nobody has ever escaped alive from the sky mines. That's a record the Vandians don't want to see broken.'

'They wouldn't come after us if they thought we were dead,' said Carter.

A brief flash of hope crossed the woman's face. The emotion was so rare here that Carter had almost forgotten what optimism looked like. 'You've got a plan?' asked Adella.

'I do.' Carter explained the bare bones of his scheme in hushed tones, watching her face light up as she dared to believe there could be an existence beyond this floating hell they had been imprisoned in.

'That could work!' she said, after he'd finished.

'Nobody's ever escaped from here?' said Carter. 'Sure people have. They must have. It's just the Vandians aren't exactly going to encourage workers to carve statues of all the slaves clever and courageous enough to break out of their damn mine.'

'How can I help you?'

'Lend me a hand sounding people out. See who wants to go with us. We'll need five or six people. And someone with experience flying transporters ... that's essential. People we know from back home – they need to be strong, mind and body. It would be fine if Duncan agreed to join. Only people we can trust. You know the rumours about informants among the miners? Maybe even Vandian agents pretending to be slaves?'

Adella nodded, eagerly. 'I can do that.'

'You can. And you forget about hiding those filthy tubers under your mattress. That's no way to think. Once you start considering that path ...'

Adella appeared abashed. 'I won't ask you again.'

'The Vandians think we're savages. To them, we're no better than those spear-carrying wild men that live north of Rodal, raiding the fringes of the league. The empire underestimates us. That's their weakness. All we need to do to escape from this floating hell is be smarter than they believe we're capable of.'

'Clean those bandages carefully,' said a voice behind them. 'Now we've got a new sky mine tethered to the station, you're going to find out how much a man sweats at this altitude.'

Carter swivelled around. It was Owen. *How long has he been standing there?* 'Seeing as how we've done such a stand-up job of taking the claim, I thought Helrena Skar might give her hitters the rest of the week off.'

'We'll see deliveries of working rations dropped off by the supply ships,' said Owen. 'That's as much of a holiday as I've ever known in the sky mines. Unless you count coming close to starving when there's no claim to work, which I don't.'

Adella removed the last of the bandages and left to wash the blood off her hands.

Carter pulled his tunic back over his wounds. 'No feast days for the Vandians, then? Don't they believe in God – not even a temple filled with heathen gods?'

'No hell full of horned stealers or heaven packed with winged ethereals. Best I can tell, the Vandians revere their emperor first and their ancestors second,' said Owen. 'A living god and a bunch of effigies to their grandparents in their shrines.'

'Hell of an ego, there,' laughed Carter. 'Vandians taken to worshipping themselves!'

Owen pointed at Adella, cleaning her hands in the basin at the far end of the barracks. 'You might want to tone down your own ego, Mister Carnehan. Hope can keep you alive up here for a little while. But once a person realises it's a false hope being dangled in front of them …'

'I have high hopes for the future, Mister Paterson,' said Carter. 'Don't reckon I've got false ones.'

Owen shook his head, sadly. 'I hope you survive for long enough to be disappointed, then.'

Carter snorted as the man walked off. *Just long enough to get off this bloody rock.*

Adella returned and asked him to help her get new bandages from the supply chambers. They were on the far side of the station, ten minutes' walk through the passages. He was becoming far too conversant navigating the maze of old tunnels. *It really is time to get out of here.* After they found the chamber, he pulled open the door and switched the light on inside. Canvas-covered crates piled high against all three bare stone walls. He pulled covers off, and as he turned, he saw that Adella had dropped her slave's robe to the floor, was standing there pale under the dim electric light. She pushed him gently down against one of the crate's canvas tops, her mouth pressing against his, brushing his upper lip.

'We can't!' protested Carter. 'You know what they've said they'll do to any woman who gets pregnant on the station.'

'But we never do,' said Adella. 'You must have heard the noises coming from the showers late at night. Everyone's doing it. The water here's laced with something that prevents women becoming pregnant, a chemical. I've heard as much from the old hands.'

'But it can't work all of the time.'

'It works,' she said, untying her hair and letting it fall behind her. 'They don't want trained miners too weak to work, pleading their belly. And what's the point of waiting? There's hundreds of ways we can die in the sky mines. This is the only way I know we can be happy. The Vandians can't take this away from us.'

'I don't know ...'

She moved closer to him. 'I trust you, Carter. You're the only man here who has what it takes to lead a breakout. And I know you're going to take me with you when you do. We're not back home anymore, are we? All the rules and the way things should be while courting ... they don't count for spit out here. We need to live while we can. Why should I die without knowing you properly?'

Adella had a point, and Carter was moving beyond the time he could resist her entreaties, the heat in his blood swelling to match hers.

'Nobody else here understands you like I do,' said Adella. 'You're the only one who deserves me. Who deserves ... this. So this is what I would like you to do ...' She whispered in his ear.

Carter did as he was bid until his head spun. He felt guilty and foolish ... flirting with danger, but the lust inside him was too overwhelming now. Carter could as much stop what was happening here as he could halt breathing. It might be wrong; but there were a hundred worse acts when they were both imprisoned to a lifetime of labour, and none of them under his control.

The next day Carter came across Kerge in one of the equipment bays, a large chamber filled with machines, devices covered by tarpaulin, others stored in wooden crates on beds of slugs made of a white substance he couldn't put a name to. The gask lay in the shadows of a large drilling unit, tinkering with the machinery, a crescent of tools spread out across a leather blanket as if the twisted man was a surgeon about to operate on his patient. A couple of slaves worked at the far end of the chamber, moving the components of a conveyor belt onto antigravity stones to carry them across to the new sky mine.

Nobody was close enough to hear their conversation, which was just the way he wanted it.

'You got a minute?' asked Carter.

The gask pulled himself out from under the drilling unit, sitting down beside his tools. 'Are you here to help construct the new sorting lines on the station roof?'

'I'm about a little mischief,' said Carter. He pointed to the little silver machine only just visible poking out of a leather tool satchel. 'Like stealing parts to rebuild yourself a new abacus box.'

'I only took components from machines beyond repair,' said Kerge. 'They were of no use to anyone except me. I do not consider that theft, only the optimum use of resources.'

Carter raised his hands openly. 'You'll get no complaints from me. I like a little initiative. Only thing that's going to keep us alive up here. Is it as good as the box you had back in the forests? You can use it to tell the future?'

'I am not a fortune teller, manling,' complained Kerge. 'This merely helps me study the boughs of the great fractal tree. The future is what you make of it. It is free will which navigates the branches. Free will is the true substance of the universe.'

'But if something was going to happen,' continued Carter, 'and it was significant enough, it would register on your sums?'

'Only in the near-term,' said Kerge, 'and even then, those events wouldn't be guaranteed.'

'Back in Northhaven, if there was a drought, we'd send people out to the forests to speak with your elders. They'd tell the farmers when the best chance of planting seeds was, so crops could make it to harvest time.'

'This is not the point of our studies. I am sure the elders were merely being polite to your emissaries. We are polite to everyone.'

'But they weren't guessing, were they?' said Carter.

'*Guessing*,' spluttered Kerge, as near to indignation as Carter had ever seen the humble gask get. 'Do you know how long it takes to master probability science? How many hours of study a gask must spend before he or she is considered even a neophyte of the greatest of disciplines?'

'Kerge, I know you've got a brain that would make the brightest engineer in Weyland weep like a fool at his own stupidity. And I've got a good use for your smarts. I need to know when the next eruption is due, when that monster of a stratovolcano is next going to blow.'

'Please tell me you are not trying to curry favour with the overseers here?' said Kerge. 'Attempting to buy your barracks extra rations by using foreknowledge? The Vandians will not free you for it, they will hold on to you all the tighter, like a prized pack animal.'

'You might not want to know how I'm planning to use what you tell me.'

'I am straining to maintain a low profile on the station,' said Kerge. 'Apart from myself, there is only one other slave here who is twisted far from the common pattern of manlings, and I am only tolerated as a useful tinkerer of machines. If the Vandians realise the true extent of my differences from the common pattern, I will end up in a zoo or on an imperium dissection table.'

'The Vandians won't hear about your talents from me,' said Carter. 'And if you like, I might be able to solve those problems of yours with a little passage out of the sky mines in the near future ...'

'I can discern no path ahead of us where an escape attempt leads to anything except death and disaster,' said Kerge. 'We must stay here and conserve our strength.'

'Hope for the best, but plan for the worst,' said Carter. 'Help me out. I just need your best guess on when Old Smoky down below is going to start spewing again. That's not too much to ask, is it?'

Kerge sighed, but reached for his abacus box all the same. 'So be it. But I see no good coming from this, and I do not need to contemplate the branches of the great fractal tree to tell you *that*. If this foreknowledge is for use in some hasty escape attempt you are concocting, I beg you to reconsider.'

Carter shrugged noncommittally. *Fine for you to talk about sitting around and contemplating matters. If Adella and I had a snug place in the repair bays fixing the Vandians' toys for them, maybe we might bide our time for a while too. But we are where we are. And whatever my future is to be, it sure won't be dying in a tunnel with a pickaxe in my hand.*

EIGHT

CITY OF THE AIR

Jacob walked back down the corridor in the *Night's Pride* with Sheplar Lesh. Like the rest of the enormous aircraft, its interior was formed from some kind of hardened paper. As strong as oak, but weight for weight, as light as the wax-paper a butcher wrapped around his wares. Jacob was lucky he had managed to convince the carrier's captain to permit Sheplar and himself access to the carrier's navigation chamber to check the course of their journey against Carter's travels. Naturally, the 'convincing' had come in the form of a generous transfer from Jacob's dwindling stock of trading coins. *This crew could give old Master Lettore a run for its reticence when it comes to guild secrets.* Their merchant carrier was heading for the Kingdom of Hangel. The only thing Jacob knew about the nation was that someone out there needed a hell of a lot of firearms, shells and ordinance. They would be in the air for four weeks, covering nearly sixty thousand miles, yet barely making a dent in the distance that they needed to cover to catch up with Carter. Most of the ground they passed over was lightly populated. A few tiny settlements. Grass plains that stretched forever like a vast yellow ocean of scrub and dirt. It made him glad he was flying over it, not riding through it. And it gave him feelings of insignificance. Not for the first time, Jacob felt doubts well inside him.

Jacob looked at Sheplar. 'What the hell can have happened to Carter and Northhaven's taken to have travelled so far in such a short period of time? It doesn't seem possible.'

'You must have faith in Khow's ability to track his son,' said Sheplar.

'Faith? Sad to say, friend, that vessel's been leaking ever since Mary died.'

Jacob rested a hand against the hull. Beyond a porthole, Jacob could see the carrier's main wings stacked above each other tri-plane fashion, connected by struts each the diameter of a lighthouse. The aircraft's hangars were visible too, slung under the lowest wing, the tiny black dots of scout planes landing and taking off. You learnt to tune out the constant humming from hundreds of propellers after a few days on board, but the rotors' vibration was always there running gently through the fuselage. The town-sized carrier was rarely quiet. Children playing; the honk of livestock in pens; orders being called between aircrew. The *Night's Pride* wasn't anything like the decks of any nautical vessel Jacob had trod. Her interior had been divided into two areas – functional sections like the bridge and the cargo holds and the navigation rooms, and open neighbourhoods where walls were painted with frescos, surfaces decorated with colourful engravings of unfamiliar gods and totems. They even had chambers where plants grew … miniature vegetable gardens flooded with light from cathedral-tall stretches of glass. Other vaults where hundreds of market stalls sat arranged across stepped levels, ladders on the walls leading up to family lodgings where passengers could glimpse vignettes of family life through open doorways. Men and women taking tea together on ornate rugs, children studying and scratching across blackboards, arguments between spouses, games of chance. A society in the sky, paying its way by transporting goods and passengers across the vast distances of the world below. There were people born in these corridors who had never been on the ground and had little desire to go there, either. The locals were polite enough towards Jacob, Sheplar, Khow and Sariel, but they talked of life on the dirt as if it was another world. *To them perhaps, it is.*

'I know it sounds contrary coming from a churchman,' added Jacob, 'but I never was that comfortable taking on faith those things which I can't explain.'

'There are many things with which I am uncomfortable, Jacob of Northhaven. The strangeness of being on an aircraft of this size. Not being able to pilot her. Not being able to grapple with the crosswinds and feel the spirits of the wind. But the rightness of the direction in which we travel, that I do not doubt. It is a true wind that carries the *Night's Pride*. As far away from home as we are, that much I know. It is a *true* wind.'

'Not much of an aircraft as far as your people are concerned, I guess,' said Jacob. 'Sure wouldn't be able to take this bird down onto a landing field in one of your canyons.'

'She is the right size for what her crew require,' said Sheplar. 'As is a flying wing for what the skyguard needs.'

'When I was living at the monastery in Rodal, Brother Frael and I would watch your flying wings skim past. He would say that you were flying with the angels. He'd use the ancient name for them, the *ethreaal*, and declare they were the same as your wind spirits.'

'There are many spirits in the wind.'

'There's quite a few angels mentioned in the good book, too.' *Maybe one from the heavenly host to look after us up here. That would be nice.*

'You have evil spirits in your faith?' asked Sheplar.

'Fallen angels, you mean?' said Jacob. 'Devilish spirits? In our church we know them as *stealers*, for the way they steal their way into the hearts and minds of men, and cause all sorts of wickedness.'

'We say much the same about the evil spirits of the wind,' said Sheplar. 'Although I think that is often too easily an excuse for a person's lack of honour. To blame your actions and omissions on the wind.'

'I reckon you've got a point there.' *Maybe one that's a little too close to home.*

'Your friend the monk sounds much like my uncle,' said Sheplar. 'He raised me inside the temple at Yundak. He was a powerful wind chanter and rose high within the order there.'

'What about your parents?'

'My mother died giving birth to me. My father was a skyguard pilot. He perished when I was seven, driving off an incursion of nomads from the north. A ballista bolt struck his plane.'

'I reckon he would have been proud to see you following in his footsteps.'

'It's a hard thing to live up to a father's name,' said Sheplar. 'Shamar Lesh was renowned as one of the greatest pilots in the skyguard. My family always expected me to follow in his path. In truth, I would rather have been a wind chanter like my uncle. A simple, ordinary life, helping those who make pilgrimages to the temple.'

Jacob nodded. Perhaps it wasn't only Sheplar's honour that the pilot was chasing on this pursuit into the infinite. It was his dead father's. Maybe that explained why a single mountain pilot had seemed so eager to take on an entire bandit squadron over the skies of Northhaven.

'A name's something you can find yourself running from, or hiding behind.' *Or something to bury in an empty coffin.* 'You shouldn't regret your choice to be a flier. Your mountains are the walls of the league, keeping us safe from the hordes and nomads beyond.'

'Walls that we live on,' said Sheplar. 'Not that we begrudge our duty. The spirits gave us rocks to live on so that we may grow hardy, and powerful winds that we may breathe pure air, and savages to the north for neighbours so that we will never grow lazy. That is what my uncle taught. What of you? Do you have family back in Weyland?'

'Carter's all I have left,' said Jacob. 'I was an only child. My father died in an accident on our farm. My mother passed soon after, not in any good way.' *No, not in any good way at all.*

'All winds must wane,' said Sheplar. 'We must live while we can.'

As the local sales agent for the Landsman Weapons Works, Hayden Gant knew a few things about guns and the men who used them. As he was bundled into his own dark warehouse and had the hood pulled away from his face, he realised that the ruffian pointing a pistol in his direction was not a novice in their use.

'I don't have keys to the safe,' spluttered Hayden. Three men stood in the dark open space, all bigger than a fella had a right to be. The moonlight through the skylight painted them in pale, admonitory colours. Two of the cut-throats lounged against a stack of rifle crates, while the third's face was almost invisible under a military cap.

'It's not your money we're interested in,' growled the man with the pistol.

'Well, if it's arms you're after, you're already standing in my damn warehouse.'

'No, we've got enough of them too.'

'Then why the hell have you snatched me up?'

'Your cargo that left yesterday. You shipped it to a crew of Tourian traders on an aircraft called the *Night's Pride*.'

'That sounds plausible.'

'It should do, since it happened. I want to know where those traders are heading with your shipment?'

'I wouldn't last long as an agent if I was to go running my mouth off about my clients' business, would I?'

The man leaned forwards with the pistol and slapped him hard across the face with it. 'How long you're going to last, that should be a pressing concern for you. And right now, it depends on whether you've got a destination for those guns you sold. Where are they going? Who're the weapons being shipped to?'

To give Gant his due, his concern for his reputation lasted until the strangers put a bullet in his left knee to match the one they blasted into his right. His worries about how he would walk again ... those disappeared right after he spilled his guts, telling his captors everything they wanted to know.

Major Alock waited by the body of the warehouse's night watchman, the guard's throat expertly slit from behind. His three troopers carefully locked the warehouse behind them, leaving the salesman's corpse lying alongside his crates and cargo.

'Guns are going to a country called Hangel for the local monarch, some grandee called the Grand Duke Pavlorda. It's southwest of here ... a couple of weeks in the air to reach it.'

'Well, lieutenant, the king charged us with looking after the pastor and his expedition. It'd be remiss of us to leave him travelling all alone in the world, wouldn't it?'

'Yes *sir*.'

Willow sat uncomfortably on a stool behind the grading line; a conveyor belt carrying a never-ending stream of rubble from the tunnels the slaves bored into the new mine. Their station lay moored to the fresh strike by a lattice of chains and swaying rope-walks; close enough to make the vertiginous crossing in a minute. After all, the slaves' time was a commodity now, and the Vandians were wasting none of it in the efficient stripping of resources from the new rock. It was a pity, Willow mused, that their owners' concern didn't extend to making the slaves more productive by introducing a few comforts – like cushions for hard seats. Or masks to hold back the choking dust that seemed to coat everything in the hastily erected structure where she had been set to work. Willow had watched the mill assembled with unbelievable speed. Metal ribs laid down like the supports of a barn, a fine metal mesh draped over it. Then the mesh sprayed with something that looked like porridge, but set as hard as stone. A couple more hours to move in the conveyor lines and the grading machinery, before running out rails from the mine head into the hall. And, just like that, Willow had the first manual job of her life. It wasn't work she could have ever imagined doing. What would Benner Landor have thought, having forbidden her any avenue of employment except occasionally helping him administer the family estate? And that only as a sideline when she wasn't being tutored in the gentle world of female accomplishments intended to bring her a suitably titled husband. Willow had been allowed to dabble in the estate, but not to do anything that interfered with her father's management. How that had eaten at her. She was every bit her brother's equal, and had shown more application and stomach for the smooth running of the family's holdings than Duncan ever had. While Duncan had been out drinking with his friends, Willow worked in the office, studying which lands suited which crops. Mastering the business of trade contracts and exports and duties, which unions were important, which tenant farmers were open to modern methods of farming and which too traditional to consider any of the excellent suggestions documented in the annals of the *Royal Farming Journal*. Yet when Willow stood in the same room as her useless brother, the only suggestions solicited, the only person that seemed to matter to her father, was Duncan. Her father had forgotten that he had built the house up in partnership with the help of Willow's mother. He worked hard to forget, that much Willow could see. Perhaps that was why Willow wandered the estate half-invisible to Benner Landor. She had too much of her mother in her; from her freckles to the rich curls of her crimson hair. Maybe Benner found too much of his wife in his daughter, and Willow's old existence had been her punishment ... sidelined and forever destined to be the spare to the heir. As good a breeder as any mare in their stables, or sow in their pens. Well, fate had surely found a way to remind Willow that a life of indolent luxury was not the worst thing that could befall any Weyland woman. What would Benner Landor say if he could see his fine, cultured daughter now? A human cog in a mining machine, sweating alongside hundreds of other slaves. Sorting rubble, scanning it with brick-sized machines and then tossing rocks back into the appropriate metal bin. One for neodymium, others for erbium, promethium, samarium and lanthanum. These were the rare ores the slaves sorted for. All the basic deposits such as iron and lead were hauled off the station for smelting. The women in Willow's grading hall only looked for the gems – quite literally.

No, Benner Landor wouldn't have been impressed to see Willow coughing from the dust, swigging greedily from a canteen to replace liquids she sweated like a pig, her nails torn and broken from handling rocks. Her simple slave's tunic streaked with dirt and grime and smelling ranker than the lowliest farmhand working the Landor fields. Her throat dry and gritty, her muscles aching from fourteen-hour shifts, her belly grumbling from the lack of food. Willow had started out from a lower base than the other slaves – women who were already used to the demands of hard manual labour. Even working in a Northhaven store meant early rises and lugging stock about; a whole day on your feet – and that was easy work compared to the farm labour which provided the bulk of employment back home. Willow had experienced none of it. Lacking a dozen servants with nothing better to do than follow after her, she struggled with the physical demands of the work. If there was one consolation, it was that at least she could set herself to the task without whining or complaining about everything she had lost. In stark contrast to Adella Cheyenne, who was trying everyone's nerves with her continual histrionics and dizzy spells as the workload got on top of her. If Adella hadn't noticed, there was a hall's worth of slaves new to the same hard labour. Swaying on the line, trying to ignore the throbbing in their heads from the sun beating down on the grading line's roof. Working in heat so thick you could slice it with a knife and ladle it alongside the thin portions of barley gruel slopped out here for sustenance. What Willow's brother and Carter Carnehan saw in this manipulative little hellion, she would never know. Sadly, for Willow, the damn woman's lack of productivity was similar to that of a Landor heir unused to anything more strenuous than a little light docket punching. So Adella had scored a seat right next to Willow. *If that isn't an inducement to up my piecework rate, I don't know what is.*

Willow should have been glad that the manipulative woman had judged this an auspicious time to throw Duncan over in favour of Carter Carnehan. Instead, it niggled at Willow that she had swapped the targets of her dubious charms. Of course, Duncan was well shot of the trophy-hunting tigress. The very thought of having Adella Cheyenne swanning around Hawkland Park being coldly indifferent to the servants while insisting on being called Mrs Landor was enough to make Willow shudder. Willow had hoped that Adella would find some amiable overseer on the station to transfer her transparent attentions to. Some clod of a man with muscles where his brains should be. Maybe Carter Carnehan fitted that model to a degree. Carter surely acted like a fool around Adella – although Willow couldn't hold that against him specifically as a crime. Almost every male in Northhaven above the age of fourteen could be wrapped around her fingers with a similar degree of ease. But Carter didn't deserve to have Adella Cheyenne stringing him along. It wasn't any more than that. Any hot flushes she felt in Carter's presence were surely the result of her annoyance at his bull-headed ways. There would never have been a more unsuitable match than one between the heiress to half the prefecture and the wild, uncivilised, penniless son of a churchman. *You're just a slave now*, a voice within Willow reminded her. Same as everyone else here ... including Carter. *Shut up.* She pinched herself, annoyed. *Even slaves have standards. Carter Carnehan means nothing to me. Nothing.*

'They've speeded up the belt again. I don't know how they expect us to sort this mess with them running the line so fast,' said Adella, her voice as sour as vinegar.

'I believe they expect us to get faster as we work longer on the line,' sighed Willow.

'It's fine for them,' said Adella, her head nodding towards the slaves sitting down the line, quick hands dancing across the grading belt. 'They're used to paupers' work in the mills and barns back home. You need to apply the right tool for the right job ... but I'm wasted here. Haven't they got a bureau that needs organising? These ores have to be shipped somewhere, and the rocks are going to need dockets and requisitions to be on their way.'

Willow swept the scanner over the rubble in front of her. Its display indicated lutetium deposits and she seized the rocks before they disappeared, tossing them into the appropriate bin behind her. Yes, this must be a far cry from the council rooms where Adella's father had secured a nice cushy sinecure for her. No men to wheedle into doing the bulk of the work for her. Adella probably wouldn't be satisfied in the sky mines until she was sitting on a plump cushion with a couple of slaves standing over her with palm leaves, fanning her useless carcass. Unfortunately for Adella, the grading line already had a supervisor. One of the old hands who had survived the last sky mine's destruction – a tall woman called Kassina Hedgepeth. She must have been fat in her previous life; only loose jowls left as a reminder of where plump flesh had once hung. In Kassina's case, her flat face, a bulbous nose that really *belonged* on a fatter woman, didn't improve her looks. Well, beauty wasn't a great deal of use for a slave: didn't stop cave-ins burying you, didn't help you sort faster, or earn you better rations.

'Grab the largest rocks first!' Kassina called towards Willow and Adella, not pausing from her slow promenade around the hall. 'I only want to see rock dust and crumbs reaching the end of this line. And yell long before your bin gets filled up. Give the runners time to wheel you empty bins before you have to halt work.' She didn't stop to make sure she had been heard and understood, marching down the line and calling for an oil can to fix a roller jamming under the belt. It would be a few minutes before the line supervisor returned into earshot, and all around them, hushed voices started talking as they worked. The men had it easier in that regard. Willow had even heard singing coming out of the tunnels. Their supervisors only cared that the quotas were met.

'Dust and crumbs,' spat Adella. 'That's all we get to eat here anyway.'

A slave walked down the line with a leather drinking sack, pushing its nozzle into each woman's grateful mouth, allowing them to take a gulp or two before moving on to the next slave. Willow tried to keep working when it was her turn, fighting back a coughing fit as the metallic-tasting liquid flowed down her throat in pulses. Then it was Adella's turn, the woman complained bitterly: how the water was too warm and was making her feel sick.

'I'll make sure yours has ice in it next time,' snapped the slave on hydration duty. It was all too easy to feel queasy here. The heat. The thin air. The light touch of gravity at altitude. The rations that never seemed to fill the hole left by the long, back-breaking work. But everyone on the line felt the same, and having to sit next to some imbecile whining about it didn't help alleviate the symptoms. *No, not one little bit.*

Adella looked daggers at the slave as she carried her water down the line. 'It doesn't matter. Carter has a plan to get back home, and then the overseers and their stupid sky miners can grub around to their heart's content after every rock that comes out of the volcano.'

'Show some caution,' warned Willow. 'Lower your voice. You need to put a brake on Carter's foolishness, or you're going to get him, yourself and everyone involved tossed off the station minus a parachute.'

'Caution won't do. We're getting out of here.'

'Adella, you have to face the facts of our situation.'

'What facts do you know? *None.*'

'I know we were on that Vandian warship for over two weeks,' said Willow. 'And I discovered from the hangar crew that the average speed of one of those metal monsters at high altitude is five thousand miles an hour. That's straight from the Vandian who trained our transporter pilots to fly.'

'So? So what?'

'Haven't you got half a brain? Take the speed and the time in the air and do the sums,' said Willow. 'That puts us at least one and a half million miles away from Northhaven. Even if you escaped the mines and hitched a ride with a caravan that was heading in the right direction and willing to harbour a runaway slave, it would take you four hundred years to reach Northhaven. Travelling by aircraft, it would be more than twenty years in the air. Can you fly? If you stole a plane, have you got a line of friendly fuel dumps along the way?'

Adella's face turned pale. 'You're wrong! That's just horseshit talked by the empire and the supervisors to put us off from escaping.'

'I know how long it takes to move a cargo around,' said Willow. 'By barge, by wagon, by train, by air.' She angrily grabbed one of the rocks in front of her. 'I may not be much good at *this*, but I know the average speed of a caravan. Lord knows, I had to plan the freight often enough for the house's harvests.'

'But Carter's got a plan ...'

'Then I hope it involves boarding the huge battleship that carried us here. I hope it involves overpowering the close to two thousand sailors that crew her decks. Because that's the only way you're returning to Northhaven in this lifetime.'

From the look on Adella's face, Willow almost regretted bursting the woman's bubble. But wishful thinking and an absence of planning wasn't going to achieve anything other than throwing them down a worse hole than the one they already found themselves stuck in.

'But he's getting ready,' said Adella. 'Stealing a transporter; getting off the station. Carter has the others from the town raring to go. Eshean, Joah ...'

'Well, you've got to talk sense into them. Because by the sounds of it, all they're going to do is get themselves dead. I understand how Carter thinks. Not a wall he comes across that won't fall with a good hard kick. But this wall has a canyon-sized drop hiding behind it.'

'We can't stay here,' protested Adella. A genuine look of fear settled across her features as the reality of their situation began to sink in. 'We're being worked to death on the line. Just cogs in a machine grinding us down. You saw the corpses of our people dragged off the new rock – how bust up Carter was left. Duncan too. They'll die before we do; leave us here alone with nobody. I couldn't bear that. In a couple of years we'll be old hands, no different to Kassina over there. Everyone we know dead, our body chewed up by work. And that's if we're *lucky* – if we survive!"

'Well, it's not a pretty thought,' said Willow.

'Any life has to be better than that. Even if we don't get home. Just living in the wilderness, not trapped inside the sky mines.'

'Maybe. But we don't know much about life in the imperium, beyond the fact they've paid for us and branded us.' She tapped her shoulder. 'The Vandians will know we're slaves wherever we go.'

'I need hope, Willow. I need hope to live.'

Yes, I could do with a helping of that myself.

'You've got to think of something,' begged Adella. 'If you know how far we've been taken, you can work out a way to get out of here. It's your brains that Carter needs.'

Not that he knows it. Despite herself, Willow couldn't help feeling sorry for Adella. How desperate must she be to consider enlisting Willow's help in escaping? But there wasn't much of use Willow remembered from her library. Maybe some platitudes by philosophers who had been imprisoned for most of their lives. About how your mind always remained free, however bad your external circumstances grew. But Adella Cheyenne didn't want to hear truisms. It was plans for a warship and the means to build it that she wanted.

'It's a miracle we need,' sighed Willow. Her brooding was interrupted by a commotion outside the front of the grading hall, a runner entering the structure and calling for the overseer. Old Kassina rushed back like a shot. A brief, hurried conversation, then she strode down the line and called orders to the workers, exhorting them to work harder and faster.

'Not any quicker,' groaned Adella. 'We're new to this.'

'New to *real* work, perhaps,' barked Kassina, overhearing the worker's complaints. 'At least *pretend* to look like you've done a full day's graft in your life. Princess Helrena is coming to inspect the initial deposits. The mistress is accompanied by two of the house's allies – her cousin Baron Machus, and half-sister, Elanthra Skar.' She strutted down the line, clapping her hands and shouting warnings about looking tardy in front of the visitors.

Princess Helrena. The bitch who put a scar across Carter's face. It was the imperial noblewoman's fault that they had ended up here. Willow felt a deep loathing rise within her. Willow wasn't used to hating, but she could learn the skill when it came to their cursed *mistress*. At the mere suggestion they would be encountering the ruthless princess again, Adella seemed to find a newly discovered reserve of speed. Her fingers flickered across the rubble, scanning, sorting and filling the bins behind the belt. 'Why us?' moaned Adella. 'Why us? With all the countries closer to Vandia they could have raided for slaves.'

I swear, if Adella were twice as smart, she'd be a half-wit. 'If you're going to play the highwayman, you don't stand outside your own house to rob travellers. Weyland's far enough away that the imperium's not going to find an angry skyguard squadron turning up looking for revenge.' *And their taste for slaving aside, we must be savages compared to them.*

When Helrena Skar swept into the hall, the noblewoman looked little different from her appearence in the bandit carrier, arriving to purchase her new labour force. A retinue of guardsmen followed Helrena, two fellow nobles accompanying her at the front of the party. One of them was a woman wearing similar finery to Helrena. Princess Elanthra, presumably, her face as cold as a block of ice. Hard edges that might have been sculpted from porcelain, a short black bob of a haircut that gave her an androgynous quality. A brooding hulk of man trailed after them. Baron Machus – his brutal features only made less dangerous by the dim look of comprehension he wore on his face. If the distance between the three of them was any guide, Willow pegged the hard-looking man as the closer of the princess's two allies. There seemed to be a tension in the air at odds with a mere tour of the spoils. The slaves who worked the line might as well have been invisible. Their contempt set Willow's nerves on edge; her toil superfluous to whatever machinations were these nobles' concern today. Was that how tenant farmers had felt back at Northhaven? Willow and her father riding past in a sleek carriage and Willow with as little care for their names as these three? *How the tables have turned.* There were doubtless more than a few working beside Willow secretly pleased to see a Landor heir brought low ... made to toil at this drudgery. Willow stared at the group. She spotted a girl of around thirteen of fourteen years standing next to a bald retainer in grey robes. It seemed an age since Willow had seen someone too young to survive the sky mines' labour camp. She had forgotten that children even existed in the world. This one was no slave or servant, though; not if the luxurious cut of her uniform was anything to go by. She wore her blonde hair in elaborate curls, cascading down the side of an elaborately engraved breastplate. The young girl peered curiously around the sorting hall, as if this was the first time she'd seen it. The man whose hand she was holding looked like a slave, though. Albeit one far better fed than any sky-mining vassal. Willow was curious about the girl's presence, so out of place here, but she concentrated on working the conveyor belt instead. The three visitors halted near enough for Willow to eavesdrop on their conversation over the grading line's clatter.

'You!' snapped Princess Elanthra at the local overseer. 'Bring me the tally for the day's sort.'

Kassina returned with a sheet detailing how much had been

separated. Princess Helrena made a point of receiving it first, only then passing it across to her half-sister.

'A tonne of terbium, another of samarium and cerium. Very good. That will bring in over seventy thousand taels at the next market release.'

'It *would* have brought in that much,' corrected Helrena, taking the tally sheet and dismissively tossing it back at the supervisor.

'What do you mean, *would*?' asked Elanthra, her tone as cutting as her sharp cheekbones. 'Have you some other way to dispose of the load, rather than through the registered brokers?'

'Oh, I have found another way,' said Helrena. 'I have a method of selling it off that means I will retain your share of the cut!'

'My share? You are missing the point of our alliance. You share from my strikes as I share from yours. We spread the risk of not returning with a serviceable strike from the eruptions.'

'Yes, risk,' snorted Helrena. 'And how will you spend the money from *my* strike? I know how you should spend it, Elanthra. Buy more fuel and actually use it to send transporters to your allies' assistance. Because my slaves had to take this sky mine all on their own. Fresh meat, barely trained, and you left me out there to swing. How much *risk* did you take doing that?'

'My slaves were in the air,' argued Elanthra. 'Doing the same as your workers … looking for a strike. We were too far away to assist you. This is outrageous. If I had staked a rock and you had returned empty handed, you would be first in the queue with your hand out, demanding your tithe of what's mined. This is a transparent ploy to renege on our agreement! You are looking to cheat me out of what is mine.'

'I'm not looking to cheat you, I *am* cheating you,' said Helrena. 'Do you think I am stupid? Did you think my spies wouldn't learn you're working with Prince Phemus. You agreed to stay out of the fray and let him steal any rock we went after.'

'And where is your proof? Does your paranoia include accusing Machus here? Have you not wondered where his slaves were? Why none of his hitters came to your aid?'

'His slaves were bringing home their own strike, a sky mine twice the size of this one. Although I am informed his rock is filled only with low-grade ores.'

'You are well informed, cousin, as always,' said Baron Machus, his voice a deep, slow timbre, as though he was working to join each word in the sentence. 'You are lucky, Helrena. But then, you always were. Less to dig out, and every tonne your workers take filled with riches.' He moved over to the sorting line directly in front of Willow and Adella, running his hands over the rubble. He lifted the scanner out of Adella's fingers, examined the readout, and then gave the device back to her. 'Samarium and cerium. God's teeth! How much is cerium worth on the metals exchange at the moment? You will more than make up for the losses incurred by the destruction of your last mine. Yes, lucky. Even your slaves here are beautiful.' He reached out and placed his ham-sized fingers around Adella's cheeks, tilting her face back and forth as if he was a traveller examining a mare at market. Wisely, other than her surprise at being singled out, Adella didn't bridle or flinch. 'You should see the dogs I have working on my station.'

Helrena shrugged. 'That's only because you've already cleared out every woman with her own set of teeth and tossed them into your harem.'

'Ah, what a waste.' From the lustful glint in the prince's dim eyes, Willow didn't think the baron was referring to the fact that the ores coming down the conveyor belt belonged to his cousin. 'You should sell this one to me. Let me scrub her up a little and see if I can't find the diamond among the discard.' He winked slyly towards Adella.

'These northern barbarians are tough workers,' said Helrena. 'But they're from the wilds. You go dipping your wick with them, who knows what medicine you'll need to cure your manhood afterwards.'

'I don't care what slaves your idiot cousin's biting the pillow with!' interrupted Elanthra. 'If you've no intention of honouring our compact, why am I wasting my time here?'

'So you can carry word back to Prince Phemus,' said Helrena. 'Tell that little turd that it will take more than sabotaging a single claim for my house to lose its mining concession. I'll pay the emperor his tithes on time. With what I'm mining inside this claim, I'll pay our father back double!'

'I demand my share!'

'I'll give you the same derisory stipend you tossed me when I was dry, and the same excuses too.' Helrena picked up a handful of rubble from the belt in her leather-gloved hand and tossed it derogatorily at her half-sister. 'Low-grade dirt for a low-grade ally.'

'You're a welching, oath-breaking bitch,' swore Elanthra. The visiting princess swung around and stalked away, her guards peeling off and flanking her as she departed.

'That was hardly wise,' growled Machus.

'Perhaps not, but it's the best sport I'm going to get this week. Elanthra doesn't have the courage to move against me directly, so instead she tries to bleed me to death. Weaken me until I become an irrelevance and my concession is given to one of Phemus's lapdogs? No! What percentage of my income do you think that dog has been promising Elanthra?'

'Enough, I am sure.'

'You are wrong, it's never enough,' said Helrena. 'You've slept with her, haven't you?'

'Of course, but only out of curiosity. I didn't get much out of it. Like cosying up to a block of ice, all bones and sharp elbows.'

'Well, then, I wouldn't repeat the experience. She can't be trusted.'

'Of course she can. As long as you trust her to endorse whoever looks like winning.'

'If she thinks I'm going to lose, she's as poor a judge of people as she was a partner.'

The two nobles walked off, ignoring the obsequious bows from the sorting line's supervisor. Willow rubbed the sweat off her brow. *We don't even exist to them. They're as careless talking around us as furniture; we matter that little.* Willow sneaked a look at Adella. She was fuming inside over bring groped like a piece of meat. Or was it just that she had been forgotten about – not a feeling that Adella Cheyenne was accustomed to, Willow guessed.

Kassina returned to her normal state of attentive agitation, prowling the belt and exhorting the slaves to throw their backs into it. She halted by Adella and Willow. 'Faster, *faster* now! I've seen cripples sort faster. Put your nose to the grindstone.'

'Why? For those three nobles?' said Willow. 'They don't even get on with each other.'

'You think if the next stake's snatched by the princess's enemies, it'll be *her* starving, girl? Mining forces are only fed when there's work to do. Those disagreements and feuds of theirs are life and death for the likes of us. We rise and fall with the princess's fortunes. When the princess and her staff are talking, you'd better be listening and learning.'

'And what would I learn?' asked Willow.

'That Prince Phemus's aunt is a woman called Circae. She's as mean as they breed them out here, and she lives to see Helrena put out of favour. She wants the imperial throne for *her* nephew. That's not a good situation for us. So throw your back into it. We take our luck with this new rock and we use it to stay alive.'

'I don't need to listen to the princess's oversized pig cousin,' said Adella, petulantly.

'Shut up and work! That sweet little face of yours. Out here, your looks are as dangerous as a purse full of jangling coins in a cave of brigands. You'd be better off without your beauty, better off with *my* face.'

'Who was the young girl standing behind the guards?' asked Willow.

'That's Lady Cassandra Skar, Princess Helrena's daughter.'

'I would not bring a girl to see this sky-borne hell.'

The supervisor shrugged. 'Why not, everything in the sky mines will be hers one day. Besides, Helrena never lets her out of her sight for too long.'

'Forgive me if I don't look upon the princess as the soft and caring sort,' said Willow.

'That child's father was Aivas Skar, one of Circae's sons. The relationship between Helrena and Aivas was not approved. Their two houses have been feuding with each other as long as anyone remembers. The old witch's son was sent to the legions in disgrace, where he died fighting one of Vandia's neighbours. Circae blames Helrena for her son's death, even though it was Circae who sought his demotion from celestial-upper to celestial-lower caste. Circae who had him exiled and as good as got him killed.'

Now Willow saw why the princess kept her daughter close. 'So, Circae wants the granddaughter in her custody? Not for the girl's sake, but as a token of power ... to deprive Helrena of all that remains of her time with Circae's son?'

'You have good instincts,' nodded the supervisor. 'Knowing what's going on behind the scenes and the factions fighting for control here, it can mean the difference between life and death for us. You're correct. Circae would have the child away from Princess Helrena in an instant if the emperor permitted it. She would teach Helrena a lesson she would never forget. But the bonds of motherhood still mean something, even in the imperium. Now, back to your work.'

Willow was disgusted. As stifling as dealing with her family had been back home, the Landors' difficulties were nothing compared to the machinations of the imperial family. What Willow had endured at Hawkland Park was mollycoddling next to this level of animosity. She set her odium aside and continued to toil in the numbing heat, turned into a sweating automaton by the drudgery. Hours of labour later, a slave slipped into the hall bearing a message for Kassina. A brief look of misery crossed the supervisor's face, tempered by annoyance at the interruption. Then she signalled to the engineer running the line to halt production and strode down the conveyor belt, clapping her hands. 'Enough! Enough! Muster outside. Sorting is suspended for a few minutes.'

There was a tension in her words that made Willow believe this wasn't a scheduled maintenance closure. *What now?* No surprises were pleasant for a slave ... that was a lesson Willow had picked up early. The double doors at the end of the structure opened and they filed out, feeling the full force of heat beyond the hall's shade. All around the sky mine's surface, slaves emerged from newly excavated mine works. Many of the men stripped to the waist, bearing the same heavy equipment they had gone down with. Behind Willow hovered their station, tethered tight to the new rock. The princess's craft was docked with the station. In the sky in front of Willow, she watched another rock drawing close, arriving slowly, manoeuvred by a squadron of transporters, cables attached and pulling it through the volcanic mist. A second vessel followed behind the new rock – a long silver arrow of destruction that looked every bit the equal of Helrena's war craft.

'Don't tell me they've found a second sky mine for us to work,' moaned Adella.

'That rock out there's mined out,' said Kassina. 'A barracks station. No work for anyone. This is a tradition ... a ritual. One still required by the emperor.'

More and more slaves left the tunnel works. Their sky mine floated in the atmosphere, exposed to winds and clouds pregnant with hot ash. Soot stung Willow's exposed skin. Face, arms and neck peppered while she waited. There was the old slave, Thomas Gale. The man in charge of managing the station for his Vandian mistress. No sign of Princess Helrena and her two allies. Whatever was about to unfold was obviously beneath the noble visitors. In the sky, the other station grew larger, its passage drawing to a halt in front of them. On its surface, she could see hundreds of slaves lined up at the edge of the mass, also waiting for something. *For us?*

'This is Station Twenty-Two, property of the House of Prince Phemus Skar,' called Thomas Gale. 'It was his noble highness's labour force who fought us for possession of the sky mine we now stand on. The slaves of Prince Phemus fought hard, but they lost, and they now occupy an empty station. They must wait in a state of idleness until the world's bounty is again showered on the imperium. By the grace of Princess Helrena,' continued Thomas Gale, 'the station and flagship of Prince Phemus are permitted entry to her territory for the prince to give the sign required by the emperor.'

Sign? Willow couldn't see any sign from the rocket ship. *What is this?* She waited with the other women from the grading line, none of them speaking. Puzzlement mingled with the relief of any excuse for a break from the grinding sort. The slaves from the rock hauled in front of them stared back just as silently, gazing at Willow and the Weylanders across the chasm of sky. After a minute passed, a flare exploded out of the rival craft's missile tubes, shattering the heavy silence. A green sun left floating down through the hot, gassy fog.

'Green – that's a third,' hissed their overseer, rubbing her cheeks. 'Prince Phemus is a hard bastard. Makes you glad that it's the princess we have as our mistress.'

A Third? Willow was about to ask what the overseer meant when she heard the first screams from the visiting station, figures tumbling down over the rock's edge. The way the slaves' legs flailed with their arms stilled, Willow could tell that their hands had been bound.

Behind the rival slave force, guardsmen with bayonet-tipped rifles marched down the rear of the work force, every third slave stabbed in the spine and thrown forward, falling into the void.

'Let no one think,' boomed Thomas Gale, 'that returning without a sky mine for the imperium is the easy option. The Vandians do not give festival days to idle slaves. This is the emperor's response to laziness and inadequacy.'

Cries and shouts rippled around Willow. Shock. Anger. Revulsion. Even the men from Northhaven booed, many of them still nursing fractured bones and missing friends taken during the fight against these sky miners, rivals who'd tried to steal the rock out from under their feet.

'Is it just hitters, or are there sorters standing over there?' mewled Adella.

'Everyone in the station takes their place,' said Kassina. 'And hopes that the lottery of the count throws the person next to them off the edge while missing them. Even pilots draw lots to see which of them are to haul the station and which must take their chances on the edge. If you fail to work hard enough, that could be *you* standing there.'

Willow held down the meagre contents of her stomach. *And they call us barbarians?* She shivered from the lesson's horror, even as she recognised the cold, terrible logic of the act. Fewer mouths to feed. And the Vandians never had to fear that failure to return with a strike was due to the slaves' desire to slack off between eruptions.

'Our work keeps us alive,' said Kassina. 'And if you're lucky, it helps you forget too.'

With the decimation of the rival slave force complete, the rival warship, station and squadron of transporters withdrew, but Willow could still hear the terrified cries of falling slaves shoved over the edge. And she knew the sound would come back to her every time she gazed into the torrid, gassy sky. That was the point of the demonstration. The slaves returned to their work, many with tears in their eyes, others stumbling back like zombies, a few shaking as though they'd caught cold even in the febrile atmosphere. She marched back to her position on the grading line as it began to rumble back into action. Old Kassina was wrong about one thing. The work didn't help Willow forget.

NINE

THE BARON'S CONSORT

Carter angrily entered the station's refectory, an oblong eating chamber separated from the food preparation area by open serving hatches through which to pass metal plates. There wasn't much preparation that went into the cooking, as far as Carter could see. But with the imperium primarily delivering sacks of grain, there was little to do beyond pouring it into vats, adding water and letting it steam up. Carter never dallied here. Too hot to be comfortable, even by the station's humid standards. If there was one small consolation, it was that the canteen was cooler than labouring inside the sky mine. Carter stared around the long iron tables and found the bench he was looking for – Duncan, Willow, Kerge, Owen and Anna seated heads down, spooning up the contents of their bowls. Carter stormed up to the table and banged its surface in front of Duncan.

'Where is she?'

The heir to the House of Landor glanced up, surprised. 'What are you going on about now?'

'Adella! Her bunk's being cleaned out. What have you promised her to move back to your barracks?'

'I don't know anything about it.'

Carter grabbed Duncan by his slave's tunic and pulled him off the bench. 'You lying piece of—'

Willow leapt up; Owen and Kerge restrained Carter from shaking the truth out of the man. 'Adella isn't bunking in our barracks,' said Willow. 'I swear it.'

'What, you think I'm hiding her under my billet?' said Duncan. 'Maybe she's got tired of you treating her like a hunting hound, fit only to lie at your feet when it suits you.'

Carter resisted the urge to plant his fist in Duncan's face. 'Where is she?'

'I have seen the female,' disclosed Kerge, the gask rubbing the quills around his neck. 'Two hours ago. She was walking with our owner's ally … the Vandian baron and his guards.'

'Baron Machus?' asked Willow.

'Yes.'

Willow groaned, her face turning pale.

'What is it?' asked Carter. 'What do you know?'

'The baron came inspecting the sorting line a couple of days ago,' said Willow. 'He noticed Adella while he here. He suggested he should buy her to Princess Helrena.'

'What!' Carter felt a wave of foreboding fill his gut.

'But the princess refused,' said Willow, hurriedly. 'She told the baron we worked too hard for us to be sold off. Called us dirty barbarians.'

'That's not a refusal!' said Carter. 'That's *haggling*.'

Owen placed a calming hand on Carter's shoulder. 'Let me have a word with Thomas Gale. If a worker's transferred off the station, he will know.'

The old hand ducked out of the canteen chamber, leaving Duncan glowering at Carter. 'She was in *your* barracks, pastor's boy. *You* were meant to be looking out for her.'

'If Adella's been taken as a house slave, there's nothing Carter could've done,' said Anna. 'We're no more than chattels to the empire. Property gets exchanged all the time.'

'She's not property to me!' shouted Carter.

'If you'd been there when Machus and his guards turned up, if you'd tried to stop them taking Adella, they would have beaten you to death, Northhaven.'

'It's not right,' said Duncan.

'We're slaves,' said Anna. 'We don't have rights. If you greenhorns keep thinking like free Weylanders, all you're going to get is dead.'

Owen returned after ten minutes. From the weary look on his face, Carter knew the truth before Owen opened his mouth. 'Her ownership papers have been transferred to Baron Machus. I'm sorry; he's already left the station with her …'

Carter scooped up one of the bowls of gruel and flung it to the floor. 'She is not a piece of property!'

Willow had tears in her eyes. 'I'm sorry, Carter, it's partly my fault. I crushed Adella's hopes. I told her how far from Northhaven we are; how long it would take to travel back home.'

'What?' Carter stared incredulously at her.

'It's four hundred years travelling overland by merchant caravan. Two decades flying on a merchant carrier. That's how long it'd take to reach Weyland even if you escaped the empire.'

'Listen to the woman,' urged Anna. 'We're trapped here, Northhaven. We're marooned and that's the truth of it. If you've got to serve as a bondswoman, being a house slave for a Vandian celestial-upper caste is as good as it gets for us. Adella won't die in a cave-in or be blown up by a misfiring blasting charge. She's never going to be lined up at the edge of the station waiting for some imperial son-of-a-bitch to signal how many have to die for their failure to bring home a rock.'

'As good as it gets.' Carter repeated her words. They were bitter ashes in his mouth.

'I thought Adella was going to talk to you,' said Willow. 'Convince you not to try to escape.'

Duncan had slumped back down to the table, all the fight departed from him. 'Adella can't be gone. She *can't*.'

Carter was spared any more accusations of failing to protect Adella. From the look on Duncan's face, it was clear she had meant something more to the man than just the opportunity to deprive Carter of a victory. *Maybe I've misjudged him?* Carter felt a twinge of guilt over the shallow depth of his feelings for Adella. If it was a competition of true love being run here, then Carter Carnehan had been outpaced.

'I was going to take her with me,' said Carter. Hollow words of comfort for the heartbroken heir to the Landor acres.

'Then perhaps it is better she escaped as she did,' said Anna. 'Because your way would have led to her grave.'

At least my way goes to an end of my own choosing.

Duncan trudged down the stone passage alongside Owen. Since Adella had been stolen from his life, the days seemed to blur into each other. Duncan's numbing workload barely seemed to register on his body. Whether he was hunched down in a tunnel swinging an axe against a rockface, hauling ore out of the tunnels, or pushing carts down to the station's supply chambers with Owen, without Adella he was just going through the motions of living. Duncan knew Willow was worried about him. The change in him was there for everyone to see. *Maybe I should be more like Carter – hard, selfish, indifferent, uncaring?* Adella's disappearance had just seemed to make Carter even more determined to break out of the sky mines. But what about Duncan Landor? Adella had been the ballast for his life at Hawkland Park. He'd been planning to escape his confined existence with her by his side – and in that foolish, childish act of whimsy, he had succeeded. Now he was stranded millions of miles from Northhaven. Duncan thought he was in a prison before, but now he knew what true servitude was. Without Adella, he drifted, lost and aimless. He might die here now, but he would never try to escape. Not without Adella by his side. He would never abandon her, not as long as he clung on to the slim hope that they'd be back together again, somehow.

'You need to get your mind off her,' said Owen, interrupting Duncan's misery. 'People leave, people die. That's our life.'

'How can I?' asked Duncan.

'You lose everyone in the sky mines, eventually. It has always been that way. Perhaps a sixtieth of the workforce I started with are alive now. Of those I count as good friends, only Anna Kurtain survives from the original slave raid.'

'How do you cope with that?'

'You must discover your duty to those around you – help them. Once you're easing others' pain, it becomes easier to forget about your own woes. I've heard what the others from Northhaven say about you … your family has a name that means something.'

'The House of Landor doesn't count for ore dust up here.'

'It counts if *you* count,' said Owen. 'What is your house? Is it the walls of the warehouses where your produce is stored? Is it the bricks of your buildings? Is it the mud of the acres that you work? No, it is *you* and your family, the people you protect in your house. It's the workers you help and the actions you take. Without people, your house is only empty earth waiting to be reclaimed by the weeds.'

The hue of illumination changed inside the passage. They pushed their empty cart through a series of blanket-like curtains, emerging into a corridor lit a dull crimson; wall lamps protected by armoured glass, cables protected behind strong metal conduits. Precautions to stop sparks from setting off their blasting powder stores.

'The mine shouldn't have run out of blasting powder so quickly,' said Owen. 'In the princess's desperation to pay the emperor his tithes, our tunnels are being blown in haste.'

'Nobody's died yet,' said Duncan.

'*Yet*. This rock was picked as a base station because of its stability.' Owen slapped the walls. 'But we haven't properly mapped out the new strike's interior. If a poorly placed charge hits a fault line, it'll split the sky mine apart and spill us into the volcano.'

They pushed through another curtain of blankets, entering a stone passage with four corridors leading off it. Numbers were painted on the walls, marking out the routes.

Owen lifted a leather satchel out of the cart and passed it to Duncan. 'The blasting caps are stored in a chamber at the end of that passage. Fill this bag with caps and then meet me back here. I'm going down to pick up the canisters of blasting powder. If you meet a storeman, have them unlock your repository and then send them down to me to unlock the fire doors to the main magazine.'

Duncan slung the satchel over his shoulder and took the passage Owen had indicated. The air was damp here. A four-minute walk down the passage which ended in an anteroom, two storerooms, big thick metal doors that wouldn't have looked out of place in a bank vault. One storeroom was sealed, but the second's door had been left ajar. *Is there a warehouse man inside, doing inventory?* Duncan pulled open the heavy door, a protesting squeal of unoiled metal, just enough to squeeze past. He found an unadorned oblong chamber with a high ceiling inside. It was filled throughout with shelves stacked with mining equipment. Duncan couldn't see any sign of any storemen, though. Normally, their ranks were drawn from slaves missing limbs and unfit for anything other than light work.

'Hello? I've come for a bag's worth of blasting caps.' Duncan heard a moan from beyond an archway in the wall. Duncan walked over. In the adjoining storeroom was a sight that made his blood freeze. Four dead Vandian soldiers, a pile of murdered slaves too – corpses pooling blood across the stone. Duncan moved warily forward. It appeared as if the men had been shot at close range, gaping wounds surrounded by powder burns. *What the hell's happened here?* The first thought that leapt into Duncan's mind was that this was a slave revolt, part of Carter's madcap scheme to escape. His second thought was that if any Vandian soldiers caught him here, they would hang him as a rebel first and attempt to get to the truth of his presence second. Finishing the soldiers he understood. But why kill the storemen? Had they resisted, too? Did Carter plan to fashion homemade grenades using the blasting powder? Storm the princess's vessel now it had docked with the station again? Take Princess Helrena hostage and demand passage home? *But Carter wouldn't kill his own people, would he? Dear God, surely he wouldn't sink that low?* And to take on the crew of that imperial war vessel, Carter would need the entire station standing behind him. A moan escaped from the piled bodies. One of the Vandians was alive! As Duncan bent down by the man's side, he saw the soldier's pistol holster and sword scabbard were empty.

'What happened here?'

'Betrayed,' coughed the guard. 'We are Cassandra Skar's bodyguard. Our officer tricked us down here. He told us Helrena was inspecting this level and wanted to see her daughter. The bastard led us into an ambush. He has the Lady Cassandra. The lieutenant's taking the girl off the station and selling her to Circae.'

Duncan felt his heart sink at the news. More of the imperials' damn politics. He didn't know whether he should be glad this wasn't Carter's madcap escape attempt, or sad that it wasn't. Another idea leapt into his mind. He could save the princess's daughter. Warn Helrena Skar. *Her only child's being kidnapped. If I can foil the scheme, surely she'll repay me with Adella's return?*

'How many took her? Where are they heading?'

'Three of them,' wheezed the wounded soldier, 'heading for our shuttle in the hangar, but,' he grabbed Duncan's arm and pointed at the dead slaves, 'they're going to blow the station, that's why they killed the storeroom staff. Traitor's wired the magazine for a remote detonation. Kill the princess, kill everyone here … make it look like an accident or a station mutiny. You have to – take the detonator from the lieutenant!'

Duncan's head spun with the news. *Sabotage.* Exactly what was rumoured to have happened to the previous sky mine. Blow the station. Destroy the sky mine tethered to it. Take down the princess and her rocket ship. That bitch Helrena and her Vandian retainers would perish, but every man and woman from Northhaven would die along with them – including Willow.

'Warn the princess,' begged the guard. 'Save the girl.'

Helrena deserves to die a dozen times over for what she's done to us, but … Duncan jumped to his feet and darted to the shelves, filling his sack with blasting caps. They weren't much of a weapon. A cup-sized aluminium disc with a rotating timer on top to set a delay for a fused detonation, a magnetic base to stick it to a canister of blasting powder. But they were all Duncan had to save everyone on the station.

Jacob stepped out of the fat cargo plane with his friends and straight into an argument. The crew of the *Night's Pride* were in heated discussions with a group of officials from the local authorities. Shouting loud enough to be heard over the shuttle aircraft's slowing rotors.

'These new fuel costs are outrageous,' spat one of the fliers. 'How do you expect us to deliver cargoes when you cheat us like this? Is it your plan for us to buy rifles and ammunition for your grand duke and transport them to Hangel as a gift for him? Are we here to trade, or to offer you free samples?'

An ornately uniformed official shrugged. 'The prices are what they are. The crops used to produce the fuel are being raided regularly now. We need the rifles to protect the farms. Then the cost of the fuel will come down.'

'We are not a charity! We do not travel the air to finance the wars of rich noblemen.'

'Then your carrier can fly in circles around Hangel until you run low enough on fuel to reconsider. Perhaps you should jettison your cargo, so you're light enough to reach your next port?'

'Criminals!'

Jacob guffawed. It looked like the locals had the advantage over the trading plane and its merchants of the air. This little city state was located in the middle of nowhere. Jacob had gazed down on nothing but endless plains and savannah during the entire journey. The very logic of Hangel's existence was little more than a staging post between where you were coming from and where you were heading to, and the fuel to make the crossing possible was the only commodity the locals possessed. *Is it any wonder that they use it as leverage?* Given the willingness of the *Night's Pride* crew to gouge them for their passage out of Weyland, Jacob wasn't too unhappy to see the boot on the other foot.

'If they decide to fly on,' said Sheplar, 'perhaps we can stay on board.'

'Yes, if they do,' said Jacob. 'I think the shouts and threats are just opening negotiations, though.' He lifted the library seal around his neck. He had already been told by the aircrew that Hangel was in the guild network. There would be a library here, as well as a radiomen's hold. The light was fading around them now. Darkness falling fast across the plains. 'Let's see if this is good for a night or two's free stay until negotiations play out ... or we find an aircraft heading south across the grasslands.'

'Ah, Hangel,' said Sariel. 'One of the wonders of the world. A jewel set in the wide expanse of the savannah. Can you feel the spray of water on your face?'

'That's just your spit, you old fool,' needled Sheplar.

'I can feel moisture on the wind,' said Khow. 'It is like a meadow mist.'

'Mighty impressive,' said Jacob. He had taken a good look at the city-state on the way down. The waterfall cascading down the rocky plateau would have been impressive enough, even if the plateau hadn't been the only landmark higher than a stand of trees on the whole journey here. Buildings had been constructed on both sides of the torrent of water, set in the rockface like mushrooms hugging a tree trunk. The entire top of the plateau had been urbanised, covered with onion-domed stone buildings and protected by a fortress-sized wall which appeared unnecessary given the height of the plateau's escarpment. The cargo plane had landed the expedition in the outer city, itself divided into two concentric rings. An outer wall protected the farmland, its crops and fields a patchwork blanket from the air. An inner wall shielded the city nestling around the plateau's steep rise. A river fed by the waterfall snaked through the enclosed land, wide enough to need bridges to cross it; silvery red, where the setting sun washed its surface with dying crimson reflections. You could tell where the money in this pocket-sized kingdom lived. The city on the plateau-top was lit up like a chandelier with electric lights powered by a crest of water turbines stretched out over the waterfall's plunge. The city above looked bright and worthy of Sariel's flattery. The wooden township below, by contrast, was dark and grim with only a few oil lanterns for comfort, hundreds of columns of smoke trailing out of crowded, bent chimneys.

One of their cargo plane pilots dismounted from the cockpit and walked away from the airfield. Jacob and his companions followed her, catching up with her naturally slow pace, encumbered by the full weight of gravity on the ground. After so long in the air, Jacob felt the effects too. Being reintroduced to the dirt after just a couple of weeks at high altitude on the *Night's Pride* was like climbing mountains with a pack full of rocks. His joints stiff and aching into the bargain.

'Some hard bargaining back there,' noted Jacob.

'The grand duke is a little too used to having his own way,' said the woman. 'But we are not his subjects. He plays us for fools at his risk.'

'You are carrying enough fuel to reach the next port?' asked Sheplar.

She merely smiled. 'I would not trust passengers with that information. But you, I think, know the winds well enough. A good wind may carry an aircraft far.'

'So it may.'

'The city's library is down below?' said Jacob, pointing to the rickety wooden towers behind the lower ring of fortifications, 'or up there?' He indicated the constellation of lights burning high on top of the plateau.

'The library's entrance is in the upper city,' said the pilot woman. 'They call it the *royal city*. The lower city is known as the *common city*.'

'I'm no royal,' said Jacob.

'You are a traveller with money? They will find you royal enough,' said their pilot. 'The lower city is mainly for gads, and those poor enough to have to live alongside them.'

'Gads?'

The woman pointed to a line of stevedores weighed down with cargo from the shuttle planes, workers struggling towards flatbed carts with their loads. On closer inspection, Jacob saw they weren't fully common pattern – at least not the sort that wore fancy official uniforms in this kingdom. They had long necks and as they tottered under the weight of their loads by the warehouse loading lights, Jacob noted their skin was patterned, too ... tiger striped yellow and brown and green. Perfect camouflage for a life in the plains beyond the city's walls, Jacob realised.

'They are natives?'

'Tame ones,' said the woman. 'Serfs and bondsmen. The wild ones beyond the city walls, you would not wish to meet.'

'You mean slaves,' growled Jacob. *The same damn evil that's snatched Northhaven's young away. That took Carter.* He tried not to think what his son might be suffering right now. His fate as a prisoner.

'We are visitors,' shrugged the woman. 'And if there is anything a trader of the air has to teach you, it is this: visitors should never judge. At least, not the kind who wish to carry on about their business, free and healthy.'

'But this is all wrong,' protested Sariel. 'The gads are a proud people. Their tribes live in peace with the citizens of Hangel.'

'Maybe they are, if you've been listening to the songs sung by caravan drivers whose ancestors last passed through here six centuries ago,' said the woman. 'The Grand Duke Pavlorda and his friends have been expanding the plantations beyond the outer wall for a long time. Into territory which the plains people claim as their own.'

'All this fool's stories are dubious,' said Sheplar. 'Please pay him no heed.'

'Nothing in the world is more dangerous than sincere ignorance and conscientious stupidity,' retorted Sariel, rubbing his beard angrily.

'There is so much open space out there,' said Khow, horrified. 'Empty land! Why must you fight over it here?'

'Be glad your people don't understand the answer to that one,' said Jacob. *Blood and dirt intermingled until it becomes one and the same. We've been dying for the same thing as long as there have been people in the world.*

'I look at these gads and I struggle to tell the difference between your people and theirs,' said Khow.

'They were probably common pattern once,' said Jacob. 'You live long enough in a place and it changes you over the eons. Like water carving a passage through the rock.'

'And a minor evolution in skin pigmentation is enough to make someone a slave? Enough of a difference to kill over?'

Jacob shivered with the damp wind. And old memories. 'Khow, old friend, oft-times we don't even need that.'

'I will be glad to return to the forests with Kerge. Glad! I will never leave the glades again.'

'I'll aim to take you that far, friend,' said Jacob. *If your homing sense leads us true.*

Trailing in the female pilot's wake, they reached a line of taxis at the airfield's edge; open carriages pulled by short, plump horses. Sharing the ride, they passed through flat agricultural land, unfamiliar crops and neatly ordered rows of bushes. It was too late for the land's farmers to be out. They were probably inside the low white buildings at the centre of their fields, windowless walls like miniature redoubts. The expedition's journey into town was accompanied by the sound of crickets, creaking carriage wheels turning and the gentle gargle of water moving across clay irrigation channels. They were at the tail end of the day, but Jacob still found himself sweating in the febrile evening air. He wouldn't fancy labouring in the full furnace of the day in these fields. Or crossing the plains on foot without a good knowledge of the local waterholes. Occasionally, their carriage overtook a wagon piled high with sacks and crates. The drivers holding the reins were common pattern, tailboards at the wagon's back crowded with sad-looking gads, sore feet in worn sandals dangling from the back as they swayed listlessly, recovering their strength ready to unload the cargo. After half an hour, the taxi reached the wall that surrounded the lower city. The gatehouse was manned by soldiers, functional padded wine-red jerkins and lobsterpot-style steel helmets protected by neck plates and cages for visors. There was none of the finery of the officers negotiating back at the airfield. Spiked mace-handles hung from their side belts, short carbines pushed into leather holster belts crossing their tunics like a sash. Jacob and Sheplar's weapons were exchanged for a brass token apiece just as was necessary in Northhaven, and he watched his twin pistols locked away inside the guardhouse with a twinge of regret. *So used to their weight already?* whispered a voice inside him. He shouldn't have missed the weapons. Not with the protection of a granite wall close to fifteen feet high, the heavy tubes of four-barrelled guns visibly poking out of the towers and the heads of sentries moving precisely along the parapet. Jacob ran a practised eye along the fortifications. This was what you might call a business-like arrangement. No part-time militia here. The soldiers were brutes prepared for trouble and ready to handle it. Jacob's opinion of the common city didn't much improve upon closer acquaintance. Narrow streets with wooden lean-tos and tenements, everything damp from the spray of the massive waterfall. The main avenue had been cobbled with stone from the plateau, but the lower city's alleys and runs-offs were mud and broken planking. Walls were black and brown and rotten, the gads shuffling along the narrow streets in muted colours, as if any dyes and splash of colour had long since run away. Threadbare cloaks, aprons and leggings the same colour as the dirt the gads squatted in, hands out reaching for a pauper's blessing. Hangel's beggars lacked even the warmth inside from chimneys spewing out smoke, the smell of burning tinder and horse dung. If there was a church here, care of the poor wasn't high on its list of priorities. Jacob could imagine the advice of poor, dead Wiggins from beyond the grave. *Not your fight. Going to see a lot more of this before we get to where we're going.* The pastor within Jacob didn't agree. The person he was returning to – the killer who owned that brace of guns – was all too willing to agree the deputy had a point and walk on by. *Which man's coming for his son? Which one can survive out here to do it?*

They reached the bottom of the plateau and the pilot woman dismounted and stepped into one of the vertical ferries, wooden platforms winched up and down the rockface. Not an option open to four travellers who needed to conserve their gold and had good legs to walk up the steep switchback steps carved either side of the waterfall. 'We'll be staying at the library,' called Jacob. 'If your carrier master decides to keep on flying south of the plains, send for us, and we'll book another passage on board the *Night's Pride.*'

She nodded curtly, and then the pilot was whisked away, rising out of sight with dozens of other passengers.

'Her clan are a canny crew,' said Sheplar. 'I think they will be flying in circles for a while, waiting to see who blinks first ... the grand duke or their trading master.'

'Whoever needs the deal more, I guess,' said Jacob.

'Am I really to climb this rise on foot, Your Grace,' asked Sariel, 'when I have so much wealth?'

'You have no money, you old thief,' said Sheplar. 'All that we carry belongs to the people of Northhaven. Maybe you can recount one of your tall tales to the platform operators, persuade them to carry you into the air for a song.'

The skyguard pilot's words proved prophetic. As they went towards the stairs carved into the cliff, shouts went up from the men operating the lifting platforms' winching gear.

'You can't go up there. That's for bearers and gads!'

Jacob turned on the first of the steps, calling back. 'Sure I can. Unless you've got a monopoly on a man using his legs, as well as the lifts heading up and down up this rise.'

'You're going to unsettle the gads,' shouted one of the men. He might have had a point there. The workers going up and down the rock-hewn steps shied away in horror, as though they expected to catch the plague from the Weylanders.

'Been cooped up in the air for two weeks. My legs need the exercise.'

'Foreigners!' yelled one of winchmen, circling a finger around his ear to indicate his thoughts about their sanity. 'You'll catch the mange off them dirty gads. There's not a hotel up there'll give you rooms.'

Jacob and the others began their climb accompanied by catcalls and jeers from the workers manning the platform gear.

'Every day I learn something new about you, Jacob of Northhaven,' said Sheplar.

'And what have you learned this evening?'

'That the best way to get you to turn right is to order you to turn left.'

'I guess there's a little truth in that,' said Jacob.

They climbed at a quick pace, overtaking gads going in the same direction on the winding, switchback stairs. The indentured labour's pace was lazy, or perhaps weary was the word that Jacob was reaching for. *I reckon when your time's not your own, you don't value it so much.* Like the gads at the plateau bottom, many of their fellow travellers shied away from the visitors, jumpy and nervous. Jacob had seen dogs like that back in Northhaven. But only the ones that lived with bad families. The hounds who felt the sharp side of a boot sooner than any kind hand or word. After the party had climbed the steps for a while, they cleared the tops of the lower town's rickety wooden roof-tops and caught a clear sight of the thundering white torrent of water falling to their side. The townspeople below might shiver and cough in the damp wash of the falls, but for the wealthy citizens above, it was clearly a delightful way to cool off from the heat of the day. He spied idlers on the balconies of their apartments, watching the fast setting sun as servants poured them drinks. The buildings resembled stone saucers embedded into the rock face so that only the front half of the structures was visible, as if giants had held a contest on the plain, throwing huge discs into the plateau walls. The manner in which the apartments clustered together put him in mind of toadstools hanging off bark. There was no way to reach the apartments from these stairs – an intentional omission. Sariel complained of growing tired, so they paused for a moment. Jacob rested against the stone palisade protecting them from tumbling over the edge. Gads slowly passed them in both directions, chattering in a language that Jacob didn't recognise, low and high tones mixed in a lyrical, sing-song tongue.

Sheplar wiped the sweat off his brow. 'I wonder what they're saying.'

'They wonder if it would be wise to offer to carry us up the stairs,' said Sariel.

'You are making that up!' protested the flier.

'I may take them up on that service,' wheezed Khow. 'Climbing a tree is one thing. Scaling a plateau this high is another.'

'All educated men speak Gaddish,' said Sariel, annoyed at being doubted. 'I was once taken prisoner by the mighty diviner Unkulu, who lived in a palace of reeds next to the great river of the plains. He kept me in a cage like a parrot, and said he would only set me free when I had learnt fifty new languages, the last being Gaddish, as it is counted as being the oldest and the noblest of all tongues. For each tongue I failed to master, he said his warriors would chop a foot off of my height. Luckily for me, Unkulu kept fifty-five wives, each offered as tribute by a different nation on the plains. How I prayed that none of them would die before they taught me my final language. I am not so tall that I could spare a foot or more of my body for his soldiers' sabre practice.'

'If we had been lucky,' suggested Sheplar, 'they might have started at the top and removed your lying tongue.'

'Pah, I always speak the truth – even when I let slip falsehoods.'

'Given you're still here,' said Jacob, passing the old tramp his water canteen for a swig, 'I'm taking it that you were up to the challenge.'

'No, indeed, Your Grace,' said Sariel. 'One of the diviner's wives, Zuri, was having a picnic by the river when she fell into the water and was crushed to death by a giant green serpent. She never finished teaching me the language of the nation of Kaaboyo. Thankfully, the next wife due to teach me was pretty Salinge, who had fallen in love with me. She stole a pair of reed wader's stilts for me, and spent the night lengthening my trousers with needle and thread to accommodate the poles. When Unkulu's bodyguards chopped a foot off my girth, I used a little road magic to make them believe that they had seen my legs regrow. After that, they treated me with a great deal more respect. Although their ruler still insisted I learn Gaddish, so that I might tell all that I meet of his skill at prophecy and foretelling. And he was uncommonly good at it. He even knew that his wife was going to die in the river, as he had sent heralds to his neighbours demanding a new bride two days before Zuri died.'

Jacob shook his head at the outlandish tale. 'Pity that diviner isn't here now. I'd ask him when we're going to catch up with my son.'

'I think he would say when we're ready to deal with the slavers who took him.'

Jacob grunted. *I got two holsters full of ready racked at this city's guardhouse.*

They continued their climb, until the landscape inside the city state's walls became as small as a toy garden. Out beyond, Jacob watched the plains for a second. Endless rolling plains the colour of burnt sienna where the last rays of sunset touched the grasslands. Jacob lost sight of it along with his night vision when lamps flickered into life along the staircase. *The city's builders must have used the stairs at one point. I doubt the lights were put in for the comfort of their slaves.* More lights glowed across the saucer-shaped houses built into the rockface. Electric lamps. A rare, remarkable thing to see. Only Khow didn't seem impressed by the sight. Maybe his people counted the use of such power as party tricks, or maybe it was the simple life they clung to in the forests. They were a people full of contradictions.

Finally, Jacob reached the top of the plateau. Stairs widened out into a public square, two stone statues of knights standing as sentinels. The upper city's walls were absent here, making a viewing gallery of the open space. There were few people around, gad servants trudging away to their households, weighed down with whatever cargoes they had been sent to fetch and carry. The first pedestrians Jacob came across were a young couple, giggling and full of the evening, waiting by a rickshaw which had thrown its wheel. The gad driving it was on his knees, pushing the wheel back in place while the boy and girl nudged each other and laughed as though they were watching a piece of private theatre laid on just for them. The pair parted with directions to the library after a little persuasion, so greatly amused by this strange group of foreigners roving the city's streets at night, that the pastor thought they might roll around on the paving stones and exhaust themselves before they bothered to answer his request. One of Brother Frael's sayings came back to Jacob as they left the couple behind. *When love is not madness, it is not love.* Maybe what the party was doing here was a form of madness, too. Human specks of dust drifting in the infinite, trying to reunite with all that they had lost. *Tell yourself that you're following Carter for love. Not for revenge. You need to believe that.* The royal city's architecture was completely different from the ramshackle tenements leaning against each other below. No wood here, but white-washed stone, tall limestone towers with proud helmeted cupolas and onion-shaped domes. Their few tapered windows fixed far higher than a man could reach, indicating a culture of privacy and secrecy. At street level, the buildings' entrances were massive and wouldn't have looked out of place inside a castle rampart. Harsh sodium light leaked underneath the portals' cracks, giving the homes a ghostly air. Moths and insects swarmed around bulbous lamps pinned into the walls along both sides of the narrow streets. The city's library, when they stumbled upon it, didn't look that much different to the entrance to Lucas's Northhaven guild hold. Its door armoured with a speaking grille set in the wall, the library building appeared little bigger than Jacob's old rectory. When a guildswoman in a blue librarian's tunic came to inspect them through the sally port, she was momentarily taken aback by these unlikely strangers carrying a guild seal. As Jacob had thought, after she admitted the expedition, they descended a circular staircase, the library closer to a mine burrowing into the hard heart of the plateau, the bulk of its chambers hidden safe underground. The reading room for guild guests was such a spit of the one in the Northhaven, Jacob half-expected Lucas to appear and inquire what had made the pastor change his mind about being far-called. Instead it was a middle-aged woman who came into view, silver-haired and stern-faced. She looked as though she wouldn't suffer fools lightly – and probably didn't take kindly to visitors turning up unscheduled with a call upon the guild for hospitality. Jacob realised that all the librarians he had seen so far in the centre had been women.

'Well,' said the woman. 'I know you're not new apprentices sent here to study with us.'

'Too old?' said Jacob.

'Wrong gender,' said the woman. 'I'm Iaroia, master of the hold here. Or mistress, if you prefer. You're not guild travellers. The grand duke only allows women to work inside the library ... one of his many sweet little foibles.'

Jacob hoped they wouldn't be staying in the city-state long enough to experience too many of them.

'Perhaps the grand duke appreciates that tomes of beauty should be looked after by creatures of similar allure,' said Sariel, making a theatrical bow.

'The locals do not sully themselves with books,' said Iaroia, in a tone of contempt that made it clear what she felt about such arrangements. 'God forbid that they learn something. Most of the librarians working here came in via the airfield as foreign postings. And your flattery would work better after a bath. Which one of you carries the guild seal?'

Jacob took it out and passed it to the woman. He introduced himself and each of the others in turn, as formality required, but didn't delve into details of the nature of their travels. She eyed the seal suspiciously, turning it over to examine both sides. 'This is from a library in the north of the Lanca ... the league? You are a long way from home.'

'And we'll be travelling a ways yet before we call it done,' said Jacob. He glanced around the chamber. 'Are we welcome to salt and roof? Rooms and hospitality?'

'*Welcome* is stretching it,' said Iaroia. 'You'll be tolerated. Borne a little better when I know what you and your little travelling circus act is doing crossing the plains with calls on guild hospitality. Not that we don't have the room. We're a lot larger than the provincial hold that gave you this seal. Perhaps seventy times more archive space here.' She stared at the gask. 'Can you speak the trade tongue?'

'I certainly hope so,' said Khow.

'Well, you're better groomed than your friends, at least, even with the spikes coming out of your hide.' She pointed down a corridor off the reading room. 'Guest rooms are on this level. You won't be allowed access to the rest of the library.' She jangled a large circle of silver keys on her belt. 'Not without these. There's a refectory next door to the bunk chamber. I'll be along with food and water in an hour. There are toilets by the refectory. No visitor baths here, though. You'll need to use the public ones tomorrow.'

Sheplar watched the guild master walk off; clapping her hands to indicate her juniors should follow after her. 'Do we need a bath?'

Jacob shrugged. 'She's a woman, isn't she? To her, we always need a bath.'

As good as her word, Iaroia returned with two librarians and platters of food after the party stowed their packs under the simple dormitory's bunks. Together, they went to the chamber next door. The librarians put the food and water on the table, while Jacob and his companions sat down. The simplicity of the refectory might have been modelled on one of the monasteries perched on the hinterland of Rodal. The fare that appeared before them was of similarly humble origins, a fact not missed by Sariel as he sniffed at the jugs of water, and poked the gruel-like meal with his fork. 'This is a dry centre of learning, Lady Iaroia?'

'*Holdmaster*, if you wish to be formal, my scraggly house-guest.

Alcohol, confined spaces and flammable paper are not a recipe for the successful preservation of knowledge, Mister Sariel.' Iaroia sat herself at the end of the bench facing the band of visitors across the table.

Sariel rubbed the surface of his long leather coat. 'Ah, the dust of travel. I must apologise, dear lady. Normally I would appear before you as a prince, not a rank shard-borne voyager.'

'A prince of the hedgerows, perhaps?' she said, using the tongue-in-cheek term for vagrants.

Khow consumed the gruel at the long table without complaint. 'We should also apologise for keeping you up after your usual opening hours.'

'Oh, these are well within our hours of work. The radiomen's guild in Hangel is only five minutes' walk from the library and they work after darkness here. The next nearest receiving station is very far away. During daylight hours, the sun interferes with their radio's signal strength. They have to operate at night when the heavens are clearer ... so we receive updates for the archives at hours few other libraries would tolerate. Another "perk" of being posted here.'

'You are not Hangel-born?' asked Sheplar.

'I was born in a country to the south of here, far beyond the plains. Denka. Very civilised, very comfortable. At least compared to life perched on this cast-off rock.'

'No locals working here?' said Jacob.

'A couple only. When you have gad servants to run after you, an austere life of service in the cause of knowledge and learning has very little appeal.'

'I don't see servants,' said Jacob. 'I see slaves.'

She shrugged. 'They don't use that term for the gads. But then, the grand duke's main source of revenue is fuel fees from aircraft that must refuel when crossing the plains. Inflammatory labels such as *slave* might put off some of our more civilised visitors. I strongly suggest you don't talk in that manner within earshot of the duke's soldiers.'

'The hell with them.'

Iaroia shook her head at Jacob's temper. 'The Grand Duke Pavlorda Bragin is a mad son from a far-from-sane family line. His paranoia has only grown worse with age. There is a plains people prophecy that during the Age of the Seventh Sun, the House of Bragin's rule will come to an end by the hand of the grand duke's own son. According to the local calendar, that's this decade. The gads are awaiting the auguries ... the appearance of the trickster angel Jok and the spirit of Ogan, the twice-born. They grow restless and the Hangels have become even more repressive and brutal in dealing with their workforce.'

'How many children does this noble have?'

'As far as his wives are concerned, Pavlorda is without issue. But he is unable to keep his hands off the palace serving girls, and many gads have borne him half-breed children. The bastards are killed, of course.'

Jacob's hands tightened on the mug of water he was drinking from. 'He murders his own kin?'

'Not only his own,' said Iaroia. 'What is sauce for the ruler must be sauce for his people. Any half-breed born within the city limits is drowned by his soldiers or abandoned on the plains to feed the first hyena to come across the unfortunate babe. Rumour has it that many years ago, one of the grand duke's half-breed children was smuggled out of the city by his mother after she gave birth in secret, and the boy was taken in by a gad tribe. That child is known as Chike Bragin and he has grown up to be a war leader who is currently giving the city a great deal more trouble than it is used to.'

'The merchant clan we flew in with are bringing rifles and ammunition for the grand duke's forces,' said Jacob.

'More weapons,' she sighed. 'Just what is needed to improve the situation. Even if every man and woman in Hangel were to carry a rifle and a bandoleer full of bullets, the plains outside go on forever, and there are a great many more gads outside the walls than there are people sheltering behind them.'

'At least the gads have the power of prophecy on their side,' said Jacob. 'Against a seven-round rifle.'

'Do not mock,' said Sariel. 'There is power in words.'

Jacob shrugged. 'Words are your trade.'

'And what is yours?' asked Iaroia, looking intently at him.

'I am – a pastor.'

'You don't sound so sure of that.'

Maybe I'm not, at that. 'Think of us as four pilgrims.'

'Well, pilgrim, as far as words are concerned, there's truth in Mister Sariel's. Chike was raised on the plains by a diviner, a great diviner. Have you heard of them?'

'Some kind of shaman, a grassland wizard?'

'They practise magic, that is true. Herbal medicine and simple science for the most part. But they can scry the future. The grand duke keeps his own stable of diviners in the palace, shamans he has captured from the tribes during fighting. The diviners are chained so they can't commit suicide. And he blinds them, as that is said to increase their power of augury.'

'A barbaric practice,' said Khow. He raised his little metal calculator. 'They must be powerful indeed, if they can follow the branches of the great fractal tree using only the power of their mind.'

'Barbaric practices? Very much so,' agreed the librarian. 'It was the great diviner that declared Chike to be the child spoken of by the Prophecy of the Seven Suns, after Chike found an old spear-bow in a cave as a boy.'

'I'm not familiar with the weapon,' said Jacob.

'A war spear as tall as a gad with a crossbow and winding mechanism built into the wood,' said Iaroia. 'All adults carry them on the plains.'

'A royal bastard raised by a wizard, a boy fated to claim the kingdom,' murmured Sariel, in wonder. 'This is an ancient story with many roots.'

'Ancient it may be,' said Iaroia, 'but the story's lost none of its potency for the grand duke. He's been driven insane trying to kill Chike and his followers, trying to prevent the prophecy coming true. And the harder the grand duke squeezes, the worse the situation becomes. An irony, don't you think? The tribes around the city have laid aside their blood feuds and differences and united behind Chike. That is something unique. I may not be a diviner, but I can tell the future of Hangel, and it will not be a happy one, whichever side wins.'

'I do not think we should linger here,' said Khow.

'On that we're agreed,' said Jacob. 'Where do the city's ticket brokers operate from?'

'There is a hotel called the Salyut on the market square; any air passage broker worth dealing with can be found inside or on the streets alongside. Seeing as you carry the guild's seal with you, I won't even charge for telling you that.'

'I need to borrow your map room, too,' said Jacob. 'Preferably also without charge. What funds we have, we need to conserve.'

'Just four pilgrims in search of a distant investment opportunity?'

'Something like that,' said Jacob. 'Although I think our ultimate business'll be paying some people back.'

'There are too many traders in the world operating in that market,' said Iaroia. She stood up to lead them down the corridor, unlocking a series of doors and taking them into a warm stone chamber filled with large wooden map tables. The surfaces were empty, but her librarians turned up with a large-scale geographical key, and consulting with Khow, Jacob worked out the chain of maps they needed to examine.

Khow leant over the key thoughtfully. 'Here. This is where Kerge has been for the last month. He has not moved.'

Jacob tracked the most direct route from their current position in the middle of the plains and began writing out the numbers of the tube rolls that would need to be brought out of archive, filling a sheet of paper with pencil-scrawled reference codes.

'You gentlemen of the road really are far-called,' noted Iaroia, reading the list before passing it to one of her librarians.

'The distance is of no concern,' said Jacob. 'It's a journey we need to make.'

'Well, you're going to keep some cobblers in business between here and there.'

It took two hand carts clattering into view, each filled with map tubes, for the surfaces of every table in the chamber to be covered. Perhaps fifty counters in all. The maps were ancient, dust-spattered things that looked as if they hadn't seen the room's electric lights for centuries. Jacob and Sheplar used spools built into the tables to trace red journey threads above the nations drafted on the thick paper, thousands of states with every type of geography ... from seas to marshes to deserts to forests to mountain ranges. Sheplar looked despondent as he examined the distance they needed to cross. Sariel was more thoughtful, running his finger across the charts as though he was dipping into the soil of each land.

'You are sure about this?' Jacob asked Khow.

'I am certain, manling.'

'If we could harness a strong trade wind and fly with no refuelling,' said Sheplar, 'following this thread would mean seventeen years in the sky. Realistically, with layovers, perhaps twenty years' journey time with merchant carriers. How can the skels have travelled so far, so fast? They should not have this level of lead on us.'

Iaroia stood by the last table they had papered with map sheets, examining their destination. 'You are certainly travelling by a strange compass. Not to mention a dangerous one.'

Jacob walked over, looking down at the land on the map. 'Is your atlas accurate, to scale? The country on this last map covers too much territory?'

'Accurate when it was drawn, and if anything, an underestimation. This isn't a country, it's an *imperium*. Vandia. The richest, most power-ful state I have on record at the hold, and then some.' She waved at her staff to fetch the gazetteer volumes for the country. 'They are said to have mines in the imperium, working mines overflowing with metals and ores.' She reached out and patted the leather money purse attached to Jacob's belt. 'The copper in your coins most likely came from Vandia, passed down the caravan routes millennia ago. The gold in the grand duke's treasury was probably pulled from the ground there. The steel in the rifles you brought in extracted there centuries ago.'

'Do they keep slaves?' asked Jacob.

'Jacob Carnehan,' laughed Iaroia, 'if what I recall from our gazet-teer is even half-correct, every nation within a hundred thousand miles of the imperium acts as their serf. You wish to safely build a tower over four-storeys tall, you need steel. You need that ... then you must deal with the imperium and their agents on whatever terms they dic-tate. You require lead for your bullets and metal for your sabres, you must offer regiments to fight for their cause. What Hangel has here and your society back in the Lanca possesses in the way of factories and mills and technology, these are but the distant, ancient wash of that wealth and power. Metals transported for centuries, each league travelled making the ore rarer and more expensive. Do the Vandians keep slaves? Why wouldn't they? I imagine they are very much like the grand duke here, except with the riches of the very gods to satisfy their demented whims.'

'I understand something of the nature of ores,' said Khow, raising his little metal calculator. 'They do not all originate from a single source. My people have chemical tests that prove that.'

'My needle-skinned guest, you are indeed learned. Yes, there are working mines elsewhere on Pellas. Too distant to be shown on the maps I possess here. I'm not sure if your lifespan is similar to those of us of the common pattern, but if you could fly far and long enough, you would one day reach a librarian's guild hold with an alternative source of metals in its maps. But for us, Vandia is the closest source. The mother lode, you might say.'

'Surely, the Vandians are a benevolent people,' said Khow. 'If they possess such wealth, they could dedicate their lives to learning and progress ... they could send their charity to distant parts of the world?'

'Ha,' snorted Iaroia. 'Have a look around the royal city tomorrow and then walk around the common city below. You will see gads sweating in the fields and in the workshops, encouraged by the lash and the cane. If you stumble across a group of Hangel philosophers sitting around the streets engaged in rarefied discourse and teasing out insights into the secrets of the universe, do let me know. I'd love to meet them. One thing I know about the Vandians is that they are normal men and women. That tells me all that I need to know about their imperium, without even consulting the archives.'

'Do you know if the Vandians have fast aircraft?' said Jacob.

'I don't need our gazetteer for that. I saw something once, when I was a girl in Denka. I was in my aunt's gardens when the clouds parted and an object came flashing past, like an arrow, although with its size and the altitude it seemed to be flying at, it was probably closer to the size of a four-hundred rotor carrier. It was made of metal, and there was fire roaring behind it. It sounded like the gates of hell had broken open and the howls of the whole underworld were echoing across the land. It crossed the whole width of the sky in a couple of seconds. That, I was told by my aunt, is how the people of the far south travel.'

'There are a people called skels,' said Jacob. 'Big ugly twisted brutes that survive as raiders and bandits. Do you know if they have dealings with the Vandians?'

'Let us see.' Iaroia waited for her staff to come back, returning twenty minutes later with a third cart, this one piled with leather-bound volumes. Everything the library contained on distant Vandia. Iaroia inspected an index tome, followed the trail through a handful of other volumes, and finally settled on one particularly heavy-looking history book. 'Oh, that's interesting.' She turned the book around towards Jacob for him to read the dense text hand-written inside as she talked. 'See here. The skels were the previous rulers of the Vandian territory ... masters of the mines that fund the imperium. The Vandians' ancestors were the skels' slaves, tribute from the nations surrounding the mines. But the bordering states grew tired of being forced to pay tribute. The countries rose up and overthrew the skels, turning their old overlords into refugees and nomads of the air. From the date here, that was over sixty thousand years ago. I wonder if the skels still nurse a grudge against their old workforce for usurping their seat at the feast.'

'I may speak too much for that,' said Sariel. 'Skels are cold-blooded devils and they resent all not of their nation.'

Jacob scanned through the entry, hundreds of additional volumes cross-referenced. Details irrelevant to his mission. Long histories of the states that had struggled and fought for possession of the mines, empire after empire. Vandians and skels merely the most recent masters of these riches. That was the guild of librarians for you, always taking the long-term view. He felt a stab of regret. *This should have been Carter's life. In a hold like this.* 'This says the skels are often found working as privateers for the imperium.' *That's a polite term for damn mercenaries. Licensed to plunder at others' expense.*

'That's the link,' said Sheplar, excited and grinning.

Jacob was about to question Iaroia further, but she and her staff were called away to take delivery of the first batch of updates from the radiomen, leaving the four tired travellers alone, surrounded by a sea of maps and piles of tomes.

'Don't piss on your own doorstep,' said Jacob, tapping the chart of Vandia. 'The imperium has its mercenary brutes flying out to capture slaves from so far away that the raided nations will never be able to band together, repeat history, and unseat the imperium. A land army marching from the Lanca would take centuries to reach Vandia.'

Khow clucked unhappily as he tapped at his calculator. 'Bad numbers. A closed branch of the great fractal tree. In a world without end ... for this to have happened to my son.'

'Had to happen to someone's son,' said Jacob. The words were cold comfort to him. To Mary Carnehan. To Carter and the taken. To distant Northhaven lying burnt with its crops fed by the ashes of the dead. Weyland would be raided for a few years or so, picked over, and then the slavers would move on. Choose another country from a thousand distant lands that wouldn't have heard of the empire attacking them. Mere primitives compared to the forces assaulting them. Leave Weyland like a fallow field for millennia before returning again. *Just bad numbers and the random roll of fate.* Jacob smashed his fist on the map table in frustration. 'Damn them! You know what this means, don't you?'

Khow rolled one of Benner Landor's trading coins between his leathery fingers. 'The rarity value of the funds we carry will be close to worthless in our destination. We cannot bargain for our children in a Vandian slave market. Not with this metal.'

'It just has to get us there,' said Jacob. 'Then I've got something else to trade. We'll be dealing in lead.' He looked at the others. Four of them. Against the weight and power of something so large and powerful, he could barely wrap his mind around the might of what they faced. Iaroia was right; they were a travelling circus act. Just dust blowing in the breeze compared to what they needed to accomplish. 'None of you signed up for this. We don't need all of Benner's money now. We can divide it among us and you can travel back home.'

Sheplar shook his bushy head of hair. 'Act well your part, there all honour lies. However strongly my heart is called back towards the mountains, I would count myself already dead if I flew for five minutes fleeing in the direction of home.'

'Spoken like a true Rodalian. And you, Khow?'

'I fear for what you are becoming, Jacob Carnehan. You are losing yourself in the vastness of the world. But I cannot abandon my child to the caprice of his captors in the imperium. I shall press on, come what may.'

Jacob sighed. Against all the odds the gask's homing instinct had been proved correct. Was Khow's estimation of the struggle within Jacob just as accurate? A dark splinter of his soul, long suppressed, whispered the answer. *Whatever it takes*. Just like the good old days. Except they had been anything but good. How could he remember the past now? How could he ever have forgotten?

'There then,' said Sariel, banging his gnarled old wooden walking staff on the stone floor of the map room. 'Anywhere I sit is where my home shall be. These odds are nothing. I have faced far worse a hundred times and considered my enemies nothing but mere spit in the wind.'

Spit in the wind? That was what the four of them were. But then hell if Jacob had anything better to do with his time.

Jacob was permitted to keep some of the volumes on the Vandian imperium to read inside the dormitory, and he fell on them with a vengeance. Long after the others had gone to sleep, the lantern above his bunk flickered with the strange artificial light generated by the plateau's waterfall. To understand your enemy was to know their weaknesses and strengths. All the volumes came with a warning on the front sheet. Vandia did not tolerate the guild system on its soil. The imperium had no need of the librarians' knowledge; not when every neighbour approached them on bended knee, offering science and learning in exchange for whatever resources the empire deigned to trade in exchange for that knowledge. They had no need of rails to cross their land when they possessed far faster methods of traversing the vast distances of empire. They suffered no network of radiomen to disseminate information which the imperial state could not control. The imperium was a vast void in the librarians' archives. Everything that was said of it or about it, ancient lore passed down second-hand by traveller caravans which crossed through the empire's territory. And they spoke of a warrior society. A highly stratified elite constructed with only one aim in mind. Keeping the riches that the Vandians had conquered solely under their control, allowing only enough resources across their borders as was required to keep foreigners from banding together. To attempt what the Vandians' own ancestors had once achieved – seizing the mines. Ruthlessly choking off resources to anyone who threatened them. Playing one country off against another. There were plenty of warlords in the Burn who knew that game. Rotating the top dog's favour among far more lieutenants than were needed for the job at hand, each allowed their moment in the sun, then cast aside or destroyed when they grew too powerful. The more Jacob read, the more he realised that there was little difference from life in the empire and life in the Burn. Only that across the ocean they killed for dust and ashes, and in the imperium they murdered to hold onto untold riches. Opposite ends of the scale, but very little difference in existence for the average inhabitant. Oddly, that thought comforted Jacob. He had survived beyond the ocean, once ... had prospered in blood and war without end. Jacob was coming home. Or was it Jake Silver who was returning?

He slept fitfully, the weight of rock above him pressing against his soul as he tossed and turned. He was buried beneath the plateau, buried with the gathered knowledge of the world. The tomes whispered to him, speaking of the power of an empire ancient, large and beyond opposition. Mary came to him in the dark of the night, calling out to him from the street outside the rectory. He pulled on his breeches and ran down to find her crying outside.

'What's wrong?'

'The children are sick, there's a plague in the town.'

'There must be a cure!' *There is*, whispered the books scattered across his bunk. *You just have to find it.*

'My three boys,' sobbed Mary.

'I'll protect them.' His hands reached down for his pistols, and they coiled around his fingers like snakes.

'Not like that,' said Mary. 'That's who you used to be. Before we married and you took my name.'

'You're meant to take *my* name.'

'But it was so black,' said Mary. 'So washed with blood.'

'I'm a pastor now.'

'The monastery couldn't clean your old life away,' warned Mary. 'Nothing could do that.' But it wasn't his wife in front of him anymore; it was his mother, stretched out wounded across the wooden floor. The local landowner had forced his cruel affections upon her one last time, despite all her protestations. She had struggled too much. Furniture and crockery lay smashed across the floor of the simple three room farmhouse. He knelt down beside her. 'Go,' she wheezed. 'Leave here. There's nothing for you on these acres.'

'There's one thing.'

'This soil isn't worth it,' she coughed. 'It's taken your father and now it's stealing me. Forget revenge. Just leave. Travel to the harbour. Let me go to heaven knowing that one true thing lives.'

He held his trembling mother until she moved no more. She had been holding something tight inside her palm. When he prised open her fingers he discovered the little metal-jacketed bullet she had been trying to locate as she heard her door being broken down. He hadn't inherited his pistols yet, so he took down the single-shot rifle from the house's wall. Good for human wolves as well as the kind that crept out from the woods on four legs. 'There's *one* thing.'

'A *one*-shot percussion cap pattern?' laughed the landowner, large on his giant horse. He must have been confident, riding out on his land. Only a single man on horseback, hanging behind him. 'Little boy, go home.'

'I don't have one anymore.'

'You won't have a life. You shoot at me with that rabbit gun, my man here will drop you in a heartbeat.'

'I wasn't fixing on shooting you.' He put his mother's bullet into the skull of the horse, watching it rear, roll and fall. *A heartbeat.* His first knife he left embedded in the guard's throat, the man falling to the side, caught dangling in the saddle as his steed bolted past. It was a good thing he had brought along a second blade. He wouldn't be seeing that one again.

'Don't!' shouted the landowner, trying to escape the terrible weight of his quivering collapsed stallion. 'I own the law in this prefecture. They'll hunt you down! I can pay—'

'Exactly what I had in mind.'

'You're just a boy, just a peasant.'

He knelt by the thrashing horse. 'You're the only thing I'm sorry about.' He quickly put the creature out of its misery. Then he turned to the trapped landowner. 'I'm the son of two peasants. So here's what I'm aiming to do. I'm going to plant you in the dirt. Not next to them, because your blood would poison the soil. Out here, where your kin will never find you. All that will be remembered is how much you were hated and feared by everyone in the prefecture. But first, you're going to tell me which of your soldiers came with you to my house.'

'The stealers take you, you little devil.'

'Good. I don't want you to make it too easy.'

'They'll come for you. All of them will.'

'I'd appreciate it. I would consider that uncomplicated.'

The landowner yelled as he tried to pull at the pistols trapped below the dead weight of the horse. But the expensive twin Landsman repeaters came to the boy, instead. Eventually. As slowly as he could make the time last. *One true thing*. His hand was on the shovel, pushing dirt into a Northhaven grave. *Two true things*. His children's graves in a rectory that was all they had known as home, wrapped in sheets inside the coffins. Shrouded to hide the swollen red lumps of the illness which had claimed their young lives. Mary's tears coming down as the shovel's head crunched down into the soil.

'They should be burying me, not them.'

'Don't talk like that, please,' said Jacob. *They should be burying me*.

'You're already buried out here,' said Mary, reading his thoughts.

'*He* doesn't exist anymore.'

'Yes he does. *He* never went away.'

'Listen to your woman,' called Sergeant Nix, from behind the churchyard wall, leaning on it with his hat at a jaunty angle. 'Blood follows after you: death just can't help it. Your children, your wife. Murdered by you, same as though you pulled the trigger. You should let your kid die alone out in the imperium, worked to death like a pack horse. Why help a slave live? Boy'll just be like you. Kill everyone he should have been protecting,'

'I never regretted killing you.'

'I'll let you into a secret, later,' said Nix. 'Sure is an honour, chewing the fat like this with you. Not often I get to meet a bigger bastard than I was. Jake Quicksilver.'

'Jake *Silver*!'

'Oh no, you earned the *Quick*. Nobody as fast as you, to reach for your pistols and kill anyone who stood in your way. You're a legend. The greatest mercenary commander ever. Battle after battle. War after war. You could have crowned yourself Emperor of the Burn. Duke of the Dead. Baron of Blood. Hell, I would have followed you before you got soft. Would have been an honour. Me and Major Alock, we were always fans of your work. A fellow Weylander abroad, making good in bad times. What wasn't to admire? Only thing I never understood, is why you left? You had the Burn trembling at your feet. So why did you up sticks and leave? Just disappeared into the night. Why?'

'Why?' called a little boy. For a moment, he thought *he* was the boy. But *he* was on his horse, uneasy at being surprised in this canyon by a thin young wretch dragging a spear after his bony body. Emaciated even by the standards of the hand-to-mouth living in the destroyed lands of the Burn. Jacob's guard reached for the rifle in his saddlebag, but he waved at him to stand steady.

'Why, what?'

'Why did you kill her?'

'Who are you talking about, boy?'

'My mother.'

'I haven't killed your mother.'

'You came to my village last week. You took everyone you could; my mother, my friends, my cousins. You lashed them to the sides of your wagons with rope. You said if any of us wanted to ambush the food supplies going into the palace again, we would have to put an arrow through one of our family first. Our people were hungry enough that's just what they did.'

He looked back towards the soldier on horseback, who nodded imperceptibly. Just another day's work. Didn't even remember it.

'Little boy, go home.'

The spear came up. It was easy to tell someone who was going to charge, by the look in their eye. 'I don't have one anymore. You burnt it to the ground before you left.'

He raised one of the shiny pistols he kept holstered. And he knew whose guns they were. And why they weighed so much.

The boy's corpse was cradled in his arms. Just like his mother's had been. Just like his children were to be in later years. 'You're me. You're me.'

'No,' said the corpse, the boy's face twisting into that of Sergeant

Nix. 'Because here's the surprise: you never killed me well enough, not old Trixy Nixy.'

'*Manling*!' It was Khow, at last, in the darkness of the dormitory, buried under the weight of the plateau. He didn't think he could be imagining Sariel's irregular snoring – this was real. To Jacob's regret, so was too much of everything he had dreamt. 'Did I wake you, Khow?'

'You were calling for someone called Jake.'

'Yes, I knew him once.'

'Was he a friend?'

'Not much of one to anybody, if truth be told.'

'I thought perhaps it might be one of your children who have passed.'

'Not one of mine, although the man should be dead, right enough. Go back to sleep, Khow.'

'I have been trying, but I find it hard to bring my mind to rest … what we have learnt today about where Kerge has been taken. I worry for his future.'

'Knowing the future: isn't that the point of your prayers? That damn abacus machine you carry around with you?'

Jacob could just see the gask raise the fingers of his leathery hand. 'There are infinite branches on the fractal tree, manling. Every decision we make leads us down a new one. It is not that my people seek to scry the future like the diviners living beyond the city walls. More that we attempt to navigate towards the kindest alternative probability available. That is why we always meditate facing in the direction the universe is moving.'

'I didn't realise. What did you do for a living, Khow, back in the forests?'

'I was an artificer, a maker of such devices as my calculator. My son was apprenticed with me; even though we always knew his fate was to be larger than our craft.'

'If you even suspected any of this—' Jacob took in the dark dormitory with his hand '—why in God's name did you let Kerge leave home in the first place?'

'That you ask such a question … you have never visited the great forests?'

'Passed by its fringes once, travelling from the monastery in Rodal.'

'Kerge was in search of his mean. That is not a task that can be denied. Among my people, open paths on the fractal tree are judged to be a good thing, closed paths considered adverse. If Kerge had stayed, his path would have grown narrow and dark, for us all. There are many shadowed paths that must be avoided. This, I think you know.'

'I'm just a simple country pastor.'

'Perhaps,' said the gask, but he did not sound convinced.

'Where we're heading, the skills of an artificer aren't going to be much help to us. You might not be doing your son any favours by remaining so calm and reasonable.'

Khow snorted. 'My people are the way we are so that we may survive.'

'I know gasks aren't immune to the poison in your spines; and you do a fine job of controlling your temper. But you're not walking among your people now. The common pattern don't snack on leaves, we're carnivores, blood and bloody to the bone. The Vandians keeping Kerge like a damn pack animal, they might need to be given a mighty fit of pique on your part to be convinced to free him.'

'I am a vegetarian because the same acids that allow me to digest leaf-matter also charge my spine toxins. The men of the forest prefer peace, but our nature is not entirely pacifistic. We will defend ourselves when we must, as any man will. And you are wrong about your people, too. You are *omnivores*. The great fractal tree has given Weylanders a choice in the path you select.'

'Us being us, I reckon we'll choose the one dripping with blood.'

'The man you called for,' said Khow. 'I hope the branch of the fractal tree you follow never reunites you with him.' The gask vanished back into the darkness of the chamber.

He should be dead and buried. Just not down here. Jacob got to his feet. A walk through the hold's corridors might be what he needed to free his mind enough to sleep. He left the bunk room and passed storage chambers with reading rooms and archives of every sort. Unheated below the surface. Cooler, certainly, than the night air outside. The corridors looped in a long circle, as though the librarians' hold had been laid out as a stone barrel, safely buried away from harm's reach.

It would be interesting to see what lay below on the other levels, but he lacked the keys to pass the stout doors barring his way. The guild would keep its secrets unseen for a little while longer. He was about to turn back when he saw Iaroia emerging from one of the passage's doors, wearing a blue night dress that bordered on the diaphanous.

'You are having trouble sleeping, Jacob of Weyland?'

'Tonight, yes. But it's not a regular complaint.' *The sleep of the innocent, isn't that what Mary always used to say.* And maybe that was the problem. He'd abandoned any pretence of that after the slavers had burnt the town.

'Then you are lucky. It's ironic, but before I joined the guild, I always read a novel to help me get to sleep. Now I do little but read and write and record, I am constantly surrounded by books, and I find it far harder to drift off than I used to.'

'Reading trade figures and political updates from distant shores would have my eyelids nodding,' said Jacob.

Iaroia stood on her toes and kissed Jacob; the touch of her silk dress like static electricity where it brushed against his skin. 'If you need to wear yourself out, there are other ways ...'

He gently pushed her back, 'You're an attractive woman, Iaroia. But I've buried a wife and I've no heart left for repeating what I shared with her.'

'A pity,' sighed Iaroia. 'Such opportunities are rare, here. The locals are dolts, and it is not the done thing with guild members you have to treat fairly as subordinates.'

'That sounds a wise policy.'

'It's honourable to grieve for someone you've lost. But it can also become an excuse.'

Jacob stared down at the head of the hold. 'An excuse for what?'

'For cutting yourself off. For making yourself cold to all others around you. And it's a cold business, I think, which you're about.'

'I reckon that would only matter if I had a choice. Goodnight, Iaroia.'

'Goodnight, Jacob.' He watched her shut the door and disappear deeper into the hold. Then he headed back towards the bunk room. He suspected he was going to find it even harder to sleep now.

*

The radio operator finished decoding the message; the device used to decipher the communication far larger than his radio, all bulky rotating discs and dials connected to its keyboard. The discs were called rotors. He had learnt that in his brief training session, after both machines had been secretly delivered to the palace. Even though the radio operator had rung the bell for a messenger to come, he still felt a frisson of fear as footsteps came up the tower. How silly was that? The radio room with its unfeasibly small set was concealed at the top of one of the palace towers, just like the aerial used to receive night-time messages. And if anybody came poking unauthorised about the quarters of the grand duke's secret police, they would get exactly what they had coming to them. But still. The guild of radiomen never took lightly to rivals crossing the demarcation line and poaching on their territory. And the strictly non-guild radio operator never wanted to be the poor sod who had to go before the grand duke and explain why all the guilds the city depended on were withdrawing from Hangel in protest. That would not be a life-enhancing choice, he suspected. He breathed a sigh of relief. It was the courier after all. A fellow officer with the secret police.

'Anything important?' asked the courier.

'Orders concerning a group of visitors that should be passing through.'

'Airmen?'

The radio operator shrugged. 'Dead men, I'd say. But that's need to know.'

'And who needs to know?'

'The chief first, then the colonel of the city guard.'

The courier tucked the message inside his jacket. 'Business as usual, then. Don't go to sleep.'

'Don't tempt me. This is the first message we've had for weeks.'

A muffled scream echoed outside the tower's arrow slit. That cry must have been impossibly loud to carry all the way from the dungeons. The two men exchanged glances.

'Won't be sleeping through that.'

'Try not to.'

No, it wouldn't do to lose a solid, peaceful job like this one.

TEN

TO SAVE A LADY

Duncan sprinted through the rock corridors, ignoring the heat, ignoring the ache in his legs, ignoring the angry shouts of workers he pushed past. Blinking sweat out of his eyes, he kicked high in the air as he ran, low gravity giving him the bounce he needed to check the corridor ahead for any signs of the Vandian traitors and Princess Helrena's daughter. If he didn't find the turncoats before they left and detonated their charges, then the soldiers and the little girl would be the sky mine's only survivors. Duncan heard a thumping sound ahead, the chamber full of air circulation machinery. He was nearing the main hangar's entrance. That was where the traitors' shuttle would be; ready to carry them away to safety, clear enough distance to condemn every Weyland slave worker to a terrible death. *If they've already left, pray that you're caught in the main blast.* Not consigned to one of the rock's splinters, thrown about as the fragment tumbled down towards the ground, getting heavier and faster with every second before the final killing impact against the dead zone. Or maybe Duncan would get lucky ... be marooned on a shard with a working antigravity stone attached to it. Waiting for a rescue that might or might not be mounted, his throat constricting from dehydration; headaches and intense kidney pain as he lingered in the dry, ash-filled sky. Not knowing if his sister was dead or alive. Taken as a slave a second time by whichever imperial inherited Helrena's sky mining charter. *Yes, that would be luck.* The magnetic detonator clutched in

Duncan's hands nearly slipped out of his damp fingers as someone came barrelling after him down the corridor. *Carter Carnehan!*

'What the hell?'

'Some of Helrena's people have been paid off by her rivals!' Duncan shouted at Carter, desperately pushing through the workers blocking the passage. 'They've wired the blasting powder stores to go off. Assassinate the princess ... murder us all in a "mining accident".'

'Where?' yelled Carter, shoving aside workers as carelessly as Duncan as he suddenly realised what was at stake.

'Making for the hangar. If they take off ...'

'Damn them all! Isn't it enough that we have to beat their rivals' slaves to take these dirty rocks for them? Now we've got to fight in their feuds?'

'Traitors have snatched the little girl, Lady Cassandra Skar. Granny wants her back, and her unwanted daughter-in-law dead into the bargain.'

Carter's face was flushed with anger. 'And the rest of us are "just too bad".'

Just too bad? That was about right.

'If they've left,' growled Carter, rounding the corner. 'There are transporters for us, too.' They were seconds away from the hangar now.

'Not without Willow!'

Yes, Duncan could see Carter agreed with him at least that much. 'I'll ram their ship,' said Duncan. 'If that's the only way.' If he could find a pilot willing to do it.

The two men pelted into the hangar's open space. Dozens of crews worked inside, hammering and patching up the simple, robust transporters. Pilots helped with the work, manoeuvring around arresting wires, overseeing engine testing. Carts laden with refuelling drums and heavy equipment lay scattered about. And there, by the hangar's opening, sat the shuttle, an elongated silver steel dart, maybe ninety feet long, with engines that could angle to lift its weight up, before powering the craft forward through the skies like a javelin hurled by a god. It squatted behind the box-like landing lens the hangar crew used to guide in mine pilots, and in front of the craft, heading for a lowered ramp, was the departing party of Vandians – three of them, an officer and two soldiers, the guards holding a girl between them. *Must have drugged her to stop her calling for help.*

With his free hand, Duncan pulled out a couple of blasting caps and tossed them to Carter, their magnetic bases making them cluster together. Carter pulled the detonators apart. 'Reckon that armour of theirs is metallic?'

'One way to find out.' If it was ceramic or the queer material the Vandians called plastic, this was going to be one short fight. The two of them raced across the chamber, the noise of their boots muffled by the repair crews' beating hammers. Duncan rotated the clockwork timer mechanism, setting it for three seconds. Just striking a Vandian could earn you the death penalty. Duncan wondered what they'd get for what they were about to do? Duncan yelled in fury when it was too late for the three Vandians to do anything about it. He slapped a charge on the back of the closest soldier's breastplate as he kicked the feet out from under the man. Carter barrelled into the second guard, a dull clunk from the charge attaching to the back of the armour. The officer had a pistol palmed in his hand, ready to use it if anyone challenged their unscheduled departure with the princess's daughter. This assault surely counted, and Duncan just managed to yank the man's arm up and the lieutenant loosed a couple of shots towards the hangar's stone roof. One of the soldiers struggled to unhook his rifle from the shoulder strap. The guard Carter had slammed into had his sword half pulled out of its scabbard. That was when both charges went off, the double blast scouring across Duncan and the traitor he was struggling with, knocking both of them off their feet. As bad as the explosions burnt Duncan, the soldiers had taken it worse. Both charges focused into the soldiers' armour, just the same as if the men's plate had been metal blasting powder barrels ... saw-teethed smoking holes left where the explosives had detonated. Duncan's ears rang as he tried to pull himself up. The officer staggered to his feet first, the pistol rising in Duncan's direction. The lieutenant's brush-mounted helmet had fallen away, but he'd been protected from the blast by his golden armour, ornamented with a circular laurel wreath above an eagle. Another charge flew through the air towards him, hurled by Carter, but the officer contemptuously slapped it aside, his attention wavering for a second between the two slaves who had dared to attack him – something that was surely unique in his career so far. Duncan used that second of indecision to snatch a fallen rifle by the barrel, swipe the weapon's butt at the officer, smashing fingers protected only by black leather gloves, sending his pistol tumbling away. Then Carter slammed into the lieutenant as the Vandian went for his short-sword, both of them tumbling back onto the shuttle's ramp. They rolled about the slope, struggling fiercely. The officer was going for something dangling from his belt. For a second, Duncan thought it might be a dagger ... but a device that resembled a trigger guard without a blade attached came up. *The detonator!* Duncan lurched forward and jabbed out with the wooden butt of the rifle, cracking it hard against the officer's head. The traitor collapsed unmoving.

'That's the best day's work we've done in the sky mines,' coughed Carter, wiping the soot from the detonator caps off his face. 'I could get real used to killing Vandians.'

Duncan moved over to where Cassandra Skar had fallen during the melee. She was breathing shallowly, but only, he guessed, from whatever sedative that had been used. Chloroform, judging by the blisters around her mouth and nose. The young aristocrat lay behind an open tool crate, and its blackened sides had absorbed the caps' back-blast. 'She's okay.'

'She's our ticket out of here,' said Carter. He had picked up the unconscious officer's detonator, as well as the hand gun, checking its magazine and counting the rounds. 'As much as she was for these three dogs.'

Duncan stared back in rising horror. 'You can't be serious?'

'You know I am. We've got weapons. We've got the daughter of the imperial bitch working our people to death out here. Let's find out how much Helrena values the life of her golden-haired whelp.'

'She's just a young girl!'

'Like the ones who died in Northhaven when the skels raided, you mean?'

'You can't do it.' Duncan pleaded through gritted teeth.

Carter raised the detonator. 'Princess Helrena's warship is still anchored to the sky mine. She's going to fly us all back home to the league, just as fast as she dragged us out here. Every last damn Weylander on the station. If she doesn't, her daughter is either going to die real slow or real fast, and her mother can visit the stealers with us, because I'll blow the station to hell rather than go back to being a slave again.'

'You've lost your mind!'

'No, Duncan. We're either going to live free or die free. We're dead men walking, all of us. It's only a matter of time.'

'What about Adella? She's been carried off as a house slave. We can't leave her behind in Vandia as a damn toy for Baron Machus?'

'One life, against the thousands being worked to death in the sky mines?'

'Is that what you call love? Doesn't she mean anything to you?'

'Adella would want us to break out. If she could send word to us, she'd beg us to escape and leave her behind. You know that as well as I do. Either of us would do the same in her boots.'

'I never knew what a cold-hearted bastard you were. I won't leave Adella behind, not if I live to be a hundred.'

'Then you can stay,' said Carter, his eyes cold and hard. 'But you won't make a century; I give you a decade or less. Hell, maybe they'll make you foreman of this floating hell for sticking with the job.'

Duncan fingered the butt of the rifle. 'You willing to shoot me to prove the point?'

'What do you think?' smiled Carter, grimly. 'It's kind of ironic, don't you think? You were willing to put steel in me back home to keep me away from Adella. Here, you'd do the same if I try and walk away.'

'Please don't do this,' begged Duncan. 'I'm responsible for Willow. I don't want her hurt.'

'You're in the wrong damn place, then. We can die fast or die slow. We can die free or have our corpses tossed off the station as wastage.' Carter held up the detonator. 'Even if I fail, dying quick is going to be a mercy to us all. And I really have got a taste for killing Vandians, now.'

It was a shared interest. Carter crumpled with the explosion of the pistol in the shuttle pilot's gloved hand, the last of the conspirators silhouetted against the cabin lights in the open hatch. The detonator tumbled down as Carter fell off the ramp. Duncan fumbled for the rifle even as the pilot's pistol swung around to point directly towards him. *Too slow by a country mile.* The pilot wasn't wearing armour, so his uniform exploded in gobs of blood and fabric as five rapid shots walked across his chest. Duncan twisted around, still trembling in shock as Princess Helrena Skar and her Vandian bodyguards came striding forward. It was the princess's pistol barrel that smoked, the stink of cordite filling the hangar, and Owen stood with the imperials. He bent down to check on Carter before turning towards Duncan. Unsurprisingly, the imperials weren't bothering to tend to a mere slave, making for young Lady Cassandra, fanning out to check the traitors were dead and the shuttle empty of conspirators.

'The blasting powder stores,' spluttered Duncan.

'Princess has her people defusing the firing mechanism,' said Owen. 'Carter?'

'Bullet grazed his thick skull. He's out, but he'll live, with another scar along his noggin to remember the day.'

'You discovered the dead soldiers?'

'Yes. And I did what you would have done if you had been thinking straight,' said Owen, nodding towards the Vandians. 'I ran like hell for the people with guns. What the hell were you thinking? Charging a group of trained and heavily armed guardsmen with nothing but detonator caps?'

'It worked, didn't it?'

'You've been working alongside your hot-headed friend for too long,' said Owen. 'You're starting to sound like him. What were you talking to Carter about before that turncoat came out shooting?'

'That we ought to check the cabin for crew.'

'Got that right.'

Princess Helrena strode over to the Weylanders, nudging Carter's prone body with her shiny black boot. The aristocrat stared down at Duncan. 'You two fools again. The skels' punishment cage wasn't lesson enough for you?'

'I saved your daughter's life,' spluttered Duncan.

'You killed four Vandians. A crime with only one punishment.'

'Only killed two,' said Duncan. 'You shot the pilot. And I just clubbed the lieutenant into unconsciousness, like a good hitter's trained to. You can find out who's behind the attempt on your life.'

She nodded, then swivelled and a shot exploded from her pistol as she put a bullet through the downed officer's forehead. *So much for taking him alive.*

Blood, brown and dark, pooled towards Helrena's boots as she turned back towards Duncan and Owen. 'I already know who's behind this outrage. That bitch Circae and the families that support her. Anybody else trying to assassinate me would have left Cassandra to die in the station alongside me.'

'They didn't touch the turncoats' guns,' lied Owen. 'Look at the rents in their breastplates. Blasting cap damage. And this pair saved your house's heir.'

'And every slave in the sky mine. Which was, I suspect, far more the point of their desperate assault?' She went across to where her men were gently placing Lady Cassandra in a stretcher, examining the young girl before having a terse conversation with the men. Helrena walked back to Duncan and Owen. 'If she was hurt, I would have had ordered every worker in this mine pushed into the sky.'

'But she's fine,' said Owen.

'Yes, she is.' Helrena waved her pistol down at Duncan. 'You shall live. It's far too expensive replacing slaves, these days.'

'I'd live better with the woman I love returned by my side.'

The princess snorted. 'I am a royal of the upper-celestial caste, troublemaker ... a daughter of the imperial emperor; do you mistake me for a village matchmaker?'

'Adella Cheyenne,' continued Duncan. 'She was taken off the station by Baron Machus.'

Princess Helrena shook her head. 'Then she is far beyond my gift. The baron is an ally. I would not offend him by asking for the return of one of his new house-slaves.'

Duncan tried to protest, but the princess raised a hand. 'You know nothing of life beyond the sky mines. If you did, you would never request anyone you cared for to be returned to labour up here. Or are you so arrogant to think that your woman would prefer to live a short and brutish existence in the name of "true love", even inside the sky mines?'

'I would,' said Duncan. 'If it were me.'

'But it is not you we speak of. It is a woman you supposedly care for. Ask me again to return her here.'

'Then promise me she will have a good life,' begged Duncan, his heart torn by indecision.

She merely smiled, and shook her head. 'Promise *me* that I will have a good life. Promise my daughter the same. You know nothing of the empire.'

Duncan could barely stop himself from weeping. 'I can't live without her.'

'Love is the greatest enemy of all,' said the princess. 'Because sometimes we will let it murder us without even putting up a struggle. Just ask Cassandra's poor father. Yes, you can live for now, slave, even as we drag these traitorous dogs' corpses away. I don't think I can spare you punishment for saving my little girl's life, though. That isn't in my gift, either.'

Owen helped Duncan to his feet as their mistress left with her child and guards. 'The gratitude of emperors and empresses is a thin soup to sup from.'

'She's just a princess, not an empress.'

'Oh, she's getting there,' said Owen. 'I have high hopes for that woman.'

Duncan felt dizzy on his feet. Not as wobbly as Carter Carnehan would when he woke up. Not half as much as the reckless fool deserved to, for gambling with the life of every prisoner on the station. 'Reckon if Helrena wins the imperial throne, she'll celebrate by setting us all free? That's the sort of thing nobles are meant to do when they take to a throne, isn't it? Open the gates to all of the prisons and give everyone a free pass?'

Owen shrugged. 'Maybe an ounce of barley extra for the gruel pot, every day for a week.'

It isn't much to stay alive for. But at least Duncan was alive to regret how little he had been left with.

There were four slaves in as accomplices on Carter's scheme. Eshean and Joah from back home – those two he knew he could trust with his back. Their transporter pilot was Alan Ferris, a Weyland man, too – an easterner from the same raid that had taken Anna and Owen. The one he'd taken the biggest risk with was Deeli Baigent, a rake-thin old hand who had only survived so long by working in the clerks' office, making sure that every tonne of ore was accounted for without anything of value being 'mislaid' by the Vandian transport crews who shipped the sky mine's bounty out. There wasn't much Deeli couldn't hustle on the station, from extra rations to fixing the slave duty rotas, and it had been the latter which Carter needed to manipulate to make his escape plan work. Carter wished there had been more people from Northhaven he could have trusted, but Duncan's cowardice in the hangar had opened his eyes to how far old loyalties could be trusted when things got tight in a hurry. *If it wasn't for that yellow idiot, everyone here could have marched off the station onto Helrena Skar's battleship for a first-class ticket home. Helrena's girl first, with a gun barrel in her ear.* Much good had Duncan's spinelessness done him. He'd heard from Owen how Helrena had refused to return Adella to the station, despite the two Weylanders foiling the noblewoman's assassination and preventing her daughter's kidnap. Trusting a Vandian to do the right thing was like trusting a viper not to bite you just because you'd avoiding stamping on it. *Poor Duncan Landor. Looking to flee his fate back home because he couldn't stomach his responsibilities. Frozen with fear in the sky mines like a rabbit transfixed by a hawk's shadow – not even able to run!* Well, there was no point in brooding over lost opportunities. You made your own luck in the sky mines, and Carter was about to set up a factory line to produce chances to get out of here for him and his gang of like-minded accomplices. Pity Willow came from Duncan's blood. The young woman shared her brother's defeatist attitude, taking every opportunity to try to badger Carter into thinking this was no time to do anything as precipitate as jumping ship. If he could have taken Willow along, his breakout might have felt a little less like abandoning everyone else to a bad fate. *It's not actually her I'm worrying about, is it?* But Willow had made it clear where she stood. If Willow loved labouring inside the sky mines so much, she would have to stick with it. Maybe he could have bound and gagged Willow ... kidnapped the irritating woman. But escaping the imperium was going to be difficult enough for those actually willing to put their necks on the line to risk it. Carter had also tried to sound out Anna about getting off the station as well, but the transporter pilot seemed reticent to abandon Owen, who wasn't minded to leave unless every Weyland soul was given the same chance, so Anna would have to take her chances up here too, and damn the promise Carter had made to Anna's brother back on the skel aircraft. Kerge's dire warnings crossed Carter's mind, too, but Carter forced the gask's concerns out of head. The twisted man had said it himself: no fate but that made by will; and if there was one thing that people agreed about when discussing Carter Carnehan, it was that here walked a strong-willed man.

'It's taking too long,' said Deeli, glancing nervously around the refectory hall. 'They should have called for us by now.'

'Don't worry,' said Carter, reaching across the table to tug at the man's sleeve. 'You fixed the rotas. All of us are off-shift and top of the list for the summons.'

'What if something goes wrong, man?'

'I've evened the odds a little,' said Carter, sharing a knowing glance with the four men. He held up a postage stamp-sized sackcloth bag, empty and coated with a black dusting. 'There was blasting powder mixed in with the pilots' tea today, as well as nettles! There isn't a transporter flyer in the station that won't be clutching their stomach and bringing up the contents of their dinner.'

'What if the stratovolcano doesn't blow?'

'You've heard the tremors down there,' said Joah, pushing his cheap spectacles up the bridge of his nose. 'The shocks started to arrive within an hour of when Carter predicted they would.'

'Well,' said Eshean. 'It was following you out from behind the safety of the town's walls that got me and Noah into this plight. The way I see it, the least you can do is lead us out of here.'

'Sounds like a huge eruption coming,' said Alan Ferris, the transport pilot's fingers drumming the surface of the table. 'I don't know where you've been getting your forecasts from, Northhaven, but that sounds like a big one, all right. I've flown enough sensor check runs to recognise the signs. There's not an insect in the sky.'

'What if the princess decides that one sky mine is enough?' whined Deeli. 'We've hardly bored into the rock tied up against the station?'

Alan Ferris snorted. 'You mean what if the ethreaal have been visiting the mistress at night and whispering that the lives of her slaves are worth something more than being worked to death, and God says she shouldn't get greedy for a second stake? How much is enough for the Vandians, you old fool? You've been here long enough to know we'll be risking our necks beating some other idiot to death over a floating chunk of ore soon enough.'

Carter tempered his own frayed nerves. He felt like grabbing the old hand and shaking him until he shut up about how many damn ways there were for this scheme to fail. Instead, Carter just poured the clerk another tepid glass of water from the pottery jug sitting in front of them. 'Drink that down and grab yourself hard. Way you've been coughing, you're not going to last too many more seasons up here as it is.'

'You think I don't know that, man? I've been here the longest of anyone. But there are worse things than dying of tunnel lung. Torture's a high craft to the Vandians, and they reserve their top artists for slaves who need to be made an example of – to stop the lower castes getting ideas above their station.'

'Cheer up,' said Carter, forcing a smile. 'We're all going to be dead, soon. And a dead slave is worth nothing, not even searching for.' *The hard part*, Carter reckoned, *would be dying without getting killed*.

A slave entered looking for Alan Ferris. Finding the pilot, the slave passed across a sheet with duty orders and a team roster scrawled across it. 'You're up.'

Alan managed to look convincingly annoyed at being interrupted while eating. 'Already?'

'Sensor line needs to be checked.'

Alan grunted. 'I can tell you a large blow-out's coming soon. Don't need seismic readouts to back up what a man's nose can tell him.'

'Sadly,' said the slave, 'Thomas Gale likes to have a little more than your snozzle to go on when ordering down-tools for everyone and hitters into the hangar. Gather your crew, get into the stink and bring us up some good news.'

'The good news,' said Alan, carefully watching the messenger depart the refectory, 'is that the team for the sensor line recovery is already sitting around this table.' He turned the sheet of paper about so they could read it.

'That's lucky for us,' said Carter. 'And I bet your transporter's been stuffed with extra water canteens and respirator cylinders, too.' He looked at Deeli.

'What, I should want to suffocate or die of dehydration? It's taken care of, man.'

'Then let's get out of here,' said Carter. 'There are readouts to be retrieved. And that's a mighty *dangerous* job.'

'That's real sweet,' said Alan Ferris, pulling camouflage netting over their grounded transporter. He clung tight to the craft's side, tremors across the land shaking the transporter like a baby's metal rattle. 'Not many hitters in the air now. Ours or the other houses' birds.' They had landed the transporter exactly where Carter had planned – in front of the standing circle near the stratovolcano's base. No sensor spikes driven in the ground here. Not now the enemy houses knew it was one of their spots. Hopefully that meant the area would be low down on the list of places to look for the party after it was posted missing.

Carter pulled his survival suit on along with the others in the gang. On the outside the fabric was a shiny foil-like metal, thin enough to crumple and fold. Inside, it was padded with a thin layer that moved like gel when you pressed a finger against it, trying to shift out of the way as though it was alive. *Weirdest suit I'm ever going to wear. Maybe it's not a fire suit today, but an escape suit.* Carter left his hood down for the moment, his respirator mask dangling from straps around his neck. He didn't feel safe wearing the suit. Certainly not protected enough to escape a full eruption from Old Smoky. Its slopes loomed above them as if they could use the volcano to climb into the sky. Thankfully, Carter had other ideas for getting out of here.

Eshean, Noah and the dockets man, Deeli, had formed a human chain, passing supplies towards the cave; sufficient air, water and food to last them as long as this might take. Their rations had been pilfered slowly and carefully; nothing that would lead the Vandians or their slave overseers to suspect an escape attempt had been made, even when they got around to taking a tally of station supplies. Carter had been champing at the bit to launch this escape, but he knew they were only going to get one shot at breaking loose, so he'd bitten his tongue, slowed down and taken the time to prepare for the task properly. Ejecta mass pattered around his sandals, a shower of ash and burning pebbles whistling down fast on streaking smoke-tails. There were still a few kinks that could derail Carter's plans; like a landslide hitting their transporter, magma flows burying it, or a direct hit from ejecta mass large enough to damage the craft beyond repair. But hell, if that happened they could just sit down and wait for rescue like good little slaves who had been planning to go back to the station all along. *Just riding out the eruption, Mister Gale. Bad luck to be caught short by it.* Sweet God, but it felt good to be doing something on his own account. Acting as a free man at last. Fear he might be caught mixed with exhilaration; a heady cocktail that left Carter shivering to hold himself together.

He ducked under the cave entrance, activating a battery lamp and swinging it around. The grotto went back fifteen feet inside, a rough, spherical space, its ground uneven and rocky. Not easy to sit on, but they would have to make the best of it. This was where Carter planned to hole up as the stratovolcano blasted its fury at the sky. He'd be helped by the short, narrow entrance. That'd protect the party from the worst of the eruption's ferocity. Fumes drifting out of cracks in the stone floor were less helpful, but they had brought spare air canisters for their masks. The men dragged their supplies inside the cave, and then walked back to the transporter to help Alan peg down the camouflage netting. The rock-patterned meshwork needed to remain intact enough to escape detection by the princess's rivals. *Sure would be ironic. Getting our heads broken by slaves from another station; murdered for a mistress we're no longer serving.* Just another thing that could go wrong with his scheme.

Rock fall had grown worse by the time they finished and were all squeezed into a tight circle within the cave. His body started to ache, and not just from nerves, the uncomfortable seat or the work of stocking this cavity in the volcano's slopes. Carter realised this was the longest period of time he'd spent on the ground since he had been taken by the skels. His body had acclimatised to the weak high-altitude gravity of the station and the sky mine tethered to it.

'What if there's a rock slide?' moaned Deeli. 'We could die trapped in here.'

'I don't think this area sees too much spew,' said Carter. 'Look at the standing stones outside. They've been here forever and they're still intact. A little magma flow solidified around their base, but that's it.

We're too far down – and the blast is going up and out. The height of that monster outside is going to protect us'

'You've got a fine brain inside that ornery skull of yours,' said Noah.

'Just don't tell anyone,' said Carter. 'I've a reputation to keep.'

'How about you let us in on the second part of your scheme, professor,' demanded Alan. 'Hiding out here and getting posted missing, presumed dead. Anyone could arrange that. But escaping across the dead zone is a whole other thing. Even with the extra fuel we've stolen, we're not going to be able to cross more than a quarter of the dead zone. The Vandians have dirt miners out there, scrabbling around for rock-fall the major houses don't catch. When we run, we're going to have an escaped slave's price on our head and not enough water in our canteens to complete a fraction of the journey, and that's if we *don't* get spotted by Vandian ships sweeping for mineral poachers.'

'Maybe you should just trust me.'

'And maybe you should just tell me – so I don't start thinking that you've lied about how you've got a fool-proof way of escaping; say, to string me and the boys along. I'm not aiming to play possum on the ground, so you can try to jump a company of heavily-armed Vandian guardsmen, hijack their patrol ship, and hope I can fly it.'

'I said I had a scheme for an escape,' said Carter, 'not a suicide.'

'We're trusting you, here,' said Noah. 'I think it's time you started trusting us back.'

'Okay then,' sighed Carter. 'We ride out the worst of the eruption down here. What's going to happen back on the station when it stops?'

'Same as always,' said Eshean. 'Scouts out as soon as it's half-safe to fly, all the men loaded into transporters. Everyone looking for the biggest claim with the best mix of ores. A bloody battle between the houses, and the lucky ones head back to the station with a fresh claim to tie-up.'

'Exactly,' said Carter. 'Too busy to search for us until the dust's settled. And by then we won't be here. We won't wait until it's half-safe to fly, we'll light out of here when it's quarter-safe to fly, and follow the ejecta-mass straight up.'

Eshean laughed. 'Are you planning to stake an early claim for the princess? Hell, you saved her brat's life and she never freed you. What's raising a flag on a chunk of gold-veined rock going to buy you?'

'Gold, no,' said Carter. 'I'm planning to stake a claim to the least viable rock we can find ... small, basalt, empty and useless. Not enough metal in it to make a wedding ring if you broke the whole thing down and ground it into dust. Just large enough to land a transporter on it. Maybe a nice hollow on its roof we can cover over with camouflage netting. And what would happen to that rock?'

'Dear God!' said Noah. 'If it had enough velocity, it'd be ignored – straight up into the trade winds, dragged out for millions of miles, maybe!'

'And we'd be sitting pretty on it,' said Carter. 'From what I've heard, plenty of those rocks stay in the air, a navigation hazard to aircraft looking to save fuel at maximum altitude. Other rocks bomb into the sea. But either way, we'd have a transporter to reach the ground safe. One of the imperium's neighbours would do for me. We can set down somewhere remote, swipe local clothes off a village clothes line to cover our slave brands, then head for any city big enough to have an airport where we can work passage on a merchant carrier. Even if we never see Weyland or the league again, we'll be *free*. Free of this hell.'

'That might work,' said Noah, his voice growing excited.

'It will,' said Carter. 'Alan, you're a pilot, your skill should be worth plenty outside the imperium. When we reach a nation inside the guild system, I can find a librarian's hold and convince its master that I'm one of their fellow-archive stuffers. They'll help us fix our position relative to home. Show us the way back. We can do this!'

A frown creased Eshean's features. 'But Carter, a plan like that – we could have taken more people. We could have broken out with a dozen transporters full of prisoners!'

'Hell,' said Carter, 'we could have taken the whole caboodle. And as soon as the Vandians catch on that one of their barracks is floating as empty in the sky as the ghost station, they'd realise the trick we pulled and send battleships chasing after rock in the air for a little target practice. This was only ever going to work with a single transporter, its crew's bones believed to be scattered out here, covered in lava.'

'You're a hard bastard, Carter. We could have taken more people ...'

'That's horseshit. Ditch your guilt right here – I could barely scrape together the four of you with the guts to try to escape.'

Deeli vigorously shook his head in agreement. 'You're right, you're right. Someone would have informed on us. An overseer, a spy, a slave. The last escape attempt was ten years before you were taken. Fella worked in the repair bays, real cushy job too. Dug a passage out of the station that only he knew about. Put a glider together inside it. He was planning to fly onto the top of a supply ship at night, leap off its hull as it was approaching a Vandian city. The soldiers were waiting for him when he landed on its hull. Someone sold him out. One of us. Vandians staked him down in the hangar and brought in a torturer. We had to line up and watch. In shifts. Took him three days to die.'

'What was his name?' asked Carter.

Tears welled in Deeli's eyes. 'I don't remember.'

Carter shook his head. Deeli was close to breaking. But perhaps that was okay, he had been here the longest of any slave. 'Doesn't matter. He was us, every one of us here. That's all we need to remember.'

'I have an extra canteen,' said Deeli, tapping a bag. 'Water mixed with mogo tuber. Strong dose, man. Die in minutes. We can take it if it looks like we're going to be captured.'

'Pour the water on the soil when we land,' said Carter. 'We're not going to need it.' He slipped the air mask over his face and hooded up.

Outside, the noise of the eruption grew louder and louder, their cave floor jouncing in the earth tremors until they had to extend their arms like frightened children and huddle together to stop themselves being tumbled around the cave. The supply crates they'd taken in for safe-keeping shook and clattered until Carter feared they were going to shatter. It was growing hotter, too, although he was too scared to sweat. Thick fumes began to fill the space, until Carter was almost sick with the rotten-egg stink, even through the respirator and silvery hood of his survival suit. He closed his eyes tight and focused on the regular click of his mask measuring out fresh doses of air. Might as well be ants caught under the hooves of a cattle stampede for all that they could do to influence their fates now.

Carter inspected the camouflage netting he had dragged off the transporter while Noah, Eshean and Deeli emptied the cave of the supplies they'd stored, rapidly refilling the craft. Every surface was coated in dust, although strangely, the standing circle seemed to be clear of a powder layer, as though there was some invisible shield protecting it. Sections of netting had been eaten away by the eruption, its camouflage surface left littered with black rock residue. Carter tipped the rubble out onto the slope. The netting was intact enough to deploy a second time. And more importantly, their transporter still looked operational enough to take to the air. Alan checked the engine and rotors over as fast as he could while calling it through. Their craft had to survive a race through the centre of the storm of ejecta-mass and come through undamaged enough to land and take off one last time. Waiting on the ground had given Carter a too-close-for-comfort insight into when an eruption started to lose force – far more precise than being holed up in the station and waiting for the storm to abate. Carter wouldn't recommend it as a way of getting the jump on the other sky miners. Not even to his worst enemy. He had sat hunkered down inside the cave for more than five hours, every minute of that time spent anticipating his end. Now he was out in the open again, shaking from exhaustion and excitement and fear. *One last stake to fight over. And the next rock is going to be all yours.*

'She's air-worthy,' announced Alan, climbing into the pilot's seat up front.

Carter swung himself onto the crew cage at the back, stowing the camo cover. 'Then the air is where we need to be.'

Noah laughed, joining Eshean and Deeli on the craft's seating. 'What do you think they'll say in Northhaven, if they see us walking back through the gates?'

'Where's everyone else?' muttered Eshean.

Carter blinked in surprise. In truth, the idea of escaping from the sky mines had been his obsession for so long – the only thing he had been able to think about – he'd never even considered what life might be like back in Weyland. 'Everyone I cared about back home is dead.' *And what about the people back on the station?* nagged the voice. He ignored it. Hadn't the other slaves had their chance? 'I don't think I'll go back. I was planning to sign up as a sailor and see the world. Maybe I'll just start from this end of the world.'

'I want to go back,' said Noah. 'See if my folks were left alive after the raid. If they are, they deserve to know that I didn't die as a slave out in the middle of the beyond.'

'I'll travel with you,' said Eshean. 'As big as the world is, there'll never be a country like Weyland or a town like Northhaven. I don't know how welcome we'll be, though, outside of our kin. Our faces are going to remind folks about a disaster that'll be long forgotten by the time we arrive back.'

Carter tried to imagine what it might be like returning to work at the librarian's hold in the valley, settling down to the suffocating routine that had driven him insane with boredom. And that was *before* he'd watched his family massacred, the town burnt – a forced witness to every pointless death in the slave pens and the sky mines. He wasn't the same man, now. Home had been taken from him. Forever.

'What about you, Deeli?' asked Carter.

The rake-thin old hand shook his head, dejectedly. 'I can't go home, man. I wasn't grabbed up in a raid, like you. My nation sells its convicts to the skels. My farm went bust in the great drought – my wife and sons passed slow from starvation and exhaustion ploughing our bare, dry fields, day after day. Didn't see much point in working on after they died. I was thrown in debtors' prison until my own mayor marched me to the auction block. If I travelled home, it would be a week or two before someone recognised me. They'd lock me up again and sell me to the first slaver that landed.'

'You can ship out with me,' said Carter. He began setting up the surveying equipment in the rear. Everything they would need to find a rock that was small, fast and as empty as a slave's stomach without a claim to work.

'Or travel to Weyland with me and Eshean,' added Noah.

'I don't want to go on the road. Just land us somewhere green and far from the imperium's reach,' said Deeli. 'I haven't got long left, now, I know that. My lungs' insides are as black as this volcano. I want to die watching butterflies chase each other over the meadows. Not sweating inside the sky mines until my corpse is tipped out on top of this never-ending bone-pile.'

'You're an easy man to please,' said Carter.

'The sky stole my life,' said Deeli. 'I want my death to belong to me. I'll be the wild man of the woods, eating berries and snaring rabbits, for as long as my body holds out.'

Below them, the rotors spun into life, a blast of choking dust blown out from below the transporter. 'Hold on tight back there,' called Alan. 'I'll be pushing the engine hard to get into the mix before any of the other houses' scouts.'

'Let's do it,' said Carter. He leaned in close to the cockpit at the front, raising his voice above the roar of the engines. 'How about you, Mister Ferris? Planning on heading to Weyland, travelling back east to the lakes?'

'Why not,' said the pilot. 'I'll have to do something with all the time I have ... now I won't be chasing rocks, ferrying hitters and blasting tunnels!'

'One last chase, first,' laughed Carter. 'And you'll find I'm not half as fussy as the princess when it comes to staking a claim.'

Alan reached for his air mask and the rest of them followed suit. Their transporter rocked in the air after it lifted away from the slopes, passing through thick black clouds rolling down the volcano in waves. They still wore their silver survival suits, useful protection against the burning gases the craft sliced through; vapour full of dust that bit like a sandstorm boiled white-hot inside a kettle. Alan used the mass of the stratovolcano's slopes to help push them into the open skies. Something about the heat of the recent eruption seemed to have thinned the air, making the ungainly transporter even harder to fly. But transporters were built as primitive aerial packhorses, not a flying wing of the Rodalian skyguard. Then they were free of the slopes, riding the sky proper, a rain of ejecta-mass rattling against the cage's roof. The rain wasn't falling, though, it was still rising, and they were chasing it up, gaining altitude at a steep angle. Carter wiped dust off his air mask's visor, gazing out of the cage's sides. The powerful outgassing from the stratovolcano had left a doughnut-shaped shockwave ... a rolling, expanding cloud-front arrowing towards the heavens. It was being filled in by steaming vapour from the sides, but at the moment, he had been given a clear view that few sky miners would have seen. Rocks, thousands of them, small and large and every shape imaginable, lifting towards a distant blue circle of sky. Fairly soon the claims would be cloaked with steam. The vapour filled by transporters from the sky mines, craft wheeling and jostling for position. Shortly, slaves would be murdering each for the largest, most valuable rocks. Maybe Duncan would be among the fighters, Owen and Kerge too. *Too bad for them; but faint hearts don't win freedom.*

Carter's eyes flicked down towards the dead zone. The barren bone-scattered land was masked by outgassing from the stratovolcano, as was the hoary old smoker's interior, but he suddenly caught a silvery glint from below. Something slipping through the smouldering cover like a shark ... a steel-hulled predator. 'Vandian patrol ship!' yelled Carter. 'Coming up below our rotors.'

'I see it!' called Alan. 'Flying at six o'clock'

'What the hell is it doing here?' shouted Carter. 'They should be sweeping the dead zone for mineral poachers, not passing through unstaked sky ten minutes before their slaves start swinging clubs at each other.'

'We have to keep on making for the rock-storm,' said Noah. 'As far as they're concerned, we're just a scout pushed out desperately early, searching for a stake for a hungry station.'

'Noah's right,' said Carter. 'Hell, we can wave at them as they fly past. They can't read minds. And we *are* searching for a stake. Nobody as eager as us in the air!'

His words were hopeful but his heart sank. He didn't believe in coincidences, and his mind was racing with all the ways this escape attempt could have gone wrong. *What could have given us away?* Carter searched the clouds below. The patrol ship had vanished from sight, but then, the incredible speed those things could move at, it could be anywhere in the air. The roar of its engine was masked by the greater thunder emanating from the rumbling monster below.

'I think it's gone,' said Eshean. 'I can't see it anymore.'

'Did any of you tell anybody back on the station about this?' said Carter. 'Sound someone out who showed a little too much interest ... but then didn't want to sign up with us?'

Deeli angrily shook his head. 'I didn't tell anybody, man. I barely trusted you when you approached me, in case you were setting up a phoney escape; a loyalty test to earn you a reward for handing me in. Wouldn't be the first time that's happened on the station.'

'No one's talked,' said Noah. 'We set this up real quiet.'

'Paper trail is covered, too,' said Deeli. 'Every piece of kit we've taken with us was allocated to genuine mining gangs months ago. Nothing to be missed.'

Carter frowned. 'Then why the hell is that patrol ship nosing around here *now*? Risking clogging their fancy engines in this almighty turd-storm? It doesn't make sense.'

'Maybe the station's worried we crashed during the eruption?' said Eshean. 'Our radio room could have sent for them?'

'And the kind empire risks its people's lives to help stranded slaves? Maybe they're transporting a suckling pig roast to us, with a crew of dancing girls to serve food and kiss our burnt knees better. Nobody on the station should be thinking about a missing crew until the princess has herself a second shiny new stake tethered next to her first. I don't like this.'

Carter liked ducking as the Vandian patrol ship shot overhead even less. The noise of its passage left his ears ringing so badly he could hardly hear the others' yells of surprise. Alan pulled the transporter to the side, heading for a roll of thick dark cloud, the transporter shaking in the patrol ship's shock wake. Behind them, the ship came roaring back, slowing and hovering on towers of flames as engines on its flank angled and held it suspended there like a hunting hawk. The patrol vessel was an ugly long elongated tube of shiny silver steel, the pilots' silhouettes just visible through the light of the bridge's windows on its prow. The lines of its streamlined hull were broken by the shape of a cannon turret, four barrels rotating towards them. Just as black cloud swallowed the transporter, the hovering patrol ship's gun starting banging shells after them, a rapid thud-thud-thud faster than any man could work the lever on a rifle. Carter didn't hear the shells whizzing past, but the scream of tearing metal from the engine housing below their craft was unmistakable, as was their sudden pitch downwards. Black clouds rushed past, the transporter corkscrewing as Alan fought for control; the party thrown about in the back, desperately clinging to seats and cage sides as the transporter gained speed. Every man was yelling and shouting, Carter's fear added to theirs. Licks of fire climbed up the back of the transporter, a streaming tail of flames from their engines. Haemorrhaging brown fuel that reeked as badly as the poisonous gas surrounding them. Nothing Carter could do but hang on, vowing that if he survived, whoever had betrayed them was going to pay for this with their life. A wrenching noise and an engine assembly came twisting past in the open air, sheared off by shell damage. Then a fierce buzzing. One of their rotors must have cleared after shrugging away the mangled mess. *We have lift again.* Carter was pushed back into the cage wall as the transporter pulled up. Alan yelled in front, screaming at his flight stick as if he could urge it to greater labours. For a moment Carter allowed himself to believe they were going to make it. If they could lose the patrol ship ... he had only shared the final piece of his escape plan inside the cave ... hitching a lift on a barren rock from the eruption. The Vandians wouldn't know his escape route was straight up and out, not attempting to flee the dead zone in the transporter. Carter could feel from the increasing gravity how close they were to the ground, and then they were fed rock, right into the craft's nose as the slope burst through the mist and met the corkscrewing transporter. Its hull rolled, Carter smashed around, striking bodies and metal. Suddenly he rolled free, hard surface burning through his survival suit. He spun out the worst of the momentum until he collided with a rocky outcrop, smashing his spine into it, leaving him gasping and stunned. *Hot, hot. Where have we come down?* A roar sounded from the sky as loud as anything he'd ever heard, passing as quickly as it appeared. Their crash site had just been overflown by the patrol ship. Carter found it hard to breathe, until he realised his air mask had become dislodged. He pushed the respirator back around his mouth, holding it in place through the silvery fabric of the survival suit. Staggering to his feet, Carter had trouble locating the transporter until he spotted it behind him, lying on its side, bent and smashed and smoking from its mangled engines. Up above, he could see sky and slope mixed through the fumes and ash-fall coming down like rain, and with a start he realised where they had come down ... they were stranded close to the lip of the crater. A minute climbing the slope, and he could stare straight down into the heart of the beast. Carter limped over towards the downed craft, seeing Noah emerge from the back, Eshean leaning against him. From the state of Eshean's left leg, unnaturally bent at an angle no man should be able to bear, Carter knew that a quick amputation was the only chance of survival the Weylander had left. Deeli had been thrown clear of the craft, same as Carter, the man trying to get to his feet. He moved forward to get a look into the cockpit at the front. Crushed and destroyed. Carter turned his face away in shock and went back towards Deeli. There wasn't enough of Alan left to fill a casket at the front of a church. *Weren't exactly aiming to take us alive. At least I know that none of us down here is the son-of-a-bitch traitor who whistled on our scheme.*

'We're finished,' moaned Deeli. 'Might as well taste my canteen now. Share the poison around!'

'Not yet,' said Carter, the words squeezed out dry and hoarse. 'We'll slip away down the slope; find some of those ground worms mining the rock-fall. They'll have transport we can steal.'

'Dead,' said Deeli, as if he hadn't heard Carter's words at all. 'Quick or slow, that's our only choice.' Carter ignored the slave and pushed him towards Eshean and Noah, more roughly than he had intended. The scrawny sky miner nearly fell over.

'You better leave me here,' announced Eshean, his face pale through the transparent visor of his hood. 'If you're planning to cross the dead zone on foot, you might as well strap that wreckage back there on your back as take me along.'

'Let's carry you anyway,' said Noah. 'It's a fine day for it.'

Below Noah's hood, Carter noticed the glass of the man's spectacles had been broken across both lenses. Shouts sounded from the thick clouds to their side, distant and muffled, and with all the survivors accounted for here ... that only left one possibility. Carter shot a look at Deeli. 'How many crewmen does a patrol vessel carry?'

Deeli pulled himself together to answer. 'There's a pilot and a co-pilot/gunner. The standard complement in the back is five guardsmen.'

'Grab the clubs from the back of the transporter. We can drop the guards in the mist, take their guns and hijack the ship.'

'That's as mad as anything I've heard,' said Noah.

'They can't see us in this damn smoke,' said Carter. 'And they're overconfident, same as the scum I killed back on the station. We can circle them, ambush them, arm up with their weapons and then we jump the patrol ship.'

'Hunters don't expect to be stalked,' said Eshean. 'It could work. Nobody fool enough to do that. Except you, Carter.'

'More desperate than foolish, today.'

'Crazy! Who's going to fly the ship, man?' whined Deeli. 'Ferris is gone!'

'I'll do it myself,' said Carter. 'If it comes to it. The imperium must keep the ships' controls simple if they expect those big lazy brutes to fly them. But we can take one of the pilots alive and tickle him with the edge of a blade to get some cooperation.'

Carter took Eshean on his shoulder and half-walked, half-dragged the man back towards the transporter wreck. Eshean moaned in agony as he was helped. 'Try real hard to keep at least one pilot alive, eh? Don't need matching splints on my legs.'

'I'll lay you up inside the cage. When we're in the mist, you yell for help, loud as you can, as if you can't move and you're bleeding out. Draw the soldiers in towards here.'

'Carter, I *can't* move, and I *am* bleeding out.'

Carter climbed into the slanting back of the craft, Noah helping lift Eshean's body up, Carter dragging him under cover. 'Won't need to act much, then.'

Carter broke open the compartment holding the heavy wooden clubs, took his and passed a handle apiece to Noah and Deeli.

'I'll have one too,' said Eshean.

Carter tossed a length of wood at the Weylander. It was going to be more use as a crutch. 'Swing hard, big man.'

'I'll cuff them with what's left of my leg if they get too close.'

Carter grunted. He didn't voice it, but part of him wished that it had been one of the other two who had taken that mangled leg. With his size, Eshean was a hell of a hitter, while both Noah and Deeli would have been better suited to filing archive updates in a librarian's hold. Alan Ferris dead and crushed in the pilot's seat. Their transporter wrecked. Carter's perfect escape plan spiked. Eshean crippled. Four of them against a company of heavily armed thugs. Kerge's ominous warnings about attempting to escape were proving to be every bit as accurate as the gask's prediction of the eruption. Their trail along the great fractal tree was narrowing to a single, desperate branch; with assaulting the Vandians sent to kill them the only direction left to travel.

Carter and his two accomplices slipped down the slope and glided into the smoke. This fog wasn't spilling over from the crater's lip, but hissing from side vents, solidified magma holes ranging in size from molehills to rocky mounts, arranged like wounds along the slope and bleeding fumes and gas. Smoke cover. The three of them stalked wide, until they trailed behind the guardsmen's excited shouts. Carter quickly lost sight of Deeli and Noah, and had to trust that they were still doing what they needed to. In the distance he could hear Eshean's pleading yells, begging for help and transport back to the sky mine. These Vandian soldiers sounded enthusiastic and pleased with themselves, hollering like they were out hunting game in the woods. What could be easier? Pumping a bullet or two into a handful of slaves who'd already been shot-up and forced down on the volcano. Given how few escape attempts had been made since Carter had arrived, this must be the highlight of the soldiers' year. This is what the bastards lived for. *Let's see if I can't dent their enthusiasm, along with a skull or two.*

A shape coalesced in front of him – the familiar sight of a Vandian's armoured back below a cape, the soldier clutching a rifle and whistling to his people to let them know his position. An intimidating size, heavily built and over six foot tall. He wore a silver helmet with a rigid red brush coming down the back of the helm – a more perfect target Carter couldn't have hoped for. Carter suppressed a yell of fury as he ran in – surprise his most effective weapon – and swung at the helm, felling the brute as his gouged helmet tumbled off to the side. An initial moan and the guardsman collapsed forward, lying face-down and still across the slope. Carter rolled him over and lifted the rifle away from the soldier's body, keeping a wary eye on the mist. The weapon didn't look much like the rifles back home – a metal stock engraved with imperial emblems, heavy, a metal magazine the length of a hand protruding in front of the trigger guard. Its safety catch was where its equivalent would be from the Landsman Weapon Works, though, and that was all he needed to know to work it. There was a sharp saw-toothed bayonet attached under the barrel for when it ran out of ammunition. Carter removed the soldier's air mask and and exchanged it for his own, making sure the pig wouldn't be coming around if he wasn't dead already. Shouts and shots sounded from inside the hot mist, hard to triangulate but very close. Somewhere, Eshean was still calling. Carter couldn't shoot blind – not without risking hitting Noah and Deeli, so he climbed the slope, the stinking fog starting to thin out. He figured if he could get on the lip of the crater and take position above the wrecked transporter, he'd have enough of a view to pick the soldiers off as they went for Eshean. There was a moan to his right and Carter swung the rifle around. Bodies on the rock, fuming mist passing over them like a river. Not the soldier Carter had just brained – another armoured Vandian stretched out, with Noah and Deeli close by, all prone and on the ground. The Vandian had been beaten down with clubs, same as Carter's. Noah had a red crater where his forehead should be, below the shattered faceplate of the survival suit. Deeli was the only one alive, just, moaning as he clutched at his bleeding gut, blood smeared across the silvery fabric as though Deeli had been swinging a cleaver at a butcher's table. The dead soldier's rifle wasn't here – must have had comrades who didn't want to leave it behind with escaping slaves stalking the slopes.

Carter knelt by Deeli, hand still on his rifle, taking his hand. 'Stay still. They'll have bandages and medicine on the patrol ship. I'll come back for you.'

'Won't — need my — canteen, now,' whispered Deeli, hard to hear through his respirator. 'You take — it.'

'Stow it. We'll be drinking wine to celebrate getting out of here.'

'Just— bones,' said Deeli, his voice growing even fainter, 'that's all — we are. My wife. My boys — me. Piles — of—'

Deeli rested his face against a rock, as if he was making himself comfortable on a pillow. He grew still, his eyes shutting and his fingers trembling no more. Carter stood up and pulled the rifle in hard under his arm. Noah's corpse stared accusingly at him through his broken glasses, saying not a thing. Guilt and anger fought for control of Carter's mind, but he shook them both away. Only a cold, detached sense of purpose left. To accomplish what he had left the station to do.

Narrower and narrower, the paths on the great fractal tree. Carter was balanced on a twig, now. 'See you soon, boys.'

He continued to climb the slope, homing in on the increasing furnace heat from the stratovolcano's crater. Black ash fell again when he came to the vent's lip, the great beast's interior masked by a vast column of smoke, waves of heat buffeting against him. Tracking along the edge he ran low in the direction of the mangled transporter. Carter had almost run past the crash site when the mist briefly cleared down below, allowing him a horrifying glimpse of two grunting soldiers, swinging their bayonets into Eshean like miners swinging pickaxes at a rock face – the Weylander stretched out in the ground behind the craft's passenger cage, already dead. Lifeless, but his body being used like a punch bag with a steady, continuous thud of blades into his chest. They were attacking him contemptuously, rhythmically, showing what they thought of slaves that attacked their masters. Desecrating his corpse. One soldier lashed from Eshean's left with his bayonet, the other swinging on the right, venting their fury on all that was left of the slave.

Carter bent down on one knee and took aim. When he pressed the trigger, the rifle surprised him. Not a single shot, but shaking with a continuous burst, the barrel rattling and bucking as he fought to keep it depressed in the direction of the two guardsmen. Whatever the hell Carter was shooting with, the two men were thrown back hard, tossed into the wreckage, their armour shredded by the spray of bullets, his rifle left clacking as the magazine complained that it was empty. Carter was getting to his feet, thinking about searching the dead guards for ammunition or just taking their rifles, when a furious red-faced Vandian appeared from the mist no more than a foot away, charging while firing his officer's pistol at Carter. He hadn't got off more than a single, wild shot when Carter's empty rifle swept around like a club and cracked into the officer's gloved hand, sending the pistol careening away into the air. Both the officer's crimson gloves locked around the rifle's stock and the two of them wrestled for the weapon – empty and useful only as a bayonet-tipped spear. Stumbling and pushing and pulling, the Vandian's eyes wide and manic through the oxygen mask built into his helmet. Like all of the thugs in armour Carter had come across, the officer looked like he'd been bred from a nation of giants. Bigger than Carter; better fed; not rangy after being sweated close to death working the sky mines; used to full gravity on the ground, too. They struggled and grappled, grunting at each other like animals, Carter desperate for the freedom evaporating around him – this brute probably just as desperate to return to his base with the corpses of all the escaped slaves piled across his patrol ship's deck.

His legs ached. Carter could feel the strength slowly draining out of him as he stumbled back up the slope, pushed, higher and higher, giving ground to the Vandian officer. Sweat poured into his eyes faster than he could blink it away. Carter tried to concentrate on the tug of war for the rifle, the weapon's stock slipping through his hands as the officer's superior health began to tell on him. Heat hammered into his spine. They were on the crater's ridge. Angry bombs of volcanic debris whistled down like mortars, tossed out of the volcano; the smallest debris from the barrage enough to decapitate the two insignificant figures struggling for life on the crater rim. Side-vents oozed rivers of lava off to their right, a bubbling grey mass flowing down the stratovolcano's slope. There was a shattering explosion as it reached the transporter and burned through the surviving fuel reservoir, then the whole wreck was carried away, slowly melting, nothing left of Eshean or the Vandians who had murdered him. Whoever triumphed here would have to sprint through hell's own garden to survive. In a final act of desperation, Carter let go of the rifle and the officer tumbled to the side as the momentum of the struggle took him forward clutching his prize; Carter pulling the short-sword out of the officer's belt as he passed. Carter cracked the bayonet aside with the blade, the officer lunging forward and back in a professional thrust that should have speared Carter through the heart. Not many ways to beat an opponent with a longer reach and only a few weak spots between his steel plate. The Vandian seemed to have reached the same conclusion. He thrust again towards Carter, his aim only thrown off by the boot-quaking bellow of the stratovolcano behind them, the quake quickening, brittle rock under their feet shattering with the force of the roar. He screamed. Falling. *Falling.* Both Carter and his quarry tumbled directly down the crater's steep interior – sword and rifle sent spinning into the boiling steam. The hot rock slope cracked around Carter's ears as he rolled and turned through the fumes, gaining momentum. The glowing white-hot dome at the volcano's centre illuminated the thick vapour cloaking Carter, even as the screaming officer was lost to his sight. While plummeting, Carter's head glanced into a lava-dome solidified as hard as granite. It was almost a mercy when unconsciousness erased the furnace whirling up towards him.

*

Jacob walked the streets of Hangel's royal city, heading towards the area of the capital where the air brokers plied their trade. Jacob took the path that circled the plateau with Sheplar, Sariel and Khow; not for the spectacular views over the country below, but so they could feel the high-altitude breeze slipping in. This road was built into the ramparts, which from their genteel state of disrepair, obviously hadn't seen an assault for centuries. Hangel simmered already, the morning sun working its way to its full height. Small wonder the streets up here were so narrow; all the better to provide shade during the day. That and making the most of the mesa's limited real estate. An embrasure protected Jacob from the fall; he couldn't see the slums below without peering through arrow slits. Just the flat immensity of the savannah beyond – a few flat stands of trees breaking up the plains, a palette of yellows and browns and oranges as far as the eye could see, right up until the horizon was swallowed in heat shimmer. The height of the upper city didn't seem any protection against mosquitoes, though. Jacob's sweating skin itched, covered in bites from a single night spent in the librarians' guest quarters. He put the discomfort out of his mind. For the first time since their journey had begun, he had a name for their destination. It might take decades to fly to Vandia, but as long as Carter stayed alive, Jacob would free his son from slavery. Whatever it took, whoever he had to face.

They passed elaborate stone staircases leading down to homes built into the escarpment, gates guarded by brutal-looking soldiers in the same uniforms as the men who had admitted them into the city. The four travellers approached a wicker chute designed to carry rubbish away from the mesa and onto the slums below. Far away enough from the merchants' exclusive residences that the smell wouldn't be a problem. A long line of servants queued up with slop buckets from the previous night. This was, Jacob suspected, a fitting metaphor for the arrangement between Hangel's rich citizenry and the masses they kept subjugated. There appeared to be a disagreement at the front of the line. It sounded as though a local choir was practising, discordant singsong complaints. As Jacob got closer he found the cause of the dispute. Among the jostling crowd a wailing newborn was being held in the air, a half-breed from the mottled green sheen of the baby's skin. One of the gad servants was attempting to toss the baby down the wicker tube, while other workers jostled and shouted, trying to save the newborn.

Jacob pushed his way through the crowd to the front. 'What is this?'

'My son,' cried a female gad. 'They are taking my son from me!'

'It has been commanded,' said the servant holding the child. 'You know the king's orders. You should not have lain with your master.'

There were chants of 'shame' from the crowd, servants moving forward menacingly, the mob's tenor growing more discontented by the second.

'And how much choice was she permitted in the matter?' asked Jacob.

'You are not a Hangel. This is not your affair, foreigner,' said the servant, glancing nervously around the mob. His adherence to the letter of the law appeared to be the minority view among the commoners. 'All half-breeds must be put to death.'

'So, you're just going to put this baby out with the trash?'

'I have no choice,' protested the servant. 'The head of my household has ordered me to get rid of him.'

'You always have a choice, friend,' said Jacob, 'take it from someone who's made a few bad calls in his life.'

'Fine for you to talk of bravery, you with your foreign accent and your travel belt jingling with money. You will be gone from here, soon. It is not you who will feel the lash on your back for disobeying your master.'

'Is this wise?' warned Sheplar, his toothy grin disappearing as he was shoved about in the near riot. 'If we attempt to right every wrong from here to Vandia, the day will never arrive when we save your son.'

'I've had a bellyful of looking the other way,' retorted Jacob. 'I don't reckon I can travel much further with my eyes closed.'

'It is why the Rodalians fly so high,' said Sariel. 'So the clouds may better conceal the sight of their backs fleeing their foes.'

Sheplar's voice rose indignantly. Khow had to restrain him from laying into the vagrant. 'I am no coward, you thieving scoundrel. Let me hear you say it!'

'A fie on all Rodalians, that is all you will hear from me.'

With the expedition's attention distracted from the terrified servant, the gad tried to reach the top of the wicker tube, but the other workers swelled forward, forming a line in front of him, their eerie wailing a match for the unhappy newborn's screams. Jacob used the diversion to snatch the child from the servant's hands, passing him quickly back into the crowd's ranks. The babe spirited away through the gathering, swiftly hidden, his mouth covered to silence his bawling. It was as though a game of pass-the-parcel had just been played.

'And what will happen to me now?' the servant bleated, waving his empty hands in front of Jacob's face. 'Is my life worth any less than the child's? My master will hear of this. Someone will betray me, they always do!'

Jacob seized the servant by his dirty robes. 'I suggest you blame the ignorant foreigners.'

The servant was about to reply when the crowd dispersed at speed around them, shrieks and yells as some of the workers were bludgeoned to the ground. A company of soldiers had appeared, two lines of them; the first swinging clubs at the gads, the second standing back and grabbing as many fleeing servants as they could, kicking the workers to the ground and binding their arms behind their backs.

A Hangel officer strode forward, pointing to the gad servant. 'What is the meaning of this disturbance?'

'I live on the Road of Eucalyptuses – my master asked me to observe the royal ordinances and dispose of a half-breed here. The mother did not want me to do this.'

'And where is the female now?'

The servant looked around at the struggling gads on the floor, being tied up. Jacob could not see the baby's mother among the pacified workers. 'She has gone.'

'And the child?'

Shaking his head sadly, the servant raised his empty palms to the air. 'They took him away – these people ...'

The officer noticed Jacob and his companions for the first time, realising that the people in front of him were no passing locals trying to discipline their slaves. His face broke into a toothy grin. 'Well then, this is a fortuitous morning's work.'

'Just trying to break up the ruckus,' said Jacob. 'Didn't realise there were soldiers on the job, nearby.'

'On the job, that is what we are,' said the officer. He drew his pistol and took a step back, the captain's men raising their rifles as they followed their officer's lead. 'But we're not looking for gad trouble-makers.'

'Brave soldiers of Hagel,' said Sariel, 'we are simple travellers in your city, passing through on the wings of the aerial traders.'

'That's right,' said the officer to Sariel. 'A dirty bard with a tramp's beard; a spiky-skinned man so many twists on the spiral removed from the common pattern he might as well be a filthy gad; a yellow-faced flier and a middle-aged preacher. Foreigners and travellers, all. Can't be many of you to the schilling in the city. We've been searching hotels for you dogs since before dawn.'

Jacob felt a sinking feeling in the pit of his gut alongside the empty weight of the holster on his hip. Both his pistols down in the outer wall's guardhouse.

'Keep your guns trained on spiky, here,' ordered the officer. 'Its spines aren't for show. You shoot one of those in my direction, and you and your friends won't live long enough to regret it.'

Jacob cursed. Whoever the locals had been communicating with knew exactly what a roused gask was capable of. That meant Weyland knowledge. And he could only think of one group back home who wanted the party dead ... but how the hell did the treacherous major have any leverage in this faraway corner of the world?

Jacob tapped his money belt. 'We could pay you to look the other way.'

The officer snorted. 'You really don't know the grand duke. But you will.' He turned to his men. 'Bind the foreigners and throw them in the palace cells along with the rebellious gads. The grand duke can have his sport with them later.'

'Not me,' pleaded the gad servant, falling to his knees. 'My master has need of me.'

'Of course,' said the officer, tapping the gad absent-mindedly on the shoulder. 'The price for failing to observe the law against half-breeds is clear. The grand duke would have *my* head if I dragged you before him unpunished.' Two of the lobster-helmeted soldiers strode forward from the company and hauled the gad up from his knees, forcing him towards the waste tube. Lifting the slave up by his legs, they tossed the screaming servant over the plateau's edge. A fading rattle from the pipe as his body collided with its edges, a fatal battering that would kill him before he ever struck the ground.

'Out with the rest of the slops,' said the officer.

'Badly done, you degenerate guts-gripers,' murmured Sariel.

'You're a brave man,' spat Jacob. 'With twenty rifles standing behind you.'

'Save your pieties, preacher. Whatever prayers you know, you and your friends are going to need to keep them for yourself.' He walked over to the dozens of gads bound on the pavement, kicking the nearest one in the ribs. 'You all think you're clever, saving one little half-breed? We'll balance out that little runt's escape by culling you for this morning's mischief.'

'This is not necessary,' said Khow.

The officer pointed a gloved warning finger in the direction of the gask. 'Shut your trap, spiky. This is *our* law. Hangel isn't for the twisted; it's a fully human city.'

'I struggle to see the humanity,' whispered the gask.

There was no more wailing or singing among the remaining gads. They were roughly pulled to their feet and made to march down the centre of the street, in full view of everyone, along with Jacob and his fellow travellers. It was amazing how far a harsh example or two stretched when it came to pacifying even the largest of populations. Tales spread like wildfire and grew in the telling. Before the end of the day there would be hundreds of slaves talking about the massacre by the ramparts. An old, long-suppressed part of Jacob recognised the efficiency of such actions. Kill one in cold blood and defeat a thousand without ever fighting the battle, on reputation alone. Was that a sliver of admiration felt by Jacob's shadow, balancing out the sickness twisting in the gut of a supposedly much-changed man?

'I'm different; not like them,' muttered Jacob. 'We're not the same.'

The officer snorted. 'You can say that again; you're a dead man walking.'

Carter hadn't expected to wake, groaning, but if he had thought about it, waking with a Vandian's tall black boot lashing into his ribs is how he might have predicted matters starting.

'Dirty barbarian slave,' growled the patrol ship's officer.

Carter rolled over, trying to recover his breath as the pain of the kick helped fire his body back to life. 'You not dead yet?'

'Shut up! You speak when I tell you to.'

Carter's eyes cleared. His head ached; his body was covered in itching red patches that felt as though his skin was on fire – burns from the fall. *The fall that should have killed me.* He lay inside a dark space lit by a smudge of light in the ceiling, running above his head like glowing moss. The cave floor was a flat, featureless grey. There didn't seem to be any way out, which rather begged the question of how he had got here in the first place. It also seemed oddly cool, given he should be swimming in magma. Or maybe roasting in hell. The Vandian officer paced restlessly around the cave. No pistol. No rifle. No short-sword. His helmet and respirator were also missing. Still had his breast armour, though.

'You're trapped too,' said Carter. The officer looked as if he might try and put a boot into Carter again, but Carter managed to get to his feet first and faced him off. 'First one was free, Captain. You want to try for two, there's only going to be one of us left in this cell. Might be you, might be me.'

'It would be me,' said the Vandian.

'How the hell did we get here?'

The officer rubbed nervously at the neatly clipped goatee beard on his chin. 'I think we're still inside the volcano. I remember rolling down the slope and then tumbling into a borehole, falling, before I passed out from the heat. When I woke up I was inside here with you.'

'And here's me thinking it was *my* head that took a beating. How can we be inside the volcano? It's not nearly hot enough?'

'There are many legends about this place, myths concerning tunnels in the volcano's crater, going underground, the gods and spirits that protect the treasure hoarded below the surface. Vandian myths and those of the peoples that lived here before us.'

'Can't be that deep underground,' said Carter. 'Gravity would crush us if we were. And living inside the volcano would be like setting up home around the middle circle of hell. What kind of spirits would want to do that?'

'Cursed demons,' spat the officer.

Carter laughed. He was having a hard time believing this was real, not the end of some fever-induced dream. Maybe he was lying on a ridge inside the crater, magma lashing below him, his brain cooking inside his skull and poisoned by sulphurous fumes. But the cell felt real enough. He brushed his fingers along the silvery survival suit, torn and ripped by the tumble down the crater's walls. *I feel real enough.*

The captain indignantly jabbed a finger at him. 'Do you find me amusing, slave? It's your fault I'm trapped in here.'

'What the hell? You're the one who shot us out of the sky! We were trying to bring in a stake for Princess Helrena when your ship appeared, cannons blazing. We figured you were from an enemy house, trying to even the odds for your own miners by taking us out of the race.'

'Don't treat me like a fool! We're not your house's troops; we are posted with the sector legion. We were flying with orders to shoot down a transporter full of escaped slaves – *your* transporter.'

So, someone *had* snitched on their escape attempt. Carter seethed with outrage. But who? It must have been one of the station workers the group had sounded out. Carter thought he had been discreet, but obviously not inconspicuous enough to avoid being carefully watched ... and sold out when the time was right. Carter trusted whoever it was had received a fine price for their treachery, because if he got even half a chance, the traitor would discover what a poor bargain they had struck.

Carter kept his anger off his face. 'Do I look like I'm insane? A transporter doesn't carry enough fuel or water to make it across the dead zone.'

'You look like a cretinous savage, because that is what precisely you are,' growled the officer. 'Did you think that flying back towards the sky mines as soon as you spotted my patrol ship would be enough to convince me that you were merely faithful workers? You were trying to run. Your transporter was flying like a brick, loaded down with stolen supplies.'

Carter scowled at the soldier, fiddling with the air mask dangling uncomfortably from his neck. It occurred to him that this cave might be a trick. Maybe the princess was holding him here, and all of this was a ruse to get him to open up to the captain? The Vandians would want to learn all the details of Carter's escape plan; get the names of any slaves back on the station who assisted the escape. Well, if so, it would be a cold day in hell before he told them about Kerge's involvement.

'Every year there is at least one mine transporter that runs out of fuel and crashes in the dead zone, its cage filled with barbarians just like you who think they can walk out,' said the officer. 'We only bother catching you fools for the example that must be made of rebellious slaves. Your execution will be your last service to the empire. Reminding every barbarian in the sky mines that disloyalty carries a steep price.'

Carter shook his head. 'Disloyalty? You people paid for my hide, you didn't purchase my allegiance. I'm a citizen of Weyland. Long live the king and God grant him wise counsel!'

'Let's see how well you mouth your insolent platitudes in praise of your warlords when you are under the supervision of an imperial torturer. They enjoy being given stubborn slaves to make an example of in front of the crowds – the difficult slaves are far more rewarding.'

Carter tracked along the cave's wall, feeling the cold material with his fingers. Not quite stone, but not quite any substance he was familiar with, either. He looked up at the cave's ceiling. 'Where's the borehole we rolled down through, then? I can't see any way in or out of here?'

'This is a larder – the demons' larder.'

'You've lost your mind, Captain Vandian, sir.'

The officer angrily pushed Carter against the wall. 'Captain Tybar, sir. But a simple *master* will suffice, from a dirty mine tunneller from the lower-hostile caste.'

Carter shoved back at him. It was like pushing granite. The captain was strong. A lot fitter, healthier and better nourished than Carter, too. 'Getting a little lower and more hostile every day I enjoy your empire's hospitality.'

Carter systematically examined their dimly lit space. No crawl spaces in or out as far as he could see. No water and not even insects to eat. They weren't going to survive long inside here. Carter approached one of the corners and jumped back in fright as a section of the cave suddenly began to fold away before his fingers, piece by piece, as if the rock was being rearranged by some manic, invisible force. A triangular-shaped doorway was left carved out of the corner. Darkness concealed whatever was beyond. He tentatively touched the edges of the opening, half-expecting to find it a living wall made of insects, the manner in which it had been clicking and chattering a second ago. Nothing but the solid surface of the cave.

'How did you do that?' demanded Captain Tybar. 'I've inspected every inch of this space looking for a crevice to crawl through.'

'It just fell away before me! There was no opening mechanism there.' He gazed in astonishment at the gap. Wherever he was, this place sure as hell wasn't an imperial military station or any dungeon owned by Helrena Skar.

'The demons of the underworld must recognise you as a mere slave,' said the officer. 'And unlike myself, judge that you present little threat to those who dwell here.'

Carter glanced witheringly at the Vandian. Without his expensive weapons, the officer wasn't much of a threat. Just a heavily built thug in a fancy breastplate. 'I'll lead the way then, to make sure my *mere* slave legs don't open the floor onto a spike-edged pit, say.'

Captain Tybar didn't protest. He still had his crimson cloak attached to the rear of his armour. Maybe the man should consider dyeing it yellow if he survived this.

A thin illumination glowed around Carter as he led the way, revealing a featureless passage running left and right – no sign of any doors or caves off it. The light of the moss was sourceless, as though the walls glimmered just enough to allow the two men to navigate. It was as cool outside their cave as it had been inside. Surely it should be far hotter if the Vandian solider was correct about where they had ended up? They pushed on, regardless. Carter in the lead, neither of them with anything to say to the other. After a couple of minutes travelling down the tunnel, he spotted a triangular doorway in the wall to the right. Tentatively, Carter stuck his head through, feeling as though he was inserting his head in the mouth of a mountain lion. A chamber, maybe three times the size of their cave. This one had hooks built into the walls that appeared as though they were designed to hang jackets from them. No clothes, but on the floor in front of the wall a pile of human-looking bones lay, as well as something more esoteric. Wings littered the floor, translucent and reflecting a faint rainbow sheen from the light above. Long, folded, torn and ragged, maybe seven wings in total strewn across the floor.

Carter knelt to examine the wings. 'Those demons of myth, they have wings like this?'

Captain Tybar shook his head. 'In ancient texts' illustrations, the demons often resemble giant spiders with the face of men. Such hell-spawn were not formed with aerodynamics in mind.'

'Said the man who flies around in a heavy steel tube with a rocket stuffed up its tail.'

'A synergetic air-breathing rocket *engine*, barbarian. These are like the wings of the *Kyrie* stained in a temple window, the warrior women who escort an emperor's soul to the lodge of champions when he passes from our mortal realm.'

'Angels ... the ethreaal,' whispered Carter. 'That's what my people call them. But these bones are human and mortal enough; old, too.'

'This is another larder,' shivered the large Vandian. 'It is where the demons store their prey.'

'Don't eat regularly if they do,' said Carter.

Driven by Carter's gloomy prognostication, the captain turned on his heels and left the room, taking the lead this time. Three minutes of exploring brought them to another entrance. This time the room's design had been constructed as a series of arches, a tunnel thirty feet long and leading nowhere, terminating at a flat wall. Bone-like ridges vaulted the chamber as though the arches were ribs in the remains of a whale. It was strange, but the feeling Carter had seen something similar to this before struck him. He ran a finger along depressions carved into the ridges, their shapes familiar. They seemed to glow faintly as he brushed them, a trick of the shadows, or the luminescent moss that covered the walls. Then it came to him where he had seen this before! 'The standing stones!'

'What did you say?'

'The stone circles, like the one at the foot of the volcano. The script here is similar to the runes carved on the menhirs.'

Captain Tybar examined the ridge. 'You have keen, cunning eyes, slave. The script is almost identical. Imperial scholars have never translated the stones' runes. It is a lost language.'

'Then these tunnels ...'

'Could we be inside a burial chamber made by the ancients who raised the circles, then?' mused Tybar. 'The stratovolcano has always been revered as an ultimate source of power and wealth. To inter great chieftains inside it would be a natural aspiration for savages.' Tybar sounded relieved, but still jumpy and uncertain. A more pragmatic interpretation of their predicament. Carter liked the new explanation a lot better than being stuck in some otherworldly Vandian realm of the dead. 'There might be tunnels here with ladders leading to the surface or caves on the volcano's outer slope,' continued the officer. 'Burial parties would not risk life and limb from the magma lake, descending the crater's walls each time they had to bury one of their chieftains. I will discover that exit.'

Carter and the Vandian exchanged suspicious glances; each knowing what passed through the other's mind. That it would be a lot easier for Carter to hijack the patrol ship waiting outside if he was facing just its pilot and gunner; with the captain lying dead in a tunnel. For a moment Carter thought that the captain was going to have it out with him here and now, but their uneasy peace held for now.

'You don't want to say a prayer, before we set out?' needled Carter. 'If this is a temple to cosy up to the gods and journey into the afterlife?'

'Keep your heathen witterings to yourself, slave,' advised Captain Tybar. 'You rejected the emperor's grace when you betrayed your caste. I am protected by his favour'

That and an inch of steel plate around your chest. 'Let's see what that's worth, Captain, sir.'

Tybar pushed Carter in front of him to lead the way. 'Burial chambers are usually protected by traps to deter grave robbers.'

'Still of service, then. Anyone would think you're afraid of demons.'

'The barbarian kind is the least trustworthy,' muttered Tybar.

They roamed the corridors and passages, a seemingly never-ending maze, Carter sniffing the air for a warm, hot breeze. Anything to indicate which direction the temple's exit might lie. No current of air obliged him. Carter was on edge, imagining hinged flagstones opening up below his feet, dropping him onto spikes or bubbling pools of acid. But no traps were triggered by his presence.

After half an hour of exploring the underground labyrinth, the two survivors came to an entrance to a cavern, far larger than any of the spaces they had explored before. Tybar seemed hesitant about exploring it, but Carter had no such qualms. He was growing thirsty, now, and tired. If they couldn't find a way out of this labyrinth, it would become their tomb all too quickly. He stepped over the threshold. The space was vast enough that the luminescent moss accounting for their light was overwhelmed by gloom at the margins, the sound of their boots on the rock floor reverberating back at them as they entered. Carter could just distinguish more bone-like arches running along the top of the chamber. They really were in the belly of the beast. The far wall had a semi-circle of menhirs driven horizontally into its surface, as though giants had played darts with the heavy stones. And if burial chamber this was, perhaps the black sarcophagus-sized blocks in the chamber's centre were where the committal of dead chieftains had been practised? Tybar walked over to the nearest block and knelt down, examining its side. Carter heard something like a faint whispering. He swivelled around. The block behind him had a simple clear glass container sitting on its surface, filled with water and resting on the block's centre. *What's going on – I'd swear that wasn't there before?* He went to inspect the container. Like a wide glass vase without any flowers. Just staring at it, he realised how dry his mouth had become.

'Don't!' ordered Tybar, standing up. 'It is a temptation sent by the hellspawn and you will pay a heavy price for drinking it.' He tapped the block's side, intricate carvings sculpted there. Carter stepped back and inspected his block. There were similar reliefs on its sides, a series of spider-like creatures with additional human limbs and torsos, as though a procession of arachnid centaurs had carefully been engraved along the block.

'These are your demons? The carvings are probably to ward evil away from the tomb,' said Carter. It didn't take much to set the Vandian off on his superstitious histrionics again. Not for the first time, he wished the exasperating officer had perished in the volcano's crater and left him to escape alone. Carter reached out and dipped a finger in the water, withdrawing it. Cold and clean, with a slightly metallic quality to it. 'In my country, stone masons carve devils we call gargoyles on the side of churches to protect worshippers from evil.'

'You are a fool!' Tybar's voice rose in pitch, almost a girl-like shriek. He appeared genuinely spooked. Carter reached across, lifted the glass vessel and swigged from it – mainly to vex the Vandian – then insolently offered the water toward the officer. Tybar swiped his hand out, knocking the glass away. It slapped out of Carter's hand and smashed across the chamber's floor, the water draining down fractures in the floor. Carter felt fury swell up inside him. 'You damnable idiot! We could have lasted a day on that!'

'You drank from it! You are cursed!'

'To hell with your Vandian superstitions. We need drink to survive. You noticed any underground streams on your travels through this maze?'

'Look at your forehead,' screeched the Vandian. 'You are sweating. You *are* cursed!'

Carter touched the skin above his eyebrows. He was sweating, but he didn't feel any… he doubled up in agony as his thoughts turned into a hail of arrows thudding into his mind, clutching out at the sarcophagus to try and keep his balance. Through the fog of pain he could just make out the imperium's officer stumbling away from him in terror. Then, as suddenly as the vice of agony had clutched Carter's mind, it vanished, leaving him heaving on the edge of the stone block.

'Possessed, you've been taken by them!' spluttered Tybar.

Carter waved the idiot to silence. He just had drunk too suddenly after too long dry, like a desperate traveller crawling through a desert, wracked by convulsions after gorging too hastily at a spring. *That must be it.*

Tybar yelped as the far end of the chamber erupted in fire, confirming every demonic fear which gripped him. The space where the menhirs had been driven into the wall was occupied by a curtain of unnatural rippling fire so intense that it flared purple and blue. 'A portal into hell itself,' moaned the Vandian.

'A portal, maybe. I can feel a breeze blowing fresh air from behind there,' said Carter. 'I think there's something on the other side, and if it's hell, it's a lot cooler than the place my father used to preach about.'

'Stand back, barbarian,' snarled the Vandian.

'What, and stay here with you? You overestimate the charms of your company. That's the way out of here, and if a hidden floor-weight triggering a witch doctor's ancient sparks and fireworks is enough to scare you off, you can leave your bones here for tomb-robbers to step over.'

'Demons will feast on you, and when they have a taste for your flesh, they will come for me.'

'I've already seen hell,' said Carter. 'And it was run by men. Anything through there is freedom, one way or another.'

Tybar glanced around, furious, searching for something he could brain Carter with. His eyes stopped on the block nearest the fire portal, fierce illumination glinting off something that had been hidden in the darkness: a pair of short-swords in scabbards left abandoned there. The Vandian sprinted across to lunge for one of the weapons, Carter fast on his heels, needing no oracle to know what the officer was going to do next. Tybar snatched his sword and tried to send the redundant blade spinning into the gloom of the cavern, but Carter leapt for it, catching the leather scabbard as it slid away and pulled the blade free. It glittered in the spark-light, as sharp and deadly as the day it had been left to accompany its last owner into the afterlife.

Tybar wasted no time; he stamped forward, throwing his sword towards Carter's gut. Carter jumped back, bending, the officer's blade stopping short of filleting him by a hair's width. The officer made a sudden back swing, unaimed and quick, catching the side of Carter's shoulder with a burning cut. Carter ducked around the block-like sarcophagus, using its bulk to block the Vandian's advance. The two of them circled each other around the tomb, the block too wide to allow a decent thrust by either opponent.

'You dare raise arms against your master? I'll kill you!' hissed Tybar.

'Just let me pass through the portal,' said Carter. 'If you're right, I'll die with no blood on your blade.'

'You're already cursed,' said the officer. 'That's why hell calls to you. You'll tell the demons where to find me when you're roasting in their flames.'

'You're a coward, Vandian. You can die in this tomb, if that's what you want. I'm getting out and taking your ship.'

Tybar obviously felt the jibe about his courage. 'Then I'll roll your corpse through as an offering!' The Vandian leapt across the block, swinging out violently at Carter as he mounted the sarcophagus. Carter backpedalled and took a swipe at the Vandian's legs, but Tybar leapt over the blade and landed to his side. Carter cursed his luck. Tybar had come to this fight well-fed on military rations, not weakened by mine labour. The Vandian still had his armour, and the short-sword was the style of blade that all the imperium's lackeys seemed to carry. Tybar must have been trained on it. Nothing like the long sabres and fencing blades that Carter was familiar with. Like trying to poke someone with a tooth-pick, or … *a dagger*. The voice of his territorial regiment's sergeant echoed in his ears. *The expected will see you dead. It's the unexpected that lays your enemy open.*

Carter swung left, a feint, and as the officer stepped to the right he pivoted and released the short-sword spinning towards the Vandian's throat. Too short to be a sabre, but a little bit longer than a dagger, its length sank into the officer's throat and impaled him above his fancy breastplate's protection. Tybar looked shocked at the unorthodox use of the blade, tumbling to the floor where his blood fountained across the block they had just been duelling across. Carter kicked the officer's sword away from him and knelt down sadly by his side. 'I would have killed a hundred like you to escape from the mines, Captain, sir. But I'm still sorry it had to be you.'

'Bar — barian,' was all Tybar managed to gurgle, before he lay motionless.

'Maybe I am at that.' Carter stood up and looked at the stones, the false fire still fizzing and rippling. It was a good show. Enough to put off most grave robbers. But Carter wasn't here by choice and all he'd managed to steal was an old blade he could barely use as a throwing knife. He raised a hand towards the exit, feeling the breeze on the other side blowing against his skin, and a strange tingling too. Was that the stink of the stratovolcano, too? But no heat. He took a few steps back and then sprinted forward, flinging himself through the veil of sparks. That was when Carter felt a jolt of pain like nothing he had ever experienced before exploding across his flesh and he suddenly realised that maybe the Vandian had been right all along.

ELEVEN

THE ESCAPED MAN

Carter woke up burning, the hot sun high above him, a wan, white disc partially obscured by steam and fumes. His back was against the rock, and he felt as if he had been sleeping on the hard surface for the best part of a month. He rolled over, groaning. The silvery fabric of his survival suit was torn into ribbons and covered in black dust. *Outside, I'm on the volcano again. And near the ground too.* His air mask dangled around his neck, not over his face. He would have suffocated at a higher altitude; passed out and never woken. Carter felt his forehead, as damp from sweat again as if he had suffered a fever, but curiously no sign of the fiery exit tunnel. He didn't seem to be burnt, so the cavern's portal must have been a false display of rapidly igniting powders after all. What he had just survived felt as unreal as a dream; half the tears in his survival suit must have come from rolling down the crater. Carter slipped a hand to his shoulder, feeling the wound from Tybar's blade. The underworld was *real enough, then.* Pity. He would almost have welcomed the possibility that fumes from the crater had leaked through his respirator, driven him half-insane, sent him fitting into visions while he scaled Old Smoky's interior. He scanned the slope. Off on the left he could just make out the standing stones through the smog; where he and his band had first holed up inside the cave, riding out the worse of the eruption. His friends' deaths were real. His crashed, lava-melted transporter was real. The company of dead Vandian soldiers they had put in the dirt was real.

His lack of food and water and a painful death from dehydration within a few days was deadly real. Mist cleared along the ground, pushed by warm winds and ... and it looked as though the transporter behind the menhirs might be real, too? *One of ours?* How long had Carter been unconscious if the mine's workers were out laying sensor lines again? *Long enough for that Vandian patrol ship to be long gone*, a voice told him. Its pilot no doubt blaming the second eruption for the loss of their guardsmen on the slopes, all evidence of the escaping slaves erased by a river of lava flowing over the corpses. What were his chances of walking out of here, as weak as a kitten, no food or water on him? Carter wished he had stashed a few supplies back in that cave. But if hopes were riches, he would be wealthier than a king. He made his choice, as painful as it was, despair leaching into his heart with every uncertain footstep forced in the transporter's direction. Shocked cries met his appearance.

'Dear God!' It was Duncan, Owen and Anna working behind the craft. The old gang, back together again.

Carter stumbled in their direction, hardly able to speak through his brittle dry mouth – his greeting croaked back inaudibly.

Duncan ran forward, unbelting his water canteen. Carter took it and drank greedily.

'Drink it all,' urged Duncan. 'We've got a second stake tethered to the station now. We're on long rations and even longer days.'

Carter swayed on his feet as he poured the flask's remainder over his sore, sunburnt face.

'Had you marked down as dead,' said Owen. 'Vandians said you'd tried to make a run for it in a transporter and they shot you down over the dead zone.'

'Looks like he *is* dead,' said Anna. 'Just dug out of his grave.'

'Escape?' coughed Carter, tasting the water over his thick tongue. 'Horseshit. Talked about it, is all. Halfway out of the dead zone is still dead. I was separated from the others on the ground during the eruption. They were back in the air on the transporter by the time I dug myself out of my cave. Reckon the boys wrote me off. They'd lifted off for the station when a patrol ship appeared and shot them to pieces. They were flying in the sky near here—' Carter jabbed a finger skyward '— not inside the dead zone. Alan's transporter went down on the high slopes and the empire's patrol ship landed nearby, then a second eruption sent a sea of lava sliding towards both craft and I was running and not watching anymore. Reckon the lava must have done for both birds and everyone on board.'

'You're the only survivor, Northhaven,' said Anna. 'The imperials recovered the transporter's wreckage and gave it back to us. No bodies for burial. The Vandian patrol ship made it back intact.'

'Damn them, anyway. Trigger-happy fools. Our people died on the volcano's slopes, not out in the dead zone. That's the truth, I swear.'

'That explains why the transporter was melted so badly,' said Anna. 'Didn't look like any fuel fire or engine explosion I've seen before.'

Carter nodded, wearily, realising how things had gone down. The patrol ship's orders must have been to shoot down the transporter when it was well over the dead zone. When the slave crew confounded expectations by flying back towards the sky mines, the Vandians had decided to keep things simple by executing the slaves on the spot, and to hell with what their informer had told them. The informer hadn't known about Carter's plan to ride a stray volcano rock to safety. Whoever had betrayed them thought they were going to try to get out the same way as every other escape, crossing the dead zone. *My plan's still intact. I can try it again.* But who would follow him now, a marked troublemaker with the scent of his friends' death clinging to him?

'Some gunner got bored and decided to shoot up a lone transporter for kicks, then,' said Owen. 'Killing slaves isn't murder in the imperium: it's a property crime against their owner.'

'They'll try and hang it on you anyway, now,' said Duncan. 'Their story is that you were escaping. The Vandians won't let a single survivor make a lie of what they say happened.'

'If I was escaping, I'd be dead,' said Carter. 'Dead in the crash or burnt to a cinder on the slopes.'

'Well, we have to take you back either way,' said Owen. 'You'll be finished down here for certain if you stay.'

'Been doing just fine,' said Carter, 'after I learnt to drink lava. But I've missed all the fun in the sky mines. Making the princess even richer every day …'

Carter's words belied his feelings. He had failed. So close to escaping the empire's clutches and his breakout had been well and truly scuppered. All he seemed to excel at was getting his companions into scrapes that saw them killed. It didn't matter how many lies he told here or back in the sky mines. The truth was as plain to Carter as the fate he was surrendering to.

Anna shook her head as she climbed into the transporter's cockpit and kicked the engines into life. 'Maybe we'd all be better off if we left you stranded in your cave down here.'

Four soldiers restrained Carter as they dragged him towards Princess Helrena. It seemed a little excessive. Especially given the beating they'd delivered when he'd unexpectedly turned up in the station's hangar. Now the princess waited at the end of the hangar with her retinue from the shuttle, station workers lined up along the parked transporters, waiting to see what his fate was to be. It was as though they had made a court of the slaves and this was to be his royal audience.

'Every time we meet,' said the princess, 'there seems to be a lesson in need of being administered across your hide.'

The soldiers forced Carter's bloody, bruised face towards the hangar's bare rock. He wanted to say something, but that would mean spitting the blood in his mouth out on her boots, which wouldn't, he suspected, exactly endear himself to the emperor's daughter.

'Tell me,' she commanded, 'how you survived your escape attempt?'

Carter swallowed salty blood; about the only thing he'd had to drink since he returned. 'There was no escape.' He coughed. 'We were checking the sensor line; sent out against our pilot's better judgement. When the main eruption caught us, I holed up in a cave that was covered by a rockslide. I dug myself out and saw one of your patrol ships blast my transporter out of the air and down into the side of the stratovolcano. The patrol ship landed nearby. Then a second eruption destroyed the crashed transporter and probably burned the patrol craft out too. It was hard to see in all the smoke, and me running for my life. I've been sheltering in caves and trying to attract the attention of a transporter in the sky since then.'

'You are a liar,' growled the princess. 'You were trying to flee across the dead zone.'

As Carter looked up, he noticed the woman's daughter stood in her retinue. Come to learn the business of disciplining truculent slaves. Her face looked as hard and serious as her mother's. She was learning her lessons well. 'If I had been, my bones would be scattered out there. I was found on the slopes, waiting for rescue.'

'Someone in the dead zone must have assisted you,' said the princess. 'Given you the water and food you needed to travel back to the volcano when you realised escape was impossible.'

'Walking out only leads to your grave. I'm many things,' said Carter, 'but not a fool.'

'You take me for one,' said the princess, her eyes narrowing below her golden helmet.

No, thought Carter, *I take you for someone who knows all about our scheme from the lips of a traitor here. And you don't want to discover your best snitch in a bunk with their throat cut if you admit it in front of us.*

'You were missing for many days,' spat the princess. 'How did you survive with no water?'

'I figure I must have been in a coma. I don't remember too much apart from wandering around the slopes, then waking up close to the spot I found the crew down from the station.' *That much, at least, is true.* It was more than odd. Carter's stint in the underworld below the volcano seemed to have ended up with him missing days, as though the passage of time occurred at different speeds below and above the world's surface. But how could that be, unless he and Tybar had been unconscious in that cave for longer than either of them had realised?

'Everybody here knows the penalty for breaking their caste and going on the run. An escaped slave is a dead slave.'

It was quite a quandary, to be sure. Carter showing up here not only contradicted the half-truth the patrol ship had made up about the escaping miners, but seemed to cast doubt on everything the slaves had been told about the low chances of surviving the endless barren plains. If Carter started raving about underworld burial temples and a dead Vandian officer, he'd be written off as a madman driven insane by vapours from the ground. Nothing good would come from that. So he had told no one about his strange adventure inside the volcano.

'If you're going to torture me, Your Highness, then don't keep your boy on the clock. I reckon that imperial torturers don't come cheap?'

'That will be a pleasure for all involved, I assure you.'

Duncan stepped out from the line of workers. 'What Carter Carnehan claims is true, Your Highness. We found him on the slopes of the volcano, nearly dead and stumbling around with half his wits taken from him.'

'Which means you have absolutely no way of knowing if the slave spent his last few days desperately hiking across the dead zone before turning back, or sheltering inside a volcanic cave.'

'I know he helped rescue your daughter when your enemies tried to kidnap her. And he saved you from assassination, too.'

She imperiously raised a gloved hand towards Duncan. 'When we first met, you narrowly escaped being ejected into the sky by the skels for trying to murder this slave. Would it not suit you to see him die today? Why do you speak up on behalf of this brazenly defiant wretch now?'

'Because he used to be a friend. And because it's the right thing to do.'

'It has been a long while since anyone presumed to tell me what was right,' snarled Helrena. She pointed at Duncan and commanded the soldiers behind her. 'Remove this insolent dog.'

Troops seized Duncan and dragged him out of the hangar, struggling and swearing until one of the soldiers clubbed him to silence in the gut with a heavy rifle butt. Willow cried and tried to break the line to reach her brother while the other miners wisely held her back. But it was too late: the princess had spotted the disturbance.

'Another woman? Emperor's blood, I thought that slave's fancypiece had been given to Baron Machus? Is this my mining station, or *his* harem?'

Carter stared grimly up from the floor. 'She's his sister; nothing to do with this. Leave her out of it.'

'Then I trust she's inherited her ancestors' stock of wisdom in lieu of her brother.' Princess Helrena turned to her daughter. 'Cassandra, you have seen as much as I have of this matter. What should my judgement be here?'

Carter watched the young royal screw up her face in thought. 'Judgements should not be arbitrary, Mother, or people will come to doubt our decrees. Arguments derived from mere probabilities are always suspect.'

'You have been listening to your tutor Doctor Horvak, a little too well, I think. Judgements should also never be perceived as weak, for that way you encourage lowers to read such traits in yourself and encourage them to rebellion.'

'Mother, this slave saved our lives.'

'In that he merely did his duty.'

Cassandra nodded slowly, earnestly, as if coming to a verdict. 'The slave's innocence or guilt cannot be determined, but at the very least he failed to prevent his work detail fleeing the sky mines. The law says he should be punished for his negligence.'

'Quite right,' said Helrena. She raised her voice so all the slaves in the hangar could hear. 'If I execute this disrespectful dog, his death would carry all the sins of the failed escape attempt. As it is, if he is to live, that burden must be shared. Half rations and rest periods for all workers from this man's barracks, and every barracks where any escaped slave was billeted!' Groans sounded from the slaves as they realised how hard their lives were about to become. She continued. 'All of you have an obligation to dissuade and report escaping workers before they abscond. For those that fail in their duty, this is as comfortable a sanction as shall ever befall you! If I were not so badly short-handed for the two mines that now require working, I would order a decimation and see one tenth of those from the guilty barracks walk the sky.' She knelt down beside Carter. 'As for you, my truculent little barbarian worker, sixty lashes for watching your comrades try to fly to freedom. And after you have taken your stripes, I would not wish to be in your sandals. Hungry slaves are never happy ones, and they blame quite freely, as you will discover.'

Carter stared at her defiantly. 'You call this justice?'

'Discipline and order,' said Helrena. 'As vital in keeping the sky mines functional as water, food and salt. Stand silently, you barbarian dogs! Here's an entertainment that will make your fast a little easier to endure, at least for today.'

Carter watched a wooden post being set up at the far end of the chamber, slaves made to do the hard work of hammering it into place, the hangar set as a stage for his punishment. The scar on his face smarted like a hot cable as he realised it was about to be joined by a few cousins across his spine. Still forcing Carter to kneel, soldiers tore off the remains of his silver survival suit, exposing his back, already burnt and raw.

'So,' said Helrena, 'you've visited the slopes of the volcano recently. That much was true.'

'I was trying for a tan. I've been getting pasty in your tunnels.'

'In the coming weeks, you will need to stay out of the sun. In the sky mines this is called a slave's massage'

Guards dragged Carter towards the frame. Lady Cassandra came up, whispering quickly and quietly in his ear. 'You will live, though.' The young royal said it as though she was betraying some confidence or secret.

'Reckon I will.' Carter trusted the turncoat who had betrayed his escape was watching this, enjoying the rewards of selling him out. Settling in for the coming show. They'd pay for their ticket just as soon as Carter was done here. His captors shoved him towards the punishment frame, joking with each other while the structure was finished off. They didn't even bother to keep their guns pointed at Carter as they waited. He was so weak he could hardly stand, let alone fight the guardsmen off. Willow had managed to join the detail setting up the structure, gazing knowingly at him with her sad eyes. She didn't say *I told you so*, but then she didn't have to. Carter's escape attempt had ended exactly where she had predicted any breakout would.

'Unhappy about Duncan getting dragged into this. Tell him that, when you next see him.'

Willow slipped him a little handle covered in a wet rag. 'Bite on the wood. Owen says you'll lose your tongue if you don't.'

'Would that be so bad?'

'You wouldn't be able to say sorry, Carter. And you'll need to do a lot of that in the coming weeks.'

'Get behind the crowd. You don't need to watch this.'

'I probably do. Maybe that witch of a princess is right – it'll make our empty stomachs ride a little easier.' She walked away, leaving Carter feeling even more miserable than before. He almost wished she'd fallen into her usual cantankerous banter with him. At least that was a game he knew how to play.

Kerge was one of the last slaves to come over, screwing the final few components of the frame in place. 'Manling,' he whispered, 'I carry news for you.'

'If it's about the poor chances of success of escaping the sky mines, I think I've already figured the odds.'

'No!' the gask bent down, using the cover of the frame to talk. 'I inspected the wreckage of your transporter after it was brought back. There was a device concealed inside it not found on any other craft here. A miniature signalling mechanism like a radio, broadcasting your position.'

Carter groaned. No wonder they had been discovered so easily. Their escape never stood a chance. Even if Carter had reached a stake small and worthless enough to escape notice, the Vandian patrol ship would have followed them straight into the air and used the rock for target practice.

'You were betrayed from the start,' whispered Kerge.

'Keep that between us,' muttered Carter. 'I don't want the son-of-a-bitch who sold us out getting wind that I know we were set up.'

'Revenge is a poor servant,' said Kerge as he slipped away with his tools.

Guardsmen strapped Carter tightly against the frame, laughing and mocking the Weylander about how fine his massage was going to be. They wouldn't have sounded so amused if they knew he'd put a spray of bullets into their comrades down on the volcano's slopes, then happily bashed in a few more Vandian skulls before flinging a blade into their captain's throat. He heard the crack of a whip unfurled behind him, testing the air. Yells and taunts rose from the slaves too, now, an angry, expectant buzz growing louder.

Revenge is all I have left. He bit down hard on the rag-wrapped handle as one of the guards began yelling the count.

One – *slash* – two – *slash* – three …

Duncan had expected to receive a piece of what Carter Carnehan must be enduring right now. But after clubbing Duncan to silence, the guards quickly dragged him to the station's surface. A large Vandian ship was moored to the rock, anchored between the station and the closer of the two stakes. Hatches lay open along the vessel's side, multiple gangways exposed with conveyor belts running from sorting lines to the ship. All the belts were stilled at the moment, the bulk of the workforce assembled inside the hangar for their hard education in the price of freedom. Engines at the vessel's stern sat cold and silent, adding to the eerie quiet as she hovered on anti-gravity stones. Vandian soldiers stood posted at each steel gantry bridging the ship. Duncan hung in the guards' thick muscled arms as they halted by the sentries, exchanging greetings. One of the soldiers muttered into a small microphone extended from his golden helmet. Whatever permissions they needed to proceed were granted, and the two brutes continued across the gantry, into the vessel, hauling Duncan along after them.

Inside, he was forced, stumbling, through metal corridors, passing Vandian sailors and the occasional house slave, all of whom studiously ignored the prisoner while giving way to the two guards. They dragged Duncan through a smaller version of the giant warship that had carried the Weylanders into their harsh new existence. Rather than being racked like meat in an automated slave pen, Duncan found himself rudely tossed into an empty cabin. Not often used as a brig, presumably, since it contained a single porthole. He turned to demand an answer from the guards, but they slammed the steel door in his face, a complicated-locking mechanism in the door clanging shut and sealing him in inside. The porthole wasn't large enough for him to squeeze through even if he had tried. His new quarters contained bunks, three berths apiece, but no sheets or personal possessions. Only bare mattresses. There was a tiny locker, which, when opened, he found was empty of everything except dust. *Spare quarters for a spare slave. Why the hell have they brought me here?* Were they going to make him toil, loading the station's bounty of ores, before tossing him into the sky? *Carter Carnehan*, he thought, *have you got me killed at last?* Duncan pressed his face against the porthole. Only a view of the station's roof. Little indication of Willow and the others going back to work. He waited and waited, but there was no answer to his concerns until the walls shuddered, the vessel cut loose from its moorings and drifting away from the station. They angled up, and Duncan felt the powerful push of the engines driving the craft higher and higher. His cabin grew warmer, sunlight outside raw and intense, pouring through the porthole. His ears began to hurt until they popped, his view through the thick circle of glass an endless bank of clouds, below. No sign of the dead zone, no sign of the stratovolcano. They were heading somewhere with a purpose. Had Duncan been forgotten? Were the crew going to turn up at some Vandian factory city with a hold full of ores, only for their skipper to remember that they had a cabin holding a slave they had forgotten to execute? A blind could be lowered over the porthole, but Duncan left it unclipped. Better a view of the endless sky than four metal walls and an empty cabin. The ship kept on flying, levelling out and powering forward, their passage uninterrupted save for a series of strange bangs, as though the craft broke the very sky by whipping through the heavens. Why had they taken him from the sky mines? How long would Willow survive on the station without his help? Brooding reflections jabbed at him like a knife. It grew dark, and in the end Duncan grew weary of watching the empty sky, only the surf of clouds and his concerns for company. He lay down on the bunk and despite his best intentions, he fell asleep, worry and exhaustion drawn around him as a thick blanket.

Duncan woke. Daylight streamed through the porthole. His ears had just popped again, and the craft felt as though it was descending. Gazing through the small circle of glass he noticed that they were crossing a body of water – either a small sea or a lake larger than anything he had ever encountered. Metal bridges crossed the waves like a wheel's spokes, vast cantilevered spans strung with a webbing of suspended cables that bore multiple purple-painted roadways. He was heading towards a distant landmass – a continent-sized island necklaced by lesser islets; the bridges' destination. The craft began to turn, riding in on roaring thrusters as gravity grew stronger. They manoeuvred over an islet below, its flattened plain criss-crossed by landing strips, hangars and a concrete fortress. An insect cloud of aircraft – tiny by comparison – alighted and took off around the metal behemoth settling amongst them. Metal feet extended from the ship's hull to absorb the impact of landing, leaving the craft squatting like a vast metal grasshopper. Duncan's cabin provided a good vantage point to watch a queue of vehicles drawing up below the vessel. Workers walked alongside the vehicles, each man a quarter of the height of the wheels, steel stairs needed to climb up to the cabs. Chutes extended out of the ship's holds and showered ores down into the trucks' bodies, a rumbling shower rapidly filling each container-back. The Vandians obviously hadn't carried Duncan here to break his back unloading cargo.

Duncan heard the cabin door unlock. Turning around, he found himself facing Helrena's daughter, the Lady Cassandra dwarfed by a Vandian soldier standing behind her.

'Out,' ordered the guardsman. 'Time to go.' The soldier stood a head taller than Duncan, his scalp shaved and shining in the glow of the passageway, a face broken by tributaries of scars. He wore the same silver armour as the other Vandian soldiers, but on his substantial frame the plate seemed a lot more deadly and a lot less ornamental.

'We're a long way from the sky mines,' said Duncan.

The little noble girl nodded soberly, as if Duncan had surpassed her expectations by working this out for himself. 'We have landed outside the empire's capital, Vandis. I don't suppose a barbarian such as yourself will have heard of it?'

'There were a few lessons hard-taught back in the station,' said Duncan. 'But your empire's geography wasn't among them.'

The brute of a soldier shot him an evil look. Same kind an overseer gave a sky miner when he caught a slave gabbing on the job.

'A horse best understands how to trot,' said Cassandra. That sounded like a quote to Duncan, even though its source was unfamiliar. He had a feeling he was going to be in for a lot of that. 'Follow,' she added, as though commanding a dog.

Duncan exited the cabin and did as he was told.

'You are to be my house slave,' said Cassandra, as though Duncan's change of position should have been obvious and communicated to him on the whisper of the wind. 'You are to be one of the servants given responsibility for looking after my person.'

Duncan rocked in surprise. *They're taking me off the station for good?* 'But I was never a teacher back home.'

Cassandra giggled as she marched through the ship's corridors, everyone giving way to her and bowing low. 'A *tutor*? How ridiculous, I already have one of those. Doctor Yair Horvak. He is a slave, too, of course, given as tribute by one of the conquered dominions that excel in science and philosophy. He is judged the finest mind in the empire. Are you so quick of intelligence?'

Well, Duncan would never have predicted this turn of events, for a start. 'I reckon not. But if you don't need a teacher ...?'

'You shall taste my food before I eat it. Check my bed for snakes and spiders. Ensure my bath has not been secretly connected to a fatal electrical source. Keep your eyes open for treason and assassins. You have already proved yourself highly adroit in that regard.'

'I guess I have.' Duncan could barely keep the grief out of his voice. When would he see Willow again? How long would his sister survive without him in that floating hell, nothing but work and death ahead of her?

'This is a promotion for you,' said Cassandra, staring quizzically at him. 'Do you not understand? You will be of the hostile-upper caste, superior to all slaves save those that serve the emperor directly.'

'I thought I was being dragged away for a flogging.'

'You showed personal constancy to one of your caste, when that could only be to your cost. You owed that man a debt, yes, the slave who was flogged? A matter of honour? It is by such devotion as yours that a house becomes preeminent. That trait can never be purchased, no matter how rich a house grows through its holdings. It can only be uncovered.'

Was that her damn mother talking? Sounded like it. If Duncan could have remained behind in the sky mines, he would have taken a flogging and be damned. 'I never asked for this.'

'If you had, you would not be the appropriate choice to serve my house. You need not fear; the last food tester to perish eating from my plate passed many years ago. Even when our house's enemies don't fear my mother's revenge, they usually cower at the thought of my grandmother's. In that, they are wise.'

Duncan recalled the station's blasting powder stores rigged to explode and murder the girl's mother, thousands of slaves sacrificed to facilitate a single assassination. *Yes, wise indeed to fear Circae.* 'She's the one who wanted to kidnap you from the sky mines?'

'Of course. I am all that she has left of my father.'

'You never get to see your grandmother?'

Cassandra leant in conspiratorially. 'No. If I did, I would slip a dagger through Circae's heart for what she did to my father.'

'What was that?'

'She stripped him of his caste and had him sent to the legions for defying her, for marrying my mother when the match was forbidden. He died outside the imperium. Not as a general, but as a common captain in the wavering-lower caste. I can forgive Circae for a death in battle, in imperial service, but how can I forgive her for that indignity? Circae may as well have made my father a horse in a cavalry unit.'

Duncan looked in amazement at the little girl. 'How old are you, Your Highness?'

'I have reached my fourteenth year.'

Duncan shook his head in consternation. *And I thought I had it rough being the son of the great Benner Landor.*

'In two years I will be of age to be challenged by our house's rivals. I will travel always with a duelling blade and pistol on my belt. Our enemies will no longer send assassins; they will send my cousins and siblings with weapons to test me.'

She was such a slight thing, petite and demure. Duncan couldn't see young Cassandra being able to lift a decent blade, let alone cracking steels in a duel. 'And no champions?'

'They are forbidden. If I am not strong enough to stand for the house, then how would I be strong enough to raise, equip and lead forces for the imperium when it comes to war? Many enemies surround the empire. There is not a nation bordering the imperium that would not try to unseat us should we permit them to grow bold, and our borders are almost as endless as Pellas itself.'

Duncan felt a weight heavy on his heart. And yet he and his sister could have happily died of old age a world away never having heard the empire's name. That would have been a good fate. The one Willow deserved. The one that every Weylander dead and dying in the sky mines deserved.

'I will stand for you all,' continued Cassandra. 'When my time comes. Behind me will stand Mother, and you, and Paetro here, and Doctor Horvak, and the shade of my father and all of my ancestors. You don't need to worry about finding a champion for me. When the day comes, Circae is the one who shall suffer. I shall make her cursed soul a gift to my father for every misery she had inflicted on us.'

The giant soldier walking by their side spoke at last. It was like listening to a granite boulder trying to converse. 'And when the time comes, Princess, you will be ready.'

'By training and blood, I shall. Father died well, didn't he?'

'Captain went down like a tiger,' said the hulking Paetro. 'Boots slipping on the blood of a mound of dead barbarians he'd laid around him, a sword in one hand, still swinging hard, a pistol in the other, trigger clicking on an empty magazine. Wasn't a fighter in the legion who ever went down grander on a battlefield than your old pa, little Highness.'

'And that is how I shall stand when my time comes.'

'Aye, you will,' growled the soldier.

Duncan bit his tongue. Back in Northhaven, for all of his father's many faults, Benner Landor had tried to raise his children to live well. Here, it seemed they were raised to die well. You didn't need to be born a slave to be a prisoner of the imperium.

The three of them left the ship through a ramp lowered to the ground from its nosecone, heading towards an odd-looking aircraft parked under the shadow of the ship's prow. The aircraft rested on a tricycle configuration of rubber wheels. Its yellow-and-black-patterned fuselage resembled a plump metal hornet, a single pilot's seat up front, two seats behind, and a third – closer to a throne – facing the other two at the rear. Its passengers would be exposed to the air on the side; heads covered by a clear hemisphere-shaped canopy; while above that, the contraption had a large double rotor, no wings and a smaller tail rotor at the rear. Paetro helped the young girl up into the rear, to take the large comfortable seat, and then turned to Duncan.

'Watch me, and learn. This is how we check a helo. And we always check a helo before we allow the little Highness to take off in it.'

Duncan watched the soldier open a panel at the rear of the craft, exposing an engine which he proceeded to detail, dipping inside with his hands to search for explosives. Then they opened other hatches, checking storage compartments below the seats for good measure.

'You'll learn the faces and names of everyone on the staff,' muttered the brute as he worked, quickly and efficiently, with a dexterity that surprised Duncan, belying his large hands. 'You never board a helo with a strange pilot, only ones on the list. That's Hesia on the flyer's stick – she's Lady Cassandra's regular pilot. She never gets sick, do you Hesia?'

The pilot removed a bulky helmet and Duncan saw that she was indeed a woman, her long dark hair tied back in an elaborately braided ponytail. It was no wonder he hadn't noticed her gender before; the pilot's helmet came with a mirrored visor that swung down to cover her features. 'Only sick of hearing your ground-pounder's war stories.'

'Aye, she's good enough to fly for us, even if she did serve with the Imperial Sky Force. Don't let her take off if it's too foggy, though. Can't read a chart to save her life.'

'At least I *can* read.'

Paetro grunted, amused at the banter. He indicated the far side of the craft, where a large weapon sat mounted on a tripod. 'That's my seat ... side gunner. In case another helo gets too close.'

Duncan nodded. Not a mistake that many got to repeat, he suspected. They climbed up into the rear of the craft, settling in the two spare seats as the helo's rotors began to rotate, spinning so fast it became a blur, and then the little four-person aircraft jolted into the air, rising vertically as if it had been plucked into the sky by an invisible hand. He followed Paetro and Cassandra's lead and pulled the seat belt over his chest, clicking it into place inside a locking mechanism. It seemed a very flimsy protection against lurching through the air, dipping over the islet's buildings before following a bridge across to the mainland. Steel ships travelled below, long sail-less things with wheels on their sides churning the water, as well as many smaller boats that might have been fishing vessels or private yachts. Fog rolled in from the water; great swathes of it, heading for the city ahead, just like their helo. They left the water behind and came across the harbour, hitting land and banking above a maze of buildings that grew taller and taller as the helo progressed. They flew through canyons of stone, vast polished granite towers rising as high as mountains. Tapered towers, hulking and massive, rises spotted with thousands of windows. Hundreds of storeys tall, so many levels that Duncan couldn't even count them, fog hiding the streets below and clouds concealing the spires above. Bridges spanned these man-made canyons at multiple heights, moving walkways filled with crowds no larger than ants, rails below the bridges where fleeting steel arrow trains travelled, suspended beneath them like bats, disappearing into tunnels cut though the buildings' sides. Duncan was left reeling by the city's scale and mass. This was *Vandis*. You could fit Northhaven and all of its puny city limits on roof of a single building here. Squeezed it under the crystal sheeting of one of the tower-top greenhouses they passed over, hidden it among the enormous fields of enclosed greenery lit by a peculiar, pulsing orange light. Duncan watched the nearest tower-top greenhouse tremble, shaking from turbulence of a nearby stream of electrical carriages; almost hypnotising, the way vehicles passed along the raised roadways, an endless river of carriages emerging from tunnels through the towers.

'District eighty is owned by our house,' said Cassandra, proudly. She had to raise her voice to be heard over the roar of the rotors. 'All of it.'

And everyone in it, Duncan thought. *Including me.*

Cassandra noted Duncan staring at the weird pulsing light from the greenhouse below. 'Crops propagate tall under electrical stimulation. We produce our own food as much as possible, so we never grow over-reliant on the grain merchants. We suffer few food riots, even during famines.'

Good to know I won't starve, here, then. Duncan cast his mind guiltily back to the orders he had heard Princess Helrena give as he was dragged out of the station. *Half rations.* And Willow had been barely keeping up with the pace of work before. He couldn't shake his fear about her fate. A premonition?

They flew through the titanic city for half an hour more, dipping between towers where blocky stone statues leaned out of the walls, watching like gods over the populace below. Other helos skimmed through the air around them – oblivious to the hordes visible packing the moving walkways below and ignoring the rivers of electric carriages queued on the aerial highways. Duncan got the impression that flying by helo, like so much else inside the imperium, was a matter of caste. Only the highest allowed to travel through the air, beyond the stench and clamour of the common herd. Fog began to filter into the void between the towering buildings, a cold, clinging vapour that chilled him to the bone. It felt odd, after the continual heat of the sky mines and the constant furnace presence of the vast belching strato-volcano. An actual chill, with slow drizzle running down the helo's canopy. Duncan couldn't remember the last time he had seen rain. Certainly not in the sky mines – not unless you included the showers of ash. They pushed on. Traversing this sector of the capital before the helo reached its destination. They had arrived back at the sea. Towers and skyscrapers fell away, concrete canyons replaced by a flat plain of formal gardens stretching out below, and then, overlooking the blue waters, a palace of sorts; a great mass of concrete domes and bulky fortifications, their ugly function barely concealed by trellises of ivy. It was built on a rise, high white cliffs, gun emplacements pointing menacingly out to sea. So, this was where Princess Helrena ruled over her wedge of the capital. Her piece of the action. There were no bridges visible on this side of the land, but a high bank of white fog was rolling in to blanket the palace.

'This is the Castle of Snakes,' said Paetro, as the helo began to descend towards an open stretch of concrete between two domes. Yellow lights blinked inside a circle, guiding them in. Other helos were visible grounded below, columns of armoured soldiers marching in eerie unison as they sang. Fog filled the parade ground.

'The poisonous kind I'm meant to check Lady Cassandra's bed for?'

The guardsman shook his head. 'Not real snakes – it's just a name, lad. The foot of the cliffs are a breeding ground for eels. In spring the water thrashes like a living thing with millions of them.'

Castle of Snakes. Given Duncan's unhappy experiences with the empire, it seemed an apt name on so many levels. The helo's rubber wheels bounced once and they settled on the ground. Duncan's new life had begun. As little choice in the matter as ever, since being beaten to the ground by skels, chained up and carried away from Northhaven. Still a slave, but perhaps something slightly more, now?

Carter swam through a daze, an endless ocean of raw, red pain bringing him buoyancy. Occasionally he would surface for a few moments of lucidity, realise that this fever was the legacy of his punishment flogging. People cared for him. Kerge maybe; others, too, taking turns in relays between mining duties; which can't have been easy, given how weary they'd be while working two rocks. A woman appeared sometimes. She might have been Willow, if her hair hadn't been burning and shifting like fire, and she wouldn't extinguish it however Carter begged. There was a cream being carefully applied to his back, burning like acid where it met his skin. A thin gruel forced down his throat. Once, he came to and heard shouting in the background. Someone arguing about the water and food being wasted on him, maybe a fight too, after that. He knew exactly where he was – the chamber where the sick and dying were isolated, in case their infections should spread. But being flogged wasn't contagious. Maybe rebellion was. Those moments of lucidity would slip through his fingers and he'd be left drifting across the heat again, as though flying disembodied through the sky mines' upper regions. In between the flashes of clarity and fever-wracked weightlessness, Carter became an observer to visions which twisted his mind with intense head-knifing agony. Sights that seemed as real as anything on the station, perhaps more real than the fever room where he had been tossed, shadowy figures moving in and out of his perception.

Skels, the twisted men; not as they were now, but as they had lived in the ancient past. A mighty horde controlling the stratovolcano. The Vandians' ancestors their serfs in the fields and mills, disposable underlings who wept under the skels' whips and goads. Riches and cities beyond imagination, jewelled mountains of concrete and glass and steel where night was remade as day by strange engines. He witnessed the revolution that displaced the skels, as bloody and merciless as any revolt in history. Millions of skels slaughtered and left to rot in mass graves, skel survivors taking to the air in giant carriers, all that was left of a once-mighty skyguard overrun by their own slave mechanics and airfield workers. Carter watched this cycle repeated between the ages and between countless peoples, common pattern humans, and men so twisted that he could put no name to them. And then, as if Carter hadn't had his fill of this grim procession of past outrages, his vision's focus widened. Some faces he recognised ... tried to reach out to. His brothers, his mother, friends and neighbours from Northhaven. Dead and alive in the same moment, time twisted. He saw Lucas Lettore in his burrow of books. He saw the old tramp who had arrived begging at the library's gate an age before ... Sariel. Carter's visions briefly coalesced. The tramp's face lingered, spinning in and out of focus.

'All the stories,' said Sariel, running a finger down his coat's illustrations. 'All the tales of the world, they're all true. If not now, before; if not now, one day soon. The *when* and the *weave* both the same.'

'I'm going mad, old man. My mind is frying inside my head.'

'That's good. Madness is the only sanity,' said Sariel. 'It will protect you.'

'From what?'

'From what? I don't remember. But it must be bad, Lord Carnehan. It might even be the truth.'

'Why don't you remember?'

'I rebuilt myself with magic ... from such a trifling speck of blood. Poor murdered Sariel. But I didn't do it properly. I am a spur-galled wimpled copy, erased and ignorant.'

'I have something for you, I think,' said Carter.

'And I for you,' said Sariel. 'It's a gift. The end of things. You have to die to live.'

'I'm getting there.'

'Stay alive for me, Lord Carnehan. We're coming ...'

'Who?'

'Hell is coming. A devil to fight stealers. In such a conflict, only a devil will answer the purpose.'

Carter begged for more tidings, but the vagrant faded from view and only his crazy tales remained twisting through Carter's visions – dolphins that danced and bees that laughed and men that leapt through the air on springed boots, heroes and villains from a thousand impossible lands before breakfast. When Carter's fever finally broke, he found himself on the bunk, sopping wet, and it was as if his body was newborn, as though he had been reincarnated in someone else's form. A water canteen lay just out of reach on the floor and he groaned as he reached for it. Kerge appeared and scooped it up, passing it to him. *Water.* Carter remembered the cold, headache-inducing liquid he had drunk in the strange labyrinth below the volcano. The sweats it generated. Was the tomb water somehow the cause of his visions? Or had he been poisoned by vapours and gases during his failed escape attempt?

'You are lucky to have survived.'

'Luck had nothing to do with it,' coughed Carter, propping himself up and taking a trickle of water. He tried to drink it slow, to avoid cramping up. 'You saved me – you and others ...'

'Willow was here, that is true. She has been swapping shifts with the sorting line workers. I am worried about how little sleep she has allowed herself. Your nation is not nearly as hardy as gask-kind. The womanling is close to exhaustion.'

Carter felt overwhelmed by a wave of guilt. The two people who had worked so hard to save him, and he'd left them behind on the station when he'd tried to break out. *Maybe I was wrong about Willow?* That was a difficult thing to admit, even to himself. He'd almost rather take another flogging than admit it publicly. 'I'm surprised my throat wasn't cut while I was asleep.'

'Not for lack of trying, by some' said the gask. 'I asked the doctor to help us keep a special watch over you.'

The slave in question was Samuel Tooky. He claimed to have been a doctor back in Weyland, but if so, Carter suspected he'd been the horse doctoring kind. Everyone on the station called him Doctor Too, for his habit of saying he'd be able to heal someone, if only he had his old surgical tools, nursing staff, or a decent pharmacy on hand, *too*. Well, at least he had proved himself useful when it came to preventing murder on his watch.

Khow pulled his silver abacus machine out of a leather tool pouch and tapped its glass readout. 'I am confused. During your fever your weight upon the world altered beyond recognition. Now it is as if you walk with the trail of a legion within your footsteps. Such a realignment should not be possible'

'I'm full of surprises.'

'I assure you, this goes far beyond your well-demonstrated talent for rash and random actions.'

'Well, I've seen a few impossible things,' said Carter. 'When I was down on Old Smoky. And I suffered a head full of them up here too.'

'And now the world is moving around you, rather than the converse.'

'My head's been left clear, is all,' said Carter. 'I know who sold us out. Who hid the tracking device in the transporter and made sure that Alan, Noah, Deeli and Eshean were murdered by the empire before we'd even bugged out for freedom.'

Kerge checked around to make sure no other slave was within earshot. 'Who on the station could do such a thing?'

'Owen Paterson. The man overheard me outlining my scheme and as good as warned me not to try to break out. When I went ahead ...'

'You are mistaken, manling.'

'The hell I am. Think about it. Paterson's been around as long as anyone. Everyone looks up to him as a leader; yet he's never been promoted into the middle-hostile caste with the other slaves who administer the station for our so-called mistress. He's just one of the boys, eating alongside us, working alongside us. Always helpful to the greenhorns, always advising caution to new workers if they look like they might go making a ruckus. Always *listening*. I just don't know if Anna Kurtain was in on the scheme with him. They're as thick as thieves, those two.'

'The two are merely veterans of this terrible place – they have survived together. Such trials create a resilient bond.'

'And who the hell survives up here?'

'Those blessed by fate and in possession of a good heart. Owen is the one who scavenged the rations and medicines that kept you alive while you recovered from your wounds.'

'To throw off suspicion, or ease a guilty conscience maybe.'

'Clear your head of this matter. I am sure you are mistaken. I have examined the station's chambers and passages, searching for concealed mechanical devices that would allow the Vandians to eavesdrop on our conversations.'

'And how many such devices have you found?'

'None yet. But—'

'But *nothing*. *Owen* warned us to watch what we say inside the station because there might be turncoats listening. He even said it with a straight face! You know what irony is, don't you Kerge? The Vandians don't need a legion of secret police sitting around bored, manning surveillance machines and listening to slaves farting and moaning, to control the sky mines. Not when they've got hungry slaves with loose lips doing the job in exchange for an easy ride.'

Carter leant back in the bunk for a second, suppressing a howl of pain when his back brushed the rock wall.

Kerge indicated a stone bowl on the floor filled with a foul-smelling paste. 'You will need to rub the paste across your spine for many weeks.'

'Do I want to know what's in it?'

'Mogo tubers mixed with fuel ether. Diluted, its toxins numb nerves and shield you from the worst of your pain.'

'Maybe I need to be reminded of the pain,' said Carter. 'I'm the only one who survived. Noah, Eshean, they all died down there. They were relying on *me*.'

'They followed their own branches, chose their own fate.'

'They never had a chance,' said Carter. 'Not from the start. You were right.'

'Time is a river sweeping all along its stream. There are currents you cannot swim against.'

'Our friends weren't the ones who deserved to drown, though, were they? It's the bastard who betrayed us and slipped that tracking device inside the transporter.'

'You must not act without conclusive proof,' said Kerge. 'Things will become difficult enough for you when you are assigned to the work parties. Starting a feud with a well-regarded worker would be counterproductive. Stay here and stay quiet. I shall fetch Willow to see you. Then, perhaps, she will allow herself some rest before her body fails her.'

When Willow did appear she seemed flushed with excitement at her charge's recovery, although if the skin of her hands was anything to go by – paler than Carter had ever seen before, almost translucent – she was far closer to collapsing than Carter, now. He could hear Kerge talking outside the fever room, conversing with male voices.

'Did you thank Duncan for me?'

'I never got the chance. He's gone.'

Carter felt a sudden shock of dread in his gut. 'They flogged him to—?'

'Gone off the *station*, not executed. Taken as a house-slave by that royal bitch. Thomas Gale told us that Duncan's been assigned to the team of slaves tasked with keeping Lady Cassandra safe.'

Carter just stopped himself snorting with laughter. 'Of all the damn jobs. I never saw Duncan Landor as a wet nurse!'

'He's already saved her once,' said Willow, brushing her crimson hair back in annoyance. 'It's not funny. It's dangerous work. The girl's bodyguards were murdered on the station, betrayed by people in her own house. How safe is Duncan going to be out there?'

'The old hands keep on telling us what a soft position being a house slave is.'

'Princess Helrena found someone willing to risk their neck doing the right thing. That's as rare a quality out in the empire as it is in the sky mines. And just as likely to get Duncan killed.'

'Did your brother do the right thing? Saving me?'

'I really don't think I'm fit to comment.'

'I'm sorry Duncan's not here for you. With luck he'll outlast us all, now.'

'It's not hard to outlast you, Carter Carnehan. Trouble follows you around like a hound on a lead. Back in Northhaven, the consequences were never going to be too serious. But stranded here, kept as slaves in the sky mines? Trouble's fatal. Almost every consequence is fatal!'

Kerge reappeared inside the fever room with a bowl of barley gruel. The smell was as good as a feast wafting towards Carter. He realised how empty his stomach had been left by the ravages of his temperature. 'You'll see Duncan again, Willow, if he's become that little girl's shadow. Helrena's always visiting the station, checking her house's riches; making sure the whip's not being spared against our spines.'

'That really doesn't make me feel better.'

'I'll make sure nothing happens to you. I never had a sister, before, only brothers. But I'll watch your back as carefully as Duncan ever did.'

'Don't do me any favours!'

Carter watched in confusion as the girl ran out, tears streaming down her eyes. 'What the hell was that about?'

Kerge rested the bowl down on the bunk. 'That? It is outside the extent of my calculations, manling.' He sighed. 'What the eyes cannot see, the mind cannot explain.'

Carter reached for the gruel. It was almost as if— No, he must be imagining it. *She probably just needs some rest.*

As large as the dungeons keeping Jacob and the others prisoner under the grand duke's palace were, little air circulated through the fetid arched chambers. And what air there was, was shared with close to a hundred gad prisoners. All of them waiting on their cruel ruler's whimsy – or perhaps just for him to finish his breakfast. Sheplar paced up and down the chamber shaking his head and muttering to himself, as if he was imagining a dozen ways that they could have avoided being incarcerated. Khow tapped on his abacus box, as though he might calculate a better fate for them, while Sariel, true to form, chattered away, adding to the heat with his jabber.

'I have never had the dubious pleasure of these ill-nurtured cells before,' grumbled Sariel. 'Previous grand dukes of Hangel have had too much decency to introduce the prince of players to their gaol.'

'From what I've seen, decency and the ruler here aren't even nodding acquaintances,' said Jacob.

'But you may be comforted to know that this is not the first gaol I have found myself imprisoned inside.'

'That, at least, is true,' murmured Sheplar, as the mountain aviator strode past.

'The Fortress of Dolar is the most impenetrable prison on Pellas, perched upon a crag so high that its prisoners must wear oxygen masks like the crew of a merchant carrier. The only way in or out is in man-sized baskets lowered on chains, the journey to the ground below taking two hours. Each cell is attended only by a deaf and mute guard who could not be bribed or cajoled.'

'A difficult place to escape,' growled Jacob.

'That was not the worst of it, Your Grace! The authorities hired the best chef in the land to work in the fortress kitchens. Each meal was a banquet so fine that the explosion of flavours could almost send you blind. You would find yourself sweating in anticipation hours before each meal. Four times a day, trembling like a drunkard for his sack. The food so exquisite, that once any prisoner had been fed in the fortress for a week, they could not bear to escape if it meant never eating there again.'

'And yet here you stand.'

'A liar and a scoundrel,' said Sheplar, passing by. It was easy to ignore his asides with the low, wailing cadence of the gad prisoners filling the arched dungeons. They sat and rocked as they sang in their own tongue.

Sariel ignored the flier. 'And it was I who gave the lie to its governor's boast of the place's inescapability. Ah yes, but it took all my ingenuity to leave that wretched prison. I kept the food the mute pushed through my cell door and scattered it by the bars of my single window, to feed the colony of hump bats – flying rodents with a sack on their back to store oxygen – that nested in the crag's caves. After the bats were addicted, I would snap one of their necks for each meal, then eat it raw. As disgusting a taste as you could imagine – but the perfect antidote for the kitchen's mouth-watering fare. Many was the time I was nearly sick into my oxygen mask.'

'But even cured of the addiction, you were still trapped.'

'Not for long. I worked the dead bats' teeth into a loose leg of my bed, fashioning a saw to hack away at my window's bars. Finally, I made a parachute out of my blanket, and when the last bar was cut … then I leapt into the moonless night and sailed to freedom.'

Sheplar merely snorted as he paced past again.

'A jump so precarious, there isn't a Rodalian glider pilot in the world who could emulate it,' added Sariel, pointedly. 'But what I had not counted on was the bats. They were so used to eating my food that a great cloud of them gathered and followed me across the sky, attracting the guard's attentions. Soon the night was filled with searchlights with the brutes shooting wildly as they tried to bring me down.' He paused a second to see if Jacob would bite for the escape's conclusion, but the pastor merely shrugged.

'Luckily,' continued Sariel, 'I had set aside a leg of honeyed ham to sustain me for my journey out of the barren forest surrounding the crag. I tossed it away and the bats followed it, along with the searchlights and the guards' bullets.'

Jacob cast an eye around the thin, miserable gads crowding the dungeon around them. 'Somehow, I don't think surviving addiction to prison rations will be a problem here.'

'Indeed, he is a miserly host,' said Sariel, casting an eye around the humid chamber. 'Leaving us to bake in his oven without even supplying the dough to knead to make bread.'

'This city's ruler knows us somehow,' said Khow from the floor. 'My numbers indicate a reversion, the inverse of an analytic function.'

'If you say so, friend. We'll be finding out soon enough, I reckon,' said Jacob.

Sariel began thumping the flagstones with his walking staff, as though he might summon his missing breakfast. Instead, the door – steel-plated wood as thick as a man's forearm – unlocked, drew open, and a team of gad slaves dragged in a heavy oak barrel. Four well-armed soldiers watched the slaves prise up the barrel lid, revealing a tub of brackish-looking water, then departed with the slaves while the prisoners lined up to use a wooden spoon to slop out rations of drink. Jacob and the others joined the line. He was impressed by the gads' discipline. There was no fighting or brawling over the precious liquid, despite the fact they would need a lot more than what was inside here to stay alive in the dungeon's oppressive heat. In fact, looking at how fast the liquid disappeared, there was a chance it would be empty by the time Jacob reached the barrel. It wouldn't be the same inside a Weyland cell, that much he knew. A figure among the queuing gads caught Jacob's eye. It was the way he tried to stay out of sight of the visitors that roused Jacob's suspicious hackles. Jacob looked closer. Something strange about the prisoner's striped yellow and brown and green skin, too; different from the other prisoners. He strode towards the gad. Confirming his suspicions, the locals began clustering more tightly around their friend, blocking Jacob's view.

'Your skin paint,' noted Jacob, 'is running in the heat.'

The other gads tried to shoo the interloper away, protesting that none of them knew what he was talking about.

'What is this?' said Sheplar, coming up behind Jacob.

'That one,' said Jacob, pointing to the gad sheltering behind his kin, 'isn't what he seems.'

Sheplar followed the line of Jacob's finger. 'Why ... the patterning on his skin is running?'

'Yes, that happens when it's been painted on.'

'A spy!' hissed Sheplar. 'A dirty informer.'

Jacob held the aviator back as he tried to push his way through the crowd. 'I don't think so. Leastways, not a spy for the grand duke, not with so many genuine gads eager to cover for him. I would say he's a half-breed. Perhaps a scout for the tribes beyond the walls.'

'This is not so,' called one of the gads hiding their comrade.

'Let's shout for the grand duke's guards, then,' said Jacob. 'If you've got nothing to hide, you've got nothing to worry about.'

The figure the natives sheltered reluctantly stepped forward. He was a tall male. His skin similar to his comrades, apart from where an indistinct mottling had been revealed around his neck, still running with sweat. Somewhere between common pattern and gad. He was a half-breed.

'You have your freedom, then,' said the gad. 'If you reveal my presence, the grand duke's soldiers will surely reward you with your liberty.'

'I doubt it,' said Jacob. 'I've yet to meet the man, but from what I've seen of his state, he doesn't strike me as the grateful type. You're taking a risk, coming into the royal city.'

'I heard that a baby had been born to a servant. We snatch them, whenever we can. Before the city law is applied.'

'I reckon you were one of them, once.'

'Your guess is a good one,' said the gad. 'I am called Zanasi by the people in the city.'

'The trickster,' said Sariel. 'Zanasi is the Gaddish god who became King of All Stories after proving to the Land Mother that he could change his shape into a hippo, a jaguar and a hornet.'

'You know our history well, old one,' said the gad.

Sariel shrugged modestly. 'I bested the real Zanasi once in a poet's duel. By rights, the title of King of All Stories belongs to me. But he wept so much afterwards, I couldn't bear to strip him of it.'

Zanasi grinned at the vagrant's cheek. 'That is wise. For when he is in the shape of a hornet, he stings mightily.'

'Yes. I am far too kindly for my own good.'

'All I can change into is a gad or a Hangel,' said Zanasi, 'depending on which dye I apply to my face.'

'You might have wanted to pick the latter for your morning's work,' said Jacob. He introduced himself and the others in Northhaven's expedition to the scout.

'A city man carrying a gad babe?' said Zanasi, staring quizzically at the strange group of foreigners after Jacob finished his introductions. 'Not a common sight. And nobody looks twice at a gad servant.'

'A common problem,' said Khow. 'To a manling, all gasks look alike. They can barely distinguish male from female.'

'There is a little truth in that,' said Zanasi. 'It was bad luck for me there were so many soldiers out early. The Hangels are normally asleep in their barracks at such a premature hour.'

'We are to blame for their early patrols,' said Jacob.

'I have heard tell of you. You are the party which climbed the servants' stairs up to the city yesterday. But I do not think the grand duke has imprisoned you for that.'

'We're just simple travellers,' said Jacob. 'But I don't think the head man wants us to get to where we're going.'

'And why would that be?'

'The why, I'm still working on. The who, that I reckon I know.'

'The grand duke rarely executes travellers,' explained Zanasi. 'He may be mad, but he is not a fool by any means. His revenues come from refuelling the aircraft which attempt the savannah crossing. He would not put his commerce at risk without good reason.'

Sheplar's ears pricked up at this. 'Attempt? The traders do not always make it?'

'They do not. The wreckage of planes that ran out of fuel litters the plains. It is said that the founders of Hangel were originally the crew of a mighty carrier which crashed on the plateau after they rode the wrong trade winds.'

'In our case, I don't think our status as foreigners is going to provide much protection,' said Jacob. *Quite the opposite. I reckon it's why we're here.*

'Where do you travel to?'

Jacob pulled out the map from the library and carefully unfolded it. He'd borrowed it with permission, planning to use the chart to book passage in the right direction with the air merchants. There wasn't much chance the mistress of the codex was going to see it returned any time soon, now. Jacob tapped the imperium's territory. 'This is the end of our journey.'

'The Far-away Heart,' said Zanasi. 'A source of great wealth.'

Jacob nodded. If you squinted, the outline of the empire's massive territory did appear a little like a sketch of a heart.

'You seek treasure?'

'I seek my son,' said Jacob. 'Slavers took him, but he's all the treasure I have. Everything else I've already given away to reach my boy.'

Zanasi looked at them oddly. 'It is strange. It is as though I have heard your story before. It seems familiar to me, somehow.'

'Déjà vu?' said Jacob.

'Perhaps you carry the blood of a diviner within your veins?' suggested Sariel.

'I am no shaman,' said Zanasi. 'That I can promise you. I have none of their blood.'

Nor did Jacob. But his bad feeling about their future grew a great deal more tangible as the sound of marching boots approached outside. A clacking noise sounded as the vault-like door unlocked, and soldiers appeared, rudely ushering the dungeon's prisoners outside, gads and visitors alike. With little light in the corridor, the torches the soldiers carried nearly blinded Jacob. He could hardly see to put one foot in front of another. Zanasi stumbled by Jacob's side along the dark corridor.

'Do you know what we can expect?' whispered Jacob.

'I fear we are to be the grand duke's breakfast entertainment,' said the gad. 'He always digests his meal better after he has murdered a few of my people.'

They were shoved out of the tunnel and onto the sandy dirt of a bright open space. Any hopes that the expedition's members were to be released faded as Jacob's vision returned. They stood on the floor of a pit that resembled a bull-fighting stadium, the gads being shepherded behind a wooden stockade, leaving Jacob and his party in the open. There weren't many seats in this arena. It seemed it wasn't intended for the general public. If you discounted the soldiers corralling the gad prisoners, the sole spectators sat behind a raised balcony covered from the sun by a white canvas shade. Taking no chances, the viewers were protected behind a canopy of armoured glass. In the centre sat a stoutish, late-middle-aged man with a shock of red hair, presumably the grand duke from the elevated position of his throne. He wore a purple tunic with a yellow wisp of a neck cloth buttoned up to the throat. He might have been handsome once but he had run badly to seed, the ravages of age and obesity beggaring his appearance. An eager gaggle of courtiers bobbed up and down behind the nobleman's seat, not quite able to see the proceedings as well as their master. Dogs leapt up around the throne, trying for a view of the proceedings as well. The grand duke cooed at them, stroking their heads affectionately. The man sitting to the ruler's left needed no introduction. It was Major Alock, his hard, stony face looked straight at Jacob and he still wore the uniform of a Weyland officer, his spine as rigid as any block of granite.

Jacob, Sheplar, Sariel and Khow were shoved in front of the raised platform.

A voice yelled from one of the soldiers behind them. 'Kneel for Grand Duke Pavlorda, most noble issue of the House of Bragin.'

The soldiers behind Jacob didn't wait; they shoved him down to his knees.

'Are these the dogs?' demanded the grand duke, fair writhing in the chair as he spoke.

'They are, Your Highness,' confirmed Alock.

Jacob stared up in hatred at the traitor who should have been helping him. 'You're a long way from home, Major. I didn't know the league kept embassies this far out.'

'You've come a long way yourself, for a man who's only travelling towards a grave.'

'Got a way to go yet, before that.'

Alock shook his head, allowing a wry grin to crack his dark demeanour. 'Well, you must have mumbled a Bible full of prayers to get this far. How the hell did you escape my men back in the forest?'

'I convinced them that stealing is a mortal sin. And that betraying your king is the civil kind.'

'Only one out of two,' said Alock. 'I'm here on official business.'

'You're meant to be helping us, manling!' protested Khow. 'That is your duty.'

'You'd be surprised where my duty takes me.'

'Like the Burn? Your men told me that you were a mercenary general on the other side of the ocean. Bad Justus. Ring any bells?' asked Jacob.

'Fully pardoned,' said the major. 'For any indiscretions, on both sides of the ocean.'

'This isn't about stealing our money, is it?' said Jacob. 'You're meant to stop us getting to the Vandian empire.'

'You see, that's what worries me about you,' snarled the major. 'First you know the right direction to travel. Now, you actually seem to know where you're going.'

'So, this fool understands too much for his own good,' said the grand duke twisting in his chair as though he itched from the heat. 'But that is only a problem while he is alive. It is time to feed my beauties.'

'What's your game, Major?' called Jacob. 'Is King Marcus worried that the might of the imperium might be directed in Weyland's direction if I reach their empire and start killing the right people?'

Alock sighed. 'You really don't know how deep you're in it, do you? The king has been *allowing* the skels to raid the country for slaves. Paid a lot better than I am for giving the skels carte blanche. Or did you think it was an accident that every military unit which could have intervened was stationed somewhere else during the Northhaven raid?'

'You are a liar!' called Sheplar. 'Rodal would never cooperate in such a dishonourable arrangement.'

'Some of the league states know what's going on, some don't.' He tapped the side of the grand duke's chair when he said *know* and Jacob suddenly understood where the little city state was getting the money to fund its expansionary war against the tribes. Major Alock leaned forward on the viewing gallery above the arena. 'Your country is even more backward than ours, pilot; and if it's happy to stay like that, so be it. The raids don't amount to much. The king only cares that he's sent enough steel and iron to modernise the nation. That's the thing about people … we can always breed more of them. But the metals that Vandia's supplying us with, they're a lot harder to come by.'

Jacob felt the anger boiling inside him. 'He'll be looking for another throne when the assembly finds out.'

'Maybe, maybe not. There are many politicians in the mechanicalist faction who are only too happy to be given what they need to produce modern mills. But you can see the king's dilemma: he needs to keep his little arrangement quiet. Where the people hear rumours about the raids, he needs our peasants thinking they're just a few random slaver attacks. Nothing they can do about it, just one of those haphazard evils that fate throws their way. This should be *easy*. The empire gets the manpower it needs without any retribution missions, without facing a pitched battle every time a skel carrier's spotted in the air. The king gets a modern state. But you, pastor, you're making it hard. You should be out west searching for your son in the Burn slave markets. Instead you're heading south, and far too well informed for your own good.'

'So, Benner Landor's hostage money was just a bonus for you and your men?'

The major shrugged. 'A man's got to eat.'

'So do my beauties,' said the grand duke, his voice growing impatient. 'It is time! Yes, yes!'

'Feed them in one at a time,' cautioned Alock. He stared emotionlessly down at the prisoners. 'Any time you fools want to tell me how you discovered where the Northhaven slaves went, you can go back to the dungeons and rot for the rest of your lives, rather than satisfying the appetite of the grand duke's pets.'

'They're not *slaves*,' snarled Jacob. 'They're family and friends.'

'Not mine, pastor. I got rid of most of my family a long time ago. Now, before we move on to the main course, I'll introduce the entrée and see if that changes your mind any.' He snapped his fingers and a naked figure was dragged out and deposited in the middle of the arena by two soldiers. 'Of course, the grand duke's pets won't eat dead meat. But it would have been rude of us to feed her to them alive when she gave us so much good sport during the interrogation.'

Jacob could hardly stand to watch as the soldiers rolled the badly scarred body over. It was Iaroia, the head of the local librarian's guild hold. They had beaten her to death. 'You murdering bastard! She didn't know anything!'

Alock raised his hands, as though he had merely been caught in a breach of manners. 'She was a librarian, of course she knew things. She gave you shelter for a night. You might have let something slip. How could I not ask her?'

Another poor innocent dead, because of him. *Because of Jacob*

Carnehan, the voice inside whispered. *When Jake Silver is the man who should have gone looking for his son. Quicksilver.* 'You're crazy, Alock! The guilds will pull out of Hangel when they hear you violated their immunity.'

'Let's just say the authorities here have a superior source of intelligence. Now, who next?' The major pointed Sariel out to the grand duke. 'There! That one's name I don't know, although I have a feeling the coins shaken from his pocket came from the Landor moneybox which mysteriously went missing. I resent scum thieving my wealth; especially after I've gone to so much trouble to steal it in the first place. He can die next ...'

Guards appeared with long lances and prodded Sariel, the vagrant waving his arms wildly as they jabbed him towards the centre of the arena. Jacob, Sheplar and Khow were driven back behind the wooden barrier where the gads stood corralled, the locals moaning and swaying, exposed under the hot sun. A series of iron gates rattled at the far end of the arena, a white-washed wall splattered with blood and dust. Jacob and his two companions were protected by the wooden palisade from whatever was caged inside there. No such protection was afforded to Sariel, however.

The guards held Jacob at bay, their spears digging into his chest and drawing blood. 'Your filthy scheme murdered my wife, Alock! You traded my son's future for a handful of metal. I'm going to kill you, Major. You and your crooked royal master, both!'

'Not today,' sneered Alock. 'I much prefer working for the state. It's a lot easier to work when everything you do is rendered legal by royal warrant. I'll leave you to last, pastor. Anytime you get tired of seeing your friends ripped apart, just tell me what I need to know ...'

Jacob spat on the floor. The second he revealed the secret of Khow's homing sense was the second Alock would order their execution. There was only one way for the major to keep the true source of the slave raids from Weyland, and that was to plant every member of the expedition in the ground. Jacob would have done exactly the same, once.

'Your milk-livered animals will not attack me,' shouted Sariel. He hobbled forward, shaking his walking staff in the air. His actions wouldn't hold back a determined predator for longer than a second or two. 'They know the prince of players too well.'

A roar of laughter emerged from the grand duke's protected viewing station, the courtiers clapping and jeering.

'I am sorry for your friend.' It was the gad scout. He gazed up at the royal viewing platform with a curious expression that Jacob recognised only too well.

'My beauties know what time it is,' hooted the grand duke. He waved his hand. One of the poorly oiled iron gates in the wall began to squeal upwards, a frantic mound of fur trying to scrabble out from the holding chamber before the gate was fully retracted. It was joined by another shape, then a third, all competing and howling to be the first to be released. 'Breakfast time!'

The gate rose halfway into the wall and the creatures had enough clearance to escape. They surged out, a trio of big cats – a similar patterning along their hides to the gads – half as tall as a man and at least ten feet long, with manes that made them seem giants from the front. Two hunters broke to Sariel's left, a third prowling low along the right, working as a pack. The first pair was just a feint. It was the lone hunter that would make the kill.

'Friends,' shouted Sariel, jabbing his cane skyward. 'My friends, you will not harm me.'

If that was the creatures' intention, they had a strange way of showing it. The creeping predator leapt at Sariel, baring a set of white teeth as sharp as a phalanx of sabres; its roar so loud and penetrating that Jacob felt his heart shuddering inside his ribcage from the power of it. Khow moaned in horror. Even Sheplar, who believed the vagrant a thieving chancer, turned his head rather than witness this unequal slaughter. Jacob could not. He had led Sariel to this fate. As surely as he steered old Deputy Wiggins to a burning inside the forest by the major's killers. As surely as Iaroia's fate had been sealed by assisting him. *I was the kind of man who would have questioned captives this way, once. Now I'm just the kind who leads them into the butcher's pit. And I don't know which breed is worse.*

Sariel screamed as he flailed at the leaping creature with his staff, the wooden rod sent flying as the massive predator ripped his right arm off and continued the arc of its leap to land in a cloud of dust behind the bard. It began triumphantly shaking Sariel's dismembered limb. The bard was spun around by the force of the attack, landing on the arena sand just as the other two cats hurled themselves on top of him, ripping his leather coat and tearing at his clothes, batting him with their clawed paws, and sending his mangled body rolling limply across the ground.

Duncan learnt his lessons well under the tutelage of the grizzled old Paetro. Paetro, it transpired, was one of the many janissaries who served in the legions. Foreign troops that took the empire's coin on the basis that there was always so much of it to go around. They worked their way up through the castes, as best they could. Some would call them mercenaries, although many might consider them pragmatists. The imperium always won every war and always would, so if you had to fight as a career, better to fight on the winning side. Duncan and Paetro's duties almost seemed to him like licensed paranoia. Gaming how to kill the girl and make it seem like an accident, then sweeping for each potential avenue for murder in advance. Accidents were the best method of assassination. Nothing to link an aggressor to the actual deed; hard to retaliate against through the legal channels of duelling or low-level warfare permitted by the emperor. Having a helo fall out of the air or a sky mine's blasting powder detonate under an enemy's boots would be an ideal kill. Stylish, even. Using a sniper who could be captured and tortured, that was counted as brutish: plausible mechanical failure, or a chance encounter with one of the island's many varieties of venomous snake, sublime. The hardest part of Duncan's training came when a surgeon in the Castle of Snakes administered low levels of poisons commonly used by assassins, peppering samples of food with toxins, so Duncan might learn to detect tampering well before it ever reached the lips of young Lady Cassandra. Duncan spent days throwing up, taking anti-venom injections and drinking purges to clear the filth from his body. By the time he finished, he could smell a table full of plates and identify the one which had been sprinkled with devil-dust or coated with poison mixed with honey to conceal its toxic aftertaste. The effects of that regime aside, he put on weight for the first time since his enslavement, sampling fare from the feasts served to Cassandra.

The young noblewoman, by contrast, never seemed to put on weight. Partly through the metabolism of Lady Cassandra's tender age, partly through the gruelling regime of weapons training she was expected to attend daily. Gymnastics to learn balance and poise. Weights to build strength. Combat practice of every sort – spears, tridents, knives, maces, sabres, foils, short-swords, bolas, pistols, ranged target shooting. Paetro supervised the combat, with experts shipped in from every corner of the empire to impart their talents. Once, for fun, Paetro let Duncan fight the young girl with wooden practice swords on the wooden slats of the training hall. Despite their difference in size, strength and age, Duncan barely walked away without his knuckles being shattered. She was like a little demon, whirling and swinging, using moves so quick and esoteric that few Weylanders would have been able to keep up. Maybe some of the trained swordsmen in the army would have been her match, but even then Duncan had his doubts. Or maybe that was just what he needed to tell himself after losing so badly to a young girl. The days were long, but after the sky mines' gruelling regime, keeping up with the young noble was quite literally child's play. And there was always the possibility, ever-playing through Duncan's thoughts, that he might see Adella again here. The imperial siblings that Helrena counted as her allies were always showing up at the Castle of Snakes to confer on strategy and scheme their schemes. Surely Baron Machus would appear one day with Adella in his retinue? But that day never seemed to come, however much he hoped for it. Perhaps it was for the best. Duncan didn't think he could bear to see Adella being pawed by another man, one of the mighty princelings who could order a slave's execution just for spilling soup over him during a meal, let alone for punching him for stealing Adella away like a rustled horse. Like a *slave*. And it might have been cowardice – or prudence – but Duncan didn't want to jeopardise his chances of getting Willow transferred to the castle alongside him as a house slave. All he needed was Princess Helrena feeling that she was in Duncan's debt again. Life inside the castle seemed different from the station. There were still the distinctions of caste here; but there was also a camaraderie and a commonality of purpose which was distinctly lacking at the raw level of existence in the sky mines. It was almost as if having gained a place at the centre of the house, no higher position existed, irrespective of hierarchy. Better a beggar here than a prince at home.

With Adella still in Duncan's dreams, and his sister's fate in the sky mines filling his mind, he distracted himself by packing his days with the routine endured by his charge. In addition to Lady Cassandra mastering arms, there were the many practical lessons of learning the house's business. Not far removed from the demands Duncan's father had once made upon his time. Attending metal brokerages and auctions in the capital, the vast wealth of the sky mines traded for scientific advances and other commodities and resources. Visiting the house's mills processing the ores that slaves gave their lives to obtain. Mile upon mile of metallic plant separating raw materials, vast glowing furnaces tended by thousands of lower caste workers, glowing ingots rolling out of the other end in a sea of steam and metallic vapour. Passing work parties in leather suits and steel helmets, battered and burnt from molten spattered metal. Walking across gantries with nervous managers reeling off lists of figures and targets, treating Cassandra and her retinue with a seriousness Duncan worked hard not to find comical. Back home, the Landor staff would have sent Duncan away with a flea in his ear if he had made similar demands on their time – not that he'd deigned to work a quarter as diligently as this solemn young girl seemed determined to. When Duncan realised that losing employment in one of the houses' great commercial concerns meant demotion through many layers of the imperial caste system, he understood a little better the managers' fawning obsequiousness. Caste was everything here. Advancement was *everything*. To belong to the wavering-lower caste was to only be allowed to travel on foot along the moving walkways of Vandis. Promotion to the wavering-upper caste meant travelling through the capital by bat-like trains hanging from aerial rail lines. Advancement beyond that meant you were permitted to drive an electric carriage, as well as live above the eighty-storey level in one of the great granite-lined towers; and that offered a view of something more than fog, the multitudes and the clamour of the streets. And above them all, the emperor's many children ruling the imperium like bandit chiefs; everything of worth concentrated in their hands. Farms, factories, land, the lives of the lower orders, all just numbers tallied against the ledgers of Princess

Helrena and her relatives. There was no national assembly here, as in Weyland, to keep the rulers honest. The emperor was a god, and his word and whims were absolute. All of the emperor's children lived in fortresses along the massive city's coastline, circling the urban masses with their forces like a ring of siege-works; the islets in the sea beyond providing airfields and naval bases that could be brought to bear on internal rebellions.

Cassandra rarely mingled or mixed with the people she ruled, passing over the crowds' heads in her helo as divorced from their pedestrian concerns as an angel in the wind. Duncan was glad of it. From what he could see of the packed streets and roadways, Vandis was more crowded than anything he could have imagined before his arrival. The capital itself an unnatural arrangement; the population breeding and expanding, never once checked by natural concerns such as how the city could possibly feed another hungry mouth. Beyond the empire's borders there was always another state dependent on the stratovolcano's resources, sending grains and food into the empire in return for whatever Vandia would trade, however one-sided the terms. And the imperium required its neighbours to pour food down the throats of its teeming, hungry, restless masses. Many inside Vandis lived without employment, subsisting solely on the empire's basic dole, made clients of whichever imperial benefactors controlled their district. Such citizens were nominally many tiers above Duncan's lowly status, but in practice these people too were slaves. Packed into the capital's concrete mountains, living without meaning or hope, distracted by vast screens hanging from the buildings; glowing picture radios showing blood being shed. Organised combats in arenas and duels between citizens. The unwashed masses had become a force within the empire, a slumbering dragon easily roused to violence; citizens descended through a hundred generations without a single ancestor having known work or purpose. Duels among the lower castes were as commonplace as the violent manoeuvring for power among the celestial-uppers; jostling in the street frequently leading to knives being drawn. Duncan had seen such duels from the safety of their helo … a circle formed in the crowd along the raised walkways; shouts and jeers of encouragement, two people in the centre warily circling each other, blades flicking out to test their opponent.

There was a sudden brutal flurry and one of the men withdrew, his victim left spread-eagled in a pool of blood while cheers rose into the air. Duncan shivered. From his altitude the duels were something desperately savage and feral. *That was me and Carter back in Northhaven, in another life.* Didn't seem like any affair which should have the word honour attached to it. Closer to rodents tearing each other to pieces in a gutter over crumbs of bread. Duncan came to the point where venturing out from the castle made him uneasy. Pellas was so big, its expanses vast and endless and green. Yet here, humanity teemed and bred without limit or good sense, suckling on the tit of the stratovolcano and the riches it vomited out. In many ways, this land's riches were its curse. Overpopulated to an unnatural degree, ceaseless masses of people, and yet the imperium still relied on foreign soldiers to aim the guns that held its capital in check; spent fortunes importing slaves to do the unpleasant labour which its own teeming hordes refused to lay their revels aside to consider. There were so many feast days in the imperial calendar, honouring the holy deeds of past emperors and empresses, that Duncan had to rely on the castle's staff to tell him which ancient emperor they had to bow their knee to in the shrine of a morning. Such devotions were as far as Lady Cassandra went in paying lip service to the imperial cult. Pieties were really intended for the lower orders. Beyond the castle, the hovering presence of helos and clouds of riot gas rising from the streets would indicate that another drunken mob had taken the daily entertainments to excess again and were being dispersed by the legions.

On top of the practical business of learning the house's estates, there were also Lady Cassandra's academic lessons. Doctor Yair Horvak supervised these. On first meeting the tutor, Horvak looked little like the scholar Duncan expected to find teaching Cassandra. A large belly that made a waddle out of every step, a wild silver beard and big bushy eyebrows that wouldn't have looked out of place on a nomadic tribesman. His one academic affectation was a monocle pushed into the bulges of flesh on his right cheek, a lens which sat there glinting over the tributaries of red veins that flushed his face and large, bulbous nose. The doctor's voluminous girth would untuck the silk shirt he wore, flapping out of a waistcoat lined with pockets, each filled with instruments jangling like a watchmaker wherever he shuffled. It was clear that Yair Horvak also worked on great scientific endeavours for the house; but whenever he tried to delegate his duties tutoring Cassandra to one of his assistants, the young noblewoman would create such a stink that Horvak was forced to return to the education of the house's heir. For her, this seemed good sport.

The first time Duncan got to speak properly to the doctor was one afternoon when Cassandra studiously occupied her desk, poring over a pile of books she had been set to read and copying out notes. Paetro cleaned a pistol at another work surface in the doctor's laboratory; his weapon carefully laid out in pieces as if his task was to learn how to reverse engineer the gun's mechanism.

'Here,' commanded the doctor, 'over here. Make yourself useful, Duncan of Weyland.' He indicated a rail above his work bench where a series of miniature antigravity stones floated, connected to each other by a crown of wires while the arrangement gave off steaming icy cold vapours. It had been assembled on the other side of the lab. Duncan walked over to the bench, and the doctor passed him a pair of steel tongs, their handles lined with cork. 'Grasp the largest antigravity stone with these and hold the circle as steady as you can. They are going to start vibrating when I increase the power into the circuit.'

Duncan did as he was bid, while the doctor moved behind a nearby bank of equipment, running his fat fingers over the controls. It took less than a minute for the stones to start shaking fiercely, the icy cloud surrounding them growing bitingly cold. Duncan used all of his strength to keep the circle of stones flying away from the surface. There was a slight cracking noise from his tongs. 'Your superconductor field's about to snap my tongs.'

Horvak worked his control panel and the shaking subsided. 'Superconductor field, eh?' chortled the man. 'And what does an unassuming barbarian have to teach me of science?'

'The rail guild operated trains in my country,' said Duncan. 'They run their trains above antigravity stones not much different from these.'

Horvak raised a podgy finger in the air. 'And no doubt a hold controlled by the librarians close by; stuffed with books full of blueprints to build such devices, if only you had more than wood and corn oil to construct their components. That was a rhetorical question, young fellow. Inside the imperium a "barbarian" is anyone unlucky enough to live at the far end of the caravan routes. It is the curse of extreme distance.'

'And is your nation counted among the ranks of the "barbarians"?'

'The curse of distance, inverted,' said Horvak. 'My country, Gankana, directly borders the imperium to the east. We have been under the imperial yoke for so long that I fear we are all evolved towards servility, now. My people are rarely taken for mill or field or mine-work, though. We are valued for our minds. Mathematicians and scientists and philosophers comprise my people's human sacrifices to the great Vandian dragon.'

'And so here you are.'

'Yes, here I am. It is not much of a choice, is it? To live far enough away to be free of the empire, yet doomed to a life of resource-starved simplicity – a living hewn with stone axes and supplied by wooden carts. Or close enough to the imperium's borders to be made a serf, yet free to exploit the imperial bounty by advancing the boundaries of science.'

Duncan indicated the circuit of antigravity stones. 'With this?'

'Further, faster, better,' said the doctor, enigmatically. 'The only science that ever interests the imperium – extending the emperor's reach.'

'Of course,' said Duncan.

'And your tone of voice tells me that you disapprove. Let us say, one small side-effect of this work will be to understand the world a little better. And that is always a worthy endeavour.'

'I understand the world just about as well I want to,' said Duncan, tapping his slave's tunic.

'Curiosity has not yet been beaten out of my people, for all of our many faults,' said Horvak. 'This is proper, given we should judge a person by their questions rather than their answers. Why, for instance, should we experience gravity as a variable force, able to crush a man as flat as a pancake at modest depths underground, while leaving us floating like a leaf on the wind at quite modest altitudes? Why should that be?'

'Because that's the way it always has been?'

Horvak grunted. 'You would make a most excellent Vandian, sir.

Only concerned with more rapidly loading cannons and how fast and far your war craft may fly. No, no. That will not do. I am certain the answers to the questions which have been puzzling me lie in the stars.'

'You are also an astrologer?'

'An *astronomer*, dear fellow. The radiation belt that surrounds Pellas is another mystery, as well as the bane of taking accurate astronomical observations. But we shall see, yes we shall. I shall push and prod and seek whatever revelations there are to be wormed out of nature's anomalous weft, warp, and weave. There is nothing that exists so great or marvellous that over time mankind does not admire it less and less.' He walked towards a wall of books, removing a tome. Then he pulled out a pencil from his waistcoat, ready to make notes inside the book. 'Now, given that you are the first Weylander to serve in the house I have come across, I shall thank you for your people's creation myth.'

Duncan stared quizzically at the doctor, not sure what he meant.

'I have yet to meet a people who do not have one. In Gankana, our priests tell of a time when our ancient ancestors were formed from clay in the image of the gods, to act as their servants. But when the god Porida's son died fighting his evil sister, Porida grew lonely, and ordered a great oven to be constructed. Into that vast oven, he marched all of his servants and borrowed the organs from his dead son, giving a gift of blood and flesh to each slave. Then he baked his servants with a holy flame until they emerged from the oven as true humans. The Gankanese were the first people on Pellas, but when the other gods saw what Porida had done, they grew jealous, and set up their own ovens to convert their servants. Thus other peoples emerged. Eventually all of the gods passed away, despairing of their foolishness in recasting base flesh to resemble their glory. Your people have such a myth that explains your beginnings?'

'Of a kind,' said Duncan. 'It's told in our Bible. Mankind was full of sin and living in cities that knew only gambling and whoring and violence. So God sent a great darkness across the land to warn the people to mend their evil ways, but the fallen men and women, busy with their revels, barely even noticed his warning. Despairing, God began to drown the cities, one by one. When it came to the last city, his angels – the ethreaal – whom God had sent to destroy humanity, took pity at the sight of the children's weeping faces. In their mercy, the ethreaal secretly bore twelve of the gentlest children away to a paradise, far across the sea drowning their homes, where they were commanded to start anew. Twelve female angels stayed with the boys, and from their children we are all descended.'

Doctor Horvak nodded; satisfied, as if he had known this would be the case all along. 'Yours is one of the more common tales. Salvation from a great calamity – there are hundreds of nations in these pages that possess an almost identical creation myth.'

'And this is part of your research?'

'More of a hobby,' said the doctor. He winked at Duncan. 'Let us say that if you want to know where you are going, sir, you must first begin with where you began.'

'It's just a Bible tale,' said Duncan. This man was eccentric, that much was certain. Blinking too much while he talked, constantly wetting his lips with his tongue as if he was sizing Duncan's frame up for the dinner plate. 'If there were any gentle angels in my people's bloodline, Doctor, I didn't come across too many of their descendants back home.'

'Nor will you here,' Horvak chortled. 'No, indeed.'

There was a clanging from outside the steel door into Horvak's laboratory. Paetro got up to open the door, revealing a steel cart from the castle's kitchens pushed by a servant – but it came accompanied by a most unusual escort. Two soldiers waited by its side; not house troops, but crimson-uniformed – without the usual armour, their faces covered by leather masks that were a simulacra of the human visage. In front of them stood a man that Duncan might have taken for the pair's officer, apart from the fact that he wore expensive civilian clothes. A dark tunic with a wolf-like emblem over his right breast, a velvet cloak lined with crimson in its interior to match his bodyguards. The leader's pale white face was round and dandyish, at odds with the stiff, high collar from which his neck emerged.

'Look now, I have brought your food,' said the man, staring intently at Yair Horvak. Duncan knew this was a person of account from the careful way that Paetro stepped aside. Paetro always moved cautiously when Helrena's upper-caste allies were about. The guardsman had a special wary stance, just for them.

'You are too kind,' coughed the doctor, the strain in his voice matching Paetro's alertness.

Lady Cassandra glanced up from her mess of books. 'Apolleon, this is my time with the doctor.'

'Ah, the acquisition of knowledge,' said the man, entering while his two bodyguards took up positions by either side of the door. 'Where would a young mind be without it?' He ruffled the young noblewoman's hair as he passed, a little too roughly to be considered fondly. 'But the emperor is growing eager to know how his projects here are progressing. So I must ask for a little of your tutor's time.'

It did not sound like a request to Duncan, and the lack of argument and ease with which Cassandra grumpily began to clear her work away reinforced Duncan's view of the stranger's high position. Apolleon halted before Duncan, examining the slave with mock amusement. 'Pon my honour, this must be the new pair of eyes arrived to watch over our young lady. The sky miner adept at the prevention of mining *accidents*. Well played.' He tapped the tunic covering Duncan's stomach. 'And a fine tongue to taste what may sit ill with our young lady's constitution. Will you sample the fare I have brought along for the good doctor, slave?'

'I am sure I would be beaten for tasting another's meal,' said Duncan. 'When my orders are to safeguard Lady Cassandra.'

'Quite so,' said Apolleon. He threw his head back and laughed coldly. 'And as you can see from the doctor's gut, he is as far ahead of us in his appreciation of food, as his mind is in the application of his genius. No. No, let's not deprive the doctor of his supper by sharing it so rudely. And now—' his hand encompassed the antigravity stones '—how fares our endeavour?'

'Slowly,' said the doctor. 'I am having issues with superfluids and their tunnel barrier limits.'

'As I said you would. But there are ways to overcome your difficulties ...'

'Suggestions from your *other* researchers?'

'Is that jealousy I detect, Doctor? Our future glories are far too bright to share with a *single* house,' said Apolleon. 'Even one with the great Yair Horvak ensconced within its citadel.' He waved perfunctorily towards the others in the room. Their time here was at an end.

The two guards stepped forward, expecting the young lady and her retinue to comply immediately. The cook left first, abandoning his cart and the room a little too eagerly.

Duncan glanced back towards the laboratory as they exited. 'Is the doctor safe in there? Those two are not house troops.'

'No,' said Paetro, 'but that is rather the point. Apolleon's guards are *hoodsmen* – officers of the secret police.'

'He's not just another princeling, then?'

Cassandra sniggered at the notion. 'Ha! He's far beyond that. Apolleon is chief of the secret service and the house's most valuable ally. When my grandfather dies, the secret police's support will be pivotal in deciding which of the emperor's children shall ascend to the diamond throne.'

Duncan thought of asking if Cassandra's mother would seek that position for herself, but he bit down the question. He might as well have asked if a fish sought water to swim in. 'I'd have expected him to be older.'

'Apolleon's rise has been the very definition of meteoric, lad,' said Paetro. 'As counsel to the emperor, his guidance is more valuable than anything your sweat ever dislodged from the sky mines. His advice is gold and that's the truth.'

Duncan gazed curiously back towards the now locked door. *So what in the world's he doing back there? Giving scientific counsel to one of the supposed greatest philosophers of the age?*

TWELVE

PUNISHMENT DUTY

Carter was surprised to discover that facing the disdain of most of the labourers on the station could lower his servitude even further. Carter might have wriggled out of being executed, but everyone on the station knew that he was as guilty of trying to escape as the workers who had died in the attempt. Now, he had been ostracised within the sky mines for having dared attempt an act everyone else was too cowardly and timid to try. Banished into internal exile for having brought collective punishment down on his barracks; he was a walking, living reminder of their cravenness. At times, it was only the slow smouldering hatred Carter felt for the people who had betrayed him that kept him alive. He was watched like a hawk now, in case he should attempt to escape again. He felt eyes on him constantly. Especially the supervisors among the old hands, the ones who had the most to suffer from losing face in front of the Vandians. The people for whom his persistence and ornery courage was the biggest slap in the face; a living rejoinder to their base survival in the mines for so long. And hiding among those ranks, Carter reckoned, were his traitors. They must suspect Carter knew his escape attempt had been betrayed. Maybe they were making their own plans to settle with him before he got around to taking his revenge. Carter grew careful, paranoid even. Trusting in no one, confiding in no one. He tasted his canteen for poison before he swigged his water. He swapped his bowl in the food hall with others when nobody was watching. He opened the blasting caps that were passed to him, checking they hadn't been overcharged to ensure a nasty tunnelling accident. Sometimes, it was only the kindness of Kerge and Willow that gave him the strength to continue. The gask still examined walls and searched chambers for listening devices; machines that Carter knew he would never find. Betrayal in the sky mines walked on two legs, mouthing platitudes about sticking together and seeing the job done as best they could while they lived. No more trips to the surface to check the seismic sensors for Carter. He served his time at the dirty, dangerous end of mining work – blasting fresh tunnels and digging passages, praying cave-ins wouldn't bury him. When Carter wasn't putting his life on the line, he was given a grim new burden to fill his time. If there had been a caste lower than slave, his new duties would've been perfect for that status. Carter was ordered to retrieve dead miners' bodies where they were killed, mangled, buried, blown up, or sometimes just dropped dead of sheer exhaustion – all hope bled from their existence. After their remains had been recovered, Carter wrapped the corpses for burial and then rolled them off the station's roof, their bodies sent flapping towards the mist-covered ground below. Sometimes the dead had barrack mates who would attend, holding a simple, quick ceremony. More often than not, the slaves had nobody, and Carter would drag the shrouds to a rocky ramp raised on the roof for the express purpose of launching the dead into the fiery, smoke-filled void below. It felt to Carter as though he was consigning corpses to hell, but he knew that nothing that came after *this* could be as base and meaningless as the existence they'd endured prior to their deaths. A deliveryman for devils and stealers. That was what his life had become. One morning he arrived at the fever room to remove a body, a woman who had passed in the night. She had already been wrapped in the simple hemp sack flannelling the station's grain was delivered in. Carter didn't recognise her ancient withered face, staring lifelessly out from a circle of cloth. An old hand. Not one of the Weylanders. There was one other occupied bunk in the chamber; a wiry, thin man, his tattered slave's tunic repaired so often that it was hard to tell where the original fabric began and the patching ended. He had been here the last few times Carter had visited; not getting better any time soon. He rose like a ghost, helping Carter lift the corpse by her wrapped legs.

'You don't have to do that.'

'I knew her,' he said, simply. 'Nobody else left to stand for her here, now, apart from me.'

'I can do the job,' said Carter. 'I'm used to it.'

'One more thing,' said the man, wheezing as they manoeuvred the shroud through the fever room's door. 'There's always one more thing in the sky mines.'

Carter knew how he felt, so he resigned himself to having company for what would pass for a funeral up top. It was strange, but he preferred ceremonies where it was just him and the body. Being alone seemed peaceful, almost as if he had known the deceased. As though the corpses were his friends. Wasn't there one of the ethreaal who was meant to attend to souls as they passed from the mortal world to heaven? He couldn't remember the angel's name. His father's sermons were lost in another time. Maybe Carter had missed his true calling back home? He should have been an undertaker's apprentice, rather than buried out in the library hold.

'Haven't you heard?' said Carter. 'I'm the reason why half the station is on short rations. They say I tried to escape.'

'You did? Well, good for you. But you went around it all wrong.' He brushed the falling ash off the shroud. 'This is the surest way to escape the sky mines.'

They climbed the steep stairs to the station roof. 'Nobody ever made it out then, the other way?'

'Not in my time. Too few of us, too many Vandians in the miles between here and freedom.'

'So how would you do this back home ... burial, a cremation?'

The man rested the body for a second and scratched his face; as though it had been so long it was hard for him to remember. 'Sometimes a cremation. More often than not, if you knew it was your time, you just left your village and walked off into the winter wilds to lie down. What you left behind was a gift for the trees and the grass and the creatures that forage among them.'

'That sounds lonely.'

'No. It's travelling. It's how you arrive in the world and it's how you leave.'

That almost made sense to Carter. *Just travelling.*

'You know how you can tell you've been in the sky mines too long?' said the man.

Carter stepped outside into the heat. Ash was falling, a thin layer of it kicking up with every step of his sandals, hot against his toes. Marker flags flapped in the wind. 'How do you tell?'

'You last just long enough to see a different country being raided to fill your station with slaves. It was Persdad the skels used to attack, once upon a time. Our land's north of the league by a few decades, along the caravan routes. Everyone in this station used to be Persdadian. But we were the last of them. Her and me. Just me, now.'

They carried the body over the stone burial ramp. It was flat on top, a steep incline down to the rocky edge of the station. A metal plate to hold the body in place until it was time to commit the corpse into the sky. 'Why did the skels stop raiding you?'

'Started getting organised, I heard, from the last slaves to be taken. People watching out for skel carriers in the sky. Alert beacons positioned every fifty miles. Setting up ballistae in the big towns, manned day and night. I think the skels are leaving Persdad fallow, now, like a farmer sets aside a field. We had an empire too; at least, we obeyed our emperor's couriers when they rode in. Just chariots and carts and spears. Nothing like Vandia here. They really do have an empire worthy of the name, don't they?'

Carter lifted the body to the top of the burial ramp. 'They're human, same as us. They can bleed and die.'

'You'll see, one day. There'll be just a handful of Weylanders left. And then a Vandian slave ship will show up with a hold full of fresh meat; green workers brushing dust off their robes from a nation on the other side of Pellas you'll be lucky you've even heard of. That's how you'll know you've overstayed your welcome in our floating paradise.'

'Based on how many enemies I've made so far on the station, I doubt if I'll be around that long,' said Carter.

'You're a good man. I've seen how well you treat the bodies. Not like the others, just like rubbish to be tossed over the side. It's a pity nobody will remember that, when the time of your reckoning comes. Our memories have already faded in the people we left behind. One day our family will pass, too, and the dark time when the skels raided will wane into legend. Eventually, even those legends will vanish. All into dust, all of it.'

'I'm not a good man,' said Carter. 'People die around me.'

'Open your eyes,' said the man. 'That's what we're in the sky mines for. That's why we were taken. To give our lives to make the imperium eternal. To die in place of the Vandians who would have otherwise worked the mines. None of this is on you. What happens here would have happened with or without your personal misery swirling in the mix.'

Carter made sure the shroud was tightly wrapped around the body. 'What was her name?'

'Jicole. You should have seen her back home. Quite a beauty. Cleverer than me, tougher too, in her way. She was going to be a harpist at the music academy. To hear her play was to think you had gone to heaven. I used to compose for her, on and off, and she would surprise me every time. Never was so much talent wasted in our sky-borne hell as the gifts of this woman.'

'You got any words for her?'

'Those will do.'

Carter gripped the lever to lower the piece of iron at the top of the ramp. 'Goodbye, then, Jicole. You're well out of here, now.'

He released the barrier and the body went tumbling down, propelled off the side, white smoke billowing around her, and then she was gone from sight.

'She's travelling, now,' said the old man. 'Travelling again.'

Carter's head began to throb, another of the cursed hallucinations that had been plaguing him since he'd escaped the stratovolcano. Mad, impossible visions of Vandia's distant past flashed through his mind. Was he going crazy, or was this a mixture of hunger, overwork, and too long exposed to the strange, rare gases of the volcano? *Perhaps I'm going insane? Could anyone blame me?* He removed his hands from his forehead. A pair of rings had been left behind on the burial platform, simple wedding bands. The old man was gone. Carter looked over the side of the station's edge; but billowing clouds had claimed the second body as readily as they had the first. There were no more of his people in the sky mines, now. Only Weylanders.

Carter slumped by the burial ramp, gripping the rings tight enough in his palm to draw blood. The pain was real; reminding him he was still alive and this wasn't a nightmare. He began to cry. *Just travelling. That's all. Just travelling.*

Jacob felt sick and guilty in equal measure, watching the massive cats tear into Sariel's broken body, the bard's corpse played with as if he was no more than a rag doll. From the grand duke's viewing platform there came the sound of polite applause, as though the old vagrant had just finished one of his tall tales, rather than been savaged for the predators' feast. The big cat which had ripped off Sariel's arm discarded it in the sand, pacing restlessly while it growled towards the wooden palisade holding the prisoners. Well-fed, the creatures were all too similar to their human masters. This pride killed for amusement, not food.

'I think the leather-skin can go next,' called Major Alock from his chair beside the ruler. 'With his poison spines, he might make more of a fight of it. Although I believe most gasks tend towards a pacifist disposition. What do you think, pastor, will your leather-skin friend give us a contest worthy of the name, or have you taught him to be a good little God-botherer? Is he going to turn the other cheek for you?'

The major looked like he might renew his taunting, but his voice dropped away. Below in the arena, Sariel picked himself up. The bard's clothes were badly ripped by his mauling, the stump of his right arm pumping blood. But not nearly enough of it, given his terrible injury, and what little there was of it as white and thick as cream. If his miraculous resurrection provided an implausible sight, it was as nothing compared to what Jacob saw below his torn clothes. Two broken white stumps protruded from his spine, as though he had once possessed a pair of massive wings crudely amputated from his back.

'They have no taste for me!' called Sariel, swaying, as though he had merely been pelted by rotten fruit by another unreceptive audience. He stumbled towards his missing limb, and picking it up with his left hand, re-attached it to the broken stump, where his skin appeared to ripple and seal around the wounded limb. 'I warned you hell-hated popinjays! The prince of players' delicate flesh makes for an unpleasant repast.'

A fierce howling rose from behind the wooden palisade, the gad prisoners going wild in a way that Jacob had never seen before, wailing and shaking the barrier, flinging their bodies about and leaping into the air. But this reaction was as nothing to the grand duke's. He leapt out of his seat, screaming and pushing his bodyguards forward from their formation behind his chair. He shoved them in front of the viewing gallery's armoured glass as though he expected Sariel to vault up and assassinate him.

'Take them away!' yelled the grand duke. 'Lock them up, all of them, before that mangy devil's flesh poisons my beauties! Bring me the diviners from their cages. Bring them before me now. NOW!'

'Kill them all!' argued Major Alock. 'I don't care what twisted people that thieving scoundrel belongs to. A couple of volleys into his skull will finish him off.'

'It is the prophecy!' yelled the grand duke, pushing the officer away. 'I need to consult with my diviners.'

'Prophecy?' The major looked shaken by the sudden turn of events.

'You fool! That mangy devil is Jok, the fallen angel. Can you not see it? Blood of milk, and wings that have been hacked away by the Land Mother as punishment for leading his kin in their unholy rebellion.' The grand duke's hand jabbed down towards Sariel, who was busy collecting his staff and ignoring the storm his unexpected survival had created. 'Your arrival is not my end. I tell you this! I am the house and the house is *me*.'

'Listen to me,' Alock barked at the panicked ruler and his entourage. 'Kill them now! If you value the supply of resources provided to your country ...'

'You understand nothing of my country, our history,' shrieked the grand duke. 'Vandia will not send its skyguard to intervene directly here. What is the imperium *here*? Nothing but the voices on the end of a crackling radio relay. Only sorcery may protect against sorcery.'

Out on the sand the predators were prodded back by lances in the direction of the wall's opening. The creature that had removed Sariel's arm was having problems complying, however. It groaned and rolled over on the ground, shaking and trembling, trying to stand, but failing to find the strength to re-join its pride in slinking away.

A fresh wave of panic rippled through the ranks of the ruler's attendants. 'You see!' bayed the grand duke, as if he blamed the major for everything that had gone wrong with the morning. 'It is just as it is written ... *And his flesh shall be poison in the mouth of the basest animal.*'

The grand duke retreated, leaving Alock arguing in vain for the Weylanders' immediate execution with the few bodyguards and courtiers who weren't retreating after their master. The major was still yelling when soldiers forced Jacob and the rest of the prisoners at spear point back towards the searing dungeons. The grand duke's soldiers had a hard job of containing the gads. They had boiled over into a state of frenzy that no amount of coercion short of murder would be able to suppress. Jacob's trip down the passage to the cells was like being caught in a riot, shoved and jostled from every side, the soldiers' yells and threats barely audible over the gads' clamour.

Sheplar pulled at Sariel's torn clothing as he was caught up in the mob. 'What manner of man are you – did you have wings?'

'Of course my people possess wings,' said Sariel, as though the mountain aviator was a dolt for not realising such an evident truth. His face turned ashen and uncharacteristically grim at what was left of his memory of those times. 'Mine were offered back as a cruel gift to me by the skel raiders, bloody saws clutched in the cursed hands that had just finished strangling my beloved. My people heal uncommonly fast, but our wings and our hearts may be easily broken and never repaired.'

'To glide on the wind without a flying wing,' said Sheplar, as though in a dream.

'I walk now,' said Sariel, sadly, as they funnelled through the dungeon's unlocked doorway. 'I walk everywhere. It's all I have left.'

'But you walk with flesh that is anathema to local predators,' said Khow, trying to stay with them in the press of gads that packed the chamber. 'That is an adaptation as advantageous as my spines and toxin.'

'I'll take the uncommonly fast healing,' said Jacob, not quite believing the storyteller's explanation for what had transpired. All around them, the dungeon filled fuller with excited locals. 'They have a saying in the army: that it takes a man's weight in lead to stop him during a full charge with bayonets. It's a lie, of course. But in your case ...'

'The prince of players is not to meet his end at the fangs of a handful of scabrous sabre cats,' said Sariel, some of his old colour returning. 'Nor at the whim of the much-diminished House of Bragin.

Standards have fallen here, yes they have. Such foul inhospitality, I have rarely sampled the like.'

Zanasi appeared from the crowd of prisoners, the half-breed scout shrinking back in the presence of the vagrant, Sariel recast by his people's superstitions into a terrible figure of legend. The rest of the prisoners were not quite so bold. They held well back, nervously singing and keening. 'You will sample it again soon, if you tarry here. The diviners the grand duke captured are held in cages, blinded with their arms and legs hacked away. Their wounds are sealed with tar and most of them have gone mad from the pain. But even a deranged diviner will eventually come to the conclusion that the best way of getting rid of Jok is to burn him at the stake and scatter his ashes before the Land Mother.'

'I told you before, noble gad, I carry the title of King of All Stories. I am not Jok, although I believe I did have to impersonate him once to escape being torn apart by horses when I was a guest of the war leader of the northern tribes.'

Zanasi merely shook his head, looking as unconvinced as Jacob, although for different reasons. 'It is said that Jok always denies his name, in fear that the Land Mother might find him again. Your appearance augurs the fall of the grand duke and the dawn of a great new age.'

'I haven't seen many great ages, except in the memories of old men,' said Jacob.

'And I doubt if this old scoundrel is to usher one in,' said Sheplar. 'Truly, did you fly on your own wings? This is not just another of your ridiculous tales?'

Sariel waved his white beard as if it might lift him high. 'We do not fly, Rodalian. We *soar*.'

'I have heard stories of such twisted people,' said Sheplar. 'But their kind has never passed as travellers through our canyons. Not in caravans or with the aerial traders.'

Sariel rubbed his forehead roughly. 'So many stories filling my head, I have forgotten what it is to ascend free. Trapped by dirt and gravity. Maimed by the skels. Is it any wonder my only comfort is my next stride, always another one to be taken?'

It was a strange turn of events. Sariel rendered maudlin by the memories of what he had lost. Their fellow prisoners had formed a circle of veneration around the bard. If you were going to imagine a saviour heralding in a new destiny for your people, a beggarly old rascal who bathed little and boasted much wouldn't have been Jacob's first choice. The only thing that hadn't changed was the fact that they were still prisoners, awaiting a fate highly likely to be fatal if Major Alock had anything to do with its outcome. Jacob brooded for half an hour before the dungeon's thick door creaked open and a team of slaves entered with a fresh barrel of water, shepherded in by a semicircle of soldiers.

'So, the grand duke wishes to keep us alive for now,' observed Khow.

None of the prisoners seemed particularly concerned by the water this time, and the soldiers fanned out, pointing their rifles in the mob's direction. Behind them, the slaves broke open the barrel, and unnoticed by the guards, began dipping their arms in towards the bottom of the tub. Jacob felt Zanasi's hand hard on his sleeve. He was being warned to pass no comment. It only took seconds … then a sudden flourishing of sharpened blades from the barrel, the slaves sealing the guards' mouths with their palms at the same moment they plunged knifes into the startled soldiers' spines. Soundlessly and almost gently, the guards were lowered to the stone floor while the prisoners kept up their racket, as unsurprised by the turn of events as if slaughtering soldiers were a regular feature of the dungeon's routine.

Zanasi was fast by the water bearers' side, Jacob and the others rushing behind him. 'So, we are to sacrifice our eyes inside the palace?'

The slave he addressed finished wiping the blood off his blade on a guard's uniform. 'More than that, Zanasi. I have tripled the potency of the diviners' drugs. They will be raving for hours, and by the time they have finished, they will be dead.'

'Better to die free than live as they do.' Zanasi clasped the slave's arm. 'Come with me.'

The slave shook his head and indicated the knife-wielding gads. 'We will stay here, and sing the songs with our brothers and sisters. When more guards come, they can join these on the floor. You must use your time well, every hour will be precious. When the Hangels follow, it will be with everything.' He gazed over wide-eyed at Sariel. 'I never thought I would live to see the day. The Age of the Seventh Sun!'

For once, Sariel wisely held his peace.

'I haven't seen much of the palace beyond these cells,' said Jacob. 'But I'm presuming it's well fortified and as tight as a drum.'

'Very,' said Zanasi. He walked to the doorway where one of the slaves kept watch, checking the passageway outside remained empty. 'The word impregnable might have been invented for this citadel. Fortunately, we have long turned the paranoia of the grand duke's descendants against the present regime.' He didn't elaborate, but quickly stepped outside the dungeon, indicating that Jacob and the expedition members should follow silently. Jacob glanced back towards the loud crowd of prisoners. None of the gads strung along. The guards' bodies were dragged out of sight, their blood cleaned off the cobblestones. Once more, Jacob couldn't help but be impressed by the discipline and purpose of this proud people. They were all sacrificing their lives, not a single argument or fistfight over who should stay and who should go. He could imagine exactly how badly matters would have run if a hundred or more Weylanders had been imprisoned down here alongside them. They crept away, following an exposed channel in the floor which carried away the prisoners' urine and night soil. It led down a dead-end of a passage, a small rusted iron drain for the waste to trickle into. Zanasi knelt down. He reached into the drain and thrust his hand in deep, searching for something. Jacob reckoned it wasn't a turd. Then Zanasi located what he was probing for. A click and a section of the stone wall swung back on a concealed metal cantilever. The stairs of a tunnel were just visible dropping away. Light so dim it was hardly perceptible, falling from a series of intermittent shafts little larger than a box of matches. Zanasi led the way, beckoning them inside. Once they had all climbed inside the narrow passage, he turned the counterweight's handle and sealed them into near darkness. The smell inside was rank; it seemed they'd be sharing their travels with the dungeon's sewer channel.

'Follow me,' instructed the gad. 'As fast as you can, while bearing in mind we will be descending for the best part of an hour.'

'In this vile darkness?' asked Sheplar.

'Consider yourself lucky you are leaving the plateau, rather than climbing up it.'

Jacob began the long climb down the steep winding stairs. 'Someone was expecting to be imprisoned in their own dungeon at some point.'

Zanasi ran a finger along the passage's rough-hewn stone. 'The corpses of the builders who dug this secret passage were dumped in the lower city's rubbish tip centuries ago. One of them wasn't quite as murdered as the guards that had shot him believed. My people have been using the passage to smuggle messages in and out of the palace from long before I was born.'

'The grand duke doesn't know about it?'

Zanasi shook his head. 'The House of Bragin's family members are almost as proficient at murdering each other in their feuding for the throne as they are skilled at slaughtering gads. The ruler who commissioned this passage was poisoned a year later by his cousin. His cousin was smothered in his sleep by his sister, and so on and so forth, down the years. I suspect the current grand duke will uncover it now, though. He will search *very* hard to explain our curious disappearance.' Zanasi gazed back at Sariel, the bard gently grumbling as he wound his way down the tight steps. 'Another sacrifice. Will it be worth it?'

'It is to me,' said Jacob. *It is to my son.* 'But I reckon your friends back there would have turned up in the dungeon with a barrel full of daggers without us.'

'How so?'

'You're not just a scout. I saw the way you looked at the grand duke in the arena, *Chike Bragin.*'

'You are sharp-witted, Jacob of Northhaven. I do not use my father's name … it is washed with too much blood and dishonour. Among the gads, I am simply Chike Zanasi. Only the grand duke issues wanted posters with the name of Chike Bragin still printed on them.'

'I remember how pissed my son was when I forced him to a trade he didn't have the heart for. I know how a disappointed son looks at a father.'

'You are the leader of gad rebellion!' exclaimed Sheplar, stumbling behind the two of them. 'You have great heart, to venture so close to your enemies.'

'Among our people, a leader who will not share his people's risks will not remain leader for long,' said Zanasi. 'And it is not a rebellion I lead. The grand duke does not rule us. The lands outside the city have belonged to the Gaddish since the rising of the first sun. It is not for Pavlorda Bragin to divide every league that may hold a head of wheat and parcel it among his favourites. It is not for the nation of Hangel to erect fences and shoot every creature that dares to cross the arbitrary lines they draw upon their maps.'

'From what you say, I'm wondering if the grand duke might be distantly related to a man called Benner Landor,' said Jacob.

'When we exit the tunnel we will be inside the lower city,' said Zanasi. 'I shall pretend to be your guide. Many travellers hire one while they layover during refuelling.'

'Unless you've got a secret passage under the wall, too, I'll thank you to "guide" us through the same guardhouse we entered by.'

'We will not need to scale the ramparts. As far as the Hangels are concerned, we are still held within their inescapable royal dungeons. And the soldiers that man the wall are dull-witted hyenas, only concerned with shaking coins out of gads passing through. But why should you care?'

'I left a couple of friends in the wall's guardhouse,' said Jacob, touching the empty belt around his waist. 'And I'd be right glad to have them introduced to our mutual acquaintance, Major Alock.'

'The officer will follow you? Pursue you, even into the savannah?'

'I'm counting on it,' said Jacob.

Zanasi sighed. 'Then our fates are bound. For the grand duke will need to take back Jok, to prove to his people that our prophecy lacks the power to end his rule. Every soldier he commands will be thrown into the fray. And he will do it within the week. All the tribes will unite as soon they hear of Jok's reappearance. The Hangels will want to crush us before we can train and prepare.'

'Such adulation,' said Sariel. 'But why should I be surprised? I have long known the power of a well-told story.'

Yet to Jacob's eyes, the bard appeared to squirm in discomfort at the thought of being the centre of one he could not so easily weave to his will.

'You are real, Jok. For all who have eyes to see,' said Zanasi.

'As is that treacherous bastard Alock,' said Jacob.

'We are not in the business of revenge, manling,' Khow warned Jacob. 'Think of your son, as I must think of mine.'

'I'm not a vindictive fellow,' said Sariel from the rear of the party, 'but any hell-hated stealer who thinks the prince of players is fit only to be served as a fine feast for a pride of sabre cats needs to be firmly disabused of such notions.'

'For once,' said Sheplar, 'I am in agreement with the smelly one.'

It wasn't revenge if you didn't seek it out. Isn't that how it worked, when the time came for a man's soul to be weighed? And one truth Jacob knew. Major Alock would track them into hell itself, and wouldn't rest until every member of the expedition was silenced for good. He would never stop. Alock was the king's hand, and the king needed his part in Vandia's slaving raids to stay secret. The expedition wouldn't be able to travel in safety until Alock and his troopers were put in the dirt.

Khow moaned in disappointment at his companions' barely suppressed violence. 'How can you be so certain the major will not abandon his pursuit and return to Weyland?'

Jacob didn't respond. A voice hissed the answer in his mind. *Because there's only the thickness of a blade of grass between what he is and what you were.*

Duncan allowed himself to feel a frisson of apprehension; in the air in the helo with the young Lady Cassandra and Paetro, passing through the mountain-sized concrete dwellings of the capital. This time they were on their way to the imperial city's heart, the Diamond Palace. Cassandra Skar had been ordered to attend her mother at an important feast day in honour of the emperor. The family rarely travelled together, Duncan had learnt from Paetro, to avoid presenting too tempting a target to the house's enemies. This way, someone would always survive to lead the house in its revenge; which in itself was enough to give most of their adversaries pause for thought. They dipped and flew through a particularly foggy day; the city's towers cloaked with white haze, broken by illumination from screens showing highlights of the previous day's gladiatorial combats. The crowd's roar filtered eerily though the gloom, distorted by stone and concrete canyons. Warning lights flickered on bridges carrying monorails, aerial walkways and electric carriage-filled roads twinkling through the mist. The air smelt of the sea that surrounded the capital; Duncan could lick the sheen off his lips and taste the salt. Once he might have felt homesick for the Lancean Ocean's similar spray, a day's travel by riverboat from his mansion. But those memories faded. This was real ... this great mass of people at the heart of the imperium. It felt like the giddy core of human existence. Operating at a scale and sophistication that made Northhaven – or any city in Weyland – seem like a collection of mud huts inhabited by nomadic savages by comparison. Lady Cassandra rode the helo robed in a high-necked white fur dress that made her look like a snow queen from one of Duncan's childhood books. Below it, he noted, she still wore a belt with pistol and shortsword, despite Paetro being similarly armed. Always ready for a fight, even on a trip to visit the emperor's home.

Duncan could tell they neared the palace when the screens' din dwindled away. A high-class neighbourhood. Propaganda and the constant distraction of violent entertainments were reserved for the teeming masses. Those in the higher castes needed little urging to cling to their power and position. The towering sides of the city fell away, a circle of parkland divided by walls tall enough to pierce the fog, battlements mounted by searchlights playing through the air. Duncan had to lean out of the side of the helo to get a look at the approaching structure. A great blue crystal needle rising ten thousand feet high, a sundial for the world's centre. It split into spires knifing the sky, its top lost to the clouds above. Around this building – surely the Diamond Palace – rose three structures half the height. Each building made of multiple steel towers, their tops combined to form a steel ring-shaped runway that could be rotated to align against the winds. The surface of the rotary elevated airport was dotted with warships landing and taking off. The vessels looked like silver needles from this distance, but when one passed overhead, he could see they were similar in size to the monster that had transported the Northhaven slaves to the sky mines. After the warships had landed, platforms retracted into bays below the airport's surface, concealing the craft. With the amount of firepower that could be launched from this airfield alone, the emperor was taking no chances with his security here. It seemed inconceivable any other nation of the world could mount a threat to Vandia's ruler, but then, perhaps it was intended as a show of force for any of the emperor's relatives who might be tempted to raise themselves through the ranks of imperial precedence by more *direct* means. Their helo banked past the steel towers holding up one of the ring-shaped runways, gun emplacements in the tower tracking their progress. Any threat the helo posed to the palace seemed mostly notional to Duncan. Even if they had been loaded with explosives and flew straight into the spire's side, they would only leave the slightest of black scratches along its glass surface, like an insect slapping into a helo's canopy. The fog carpeting the parkland swallowed them as they sank lower. Their three wheels bounced down on the tarmac of a landing field filled with hundreds of stationary helos. They left their pilot, Hesia, with the craft. She sat in the cockpit playing with a jab-stick, a common street weapon in the capital's streets. A blunt knife-sized rod that could deliver a paralysing burst of electricity into a quarry. Duncan, Cassandra and Paetro entered the base of the Diamond Palace through the closest entrance, an atrium filled with a wall of lifts at the far end of a marble-floored hall. Before they were allowed to go further, the three of them had to submit to identity tests – even Lady Cassandra. A needle nicked their arms, drawing blood; the results shown on a screen visible only to a group of soldiers manning the turnstile outside the lifts. It took a minute, but they were allowed through. Duncan found it vaguely amusing that he was on file somewhere with the imperial security apparatus and judged fit as a mere house slave to accompany the young princess. If he had turned up here as Duncan Landor, son of one of Weyland's wealthiest landowners, he would have been shown the interior of a cell. As part of Cassandra's retinue, he was allowed to enter even the heart of the imperium. That lesson wasn't lost on him. A crimson-uniformed retainer in the lift took the three of them to a ballroom.

Duncan was just one of many visitors on a transparent-floored gallery, the middle tier of about ten similar balconies overlooking a vast central space. It was a dizzying sight. Thousands of guests above and below, milling and circulating, slaves with trays of food and drink moving among them, the crowd's voices joined in a single droning hum, rising and falling. Every hue of uniform and dress was on display, although Duncan didn't doubt that below their finery the guests were as thoroughly armed as his young charge. He double-checked his footing in the transparent floor as though his feet might find a missing panel and fall through. Tall window-walls behind showed they were more than halfway up the Diamond Palace's height, one of the tower-borne airfields below them, the lights of the fog-shrouded city just visible glimmering beyond. It was as though the rest of the capital was merely a hallucination created by and for the palace's dreamers. Crimson-uniformed soldiers in leather masks lined the window, spindly rifles as long as lances and white ceramic shields with the wolf's emblem adorning them. They were the same breed as the guards who had accompanied Apolleon to the Castle of Snakes' laboratory. Hoodsmen, the emperor's secret police. The group moved across the floor, stopping for the young princess to make small talk with other guests, Duncan checking the food from plates borne by waiting staff before he allowed it near Cassandra. Given how many hundreds of serving slaves were at work across the floor, with more emerging from service elevators every minute, and how fussily the courtiers grazed from the fare, it should have been almost impossible to ensure a specific guest received a specific serving. But almost impossible was still *nearly* possible. And Duncan knew enough about the house's enemies to understand that there wasn't much they wouldn't stoop to in their efforts to remove Helrena and her young heir from the game of imperial politics. Duncan had grown fond enough of the young princess that he didn't want to see her become a casualty in the perpetual struggle for the diamond throne.

Duncan leant in towards Paetro as the girl's attention was engaged on a richly dressed couple, a gaggle of advisors and bodyguards waiting dutifully behind. 'Everyone else has a larger retinue.'

'More people to trust,' said the soldier. 'More ways in.'

'With all Helrena's wealth, why doesn't she just move to the provinces? Go somewhere she can raise Cassandra in safety?'

'Her wealth depends on her imperial licence to work the sky mines, lad,' said Paetro. 'You move away from the capital and the influence of the court, you will discover how quickly your wealth becomes someone else's. Without money, you cannot fund a household guard and adequate security. And you will find distance offers little protection against ancient grievances and feuds. Believe me, if you leave, you are not running to safety. Quite the opposite.'

Duncan looked at the great crystal windows with their imposing view over the fog-shrouded city below, each pane elaborately engraved with scenes of victory triumphs from imperial history. 'This isn't a palace; this is a luxuriously-appointed prison.'

'Perhaps it is,' said Paetro. 'But when you're trapped on the board, better a knight than a pawn, eh?'

'What are you doing here?' asked Duncan. 'You had a choice. You could have stayed happily at home and never set foot inside the legion.'

He shrugged. 'My birthplace was boring. Life in the legions paid well and offered a promise of excitement. That's where I met young Cassandra's father. We saved each other's lives more times than I can count. And I promised that I would look after his daughter if anything happened to him. Try and keep his wife alive too.'

'What was Cassandra's father like?'

'Dangerous. He thought that rules didn't apply to him. That he could grab the stuff of life, twist it, move it and change it. But rules are like gravity, they always drag you down in the end.' He glanced at Duncan and frowned. 'And when I see that look on your face, it reminds me a little too much of him. Aren't you enjoying the party?'

'That's the trouble, I think I am.'

'This is where history is made. You're standing at the very centre of the universe. Being part of it can become addictive. This is the game ... the greatest game, the *only* game. What would you have been at home?'

'If I had stayed, whatever my father had told me to.'

'I know you well enough to know that you weren't staying,' smiled Paetro. 'You're too similar to me, lad. I could have joined my brothers selling groceries in the market. Two pounds of apples, madam, or would you care for some potatoes today, perhaps? Is it time to sweep up the shop yet, or tally the stock? Every week identical to the next. That's all you left behind. Drudgery and boredom. Yes sir, no sir. Another daily compromise on the road to hell. Instead, I cleared off over the border and signed up. In the capital you could live to see Helrena become empress one day, and Cassandra succeed her ... the fate of nations forged. Having helped raise the future ruler of the world. How many people have done that? Young Cassandra as empress. Wouldn't that be a thing to see?'

Duncan said nothing but the pang of guilt he felt inside answered for him. *It would be.*

Paetro nodded, contented. He understood. 'Wars and plots and rebellions and intrigues on the same scale as this city.' He stomped his boot on the floor. 'We're walking on glass, here, lad. And that's *always* interesting.' His eyes narrowed as another retinue approached where they stood. 'And here's a cure for a dull life if ever I saw one. Circae!' He mouthed the last word like a hiss.

The couple that Cassandra had been talking with retreated a respectful distance as they saw who was bearing down on them. Paetro moved to Cassandra's back, as did Duncan. The young princess's grandmother cut quite a figure, sweeping forward in a purple silk dress swollen by a whalebone waist frame, a moon-shaped fan behind her dark hair, raised like a tower in elaborately tied bundles. Her face was pale, as was the fashion in the capital. Only those without wealth laboured anywhere a tan could be gained. Circae looked younger than her years, but an air of haughty superiority stretched her skin taut, marring whatever beauty had survived the march of time. She led a group of at least ten courtiers and guards closely attending her train, strutting as though they were the gathering's centre of attention. Judging by the nervous and knowing looks the retinue were given as they passed, fans raised as cover for onlookers to gossip behind, they may well have been.

Circae halted before Lady Cassandra, her attention focused like a beam on her granddaughter – completely ignoring Duncan and the girl's large bodyguard. 'Ah, the newest jewel in the house's crown. And the only one worth possessing. I am so glad to see you at court, my dear. Your mother keeps you far too isolated. We should see you here with a greater frequency.'

'I will take my place at court one day,' said Cassandra. 'When I am of age.'

'Your fate is to end up more than the caretaker of the Castle of Snakes,' said Circae. 'More than a gang-master to a mob of unmannerly sky miners. Half your blood is mine. And that is by far the greater half of you.'

'Whenever I fail, I resolve to train more. And I know which half has missed the mark and which half has committed to fight harder.'

'Do you know? I believe you may be confused,' said Circae. 'But in time you will understand, truly. You are not to be your mother's creature. I will not allow it.'

'I will choose as my father chose.'

'Your father ... my son? You did not know him, little lady. You do not know the man he was. He only had one weakness, and that was the one common to most of his gender ... a low tolerance for the siren's song. Your mother found that weakness and twisted it like a dagger until he died.'

'He died because he was exiled to the legions. You stripped him of his caste,' accused Cassandra.

'His actions did that for him,' said Circae. 'But many men are weak. We cannot blame them too much. They look for glory on all the wrong battlefields. They look for love in the wrong hearts. I see too much of it in my position. You will understand more as you grow older.'

'I know all that I need to, now,' said Cassandra.

Circae smiled coldly. 'There's always a little more to know, to secure power. When you can admit that, you will have discovered your legitimate blood and your true path.'

'We shall see.'

'You are all I have left of my darling boy,' whispered Circae, so low that Duncan had to stretch to hear it. 'Remember that. Any poison your mother has filled you with cannot change this fact.'

Cassandra snorted as the old woman bowed her head and moved away, her entourage scrambling eagerly after her. The middle-aged couple the girl had been talking to previously came back, eager to hear what had been said.

'Why is Circae so powerful?' Duncan asked Paetro as they stepped back again. 'If she has no stake in the sky mines?'

'Circae is the mistress of the imperial harem,' said Paetro. 'If you are a minor house and you wish to become a major one, there is no faster way than having a daughter accepted for marriage with the emperor. And when the daughter sires a child, she sires a potential heir to the diamond throne. The mistress of the harem selects from among every ambitious daughter of empire who seeks to be elevated to such a position. Of course, when a woman catches the emperor's eye, he can order her installed in the harem whether the mistress cares for the lady's bloodline or not. And in that category, you have Princess Helrena's mother, Mina. They were the fiercest of rivals. Circae loathed Mina for her influence over the emperor, which was beyond her control, almost as much as she hates Helrena for stealing her son from her. Mina was a great beauty, but from a very minor merchant house from the east, a recently conquered territory barely fit to be considered for citizenship.'

'The mother is no longer alive?'

'Mina died giving birth to a second child. The babe died shortly after, also. He would have been a younger brother for Helrena if he had lived. It was never proved, but there are strong rumours that one of Circae's assassins arranged for a fatal nerve agent to be mixed with the drugs that were used to ease the pain of childbirth. The tampering did for both poor Mina and her child. It is an insult, too, you see, to kill in such a way. You only poison those you consider of low born blood.'

Duncan watched Circae and her retinue disappear, swallowed by the crowds. For Cassandra to have such an implacable enemy so young. His heart ached with the unfairness of it. The burden was a weight the girl shouldn't have to bear at her age.

'Helrena spent most of her youth narrowly avoiding being murdered by Circae's killers,' added Paetro. 'That she has survived and prospered and become one of the emperor's favourite children is, well … as tough as I am, I am not sure I could have achieved half of what Princess Helrena's secured if our positions had been reversed.'

Duncan nodded. The history between the two families explained a lot. 'It is why Princess Helrena values loyalty so highly.'

'She knew precious little of it during her youth, that's for sure. She recognises the real metal when she strikes a vein of it.'

'And I thought my father had rivals back in Weyland.'

'The stakes are far greater in Vandia,' said Paetro. 'And likewise the evil our enemies will stoop to, to scoop the pot. Nothing would make Circae happier than murdering Helrena and becoming Cassandra's guardian. It would be the culmination of her miserable, scheming life, lad. But we're here to help ensure that never happens, eh? You catch the poison that comes her way, I'll catch the bullets.'

Lady Cassandra strolled over to the two of them. 'Let's go to a higher floor. The air here has been tainted by the imperial whore-herder.'

'I think I saw your mother up there, little Highness,' said Paetro. 'The tribute ceremony will begin shortly and there'll be a fine view of the diamond throne.'

'Who is paying tribute?' asked Duncan.

'Why *everyone*, silly,' said the girl, who found Duncan's patchy knowledge of Vandia a never-ending source of amusement and teasing. 'Every state that borders the imperium and all the countries in communication with Vandia who would trade with us for our wealth.'

Duncan followed the young noblewoman to the bank of lifts. *Everyone indeed.*

After they had gained the balcony's railings, the view of the main chamber from the upper level was incomparable. An orchestra struck up a forbidding-sounding martial tune, amplified by speakers throughout the space. At the same time, a deep voice began announcing the emperor's many titles. A bay in the wall at the far end of the chamber opened. The diamond throne and the man who occupied it rumbled forward on steel tracks, while long banner-sized screens drew down from the ceiling, one behind the throne and a screen on either side. Their purpose was to show the emperor close up in all his glory, receiving his dues from the world. Emperor Jaelis possessed a stern demeanour that even his cunning fox-like eyes couldn't offset, a short silver beard and a bald round head that appeared to have been shaved. His large frame filled the ruby-red throne. The emperor's throne resembled a crystalline cave that had been allowed to solidify around his body, one mineral-laced drop at a time. It twinkled and glistened from a bank of uplighters in the floor, giving the impression of Vandia's supreme ruler being borne into the throne room on a constellation of stars.

Emperor Jaelis looked bored to Duncan's eyes. And somewhat out of place. As though a gladiator had been wheeled in to celebrate his arena victories; brutal power running slightly to seed, a range of expressions plucking at the edges of his ruddy face. A personal guard of hoodsmen marched alongside with their faces concealed by masks, their black shields mounted with a golden double-headed eagle. And one of the screens showed a glimpse of someone familiar. The same man who had visited the Castle of Snakes' laboratory, demanding an audience with Doctor Yair Horvak. Apolleon Skar. He pointed into the massed ranks of dignitaries waiting to offer tribute, muttering in the emperor's ear while the ruler nodded on his thick neck. They were faced by hundreds of ambassadors and foreign nobles assembled as neat as any legion's formation, the regularity of the supplicants' lines at odds with the varied cut of their multi-coloured clothes and uniforms.

Duncan noted that Princess Helrena had appeared beside her daughter; five or six people behind her that he vaguely recognised from the castle, Doctor Horvak the only one he could name. 'The glory of Vandia,' announced Helrena, with a touch of sarcasm, to Duncan's ears. She leant down by Cassandra. 'Watch the tribute-giving. See who is eager. See which states are too generous and which stingy and sullen … like dragging metal teeth from a mouth. Their behaviour will be as good as an atlas of where we can expect to see rebellions crushed in the coming year. Where we will find parties eager to trade with our house. Who are to be our allies and who our foes.'

'Only the foes outside the empire,' said Cassandra.

'Yes, I saw the harem's witch snapping her claws at you. You handled her well enough. Circae will only ever be our foe. There is, at least, a comforting constancy in her malevolence.' Helrena looked over at Duncan. 'And how does the Diamond Palace and our imperial master find Duncan Landor?'

'I am not a physician, but your father does not look well.'

'We have Doctor Horvak for that, but you have a keen eye. The emperor has recently taken his medicine, I would say. The twitching around his cheeks gives him away.'

'What is it?'

'The worst kind of sickness – one of the mind, not the body. He is forgetful and turns furious over small matters. Very unpredictable. He was always quite wild and impetuous, but this is something else again. Only Apolleon seems able to soothe his ill-humours now.' She looked down the glass railings at the crowd of courtiers and nobles watching the emperor's arrival. 'They know, too. You can almost taste their eagerness, can't you? It may be a few years away, but my father will appoint his successor … a new emperor.'

'Or an *empress*?'

'You should never name an ambition. You may scare it away.'

'I would not want the throne, if it was me,' said Duncan.

'Then you are wise indeed. But the only thing more dangerous than having the position is *not* holding it.'

Below, the booming voice on the microphone switched from announcing the imperial titles to listing the countries coming forward with their gifts. States and provinces and nations without end, all of them unfamiliar to Duncan, as was much of the tribute being offered. Supplicants proceeded down a red carpet, approaching the imperial personage, surrounded on either side by ranks of fellow grandees. A few parties had brought along samples of their gifts – mainly scientific curiosities like engines inside frames that rocked as flame boiled out of their rear, globes that projected flickering spectres in the air, or vials of new medicines held in crates that leaked freezing gases – but most contributions were too large to fit inside the palace – millions of gallons of fuel ether and thousands of tonnes of grain being promised. All conferments were offered in the same obsequious manner, however, with the nation's representatives on the floor in front of the diamond throne, their noses rubbing against the glass floor. Then Emperor Jaelis would give a bored flick of his fingers and the next gaggle of supplicants would rush forward, genuflecting and bowing.

So it went, until a group of purple-robed grandees ushered forward a stumbling figure. At first, Duncan thought it was a man clad from head to foot in plate armour, but as the form lurched forward, he realised that this was actually some kind of automaton. Courtiers on the balcony levels cheered and clapped the ingenuity of this device, but it seemed to react to their applause by veering off, ploughing into the waiting dignitaries, where it carved a violent path through their bodies, steel arms lashing around and breaking human skulls and cracking chests. A company of the emperor's soldiers were soon all over it, lashing at the plating with their rifle butts and pouring fire into the automaton until its metal body stopped twitching. Emperor Jaelis leapt out of his throne, a heavily ornamented silver pistol pulled from the patent white holster that crossed his uniform. The screens showed his reactions in close-up. He waved his gun in the direction of the party that had brought the humanoid device, yelling abuse towards the visitors. Jaelis drooled and his head twitched uncontrollably as he lost his temper; an unsettling sight in someone who was meant to be absolute master of his vast dominions. A couple of ambassadors broke and ran but Jaelis shot them in the back as they sprinted down the central carpet, his pistol ejecting spent cartridges. A silence fell across Duncan's balcony as the cartridges chinked against the floor. The remaining diplomats had fallen to their knees, begging and howling, but it wasn't enough to spare them. Striding up to the visitors, the emperor shot each of them in the head, bodies jouncing back as they collapsed and lay unmoving, blood pooling out towards the crowds on either side. Duncan tried to turn his head away, sickened. But he found he couldn't. The terrible theatre down below had too powerful a hold. The mighty emperor Jaelis was reduced to kicking the corpses in the ribs, purple-faced and swearing, until Apolleon caught up with Jaelis and managed to placate the brute enough for him to return to the diamond throne.

'That could have gone better,' muttered Paetro.

Duncan watched the dead bodies dragged out of the chamber by hoodsmen. 'He should have spared them?'

'He should have ordered his guards to imprison the fools, lad. Kept his dignity. Questioned the diplomats and determined if that was an accident or an assassination attempt gone wrong. They're only good for worms now, and we won't have won any friends in their country.'

As the tribute ceremony recommenced, the applause and ovations sounded hysterically overdone, supplicants coming forward even more nervously. Now the emperor had been roused into a killing fury, his hands bounced angrily around the throne, with little seeming to satisfy or impress him. The diamond throne seemed too small to contain Jaelis's rage. His dark mood infected the rest of the guests, as well. Duncan realised why so many of the local nobility stood on the tiered balcony floors above the throne room. It was a lot easier to stay out of the way of any crossfire. Somehow, the distance didn't seem enough to protect him; but Duncan guessed that it would be dangerously impolitic to be seen to leave now, as much as he wished he could. What a stupid end to Cassandra's young life that would be ... catching a stray bullet fired by her homicidal grandfather. Duncan's attention on the ceremony wavered as another party came up to the railings. Baron Machus led the group, and in his retinue Duncan spotted the woman who had been haunting his dreams. Adella! He felt a sudden surge of elation at seeing her face, again. Even in these laughable circumstances, with the woman kept as the virtual prisoner of Helrena's oaf of a cousin. Helrena began talking to her relative, Lady Cassandra listening intently to what was being said. Duncan found a moment to slip over to Adella. She positively glowed in a red gown, all pleats and folds, slit at the side to reveal her long legs; her hair bundled high in the same fashionable style as Helrena's vindictive mother-in-law. When she spotted Duncan, a strange look crossed her powdered white face – embarrassment mixed with chagrin. She should have felt none of those things. Duncan understood that Adella had as little choice in the matter of where she ended up a slave as he did.

'What are you doing here?' blurted Adella, as she backed away from the prince's entourage.

'Princess Helrena took me for a house slave,' said Duncan. 'After I saved her daughter from a kidnapping by Circae.'

'I thought you must be dead,' said Adella. 'I heard from one of the baron's servants that there had been an escape attempt in the sky mine; how everyone involved was killed by the Vandians.'

'It was Carter, along with Noah and Eshean and a couple of old hands from the station. Only Carter survived – although how, I'll never know. We found him wandering around the volcano days after he should have been dead, no water or food on him, claiming he'd watched the others try to fly to freedom on a transporter during the eruption. He always did have the luck of stealer, that one. Carter had been hinting to me that an escape was in the offing, but I told him I'd have nothing to do with it. Using an eruption for cover was clever, but the dead zone got its name for a reason. Besides, I could never leave without you. I would rather have died in the mines than leave you behind!'

She wiped a tear from her eye; and Duncan couldn't bear to ask if it was for him or Carter. It was stupid, feeling jealous of Adella's affections towards the preacher's son. She had been made the property of a Vandian noble, yet Duncan could muster few feelings of jealousy towards Baron Machus. The baron was only a boorish thug, his fists out to paw at whatever he found pretty and diverting. While Carter, whipped and probably starving and broken by now for his part in the escape attempt, far away in the sky mines; Carter, he could feel envy towards. Because Adella had chosen him voluntarily. Not forced into his service as a slave. But freely chosen the man.

Duncan reached out for her. 'I'm still alive and now I'm here in the capital with you.'

She shrugged his hand off her shoulder. 'I'm glad, but you mustn't do that around Baron Machus. He would have you whipped to within an inch of your life just for looking at me.'

'It would be worth it.'

'You have to think of yourself now, Duncan, not me. Everyone we know is trapped inside the sky mines, toiling in that floating inferno. And we can still be sent back there if we fall foul of the wrong people.'

'I'm going to get Willow out, too,' said Duncan. 'Try and find her a place inside Helrena's household.'

'Good. That's all we can do now ... survive. You have to forget me.'

Duncan's heart was breaking. 'How can I ever do that?'

'That's what you need to figure out. Nothing good will come of you having feelings for me.'

'I don't know if I can?'

Adella shrugged. 'You must. Think of Willow back on the station if it helps. Nobody else will save her from being worked to death.'

Duncan felt his body slump at her words. This was his life leaking out of him. 'And what about you?'

'It isn't so bad here.' Adella indicated another three young beauties in the prince's retinue. They were dressed similarly to Adella; except their gowns were yellow, green and purple. Each appeared to be of a different nationality, like a set of exotic dolls collected by the noble oaf. Adella's voice lowered. 'Machus is easily bored and easily diverted. His ambitions outstretch his intelligence by a wide mark. He cares nothing of class or status or breeding in the women he surrounds himself with, we're just pretty baubles that glitter for him. Half his wives were slaves when they were first taken into the household.'

'You'd marry him!' Duncan was shocked at the notion, despite himself.

'And how much choice would I have in the matter? Easily forgotten and easily discarded is as good as it gets, here. I have food and I have an easy life. That's more than most possess, even the lowborn citizens here.'

'I've seen how crowded and violent it gets out in the capital's streets,' said Duncan.

'Then you know. Think with your head, not your heart. If you ever loved me, promise me you'll stay alive for me and for Willow.'

'I will,' whispered Duncan. It was agony watching Adella slip back towards the coterie of women in the prince's train. She was alive. That would have to be enough for them both, for now. Adella didn't even dare to glance back as the prince's group walked away.

Paetro appeared and pulled Duncan back towards their party. 'Do you know that woman?'

'She's called Adella Cheyenne; she's from Weyland too. We were captured and transported to the sky mines together. She caught the eye of the baron there and was taken for a house slave.'

'I know who she is,' said Paetro. 'You should choose your friends more carefully.'

'What do you mean?'

'She was not *taken* by Machus, lad. She was *given* to him after she earned her freedom from the sky mines. Princess Helrena does not allow such slaves in her household. If you can sell out your own tribe, you're perfectly capable of selling out your mistress if the temptation arises.'

'Adella's sold nobody out?'

'Why do you think the woman was removed from the sky mines? There was an escape attempt; a group of miners who stole a transporter to attempt the dead zone crossing. She was aware of it and she betrayed the plot. The conspirators were watched and executed when they tipped their hand. For the woman's collaboration she was promoted to the position of house slave, as required by imperial law. But we are not required to take such slaves in personally. Helrena should have sold the woman at the market, but Machus wanted her. More fool him. It is always easier to betray the second time around ...'

Duncan rocked on his feet from the sheer shock of the soldier's disclosure. The tears that had come to Adella's eyes when she realised that Duncan and Carter were alive. Had she really believed them both dead ... by her own hand? And by her own treachery?

'You must be wrong,' Duncan spluttered. 'Adella couldn't do that, she wouldn't. She loves us, both of us ...' *It was a mistake. A terrible mistake.* 'That must be a tale the baron concocted to justify seizing Adella and taking her away.'

Paetro shook his head, sadly. 'That is not how things are done in the imperium. In adversity, you often learn what mettle you and those around you are made of. In the legion, it was never the ones you thought would break and run that disappointed you. Battle made mice of many lions and the reverse, as well. You can only know which kind of man you are when you reach that point.'

'Adella loved us,' sobbed Duncan. The truth of what had happened dawned on him with a terrible clarity, a truth as crystalline as this strange palace. It all made sense. The peculiar sequence of events. How the escaping transporter had been located and destroyed with such ease in the middle of an eruption, when the patrol ships usually gave the stratovolcano a wide berth. Adella disappearing from the sky mines shortly before the escape attempt. And here she was, safely ensconced with the baron's household, believing both Duncan and Carter had perished in the escape attempt she had snitched on. And they would have died, too, if events had gone differently by a hair's width. If Duncan had taken Carter up on his thinly veiled hints of seizing their freedom. If the pastor's son didn't possess the devil's own luck. To escape the sky mines Adella had sentenced both men who loved her to death. Willow too, by proxy, without Carter or Duncan to look after her. He found that harder to forgive than his own narrowly averted fate.

'There are things that people can love more, lad,' said Paetro, unhappily. 'Like living. You'd be surprised by what a man will do to live. And a woman, too.'

Zanasi looked grim. A gad scout had entered the encampment on the flat, rolling savannah shortly before, and he must have brought bad news. Whatever the intelligence was, it had yet to infect the almost celebratory gathering ordered by the tribal elders. Jacob had only been out in the grasslands for the best part of two days ... and there were still new tribes arriving hourly, drawn by the news of the so-called Jok's arrival. Tonight was the gathering of their elders, what passed for a grassland parliament out here in the wilds. For some among the expedition, matters were proving a little *too* celebratory. Sheplar had revealed a mighty appetite for the raw honey wine served by their hosts. He was currently being ministered to by Khow, who was mixing a woodland remedy as best the gask could from local ingredients. Jacob wouldn't have pegged the mountain aviator for the type, but people surprised you that way, sometimes. At least it wasn't a habitual weakness. Maybe the shock of Sheplar discovering he could once have been outflown by the beggarly bard had proved too much? Nothing shook a man so much as having his preconceptions overturned.

Jacob stopped Zanasi as he paced past. 'What is it?'

'News from Hangel. The grand duke has finally given up searching the city after discovering the escape tunnel under his feet. He has dulled his anger at being duped by murdering every prisoner in the dungeons. The slaughter wasn't enough for his tastes, so he proceeded to order one in every three gads inside the royal city thrown over the mesa's side. In the lower city, his men are now torching the homes of all suspected sympathisers. Males, females, children – there are none being spared.'

'I'm sorry,' said Jacob. 'If Major Alock has his way, Hangel's army won't linger long carrying out revenge attacks. They'll be coming out of the city.'

'I agree. What do you think our chances are against their forces?'

Jacob glanced around the village and the hundreds of campfires burning on the plains beyond. So many fires it was as though a constellation had been laid down on the dark savannah. *But numbers aren't going to be the issue.* 'They will be advancing with riflemen. Your spear-bows are fine for bringing down prey out here, but your rate of fire isn't any better than a crossbow, with a range a quarter that of an old breech loader. If Hangel's army is sensible enough to engage at a distance, they'd slaughter every warrior here and suffer only powder burns on their fingers.'

'To date, we have fought them by remaining concealed in the grass, two or three warriors at a time. We attack with poisoned bolts from cover and then retreat as far and fast as possible, allowing the regiments of Hangel to empty their long guns into the dirt. When their farmers steal our land, they never forget every day they leave their homes may be their last.'

'Harassment from the fringes is fine, but when Hangel's army comes out in force, your only real choice will be to retreat.'

Zanasi sighed. He rubbed his face, now scrubbed clean of all the pink dye he had used to conceal his half-gad heritage. 'It is not just rifles my cursed father possesses. The grand duke's mills have been turning out cannons and bombards as well as war wagons, great iron carts which resemble armoured turtles, mounted with weapons and driven by foul-smelling engines. Hangel has not used them yet against us. No doubt the grand duke thinks they are still his little secret. If so, he would have been better off not working so many slaves to death during their manufacture.'

'We call them tanks. I saw one once, broken down and rusted, a real ruin. Not fit even to be smelted down into swords. Tanks consume an unholy amount of metal during construction.'

'*Tanks*. A fitting name. Would that Hangel's tanks were so corroded ...'

No. The imperium would be supplying high-grade metals to its covert ally. It seemed the same evil that had claimed Carter had crept out towards them here, advancing like a restless shadow over this beautiful landscape. 'They're best used in squadrons, like cavalry, and flanked by boots on the ground.'

'Jok says that you are a high priest among your countrymen, a *pastor*. It is a martial order you serve in?'

'Just well-travelled, friend. None of this is God's work, I'm damned if I'll say that. This is the business of men.'

'You sound like your gask brother.'

'Well, he's right.' *And damn me if this coming fight isn't like another old comrade. One I'm far too glad to greet.*

Zanasi gazed down at the twin pistols just visible from under Jacob's duster. 'Your weapons resemble an ancient plough, worn as thin as a bone blade through repeated use.'

'Maybe they've had too many owners.'

'Jok has forgotten who he is. And so, I think, have you.'

'I'm just a man trying to save what's left of his family.'

A whistling noise sounded from behind a ring of simple circular wooden huts, something wooden being whirled fast on the end of a twine. 'The diviners are ready. Are you ready to meet *my* people's priests, pastor?'

Jacob followed the war leader towards the council. 'More so than Sariel is, I reckon.'

The old bard was already in front of the diviners, still trying to claim his title as King of All Stories rather than the messiah the tribes had him pegged for. Sariel's torn clothes had been darned and mended by the locals, and he looked even more beggarly with patches of zebra leather across his cloak as he stood with his back to the campfire, a semicircle of the grassland shamans seated cross-legged in front of him, their faces concealed by wooden masks glowing like devils in front of the fire.

Zanasi knelt on one knee in front of the diviners. His attention seemed focused on the gad in the centre, his face hidden like the others by the wooden mask, but his body bent and ancient even by the standard of the tribe's elders. His tiger-patterned skin salted silver wherever it was visible under the crimson robes.

'Narlrem,' spoke Zanasi. 'As you have commanded, I bring before you the companion of Jok ... Jacob of Weyland.'

'The companion of the *prince of players*,' protested Sariel.

The ancient diviner, head of the council, swayed where he sat. 'This man is both more and less than that. He is companion to Jok. He is Ogan, the twice-born.'

Twice-born? There was an element of truth to that, although *once-almost-dead* would have been a more accurate description. But the locals desperately needed their prophecy to be true and would distort whatever they saw now through the lens of belief. Jacob had an inkling of how Sariel must be feeling right now.

'I'm not a spirit,' said Jacob. 'Just a man who's lost everything and is working to save what he has left.'

'We all carry spirits within us,' said the diviner. '*All*. Zanasi's spirit is the finder of things. He discovered the golden spear-bow put aside by the sleeping warrior. He discovered Jok in the fastness of the Hangels. And he has also discovered Ogan, the twice-born, who walks unwillingly in the shadow of Jok's greatness.'

'If you believe that ...'

'We know it to be true. And the Hangels believe it. Or they would not now be mustering a force to fight the final battle foretold by the prophecy.'

'It'll be final, all right,' said Jacob. 'Your arrowheads against their repeating rifles ...'

'You shall walk the paths of the future,' said Narlrem. He beckoned behind him and a gad came forward from the crowd surrounding the council. The villager carried two wooden bowls filled with a green paste that looked about as appetising as the crushed insects the gads thought a delicacy. 'It is said that the twice-born will see the future, while Jok will see the past. Both must remember for the Age of the Seventh Sun to begin.'

'I have partaken of many foreign feasts before,' moaned Sariel. 'I have eaten dragon's eggs as large as boulders to keep Queen Carmella happy at her breakfast. I have eaten worms from the Caverns of Rerald, miraculous creatures which breed and multiply inside your stomach; so you may only eat a single meal and never go hungry for the rest of the year. All without complaint. But here I must draw the line! And you have none of your fine honey wine to wash this pulp down with?'

'You need a clear head to see the past,' intoned the diviner. He stared meaningfully at Jacob. 'As well as the future.'

Sariel reluctantly took the first bowl, while Jacob lifted his from the villager's hands. The tribes needed to believe what they needed to believe. And the gads were still Jacob's best chance of killing Major Alock and his troopers before the damned officer executed his secret orders. The strange whistling noise sounded again behind the

431

diviners as villagers whirled wooden sculptures around on the end of twine. Others sang and danced. Jacob scraped the paste into his hand and tasted it. The mixture had a fiery kick, as if the locals had blended chili-peppers into the goo. Jacob had only tasted something this hot once before, and that was the white radish-like mustard the Rodalians served with rice. His cheeks and forehead began sweating. Beside him, Sariel moaned and begged for alcohol. But the bard's complaints were growing distant, as though he had retreated into an echoing cave. The world swirled around Jacob, colours distorted and running together, a rainbow-whirl. It was as though he was seeing sounds, the windmill whirl of the natives given colour, waves that flexed and flowed through the dark sky. Grass warmed his back and the stars in the sky danced for his pleasure as they spread out, the heavens growing lighter and lighter. Across that blank vault he saw many futures. Or perhaps potential futures; the branches of the fractal tree Khow spoke of. Warriors hiding in the grass flushed out by columns of tanks, enormous iron platforms like galleons-of-the-land, rumbling forward and belching corn smoke from their exhausts. Metal flanks pierced by cannon ports and rifle embrasures, clouds of gunfire as fleeing gads were slaughtered by volley after volley. Hundreds of variations of the same slaughter, all ending with bloody warriors mangled under clanking caterpillar tracks. Jacob turning tail and running. Hiding inside the wreckage of one of the crashed carriers that lay rotting in the grasslands. Chased through what was left of the wooden airframe until there was nowhere left to hide. Or managing to escape. Caught in another country. Captured in the south, the east, the west. Major Alock's implacable features visible standing over Jacob, a rifle lowered above Jacob's face, pushed against Jacob's chest, pushed into his duster's back, a corpse rolling over, and over … and somewhere distant, his son dying and dying and dying. He was still yelling when the visions' burning heat calmed and left him lying in the distant savannah; his groggy cries echoed by Sariel's. The camp fire had died, still smoking gently, as the grey night sky turned to dawn's first gleaming. Jacob's grass bed was damp with the dew. Only the old diviner, Narlrem, remained. The rest of the council and villagers had departed with the night.

'It is a hard thing to experience your death so many times,' said Narlrem.

'You've got that right,' said Jacob, pulling himself upright.

'Diviners learn to control the dreams. It takes many years.'

Jacob's body ached, every muscle and sinew spasming after a cold night on hard ground. 'Once is enough. Reckon I'll stay a pastor with my church.'

Sariel came out of his own fug. 'Sack, I need sack – sweet mercy, but bring me your honey wine. You have poisoned the prince of players! So much lost and what is left clamouring inside my motley-minded brain. It's killing me.'

'You have merely remembered a little of yourself, Jok,' said the diviner.

'I need to forget,' moaned Sariel. 'I need to travel. I must leave.'

'We will help you, Jok. There are others paths that may be divined beyond the future and the past. The shamans remember them, even if you do not,' said Narlrem, enigmatically. 'When your part in the prophecy is exhausted, there may be time to assist you.'

The ancient diviner extended a hand and pulled Jacob up with a wiry strength that surprised the pastor. Jacob went across to the burnt-out fire and pulled a smouldering stake of wood free. He used it to draw a sketch in the dust of the blackened ground. Jacob finished drawing and looked into the ancient gad's intelligent eyes. 'You come across any of these in the grasslands?'

'Occasionally we do.'

'See if your people can bring me one that hasn't been ruined by the rainy season.'

Narlrem nodded, seemingly content. 'Then you have found the truth. You are indeed Ogan, the twice-born.'

'Second time lucky, friend,' said Jacob. *Damned if I'm going to go down a third time without a fight.*

Willow found Kerge in the one of the communal wet rooms, tinkering with a rickety set of pipes that led to the water tanks near the station's roof. If repairing the ancient plumbing was a menial use of the gask's talent with machinery, he did not show it. Kerge tackled the job with the same curiosity that he seemed to bring to all tasks.

Willow wiped the grime and dust on her hands across her dirty slave's overalls. 'I'm looking for Carter.'

Khow reached up to the ceiling, sealing one of the joins. Every drop of water was precious. They couldn't afford any wastage on the station. 'He is not here.'

'I can see that.'

'I thought Carter was going to come off-shift at the same time as me. I'm worried about him.'

'Each of us must find within ourselves what we require to keep going.'

'That's what worries me,' said Willow. 'I'm not sure Carter has anything left. I have never seen him like this. It's as if he's broken, as though he's given up.'

'He has not,' said Kerge. 'He is allowing himself to feel the pain of others, perhaps for the first time in his life. Another three workers died this morning during a cave-in on the new rock. Too tired to accurately set their blasting charges. Carter removed their corpses and gave them burial.'

If you can call sliding bodies into the sky's fumes a burial. Even a pauper back home gets more than that. 'Carter hasn't been the same since he was found wandering down by the volcano.'

'In that you are correct. His weight on the world makes no sense to me anymore. He is moving beyond my calculations.'

'He always was beyond mine.'

'No,' said the gask, his voice turning sombre. 'I am serious. There is a strangeness inside him, increasing beyond anything that a man-ling should be able to survive. He is not just changing, he has *been* changed. I believe something terrible happened to him on the surface.'

'I don't need your people's faith to know that. Carter saw our friends shot to pieces by a Vandian patrol. What could be worse than watching people you care about murdered in cold blood?'

'See if he will tell you when you come across him. To me, he will not speak of this.'

'And you think he will to me?'

Kerge removed a spanner and tightened the pipe's joins. 'Asking costs nothing.'

'I'll find him quicker with your help,' said Willow. 'You always seem to be able to track people down on the station.' *In a way that's almost uncanny.*

Kerge tapped the broken plumbing system. 'Little wonder. Your people smell ripe, even when the showers *are* working.'

'Maybe I'd perspire a little less if I sweated deadly toxins out of my pores,' said Willow. She didn't pursue the conversation. It was obvious to her that the gask was trying to keep his people's secrets from reaching Vandian ears. 'Help me out, Kerge. Please. I really am worried about Carter. What if he decides to follow one of the bodies into the clouds?'

'He is not currently on the roof,' sighed Kerge, kneeling on the floor and packing away his tools. 'Come. I will be your guide, just this once.'

'Thank you.'

Kerge was as good as his word. They discovered Carter in the eastern end of the station. Willow spotted Carter first. Hanging shiftily back inside an empty junction chamber, three tunnels leading off the cave. This was a strange place for the Weylander to be, looking suspicious. A section of the rock where new tunnels and chambers were bored during the slaves' 'idle' time. Enlarging the station for future operations and digging practice tunnels during training. With every slave pulling double shifts, this end of the station saw few workers now. Apart, perhaps, for one exception. Men and women were rumoured to use the empty chambers and passages for assignations out of earshot of their barrack mates. Surely Carter wasn't out here for that? Willow felt a flash of intense jealousy. With Adella long gone, Carter really shouldn't have any other women on his mind. Willow almost decided to abandon the fool here and head back, but she let her anger get the better of her. She marched towards him, about to raise her voice, to let him know just what she thought of a man who let off steam by going in search of the type of women who ventured out here; but as soon as Carter saw her, he grabbed her by the shoulders and threw a hand across her mouth.

'Be quiet!' whispered Carter. 'You'll scare them off!'

Willow heard Kerge coming up behind her. She yanked Carter's fingers away. 'You flushing out unmarried fornicators? Is that part of your duties too, now?'

'There's not much of that going on here,' said Carter. He glanced at Kerge. 'I told you I would track down the people who sold out my escape. They're along here.'

'How can you be so certain?' asked Kerge. 'This is becoming an obsession for you, manling!'

'I've been tracking the traitors, seeing where they go and who they meet. The rota's been fixed so that all the informers come off-shift at the same time. Then they head down here and discuss the station's business. Who's looking for supplies they shouldn't be. Who's been overheard talking about escapes and revolts. Who's been acting suspiciously. Which slaves might need to meet with a mining accident or be made an example of.'

'Nobody on the station would do that,' said Willow, shocked.

'Kerge came across a tracking beacon hidden on our transporter,' said Carter, obviously struggling with excitement to keep his voice low. 'Just our bird, nobody else's. Someone sold us out to the Vandians ... after that, the informers were watching and following me every step of the way.'

Willow looked uncertainly at the gask. 'Is this true, Kerge?'

'I did indeed retrieve such a radio device from the wreckage. The presence of informers inside the station seems the logical conclusion. I thought I would discover a mechanical surveillance system concealed in the station, but there is none here within my understanding.'

Carter agreed with the gask. 'That's as good as saying there is none.'

'Who?' hissed Willow, barely able to register the implications of what Carter had suggested. 'Who would give you away?'

'Anna Kurtain, Owen Paterson, a couple of the other old hands too. The ones who always seem to survive, no matter what's chucked the station's way.'

'You have to be wrong,' said Willow. 'Owen and Anna helped scavenge the food and medicine that kept you alive after your flogging. They could have let you die from your wounds.'

'Can you think of a better way to throw off suspicion? You think the traitors are going to cackle in triumph like pantomime villains during every execution and punishment beating? They pass you the gruel bowl and smile before they poison it.'

'There must be another explanation.'

Carter pointed down a tunnel on the left. 'It's a secret council they're having down there.' He lifted up a pickaxe handle he had left propped up against the bare rock wall. 'If they're romping around naked, drunk as skunks with their slaves' rags on the floor, I'll make my apologies and leave, rather than letting this do the talking.'

'Violence is never the solution,' said Kerge.

'It might not be yours,' said Carter. 'But every corpse I've rolled off the station can be traced back to the informants, one way or another. Good people killed by overwork and short rations, because those bastards betrayed us.'

'And how badly will the Vandians punish everyone if you murder their snitches?' argued Willow.

'I don't mean to kill them,' said Carter. 'That would be far too quick. But I'm planning to leave them with some lumps to help remember the people they betrayed. And then I'm going to tell everyone on the station exactly why they're being worked so hard and starved on half rations. Let's see how Owen likes surviving in the sky mines as an outcast.'

'That's as good as a death sentence,' said Willow. 'Someone will slit their throats sooner or later.'

'Then that's what will happen,' said Carter. 'And it won't be murder, it'll be justice.' He looked at Willow. 'Don't you feel anger at what's been done to us? Don't you wake up angry and go to sleep enraged?'

'I feel sad, mostly. We're turning on ourselves, now, biting at our own wounds. I thought you were broken, Carter Carnehan. I thought you had given up on life.'

'I came real close to it … a whisker either way, and I might have jumped. When the darkness lifted, I realised my hunt would go a lot easier if the informers believed they really had broken me. A shattered soul doesn't seek redress for being betrayed.'

Willow didn't know if she should feel relief or distress that she had been so easily taken in by Carter's act. 'If you're going down there, I'm coming with you.'

'Don't be foolish. I'm meant to be looking after you.'

'Duncan isn't here and you're neither my brother or my keeper, Carter Carnehan. You can turn around and leave, but if you choose to go through with this, I'm going to be your shadow.'

Carter looked in desperation at Kerge. 'Sweet mercy, take her back and let me get on with what I have to do.'

'I can hardly do that while I am also accompanying you … if only to moderate the worst of your people's behaviour.'

Carter shook his head in fury, but he had realised he couldn't create more of a scene without alerting the traitors he hunted. 'Come then, damn it, and the stealers take you as they find you.'

Annoying Carter was good sport, if hardly a taxing activity, but Willow soon had other things on her mind. They passed into near darkness. There weren't many lanterns pinned along the walls, wasting power, not with so few workers to benefit from their light. This passage's surfaces hadn't been flattened off, and crags and outcrops tried to trip Willow up, both her hands held out in front of her in case she smashed her skull into an overhang. They advanced in complete silence, Carter in front and the gentle sound of the gask's breathing behind her. The passage reeked of urine and other less salubrious things. Willow had no trouble believing the things that people said happened down here during the dark of night. After five minutes of edging and half-feeling their way forward, the end of the tunnel grew lighter. Someone had brought a mobile lantern, low voices echoing softly as they talked. It was a long way from the rest of the station and there was no good reason for people to be furtively gathered ahead. Willow felt the fear rise tight in her belly. How fiercely would such schemers fight to stop their secret being revealed? At least she would emerge from the darkness, the conspirators' night vision adjusted to their lantern's illumination. And Willow would have the element of surprise on her side. The tunnel curved off to the right, an intense yellow light beyond. Carter halted and Willow and Kerge stopped behind him. She followed Carter's lead and edged around the corner to see what they faced. Just as Carter had predicted, Owen and Anna were inside an oblong-shaped end-chamber, sitting on empty supply crates. A couple of old hands Willow vaguely recognised, senior Weyland men, and a woman who, to her regret, she knew all too well. Hoary old Kassina Hedgepeth, the sorting line's bad-tempered overseer. All of these people were billeted in different barracks. The only thing they had in common, the fact they had survived while the majority of the slaves taken alongside them had long since perished.

Willow noted two pickaxes propped against the wall. They were comfortable here, they felt secure. The group were too far away for Willow to overhear their conversation properly, but words drifted to her as echoes as the conspirators talked animatedly, hands waving, casting quick shadows on the ceiling from the lamp in their centre.

'Too busy — stealing.'

'Going — to — caught.'

'— to act — now.'

'I told you,' whispered Carter. 'Does that sound like a knitting circle in there to you? We'll get the truth out of them. Rush them when I move in.'

How many times had these secret meetings been held? Willow felt sick that people she trusted could betray their own countrymen with such ease.

Carter rushed in yelling, his club connecting with the gut of the nearest seated man, sending him sprawling off the empty supply crate. He converted the momentum into an upper cut, catching the second old hand under the chin with a fierce crack that left the man toppling towards the lantern. Willow sprinted towards the two pickaxe handles even as Carter felled the first conspirator, grabbing one and tossing the other towards Khow. She didn't know which of them looked the most uneasy about wielding a weapon, her or the gask, but at least the weapons weren't in the hands of the people plotting inside here. Anna, Owen and Kassina leapt to their feet, startled, the look of shock on their faces at being discovered telling its own story.

Carter waved his club in the direction of the remaining three plotters, stepping near the last man standing ... Owen Paterson. 'I know what you are and what you've done, and I'm here for a reckoning.'

The two women retreated to the walls of the chamber. The fury Carter was in, he might give them a taste of the club, too. Willow blocked the tunnel exit, just in case they ran for help.

'That's too bad for you,' said Owen.

'You think?' Carter drew his makeshift bludgeon back, ready to fell the conspirator. 'I'm the one holding the club.'

'But that's the thing, you've brought a club to a gunfight,' said Owen, nodding towards Anna Kurtain.

Willow groaned. The transporter pilot pulled a Vandian pistol out of her slave's tunic, its barrel wavering between Carter, Willow and Khow. It looked old and rusty, just the kind of hand-me-down that the imperials would pass to their more trusted collaborators, but Willow didn't doubt for a second it was still serviceable.

Anna pointed the pistol at Carter. 'Move back and drop the club!'

'I'd suggest you obey her,' said Owen. 'You wouldn't be the first person she's killed in the sky mines to protect me.'

Willow gasped. So, the rumours were true. There really were collaborators on the station, keeping an eye on operations and making sure any trouble was brutally crushed before it spread.

Reluctantly, Carter let the club fall to the floor and stepped protectively towards Willow. Kassina Hedgepeth advanced on Willow, seizing the club from her hand before snatching Kerge's too. Then the humourless old overseer stepped back, leaving a nice clear field of fire for Anna. 'They know about you, Paterson. Put a bullet in their heads and let's roll them off the roof before we're missed for our next shift.' She looked with contempt at Carter. 'Everyone will think he leapt off, anyway.' She pointed at Willow. 'Lady Muck here, mooning after this fool, maybe she jumped off after him. And nobody will miss the gask – he's twisted, not even common pattern.'

Willow glared with loathing at the overseer. 'He's more human than you are.'

'This is unnecessary,' said Kerge, even his normally reasonable voice sounding strained and uncertain.

Anna's arm straightened, getting ready for the killing shot. 'None of you can leave here alive.'

'Get it over with,' snarled Carter. 'I've had all I can stand of your traitors' stink.'

Willow shut her eyes. She wasn't sure whose hand reached for whose first, but her fingers were finally curled around Carter's. Far too late for either of them.

Major Alock examined the map on the folding table, Grand Duke Bragin sitting on his mobile throne, twitching and squirming, while the soldiers who had carried him in front of the command tent hovered vigilantly by his side. As always, the ruler's damned hounds followed the man like a moving carpet, leaping up at officers' legs and urinating against the vehicles' armoured sides. Normally his sedan chair would have been carried around by slaves, but nobody in the regiments of Hangel trusted the gads to stay loyal – not even as water and ammunition carriers. The crews of the armoured force and infantry accompanying them were solely Hangel. Out on the plains the engines of the waiting lines of armour lay switched off, troops stretching out canopies as shade from the relentless sun.

A junior officer pointed to an area of the map with his swagger stick. Swaggering was something that seemed to come naturally to Hangel's army. It remained to be seen how well they would fight. 'This village is where the scouts tracked the gathered tribes.'

Alock exchanged a glance with his own lieutenants. 'And you are certain the escaped Weylanders are still with them?'

'They're parading Jok around as though he is a siege cannon that will bring them victory.'

'He is a dirty old thief,' said Alock. 'And I don't care what twisted people he belongs to. When I've chained each of his arms and legs to a tank, I'll see how well he heals after he's been ripped apart.'

'You will not need to,' hooted the grand duke. 'My diviners have foreseen his end. He and the other foreigners will be obliterated in a fiery explosion. The gad village burnt to the ground. The plains filled with fleeing gads! Victory is certain! My armoured squadrons are unstoppable!'

Alock grunted. He didn't put much faith in the ravings of the demented, tortured witch-doctors Bragin kept caged like parrots. Trundling the prisoners out and drugging them so heavily they had all died. There had been hell to pay for that error. Those creatures would have said anything to keep the grand duke happy before rolling around their cage floors in agony and expiring. *Of little matter.* After this battle, the grand duke would have many more shaman prisoners to play with and amuse him during his idle moments. Major Alock glanced over at the tank squadrons, each vehicle mounted with massive cannons, metal ramparts filled with riflemen. Infantry regiments drawn up in the shadow of the vehicles they flanked. There were hardly any troops left in the city, but that was not a problem. After the cull, there weren't many gads left either. The price of slaves was going to rise in the coming weeks, and if Alock and his troopers played their cards right here, they would take enough trading flesh in the aftermath to make them all rich men. It would make up for losing one of Benner Landor's money chests to the so-called 'Jok'.

'Divide the armour into three columns,' advised Alock, tapping the village on the map. 'One large force in the centre, two supporting columns on either side. Let the centre column drive forward and engage those too slow, drunk or stupid to retreat. Then the two supporting lines will advance and close around the fleeing warriors, cut them off, and slaughter the tribesmen from all sides simultaneously. If the tribes crack early, form a line and crush them as they retreat.'

'We should engage from a distance, instead,' said a Hangel general. 'Form an arc in front of the village and bombard them until they break.'

'Break and *scatter*,' sighed Alock. He didn't need a diviner to tell this buffoon had come up through the ranks as an artilleryman. 'If the natives are routed and you are not prepared, your descendants will go to their graves still facing hit-and run-attacks by guerrillas. The witch doctors' prophecy is a blessing, not a curse. It has actually made your enemies stupid enough to muster and face Hangel's regiments. Arrowheads against steel armour and repeating rifles. The imperium has given you the blueprints and steel for *mobile* weaponry. You have not cast accidentally-travelling cannons; you should never fight your next war with the tools of the last one.'

'Who are you to lecture me?' protested the general, his ruddy self-satisfied expression vanishing.

Alock drove his fist into the table. 'These are aggressive weapons. They are used to drive and smash. Caution only favours the enemy. So attack, attack, attack!'

Grand Duke Bragin's dogs started barking and running in circles at the excitement. 'Yes, that's the spirit. The gads back in the city gave us no trouble, and my men were on foot, not protected inside my new steel fortresses.'

'With respect, Your Majesty, these are warriors of the gad,' said the general, 'protecting soil they believe to be holy. No soldier that has experience hunting them through the grasslands would ever under-estimate their talent for warfare.'

'Holy soil!' screeched the grand duke. 'Let us consecrate it, then, with their blood. Destroy them. Crush them. Let the Age of the Seven Suns end mangled next to their corpses, let it end crushed beneath our tracks. We shall strike as the Weylander has suggested. Go back to the squadrons and bring your engines to life.'

Alock left the gathering with his troopers, the hounds' barking disappearing behind him. It was hard to tell who the biggest lapdogs were among the dilettante rankers. Hangel's fighters had cut their teeth smashing slaves' faces into the ground, and that was easy work. Not the standard he had trained to. But the grand duke had the tools and numbers to do the job, and to the major that was ultimately all that counted.

'What about the pastor and his people?' asked a lieutenant.

Alock tilted the rim of his hat up. 'They've proven too slippery. I'm growing bored with life on the road. Screw an interrogation. I don't care if God is personally sending angels to whisper the emperor's plans in Father Carnehan's ear each night. The pastor can take his secrets to the grave. Find them. Kill them. Bullet or blade, no difference to me.'

'I enjoy the simple plans,' said the lieutenant.

And so, in truth, did Alock. Brutal, but effective, as long as you possessed the might to drive it through; like the joyous sound of running a sabre through a man's chest. Forgoing his prisoners' interrogation meant abstaining from their torture. He would have enjoyed the opportunity of making each of the troublesome expedition members really *feel* their deaths. The major listened to the call of engines rumbling into life across the plain. A concert to his ears, and this was just the beginning of the first movement. What a glorious trade. Killing was all the major existed for. He just didn't seem capable of feeling much else. The feeling of power as his victims begged for life, bringing him for just that brief second the power of a god with control over life or death. And in the end, it was always death. Because nobody in power paid good money to keep their enemies alive.

THIRTEEN

THE STONE GARDEN

Duncan passed below an arch in the hedgerow, beyond which Princess Helrena was meant to be resting. Inside the part of the castle's grounds called the Stone Garden, after the ancient circle of standing stones that formed the centre of the ornamental park. Duncan was close to the edge of the cliff. In the distance he could hear waves breaking against the rocks. A regular crashing rhythm intermingled with the crackle of the lightning fence – great steel spikes as tall as church spires exchanging vaulting spikes of electricity between each other. Ready to fry any assassin or rioter who made it over the outer battlement, past the guard posts, and navigated the mine field beyond that. Even here in the gardens, you were always reminded of the defences protecting the Castle of Snakes. When Duncan had first arrived as a house slave, he had thought those precautions paranoid. Now he had seen a little of the nature and number of the enemies Helrena and her family faced, he knew it was merely what was necessary. He wondered again why he had been unexpectedly summoned to see the head of the house. The princess should be far too distracted to waste time with him. There was meant to be some grand gathering of Helrena's allies convening later to discuss the emperor's deteriorating health and how best to prepare for the struggle for the throne. But there was a part of Duncan that no longer felt curiosity, or much else at all. He was just going through the motions. It was as though a grey veil had been drawn over his life, eliminating every vestige of colour and brightness. It didn't matter what young Lady Cassandra ate now – the food Duncan tasted for her might as well have been ashes in his mouth. Poison would have been a welcome distraction. What was the point of Duncan now? Before his capture, he had been dedicated to making a new life with Adella, proving he could be someone outside his father's shadow. Showing he didn't need all that wealth and power. What a joke! Instead, he had ended up stranded at the other end of the globe, drawn into the lethal intrigues of foreigners, and with the woman he had thought was his life throwing him under the carriage's wheels to save her own skin. If there was a bigger fool in all the nations, then the world was far too large for Duncan Landor to bump into him.

He'd reached the heart of this place. There was the stone circle the garden had been named after, ancient black monoliths brooding and scarred by the ages. A large circular aviary the size of a house had been raised behind the stones, with Princess Helrena in front of it. She was on a folding seat with an easel in front of her, painting one of the birds. Duncan checked around. There appeared to be no bodyguards present. So, this is where she came to be alone with her thoughts. Not much use to Duncan: he wished his thoughts would stop chasing him. Towards the back of the gardens a concrete dome rotated on a steel disc, its clanking noise catching Duncan's eye as four massive barrels tracked something flying near the castle's air space. He pitied anything that tried to kill Helrena Skar here, inside her territory.

'Do you sketch and paint, Weylander?' asked the princess as he walked within earshot.

'Not one of my talents,' said Duncan.

'A pity. In the empire, it is regarded as an essential part of nobility. We master weapons, strategy, politics and combat alongside such arts as poetry, illustration and calligraphy. Even flower arranging. It is considered a mark of refinement.'

'I've got a flower arranging tip for you,' said Duncan, pointing to the rear of the formal gardens. 'Your woodland aspect would look a lot better if it wasn't overlooked by quite so many gun emplacements.'

'Your insolence has been absent of late,' said Helrena, placing her brush down by the easel. 'Normally I would applaud, but your maudlin demeanour has been noted by my daughter, and it is now infecting her. Cassandra is normally far more resilient, which means, I suspect, that she likes you more than she should.'

'Cassandra reminds me of my sister, Willow, when she was younger,' said Duncan. He was too diplomatic to say her better parts. Being raised amidst the snake pit of imperial politics, it was a miracle the young noblewoman hadn't crumbled under the strain.

Helrena stepped aside. She had painted a green bird inside the cage, flashes of brilliant red in its plumage. 'Paetro tells me your dark mood is because of the woman, the one we sold to my cousin.'

'Sold her? You should have made her a full citizen. She earned it.'

'If you live long enough, everyone will betray you,' said the princess.

'I don't believe that.'

'You don't want to believe it, but part of you knows it is true. It is something my mother used to say to me. It proved all too prophetic in her case. She was poisoned in a hospital's delivery room by the friend she asked to attend the birth.'

'I was told your mother's death was not proven as murder.'

Helrena stood up from her seat in front of the easel. 'No, never *proved*. You do not kill a wife and unborn son of the emperor with impunity, even if you are Circae; even when my father has so many children and concubines. But I doubt it was any coincidence that following my mother's funeral, my mother's "dear friend" rose far and fast among circles of influence controlled by Circae.'

'This place,' said Duncan. 'This city. There's too much power and wealth here. It twists and distorts everything. Lives and values alike. Nobody should have to leave the world like that. I told Paetro you'd be better off taking Cassandra and fleeing for the provinces.'

'You lack the experience of my life to judge.'

'I had a taste of it at home. Not on the same scale as the empire, but a taste of it all the same. Money and influence; everyone fawning over you because of who your parents are. Your jokes are funnier, your decisions are better than anyone else's – however stupid. I was planning to leave; just up sticks and take myself and Adella somewhere far away, another league nation, one of our neighbours. I would have walked away and not given what I'd left behind a second glance.'

'There is no country so barbaric or so far from the imperium that it is not within range of our ships,' said Helrena. 'You of all people should know that. Those who would destroy my house would celebrate if I fled ... before exploiting the opportunity to settle old scores far away from my forces and friends. There are some things you can never run away from; you just have to turn and face them.'

'Another of your mother's sayings?'

'Something Cassandra's father used to say.'

And from what I've heard, it got him killed as well. 'And here was me thinking *I* was the slave here.'

'You are,' said Helrena. 'And as the mistress of the house, it is my duty to make sure you do not wither away from a broken heart and distract my daughter from her education.'

Duncan shrugged, sadly. 'There are a lot of things the owner of slave can command him, but "be happy" isn't one of them.'

'Let us see,' said Helrena. She pushed Duncan down onto the chair and kissed him with the kind of ferocity that should have been reserved for combat. *Maybe this counts?* 'Be happy!'

He drew back on the chair, shocked, his eyes casting around for the guards that would give him a beating for such a gross breach of caste protocol. 'I could be executed for that.'

'On the contrary, the road to execution lies in refusing to obey me. A few years ago I came to the conclusion I did not need the complications that arise from nobles of the upper-celestial ranks mistaking a physical union for a political one. I trust the decade's difference between us does not wilt your desire ... I prefer to take my sport with younger, more vigorous lovers. Do I really need to command you to your station?' She ran her hands down his trousers. 'No, it would appear not.'

'Back in Weyland, this is what they call catching someone on the rebound.'

'Your people have such a barbaric turn of phrase.' Helrena undid the ribbon from her elaborate pile of hair, her fingers reaching behind his back and tying his hands together. 'But then, I suppose you used to strut around as a brutish barbarian lord among your people. I think I will need to protect myself from you.' He tugged at the bindings, but whatever knot she had used, his hands were well secured; there would be sailors in the Lancean Ocean envious of her talent. Then she drew her dress up and took Duncan as her seat. 'So, Duncan of Weyland, you are *on the rebound*? I think with right encouragement you shall bounce back admirably.'

Duncan had no choice but to look at her as she dragged her fingers through the hair at the back of his head. 'What if I told you I didn't think this was going to make me any happier?'

She kissed him hotly on the lips, before whispering in his ear. 'Do I look like that would make the slightest difference to me? I am quite selfish that way.'

By the time Duncan had been finished with, he had to admit, the imperium possessed interesting techniques to compel a slave away from misery. At least for a little while.

Duncan waited with Paetro outside the Castle of Snakes' largest hall. This was the focus of the conference being hosted for the house's allies. Lady Cassandra had been allowed to sit in on the preliminary discussions as part of her tuition, but the hour approached when the main meeting would start. No doubt she would be particularly prickly when she had to turn to her dry lessons with Doctor Horvak instead. At the moment, Cassandra was inside, listening to the raised voices Duncan heard arguing. He couldn't discern any details, but then he didn't need to. The tone spoke volumes. Self-regarding opportunism dressed up as politics. The corridor outside had filled with dignitaries and their bodyguards. They had been deprived of their ranged weapons and carried short-swords only, but Paetro still appeared ill-tempered with so many strangers allowed into the castle at the same time. He saw threats in every shadow.

'The airfield must be reaching capacity,' said Duncan.

'That it is, lad,' said Paetro. 'But there's one amenity our "honoured guests" won't find inside the castle that I wager they'll have in theirs.'

'What's that?'

'A chamber with a harem. And a wise man might ask why that was.'

'Maybe because silks, perfumes and cushions wouldn't suit this place.'

'I'm merely passing the time, is all; chewing the fat. Aye, it's hardly for old Paetro to gainsay the mistress's commands, except to point out that in this house, the position of consort tends towards a shorter term than the role of food-taster.'

Duncan shrugged. 'The role of a slave here seems to involve obeying commands.'

'Princess Helrena needs to spend more time in the fencing hall, sharpening her combat skills. Not jawing with these celestial-caste aristos ... or any *other* distractions.'

'She's sharp enough as she is.'

'Do you think so? There're rumours that Circae intends to have one of her allies issue a challenge against our mistress. As soon as they can manufacture a casus belli that satisfies imperial law, it'll be sabres or pistols inside an arena. You mark my words.'

'Would the fight be broadcast on the screens?'

'That it would, lad. The lower castes are mad for it, the chance to see their rulers' blood spilled in the sand. Two houses going at each other. The biggest riots always break out in the losing district; it's almost a tradition here.'

'Why do they run the broadcasts, then?'

'Draining the boil, lad, draining the boil. You control when trouble breaks out, scoop out the worst offenders with riot tractors, and haul in hardy "volunteers" for the legion on the side.'

'You served with such men?'

'Best fighters we ever fielded,' grunted Paetro, before turning his attention towards a soldier walking up to them. The guardsman bowed, passing Paetro a readout from the castle's radio room. Paetro read the orders and snorted. 'Lady Cassandra's visit to the new power plant this evening has been cancelled ... teething problems. I wouldn't want to be the overseer across there. Find Hesia and tell her she can run some helo maintenance after all.'

'What if there's a delivery from the kitchens?'

Paetro jerked a large thumb towards the doorway into the conference, soldiers with rifles standing at attention on either side. 'Nobody's interrupting them for food. Head back to the doctor's laboratory when you're done. It'll be science, history and supper for the little Highness, in that order.'

Duncan turned and was about to obey when he saw Helrena sweeping down the passage, exchanging greetings with the crowd of nobles.

It was hard to tell who the visitors were more obsequious toward: the princess, or the deadly head of the secret police, Apolleon, trailing by her side. If Duncan felt awkward around Helrena, she showed little of it, acting as though nothing had passed between them. *That's probably because for her, nothing has*.

Helrena brushed past Duncan as though he wasn't there. Unfortunately for him, the pallid, foppish Apolleon showed no such compulsion in avoiding toying with her servants. 'Ah, our sturdy young sky miner. Still keeping Lady Cassandra safe, I trust?'

'Such is my duty, sir.'

'Indeed. And very *diverting* it must prove for you.' The way the head of the imperium's secret police rolled the word around his tongue, he might as well have been an audience applauding inside the Stone Garden. He clasped Duncan a little too warmly on the shoulder and moved off. The false bonhomie meant Duncan was greeted as a duke while leaving him feeling as insignificant as any slave in the capital. That was a definite knack, a skill not easily acquired. You had to work at it. Duncan sighed and left to locate their helo pilot, Hesia.

All afternoon the Castle of Snakes' passages had been packed with staff busily working – looking after visitors and their entourages, making sure that every corner of the castle was presentable. Duncan headed for the domed hangars overlooking the airfields. Their hangars joined the complex's eastern side like massive concrete toadstools, sheltered from the sea by a line of defensive towers and bunkers. Duncan could hear the air-slicing thump of helos still landing outside. More of the nobility that suckled on the house's mining wealth, arriving to argue about carving up the larger pie that would become available along with the imperial throne. *Damn, but it's busy*. Visiting pilots escorted in the direction of the military canteens, ground staff dragging cables and equipment pods out, servants waiting to guide new arrivals through the maze of concrete tunnels and guard posts. Duncan moved out of the way as a vehicle hauled a large steel fuel tank past, slowly manoeuvring through the crowds. Someone wanted visiting aircraft to be able to take off promptly. It was a fine idea, growing even more attractive to Duncan when he spotted who had just landed outside. Baron Machus! Helrena's cousin swept through the hangar accompanied by a full retinue of advisors and soldiers. And the current favourites from Machus's harem to flaunt his virility in front of his fellow nobles … Adella at the back of the prince's entourage. As Adella passed through the hangar she was talking with the pilot Duncan had arrived to see. *What's the devious bitch up to now? How does she know Hesia?* As Duncan watched, Adella passed what might be a brooch to Hesia, and the pilot pocketed it. He didn't think he could stomach talking to Adella again, not now he knew that her luxurious dress had been paid for in Weyland blood. Duncan and Carter's blood, too, for all she had known at the time. He ducked behind a parked helo, ignoring curious looks from a pair of mechanics in brown boiler suits delving inside its engine panel. Duncan observed Adella trail the group. Machus and his retinue disappeared down a passage, and then Duncan headed for Hesia. The female pilot had stopped in front of a helo, talking to its ground crew. It was one of the bigger aircraft, with twin rotors on top, designed to lift a company of house troops. He went up to her and pulled the woman aside.

'You know who you were just talking to?' asked Duncan.

'Hard not to,' said Hesia. 'I flew her to Baron Machus's district the day she arrived here.' The pilot tapped her flight overalls. 'She saw me drop my brooch on the field. Clasp's broken. You've heard how the woman got her ticket out of the sky mines?'

'Yes. And it might have been *me* the guards executed,' said Duncan, 'if I had joined the escape attempt.'

'Best decision you ever made,' said Hesia, pushing her long hair back over her shoulder. 'I've flown supply runs across the dead zone. Unless you're on one of our ships, you're never getting out, not unless you count being made a corpse as escaping.'

'You live long enough and everyone betrays you in the end,' said Duncan, sadly.

Hesia put her hand on Duncan's chest and landed a quick, passionate kiss against his lips. Duncan glanced around to see if anyone had spotted them. 'Damn, but is Doctor Horvak testing a special scent in my quarters that I haven't been told about?'

The pilot smiled, coyly. 'Just thought I'd taste some of that celestial-caste honey while it's still on offer. See what all the fuss is about.'

His face flushed red. 'Is there anyone in the castle who doesn't know?'

'Don't worry, Weylander, it'll be me that flies you to the slave market after that scent's novelty has worn off. And it always does.' She prodded him playfully in the shoulder. 'Count on it.'

'You've got the rest of the evening to get over me. Cassandra's flight has been cancelled. Paetro says it's time to give the helo a full maintenance check.'

'Lucky me. Stepping out with a grease can and a set of spanners.'

Duncan nodded goodbye to the pilot and walked away.

'Don't be too judgemental about your country girl,' Hesia called after him. 'You've served in the sky mines, so you know how it goes out there.'

Duncan turned back. 'Would you trust Adella on *your* crew, if she'd been given a position inside the castle?'

'Well, I believe Machus deserves her more than we do. They suit each other, don't you think?'

Duncan couldn't disagree. Helos still touched down beyond the hangar's blast doors, the gust from their rotors helping to cool the heat on his cheeks. He left for the doctor's laboratory before someone assigned him a party of visiting nobles to nanny. Lady Cassandra was already at study by the time he arrived inside the lab, and, as he had predicted, in a churlish mood having being made to vacate the gathering just as the major players replaced the minor nobles around the table.

'What is the point,' she complained, 'of being taught politics and oratory, if when I have an opportunity to see the heads of great houses deploy such skills at first hand, I am sent away like a scullery maid to my books?'

'I doubt if there are many scullery maids with access to a library as fine as mine,' said the doctor, sounding a little peeved. 'And who is to say that there may not be the chronicles of greater politicians than our current crop of leaders buried among your tomes?'

'My mother,' said Cassandra, tartly. 'What do you think, Paetro? Would I not be better in the real world, seated downstairs around the table with my equals?'

The bulky guard winked at Duncan. 'I think the real world prefers to share their strategies in private. Master patience, little Highness. Your place at the table will come with age.'

'I may choke on book dust first,' she muttered.

'Please,' said the doctor. 'You've arrived late for your studies. I hadn't expected you to be allowed to attend the start of the gathering. Time to apply yourself now.'

Cassandra was due a three-hour session of tuition, and Duncan knew that they had reached the halfway point when the food cart arrived from the kitchens. It was fancier than the normal fare delivered during study sessions. Hot fresh crab taken from the bay outside, stuffed with a multi-coloured assortment of cold fish – considered a delicacy in the empire, if a little too slippery for his tastes. Duncan suspected the kitchens were overworked with extra guests and notables cramming the castle. The princess and her staff had been served the overflow from some head of house's idea of a meal; dished up on engraved gold platters, and with portions that could have fed an entire barracks in the sky mines. Duncan tried to ignore the mixture of guilt and worry over what his sister would be enduring right now. He found it hard to remember how hard and endless working days had been on the station. But he would never forget waking up every bit as hungry as he had gone to bed. *Please let Willow be safe. Please let someone back there be looking out for her.* But that should have been his job.

Paetro interrupted his thoughts. 'Come on, lad. Everyone here is hungry. First mouthful ... the young Highness needs to check you don't turn blue and keel over on us.'

Duncan did as he was bid, and when he didn't expire the others in the room began tucking in. The two lab assistants helping the doctor fell on the meal as though they hadn't eaten for a week. Duncan wished he had their appetite. He had been off his food of late.

Doctor Horvak leant in towards Duncan, speaking low enough that the others couldn't hear. 'Paetro and Lady Cassandra have never been slaves, but I know that look. The ones you had to leave behind?'

'Yes,' said Duncan.

'At least I can comfort myself that my wife and daughters are safe as citizens of my country, even if it is firmly under the Vandian yoke,' said the doctor. 'Yours are slaves in the sky mines?'

'My sister, Willow.'

'Women are far more resilient than we are, Duncan of Weyland,' said Horvak. 'She will survive, I am sure of it. Come with me, young fellow. Honest work is always a cure for melancholy.'

Duncan didn't say anything. Doctor Horvak might be a serf here, too, but at least the scientist had a country and a family and memories of them worth keeping. What did Duncan have from his old life? It had all been a lie ... everything so obvious in hindsight. How the workers at home must have laughed at him behind his back. Adella's feelings solely towards the Duncan's title, heir of Hawkland Park. An inheritance he had treated as valueless; wealth and power as empty as his father's dreams for endless expansion across the north. And when Duncan's name was rendered worthless, Adella had abandoned him for Carter's dubious protection, before exchanging the pastor's son for the infinitely more comfortable and reliable security of Baron Machus's bed. Maybe it would be better if Willow *was* more like Adella. At least then he could have more faith in his sister's survival. Duncan followed sadly after the scientist as they left the others to finish eating. The doctor unlocked a glass door at the far end of the chamber. It led into a short corridor and a second glass door peering into an area that resembled a greenhouse, rows of plants growing tall under bright lights, steam misting the glass. They had come to the back of the castle, windows overlooking towering cliffs and the dark sea beyond, spray thrown up against the hold's high concrete walls. When the doctor closed the door to the hot room there was a strange hissing noise under Duncan's feet.

'The air smells odd in here?' said Duncan.

'It's pressurised,' said the doctor. 'In a similar manner to an aircraft's interior as it travels through thin atmosphere.'

Duncan gazed along the rows of greenery – planting trays drip fed by rubber hoses and the smell of wet vegetation strong in the room. Behind each tray stood a set of glass canisters, coiled tubes feeding multi-coloured chemicals into the soil. 'Why would you look to grow plants on a merchant carrier? You can send transport planes down to the ground to trade for food more cheaply.'

Doctor Horvak tapped the side of his nose. 'Ah, but who knows how far we may need to travel one day?' He pulled a cork clipboard off the wall and passed it to Duncan; a pencil attached to its edge with a length of string. 'Mark the sizes on the right-hand column as I call them out.'

Duncan complied, the doctor walking the line of vegetation, muttering as he tapped the glass canisters, placing a measuring tape by the side of each plant – everything from cucumbers to cabbages growing in the soil – and then announced heights for Duncan to scribble down. They'd undertaken the exercise for ten minutes when Duncan heard what sounded like a distant thud, panes of glass in the wall rattling and dislodging flurries of dust above his head.

'What was that?'

'I'm really not quite sure,' said the doctor, sounding perplexed.

Behind them the door was thrown open by Paetro, a hiss of escaping air – the outer portal hadn't been shut properly. 'My experiments!' called Horvak.

'Hang your experiments, Doctor,' said Paetro. 'That was an explosion.'

Duncan dropped the clipboard. 'A bomb? The meeting—!' If Helrena's enemies had succeeded in infiltrating the gathering, they'd be able to wipe out the house's leadership and its allies in a single stroke.

But Paetro wasn't listening to Duncan – he stared in shock at what lay beyond window. 'Get inside, now!'

They were barely inside the corridor, the burly guard half-dragging, half-pushing Duncan and the doctor forward when a shattering explosion echoed behind them, splinters of glass jouncing down the corridor. Paetro had his pistol out, slamming the inner door shut. 'Glider chutes,' snarled Paetro. 'Carrying at least a company of commandos in on us! There's an assault ship out at sea.'

Sirens began to wail in the passage outside. Lady Cassandra jumped to her feet. Paetro dipped down into his boot and pulled out a small concealed pistol, tossing it across the room to her. Duncan felt a flash of annoyance that Paetro hadn't thrown the weapon to him. Wasn't he meant to be protecting the young noblewoman too? Was he that useless?

'Why aren't our air defences shooting them down?' demanded Cassandra. 'I can't hear our guns?'

'As an educated guess, little Highness, the explosion we heard will have something to do with that.' One of the doctor's assistants panicked and scurried towards the door, but Paetro grabbed him by the collar, hauling him away from the exit, shoving the man back towards the plate of food he had abandoned. 'Nobody goes out there. Some of our so-called allies at the meeting have betrayed us. That's the only way our castle's defences are silent.'

'We need to head down to the shelters,' cried the lab assistant. 'We'll be better protected underground.'

'Please be quiet, Tarius, I need to think,' said the doctor, a lot more calmly than Duncan felt. The scientist moved behind the bench where his super-conductors floated in an icy mist. 'Yes, yes, Paetro is correct. If hostile forces have infiltrated the castle, the shelter's stairwell will be the perfect position to ambush the house's leadership. We cannot safely retreat below ground.'

Duncan's mind raced. If Circae was behind the attack, then she might very well want to seize custody of Cassandra. If another enemy was behind the assault, then the house's heir would be at the very top of the list of high-level targets to assassinate. Either way, they were in deep trouble. 'Do you keep any weapons here?'

'I have the blueprints for a few,' said Doctor Horvak. 'But they're not of a scale to prototype inside my laboratory; and if we were to use them, we wouldn't have much of a castle left to take refuge in.'

'Lend me your back, lad,' said Paetro, picking up one end of the heavy testing bench, still covered in plates and half-eaten food. Duncan took the other side, lifted, and they dragged it towards the entrance. At least the door was constructed of heavy oak plated with steel. Locked and with the makeshift barricade behind it, they had bought themselves a little time. But time for what?

'My mother ...' moaned Cassandra.

'There are dozens of guards at the gathering,' said Duncan, trying to comfort her. 'Well armed and ready for trouble.'

'Our best soldiers,' added Paetro. 'Picked more than a few of them myself. They'll stand, they'll stand.' It sounded to Duncan as though he was trying to convince himself.

'What if the sound we heard was a bomb exploding in the meeting hall?' fretted Cassandra.

Duncan's heart went out to her. She had already lost her father to the imperium's internecine feuding. So young, she didn't deserve any of this. *Do you? Do any of us here?* He remembered how inconsolable he had been after watching his mother buried in Northhaven. Months of terrible darkness, hours the same as weeks. All happiness drained from his life, and Willow's, too. What if that explosion *had* been the sound of Helrena being murdered? Would Cassandra be expected to assume the suicidally dangerous mantle of head of household? How long would the poor girl last in that cursed role? Duncan vowed he would help Cassandra survive, however difficult the task might be.

'Don't focus on what you can't do anything about,' barked Paetro at the young noblewoman. 'Your pistol, check it, check the clip. What if I've passed it to you empty? Remember your training. You too, lad, search the science centre with the others – scalpels, acid, anything that you can poke, burn or pierce with, my braves.'

One of the assistants looked up, distracted by Paetro's orders. He was standing bent by the greenhouse corridor door. Duncan could hear an odd whipping noise beyond. 'There's something—' The man's words ended with the thud of bullets removing the top part of his skull. His body tumbled in a blast of shattered glass; the plant lab's door's remains scattered as blood-spattered shards across the stone floor. The shots sounded wrong to Duncan, deadened, spitting too silently to have come from any firearm.

Paetro was by the side of the wall in a second, crouching low and firing down the plant lab corridor. 'They're sliding down the battlements on rappel lines!' The bodyguard ducked back as more silenced weapons rattled down the passage, bullets cracking against their room's far wall. Paetro's pistol answered, sounding as a gun should, its barrel bucking after each thunderous eruption. Duncan sprinted to Cassandra, taking cover behind one of the doctor's experiments. She was saving her ammunition for when the attackers entered the laboratory. Yair Horvak's remaining assistant wrestled the doctor behind the furthest bench, trying to keep him safe.

Paetro loosed off another shot. 'Be hanged! Young Highness, it's not commandos down there. They're *murdisto!*'

Duncan desperately cast his eyes around for a weapon. Long shards of glass from shattered chemical vials lay scattered across the floor, but they had fallen under the chattering volley of fire aimed into the chamber. Attempting to stab men armed with automatic rifles wasn't going to keep Cassandra safe for long. Duncan pulled the girl lower as a ricochet whistled across their bench's work surface. 'We'll be fine.' *And for my next lie ...*

'It's assassins we face,' said Cassandra, her voice quavering as she tried to hold it steady. 'Not soldiers. The murdisto are specialists; their tongues removed so they cannot betray their employers.'

'Remember what I told you,' Paetro yelled back, aiming another shot in their attackers' direction. 'How they fight – their techniques and weaponry.'

'If they've come to take me alive,' whispered Cassandra, grabbing Duncan's sleeve, 'they will enter with ceramic daggers and bullet-bucklers, high-power magnetic shields strapped to their limbs that can repel firearm projectiles. It is a fighting style they are renowned for.'

Duncan reached up to the bench's surface and found the tongs the doctor had used to push around his freezing magnets. He leant out with the tongs and located the longest shard of glass lying in the swelling chemical puddle on the floor. Bullets sprayed around, missing the tool and his hand. Duncan scraped the glass towards him. He had it. He tore off a strip of his tunic and tied a makeshift hilt around the crystal blade: now he could grip it without slicing his hand to pieces. 'Their shields won't be able to repel glass.'

'They are very skilled at knife fighting,' whispered Cassandra. '*Highly* expert. Don't let yourself be killed for me, Duncan of Weyland. This is my fate; it doesn't have to be yours. Please try and save yourself and the doctor.'

Duncan leant closer to the young girl, blue sparks arcing over his head, damaged cables quivering dislodged on the experiment bench they sheltered behind. 'I'll let you into a little secret, I haven't got a whole lot else to live for besides you. So when those hired killers come charging in here, I reckon I'll give Paetro a hand, if it's all the same to you.'

Cassandra pulled back the triangular slide on the rear of her pistol. 'Let us make a good end of it, then.'

A voice sounded down the corridor from the shattered plant station, confident and aristocratic. 'Lay down your arms, and we won't kill you!'

'You can talk? Aye, you must be these dogs' owner, then. I'll tell you that I was in the legion,' called Paetro. 'So I've seen before how well your friends back there "don't kill people" who surrender to them. It must be all their country's high mountains, that thin air making them forgetful! Besides, I developed a taste for hunting murdisto clans down, so why don't you release your hounds and we'll do this the traditional way?'

'Maybe we should do as they say,' said Cassandra. 'They might wish to ransom me.'

'It's not for us to trust the good intentions of vicious scum like this, lass,' said Paetro. 'Just remember your training. Come on you bastards, are you trying to bore us to death in here?'

'Your house is finished,' called the voice down the corridor, furious. 'Join it!'

An eerie whining began at the far end of the corridor, growing louder with each second. Paetro slapped a fresh clip in his pistol.

'They're charging their shields,' said Cassandra. 'They'll have two minutes of protection.'

Duncan had the feeling it was going to be the longest two minutes of his life. Probably the last, too. Then that terrible whining built to a crescendo advancing towards them. Paetro bent around the wall, emptying his magazine down the passage. Each shot was met by an electrical howl and the sound of bullets ricocheting around the corridor, before the last remnants of their inner door exploded as a dozen assassins surged into the laboratory. The attackers wore armour formed from dark brown leather scales, wooden face masks carved as leering goblins, arms and legs weighted by circular domed metal shields strapped to each limb. No bigger than plates, the bucklers crawled with blue electrical energy, each shield singing as the assassins charged forward, deflecting shot after shot, Cassandra's pistol laid across the table, each volley expertly aimed. It was as though the assassins could catch bullets and pluck them from the very air. Paetro's weapon fell silent, his clip exhausted, and the bodyguard drew his knife, arms a blur as he traded blows with the nearest assassin. Duncan saw a leg swing out and catch Paetro in the gut, sending him slamming back into the wall, and then the attackers were all over Duncan and the young princess, her ammunition exhausted too. Without a weapon, Cassandra jabbed and kicked, every lethal move and technique he had watched drilled into her during the training sessions. Duncan lunged for the nearest assassin with his shard of glass, aiming for the man's neck. But the killer snaked to the side, leaving Duncan reaching for air, a boot kicking his feet out from under him and sending him stumbling to the ground. Cassandra had noted his predicament, slapping back the man attacking her and twisting her body around in the air to land interposed between Duncan and the other raider. *Who is protecting who here?* Both assassins flicked their daggers at Cassandra, the young girl darting back, turning their hands with her fingers, nearly overwhelmed by the killers' speed and skill.

'Table,' yelled Duncan, reaching for a torn cable under the bench. Cassandra rolled over the work bench, and as she touched its surface Duncan jabbed the sparking wires into the chemical lake across the floor. Energy danced across the wet flagstones, both assassins quivering and shaking before the blast of electricity sent them flying back into the wall. Cassandra rolled off the bench behind him, already engaging the men attacking Paetro. A scream sounded at the back of the room, drawing Duncan's attention. Three assassins – and one of them had stabbed the last laboratory assistant in the throat, the other two pushing the struggling Doctor Horvak onto a table and binding his arms behind his back with black plastic cables. They could have rushed Duncan and the young noblewoman from behind, killed both of them, but instead … Duncan suddenly realised who the real target of this raid was. *They want the doctor alive.* The murdisto who had just dispatched Horvak's assistant pulled the bloody dagger out of the scientist's throat and turned back towards Duncan, noted the rubber cable hanging from Duncan's hand, its sparking tip pointed in the killer's direction, and laughed. Then the assassin contemptuously tapped his blade against the shield on his arm before charging at Duncan.

Out in the almost endless grasslands the sloped steel prows of the grand duke's tanks were visible. Dipping up and down over the rolling prairie slopes, cannons saluting the sky before they plunged down again. Seeing them, Jacob felt real apprehension. These vehicles were far bigger than the tiny destroyed tank he had once come across rusting away to nothing – more like galleons on tracks. Multiple gun turrets and ramparts up top holding infantry companies. Razored spikes and sharp ploughs for prows, their sides dotted with rifle ports. Three sets of tracks rumbling relentlessly on each tank's side. A dozen exhausts sloped out of their rear, dirty black smoke pouring out as the armoured squadrons flattened grass and the few stands of trees that stood in their way. A small fortune in metal, and perfectly designed for warfare on the plains. *And what do we have to face them? Blood and bones.*

Zanasi stood by Jacob's side, the gad war leader's armour strapped over his long limbs, withered and worn leather like dark wrinkled walnut shells. Dozens of warriors stood behind Zanasi, watching silently and grimly, Sariel among their number. The bard rubbed his snowy beard and stood on his heels to see over the dry chest-high grass. Animals poured past their position; antelopes fleeing the strange machines in terror, clouds of egrets rising into the sky. Sariel groaned. His feelings towards what came at them today sounded a lot like Jacob's.

'They are advancing as you believed they would,' said Zanasi. 'The middle force forward, while their left and right flank slows and widens their sweep. Is this one of the things you saw during your divination?'

'No,' said Jacob. 'That manoeuvre is called the trident. Cavalrymen use it to attack a dispersed infantry formation holding firm against horsemen.'

'Cavalry enjoy the charge,' said Zanasi.

Jacob smiled, but only to silence the nervous drumbeat of his heart. 'Don't they just. They're fools for the rush.'

An artillery bombardment whistled overhead, shells exploding in the village behind Jacob. Gouts of dirt and broken timber rose into the air. But little broken flesh. Anyone not in the fight had departed hours before. That included Sheplar, of limited use as an extra gun without his Rodalian flying wing, like the pacifist-natured gask, Khow. Jacob regretted that his attempts to salvage aircraft parts from the carrier wrecks and provide the mountain aviator with a small craft had failed. They really could have done with a scout in the air right about now. Sariel had been made to stay, of course, despite every stream of protest and exertion of his imagination to counter the rationale for his presence. It would hardly do for the tribes' totem to be seen fleeing the field before the battle had even started. At least Hangel didn't possess the shells or bombards to launch a proper rolling barrage to cover their tanks' advance. *Thank heavens for small mercies.*

Gaddish tribes divided their forces into companies of a hundred warriors apiece, rather appropriately called spears. Hangel's tanks were now close enough to the first spears for the locals to launch their counterattack; rising from the grass where they hid. A wall of oval shields woven from river rushes rippled towards the tanks, with a rolling crack – like snapping wood – as Hangel's rifles opened fire from gun ports, massive explosions turning the ground into blackened geysers of dirt and flame when the tanks' big guns joined in. A gad shield was designed to catch and trap a spearhead. Against rifle volleys they splintered hopelessly, warriors clutching shield fragments as they were flung back, a bloody felling out on the plains. A second spear joined the attack, then a third and a fourth, attempting to overwhelm the armoured column's guns. Soon, dozens of spears were rushing in from every direction. Crossbow-sized bolts rained down from the gads' spear-bows, falling short of the vehicles in most cases. Where they hit, they clunked uselessly off the thick metal tank armour. Beside Hangel's vehicles, the grand duke's infantrymen knelt in two ranks, pouring massed volley fire into the attackers' ranks. Their biggest problem was reloading fast enough to slow the charging waves of gads. Seeking to keep their fire from faltering in a close quarters' melee, the troops retreated up ladders along the vehicles' sides, taking position on the mobile fortresses' ramparts. Every time the tribes' warriors came within footsteps of the tanks, they fell back clutching their bodies as a storm of bullets cut them apart, more soldiers emerging from gantries along the tracked fighting machines' topsides. Tank crews hurled grenades down into the grass, blasting apart any natives who had survived the furious, doomed charge, other tank-men pulling rifles to their shoulders and working the levers as fast as possible, pumping shells into the tribal warriors.

'Their steel beasts are every bit as effective as you said they would be,' growled Zanasi.

'Pull your spears back,' advised Jacob. 'You're getting slaughtered out there.'

'I have commanded many armies in my time,' said Sariel, 'but there was only one force that fought in a cause as hopeless as this. The great siege at the Walls of Rodach. Just a hundred of us against the endless forces of the Emperor Sayarsa, that brainsickly ill-breeding apple-john. We blocked the advance of so many troops we believed an earthquake was erupting under our feet – yet it was only their legions' boots.'

'Call our brothers back!' ordered Zanasi. One of his warriors lit the taper underneath a bolt wrapped in rags, and then he pointed his spear-bow at the sun. He fired his projectile high into the clear, cloudless sky, and a red trail of smoke scratched the air above them. Cheering could be heard from the grand duke's soldiers as hundreds of gads turned and ran; long loping strides with the crackle of rifle fire against their backs, cutting warriors down as they fled. Out on the plain, the two exterior 'spikes' of the trident pulled in, tank columns aiming to roll over every gad concealed in the prairie and massacre them in a crossfire. The distant boom of artillery eased as their tanks' prows crushed fleeing warriors; hard for cannons to distinguish friend from foe without butchering their own.

'We are undone!' moaned Sariel.

'Give them time,' said Jacob.

'Time for what?' demanded Sariel. 'Are our gad brothers expected to run faster than those fierce engines? I have told you – I have told everyone who will listen – I am not Jok! I cannot turn the savannah into an ocean and drown these ragged warts of Hangel.'

'*Time* for their trident to become a scythe,' said Jacob. 'When your enemy flees before you, you need to eliminate them quickly before they disperse into the wind.' He pointed at the advancing vehicles. All three columns of tanks were sweeping out into a massive curved line, a long rumbling hook of armour, companies of infantry marching and firing between each tank. With the smoke of gunfire from the rifles and the tanks' rocking, booming cannons, there was hardly an inch between each vehicle for a warrior to duck and hide in the grass. 'You see … just as a cavalryman would do it.'

'You predict a fate we cannot avoid,' moaned Sariel. 'Those pigeon-livered lackeys of the grand duke are too comfortable in their steel turrets. We are lost!'

As if underlining the bard's point, the long grass whipped around them as the village came within rifle range, bullets shredding the sward. They stood directly before the storm now. Jacob should have been terrified, but most of his fear was replaced by something he barely wanted to give a name to. Excitement? Anticipation? Longing? Courage was a cup you only drank from once. Because once tasted, there was only one place to refill it, and that was here. *You've been hiding under your church's simple cloth. The wrong man for the job. Smell it, taste it. Tell yourself the lie that you never missed this.* A bullet whisked along Jacob's ear, close enough for it to pass whining like a hornet. The invaders had found the gad war leaders' range. And this was the signal for something more than the tribes' imminent end. Zanasi's warriors stepped aside as a team emerged carrying a device that resembled a dented barrel on a tripod, wooden slats across its front.

'A bombard?' wondered Sariel. 'No! That thing is no mortar?'

Jacob knew exactly what the device was. After all, he had drawn a sketch of it in the dirt for Zanasi. And the war leader's followers had managed to find a few rotting among the ruins of crashed carriers. 'A plane-to-plane signalling lamp,' said Jacob. 'What aircrews call a Morse-maid. You can use one to transmit more complicated messages towards the horizon than firing smoke arrows.'

'A fire arrow calling for retreat would suffice,' complained Sariel.

Having set the tripod up, the gads rotated it, and then worked the shutters mounted in front of the lamp. A distant flash of light from oil-fired mirrors answered their signal, far out in the savannah. Jacob and his allies only had seconds left. Officers riding tanks down on the village would realise that this was something new to the tribes. And they would wonder what the signals meant. Jacob didn't want to puncture their overconfidence until ...

A line of fire erupted along the length of the advancing tank line, explosion after explosion sending the massive vehicles careening off course, the air filled with steel fragments and smoking tank tracks. Sariel glanced wildly around him, trying to locate the artillery that had launched such an impossibly coordinated bombardment. But Jacob knew the bard wouldn't find what he was looking for. Such accuracy was beyond cannons, even if the natives had come into possession of a battery of big guns. The entire armoured column stalled, and where vehicles were still moving, gads rose from the grass, sprinting towards the tanks with iron spheres, fuses burning, leaping up ladders and hurling grenades into the ramparts and tossing them through open hatches. Explosions and screams echoed inside the grand duke's galleons of the land. Companies of warriors rose up in front of the checked vehicles. These gads carried spear-bows, but the tribes' traditional weapon remained strapped to their backs for close quarters' combat. Instead they clutched modern rifles, steel barrels bucking as they emptied their magazines towards the invaders from Hangel. The brutes had never faced fighters as well-armed as themselves. Startled infantry companies crumpled, turned and ran as a wave of warriors charged the halted invasion force. Unfortunately for the invaders, they were now fleeing into a wall of warriors advancing from behind, more gads armed with rifles. The same fighters who had come crawling out of the grass behind the artillery crews to slit their throats. Every tribe that had arrived to marvel at their reluctant saviour, Jok, was there. Every clan tired of being hunted and chased from their own lands as though they were little better than rodents scavenging from a grain bin.

'Mines, grenades and rifles!' said Sariel, shocked by the scale of the sudden turnabout.

'The tribes put the signal lamps to use before the battle,' said Jacob. 'They made our old friends on board the *Night's Pride* a better offer for their cargo.'

Sariel glanced up at the sky, as if he might still see the propellers of the great merchant carrier turning in the heavens. 'What have you promised the gun runners?'

'Nothing our people will miss,' said Zanasi. He raised his spear-bow at the broken, burning wrecks littering the savannah: a small fortune in metal salvage for the brokers that feasted on the ruins of battle. 'Not once the House of Bragin has fallen.'

'Is this victory what you saw in your vision?' asked Sariel.

'No,' said Jacob. *I saw the death of my son.* Jacob stalked towards the burning tanks.

Sariel called after him. 'Where are you going?'

'Got to make a start.' *By making an end of Justus Alock.*

Sariel attempted to catch up with him. 'You do not defeat your enemy by becoming him.'

'It's a little late for that,' said Jacob, stepping over a gad's corpse. Of all of the bard's stories, that was the greatest lie of them all. *It's exactly how you win a battle.* How could Jacob ever have forgotten? 'We need to do this. We have to. For my son.'

It wasn't only the beggarly bard who lied to himself. Jacob started to sprint, joining waves of howling tribesmen. Identifying Hangel's command vehicle wasn't difficult. Twice the size of the others and with enough flags and pennants tied to the top to do a market fete proud. Tank-men hung limply out of its hatches, entrances spouting smoke, corpses being checked by warriors who carefully stripped the dead of pistols, blades, ammunition and personal possessions. What was the value of such trinkets among the tribes? Everyone who had taken part in the battle would be going home to their villages rich. Zanasi and two of his bodyguards followed hard on Jacob's heels, and for much, he suspected, the same reason as the pastor. Jacob climbed up a ladder in the command tank's armoured side. The metal was hot. Flames burnt below, crackling in the dry grass where mines had detonated and destroyed the vehicle's tracks. Victorious gads danced on top of the tank, bounding excitedly around the ramparts and hanging off the turret cannons as though the guns were part of a playground.

On the floor of the rampart a soldier lay against the metal, his body twitching as he bled out. Not quite dead. His body had absorbed the best part of a grenade used to clear the top of the tank. The man tried to raise a hand towards Jacob. 'Am I — going to die?'

'I reckon you are.'

'Help me!'

Jacob stepped over the expiring man. 'You're way beyond it. Just look at the sky, don't think about the pain. Look at how the sky's clear and blue.'

Zanasi followed after him, stepping over the dying soldier with his bodyguards. The war leader exchanged words with one of the gads who had taken the tank before returning to Jacob. 'Inside.'

A hatch was thrown open and Jacob climbed down into the interior, following the war leader and his people. A passage lined with rifle slits, more dead soldiers and then, in one of the compartments off the walkway, a room as richly appointed as a boudoir. Tapestries hung on the metal walls, a table filled with crystal decanters and drinks. A couple of gads stood sentry outside, keeping its single occupant quiet.

466

They hadn't needed to work very hard. There wasn't much fight left in the man – not now his regiments had fled and fallen.

'My son,' mewled the grand duke, seeing Zanasi. 'Dear Chike. My long-lost flesh and blood, tell me this is a dream. The diviners told me they saw the tribes breaking and running, your village burning. This can't be my end, it was never foretold.'

'Our village has been burnt to the ground,' said Zanasi. 'Your artillery's incendiary shells proved more than effective. And many of our spears did break and run. As they were instructed to, to entice your forces onto our minefield.'

'And *you*, you're alive?' said the grand duke, noticing Jacob for the first time. 'You're meant to be dead; your body obliterated in an explosion!'

'I guess even a soothsayer can make a mistake,' said Jacob, 'or tell a fool a lie.'

'We can rule together,' whimpered the grand duke, extending a hand towards his son. 'You by my side. You have proven yourself worthy of my name.'

'Your name is worth the handful of ashes you can scoop from my village. Hangel has fallen,' said Zanasi. 'The gad servants you left alive forced the city gates early this morning, before dawn. Your secret police and the dregs of the army defending the plateau proved inadequate when faced with slaves carrying the same weapons as Hangels. The great diviner Narlrem now sits on your throne. He will make a far wiser king than any who carry our cursed blood in our veins. Our peoples shall live together in peace, as we did in ages past; the gads of the plains and the Hangels of the plateau.'

'No!' The grand duke was clutching the cushions spread across the floor, his body twisting and turning in agony.

One of the warriors by Zanasi's side grunted and raised his spearbow, but Zanasi rested the flat of his palm on the weapon and pushed it aside.

Grand Duke Bragin stared up incredulously at the war leader. 'Mercy? You mean to show me mercy after all I have done to you?'

'Your regime is finished. Your laws discarded. You shall live in the slums where your slaves were quartered. Your sceptre will be replaced with a hoe. Your crown will be exchanged for a ploughman's straw hat, and you shall live among the ashes of all that you have lost for the rest of your years. That will be my mercy, *Father*.'

'You dirty half-breed!' Grand Duke Bragin's hand came up from below the cushion, a tiny sleeve pistol no bigger than a fire-lighter clutched in his fingers. The gun barked and its single shot struck Zanasi, sending him tumbling backwards into the compartment's tapestry-lined wall. Both Jacob's pistols were out, five shots walked across the grand duke's chest before the pastor was even aware of the guns' cold jolting weight in his hands. Hangel's ruler shuddered for a second, and then the small pistol pitched out of his hand. He lay motionless, the floor of cushions absorbing his pooling blood. Jacob pulled the seal of the Guild of Librarians from his chest and tossed it contemptuously onto the body. 'Pass that to Iaroia when you see her.'

'His life was not in your hands,' groaned Zanasi, trying to pick himself up.

Old instincts. It had not even been a conscious decision. Jacob examined the war leader alongside his men. Zanasi had taken the grand duke's bullet in the lower shoulder. They began staunching the blood with a tourniquet and Jacob reckoned the gad would live if his wound didn't become infected. 'You have my apologies. That's the thing about wars … once they've begun; the solution for everything starts to look like a bullet.' Jacob looked over at the two bodyguards. 'Take the ball out with a spearhead heated with flame; seal his wound with a clean blade made even hotter.'

The two warriors lifted Zanasi up as Jacob opened the door to explore deeper into the command tank's interior. 'Let my spear search inside, Jacob of Weyland. You may yet keep your soul.'

Jacob shook his head as he stepped out of the compartment. 'Lost most of that the first time I died.'

'Ogan the twice-born,' moaned Zanasi, as though he incanted a prayer, or recognised the presence of a dark deity.

And you can't murder a dead man, an old voice echoed inside his mind. But was that for Jacob, or the killer he was hunting down?

He found what he was looking for in the tank's main map room, the smell of cordite overwhelming in the confined space, bodies from both nations lying across each other, united in death. Major Justus Alock was one of them – but he'd not quite met his end yet. Two natives had fallen across his legs. Alock hadn't needed their weight to trap him – the spear-bow bolt pinning his chest to the wall had proved adequate to that task. Tough bastard, though. Still clinging stubbornly to life. He might even live if he was dragged to a surgeon's station. Jacob let his hand drop where it had been hovering above his gun belt. The major's pistol lay out of reach where he had cast it, empty of shells, towards the gad who had left his spear-bow bolt embedded in the Weylander's chest as a dying gift.

'I didn't believe in the shamans' powers,' coughed Alock. 'Damn them for witch-doctors. But you, you knew exactly what we were going to do.'

'That's because I've seen you do it before,' said Jacob. 'Wasn't magic. Out in the Burn. Six hundred heavy cavalry, a perfect trident formation, coming down on us like thunder. You were leading them against the free companies hired by that fat idiot King Merara.'

'You're lying! You've never travelled further than the pew of your church.'

'I didn't recognise you at home, either, when we met in the palace gardens. We both had working names back in the day, Bad Justus. Just two dots at opposite ends of the battlefield, hidden in the smoke and the horror. Wading through corpses and making more for the warlords. No, I can't say we ever met face to face.'

'You're only a pastor!' protested Alock, moaning as he leant weakly on the spear shaft. 'A hick local. You're a churchman. Show me a little of God's mercy.'

Mary's voice sounded in his mind. *Mercy always bears richer fruits than justice.* But then, she had never been pursued by Bad Justus. 'Do you believe we can change, Major? Men like you and me?'

Alock looked up at Jacob, the only answer the barely veiled hatred in his face, cold and hard. That was one emotion he could feel just fine, even dying.

'No. I didn't think so either.'

'You're no better than me,' spat Alock, blood pooling from the corner of his mouth. 'You're no holier than a stealer.'

'There's one real crucial difference,' explained Jacob, easing one of his guns out from his belt. 'Your pile of corpses isn't going to get any higher.'

The single shot from his pistol echoed loudly around the tank's interior. Then he slowly holstered the pistol and shut the door on the tank's map room. For Jake Silver, for *Quicksilver*, by the time that man had finished with the people who'd murdered his wife and destroyed his home, he'd need wings to fly higher than the mound of bodies left behind.

Jacob climbed down to the prairie grass. Sariel had caught up with him, waiting in the grass, staring in revulsion at bodies scattered around the destroyed tank. Dead gads, blown apart and shot to pieces. Infantrymen from Hangel pin-cushioned by spear-bow bolts and filled with bullet holes from Weyland-bought rifles. There wasn't much to distinguish between them once they were gone. Just meat for the hyenas. And damned if any beast would taste the difference and complain.

'Nothing except a battle lost is half as melancholy as a battle won.' Sariel rubbed at his eyes as though he could blot out the sight of carnage. 'My mind is burning. I'm not sure who I am, anymore. And I'm not certain who you are, Your Grace, if a churchman you ever were.'

So who the hell am I? 'I'm back.'

'Sweet mercy, I wish I were.' Sariel fell to his knees and threw up over the ruined caterpillar track lying broken across the ground, his stomach heaving in the uncaring heat.

Carter couldn't take his eyes off the pistol barrel in Anna Kurtain's hand. He heard the old female overseer's exhortation to gun down Carter and his two friends and toss their corpses off the station.

'Don't kill Willow,' pleaded Carter. 'You want to shoot me, go ahead – but Willow isn't going to betray you. Kerge won't snitch either ... his people are so strange, no worker would listen if he did.'

Carter felt Willow squeeze his hand. 'Don't you make promises for me, Carter Carnehan, not to these filthy traitors.'

'Nor on my behalf,' said Kerge. 'If I can talk plainly enough for you to comprehend me, manling.'

'It's ironic isn't it?' said Anna. She turned the pistol towards Carter's head. 'You arrived here having promised my brother you'd take care of me, and here I am going to take care of you. Nothing personal in this, Northhaven.'

'Wait a minute!' barked Owen. He pointed towards Willow. 'Why did you call us traitors?'

'What else should I call you?' said Willow. 'Selling out your own people to the Vandians for extra rations and light duties.'

'Or maybe you're the Vandian infiltrators people in the barracks whisper about,' spat Carter. 'That wouldn't make it treachery – you're just doing your bit to make your foul, fat emperor even richer.'

'We're not traitors!' said Owen.

Carter raised his fist at the man. 'Maybe you're a knitting circle after all, then? Crawling into the dark to swap tunic patterns? I've been following you for weeks; seeing who you meet and how you operate. You overheard me talking about the escape. You made sure a tracking beacon was hidden on my transporter. And when we ran for freedom, your masters in the slave patrol were waiting to gun us down in cold blood. Good Weyland blood shed, so you and your friends survive while the rest of us waste away. I've buried our people, one body at a time. So it really doesn't matter to me if you were born in the imperium or born back home.'

Anna's pistol trembled in her hand. 'You said you knew who Owen is. What's going on here?'

'Damn fools,' swore Owen. 'They're not here to claim the reward. You really don't know what's going on here, do you?'

'You always did like the sound of your own voice,' said Carter. By his side, Willow appeared equally puzzled. 'But damned if I know what you're talking about. What reward?'

'The reward on bushy tail's head here, if someone snitches on him to the Vandians,' said Anna. 'Hands him over to the imperium.'

The other conspirators shifted uneasily, even the sorting line's overseer, Kassina Hedgepeth. She spoke up. 'Every few years we have to get rid of someone who works out the truth and decides that there's a deal to be done if they head to the radio room and blab to the imperials.' Kassina pointed to one of the men holding a club. 'That's why Burnet is in the circle. He works in the radio centre. Sending out supply requests and monitoring what the snitches are broadcasting back to the empire.'

'I frequently find myself confused by your nation's irrational beliefs and unpredictability,' said Kerge. 'But in this matter, you have truly surpassed my understanding.'

'I'm with him,' said Carter. 'What in God's name are you talking about?'

'Maybe we should kill them anyway,' said Burnet. 'How do we know they won't talk?'

'The same could have been said of you, once,' said Owen. 'We have fallen far, but not so far as to take innocent lives.' He stared at Duncan, Willow and Kerge and sighed deeply. 'Sit down. We will talk of why we are here. You and I, and all of the slaves from Weyland working and dying in the sky mines.' Carter did as the man ordered, Willow following hesitantly along with the gask. He noticed that Anna still kept her ancient pistol to hand, though.

'Years ago, when I was a child, agents of the imperium arrived in Weyland,' said Owen. 'They had a deal to offer our king: large amounts of metal and other resources in return for the one thing our country had in abundance ... human flesh. Slaves. The pact had to be secret to prevent the king from being strung up by mobs of his understandably disappointed subjects. Weyland was to be treated like a chicken coop, the empire's licensed raiders dipping their scaly hands in for fresh meat whenever the imperium needed labour. The pact would last for twenty years. Slave raids would be unopposed by the military and news of the attacks kept as quiet as possible. Then the slavers would move on to another nation that had been bribed to offer human sacrifices in return for a tiny sliver of the imperium's vast wealth. Weyland would be left rich ... if slightly poorer in population.'

'What are you talking about?' spat Carter. 'We're a member of the league. If the navy finds a ship carrying slaves we free them and burn the damn boat!'

'And Weyland's king had much the same reaction. The imperium's agents were thrown out on their ear and told never to return on pain of death. If any slavers given letters of marque by the empire dared to darken our skies, Weyland would invoke the pact of the league. To attack one is to attack all. The Rodalian skyguard would be ordered to pursue every hostile carrier violating our airspace; our cities and towns would be transformed into armed camps, protecting every prefecture as best it could.'

'That was not the Northhaven I was raised in,' said Willow.

'It would have been,' said Owen. 'But the king's brother heard about the terms of the deal. And when he did, he thought the king a sentimental fool. Let us be kind, maybe the brother told himself that with such resources at his command he could industrialise the country. Bring a similar standard of living to Weyland enjoyed by the richer countries of the south. And all he had to do was to make sure that the king and his more "immediate" heirs to the throne died in an avalanche, when such accidents were common in winter. He didn't even need the help of the Vandians' network of spies to arrange it. The royal guardsmen on duty were the brother's men, the rest of the staff at the winter lodge either bribed or silenced.'

'You're talking about the *last* king,' said Carter.

'And the brother is the man we now call King Marcus.'

'So that's why we're here?' said Carter, furiously. 'Why our regiment was out at sea on manoeuvres with the navy and the skyguard when the skels attacked us? Traded like horse flesh on market day by our own damn ruler!'

'Look on it as Weyland's small contribution to running the sky mines,' said Owen, irony but no trace of humour in his voice. 'Repaid in kind by the imperium, and all for the greater good.'

'How can you be so certain of this?' demanded Kerge.

'Because there were three survivors of the avalanche,' said Owen. 'Three young boy princes. They were discovered long after they should have been dead, by a guardsman who was a little less bribed and corrupt than the rest of his company. He couldn't let the children live, but he couldn't bring himself to slit their throats either. So he washed his hands by arranging for them to be in the next town raided by the skels, after which they would never be heard of again.'

Carter could hardly bring himself to ask the next question. 'And …?'

'Two of the princes died when the last sky mine was blown apart. Sabotaged, in all likelihood, by Helrena's rivals.'

'And the third,' said Anna, 'is protected by a circle of loyal Weylanders who keep his identity hidden. From traitors and snitches. From the Vandians who'd execute him in a second if they ever realised who he really was. The same circle who try to make sure we don't all die out here from hunger and overwork; say, by trying damn fool escape attempts with not a chance of success.'

'We didn't betray your escape, Carter,' said Owen. 'I warned you off it because it was obvious you were going to get yourself killed and bring punishment down on the rest of the station. Nobody can cross the dead zone in a transporter. The volcano's plains are littered with the bones of slaves who spent their final days drinking engine oil.'

Carter looked around the small cavern in shock. At these people who had survived against all the odds inside the sky mines for so long, ragged and hungry, but still bound together with a singular purpose.

'So, Mister Carnehan,' said Owen. 'That's why we are here. Both in the narrow sense of this cave and the wider sense of our predicament as slaves of the imperium. And that is the nature of the conspiracy you have unravelled so keenly. What do you have to say?'

Carter fell to his knee and bowed down before Owen, Willow touching the rock by his side. Not before Owen Paterson, but before Owen Hawkins. The true King of Weyland. 'Your *Majesty*.'

Duncan remembered the advice of the territorial regiment training sergeant as the assassin closed in on him, the paltry electrical cable sparking in his hand his sole defence; the one way to disarm an expert knife fighter that an opponent never expected – mainly because the move was completely insane. He ignored the grunts and yells behind him as Cassandra and Paetro struggled against impossible numbers, lunging forward and feinting with the cable, using the split second of uncertainty to catch the assassin's blade in his shoulder. Raw red pain flared as the dagger drove home, passing through his flesh and glancing against his scapular. *Better the shoulder than your heart.* His attacker couldn't withdraw the blade quick enough to stop Duncan breaking the man's hold on the hilt, then shoving the cable into the killer's chest, the assassin's turn to yell as Duncan hurled him backwards with a thousand volts coursing through his body. The killer hit the wall, pitching forward as the surge of energy dissipated, collapsing at the feet of his two clan brothers hauling a struggling, belligerent Doctor Horvak towards the plant lab. Their masks glanced down at their dead comrade, a goading present laid at their feet, before moving up towards Duncan. Both blades came up as one, signalling their contempt at delaying the inevitable just as the laboratory's main entrance exploded. Duncan was thrown to the floor by the shockwave, the assassins scattered and the doctor's bound form landing hard against him. Duncan's ears rang like a cathedral bell tower in full peel, his vision blurred. His thumping mind tried to focus on a group of hoodsmen rushing into the room, their leader, Apolleon, converted from a sly courtier into a terrible fury, leaping and thrusting with twin daggers, disordered assassins falling to the secret police's blades. Duncan could see from where he had collapsed that Paetro and Cassandra had also fallen to the floor. *From the blast, or put there by the assassins' blades? Please let them be alive.* Duncan tried to pick himself up. Doctor Horvak's body trapped his legs, the scientist moaning as Duncan attempted to push him off. *Not dead, not yet.* More murdisto joined the fray down the plant lab's corridor, far enough from the blast to still be combat effective, three or four killers rushing the counterattack's commander. Duncan must be badly concussed. Apolleon moved far too fast, his daggers growing longer, becoming part of his arms, twin sabre limbs, impaling and decapitating men quicker than Duncan's blinking eyes could comprehend. Murdisto assailants fell away, cut apart by the crazed butcher. Duncan finally managed to wriggle out from beneath the doctor and crawled towards Cassandra, the boots of Apolleon's men dancing by his side as they thrust and parried with assassins, corpses from both sides tumbling around him as he inched towards the young girl. The house's defenders finally turned the assault, pushing the raiders back down the corridor, a distant whine of the assassins' shields deflecting knife and sword strikes, howls and cries as they retreated. Duncan reached Cassandra and rested the back of his hand against her mouth. He could feel the intermittent sigh of warm breath. *Still alive!* He ran his hands across her body. All the blood on Cassandra's clothes appeared to belong to the assassins rather than the young noblewoman.

Paetro emerged out of the blurred edge of Duncan's vision, bleeding from multiple wounds. 'She lives?'

'Yes,' coughed Duncan, his throat on fire as though he had swallowed the explosion.

'Thank the stars!' gasped Paetro.

Duncan turned to gaze behind him. Apolleon knelt beside one of the assassins. And Duncan swore that for a brief second the nobleman's right hand had been a silvery spike withdrawing from the corpse's skull. He blinked, not believing the evidence of his eyes. When Duncan looked again the secret police chief appeared as normal as any of them. Two of his hoodsmen held Doctor Horvak in their arms, keeping him upright while they cut the bonds from the stunned doctor's hands. A team of medics ran in and began carefully examining the scientist. Shots sounded from the direction of the greenhouse, the slow measured burst of an execution being carried out.

'Don't you want to interrogate the prisoners?' said Paetro.

'They don't have tongues I can order pulled out. I know all I need to know,' said Apolleon. 'Circae does not understand the game she is playing. But she *will*.'

Duncan thought of the nobleman's twisted hand, reaching deep inside the corpse's skull. Could a dead man's mind cling to his secrets, before he became food for the worms? *I know all I need to know*. What manner of dark sorcery probed a mind so easily?

Paetro stalked out to the plant laboratory, returning seconds later with the news that the officer he had been trading insults with had fled down the rappel line. Then he limped back towards Duncan and Cassandra. 'You arrived just in time to save the young Highness, my lord Apolleon. Another few seconds and we could have been measured for burial shrouds.'

Apolleon looked down at the young noblewoman, as if noticing her for the first time. 'Of course.' He turned to the medics attending Doctor Horvak. 'The doctor is uninjured. See to *her*, you dolts.' He turned to Paetro and Duncan. 'But you are too modest; we only just arrived in time to finish off the raiders. This valiant defence was led by Lady Cassandra's gallant tutor and her staff.' He announced his verdict as though rewriting history, before staring sadly at the bodies of the two lab assistants. 'And many of you paid the price with your lives.' There was something about the way he said it that made Duncan's skin crawl. As though the two men had been ants scraped off the underside of his boot.

Paetro picked his pistol up from the floor. 'Aye, we merely did the duty we were sworn to.'

Paetro stood by Duncan while the medics examined Cassandra. Doctor Horvak assisted the team, irritably brushing off concerns about his own health as he located a black bag full of surgical instruments and medicines. The girl started to come round and Duncan gently wiped the grime of the explosion off her face. 'I told you that we'd be fine.'

'Are we with our ancestors now?' she whispered.

'Still soundly in the mortal world,' said Duncan.

'I thought I might see my father again.'

'We are all here to look after you,' said the doctor. 'Myself, Duncan and Paetro.'

'I've decided to cancel your lessons for the rest of the day, lass' said Paetro. 'That's something to be pleased about.'

'This is the doctor's chamber ... are my books here?'

She sounded far more concussed than Duncan; he looked worriedly over at Doctor Horvak.

'You need to rest. Your head glanced hard against a bench when you fell,' pronounced Horvak. The doctor gave Cassandra an injection to help her sleep while they anxiously waited for a stretcher to carry her to the castle's infirmary. Duncan found Apolleon looking at him in a peculiar way. Did he suspect Duncan had caught sight of something strange during the fight? That might not be a particularly safe situation for the Weylander. 'Is Princess Helrena alive? We heard a blast.'

'Such loyal *concern* from our plucky sky miner! Your mistress is unharmed. You heard the castle's gunnery control system overloading,' smiled Apolleon. 'The hold's security is far too tight for a bomb to be smuggled inside the gathering.' He tossed something that resembled an open shell down to the floor. Duncan looked again. It was a little black brooch! 'There was a roll of magnetic tape concealed inside it, designed to overload the defence generator. An inside job. My agents caught the woman responsible fleeing the central computer chamber. She serves as your young lady's pilot, I believe.'

Paetro groaned. 'Hesia! No? How can you be sure it was her?'

'Oh, we will be *quite* sure,' smiled Apolleon, coldly. 'All we require is time.'

'You must be mistaken,' said Paetro, his face uncharacteristically pale and uncertain. 'If Hesia wanted to betray the young Highness, all she needed to do was fake engine trouble and land her helo at an ambush site.'

Apolleon indicated the damage around them. 'Can you conceive of a better way for Circae to undermine Princess Helrena than snatching her granddaughter under the noses of the house's gathered allies? What a message to send. Stand against me and I can attack you without mercy anywhere and at any time. You are never safe. Ah, dear Circae. There is a woman who understands imperial politics.'

If Duncan hadn't already been on his knees, he would have dropped to them. *Adella*. Adella was the one who had slipped Hesia the brooch, to silence the castle's automated defences. She had been willing to sacrifice Cassandra and Duncan's lives for her new master. Merely collateral damage as the assassins silenced every witness to their real mission ... abducting Doctor Horvak. Duncan hadn't believed his hatred for her could grow any deeper, but he was shocked to find that among the ruins of love, there were still depths left to plumb. He could have almost forgiven Adella's treachery in throwing him to the wolves a second time. But for trying to kill Cassandra? Never.

'It's Baron Machus,' rasped Duncan. 'He's the one who sabotaged the castle's defences.'

'And how do you know *that*?' said Apolleon, the menace in his tone obvious.

'I saw one of his entourage pass that brooch to Hesia. Hesia told me it had fallen from her uniform on the airfield where Baron Machus noticed it had come off.'

'Ever the gallant.' Apolleon jabbed a finger at his hoodsmen. 'Locate the baron and his party and ensure they are detained!'

The agents sprinted away as ordered, returning five minutes later with a sense of foreboding that Duncan could detect even below the anonymity of their masks. Bowing to the head of the secret police they gave their report. When Apolleon turned back to Duncan, Paetro and Horvak, he appeared unexpectedly sunny. 'So, as reliable as any confession. Baron Machus and his people were called away to "urgent business" at his fortress five minutes before the assault began.'

Paetro shook his head in fury. 'The princess's own cousin ...'

'Every family is unhappy in its own way,' said the doctor, gravely.

'A very distant cousin,' said Apolleon, 'with, it seems, quite extravagant ambitions. The cretin has finally over-reached himself.'

Duncan could barely look at the head of the secret police in case his eyes betrayed what he had seen. This cruel nobleman carried far too many secrets. All the science of the world offered as tribute to the imperium. And what weird science had Apolleon plundered to transform himself into the deadly creature Duncan had glimpsed? Or had his mind been overcome by chemicals spilled across the laboratory? God knows, his head was throbbing hard enough. One thing at least was certain. Circae knew exactly what she was doing. She hadn't been targeting her granddaughter; she had been seeking to disrupt whatever mysterious scheme the doctor was engaged in for Apolleon. But Duncan could hardly question Circae about the nature of that mysterious project. And as for Apolleon, the quicker the ruthless nobleman departed the castle, the safer Duncan and his friends would be.

FOURTEEN

A TRUE HEART'S WANT

Willow walked back to her barracks in a daze, passing through the maze of passages. She didn't know which she should be more shocked at. The fact that one of the station's slaves was the true heir to the throne of Weyland, or that when it had come to it, Carter Carnehan had been willing to sacrifice his life to save hers. The plotters had scattered back to their duties. Kerge returned to his repair bay. Only Carter walked with Willow. He had changed. The sky mines altered everyone, of course. Or perhaps the deaths and hardships just stripped away the lies and falsehoods people surrounded themselves with, revealing their true identity beneath their layers. That was a mining of sorts, too.

'So you still don't know who betrayed your escape,' said Willow, if only to break the pensive silence between them.

'I'm not sure I care anymore,' said Carter. 'I was so certain Owen and Anna sold us out. I would have brained the lot of them, and for what? What would I have achieved? Cracked the head of a man who should have worn the crown back home?'

'Anyone could have betrayed you,' said Willow. 'Maybe one of the others trusted too easily. Talked to the wrong person or was noticed stealing supplies for the breakout.'

'I led them to their deaths,' said Carter. 'Eshean, Noah and the others. I nearly got you and Kerge killed back there, too. We could have charged in and Anna could have gunned us down with that antique pistol, thinking that *we* were the turncoats.'

'But we're still alive,' said Willow.

'And so is Owen,' said Carter. 'I lost my two brothers to the plague. He lost his to his uncle's treachery. And we're both here as slaves, no way of ever getting home. Where's the difference between us?'

'There's one difference. The Vandians don't care who you or I were back home – daughter of a Landor or a pastor's son. But if the empire ever finds out who Owen is, they'll execute him immediately to protect their tame pretender.'

'Give me time,' said Carter. 'Maybe I'll get Owen and Anna killed in my next doomed escape scheme.'

'Self-pity isn't an attractive trait,' said Willow. 'You like fighting and you don't give up.'

'That's just a polite way of saying I'm pig-headed and stubborn.'

'It's kept you alive,' said Willow.

'No,' said Carter. 'People do that. *You* do that.'

'Now you sound like Owen.'

'Whatever else I am, I'm not a king.' He slowed Willow in the corridor and uncertainly pulled her towards him before kissing her. She nearly slapped him in surprise, before her displeasure melted away and she yielded. It was almost as she had imagined so many times over the years. 'What was that for?'

'I wanted to see if you really were mooning after a fool,' said Carter.

'And what's your verdict?'

'Well, I've certainly been a fool.'

'That, I find hard to disagree with,' said Willow.

'It's not because you thought we were going to die back there?' asked Carter.

Carter sounded as though the answer might actually matter to him. Maybe he had changed more even than Willow had realised. 'No, Carter Carnehan. I believe I know myself well enough to say I've been in love with you a little longer than that.'

Carter looked as though he was about to cry. It seemed to be a good evening for surprises. 'Are you sure you're the real Carter? You're not some peculiar fire goblin who swapped bodies with him down by that volcano?'

'I can't protect you,' said Carter. 'I can't save you from any of this. I don't think I can bear knowing that. We're trapped here until one of us ends up in the fever room, or dragged out broken from under a rock fall, or plummeting into the heavens from a shattered sky mine, or—'

'Or something real in your life for once?' smiled Willow. 'Of all the things to be scared of – not the empire or their guns or their whips. Here, or at home, nobody ever knows how long they will have together.'

'For me, it might not be that long,' said Carter. His eyes were red and wide, as though he was about to confess to a terrible crime. 'I don't know about fire goblins on the surface, but I saw some things during the escape attempt. Mad, impossible things – a labyrinth where time moves slower; with a portal of fire, discarded angels' wings, and water and short-swords that seemed to appear when you will them into being. And ever since I was found on the slopes I've slowly been going mad, my head filled with visions and nonsense. Vandia's past, the nations that have fought and died to seize control of the strato-volcano. It's like all of the world's been packed inside my head and is wrestling to get out. All the souls of the millions of slaves who've died out here in the sky mines. There are so many bones across the plains, and I've been adding to them every day, rolling the corpses of our dead into the sky.'

'Your mask was damaged and your filters exhausted during the escape; that's all,' said Willow. 'There are tunnellers who end up in the fever rooms like that; they've breathed in a little too much volcano gas.'

'What happened on the surface was real,' said Carter. 'And the sights I see in my visions seem real too when I'm experiencing them, as real as you standing here.'

Willow kissed him again. 'Well, I'm probably the mad one to feel like this about you. So there it is … we deserve each other.' In truth, she never thought she could feel so happy. If she could travel back to the cells of the skels' slave carrier and tell herself she might one day feel like this, she wouldn't have believed the words coming from her own lips. The sky mines and the imperium and their internecine struggles, they could go to the devil for all that Willow Landor cared. She had everything she needed right here.

'I don't deserve you,' said Carter. 'But maybe I will, one day.'

'And what day would that be?'

'The day after we escape,' said Carter.

'How?' asked Willow, fighting to keep the scepticism from her voice. They passed through the station's main tunnels. Workers moved about, stowing equipment and heading for the canteen chambers and their barracks. She lowered her voice so that only Carter could hear. 'You heard what Owen said. Nobody has ever flown out of the dead zone on a transporter, no matter how much extra fuel you load onto it.'

'My plan didn't just involve a transporter flight,' said Carter, his old reckless confidence seeming to return. 'And I was thinking too small, before. I should have taken everybody. Seized the radio-room, smashed the equipment and to hell with any snitches. The empire can't chase everybody at once!'

'Please tell me that you're seeing things now,' said Willow. What rash plans rushed through his mind? *Maybe he is slowly going mad?*

'I'm seeing the way things can be. All I have to do is get Owen and his knitting circle on our side.'

She glanced around the corridor, watching the slaves walk past them; every one of the workers potentially the informer who had wrecked the first escape attempt. *Maybe.* 'You need to be careful.'

'I'm taking you with me,' said Carter. 'That's why I failed the first time. My plan wasn't honourable.'

'Honour is a poor shield against an empire's bullets,' warned Willow. Someone called out along the passage and she turned as she realised it was her name being shouted. By Thomas Gale, the head of the station. He came down the corridor towards her and Carter, but it was the company of Vandian soldiers behind the old man that caught her attention. Her heart missed a beat. What if they were here to punish Carter again? Maybe some officious imperial bureaucrat had judged the number of strikes taken during the slave's flogging too lenient and increased them. It was obvious Carter was still wracked with pain and turning feverish at times; he believed the gibberish he

483

had just told her. How could Carter possibly survive a second whipping?

'He's too weak!' she cried, practically throwing herself at the station coordinator.

'Who's too weak?' asked Gale.

'Carter,' said Willow.

Gale seemed to notice the man behind her for the first time and his face creased into a snort. 'Good, maybe he'll make a little less trouble for the rest of us in future. But I haven't come on fever room duties; it's you I'm looking for.' The closest soldier stepped forward with a small steel machine and scanned the tattoo on her arm. 'This is the one!'

Willow gasped as two of them seized her and started to drag her along the corridor. Carter shouted something and tried to stop them, but one of the men slammed a rifle butt into his gut, felling him. It was all happening too fast.

Carter tried to get up. 'What are you doing?'

The soldier with a rifle forced him back down. 'Obeying orders, slave. Not questioning them.'

'Where are you taking her?'

'How would I know?' snarled the soldier. 'This station is behind on its quotas. She your sweetmeat, is she? Maybe she's going to be fed into a smelter to encourage the rest of you to get off your lazy arses and swing the lead.'

Carter leapt for the soldier, but one of the guard's friends drew his pistol and cracked its handle across his face. Willow winced at the cruel sound of the impact. He went down to the ground again and looked like he would stay there.

'Leave him alone! He's done nothing!' Willow shouted at Gale.

'Everyone's done something, my dear,' he smiled apologetically, indicating this was all outside his control. Which, in truth, it probably was.

Willow struggled, trying to look back towards Carter. *No, no, this isn't happening. Not now.* She just managed a glimpse of Carter, collapsed on the bare stone floor of the passage, one of the guards giving him a sound kicking in his ribs for daring to intervene in their business. Then she was dragged up the stairs towards the surface. This wasn't how it was meant to end! She had waited most of her life for this moment, to be with Carter, and now it was stolen from her. The moment belonged to the imperium; her body and life, the empire's possessions.

It was warm inside the castle infirmary, a constant temperature, but Cassandra's hand felt cold to Duncan. Her eyes fluttered open. 'You're still here?'

'I am,' said Duncan.

'I asked one of the nurses to collect something from my rooms. A gift for you. Reach under the pillow.'

Duncan did, finding the cold steel of a heavy circular medallion. 'Is this a campaign medal? Paetro had something similar. In fact, he has quite a few.'

'This was gift to me from my father, before he left the last time. You wear it over your chest. It's for luck.'

'If I take it, where will your luck come from?'

'My luck sent you to me,' Cassandra smiled. 'So I suppose I don't need it anymore.' She drifted back into a shallow sleep. Duncan sensed Cassandra's mother standing in the infirmary's doorway before he saw her, a brooding silent presence behind the respirator's hiss next to the bed.

'How is she?' asked Princess Helrena.

'Doctor Horvak believes she will be fine.'

'Perhaps you were right, Duncan of Weyland. I should have sold my holdings and fled as far as the money would take us.'

'No. I was wrong. If your enemies can reach inside your castle with all its defences and soldiers, then they would come for you and Cassandra anywhere you ran.'

'Circae might forget, given enough time and fresh distractions. When you live in the heart of the imperium there is always another enemy stalking you, a more immediate threat to deal with.'

Duncan noticed that the princess's clothes had brown powder burns. 'You were in the fight?'

'Five companies of assassins landed in addition to the cadre that attacked you. Three were diversions, two tried to assault my allies at the gathering. We are still sweeping the castle and grounds. Give a murdisto an inch of shadow and they can hide in it for days, as still as a stone. I wouldn't wish to greet one of them in a week's time when I am resting in my bath.'

'Find them all and kill them,' said Duncan, the venom in his voice surprising him even as he spoke the words.

'Apolleon says you fought like a tiger to save my daughter. The doctor tells me he saw you dispatch two assassins with an electrical cable. You were not trained to face murdisto, you were not even armed.'

'It was my duty.'

'I might accept that from Paetro, but not from you.' She leant in to kiss him. It wasn't like before. There was none of the passion, but little of the cruelty either. If a kiss could be said to be sad, then this was such a caress. 'Cassandra is all I have in the world. All I have left of what once mattered most to me. When you saved her from abduction in the sky mines, you were protecting your life and all of your countrymen on the station. But this time you shielded her when you could have run, when you had every excuse to take flight.'

'I'm fairly sure that makes me a fool,' said Duncan.

'Then perhaps I am, also.' Helrena passed him a small silver tube.

'What is this?'

'Your second gift of the day. It contains your papers of freedom. You are now listed on the imperium's rolls as a citizen. There is a second set inside for your sister, in the sky mines. A ship has already picked her up from the station and is flying her here.'

'Willow!' Duncan was stunned to silence. He was free, and so was Willow? He could hardly believe this wasn't a dream. Perhaps he was actually inside the infirmary, wounded and made feverish by the assassins, and this was the result? But it wasn't imagined. He knew reality, and this felt like the most real thing that had happened to him since the skels turned up to raid the town for slaves. He had his freedom and so did Willow!

'I hope you will stay here with us,' said Helrena. 'To help protect Cassandra. We can find a position on the staff for you sister, too. If you really wish, you can wait for a ship to head out in the direction of your homeland. That may take six months and I would not recommend staying in the capital outside of my house's protection. Circae is quite vindictive. She will certainly hear of your part in the castle's defence and seek to pay you back for it. She'd order your sister garrotted in front of you just to revel in your pain.'

'I don't know what to say.'

'Then you might as well tell me you will stay. It is a curious turn of events. My cousin, whose family owes everything to my house and my rise in the empire – who would be nothing but backwater traders without me – has chosen Circae's faction. Yet you opt to stand with me. With such insanity, saying you will remain will create some small semblance of balance in the world.'

He gazed at Cassandra. She seemed so peaceful at sleep. 'That's not why I saved her. For my freedom, I mean.'

'I realise that. By rights you should be dead.' Helrena snorted. 'Facing murdisto with a loose cable? Send me lucky generals over sensible ones – which emperor was it who said that?'

'Doctor Horvak will know.'

'I am sure he will. He knows almost everything else.'

'You should free the doctor, too.'

'I would gladly send him to have his slave tattoo removed, but he might return to his country. I could allow that, but Apolleon most certainly would not.'

'He's not … *right*. Nothing good will come from dealing with that man. Not for you, your house or Cassandra.'

'Be careful you don't notice *too* much,' said Helrena. 'There are many things you don't understand about what my house is planning; and you will sleep better and safer for your ignorance. Besides, I don't have so many allies at court that I can afford to be selective. And the only thing worse than calling the head of the secret police your partner is calling him your enemy.'

'He's evil. Can't you sense it?'

'Let us say that he does bad things for a good cause. Better he is that way, than the reverse.' She brushed Cassandra's hair out of her eyes and stood up to go. 'Let me know your intention after your sister arrives and you have talked matters over with her. For my daughter's sake, I hope you will find that Duncan of *Vandia* has a better ring to it than your barbarian backwater.'

'And for your sake?'

'There are things I cannot say or promise anyone,' said Helrena. 'That is how matters are and how they must be, whether you are a slave or a citizen. You are younger than I, but you are an adult. You understand this.'

'And if I was a prince of the imperium?'

'Then one of us would probably end up getting killed,' Helrena sighed. 'That is the way matters usually end.' She shut the door to the medical bay, leaving Duncan alone with his thoughts. He had a world more to think about than when she'd come in.

Jacob and the other expedition members halted, their gad hosts indicating they had reached the place that they had been travelling towards; a thick stand of trees on the prairie the only landmark aside from the ubiquitous tall dry grass. Jacob wasn't sure what to expect. The great diviner Narlrem had told him the travellers were to be rewarded for their help in ushering in the gads' long prophesied new age. Jacob had hoped that meant Hangel's new rulers had paid for air passage south on a merchant carrier. But this was too far away from the plateau's airfields for anything but a forced landing in the grass. Now Jacob suspected this was merely another ceremony where they would be honoured with crowns of dried flowers and fine words. He should have guessed from the number of shamans and tribal chiefs accompanying their parade out of the city gates and into the wilds. He tried not to let his disappointment show. He was itching to be in the air again, closing the distance between him and Carter.

'This way,' said Zanasi. He led the four travellers towards the trees. 'If you leave here,' said Zanasi, talking directly to Jacob. 'What will you do?'

Jacob didn't like the way the war leader had intoned *if*. 'You know what I'll do. Find my son.' *You'll do whatever it takes*, said the voice within him. *Kill anyone and everyone who gets in your way*. He reached inside his duster. The pistols were both there; and the travel pack's weight on his back, too. Maybe the expedition would be better off heading away right now, and let the gads sing to the sky.

'And what if you find more than that?'

'My son. The rest of my people taken in the raid if I can. That's all that matters to me.' *You're a liar. You're going to kill them all. Everyone who played a part in Mary's death.*

'We shall see,' said Zanasi.

'We're all still friends, aren't we?'

'In this life, twice-born.'

'That's good, because any other way at least one of us would have cause to regret it.'

As they got closer, Jacob saw the glade had grown up around another of the stone circles, dark stones brooding under the leafy canopy's shade. Jacob felt the same sense of foreboding he had back in Weyland when coming across these ancient structures. Vines circled the trees, surrounding them as thick as coiled rope, but none dared touch any of these menhirs laid long before the memories of man. The stones stood untouched, remote and alien, beyond the reach of entropy.

'This is another one your ceremonies?' asked Jacob.

'It is,' said Zanasi. 'Although none of our diviners have practised this ritual in living memory.'

'Prophecies are not rendered tangible every week,' said Khow. He examined his abacus box, tapping the screen. 'Most unexpected. It has stopped working.'

Jacob pointed at the cover of the tree. 'No sun.'

'I do not understand how its battery can be drained of charge?' The gask shook his metal device, annoyed.

Natives entered the space and sat down, surrounding the standing stones, forming a larger ring around the glade's fringes.

'This ancient place is a map of woe,' protested Sariel. 'Why have we come here, noble gads?'

The great diviner Narlrem appeared in the clearing, his people clearing a path for the recently crowned ruler of the land. 'We promised we would help you, Jok. And for the gads, nothing weighs heavier than a promise given. Ignore your fear. Embrace the stones.'

'I remember these circles,' said Sariel, reluctantly laying his hands on the nearest stone's runes. 'Such rocks sing to me, sometimes. I do not care for them or their idle chatter.'

'It is a song you helped to create, Jok,' said Narlrem. 'But your mind is so occupied and broken that the part of you that remembers their rhythm lies buried deep.'

'Do not speak of them! They are very dangerous. They call foul things.'

Sheplar leaned in to Jacob, whispering so that only the pastor could hear. 'Well, they certainly called us here.'

'Dangerous they may be,' said the new ruler of Hangel. Narlrem appeared uncharacteristically grim, his eyes wide and sad. 'But we are to help you remember the many paths and the infinite maze.'

'How is this going to assist us?' asked Jacob, growing impatient.

'You must hear the song,' said Narlrem. 'Sit within the circle. Each of you must lay a hand on a stone. Jok, try and think of who you were before you were destroyed by the Land Mother. Khow of the gask-kind, hold your child inside your mind, focus on his captivity.'

'And what must I think of during this ritual?' asked Sheplar.

'You and the twice-born must clear your minds as best you can. We need to focus solely on Jok and your gask companion.'

'Return to me my wings and I will happily fly away from these plume-plucked barnacles,' complained Sariel.

Jacob did as he was bid, sitting inside the stone circle with the expedition members while the council of diviners passed wooden bowls around the gathering. The gads dipped their fingers into the same evil tasting paste that had left his head spinning out on the plains. He laid a hand on the nearest stone. Its surface was cool in the shade of the trees, perhaps colder than it should be. A primordial shiver crept down his spine. Beyond the stones the diviners had joined hands and swayed in unison, the other gads incanting a deep, moaning refrain. If this were a blessing, it couldn't be counted a joyous one. It sounded like a death dirge to Jacob's ears. But the gads were a superstitious people, and Jacob needed all the help he could get, however tenuous.

'Their song will destroy the stones,' muttered Sariel. 'It always does.'

Making a lie of his words, the gads' singing appeared to have a more subtle effect than destruction. Alien runes cut into the stone began to glow gently as though they had been filled with luminescent lichen, reacting to the gads' lament by pulsing into life in the half-light. Under Jacob's hand the stone surface tickled his palm, vibrating, an itch growing stronger and stronger. He tried to pull his hand away from the rock but it was as though his skin had melted into the stone – as if he was becoming stone himself. Jacob tried to shout, to protest, but the vibration became too strong, his throat's dry shout lost to it, stone and skin quaking and trembling, every iota of his being converted into an excited shudder. Outside the circle, the distant chanting joined with the stones' song. A protective bubble had formed around the stone circle, protecting the gads from the ferocity of the energies being unleashed within it, the victims sealed off. Fire seemed to rotate around them. Jacob moaned in terrible agony, even that noise lost. *A trap after all, then.* That's what you got for trusting in the kindness of strangers – letting your guard down for a second. Jacob felt as if his head was going to explode, his last thoughts only regrets. *Carter, my son!* All the lost chances passed between them, the mislaid opportunities that had filled Carter's life and ruined his future. Jacob yearned to travel back to that moment, so long past, on Rake's Field and take a different path. Make peace between Carter and Duncan Landor; force his son to see sense over Adella and Willow. Pack his family off for a trip to the coast before the slavers struck. So many paths, so many choices, and how few of them ended up *here*. It was as if Jacob walked the paths of the great fractal tree that the gask spoke of. He fell to his knees, his hands fused with the stone. Sariel, Khow, Sheplar, their bodies hummed, shaking so fast they were blurring. Plasma danced off the stones' surface, coiling fingers of star-stuff, as though the sun itself bled through these rocks. Then a fierce discharge claimed everyone inside the circle. And the very final fragment of the diviners' visions was at last given truth. *You're meant to be dead; your body obliterated in an explosion.*

Duncan had expected Willow to cry when she stepped off the helo and onto the landing field. When she saw her brother was still alive … let alone when he gave her the joyous news that she was now a free woman. What Duncan hadn't expected was her to launch herself at him, swinging at him and nearly knocking him to the tarmac. He had played this moment inside his mind a dozen times, but it had never ended with him falling against the cold steel of the helo's hull, the surprised pilot walking away, only glancing back as Willow tried to hammer Duncan with her fists.

Duncan grabbed Willow's arms, pushing her back and trying to hold her still. 'What the hell are you doing?'

'What are *you* doing? Dressed here like some imperial lord while our friends are starving and dying in the sky mines? What about Carter and Kerge and Anna and everyone else? So they have to keep swinging a pickaxe at the princess's enemies, while you and I eat off the gold plates they're being murdered for?'

'I can't help them,' said Duncan. 'I can't help *everyone*.'

'You're a Landor, all right,' said Willow. 'You've helped yourself just fine.'

'Don't you understand,' spluttered Duncan, 'what a feat it is to be raised from a slave to a citizen? How hard and rare that is? Not just for me, but for *you*. We can stay here; see a whole new world – an empire so large every nation of the league could be squeezed into a single imperial province. Or we can travel home. Back to Weyland.'

'And how would I ever look our farmers in the eye again, knowing I had left their sons and daughters to rot to death under the whip?'

'Tell them you escaped,' said Duncan. 'Isn't that the truth? We *have* escaped!'

'I haven't escaped! I'll never escape this foul place, not if I lived to be a hundred as a hermit in the Rodalian mountains. Part of me will always be trapped in the sky mines. You might as well ship me back to the station. I'd sooner take my chances with our people than accept anything from a single dirty Vandian.'

'That's not your decision,' said Duncan. 'One thing's the same here. I get to inherit the house, and you get to do what I order.'

'You can stick it,' said Willow. 'Your inheritance and your fine Vandian clothes, both. You're not free. You're a greater slave than anyone back in the mines.'

'For God's sake,' said Duncan. He pointed to the woman from the castle that was meant to show Willow to her rooms. 'Escort her inside until she's come to her senses.'

Duncan heard Paetro chortle behind him as his sister was led away shouting abuse back to him. 'It's not funny. What just happened here?'

'In a woman's mind? Who's to know, lad. But with the best will in the world, it was always going to take her time to adjust to the news.'

'I thought she'd be grateful – I thought she'd be happy!'

'She's out of that hell anchored above the volcano,' said Paetro. 'You did the right thing by her, whether she's grateful for it or not. Whatever your sister feels about freedom, it's beyond your influence. The best a man can do is only what he knows to be right – how the rest of the world reacts to it is up to them.'

'I'll visit her later; after she's had a chance to calm down,' said Duncan.

'One thing I learnt in the legion,' said Paetro, 'it's that everyone around you has to take responsibility for their own fate. You can lead people to battle, get them to the right place at the right time, but you can never make them fight. You contest your own little corner of a campaign and trust everyone else will do what they need to … to survive and win through.'

'Does Willow really expect me to wave a magic wand and set every slave in the empire free?'

'Not even the emperor could emancipate the slaves,' said Paetro. 'Not with all of the imperial houses relying on them for labour. Old Jaelis Skar would be out on his ear the moment he reached for pen and parchment to sign such a decree.'

Duncan cursed her under his breath. Who did Willow think she was, arriving here and making him feel like a traitor after all he had done for her? Maybe he should have let her sweat in the castle for a month or two as a slave? Then she might show a bit of gratitude for being raised to a citizen.

'No, I like her,' said Paetro. 'Your sister has fire. Maybe the princess could petition the emperor to strip Machus of his title and make your sister a baroness instead!'

'I suspect Willow's going to be insufferable enough as a citizen,' said Duncan.

'Come away, lad. Lady Cassandra intends to visit Hesia before she's transferred to the secret police's tender mercies. I want to see what Hesia has to say for herself, first. I don't want the young Highness any more upset over the attack than she already is.'

It was true; Cassandra had taken the betrayal by her personal helo pilot badly. And she wasn't the only one who wanted answers. 'I thought Princess Helrena would insist she interrogated Hesia first.'

'The only thing Hesia has to tell us is *why*. And that won't help us sleep better at night, not when we already know the *who*. The princess is happy to let the imperial torturers get their hands dirty.'

Except that Hesia would tell her interrogators about Adella's involvement in the attack on the castle. It shouldn't have mattered to him. Adella deserved everything Helrena was going to throw in the direction of her treacherous cousin. After Baron Machus lay dead, Adella would be without a master or a protector. She could be sent back to the sky mines for all that Duncan cared, along with a message that she'd betrayed the Weylanders' escape attempt. 'Cassandra wants to know why Hesia sold us out, even if her mother doesn't.'

'So do I,' sighed Paetro. 'But I have other reasons.'

He didn't elaborate on them as they travelled inside the castle, down the deep, damp concrete passages that led to the hold's bunkers. And its cells. They reminded Duncan of the slave pens back on the skel carrier. Hesia squatted in a cage on her own. Her face was badly bruised, purple marks and swellings everywhere. It appeared Apolleon's hoodsmen hadn't been over-gentle when they captured her sabotaging the castle's gun control system

'I wondered when you'd come,' said Hesia.

'And here I am,' said the bodyguard. Paetro sat down on the edge of a bare table. The gaoler nodded to the pair of them, announcing he was going to leave for a couple of minutes to collect his lunch.

'Cassandra wants to come and visit you, too,' said Duncan. 'She needs to know why you did it.'

'She can wait until the imperial torturers have finished with me,' said Hesia. 'Then she can read their report and be sure.'

'*I* want to know,' said Paetro. 'Imperial torturers be hanged! Aren't I worth an honest answer; or has Circae bribed you too well to talk, even now that you're captured and blown?'

'My sister has bone cancer,' said Hesia.

'Your *sister*?' said Paetro, incredulously.

'Yes,' said Hesia. 'Aradela doesn't have more than a couple of years left. And the only cure for it is in the hands of the imperial surgeons. A treatment reserved, like everything else, for the upper-celestial caste.

Circae's agents found out about her illness and approached me. Circae said if I brought down the defence grid during the gathering, she'd arrange for one of the surgeons to save Aradela's life.'

'You should have told me! Princess Helrena could have helped you, helped *her*.'

'What, help the relation of a lowly helo pilot, someone who doesn't even serve in the house? The low-caste daughter of a soldier and a freed slave? You know the imperial medical college is only allowed to operate on the celestial-upper caste. But Circae has something on one of the surgeons. She'll force the cure out of them. What would the princess do? Petition her father to make Aradela a countess so she can get the care she needs? This was the only way.'

'You betrayed your *house*.'

'Family, house, empire, gods,' said Hesia. 'In that order. Who taught me that?'

'You're a damnable fool!'

Duncan raised his hand towards her, but she spurned his act of sympathy, pulling back away from the cage's steel bars. He glanced over to the armoured lock-box on the wall that held the cell's keys. *What would I have risked to save Willow if she was sick? As much as this?*

Hesia turned her back on both of them, 'I was raised that way. I'll die, but she'll live.'

'You expect Circae to keep her word?' said Duncan.

'The old witch wouldn't last long at court if she didn't,' said Hesia.

'It won't matter,' said Paetro, annoyed almost beyond words, gripping the bars of the cell so tight his hands turned white. 'When Apolleon's torturers have finished with you, they'll know why you betrayed the mistress. Do you think Apolleon will let Circae keep her word? He'll arrange an unpleasant accident for Aradela to send a warning about the cost of betrayal. Aradela'll end up raped and strangled, or with a blade in her back during a city riot. That's all you've achieved for her. A quick nasty death rather than a long, slow one.'

'I wasn't *intending* to get caught,' retorted Hesia. 'Leave me your knife and I'll end matters honourably. I'll make sure I never reach the secret police alive.'

'Aradela,' groaned Paetro. 'Why, why did it have to be her? She should have told me.'

And then it hit Duncan. *The low-caste daughter of a soldier and a freed slave.* Hesia's sister. But Paetro's *daughter*. And now he was going to lose both of his children at the same time.

Paetro's hand went to the dagger hanging from his belt. Then he shook his head. 'My duty, lass, to the house. To hand you over to Apolleon's people.'

'Leave me your knife!' she begged.

'It's too late for that,' said Paetro. 'You've made your choice and now you must live with the consequences.'

They went into the passage outside to wait for the gaoler to return with his food.

'Paetro—' said Duncan.

He raised his hand as he strode away, brooking no argument. 'There's nothing more to be said. The young Highness isn't to be allowed down here. We'll tell Lady Cassandra she sold us out for money. It's better she grows up hating Hesia than feeling pity for her.'

'You're sure about that?'

'Aye, of course I am,' said Paetro. 'I wish to the gods *I* still believed she'd betrayed us for the money.'

'I'm sorry,' said Duncan.

'And a helo stick is meant to be a solid, safe job,' said Paetro. 'The legion does the dying while the pilots do the flying. That's the saying.'

Duncan could still hear Hesia begging and shouting for a knife, but at least they didn't have to look at her anymore. When the gaoler returned, he was late, breathless, flustered and empty-handed.

'What's the matter?' asked Duncan.

'Damnedest thing,' said the gaoler. 'A patrol's caught a gang of vagrants in the gardens. Must have wandered in during the attack while the defences went down.'

'Vagrants?' said Paetro. 'The guards were meant to be searching for murdisto.'

'Well, this lot are no assassins,' he laughed. 'Tinkers and travellers more like. They were found blotto, drunk out of their gourds and totally passed out. They'd made a camp in the centre of the Stone Garden, set a fire in the centre and nearly burnt the place down!'

'There'll be hell to pay for the guards on the ramparts,' said Paetro. 'And the sector police in the district, too. If they can't even keep a gang of drunken beggars out.'

'Peace, Paetro, our boys *were* shooting towards the sea and the sky at the time, rifles and no radar,' said the gaoler. He moved against the wall as the patrol came marching down the stairs, flanking the captured vagrants.

Paetro muttered something about that being the point of an effective diversion, but Duncan had stopped listening to his friend. Among the vagrants was someone he recognised. Someone who shouldn't be within a million miles of the Castle of Snakes: Jacob Carnehan, the pastor of Northhaven! He looked a state, his clothes dirty and travel-worn, his face gaunt and ill-shaven. But he had undergone a more fundamental change than that; the soft contented glow the man had carried around like a halo was gone. In its place was something sharp and dangerous, the still calm replaced by a barely suppressed fury. Jacob Carnehan didn't look like a vagrant. He looked like a madman escaped from an asylum, his veins filled with brimstone and a wrath that had addled his mind.

'Landor!' cried Jacob. 'Duncan Landor!' The pastor sounded groggy, as though he had been drinking. But as far as Duncan knew the churchman was teetotal. And that was the least bizarre part about his near miraculous appearance here.

The soldiers didn't stop. They shoved the prisoners along the corridor and into the holding chamber. There was a gask among them; an old white-bearded man who fairly deserved the label of tramp, and a pilot in the uniform of the Rodalian Skyguard. Had the Rodalian flown them here? It wasn't possible, was it? Too great a distance lay between the empire and Weyland. It should have taken decades for them to reach the capital, even if they rarely touched down to refuel.

'How does that tinker know you?' said Paetro.

'He's from home,' said Duncan, trying to rediscover his voice. 'From … Weyland …'

'Too old to have been taken as slave for the sky mines, I reckon,' said Paetro. 'Have the skels been raiding for the other houses? Selling our wastage on the sly?'

'I really don't know.'

'Do you think he came looking for you?'

'Let's find out,' said Duncan.

They went back into the cell block. Old man Carnehan was being pushed into a cage next to Hesia, the other prisoners already tossed inside. Duncan could hardly believe the pastor was here. It had been an age since he'd had a reminder of home, by something as concrete as this, a new face. A reminder that Duncan had once possessed a life far removed from slave and citizen of the imperium. He no longer felt homesick for Northhaven. He could barely even remember it now.

Paetro strode up to the patrol's sergeant. 'Any clues how this lot got here?'

The sergeant pointed to the men's personal possessions, travel bags and a walking staff and gun belts hanging from hooks on the wall. 'Travellers with a merchant caravan, maybe? They were carrying basic revolving chamber pistols, barbarian trading currency and everything you'd need for a life on the road ... fire-starters, bed rolls, snares and fishing hooks. That prickly-looking twisted fellow has a hand-held computer which is unusually advanced. Thought it might be an artillery fire control, but it only has mathematical functions as far as I can see.'

'What are you going to do with them?' asked Duncan.

'Find out how they jumped the wall, what drunken route they weaved through the minefield, and then give them a few good stripes for their cheek,' said the sergeant. 'Fifty lashes apiece should send their caravan master the message that a house's hold isn't a free camp site. Teach them to keep a tighter leash on their scroats.'

Duncan walked over to the cage. Jacob Carnehan clung to the bars like a wild animal, his eyes filled with an icy madness that Duncan didn't think any human could hold. 'Where are they, where're the others?' he demanded. 'Where's Carter and the people the raiders took?'

'They're not here,' said Duncan. 'Just myself and Willow, you remember, my sister?'

'Where's *Carter*?' He said it like a man dying of thirst in the desert mouthing the word *water*.

'They're working in the sky mines,' said Duncan. 'The empire has a giant volcano where metals and ores are still pumped out from the world's deep heart. There are mining stations and stakes tethered above it on antigravity stones. Everyone from Northhaven is serving there.'

'Serving?' snarled Jacob. 'How much choice do they have in that?'

Paetro pulled Duncan back a step. 'Careful there, lad. You're close enough for him to snap your neck.'

'He's a pastor,' said Duncan. 'He's not dangerous, I promise you. What in the world are you doing here, Father Carnehan – inside the empire? How did you even find me?'

The gask came forward to the bars. 'We are an expedition of mercy, manling. Funded by the town and the people of the great forest to track down everyone seized by the slavers. We have money to purchase those taken, to buy them back from their new owners.'

'You,' said Duncan, still stunned by the shock of seeing Weylanders in the castle. 'You're Kerge's father?'

'I am!' said the gask. 'I have come for him!'

'Your people are owned by the mistress of this house,' said Paetro. 'And you've come a long way for nothing, my quill-skinned friend. Because their labour means a lot more to her fortunes than a camping pack filled with exotic trading coins.'

'Your father sent us, boy,' said the pastor, his hand reaching out pleadingly to Duncan. 'Check the stamp on those coins. It's Benner Landor's money we've brought to buy our people back with!'

'How did you get here,' demanded Paetro. '*Here* and the empire?'

'We started out flying on merchant carriers. On one of the ships we met this old rascal who had dealings with the skels, scouting soft targets for the raiders. The old coot told us all slaves taken by the skels eventually ended up in Vandia. A few months later we came across a guild library in the wilds,' said Jacob. 'The library had plans for a craft powered by rockets, one that could travel faster and further than anything we thought possible. We spent most of the Landor fortune building it. But the ship ran out of fuel and crashed on the empire's borders. The rest of the way we travelled using Khow's homing sense. But the damn gask's led us to the wrong Weylanders!'

'His nose's led you to the wrong country,' said Paetro, uneasily. 'The imperium takes slaves from a respectable distance so it never has to deal with strays, rescue missions and expeditionary forces. You're the first who've made it this far. And I reckon you'll be the last too.'

So the pastor came here searching for the wrong Weylanders? Duncan felt the anger rising inside him; so strong it threatened to overwhelm him and choke his words. 'Where's my father?' demanded Duncan. 'You're it? You're the entire expedition? The town's pastor, a single mountain pilot, a woodland gask and this filthy old tramp? Where's my *father*? He lost his only son and daughter … where is *he*?'

'We started out with a company of the king's guardsmen,' said Jacob, 'but some of them were killed and the rest deserted along the way. We had Constable Wiggins with us, too, but he was murdered by savages during the journey.'

'To hell with the king's men!' shouted Duncan. 'Where's my bloody father? Was he badly wounded in the raid? Did he lose his legs?'

'His people needed him back home,' said Jacob. 'The workers, everyone who relies on your house for their work and livelihoods. Benner funded our outfit and we've come on his behalf.'

Tears rolled down Duncan's cheeks. 'We needed him. Willow and I needed him *here*. You came! You came for Carter! Even this gask came for his son, didn't he?'

'We would never have made it this far without your pa's assistance,' said Jacob.

'He didn't give you his money for us,' said Duncan. 'That was just a cheque he wrote so he could forget all about his children, wasn't it? He knew you were going to die! Nobody escapes from the sky mines … nobody ever turns up here searching for slaves.'

'We're not dead yet,' growled the pastor.

The pastor didn't answer Duncan's accusations. But then why should he? Jacob Carnehan was a churchman. He only told the truth. And what he'd left unsaid was enough to make Duncan's mind up for good. 'I'll see what I can do for you, Father Carnehan. You can take Willow back home with you if she wants to leave. I'll pay for your passage myself. But I barely had a home worthy of the name to return to even before I was snatched by the skels. This is my place now – I'm needed here. I've seen wider horizons than the tiny little corner of our undeveloped backwater. Northhaven would seem small now.'

'You're needed here? I *need* my son!'

'He will never be freed,' said Duncan. 'Carter's still alive. That'll have to be comfort enough for you, Father; and for everyone else in Northhaven. Tell them back home that quite a few of us are still alive. I doubt if anyone at Hawkland Park will be interested in the news, but there'll be families on the hill that will care to know. And you tell my father that I'm not a slave anymore. I'm a citizen. I'm my own man. And I freed Willow too. I did it without him, without Landor money, or his name, or his precious house.'

'You're a renegade,' snarled the pastor. 'That's what you call a man who sells out his own people to join the enemy.'

'I'm the man who's going to try and save you and your friends' lives,' retorted Duncan. He looked with astonishment at the churchman. Jacob Carnehan's features twisted and contorted. Nothing like the stern, straightforward man who preached peace and gentleness in Northhaven. 'You can thank me for it later.' Duncan turned his back on the cage and stalked away with Paetro. Behind him, the churchman howled and shook the cage's bars as though the prison chamber *was* an asylum. Duncan couldn't help but feel pity for the pastor. The journey, its travails and the battles his party had fought on the way had clearly left him deranged. But there was little Duncan could do. Not for the pastor's peace or those still trapped inside the sky mines.

'That was a hell of a trip they must have undertaken,' said Paetro. 'All this way for nothing. The first to have made it. That's the stuff of legend, lad.'

'He's a priest. Perhaps he prayed for a miracle,' said Duncan. 'But I don't think his master is kind enough to grant two.'

Paetro glanced forlornly back towards the holding chamber. To where his daughter awaited her torturer's arrival. 'Aye, there's truth in that. The gods love nothing better than to play with the fates of honest families. It's always the ones like Apolleon, Circae and Machus who're given wings to fly above the rest of us.'

'Jacob Carnehan was lucky getting this far,' said Duncan. 'But it's run out now.'

'Chance, you say? I'm not so sure. You're certain he's a priest?'

'Of course. I've sat in his church enough times to know he can preach until his congregation's eyelids start to nod.'

'I've seen a man stare at me with those kinds of eyes on the battle-field,' said Paetro. 'Never inside a temple.'

'You can give Lady Cassandra the bad news,' said Duncan. 'I'll see how my sister's taking hers. My father sent those idiots out here? I'll send him Willow back for his money.'

'You don't want to swap?' asked Paetro.

'Are you serious?'

'The young Highness will take the word about Hesia better if she hears it from you,' said Paetro. 'And telling your sister she's going home … well how bad can that be?'

You don't know my sister, thought Duncan. But he acquiesced. In truth, he was glad not to have to see Willow again for a few hours. He'd had more than enough of witless Weylanders judging him, when he was trying to do his best for the cretins. Maybe Willow and the pastor would have been happier if Duncan Landor had stayed in the sky mines to be worked to death? Stayed a slave rather than earning his freedom; confounding their low expectations of him. Poor useless Duncan Landor, who was no good to anyone without his family's wealth and reputation backing him. A purposeless tool to be discarded by women like Adella as soon as a surer bet appeared. What Duncan had achieved, he'd earned on his own. With nobody to help him. They should have admired him for it, not been filled with jealousy for his feats.

FIFTEEN

UNHAPPY ARRIVALS

'Oh, my dear vile-tilted crown,' said Sariel, clutching his head in his hands. 'My mind feels as though it has been torn in twain. It was a shaky bridge he established ... curse the great diviner.'

'How did it happen?' demanded Jacob. 'I remember the gads' stone circle, their ritual. Then being woken up here, inside another circle, in the grounds of this giant Vandian fortress.'

'You were thinking of them, weren't you?' said Khow. 'This young manling Duncan Landor and his sister.'

'Yes, they were on my mind,' admitted Jacob. 'The very last thing before I passed out. My boy Carter had quarrelled with Duncan over a girl and they'd fought a duel. A little while later the skels arrived for them both.'

'Your thoughts were the homing sense that directed us here. My people have always known the stones were ancient, beyond our understanding,' said Khow. 'But this? They are gateways, are they not? They pass information.' The gask talked to Sariel, but the old bard affected not to have noticed his cellmate. They spoke low so the gaoler couldn't listen in on their conversation, but still, Sariel had heard the question well enough.

'We're not damn information,' said Jacob. 'We're people!'

'In a manner of speaking,' said the gask, 'we are merely points of data. And in a manner of speaking, the entire universe is. Otherwise my people's calculations could not be brought to focus on mortal matters. Think of the stones as a radio set, but a radio that allows people to be transmitted from one location to another.'

'You're right about one thing, this is beyond your woodland magic,' said Jacob. 'Sariel, the gads seemed to think you know about the stones and their use ...'

'I knew once,' whispered Sariel. 'But the sorcery that controls the runes has been burnt from me. It comes and goes like a dream.'

'A dream you must remember!' said Sheplar, the pilot lifting Sariel off the cell's floor and shaking him in frustration.

'It is a nightmare. Leave me alone! There are things best forgotten.'

'Come on, old man,' urged Jacob. 'We need your help. If the stones carried us here, they can carry us back home too.'

'I don't want to,' whined the bard. 'How do you think I ended up with a fraction of my memories and the rest of my head filled with naught but echoes? There are demons that haunt the passages those stones use to pass travellers across the world. Terrible entities. You call them stealers! Devils ... evil and capering and endlessly hungry. They caught me using their strange bridges and they almost burnt me to ashes. That's why I wander the land ... why I can never slow, so they might never catch up with me. I am marked by the stealers for the sins of my trespass.'

'Just tell me about the damn circles!'

'Sometimes the stones open a gate for me, sometimes they don't,' said Sariel, tugging frantically at his beard. 'The stones have a will of their own. You can only use the stones as a portal to depart once. Each circle draws power from the underworld, immense and terrible energies. The stealers feel it ripped from their hellish plains and trace the energy's thread to the circle, then they overload the stones in a fierce explosion so there is one less source to rob them in future.'

'So we can still use those stones out in the grounds to escape?' asked Jacob.

'Maybe, maybe,' said Sariel. 'But the stones outside will be destroyed by the stealers soon enough. Exiting a gate doesn't rob the stealers of their power, but it does leave a ripple in their world, a current they can track. It may take a day or two, but the stealers will hunt down the stones we exited by and overload them too, place the circle beyond our use.'

'Then we have to make sure the Landor boy releases us to his sister's care before then,' said Jacob. He wasn't sure what to believe of the tale the mad old bard had told them. But there was one thing that certainly wasn't one of Sariel's crazy stories. They had crossed an impossible distance faster than anything alive should have been able to. Maybe they had trespassed into hell to reach Vandia? Jacob would gladly strike a deal with the stealers to get Carter back. *You might yet have to.*

'We must escape,' begged Sariel. 'The stealers will come in search of me. They loathe the prince of players for tapping into their dark powers. They will hunt me and try to incinerate me again.' He gazed out at the gaoler lounging behind his table, tucking into a plate of steaming meat. 'They could come to us as anyone. That is why they're called stealers … you can't trust your friends, your family. It is the faces and bodies of those closest to you that they steal to cavort in.'

'And their souls,' said Jacob. 'And we're here to save my son's. Damned if I'll be packed off home by that Landor whelp like a piece of unwanted baggage.' He remembered a passage from the Bible he used to work into his sermons. *Beware the devils that steal into your heart and turn your hand to evil. Beware such stealers and turn your hand only to good deeds.* If that was a warning for him, he was about to throw it out of the window. Nobody was going to stop him getting to the sky mines. Not Duncan Landor or the Vandians. And good deeds weren't what it was going to take.

'There will be nothing left of me this time,' moaned Sariel. 'Nothing left of my mind once they have crushed me again.'

'Stop bleating, smelly one,' said Sheplar. 'It will not free us from here.'

In the cage next to theirs, its sole prisoner, the woman, called out to their gaoler. She sounded loud and desperate. 'Lend me your blade. You used to be in the legion, didn't you? Grant me a clean death.'

'And reserve a bad one for me, when the torturer arrives and finds only a corpse to question?' He laughed. 'Better you than I, Hesia!' She fell back to the floor, hugging her legs.

'Misery loves company,' said Jacob, shaking his head. The woman had looked wretched enough before. Jacob and the expedition had been the main audience when a young girl had slipped inside the cell block … the chief imperial's daughter, as it transpired, obviously used to getting her way, shrieking and crying about the imprisoned woman's base treachery. Until a party of guardsmen turned up, summoned by the gaoler to whisk Lady Cassandra far away from the dungeon level. Jacob sighed. So near, only to end up trapped here. Waiting on the good graces of Duncan Landor to convince his new friends the expedition posed no threat and deserved to be allowed home. *We'll be lucky if they don't turn up with a firing squad.* He paced the cell, waiting hours for Duncan to return. But when a new visitor did arrive inside the holding chamber, it was Willow Landor, her face streaked with tears and red from crying.

'Dear god! Father Carnehan, it *is* you. I thought that they had made a mistake – that Duncan had asked the Vandians to mock me, telling me a pack of complete nonsense. But you're here!'

'So it seems,' said Jacob. 'We've come for you, for Carter, for everyone.'

'The Vandians won't free the sky miners for money,' said Willow, her eyes glancing between the prisoners in the cage. He could see the hope dying in her eyes. Just the four of them against an empire. 'As slaves we can mine more trading metal in a single hour than you can have possibly carried here.'

'We used our funds getting to the empire and the rest was stolen,' admitted Jacob.

'It's a wonder you are here at all. Duncan's soldier friend told me you built a rocket-powered aircraft, similar to the Vandians' vessels. Is it still operable?'

'Would you want to come back with us?' said Jacob. 'Your brother seems to have turned native.'

'He thinks he's a Vandian lord now,' said Willow. 'He's a fool.'

'And Carter's alive?'

'Yes,' she said, holding back her tears again. That was when Jacob knew he could trust her. There were a lot of things you could fake. The lie behind their strange arrival, maybe, but not what this girl felt towards Carter. 'He's in a bad way, though. They flogged Carter for trying to escape and have been punishing him ever since. It's not just his body that's broken either. He believes he's being sent visions, seeing terrible things. I think captivity is driving him insane.'

Jacob glanced back to Sariel, moaning and shaking on the floor. He imagined Carter, freed and broken, wandering the world far-called, tramping down an endless road in search of a long lost life like poor, mad Sariel. Looking for his mother and his dead brothers. Comforting himself with alcohol. Never finding them. Tears came to Jacob's eyes. He wished Mary was still here. She would know what to do, how to heal him. Jacob understood what was needed to free his son, but how to mend what had been broken? He reached through the bars, touching the girl's fingers. 'Nothing we can't fix, Willow.'

'No touching!' shouted the gaoler. 'Back there, he could snap your neck in a second.'

Jacob stepped away, something round and hard pushed into his palm. He gazed down. It was a small round brooch.

'Damn you!' swore Willow. 'I came here to reassure you and you dare to steal from me!'

The guard drew a metal rod from his table, a rubber-insulated shaft of barbed steel that started sparking as soon as he pressed a button on its hilt. He strode around Willow. 'You damn tinkers, you never learn,' he snarled. 'If it's not tied down, you'll steal it. Out of their reach, madam. A broken rib or two might teach these dogs to respect our house.' He slapped his stick against the cage, and its bars sparked with energy, Sheplar yelping as he removed his fingers from the metal.

The gaoler laughed, but the sound turned to a croak as Willow sapped him from behind, a little black sack weighted with lead dangling in her hand. He tumbled limply against the cage to fall still against the bars.

'Give me the brooch,' ordered Willow. Jacob passed it to her and she tossed it to the other cage where the woman imprisoned inside caught it,

'My father sent you?' said Hesia.

'He told me you would recognise it,' said Willow. 'And that you'd take a chance at exile over an appointment with an imperial torturer.'

'Yes,' she said, without hesitation. 'I will, to save my sister's life.'

'A few more than that,' said Jacob.

Willow dipped down to the gaoler's belt, removing a silver card tied to a keychain. She ran the card through a steel box against the wall, its hatch springing open and revealing the keys to every cage. Willow walked to the cell holding the Vandian woman first. 'Your father told me there's a fast long-range munitions ship on the field next to the kerosene-liquid-oxygen tanks, fully fuelled and due to leave soon. You can fly it to the sky mines?'

'Cross the dead zone? But there's nothing there. The southern border's closer.'

'We're going north,' said Willow, firmly. 'Agree, or you can stay and your father can find another fool to take the blame for springing you.'

'So be it.' Hesia stared across at Jacob. 'But I'll have your word in return that you won't let the empire take me alive. Put a bullet in my head or a blade in my heart if it comes to it.'

Jacob nodded grimly from inside his cage. 'You won't fall into their hands alive ... my word on it.' *That won't be the difficult part in all this madness.*

Willow released the Vandian and then opened the Weylanders' cage, Jacob and the others spilling out. Jacob lifted his gun belt off the hook on the wall and recovered his travel pack as his companions collected their possessions. Khow fiddled with his abacus box and had to be chivvied towards the chamber's exit, vainly trying to calculate their fate as Sariel and Sheplar waited to brave the fortress proper.

Hesia found a domed pilot's helmet on a shelf, strapping it over her head and pulling down a mirrored visor to conceal her bruised face. She opened a locker with spare guard uniforms and tossed them at the Weylanders. 'Put these on. The castle is still packed with guests who've travelled here for a diplomatic summit. If we are stopped, you are servants heading to the landing field to make your master's craft ready to depart. We have at least an hour before the next gaoler's shift starts.'

Jacob was impressed she had watched the guards. He hadn't spent enough time inside the holding area to work out the pattern. They had only just stepped into the corridor when Jacob halted them. 'Forgot something. Wait here a second.'

Jacob ducked back into the chamber, dragging the unconscious gaoler into a cage. Then he slipped his knife out, placed his hand hard over the man's mouth and plunged the blade deep into his heart. The man trembled slightly in the second it took him to die; the gaoler's last breath warm and faint against Jacob's fingers. He could never be allowed to tell his mistress of Willow's part in this. Let them wonder if she'd been abducted during the prison break. How many times had Jacob crawled across battlefields in the Burn to silence sentries like this? Years before, but now it was as though he had never buried his recollection of the act. *His* memories again, not those of another man. Jacob pulled the dirty white collar of a pastor from his shirt and tossed it into the pooling blood. The Vandians had stolen the quietest part of his life, ripped it right from him. Now they would face the rage that filled that silence. Jacob locked the door to the cage and re-joined the others.

'You found what you forgot?' asked Sheplar.

Jacob grunted and they moved off. *My soul be cursed, but I believe I have.*

Duncan went searching for his sister, leaving Lady Cassandra with Paetro; the young noblewoman hard at work in a draughty hall with one of the empire's most famous gymnasts, balancing on a wooden horse while the tutor strode around her, barking out commands. It was typical of Willow to get lost so soon after she had arrived. True, the Castle of Snakes sprawled across the cliffs overlooking the sea, corridors and passages and chambers across multiple levels, below and above ground, but she should have wit enough to ask one of the house's many retainers how to find her way back to her rooms. He reached the hangars with a view to going outside and checking the gardens when he noticed that Princess Helrena had arrived to greet new visitors. Duncan cursed his luck. Apolleon again, a retinue of hoodsmen standing menacingly at the man's back. Whatever the head of the secret police wanted this time, he was going far beyond civility in demanding it. He appeared to be having a heated argument with the princess. With Apolleon's party positioned in the middle of the open blast doors, the only way to avoid him would be to turn back. Duncan decided to walk past and hope he wasn't noticed.

'Where is he?' insisted Apolleon. 'The man you found in your garden?'

'Man? You mean *men* … the travellers?' said Helrena. 'How do you know we caught a gang of tinkers in the grounds? And why are you wasting your time with such trivialities?'

'*This* man,' said Apolleon, flourishing a sheet of paper. It contained a sketch of an old bearded man who looked a lot like the vagrant who had arrived at the castle with Jacob Carnehan. 'He is a criminal, a wily, dangerous foe of the imperium who has been on the run since before you were born.'

'Dangerously drunk, perhaps,' said Helrena. 'They were in a stupor when my guards came across them and tossed them in a cage. I cannot confirm this man is the one you seek. I do not trouble myself with trespassers and itinerant squatters.'

'You underestimate this radical at your peril,' warned Apolleon. 'He has as many aliases as you own slaves. This is *Sariel Teller. Sariel Player. Sariel Skel-Bane.* He has a knack of wriggling out of chains and slipping past sentries like a ghost. Send a company of soldiers to secure him … fully armed and armoured.'

'For one dirty old man?' said Helrena. She was looking at the nobleman as if he had lost his mind. 'I have never even heard of this criminal?'

Apolleon was practically shaking with anger, or was it fear? Surely he wasn't scared of the elderly hobo Duncan had glimpsed in gaol alongside Jacob Carnehan? Northhaven's expedition was a joke; a handful of expendables dispatched to a faraway death to assuage the guilt of Duncan's father. What in the world could scare one of the most dangerous men in the imperium so badly? 'Do not question me. Do as I say! He should be dead. He *will* be dead!'

Helrena turned to her retinue. 'Call the cell level, have them manacle the travellers and dispatch my private guard to bring them before us.'

Poor, unlucky Jacob Carnehan. First most of his parish had been burnt to the ground, then his son had been enslaved, now he was going to be thrown to the not-so-tender mercies of the Vandian secret police. Duncan decided to idle behind the nearest helo and see how matters played out. Helrena didn't look pleased in the slightest. Not at her rude treatment at the hands of a supposed ally, nor at the implications that the secret police had an unlimited number of informers among her staff. Maybe the old vagrant Apolleon hunted had been hiding in exile inside one of the empire's neighbours when Jacob's craft landed for supplies, and the outlaw had seized his opportunity to join the expedition? If so, his urge to see his homeland again was going to cost him his life. But would it cost the pastor's, too? Duncan sighed. He had hoped to help Jacob Carnehan return home. But if Apolleon got his hooks into the Weylander, then Carter's father would be far beyond Duncan's help.

A soldier returned a second later, whispering in the princess's ear. Helrena's face turned white at the news. 'All the travellers are gone! And Hesia with them! Is this Circae's doing?'

Apolleon roared a yell of anguish at the hangar's roof. 'I warned you! Seal off the castle, lock down the landing field. Search every turret and room, every inch and corner of the castle until you find him.'

It wasn't just the head of the secret police that was discomfited by the news of the escape. Duncan slipped out of the hangar, his walk becoming a sprint as he ran across the gardens and cliff defences, desperate to find his sister clearing her head in the open air. But Willow was nowhere to be found. All around him sirens began to wail. On the battlements of the wall facing the city's towers and spires, across the hangars and the hulking concrete fortifications of the Castle of Snakes. Duncan checked the small woodland, the Stone Garden, the walks along the cliff defences, the gun emplacements facing the whipping sea. Patrols began to comb the grounds alongside him. Duncan was still searching half an hour later when a guardsman came dashing past and recognised him, stopping to jab a finger back towards the castle.

'Orders from the princess. Head to the airfield and find the transport Paetro's riding.'

'And then what?'

'Climb in the helo alongside him. Apolleon is sending his personal warship to the landing island. We're stripping the castle of every able-bodied man and joining his people on board to chase a skyjacked ship.'

'Skyjacked?' Duncan's gut twisted at the news, all the horrifying implications flashing through his mind at once. *Willow. Damn you!*

'One of our supply runners has vanished, its pilots found stuffed dead under the field's fuel tanks. As soon as we know what direction it's headed, we're following.'

Duncan turned away so that the man couldn't see the painful web of emotions playing across his face, and then scurried towards the castle. He could guess which direction the stolen ship would be heading. *The sky mines.* And he knew why Willow was missing, too. In her fit of jealous pique, she'd finally found a way to ruin everything Duncan had achieved here. He'd won Willow her freedom and *this* was how she repaid him? And now he was being ordered to hunt down his own sister, while her selfishness meant Paetro would be forced to stalk and shoot his own daughter, all in the name of duty. And for what? So Carter Carnehan could enjoy a pitiful last hour in the company of his father before the entire might of the imperium bore down to slaughter a ragtag band of slaves and outlaws? *Willow.* Even here, the Landor name and the Landor line could reach out to curse him. He felt like letting rip to the sky with a similar roar of rage to Apolleon's. Instead he sprinted towards the airfield, towards the whipping noise of a dozen squadrons of helos rising into the sky to start the pursuit. *You've brought this on yourself, Willow. Everything that happens. It's all on you now.*

Jacob was finally able to rise out of the padded chair in the cockpit, muscles aching and pulsing in protest. He had never thought it possible to travel so fast that his body became as weighted as if he had been recast in lead, the air itself exploding as their vessel speared above the imperium. At least the extreme speed had stopped Sheplar appearing from alongside Sariel in the cargo hold, to annoy the female pilot with endless questions over the ship's design and the function of every knob and switch on her control panel.

'I'm decelerating,' announced Hesia. 'Dropping filters over our engine intakes.'

Jacob saw why. A rolling grey cloud lurked beyond the cockpit's canopy, the patter of ash and dust starting against their airframe and growing louder. 'Sweet mercy! What is that?'

'A proto-eruption,' said Willow. 'They can rumble on for weeks before the stratovolcano starts to blow in earnest.'

'And my son is on a mining station tethered above *that*?' The land they'd already passed over was bad enough. Scoured of all greenery, empty river beds and mile after mile of smoking rock. Only the occasional ground-based mining operation to break up the landscape, vast steel fortresses on tracks slowly picking their way through the volcano's lesser mineral fall. The blackened hellish vista seemed limitless, even at the almost inconceivable speeds they had been hitting.

'That's why the empire uses slaves here,' said Willow. The girl was so matter of fact and cold she made Jacob grimace. He'd had a chance to have a closer look at her now. Willow was a lot gaunter than he remembered her. Her brother had regained his frame living high on the hog with the Vandians but there wasn't much of a healthy sheen about Willow Landor. She still had the hungry, quick eyes of a slave; flitting around the Vandians' ship, restlessly searching for the next threat. He had seen that look before, among the starved peasants of the Burn. Cannon fodder who expected nothing more from a new encounter than theft, murder or a flogging.

'Dropping altitude,' announced Hesia, and Jacob felt the deck fall away from his boots. 'I'm hugging the deck. Trading speed for stealth. We shouldn't meet any slave patrol ships flying so low. They'll have gone for height, trying to get over the worst of *that*.'

'Just take us to the station,' said Willow.

'And there are no guards in the sky mines?' asked Jacob. 'No soldiers?'

'Not unless the princess managed to send them ahead of us,' said Hesia. She indicated the lifeless plains flashing past below. 'Hunger and thirst make the best sentry of all. No work, no water.'

And his son had been marooned out here all this time? They might as well have stranded Carter in the central circle of hell.

'Carter will be safe,' said Willow, picking up on his worries. But she sounded too much as though she were trying to convince herself.

'I can sense my child,' said Khow, excited. 'Kerge is close. It is as though I could reach outside and touch him.'

Hesia jerked her thumb towards the hatch at the rear of the cockpit. 'Go down to the cargo hold and bring your kite-flying mountain man up here. I need him to sit on the scope and keep an eye behind us.' Willow heeded the pilot's instructions and left to retrieve the Rodalian.

Jacob felt a bite of fear. 'We're being pursued?'

'Not yet, not the way I'm bouncing us about. But they'll piece our route together soon enough, if only from plantation owners arriving at garrisons and demanding compensation for us stampeding herds and shattering farmhouse windows.'

Their jouncing grew worse, the bombardment of grit swelling louder and larger. Hesia activated a steel mesh that folded down across the cockpit glass. The ship's triangular wings were visible beyond the canopy, shrugging off debris like a cloud of rain.

'We'll hold?' asked Jacob.

Hesia shrugged. 'We're not rated for the dead zone. This bird was scheduled to fly to the house's holdings in the eastern provinces. Munitions and weapons for our line of forts out there. Just an engine, long-range fuel tanks and a large cargo hold welded together. Our armour's to protect us against rifle fire from the ground, not this. There's one piece of good news: if we're holed, the weight of explosives on board means that at least we'll have an instant death.'

'I haven't travelled this far to be blown to pieces an hour before I reach my son.'

'No? Well, the people in the capital might not care about a few runaway slaves and foreigners, but I've betrayed my house twice. For me, there's no distance Helrena Skar won't travel to settle that score.'

Jacob could see the stratovolcano's lower slopes moving towards them through the dark shower, sandwiched between the ground below and the black clouds above. If this was just the opening salvo, how bad would the storm grow when the volcano moved towards a full eruption? The volcano's rise came closer and closer. Hesia banked her craft with a view to climbing towards the sky mine.

'Manling!' said Khow from the back of the cockpit. He pointed out of a side-port towards the ground.

Jacob went to the gask and followed the direction of his leathery finger. Khow had picked out a feature by the base of the volcano. A circle of menhirs below, the ancient standing stones seeming at home in this bleak, deadly land. 'I see them.'

'Will the stones activate for Sariel,' wondered Khow, 'without the assistance of the great diviner?'

Jacob glanced towards the cargo hold. He could hear Willow and Sheplar climbing up the metal stairs. It was a good question. With more riding on the outcome than Jacob wanted to dwell on right now. Sariel hadn't been himself since they had arrived in Vandia. His stories had dried up, few tall tales and boasts. The bard had drawn into himself. It reminded Jacob of Carter's brothers in the last days of their fever. You always knew you were in trouble when a sick child stopped complaining, growing worryingly silent.

'And even if the stones are still active,' added Khow, 'if Sariel cannot control them properly, we could end up anywhere in the world.'

Jacob cleared his throat. It had turned dry and worried inside the Vandian vessel. 'Anywhere in the world that isn't the empire. I can live with that, friend.'

Sheplar took the gask's seat, following Hesia's instructions for operating the radar. Kerge left for the cargo hold to help calm Sariel. Relying on the unstable bard to escape Vandia? Jacob prayed the gask proved successful.

Hesia had flown supply runs to the sky mines often enough to be able to locate the station, even in the thick hot clouds and debris. A couple of minutes later the station came into view through the squall of gas and super-heated debris.

'Trying to raise their radio room,' said Hesia. 'No response. It must be down for maintenance.'

Jacob looked out of the canopy at the massive rock emerging from the burning soot, blue power lamps glowing on antigravity stones studding its sides. It wasn't a single rock outside, but three of them tethered together by a web of steel cables. Willow joined him by the window. 'We're in luck. No ships moored up. Sometimes the Vandians take shelter if there's an eruption on the way.'

Hesia pulled back on her flight stick. 'We're too big to land in their hangars and too small to dock alongside. I'll set us down on the station roof. I can see some slaves waiting for us topside.'

'We're not on the resupply schedule,' said Willow.

'Let them wonder,' said Jacob.

'Most of our people will be busy preparing,' said Willow. 'We chase an eruption's tail into the clouds to try to stake the best rocks. There's a lot of competition between rival houses for the best strikes. It's a bloodbath.'

Jacob had the feeling matters would be getting a lot bloodier today. Their reception committee retreated on the station's surface, the ship's engines rotating into landing position and blasting rock before it settled down.

'The man at the front is Thomas Gale,' said Willow, gazing at the ground from the cockpit. 'He administers the station for Helrena Skar.'

'Then he can administer my son to me,' growled Jacob.

Jacob left the cockpit and climbed down to the cargo hold. He and the others crowded around the back of the chamber, surrounded by metal crates lashed to the steel deck with black straps. Hesia dropped the loading ramp. A wave of heat flooded in from outside, choking dust and ash drifting in. Jacob stepped outside, covering his mouth and nose with his hand. It was worse outside, dust obscuring the air vents and stairs down into the station. The man that Willow had identified as the chief slave raised a hand in greeting and came forward with his entourage following slowly, figures obscured by the squall. They probably thought that Hesia's vessel had landed to ride out the worst of the storm. Would they be happy to hear that he'd come for Northhaven's abducted slaves? *Easier for them if they learn to collaborate with a new master.* A few trustees with wooden clubs weren't going to stop him now.

'Halt there!' shouted Thomas Gale, pausing a few feet in front of Jacob.

As the slave raised his hand, a company of men sprang up from under rock-coloured camouflage cloaks. They wore Vandian armour, large black rifles pulled tight against their shoulders, a ring of soldiers surrounding the expedition members. Jacob glanced carefully to either side, counting at least a dozen gun barrels pointing at them, without factoring in the men behind him. Jacob heard Khow groan, the gask realising at the same time as the pastor why the radio room had been silent on their approach. Clever, hiding the patrol ship so they wouldn't be expecting trouble. All this way; all the countless leagues and dangers passed. Almost close enough to shout to Carter and hear the response, and they had blundered straight into the middle of an ambush. His fingers twitched for the comforting weight of his pistols, wavering near his gun belt. Even in his young days, even then, the man known as Jake Quicksilver couldn't have taken so many down at once. And he wasn't a young man anymore. He was tired and had just lost everything. *Again.*

One of the Vandian guardsmen walked up to Jacob, an officer's pistol in his gloved hand, pushing the barrel hard into the side of the pastor's temple. 'You can reach for your guns if you want to. I'd like to see what happens.'

'One of us would die,' growled Jacob. *Wasn't that the way it always ended?*

Duncan sat with his back against the wall and an arm in front of him to stop him falling out of the seat. There were hundreds of troops inside the chamber, Paetro next to him. Apolleon's warship was a monster, twice the size of the vessel that Princess Helrena had used to transport the slaves from the skels' raids back to the empire.

'I'm sorry it's Hesia we're going after,' said Duncan.

'Nobody knows the escaped prisoners are Weylanders,' said Paetro. 'Or that your sister's been taken by them yet. Except for you and I ... and I won't tell.'

'Thank you.'

'You don't control what your family do, lad,' said Paetro. 'I understand that better than anyone.'

He had that right. 'I can't believe we're shipping out after a few fugitives with so many soldiers.'

'The mistress didn't want to do it,' said Paetro. 'Stripping the castle's garrison to the bare bones like this. She still thinks Circae is behind this; a few murdisto on the loose we never accounted for. Maybe a feint to draw us away from the capital and silence Hesia before she's broken on the torturer's table. But the mistress has no choice in the matter. Not with Apolleon acting as crazily as he is.'

At least Lady Cassandra was on board too, strapped next to the princess on the command deck. The girl would be far safer with the house's fighting men than alone inside an empty fortress. 'You saw who we're after. This Sariel is just a raggedy toothless vagrant. If he ever was a dangerous outlaw, those days are long behind him.'

'Be glad that Apolleon's so obsessed with catching him,' said Paetro. 'He doesn't give a fig about your countrymen. Maybe we can yet extract your sister out of the fire, no questions asked, if the chance presents itself.'

'I wish we could do the same for Hesia.'

'Wishes won't bend fate,' said Paetro. 'If my girl's any sense, she'll find a fast high trade wind and ride it until her fuel runs out. But she'll never be safe. Even if Hesia gets away, she'll have to live every day not knowing if this is the morning when someone comes calling for the bounty on her head.'

There was a kick of acceleration, the bench shaking as the warship picked up speed. 'Aye, they've got a direction now. The chase is on.' He didn't sound happy about it. Paetro grunted. 'If we look like we're about to capture Hesia, I'd ask one favour of you.'

'Name it.'

'Make sure she isn't taken alive.'

Duncan looked at the ageing soldier with shock.

'I received orders from the secret police before all of this blew up. They told me to assist the imperial torturers when they arrived for Hesia. It's how the bastards work. Someone who knows the victim well enough to confirm she's telling the truth or merely saying what the torturer wants to hear when the pain gets too much for her.'

'They'd make you do that?'

'I'll do my duty for the house and the young Highness,' said Paetro. 'But the hoodsmen can kiss my arse. Hesia knows enough not to let herself be taken alive, but if she fails …'

If she fails. Duncan nodded. 'My word on it.'

'It's a hard day's duty,' muttered Paetro. 'Chasing our own.'

Duncan sympathised. He thought he had escaped the shadow of the sky mines. But here he was, heading back towards the monstrously large stratovolcano. How many people dead, all because they had followed that fool Carter? Now Carter's father had trailed his son to the empire and placed Willow in peril because the self-righteous churchman didn't know when he was beaten. The world would be better off without the Carnehans. And it looked as though the world was about to oblige.

Jacob could see precisely how he would do it in his mind's eye. Pushing the officer's pistol aside and using the guardsman's body as a shield as he swivelled, one pistol and then another, rotating and shooting, allowing the Vandian to absorb the return volley. Sheplar, Sariel, Khow, Willow and Hesia … they would all be caught in the crossfire. How many of his companions would be dead on the ground before his pistols were empty? One shot, one kill, and would he have enough ammunition to account for every Vandian, even if he didn't miss once? *Time to find out.* Jacob was a heartbeat away from reaching for his pistols when Willow called out in shock. 'Owen?'

'Willow?' spluttered the officer.

'You know this Vandian?' asked Jacob.

'He's not a Vandian,' said Willow. 'He's a slave here, a Weylander, like us! What in the world are you doing?'

Owen's pistol wavered uncertainly in his hand. 'I could ask you the same question. You miss the sky mines so much that you got yourself dismissed as a house slave?'

'We've come for Carter and Kerge,' said Willow, thrusting her hand towards their supply ship. 'And anyone else who wants to escape.'

Jacob used the second of hesitation to grab the man's arm, spinning him around and turning the pistol against his own head. The circle of soldiers surrounding them stepped forward, bayonet-topped rifle barrels jabbing forward like spears. 'Any of you want to shoot, your friend here takes the first bullet through his brain. Now, answer the lady's question. If you're really slaves, what the hell are you doing dressed as imperial guardsmen?'

'We're escaping,' said Owen, struggling under Jacob's grip. 'The whole station! We've already seized a patrol vessel that arrived to wait out the eruption. These uniforms and guns came from its crew. We thought you'd landed to investigate what happened to the first ship.' He stared across at Willow Landor. 'We're using Carter's escape plan. It's a fine one, Willow. Good enough to get us all out of here at once.'

Jacob glanced across to where the supposed head man stood. He noticed how the slaves behind the head man had rifles too, pointing at the collaborator's spine. Jacob made his decision and released the miner masquerading as an officer. Things hadn't changed so much, then. Even out here, Carter was still making trouble for everyone concerned. 'Where's my son? Where's Carter Carnehan?'

Owen gawped at Jacob in shock. 'You're his—?'

'I'm a Weylander, just like you. Now, where's my boy?'

'It's true,' said Willow. 'This is Jacob Carnehan … Carter's father. His group have travelled all the way from Weyland searching for the people taken from Northhaven. Where's Carter? If this is his plan, why isn't he up here with you?'

That was the question on Jacob's mind, too. His son wasn't the sort to avoid a fight. Owen could hardly meet the girl's gaze. 'He's dying, Willow. I'm sorry. He's in the fever room, in his final few hours. The soldiers beat him real bad for trying to stop you being taken from the station. Carter only told me his scheme for getting out of here when he realised he wasn't going to live to try it himself. He's got broken ribs and a fever, but that's not the worst of it. The doctor reckons his brain's bruised and swelling inside his skull. It's a miracle he's still alive.'

Willow looked like someone had pierced her through the heart. For Jacob, someone had.

'No,' gasped Willow. 'He can't be. He's too strong! He's—'

'Take me to him!' ordered Jacob.

'He might not recognise you now,' said Owen. 'The doc said we couldn't even load him into a transporter without finishing him off. But I'll show you down to where he is.'

Jacob felt a hand on his shoulder. It was Sheplar Lesh. 'I'm sorry.'

'Just keep the supply ship ready to fly,' muttered Jacob, saying a silent prayer to a God he didn't even work for anymore. 'Keep your eye on the scope with Hesia. Whatever happens, we're likely to need to pull out of here fast.'

Owen led the way deep into the station. Jacob barely even heard the man as he described how the slaves were going to use all the station's mining transporters to land on volcanic debris, ride the rocks into the trade winds and scatter to every corner of the empire and beyond. The greatest escape the sky mines had ever seen. That Carter had come up with the plan only made his wretched fate all the crueller. This man was full of praise for Jacob's son. How Carter bounced back every time the Vandians beat him down. How Carter had given the rest of them hope for the first time in the station's history. It sounded a lot like an obituary … or words carved on a gravestone. Sariel and Khow helped Willow as they stumbled towards the fever room. She could barely see, the tears streaming from her eyes. Inside the fever room there were two reunions: Khow's son tending Carter, the young gask seeing his father enter the chamber, the two of them running into each other's arms. By contrast, Carter was rushing nowhere. The only patient in the chamber, he was laid out on a mattress, naked apart from the sheets surrounding him like a toga; his bedroll circled by jugs of water, home-made poultices and flannels to wipe the sweat off him. *Dear God. How thin and wiry he looks.* There were scars on his back, hardly healed red weals criss-crossing. Carter's face purple with bruises and swollen where he had taken the beating, a less recent scar cut across the side of his cheek as though he had been duelling. What had they done to him? His son. All that was left of his family, broken and laid out here to die. There was another slave inside the room who Owen introduced as Doctor Tooky.

'How long does he have?' asked Jacob.

'He should have passed already,' said the doctor, simply. 'If I had a surgeon's table, anaesthetic, sterile instruments and trained nurses too, I could open his skull too and try to ease the swelling that way. As it is ...'

As it is. Jacob had seen enough dying men before to recognise when it was nearly over. On the battlefields of the Burn. On the beds of his parishioners. Willow fell in front of the mattress, on her knees, moaning as though the sick bed was an altar and she could resurrect his son. She might have been repeating *please* over and over again, but it was hard to tell.

'I'm using painkillers from the patrol ship we captured,' said the doctor. 'He's not feeling much, now. That's all I can do for him.'

Jacob knelt by the bed. 'Do you have anything that can wake him up?'

'I do,' said the doctor. 'But it won't help his body last any longer.'

'Use it,' said Jacob. He could feel his face growing as pale as a corpse himself. 'I want him to know I came for him.' He glanced over to Willow. '*We* came for him. Before he passes. He deserves that much.'

'As you wish,' said the slave. He went out and returned with a glass hypodermic filled with a thin green substance. After he injected

Carter, they waited for a minute, and then his eyes began to flutter before opening.

'Willow, I'm hallucinating again? You're not here?' He reached over to her to feel her fingers and then looked over at Jacob. His voice sounded faint and dry. 'Who are you?'

'I'm your father,' said Jacob, gently.

'No, you look something like him, is all. But he's not here. He's dead.'

'It's me, Carter. I've come for you. It takes more to kill me than a few skels and their imperial friends.'

'It's me that must be dead,' coughed Carter. 'You should be far away. You look so thin. So different.'

'You might say I've been far-called as well,' said Jacob. He clutched Carter's other hand. 'And you're a fine one to talk.'

'It *is* him, Carter,' said Willow. She indicated the others standing in the room behind the doctor. 'Northhaven mounted a rescue mission. They've arrived to take us home.'

'You have to go, then,' said Carter. 'And live for both of us.'

'Don't say that,' cried Willow.

'My mind's burning up,' said Carter. 'The things I've seen. Too many people and places and times. Too much. I can't separate any of my thoughts. It's as if my memories have been poisoned. Did I watch Mother die, or was that something else I imagined?'

'She's dead,' said Jacob. 'I'm sorry.'

'She'll be here soon,' said Carter, trying to look around. 'Owen, when's my mother arriving?'

The young gask was by the boy's side, kneeling next to Willow and mopping his brow again. 'I told you I felt my father's presence close by.'

'Thought you were joshing me,' said Carter, trembling. 'A spoonful of hope to keep me going.'

'Your son's presence in the world is not as it should be,' Khow told Jacob. 'He feels wrong.'

'He's *dying*,' said Jacob.

'His numbers are part of the sickness, I think,' said Kerge, tugging at his father's arm. 'I do not know how that is possible, but it is.'

'It is not an illness,' said Sariel, stepping forward. 'He has been touched. He is a messenger, ridden by spirits.'

'Sariel?' said Carter. 'Now I know I'm trapped in a fever dream.'

'You know him?' said Jacob, shocked. He wasn't sure if he was talking to Carter, the old bard or both of them at once.

'Sariel visited the librarian's hold in Northhaven,' Carter coughed.

Jacob looked suspiciously at the old man. 'You did?'

Sariel limped forward, clutching his walking staff. 'I have been to so many places. They all blur together. But I remember you, young Lord Carnehan. I remember all those I have knighted, it is a sacred duty for me.'

'I don't understand?' said Jacob.

Sariel touched his leather coat, brushing his hand over the hundreds of drawings illustrated there. 'Lord Carnehan's mind is like my story coat. Overflowing.'

'I do not understand, either,' said Kerge, waving his abacus machine at the elder gask. 'Father, this manling's presence is not coherent.'

'That's because I'm not quite a manling,' said Sariel, 'although I'm afraid I am quite broken.'

Kerge shook his head and started tapping at his abacus box again.

Sariel removed Jacob's hand from Carter's and reached out to feel the boy's forehead. As their skin touched there was a brilliant flash followed by a detonation, the shockwave of a shell-burst. There wasn't any heat: an ice-cold gale exploded through the chamber, overturning everyone and everything except Sariel and Carter, who remained anchored in place as though they had been carved from stone. Jacob was flung back into one of the fever room's empty bunks, Willow thrown in the opposite direction, both gasks and the doctor and Owen tossed to the far end of the bare windowless chamber in a storm of pottery and bedding. Sariel and Carter glowed like twin suns, too bright to look at without black spots rippling across Jacob's vision. It was as though the ward had been filled with a flight of arrows, each of the darts a thought, strange and alien and pure. He saw the stone circles and the world, so large, league after league and nation after nation without end. Too intense for his mortal mind. Jacob's head pulsed behind his ears, as though someone was cutting into his skull. The others' thoughts leaked across his, water from a rack of jugs, all broken and pooling into the same puddle. *Digging tunnels in the sky mines and light falling through trees in the gasks' forest and cutting off mangled legs with a hot saw and the corridors of the Landor estate and the weight of an avalanche striking and burying everyone and Sariel and ...* Jacob screamed. Then as quickly as the pain had struck, it receded. Jacob gasped hard, attempting to breathe; his chest spasming as the light filling his head fled, Carter still wrapped in sheets and the bard kneeling before the bed. Everyone except those two pulled themselves back on their feet, badly shaken.

'What the hell was that?' demanded Jacob.

'I took Lord Carnehan's stories from him,' said Sariel, turning. 'He doesn't need them anymore.' He grinned wickedly at Jacob. It was like staring into the eyes of one of the gargoyles clinging to the side of a cathedral. 'You might say that I *stole* them.'

Jacob drew his pistol. 'If I didn't need you to open the stone circle, I'd damn well kill you right here!'

He looked to the side as he felt Carter's hand tug on his sleeve. His son was standing up! 'You're not my father, are you ... why are you carrying a gun?'

'Your son has come to no harm, Your Grace,' said Sariel. 'Lord Carnehan's stories were stored in the correct order, not fragmented and reconstituted from echoes as mine were. You might say that his sickness was my cure, while the converse is also true. Besides, what better use for a librarian, than the transmission of knowledge? You are lucky, my lord. You would not have survived the paths you walked without my blessing back in Northhaven.'

'Two,' said Jacob, looking in astonishment at his son. 'I'm carrying two guns, Carter. Because we've travelled through hell to reach you and it took more than a sermon a week to reach Vandia.'

The doctor was by Carter's side, feeling his skull and forehead. 'His swelling has gone? And the fever has broken? It can't be possible!'

Carter groaned and nearly dropped to the floor, his fall halted by Willow running forward and leaning against his weight. 'But his ribs are still broken.'

Carter touched his swollen purple face. 'My mind's clear. For the first time since the volcano. Sweet mercy, thank you, Sariel. I'd forgotten what it feels like not to have an irate swarm of visions buzzing inside my brain.'

Jacob looked suspiciously at Sariel. God wasn't to be thanked here, he suspected. Maybe the opposite. What had the gads called Sariel? *Jok the trickster, Jok the fallen angel?* For the first time since Jacob had begun this long journey to recover his son, he felt real cold fear stabbing deep inside. Not fear like before of dying before he ever reached his child, but dread of something unknown and incomprehensible. Now he understood why he'd sensed the gads' shamanic council considering the stone circle as a means of eliminating the expedition, rather than of sending them on their way. Was this how evil passed through the world? Not as the horn-headed stealers of biblical legend, but under the guise of confused, avuncular mischief, so easy to underestimate, so simple to ignore? Jacob gazed back in time and saw events of the journey with different eyes. Finding the stone circle, still hot and burnt, when the train out of Weyland halted for that odd missing rail. Sariel's well-timed entry onto the express. Jacob's pistols mysteriously turning up in his tent during Wiggins' torture and Jacob's knots retied so he could slip them. The theft of their money box before the bard conveniently bumped into the expedition at the aerial port. *It was all Sariel.*

'You will never forget, Lord Carnehan,' announced Sariel. 'You will always carry a shadow of what has passed through you. It will linger like a stain on the soul. You are hardly much of a story-teller, not compared to the prince of players.' He brushed his leather coat, slyly satisfied with himself. 'And if you are happy to forget, I am more than happy to remember.'

'What the hell are you?' said Jacob.

'I should say that remains to be seen,' said Sariel. 'There are many stories, and the prince of players features in so many of them. I have so many names. But I can promise you one thing—' he looked around craftily at the group in the fever room '—those who ripped my wings off and burnt my body at the stake will be given cause to wish I had *stayed* burnt and lost!'

'I saw the stones,' said Owen, amazed. He walked up to Sariel and touched his leather cloak, covered in stories, captured over the years like souls. 'I *saw* them.'

'An ancient way of travelling,' said Sariel. 'Though not without dangers these days. For some, of course, there will be additional dangers of returning home. Such as the regrets of an uncle discovering a nephew with a stronger claim to the throne is quite not as dead as he believed. You would be better off riding the eruption to distant provinces as you had originally planned, Owen Hawkins. There are few kind fates awaiting you in Weyland. Too many of the industrial lords owe their wealth to your uncle's scheming.'

'How—?'

Jacob looked on in amazement, memories of an avalanche claiming the royal family unfurling as though they were his own, the shadows of a palace and a privileged life in the heart of the capital hovering close behind. All ripped away and lost along with his family, before ending up inside the sky mines.

'I would know you even without the tales I removed from Lord Carnehan's mind. I passed through the court when you were five, and you have not changed so greatly since then. At least on the outside. There is little of that spoilt arrogance about you, now. Maybe you could find it in your heart to thank your uncle for his scheming ways? That would be a more interesting ending to your tale.'

'Maybe *after* I have buried him,' said Owen.

'Now that's more like the boy I recall,' smiled Sariel.

Khow yelped at the other end of the bed, shaking his abacus box. Wisps of grey smoke rose from the device's back.

'Stories possess a weight beyond mere numbers,' Sariel told the gask. 'I would advise against factoring me into your equations, again. Recurring loops are not good for little thinking machines.' He bumped his staff on the floor and the smoking stopped. 'Now, shall we put all those transporters idling in the hangar to good use? Those who wish to go up can go up, and those who wish to go down can go ... sideways.'

'You've remembered how to use the stones properly?' said Jacob.

'Perhaps more importantly,' smiled Sariel, 'I have remembered *why* they were used.'

'You can take us home? All of us?' asked Owen, looking overwhelmed by the shock of the sudden explosion and all that he had seen inside his mind.

'I can take you back to Weyland,' said Sariel. 'But I can't take you *home*.' He looked at Jacob, rubbing his beard thoughtfully. 'It's not there anymore. You understand that, don't you? You've walked this path once before.'

'And I survived before, too,' said Jacob.

'Think before you ask to return. The Vandians will contact the king and every agent they have inside the league nations. You'll be a hunted man for the rest of your life. You and everyone else. King Marcus won't suffer tales of his subjects stolen as slaves by a distant empire. Not when everyone believes they were random raids by the skels. It's a *very* large world. I could take you to some harmless land where even the radio signals passed between the holds won't catch you up for a thousand years. Nobody to care who you are or *were*.'

'Just return us to the kingdom,' snarled Jacob. 'Vandia is far-called enough for me.'

'Well, you've returned me. So I shall return you. That's only fair.' Sariel leant in close, whispering low enough that only Jacob could hear, 'And you haven't watched the king and his allies die yet, have you, for murdering your wife? That would be a fine sight to see, wouldn't it?'

Jacob recoiled. It was as though the bard could reach inside his head and pick out his thoughts. Sariel swept grandly out of the fever room, Owen, the two gasks and the doctor behind him. Jacob helped Willow carry Carter out, his son limping, still weak and sweating. Not dead. Not yet. Jacob's prayers had been answered. But he dearly wished the answer hadn't come from the bizarre bard in their company.

'You and Willow could take Sariel up on his offer,' said Jacob. 'Go somewhere so far from home they'll never find you.'

'Weyland is my home, as much as it yours,' said Willow. 'And my father deserves to know that Duncan and I survived.'

Maybe Benner Landor had paid for that much. But Jacob suspected her homecoming wouldn't be anything like she hoped.

'Anywhere that's not the sky mines,' coughed Carter. It seemed colder in the passage outside the fever room. Slaves rushed along the corridors, stripping everything they could carry and hauling it towards the station's hangars. 'Anywhere Willow goes, I'll travel there, too. But I'd like to see Northhaven again. I've seen more than enough of the rest of Pellas for a lifetime.' He gripped his father's shoulder tight. 'Thank you for coming for me.'

'Carter, you only thank someone when they had a choice. And you never need to say it to family. I taught you that much.'

Jacob's son stared at the two pistols belted under his duster. 'You taught me a lot of things.'

'You may have to learn a few new rules, and forget a lot of the old ones, if you're set on returning to Weyland.'

'We had to fight here,' said Carter, the pain and horror leaking through his voice. 'They forced us. Slave against slave to stake the best rocks inside the sky mines for the house.'

'Choosing who you fight is the privilege of kings and emperors,' said Jacob. His eyes narrowed. But it was only enjoyed by the *live* ones. 'For everyone else, it's just someone charging at you with a sword or a bayonet and the decision you have to make in that second.'

'I *hated* it.'

'Then you've already learnt your most important lesson. It's when you start to revel in the fight that you know it's time to quit,' said Jacob. It sounded as though Carter wouldn't be picking any more duels when he reached Northhaven. His son had travelled a long way to learn that lesson. He was a man now.

'Going back is the right thing to do, isn't it?' said Willow. 'Or this will just go on. Others from home forced to come out here, instead of us.' She didn't sound sure about it. But then, Willow was no fool.

'The right thing, maybe,' said Jacob. 'But not the easy one.'

Carter tried not to wince as he had to limp down a set of stairs towards the station's hangars, the pressure on his cracked rib as he walked. 'I saw so much *blood.*'

Jacob knew Carter wasn't talking about the sky mines, but what he had glimpsed in their sudden strange pooling of memories. Sariel was right about one thing. King Marcus and his allies would be hunting the survivors, even before he heard the rumours that a rival to the throne had arrived in Weyland. So much blood. *There'll be more.*

SIXTEEN

EMPTY STATIONS

Duncan saw Paetro swing back into the compartment, staggering as the massive ship pitched to the side. Duncan waved at him, still clinging to his seat's acceleration arm, even now that their vessel had slowed to normal cruising speed. To either side the house's soldiers grumbled and groused about the wisdom of this mission. 'What's going on?'

'Our guardsmen have just returned. The mining station is empty, completely abandoned – not even a skeleton crew, as best they can tell.'

'As best they can tell?'

'They didn't search every passage and chamber. Supply ship's been on the station, all right. There are snares and tripwires everywhere, rigged to mining charges and some of the house's explosives destined for our forts.'

'Where've the slaves gone?'

'Half the house's transporters are in the air, riding for altitude, even though it's suicidally early to be trying for a new claim. We're brewing up to a full eruption outside now.'

'I noticed,' said Duncan, the shaking of the deck under his feet growing stronger. 'What about the stolen supply ship?' *And more to the point, Willow … as well as Paetro's daughter?*

Paetro shrugged, confused. 'A scout helo's spotted our ship on the ground, alongside the miners' remaining transporters.'

'But that doesn't make sense? They don't need to recover seismic ground spikes to see what's coming – they're in the middle of it, they'll die down there?'

'*We'll* die down there!' said Paetro. 'Apolleon has lost his bloody mind, lad. The man's obsessed. He's ordered the ship to head towards the volcano when we should be docking here to ride out the worst of the eruption. Apolleon's convinced the outlaw he's hunting is some-where down there. In search of a lava bath, maybe. Princess Helrena has ordered us to take the young Highness to the landing bay and buckle up inside a troop transporter. Bail before we're hit, if we need to. The mistress would be within her rights to relieve Apolleon of his command and turn us about. But we'd have a fight on our hands with the hoodsmen on board, and that'd be nothing next to surviving the political hit.'

Better that, than the kind of hit Old Smoky might deliver, Duncan mused. 'What about Willow and—?'

'I don't know.' He sounded weary. 'Hesia's flown across the dead zone for the house. She knows how dangerous it is here. If she's got any sense she'll be blasting away at top speed along with your sister.'

And how much sense did Willow possess? Or Jacob Carnehan, and, by now, that fool Carter too? He groaned. Duncan, Cassandra and Helrena were meant to be safe on board one of the most powerful warships in the imperium. And they would be, too, if the lunatic in command wasn't planning to fly them over a stratovolcano heading for full rupture. 'What's going on here, Paetro?'

The bodyguard shrugged. 'Make me a colonel of the secret police and I'll do my best to find out for you.' He turned to the troops in the chamber and shouted at them. 'Oxygen masks and heat suits, my braves. Rifles and full armour. Down to the launch bay and get ready to earn your salary. You'll do a man's work today!' Paetro did his best to ignore the groans of disgust and a few unruly shouts back. 'Aye, that's right, I'm serious. Have you ever known me not to be? Move, move, *move*!' He turned to Duncan. 'Our job's the same as it ever was. Keeping the young Highness safe.'

Duncan left the compartment and headed away to the bridge, trying to walk the ship's deck as she listed at a twenty degree angle, the engines' roar outside the hull deafening as she attempted to cor-rect her flight amidst the maelstrom.

Carter crouched down close to the ground, trying to shield Willow from the worst of the scorching ash rain. The standing circle lay directly behind them, the plain in front of the stratovolcano littered with grounded transporters and the stolen Vandian supply ship. Many miners hunkered down as best they could while Sariel worked to achieve what he had promised them – opening a portal to Northhaven. A few slaves unloaded crates of weapons and guns from the hijacked ship. Right now, Carter wished he had followed the transporter crews who had stuck with his original plan. Fleeing for the rocks and riding the trade winds to freedom. It was mostly the foreign slaves with homes close to the empire's borders following his scheme. The majority of those who had stayed were Weyland born and bred. Too late to try and take off now. The air thick with debris. Any transporter hovering for more than a couple of seconds choked on the dust and came sliding back to the ground. They were grounded, and the only way out was a mysterious gate he had glimpsed in his mind for a few seconds. *The portal has to be true, doesn't it? Not part of my madness. Outside of commandeering a Vandian warship, it's the only way my father and the expedition reached the sky mines this fast.*

'I can hear something?' said Willow, her voice muffled by a survival suit.

'Same sound we heard on the skel carrier,' said Carter. 'There's a Vandian ship in the clouds.' He didn't add that the fact they could hear it over the volcano's violent upsurge meant it was going to be one hell of a large vessel.

'Course there's a ship. Wherever you can find Carter Carnehan, you'll find trouble skimming fast behind.'

Carter glanced behind him. It was Anna Kurtain. 'So this is how you're aiming to keep me safe, Northhaven? Ducking rocks and dodging lava, waiting for the full blow to land on top of us?'

'I'm doing my best,' said Carter.

'I can tell. You know, your father isn't much like you described him back on the station.'

Carter had to agree with her. His father looked the same, talked the same and walked the same. On the surface everything that counted should have been constant – whereas, in reality, *nothing* that mattered was. It was as though his father's blood had turned to flint in his veins. Turning him stony, hard and hazardously sharp.

Anna laughed. 'Don't get me wrong, he's your father all right. Arriving here with a crazy-arse story about magical shortcuts home and a ship with enough guns, grenades and ammo to start his own private war against the empire. Who could he be but a Carnehan?'

Carter shrugged. Now all that came when he heard his surname was his mother's face. 'It's how the rescue party reached us. I've seen it. Owen, too.'

'Why do you think I'm here? I've followed Owen through hell most of my life,' said Anna. 'We all have. He kept the miners together and as many of us alive as any person could hope to. Even when the old rock was blown to pieces. Even after we lost his brothers. A couple more hours down here doesn't make any difference to me. This is all I ever wanted, Northhaven. A chance to make a difference and choose how to do it away from there—' She pointed up towards the black rolling clouds. 'You've given us that. So as far as the promise you made my brother goes, this is as good as it gets. The rest will have to sort itself out on its own. I just thought you should hear that.' She stared across the desolate plain towards Owen, the man walking among the sheltering slaves. Reassuring them, pointing back to the standing stones and talking of the portal. Carter recognised that look on her face. He wondered if the prince-turned-slave knew how Anna felt about him; if Anna didn't tell Owen soon, she might not get another chance. The dead zone seemed hungrier than usual for Weyland bones.

As Anna walked away, Carter heard his father complaining to Sariel. 'You told me you could open a damn gate down here?'

Sariel appeared blithely unconcerned by the urgency of the task he attempted. 'Opening it won't be a problem. Arriving at the other end without resembling jam is quite another matter. The gate mechanism is being interfered with from afar.' He pointed towards the shadow of the massive ship just visible battling through the volcanic clouds. 'But not *very* far. I warned you back in the cell that the stealers would come for me when they traced the stone circle we used to exit. One of *them* is on board that vessel, a motley-minded measle hunting me.'

Carter bit his tongue at the first sight of the warship. They were so close. All they had been through, all they had endured and survived. Sariel had to get them home. He *had* to.

'And here was me thinking you might be counted among their number,' said Jacob.

'There's no need to be insulting,' replied Sariel. 'I could pass through the stones and shield a handful around me. Yourself, your son and his friends, perhaps. But not everybody here. Do you wish to cut your losses and run?'

Carter saw his father waver. For a terrible moment he thought that he was going to accept Sariel's offer, but the pastor wearily shook his head. 'I gave my word to the people of Northhaven that when we left, we would be travelling here for everyone. Not just for my son.'

'Are you sure I can't *tempt* you, no? And what is a man's word but wind passing through the lips,' sighed Sariel. It sounded like a quote. 'As you wish. It will take time, however. Let us give the stealer something to worry about other than targeting us during this earth-vexing turd storm.' He raised his staff towards the stratovolcano and started chanting in a language Carter didn't recognise. The eruption appeared to grow stronger, a mortar hail of steaming rocks raining down on the slopes and around the immense black plain of the dead zone. Debris exploded all about them.

Carter ran towards the old bard with Willow. 'Get down!'

Sariel shrugged the two of them off as if he hadn't heard Carter's warning. 'When they ambushed me last time, there were a hundred stealers against six of us. And it took a full hundred of the spleeny lily-livered giglets to do the job properly. So, their toy empire is getting greedy? It wants a little bit more? *Here it is!*'

He thumped his staff into the ground at the moment a massive earthquake rode up towards the volcano, the cinder-shrouded terrain shuddering below their boots, an avalanche of stone shrugged off the stratovolcano. Willow tumbled over and Carter followed a second later, both of them sent sprawling into clouds of black powder. A colossal outrush of lava breached the slopes and sprayed across the ship as Carter fell. It was as though the vessel had been struck by a giant's lance formed from pure fire, the warship's hull crumpling and screaming as though alive, the vessel severed into two sections. Clouds of rotor-driven aircraft buzzed out of its hangars, abandoning their carrier like angry wasps swarming out of a broken hive. They emerged choking on the hard hot rain of rock, gas and magma; engines and rotors every bit as useless in this environment as the slaves' mining transporters. Most of them ditched for the ground, only flying far enough to clear a ripple of explosions running down the huge warship. The Vandian vessel finally lost whatever trick of aerodynamics kept millions of tonnes of steel hovering in the air on a wall of jets, the forward section of the ship ploughing down into the dead zone, the aft half whipping around as its engines exploded and drove it spinning away into the poisonous clouds.

Carter wiped the dust off his heat suit's mask, helping Willow rise from the ground. 'He didn't just do *that*, did he?' she shivered.

'He can't have done,' said Carter. *Just a coincidence.*

Sariel strolled back towards the obelisks, nodding to the pair; as casual as a greeting to neighbours promenading around a park. 'There's a reason why you construct a circle at the base of a volcano. And it's not merely for easy access.' He gestured at Khow and Kerge, the pair of gasks sheltering behind a rise. 'Ah, my two spiny companions. Come here and bring your fusty little machines with you. You will find the twists and knots in the fabric of fate surrounding the stones. Map the discontinuities for me. Discover the pattern behind their creation. I need to bypass the stealer's loops to open the gate cleanly.'

The two gasks reluctantly abandoned their shelter and followed Sariel into the stone circle. Carter turned his attention back to the plain. Their pursuers were disciplined, Carter gave them that. The troops from the crashed helos rapidly formed up into companies, others creating a skirmish line and marching straight towards the standing stones. Steam, the ash rain and thick, deadly gas covered their advance, the exact numbers and forces arranged against the slaves lost in the swirl. Is that how it would play out? Like Carter's escape attempt. Weylanders and Vandians lost in the volcanic fog, doing their damnedest to maim and kill each other. No, there was one important difference this time: Carter stood alongside his friends and family.

Carter's father shouted to Sariel. 'Help us!'

'I have my hands full here. And unless you can swim through lava better than a Vandian ... no? Well, then. Your nation is well-practised at killing each other. Now seems the perfect time for a little more of the same.'

'These people are worth more than a tall tale by the fireside in the future,' scowled Jacob.

'Time to prove that theory, then. If you see something resembling a man mated with a giant spider, sharp bony limbs, decapitating people, do please let me know,' said Sariel. 'I can always make time for old friends.'

'All men form a semi-circle around the stones,' Owen shouted. 'Pass out the rest of the ammunition and rifles from the Vandian ship. All women to take shelter between the slope and the circle.'

'Forget that,' ordered Jacob. 'Rifles and rounds for the women, too.'

'This isn't the Burn!' snapped Owen.

'Maybe not, but you know what the empire will do to rebellious slaves, and our women will die foulest of any Weylander.'

Willow picked up a rifle from a supply crate. 'We'll fight, Owen. We have to.'

Carter tried to say something but Willow cut him short. Owen looked as though he was going to protest again too, but the sorting-line supervisor, Kassina, stepped forward and lifted a weapon out of one of the crates. 'With all due respect, Your Highness, you can shut your bloody trap. I brought more rabbits back to the pot than any man around the lakes with a hunting rifle. Kept you alive all these years up there as a slave, too. Damned if I'll act any differently now I'm a free woman again.'

Weylanders came forward, men and women alike in a long line, rifles and clips passed among those who hadn't already taken weapons.

'Form two lines around the standing stones,' barked Jacob. 'Anyone with Vandian armour up front. Unarmoured folk as the rear line. Best seven shots up on the slopes to act as snipers. Find large, hard boulders to shelter behind. Open fire at three hundred yards and closer. Any target further than that will be wasted ammunition.'

A cough sounded. Carter turned around. It was Sheplar Lesh. He stood beside the Vandian woman who had flown his father to the sky mines. The Rodalian pilot bowed towards Carter. 'With a kind wind, my debt to you and the raid's survivors will be paid by the day's end. My name and honour restored.'

Carter glanced around at the poisonous billowing clouds rolling down the volcano's slopes. 'There doesn't seem too much chance of a kind wind today. But I reckon your name was carved on a Rodalian temple stone the moment you left. You've got no debts to me that haven't been paid a hundred fold by bringing my father to me alive.'

The female pilot passed Willow a spare pistol to go along with her newly acquired rifle. 'Save the last bullet for yourself.' She looked at Carter. 'And if she can't do it, *you* should. Those aren't legion soldiers mustering out there. That's the secret police's flagship that went down on the plain.'

Carter watched the two aviators weaving through the storm of hot dust, taking position behind a cluster of rocks. He felt Willow squeeze his hand tight. *I can't. Don't ask me to do that.* 'I don't know if—'

'It doesn't matter,' said Willow. 'Just being here's enough. Alongside you.'

He stared at the stone circle for a second, Sariel and the two gasks like penitent priests attending a human sacrifice, lost among the swirling dust. It seemed a crazy hope. Passing through the stones. 'You were freed, Willow, you're not even a slave, and you still came back for me ...'

'It's like your father said back in the fever room. I guess I didn't have any choice in the matter, either.'

Maybe not having any choice was the most important part of living free. Carter looked at the Vandian rifle in his hands. More use to him as a crutch. He didn't want to fight. He barely felt strong enough to raise a gun, let alone absorb its recoil along his shattered ribs. He was sick of battle. But right now, at this moment, there wasn't an enemy he wouldn't face or a number he wouldn't take on to keep Willow out of the empire's hands. 'That rock over there looks large enough to shelter the both of us.'

His father's voice cut through the storm with a power of its own. 'The Vandians are coming to take you for slaves. But you're standing here to take your freedom.'

'He's right!' shouted Owen. 'When the empire's pet raiders captured you, they were scooping up carpenters and butchers and farmers, scared and surprised and raw. But they're advancing on survivors today, survivors who've eaten and lived on rock, who are armed and steeled. Let every Weylander here send the emperor back a hundred of his own and count it a bargain ill-met. We've lived through hell. Today we'll give it back to them!'

Ragged yells and cheers echoed down the line.

'For Weyland!'

'For the true king!'

Carter pulled his rifle tight against his aching shoulder and stole a glance at Willow. 'No. For you.'

He sighted the weapon. Vandian soldiers hopped between boulders, covering each other as they zigzagged ever closer. *Near enough.* Empty casings showered out of the side of the unfamiliar weapon as Carter opened up, its chatter lost among an outbreak of rifle-fire all around the circle. Hot casings jounced off his survival suit from the ejection port of Willow's gun as she swivelled it left and right. Vandians dived down ahead. Bullets whipped and whistled off rocks around them, geysers of powder across the boulders mirroring the eruption fountaining above, sharp stone splinters filling the air. His Vandian rifle was better at absorbing recoil than any firearm from Weyland. It only felt like every second shot was shattering Carter's ribs.

Duncan blundered through the smoke. How long had he been out cold? The wreckage of his helo lay behind him, bodies scattered around the vehicle's twisted rotors, what was left of its fuselage on fire – either from the crash or magma and hot ash igniting the fuel tanks. The helo was one of many. Entire squadrons were stretched out broken and smoking across the dead zone. *It's lived up to its name today.* The landscape looked as though an entire legion had decided to camp here and use their aircraft as bonfires. Cassandra wasn't inside what remained of Duncan's troop transporter, not one of the broken bodies. He had already checked for her. Ahead, he found Paetro, turning over fragments of wing and aluminium fuselage.

'Where is she?' called Duncan.

'Not here,' said Petro.

Duncan turned back towards the forward half of the warship, crew climbing out of rents along the severed remains of the once mighty vessel. All of this, for one high-caste fool's obsession with an ancient outlaw who must have been close to dying of old age? He hoped that

Apolleon lay impaled on a girder in the wrecked bridge for this. He prayed that Helrena didn't. He was torn between searching through the damaged vessel's wreckage for the princess and combing the battlefield for her young daughter. 'Would Cassandra have gone back inside the ship? Looking for her mother, maybe?'

Paetro shook his head. 'If she's not trapped below the wreckage, the young Highness will follow her duty. She can hear where that is, even over this eruption. Same as it ever was. Just follow the sound of cannons.'

There weren't any cannons. But with the random barrage of burning rocks falling, neither side needed artillery. Duncan stared at the distant standing stones; a rattle of gunfire exchanged not so far from where he used to conceal the sky mine's seismic recorders. He could barely see the battle, a driving wind of hot ash obscuring the plains, beating against the visor of his mask. The smell of sulphur was nearly overwhelming, even through its filters. 'This is madness!'

Paetro levered up a broken wing, checking below. 'Whatever mutiny broke out on the station, those workers are grounded down here now, same as us. Nowhere left to go, nothing left to live for. They'll fight to the last, I can tell you. I would do the same.'

'Willow and Hesia?'

Paetro placed a hand on Duncan's shoulder. 'Trust they're on one of the birds in the air heading for clear sky.'

Duncan couldn't be sure where his sister was, but he knew who was making a last stand in the lee of the volcano. *Carter Carnehan*. This mess had his signature all over it. Carter's father had showed up and his son had seized the munitions ship, trying to make a break for it using the fresh eruption as cover, just like he had before. Except this time, he'd incited most of the station to follow him, only to discover there was a reason nobody tried to fly during a full blow. And now here they all were, grounded and surrounded with nowhere left to go except towards a mass execution for mutiny. Yes, Carter would be over there somewhere. Duncan had never met anyone so eager to die. And if he got Willow killed, Duncan would slip the noose around the wild man's neck himself and ask to pull down the lever for the hatch in the hangman's platform.

Paetro unshouldered his rifle and checked its clip. 'I gave that girl's father a promise in blood I'd keep her safe. Let's not make me a liar this day.'

Above them the slopes of the stratovolcano shuddered after each explosion, discharges echoing across the plains, huge rocky masses driven out at inconceivable pressures. Residual clouds of gas even thicker than the current smoke cloaking the dead zone began to spill down. The two of them followed the sound of gunfire, lost and muffled amid the billowing murk.

Jacob ducked behind the boulder as bullets scoured its surface, shots coming from at least two directions. Owen dived close behind him. He heard a hissing sound as rolls of poisonous gas spread out from the slopes, heating and cooling by turns as clouds crept across the ground. It blotted out the sight of the shower of burning rubble falling around them, but not its sound ... a clattering rain of pebbles. The pastor could only tell front and rear from the whistle of bullets coming at him.

'I remember stories from my father about his campaigns – the fog of war,' Owen gasped. 'I don't think he meant this.'

'Give me a savage northern nomad clan any day,' said Jacob. 'The imperium's men are too well armed and trained.'

'I think I'd settle for the hinterlands of Rodal over the dead zone, too,' said Owen. He slid his rifle's bayonet out of its clasp under the weapon, thrusting it down onto the barrel. Not as accurate now with the extra weight, but damned if the exiled noble could sight on what they were shooting at anyway.

Jacob put a return volley into the choking clouds. What was it the officers told the young men back in Northhaven's territorial regiment – any fool can hold a rifle? No shortage of fools here. Ironically, it was probably only the eruption that had allowed them to last this long. When a man's field of vision was reduced to a couple of yards, there wasn't much chance to bring trained marksmanship into play or to signal disciplined manoeuvres. Just the basic savageries of attack and defence. Hack and shoot, bayonet and sword. But even in this murk, the Vandians' superior numbers were beginning to tell. Miners left dead around the rocks, wounded people pulled moaning to the rear, teams hauling crates of clips through the defence line, tossing ammunition to the beleaguered defenders. There was a cry to his left, a charging Vandian left impaled on the bayonet below Kassina's rifle. She kicked the attacker off her blade, sending the corpse tumbling to join another soldier she had shot through the oxygen mask. As good as her word to the throne's true heir. Kassina ducked back below the boulder, another miner shooting in her place while she reloaded her rifle. *Too few of us, too many of them. If they decide to press the attack ...*

Out in the clouds came a sound to make a man doubt his sanity. A deep, lingering screech that shook Jacob's heart in his chest and made his spine run cold – something which had no place among this burning hellscape. Quite unlike the muffled yells of dying miners and shot Vandian soldiers lost in the volcanic outgassing. Some*thing* was hunting out there. The supernatural noise came again and Jacob had to resist the urge to flee with every fibre of his being. He glanced around. He had lost sight of Carter and Willow. Jacob had lost sight of everything apart from this boulder, its neighbour, Owen, and the fierce spray of gunfire breaking against their position.

'Is that sound the thing Sariel talked about?' asked Owen.

'Unless you got mountain lions living up on the slopes with sore throats from all this smoke ...'

'Demons don't exist,' said Owen, sounding as though he was trying to convince himself. 'Stealers are just a Bible tale.'

Jacob slipped out the Vandian short-sword he'd commandeered, laying the steel against a ridge in the boulder. He would have preferred a heavy cavalry sabre, long and sharp, but beggars couldn't be choosers. 'Said the man praying for a sorcerous portal to open to carry him home.'

'Say a prayer of exorcism,' pleaded Owen.

There are never any atheists sheltering behind the shield line. 'The Lord bless our aim when we stand against darkness.' The last line from the text came unbidden to Jacob. *And let us never slip into the darkness ourselves.* He heard a mortal bellow. Charging men, figures sprinting through the black mist. Angry cries and unrestrained shooting to comfort their rush against death and the defenders' return fire. Dozens of Vandians appeared as though they had materialised inside the smoke, screaming a battle charge and rushing the defensive line. Jacob raised his rifle and aimed bursts at as many soldiers as he could sight down on. More attackers appeared behind the first line, and his juddering rifle clicked empty in protest. Damn the fancy machine weapon. It practically vomited ammunition. A Vandian came crashing over the boulder and the short-sword was in Jacob's hand as he plunged through the man's visor. His first foe had a comrade behind, raising a rifle to shoot, but the soldier went down in a burst of fire. Carter and Willow appeared through the fog, and from the smoking rifle barrel, it was Jacob's son who had just saved his life. Carter and Willow dived behind the boulder, Jacob using the spare second to slap a fresh clip into his rifle. Below their feet the ground began to shake again, a roaring from beyond the clouds signalling the sky mines would receive a fresh bounty soon. *They can keep it.* Within the smoke Jacob could hear semi-molten rocks detonating around the plains like a thunder god's wrath. If one of those landed on top of the standing stones, the Vandians wouldn't need to assault the position. They could retreat to the shelter of their crashed warship and return to scrape away the rebellious workers' remains after the eruption died away.

'Pull back towards the stones,' Jacob told his son. 'Wait for the portal to open.'

'I'm not leaving you here!'

'And I haven't travelled all the way to the empire to leave your body for the crows,' spat Jacob.

Carter stayed firmly put. 'Do you see any crows flying through this?'

A second wave of Vandians broke through the thick mist, even more soldiers than before, rifles blazing as they sprinted forward, razor-edged bayonets extended and levelled at their rebellious slaves. All of the defenders opened up, but there were too many attackers and too few Weylanders. Soldiers breached the line, leaping over the boulders, thrusting steel into sky miners' chests and heads. Jacob drove his rifle butt forward, smashing it into the visor of the closest Vandian ... then abandoned the weapon – it was far too unwieldy to bring to bear in close-quarters combat. Both pistols were in his hands, soldiers spilling down as he walked his guns around the attacking mob, a bullet apiece at close range. Time always seemed to slow for his pistols, unnatural clarity, wounds appearing, soldiers doubling up, each spinning arc of lead with a blood-spattered home that seemed to call it in. Then his guns fell silent, their smoke lost in the eruption. Time's tread resumed. Bodies lay littered around Owen, Willow and Carter. Around Jacob, a larger mound of corpses. He saw the look of shock on his son's face before he noticed Owen had been wounded in his side – a Vandian bayonet wound from the size and speed of its staining blood. Owen slid down the boulder clutching his side.

'Help Owen behind cover of the stones,' ordered Jacob.

'I won't abandon you!' said Carter.

'I remember your mother teaching you chess,' said Jacob. 'A knight should always try to save a king.'

'Don't ask me …'

Jacob took his son's arm and whispered, 'He's these people's best chance of avoiding a death warrant signed by King Marcus. And Willow, I reckon she's *your* best chance of a real life. Take them both and live.'

There were tears in Carter's eyes. 'Don't you die. I'll wait for you as long as I can by the stones.'

'Don't tarry too long, boy.' Jacob watched Carter and Willow haul the heir to the throne away between them, half-dragging him into the murk. Jacob pushed fresh shells into his pistols' chambers and collected the corpses' rifles, laying them around the boulder to save reloading. He was joined by Kassina, ducking low and clutching her gun.

'They're all dead over there,' she said.

'I'm still alive,' said Jacob. 'Just.'

'So you were a preacher back home? Your sermons must've been the hell-fire kind.'

'Quite the opposite. I valued my peace.'

She raised her mask and spat against the boulder, watching the liquid steam away. 'Travelled a long way to be disappointed, then.'

'Found my son. Found a king I wasn't expecting, too. Maybe being far-called was worth it.' He tried not to think of all that he had lost on the way.

Kassina worked her way through the spare rifles, checking their bolts and magazines. 'Glad you think so. I could put a bullet in a Vandian for every day they've kept me as a slave, and I'd still choose home over this place.'

A figure appeared at speed from the gloom to their side. It was Khow, the gask running low and clutching his abacus machine. He halted in front of them, recovering his breath for a second before speaking. 'The gate will be open shortly. Kerge and I have traced the ruptures preventing its activation. Time to pull back, manling.'

'Where's Kerge?'

'Spreading word to retreat among the other fighters.' As Khow finished speaking there was a strange noise behind them. An orange glow pulsed through the hot black fog, a spear of energy just visible lancing towards the sky and flickering as it held steady. 'We are successful! Sariel believes we have a little more than five minutes before the stealers break his control over the stones and overload the circle. All must pass through before then.'

'Now I've gone and seen everything,' whispered Kassina, staring at the lance of light.

As though summoned by the activation, the eerie fog-shrouded screeching resumed, a wave of Vandian soldiers breaching the mist, rushing towards the remaining defenders … or perhaps trying to outpace whatever lay behind them.

Jacob grabbed a rifle, bringing it to bear. He shouted to Khow. 'Go get your son!' His first burst downed a pair of sprinting soldiers. Kassina's weapon rested on the rock to his left, short controlled bursts pivoting left and right. There were soldiers all over the plains, swarming towards the rocks. Too many defenders had already heeded the gask's instructions to run for the gate. Not nearly enough rifles to stop this wave. Khow stepped forward, raising his arm and downing the nearest attacker, the soldier screaming as nerve toxins on the gask's spines burned through his body. Khow roared. He no longer sounded like a twisted man … more like a maddened bear. Khow's body whipped with pent-up energy, a cracking noise similar to a catapult firing. Attackers screamed as they were struck. The gask grabbed one of the violently convulsing soldiers, using the man as a shield as he flicked spines at the assault force. His muscles popped, spines fleeting off his hide. Khow loped through their ranks with an oddly graceful and sinuous movement, in stark contrast to the ferocity of his roars and the death of any soldier on the receiving end of his poison. Dead Vandians tumbled around him, their last steps juddering as paralysis set in, convulsing and twisting down to the rock. Rifles fired into the air or at the ground as the squad discovered they could no longer point their weapons; fingers rictus-tightening against triggers. As suddenly as the charge had started, it was over. The gask retreated back over bodies shaking in their final death throes, heading for the shelter of the boulder.

'I thought your people couldn't fight,' said Jacob.

'We loathe stealing life,' said Khow. His voice shook; *he* was shaking, trying to re-establish his self-control. Overcome the urge to turn Jacob and Kassina – all too similar to the predators who had just tried to murder him – into pin-cushions. 'That is not the same as lacking the ability to defend ourselves.' He regained a measure of restraint, his voice growing level. 'It is shameful. But I must protect my child.'

'I never want to see an army of your people,' said Kassina, pulling out her clip to examine how many bullets were left.

'Nor do I.' Khow stared down at the ground, disgusted, and seeing the broken dome of a human skull embedded in the solidified lava. 'We stand on death just by being here. How I wish for the peace of the forest and the trees and—' His words were cut off by a shrieking fury forging out of the eruption. It came at the same time as another quake, the ground shaking as a creature the size of a horse charged out of the darkness. Moving at such a clip that Jacob only had a second to take in how wrong the thing was. This steed had six legs, each a bent spear cracking the ground, the central bulb of its body jet-black; a man's torso, head and arms like a centaur where a spider's eyes would have been. It leapt shrieking over the boulder. Kassina was closest, her rifle already rising, a burst of gunfire tracking its leap. A spear-like leg flicked almost contemptuously out while the creature passed, as though slapping a child. Kassina's body spun to the ground, face frozen with shock as her head curved away from the rest of her neck. Both Jacob's pistols were in his hands, shooting as fast as he could squeeze the trigger, but for the first time in his life, his pistols' target was not where his shells struck; the monster leaping to the side even as it turned. It shrieked and skittered forward, the evil noise paralysing Jacob. Suddenly his hands had forgotten how to move. In that second of hesitation it charged; Khow pushed Jacob out of the way and filled the air with spines, a cloud of poison toxin expanding out towards the … *stealer*.

Khow sprinted forward, still shooting spines and roaring. The stealer charged, howling, leaping to the side and impaling the gask through his chest with a leg. The limb broke inside Khow's body, only five legs remaining as the stealer rolled away snarling. Khow's momentum took him two more steps forward and then he collapsed onto the dark rock, sprawling down with the lance-like limb jutting out of his spine. The stealer turned, sliding on the bloody ground, trampling the corpses of dead miners and fallen Vandians, like an ebony bull ready to charge and gore Jacob. Its body had been badly peppered by Khow's spines. The stealer didn't look paralysed. Judging by its distorted human face, it seemed enraged.

Jacob's hands were his own again. They came up clutching twin Landsman navy pattern single-action pistols. 'So you're a demon? These are mine. Let's get acquainted.'

'That's hardly fair,' drifted a voice from the fog. Sariel emerged. 'Playing with your food again, Apolleon?'

The face above the beast grinned, hissing through its teeth. '*Sariel.*'

'You're about ninety-nine demons shy of the toad-spotted bush-whackers you needed last time,' said the old bard, advancing slowly, carefully. 'Not to mention all those hell-hated skels you had running around in your service. But desperate times, I suppose? Did you keep my wings, the ones you ripped off my back? As a trophy, perhaps.'

'You should have stayed dead,' hissed the stealer.

'Good advice,' said Sariel, looking at Jacob and motioning him to move towards the gate with his fingers. 'The real question here, is can you hack me apart faster than I can heal? Just one of you? I don't think you can.'

'You are not yet complete,' snarled the stealer.

'Your death shall be medicine enough for me,' said Sariel. He slapped his staff against the rock and its wooden surface seemed to ripple, turning into a shining silvery metal. He spun the staff around, an almost hypnotic windmill motion. Not for walking, anymore. The old bard advanced on the stealer and it retreated, circling the man. The stealer leapt into the air, all of its legs thundering down like a rear-ing horse. Sariel dived and rolled under the limbs, his staff whirling and deflecting each pincer. The stealer flipped in the air, landing and swivelling, forelegs striking forward – but Sariel had backpedalled. The creature's legs smashed against a boulder, shattering the bare rock into pieces. It renewed its paralysing howl and charged, both figures sliding back into the toxic mixture of volcanic steam and gas. The battle sounded like a clash of steel sabres, staff against javelin-sharp legs, increasingly muffled as they vanished.

Jacob stood there for a second. His guns hung useless in his hands. The rattle of smoking rock falling through the darkness. Only a few shots in the distance. A brief lull in the assault and the eruption, both. There was another roar behind him. A mortal one, this time. Kerge appeared with a patrol of sky miners, still spreading word among the defenders to fall back to the gate. The young gask had discovered his fatally wounded father. Jacob holstered his pistols, picking up one of the rifles resting against the boulder and ran to Khow's side.

'Why this fate?' cried Kerge, kneeling by his father.

'It is the natural – order of things,' groaned Khow. 'For me to follow the final path – before you.'

'You saved my life,' Jacob told the old gask.

'And you shall – save my son's, yet,' said Khow. 'His is the golden mean.'

'You can live,' cried Kerge.

'I shall,' whispered Khow. 'In – you.'

'No!'

Khow pulled Jacob close to his mouth, whispering. 'Manling, the universe *moves.*'

'What, do …?' But it was too late. Jacob's gask friend had passed from this vale. Khow lay still against the hard black ground, quills flattening against his leathery skin. Kerge tilted his head to the dark sky and wailed, an awful cry of agony and pain, one that cut to the very bone. It would have lingered with Jacob a long time if he had been planning to live.

Jacob pulled the young gask to his feet and addressed the two sky miners. 'Escort Kerge to the gate. Carry the body with you too, if you can manage. Take them both through the stone circle.'

'It's time to pull back,' one of the miners told Jacob.

Jacob pointed into the black clouds, the enveloped sound of shots and yelling soldiers growing closer. 'I'm looking to cover your retreat. Otherwise the stones will be overrun long before you're clear.'

The men didn't argue. They hurried the shell-shocked young gask away, hauling Khow's body between them. Khow's body deserved to be buried in the forest he had loved so dear; that was his people's rite. This was Jacob's. Blood and flames and fatal skirmishing inside the dark fog. He belonged here. Jacob pulled up the enemy's strange machine rifle. Aimed it at the line of attackers emerging out of the murk. He was about to fire, but his finger hesitated on the trigger. There was something wrong about one of the advancing figures, too small, a trick of perspective in the shifting smoke or ...?

Hesia sprinted to his boulder, flinging herself against the rock and firing into the fog at the attackers shifting through the mist.

'The gate's open!' Jacob shouted to the pilot. 'Run.'

'I know,' Hesia laughed, pulling him down below the boulder. 'But no retreating yet. Time to take cover.'

Out in the dead zone a whining sound approached, something huge spinning and cutting through the clouds, dropping closer and closer. Jacob resisted the urge to peer over the boulder as a massive explosion shockwaved above his head, the stone's edge splintering into the shredded gas. A shower of enemy bodies hit the ground, the volcano renewing its eruption far above, as though an ancient fire god had grown jealous of these mortals' shallow imitation of its fury.

'Your crazy mountain man wasn't much of a pilot,' said Hesia. 'But then, he didn't have to be to crash the munitions ship into the hoodsmen's advance.'

'Sheplar!'

'I showed him where my parachute's stowed,' said Hesia 'But given his luck, he'd probably bounce without it. *Now* it's time to go!'

'Wait here. I have to check something, first.' Jacob climbed over the boulder and slipped across the plain. He found the figure he had been looking for and wiped dust off the mask's visor. The same young imperial noblewoman who had come down to the dungeons to scream at Hesia. Lady Cassandra. He felt for a pulse. *Unconscious.* Her hearing wouldn't be so good when she came around, but then she didn't need her hearing to be a hostage. He hefted her body up and walked back towards the boulder.

Hesia climbed over to see what he had discovered. 'Who is that?'

'An old friend. Yours, not mine.'

Hesia gazed down through the visor. 'Lady Cassandra!' Her head jerked up, startled, towards a shout in the fog followed by a burst of gunfire. Hesia tumbled to the ground. Dead? Jacob turned instantly, drawing with his free hand, shooting a couple of approaching guardsmen, and then vaulted behind the boulder, pulling his hostage after him.

Jacob yelled from cover. 'Draw back! I've got your princess's daughter with me. If you want her to stay alive, you'll pull out every fighter here and hunker down inside your wrecked warship.'

'Father Carnehan?' called a voice. *Duncan Landor!* Jacob peered over the boulder. Two soldiers left. One was his son's friend. And the man with him looked a lot like the hard brute that was Hesia's father.

'That's your daughter lying out there, Vandian.'

Paetro darted forward, kneeling and turning the pilot's body over. 'Ah, lass. Why did you stop and stand? You should have run and kept running!'

Hesia slapped him in his gut with her jab-stick. 'And you should have shot me in the head, Father.'

Paetro collapsed, jerking as electrical energy coursed across his body. Jacob holstered his gun and slid back over the rock with Lady Cassandra in his arms.

Duncan had a pistol in his hand, pointed trembling towards Jacob. The pastor kept the young girl's limp body in front of him as a shield, while Hesia recovered her gun from where it had dropped in the ash. And he had thought *his* son could act like a fool.

'Let her go!' yelled Duncan.

'I can't do that,' said Jacob. 'Tell me she's not the emperor's granddaughter. Tell me that if I hold a gun to her head, the imperium's agents and allies back home won't think twice about shooting at me, just the way you're hesitating right now.'

'For the love of God, Father Carnehan, she's just a girl!'

'And for the love of God I could show you the graves of a dozen far younger than her back in Northhaven. Their only crime to be too young to work inside this mortal circle of hell … and too slow to outrun the skels that caught and decapitated them.'

'She's innocent of all of this.'

'She *is* this, Duncan. Every weave and thread of her clothes and every ounce of that massive carrier that brought you here to try and kill us. Come home with us. Your sister's waiting for you over there. I gave Benner Landor my word.'

'My *father*!' Duncan almost choked on the word. 'You're trapped! You've got nowhere to go. All you and Carter are going to achieve here is to get Willow killed.'

'There's a gate inside the stones – a portal running all the way back to Northhaven. You only have to step through and you'll be breathing Weyland air.'

'*You*'ve been breathing too many volcano fumes.'

'How do you think we reached the empire so quickly, boy? My story about building a fast aircraft was just that, a story.'

'I don't care if you were blessed by fairies in the gasks' forest and slid down a magic rainbow to reach Vandia,' cried Duncan. 'My life's here now, with *her*.'

'Let Lady Cassandra go!' Hesia stood above her father, the man still moaning on the ground. Hesia's pistol pointed towards Jacob's ribs – the imperial pilot to the left, Duncan standing to the right. Hesia had a good clean shot right past his human shield if she took it.

Jacob grimaced. 'You're thinking they'll pardon you for this? You're having trouble remembering whose side you're on.'

'No. And I'm not planning on staying in the empire,' said Hesia. 'But I'm not about to let you capture Lady Cassandra and drag her with us into exile, either. Duncan is right; she's innocent of any of this. I had my reasons for what I did. I'll wear the title of traitor for it for the rest of my life. Damned if I'll put that little girl's life in danger again for nothing though.'

'You're mistaken. On both counts. It's not for nothing. I'm taking her with me.'

'You think I won't shoot?' hissed Hesia.

'No, I'm actually quite certain that you will. This is the last chance for both of you.'

'Just lower Cassandra to the ground,' pleaded Duncan. 'Let her go, Father Carnehan. If you do, I'll turn my back and you can all run as far and as fast as you can travel. I won't shoot at you ... you have my word on it. I only want Cassandra with me, unhurt.'

'There are two of us,' insisted Hesia. 'We've already drawn on you ... and both your guns are holstered. You're just a country priest searching for your son, and now you've found him. There's only one way out of here for you now. Lower the girl to the ground and we can make a run for the gate.'

She had a point. There was only one way out.

'Father Carnehan—' implored Duncan. 'I'm begging you!'

'Jake Silver,' whispered the pastor.

'What?'

Quicksilver. The two guns were in his hands, exploding and rocking. Cassandra Skar tumbled towards the black ash-covered rock. Two more bodies crumpled into the dust. Hesia tried to gargle, but it was impossible to make a clear sound with the best part of her throat missing. The shot meant for her had flown high. Must have ricocheted off a fragment of raining rock. Duncan Landor had collapsed, sprawled silently on the ground with a bullet through his heart, exactly where he had aimed it. Still on the ground, blood spreading across the silver foil of his survival suit.

'Dirty bastard,' moaned Paetro, crawling towards his dead still daughter. 'My girl, my beautiful little girl. Hesia flew you here. She saved your worthless life.'

'Good people die in wars,' said Jacob. 'On every side. That's why I've found it far better to swear off them. But then I didn't start this one. Your people did.'

'*Bastard*,' moaned Paetro. 'And Duncan, the poor lad was one of your own.'

'Not at the end. Not when it counted. But I'm leaving you alive,' said Jacob, standing over the writhing guardsman. 'So you can tell the girl's mother and grandfather *this*. Whoever they send, however many they send, it doesn't matter to me. I'll kill them all. I'm going to start with the emperor's lackeys in my country, but their blood's not nearly enough to pay for slaughtering my wife and taking my son. Your stooges are merely going to be what I need to get started. After I've finished with the empire's local puppets, I'll slay all the skels under the sky. When I'm done with that piece of work, I'm going to be just about getting warmed up. You tell your princess and your emperor I'm counting on them sending a lot more like you. Every soldier and every machine rifle and every fancy, fast ship you can smelt out of this big bloody smoking monstrosity you've murdered so many decent people for. Because you're all just too damn far away from Weyland for me to kill properly. So I'm relying on you to make sure your mistress delivers them up to me. You'll do it, won't you? For your noble-blooded little lady here, and your dead, renegade daughter?'

'I'll kill you!' shouted Paetro, trying to stand.

Jacob kicked the officer in the gut, sending him sprawling back onto the ash. 'Good luck then, Vandian. Even I couldn't manage that. And curse me, but I tried.'

He hefted Cassandra Skar's limp body and walked away into the deep, burning darkness.

Carter waited with Willow by his side, desperately keeping his promise to his father. Willow stood on a boulder, scanning the murk intently. She wasn't just looking for the pastor of Northhaven. Willow was convinced she had glimpsed her brother's face behind a mask out there in the melee. Carter hadn't seen Duncan Landor. Only dozens of Vandian guardsmen with rifles attempting to kill as many rebellious slaves as possible. If that had been Duncan, then she'd already lost her brother. The stone circle stood behind them, Carter urging the last few stragglers into the spinning circle of fire in its centre. Bodies seemed to dissolve as they struck its orange light. It was a measure of the desperation of their situation that most fled into the portal without a word of argument. But then, the slaves had watched Anna help Owen through first with Doctor Tooky in attendance, and if their leader had passed inside, that was enough for most of them. They marched in, the bravest first, the reluctant later – and the dead last of all. Poor Kerge and his brave father's corpse. *Please God, don't make me carry my dad back that way*. Sariel had disappeared shortly after he activated the stones, warning only that entering the circle was a one-way trip. Now Carter couldn't even ask the old bard how much longer the gate would remain open. He felt safer than he had any right to. As if the circle of stones was a beacon of light, warding against danger. Even the clouds of thick volcanic ash seemed to twist around the pillar of light and fire, giving those sheltering below a wide berth. But his anxiety remained … the terrible fear that its light would wink out and they would be left stranded here. Carter delaying for his father and Willow refusing to go through without him.

'There!' shouted Willow.

Carter scanned the waves of billowing black smoke. A figure? His heart leapt, before sinking as he realised it was Sariel, not his father. The old vagrant limped slowly forward, his wooden walking staff in one hand, the other hand securing a body slung over his back. He carried the Rodalian flyer, Sheplar Lesh. It was hard to tell whose clothes were more torn and blackened between the pair.

Carter helped Willow take the pilot from the old man's arms. Sheplar was unconscious, his face a red mask of blast cuts. 'You look like you've been dragged backward through the infernal regions.'

'Merely paying my respects to one of its callers, Lord Carnehan.'

'Where is my father – did you see him?'

'I caught sight of him once briefly,' coughed Sariel. 'But then this base Rodalian rascal dropped a munitions ship on my head, having first secured his safe survival with a parachute. As to where your father is now, see behind you …'

Carter nearly choked when he saw his father emerging from the broiling gas clouds. The pastor's mine survival suit was wreathed with steam, the ground black and burning with every step the man took. His father appeared to have rescued someone too, a small body stretched across his arms. Too compact to be Duncan Landor, surely?

Willow ran towards the pastor. 'I thought I saw Duncan out there on the plains. During the attack?'

'Afraid your brother decided to stay put,' said Jacob, halting before them. 'But this one's coming back with us instead.'

Carter saw a face through the air mask and suddenly realised just who it was his father carried. 'That's Lady Cassandra Skar, Princess Helrena's heir. She's the emperor's granddaughter! You do know that?'

'I'm counting on it,' said Jacob. 'Careful assassins do a poor job. And we'll need the aim of King Marcus's killers to be off for everyone who's survived the empire's hospitality.'

'Dump the child on the slope for her guardsmen to find,' urged Carter. 'We don't need her as a hostage.'

'Poor little thing ... surely we can leave her behind?' said Willow.

'I'll tell you how this'll go,' said his father, 'without this daughter of Vandia. We'll be back in Northhaven and there'll be a bandit raid. Except they'll be the best-armed and best-trained bandits you've ever heard of. The town'll be thoroughly burnt this time, the old and new town. Everyone slaughtered. All the people you brought back counted among the corpses. So you can choose. This little Vandian girl's freedom, or the lives of hundreds of blameless people you've survived alongside in this hell.'

'It's not *right*,' said Carter.

'I can't offer you shades of right today,' said his father. 'Only a choice between wrongs.'

Willow squeezed Carter's arm. 'Maybe we could travel to a country far away from home, after all? It wouldn't be so bad.'

'Not so bad for us,' said Carter. 'What about everyone else? You were right, Willow ... there's not another soul in Weyland who deserves to leave their bones here. The empire's stolen so much of our lives, how can I let them rob us of our chance of returning home, too? I don't think I can run away; not even if there's another fight involved.'

Sariel walked forward and slapped Jacob on the back. 'Ransom. Very good. Quite the prize. Wouldn't it be an irony if you left the centre of the world's riches a poorer man than you arrived?'

'Did you finish that filthy stealer?'

'I was about to,' said Sariel. 'But someone carelessly dropped a vessel full of explosives on me. The unchin-snouted flap-dragon scurried away in the blast's aftermath. Apolleon doesn't heal as well as I do, so at least we won't be encountering him in the next few hours.' Sariel indicated the stone circle, the pillar of fire stretching from the menhirs to the poisonous, rolling clouds trapped below the sky. 'There are, however, a horde of his unhappy friends currently crashing against the walls of our world, trying to overload the stones. It would far better if we start our journey before my concentration falters and they succeed.'

Jacob limped towards the open gate, carrying the hostage. Carter walked after his father, Willow at his side. He had a nagging premonition that this was only the beginning.

EPILOGUE

The farm boy walked home towards the town, Landor coins in his pocket and Landor wheat heads stuck against his simple woollen shirt. He'd been working late in the summer heat. The days were long and so were the hours, attempting to bring in the harvest with so few hands. But the pay was better than it had ever been, so who was he to complain? A fabric bag dangled from the end of the wooden stick slung over his shoulder. This morning it had contained his lunch. Now it was full of vegetables and a good-sized hunk of bacon. A little off-the-book extra from a farm manager eager to make sure he turned up at the fields next week, rather than arriving at one of the rival farms for day-work. He tramped down the road, humming to himself, pine trees on either side, the red threads of evening staining the sky and chasing the setting sun lower. Up ahead was where the mountain road to Rodal joined the king's highway. That was when he heard it. A mad sound. As loud as a festival in full swing, but crying and weeping mixed in among all the songs and cheering. Heading down the mountain road and getting louder. He stopped, startled, at the sight that greeted him. Hundreds of young men and women. A caravan without a single wagon, cart, horse or pony on the road. Clothes as outlandish as any travellers' he had seen. Some in silvery suits, men with metallic-trousers and bare chests where they had torn off their clothes, women in dirty grey tunics, others in metal armour, strange black rifles hanging from nearly every shoulder like the weirdest shooting party ever to tramp across a Northhaven woodland. He waited uncertainly for the shambling mass of people to turn the corner and lead the way to the town ahead of him. An old man sauntered slowly down the mountain road with a few stragglers strung out behind him. If this elderly coot was a traveller, he was the poorest sort. Definitely a vagabond. He saw the boy and raised his gnarled walking staff in greeting.

'Have you hiked in from Rodal?' asked the boy. 'Pilgrims from one of the mountain temples?'

'These wayward knaves have wandered down from somewhere a little higher than Rodal,' said the old man. 'And a little further too.'

'Never seen any caravan like this,' said the boy, his voice cracking in wonder.

'Oh, there's a quite the tale behind it,' agreed the old man. 'It deserves to be told. It *needs* to be told as far and as wide as Weyland's borders. Whispered in every ear and spread across every league of the land. Because if you can't learn from history, you are surely doomed to repeat it.'

'Maybe later. I have to get home. Ma's on her own. She needs my help to prepare supper.'

'Surely she can wait? My story concerns the true heir of Weyland and an evil king, distant lands, unwise rulers, slavery and battles, and the terrible travails of ordinary folks not so very different from you. It also features the prince of players, of whom it is said no more noble a figure ever—'

But the boy wasn't listening anymore. He had seen two ghosts shambling down the mountain road. Two ghosts that looked a lot like his dead older sisters. He ran towards them, the old vagrant's last words lost to the wind and empty road around him.

'—and suddenly ... Ma wasn't quite so much on her own.'

Duncan struggled to consciousness as though he was drowning in a sea of acid, straining through a dark surf of pain – every last iota of agony, all his. Surgeons, doctors and medical staff everywhere, a quick glimpse of Paetro's familiar face among the white masks and strangers, soldiers lying on medical stretchers under bright white lights. Screams, moans, the hiss of strange machinery trying to pump and inject life back into dozens of burnt and dying fighters. And there was a woman's voice, yelling, one he dimly recognised even through his drug-infused befuddlement. *Helrena*. Straddled across an operating table near Duncan's, her limbs flailing, orderlies trying to hold her down as surgeons picked metal from the crashed ship jutting out of her flesh. One of the doctors called for an anaesthetist, but he could barely be heard over the princess's howls for her daughter – for *vengeance*.

Paetro's deep reassuring timbre spun out of the confusion, but Duncan couldn't quite focus on the man – perhaps the surgeon's blade slicing into him, the pleas for something called a ventricular suction pump, were too much of a distraction? He tried to peer through the bobbing white forms busy around him, surrounding where he was lying down. 'It's a disaster, lad. A bloody nose and no mistake. Half of us blown to pieces and our sky mines empty, the rebels fled.' *There*. Duncan found the soldier at the other end of the trolley, distorted by dizzying waves. Paetro clutched tightly to a crumpled, blood-stained medal. The same one that Lady Cassandra had given away. It seemed its luck had held good, at least as far as deflecting the bullet meant for Duncan's heart was concerned. But the young girl's luck …? If Duncan could have overcome the disabling pain, he would have wept.

'Aye, there'll be a reckoning for this debacle,' Paetro continued. 'First from the emperor … looking for someone to blame. And we have to survive it. *You* have to survive it. If we're going to see the young Highness back home safely. And pay them back for this damned humiliation. I want to be there for that.'

Duncan tried to say something, to reassure his friend, but it escaped as a guttural choking sound and the taste of blood.

'—defibrillator.'

'—going into seizure,'

A trapdoor opened along the operating table and Duncan plunged into total darkness.

Turn the page for a sneak preview of
the second novel in the Far-Called series:

Foul Tide's Turning

ONE

WANDERER'S WELCOME

It was cold coming out of the east in winter, a harsh biting chill that even the flames from the burning, overturned wooden coach couldn't cover, nor the whipping snowstorm conceal. Young Thomas Purdell – Tom to those in his confidence – suspected he might not live long enough to warm himself over the wreckage's inferno, though; not the way the bandits were working their way through the surviving passengers. So far, they had only slit the throats of those travellers who'd put up a struggle when resisting the sudden attack. Tom was far from hopeful he was out of the woods yet. It was hard to question a dead man or woman; and this attack wasn't quite as it appeared on the surface. Not that the wilds of Northern Weyland weren't infested with bandits and marauders. But such men usually rode with cheap nags and old single-shot rifles. These eight killers were suspiciously well-equipped with lever-action rifles from the Landsman Repeating Arms Company, and though Thomas wasn't much of a judge of mounts, their horses were healthy grain-fed sorrel-coloured steeds rather than the usual nags rustled as prizes by the likes of *these*. The dirt and well-patched clothes were fully in keeping with their supposed ignoble profession, however.

'You've not got much on you,' noted the bandit chief, placing himself in front of Tom. He carried a short sabre on his belt that lent him a piratical air.

Tom glanced at the prisoners on either side of him; a well-dressed traveller on his left, with one of the coach's surviving drivers to his right. They cowered, not meeting their captors' eyes, and about as much use to Tom as trying to warm his hands on ice-cubes. As useless in a fight as the two women, a pair of sisters, from the southern city whose name he had already forgotten. Staying very silent to avoid attracting attention; as the only two females on the coach, they had already failed in that task.

'I'm a simple journeyman from the Guild of Librarians, travelling to my new order,' said Tom. 'What wealth the guild has sits on its shelves. Archives,' he added, 'that are very well protected inside our guild holds.'

'Anyone would think there were thieves abroad,' laughed the chief. He waved a leather tube, the wax seal at the end broken. Tom groaned aloud. That had been well concealed inside his luggage tied on the coach's roof. Not well hidden enough, it seemed, from the expert fingers of these dangerous, desperate men. Tapping the tube against his palm, the bandit removed a thick paper scroll and turned it around to reveal ... a list of numbers scratched by hand in black ink. 'And what the hell is this, then?'

'A cipher.'

'I know it's a bloody cipher. What's it say?'

'I don't carry the means to decrypt it,' said Tom. 'In all likelihood, it's just a message of greeting from the Master of the Codex at my last library to my new master. The old girl was never happy with my work. She's probably just telling Master Lettore that I need to be watched like a hawk in case I slack off.'

The bandit leader snorted. 'That's not going to be a problem for your guild boss anymore, *simple* librarian, trust me. If you know anything about what's really written on this, I could make things go a lot easier for you.'

'It's encrypted,' said Tom. 'And you don't send the key with the man. It's not how the guild does things.'

'Pity,' said the bandit. Tom didn't get the feeling he meant it was going to be a pity for the raiders. He swivelled toward the prisoner kneeling next to Tom, a slick dark-haired passenger with a jutting chin and a tanned neck enclosed by a starched white collar and dark red tie. 'What about you, fancy pants? Where you travelling?'

'Northhaven prefecture,' said the passenger. 'I'm a salesman for the Turnage Machinery Manufactury. I'm looking to sell horseless ploughs and subsoilers to the landowners up that way.'

There was a ripple of discontent among the bandits at this news. 'Ah,' said their chief. 'You'll have to forgive my boys. Many of them were labourers on farms in the eastern plains … until their landlords cleared them out and stole their fields away from them when they couldn't make rent. What a hoot, eh? All those machines that can work land using just a tenth of the labour; such generous harvests they produce, and your family still dies of hunger when you can't find work. I think that's what they call irony, isn't it?' He kicked Tom in the ribs; painful, but meant as a gentle nudge. 'What do you say, Mister Guild of Bloody Books? That's irony, isn't it?'

Tom nodded. 'That's one word for it.'

'Yeah,' said the chief, tugging a thumb behind his leather bandoleer. 'I thought it was.'

'Why are you doing this?' asked Thomas Purdell. 'Attacking a coach on the road? If we had money, we'd be travelling with the Guild of Rails on a train. If we had *real* money, we'd be flying in by air.'

'If I had wings, I'd attack merchant carriers in the sky. If I had a hundred more men and powder to blow the rails, I'd bushwhack a train and damn their high-and-mighty guild. As it is, you grass-suckers are my marks today. You see, there's always someone worse off than yourself,' said the bandit chief, pulling out his sabre. Its steel almost glowed in the white of the snowstorm. 'The trick is to make sure that those worse off stay that way, while stuffing your own pockets at your victims' expense. Just ask those landowners out east. Besides, it's not only money that travels by road. Sometimes secrets do, too.' He nodded at his men. There was a scream from the two sisters as the bandits dragged them closer to the burning coach, ripping the women's dresses as they hauled the pair away. It looked like the marauders intended to stay warm by the coach's wreck, at any rate. Tom cursed the old harpy of a guild mistress who had forbidden him to travel armed with a pistol. *Librarians are not soldiers*, she had archly instructed him. *Knowledge is our weapon*. Maybe he could try braining the bandit chief with the single book he had brought with him as a gift to the new library. *The Philosophies of Holtus*. God knows, Tom had found it hard enough to penetrate the words' meaning ... maybe their weight would concuss this fiend long enough to make a break through the snow.

The travelling salesman tried to get to his feet, mumbling a protest about his ill-treatment after handing over his coins, but the bandit chief merely plunged his sabre into the multi-coloured threads of the man's tweed jacket, a spreading stain of crimson added to the rich fibres. Tom stared down at the salesman's corpse as it collapsed to the hard, icy ground. Neatly and efficiently done.

The bandit chief winked at Tom, as though they were just exchanging pleasantries at a local tavern. 'That's man's work, sticking someone to put them in the ground. Haven't designed any dishonest machine to do that yet. Why waste a bullet, eh?'

Tom heard the words whisper out of the white, like the jagged ice pushing in on the snowstorm. '*It's not a waste.*' Just as Thomas Purdell thought he might have imagined the words, the sabre clattered to the ground, falling out of the bandit chief's fingers; the marauder staring in shock as a pool of bubbling blood spread across his chest, a mirror image of the wound he had just inflicted on his hapless prisoner. A snow-swallowed silhouette moved at the margins of the blizzard, barely visible, and Tom was deafened by the rippling explosions of two pistols being fanned simultaneously, little arrows of flame marking each shot. A grey ghoul emerged from the white-out, cloaked in wolf fur, twin long-barrelled pistols smoking, burning gunmetal leaving a trail of vapour drifting behind as though the weapons had sucked up the souls of the departed only to expel them through its barrels. But this wasn't a ghoul. It was a man concealed by a fur cape, only the face really visible. Why was there no return fire? Tom cast his eyes back. Four bandits lay scattered across the snow, crimson blemishes spreading where the men had fallen, three more had tumbled into the blazing shell of the coach, the two sisters shivering in the gusting wind, speechless, too shocked even to scream at the sight of the raiders charcoaled in the wreck's flames. Thomas Purdell hadn't registered enough shots to match the number of fatalities. But he must have, unless the man cloaked in wolf fur had found a way to dispatch multiple victims with a single bullet. It had all occurred impossibly fast ... or maybe it was just impossible.

'There's a fork down the road which you passed a little while before the raiders hit you,' said the figure. This man had the kind of voice a ghoul should possess. Deep, sonorous, commanding. He crossed to the trees where the coach's surviving horses had been tied up by the bandits, released them and led them back to the driver. 'Follow it for ten minutes … you'll arrive at a farm run by a family called the Proillas. They're good people. They'll take you in until Northhaven Township sends a patrol out here to escort you in.'

The figure walked back into the white-out and returned, listing on a horse as if he was communing with the storm. Concentrating, in the event more raiders stalked the night. Tom watched the man pass before turning to their surviving driver. 'Is he a scout for the army?'

'That's the pastor of Northhaven,' said the driver.

'Pastor? You mean a churchman? What kind of churchman is that?'

'The kind that's been through hell, I reckon,' said the driver. 'A while back the town was hit by slavers. They killed half the folks and stole most the rest young enough to be worth stealing, murdered the pastor's wife and kidnapped his son. It was the pastor that went after the missing people. Went out as one man. Came back as another.'

That was a familiar tale. 'What's his name?'

'Jacob Carnehan.'

'He's the man I was sent to find,' said Tom. He grabbed one of the horse's reins from the driver's hand, mounted it and rode into the snow after the pastor, catching up with the churchman shortly after. Despite the fierce weather, he didn't seem to be in any hurry; just advancing through the storm as though it belonged to him. 'My name's Tom Purdell and I have a message for you. It needs to be taken to the librarian's hold in Northhaven to be decrypted.'

'You knew the message was for me? You should have told the bandit's leader. He might have spared your life.'

'He wouldn't have,' said Tom, swaying uncertainly on the horse he'd borrowed. It was still skittish; after being halted, cut from the train, rustled and made a witness to two massacres in a single evening, Tom could hardly blame it. In fact, he knew how it felt. He took a closer look at the man he had been sent to find. As straight, tall and sharp as a razor; a big man in his late middle age with hard, knowing eyes fit to unpeel a man's soul. His movements were careful and close, spare and measured. But he could explode into violence at speeds that should be impossible to anything mortal. Tom had already seen that. *Can a devil be a churchman ... can a stealer?* Things here weren't exactly what they seemed.

'No,' said the pastor. A voice that was used to being obeyed, the word dragged over gravel. 'He wouldn't have. You're not stupid, boy. I'll give you that.'

'Foxy enough to know those raiders had been told to raid the coach and search it for messages,' said Tom.

'It's not foxes that are needed out here,' said the pastor. 'It's wolves. Wolves to eat wolves.'

'I'm just a simple librarian.'

'I believe that as much as the bandit leader back there,' said Jacob Carnehan.

'You're a distrusting man,' said Tom.

'I'm *alive*,' said Jacob. 'And fixing to stay that way.' He spat down onto the ground; it froze on the way. 'You won't be able to get to the library until tomorrow morning, not without freezing to death. You had better come in to Northhaven with me. You can stay at the rectory.'

'My credit's good for a hotel in town,' said Tom.

'And I might wake up tomorrow to find you in a ransacked hotel room with your throat slit and your message vanished,' said Jacob. 'The kind of news that can't be passed down open radio relays for fear over who might intercept it, that's the kind that has a way of attracting trouble.'

'I'll be safe in your rectory?'

Jacob's eye's narrowed to dark slits. 'The protection of the good lord, guildsman, do you doubt it?'

Tom's eyes drifted down to the twin pistols on his belt. *And his tools.* 'I'll stay with you, don't worry. Is it true, Father Carnehan? You were one of the people who brought back the true king.'

'*True* king?' said Jacob. The pastor grunted. 'Seems there are two men who claim that title these days, which one of them did you mean ... Marcus or Owen?'

Thomas Purdell knew when he was being teased, or perhaps tested.

'Prince Owen, of course. His uncle has to renounce his claim to the throne.'

'I don't suppose the people's assembly is any closer to deciding the matter of who should wear the crown?' said Jacob.

'They're still debating,' said Tom.

'That's what assemblymen do best,' sighed the pastor.

'The assembly is split down the middle,' said Tom. 'People are talking about a war, a civil war now. Both sides are at odds.'

'Won't be anything civil about it, if war comes,' said the pastor. 'Family against family, house against house. There's no feud quite so vicious as a good clan feud.'

'You didn't answer my question,' said Tom. 'Were you one of the people who found Prince Owen at the end of the world and brought him back?' *Far-called*, that's what people called it. When you went travelling across a world without end, not knowing if you would ever return alive. Or ever want to.

'I left my home to do two things, Mister Purdell. The first of which was rescuing my son from a slow death in a foreign hellhole,' said the pastor, 'and that I did. A lot of enslaved Weylanders escaped during the same slave revolt.'

'Some say the prince is insane ... mad.'

'*Some* do? *They* wouldn't happen to be newspapers controlled by the uncle who took the throne when the young princes conveniently disappeared, would they? Held as a slave for over a decade, watching his brothers worked to death in a mine under the whip? Wouldn't you be mad about that? I'd say Prince Owen's mildly irked right now. When he gets mad, then the country might really be in trouble.'

There was a fury in Jacob Carnehan's words, every bit as cold as the blizzard swirling around them. 'You said you went out to do two things, Father. I know you found and freed your son. What was the second thing?'

'Oh, the second's a-coming,' said Jacob. 'And I'll let you into a little secret, guildsman, by way of thanks for the encrypted message you're carrying. I won't have to travel far for it. This time, it's coming straight to *me*.'

Tom's eyes drifted down to the holstered pistols, steel barrels still warm and cutting a fine mist in the cold. And he thought of the eight dead bandits lying back on the road around a burning coach. Gunned down so fast and quick. *Like quicksilver.* Tom had never seen anything like that before, never even *read* of anything like it. And reading was, in theory, meant to be his trade. How many killers' corpses would you trade for a murdered wife before you counted yourself satisfied? Tom reckoned it would depend on the man. He stared at the shadowy silhouette riding the road ahead, being knifed at by biting snow, and he saw the pastor as he truly was for the first time. *A shadow on the world, making shadows.* Safe in this man's rectory? Like hell. Thomas Purdell suddenly realised he was caught at the heart of the storm.

DARK
SERVICE